THE PLAYER

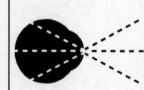

This Large Print Book carries the
Seal of Approval of N.A.V.H.

THE PLAYER

BRAD PARKS

THORNDIKE PRESS
A part of Gale, Cengage Learning

GALE
CENGAGE Learning·

Farmington Hills, Mich • San Francisco • New York • Waterville, Maine
Meriden, Conn • Mason, Ohio • Chicago

GALE
CENGAGE Learning®

LIBRARY OF CONGRESS CATALOGING-IN-PUBLICATION DATA

Parks, Brad, 1974–
    The player / by Brad Parks. — Large print edition.
        pages ; cm. — (Thorndike Press large print mystery)
    ISBN 978-1-4104-6969-4 (hardcover) — ISBN 1-4104-6969-7 (hardcover)
    1. Ross, Carter (Fictitious character)—Fiction. 2. Investigative
reporting—Fiction. 3. Environmental protection—Fiction. 4. Organized
crime—Fiction. 5. Large type books. I. Title.
PS3616.A7553P58 2014b
813'.6—dc23   2014007331

Published in 2014 by arrangement with St. Martin's Press, LLC.

Printed in Mexico
1 2 3 4 5 6 7 18 17 16 15 14

*To Ga, ninety-five and still
the classiest grandmother ever*

During seventy-seven years of scrupulous living, Edna Foster had survived whooping cough, encephalitis, breast cancer, one breech pregnancy, and two husbands. She figured she could handle the flu, no problem.

It struck on a Wednesday, the first day of spring's warmth had made it to New Jersey and visited her neighborhood in Newark. She had opened up the windows in the morning, tolerating the noise from a nearby construction site because she was ready for some fresh air after a long winter. By afternoon, she had caught a chill and shut the window. By nightfall, the chills had developed into a full-blown fever, with muscle aches and diarrhea to go with it. She called off the Bible study scheduled at her house that evening and consigned herself to bed. Too much fresh air, she supposed. By the next morning, she felt better.

The flu came back a week later. She hadn't

opened the windows that day, but she had been digging in her garden. She chastised herself for not dressing more warmly as she suffered through another miserable night. But, again, the sickness took only a day to run its course.

Perhaps a month after that, she broke her tibia. She hadn't been doing anything more strenuous than walk through her living room when it happened. She had to drag herself to the phone to get an ambulance.

The doctor in the emergency room set the fracture, put it in a cast, then sent her home with crutches and enough Vicodin to get her through the discomfort. Edna used the pain-killer sparingly for a few days, then flushed it down the toilet. She never drank or smoked — she was a good Christian woman, after all — and she didn't like how the drugs made her head feel fuzzy. Plus, there were too many junkies in her neighborhood. If word got out Mrs. Foster had pills, one of them would get it in his fool head to break into her house for them.

Without the painkiller, her mobility was even more limited. Her legs and ankles swelled, which she attributed to inactivity. She tried gritting her teeth and forcing herself to move about, if only to get her blood moving.

That's when she broke her arm. She had

8

been crutching around her kitchen when her ulna just snapped. She crumpled into a heap on the floor and, unable to reach the phone this time, had to wait six hours until a neighbor came by to check on her.

The broken arm led to another hospital visit, another splint, and more Vicodin, which she promptly flushed.

Now fully laid up, the swelling got worse. She also kept coming down with the flu — at least once a week — which only added to her suffering.

But that wasn't all. Her skin felt itchy, no matter how much she moisturized it. She had a bad taste in her mouth almost constantly, even when she had just brushed her teeth. She developed back pain that ached nearly as much as the arm and leg fractures. Her lungs sometimes felt like they were on fire.

Her granddaughter, Jackie, the pride of the family — she was a college girl! she was going to be a doctor someday! — tried to force her to go to a physician. But Edna wouldn't have it. She was through with doctors. They would just give her more painkillers, and she didn't want any of that garbage. She would get by with her Bible, prayer, and some old-fashioned mental toughness.

Then her mind started to go. Edna had always taken her sharpness for granted —

she was only seventy-seven, after all — and usually completed the *Newark Eagle-Examiner* crossword by seven thirty each morning. Yet, suddenly, she found she couldn't concentrate long enough to do even the simplest word games, the ones meant for children. She started blanking on simple things, like what she had eaten for breakfast or what day of the week it was. She had dizzy spells even when sitting down.

It was forgetting to flush the toilet that really got her in trouble. She barely urinated anymore, and what came out was often dark with blood and protein. She hadn't told anyone — her pee was no one else's business — but then Jackie walked by the unflushed toilet, saw the brownish water, and threw a fit, ordering her grandmother to go to the hospital immediately.

Once admitted, they quickly diagnosed Edna Foster with advanced-staged renal failure.

They put her on dialysis immediately but, again, Edna wasn't having it. She was in so much pain — her leg, her arm, her back — that sitting next to that machine for hours on end was unbearable. Her mental acuity was coming and going, but in her more lucid moments she managed to convince two doctors, a hospital administrator, a social worker, her pastor, and, most important, her granddaughter, that she didn't want dialysis anymore — and that she understood the consequences of that decision. She had been preparing to meet Jesus her whole life, she told them. If He was ready for her, she was ready for Him.

Finally convinced, they sent her home and, with help from Jackie, she got her affairs in order. During what turned out to be the final week of her life, she kept her Bible with her at all times. She slept most of the time, but when she was awake she asked Jackie to read some of her favorite passages. Often they were from the Book of Luke. He was a physician, after all. Just like Jackie would be someday.

The end, when it came, was merciful. She lapsed into a coma one night and slipped away two mornings later, around breakfast time. The ladies from her Bible study group speculated that Edna Foster was walking with the Lord by lunch.

CHAPTER 1

Even in an era when American print media has plunged into inexorable and perhaps terminal decline, even at a time when tech moguls are buying up venerated news-gathering organizations with their equivalent of couch change, even with the likelihood of career advancement dimmed by the industry's collective implosion, there are benefits to working for a newspaper that cannot be quantified by simple measurements like salary, benefits, or future prospects.

Kook calls are definitely one of them.

We get them all the time — from the drunken, the deranged, the demented — and they come in enough different flavors to keep us constantly entertained.

Some are just mild, low-grade kooks, like the ones who have newspapers confused with talk radio. They'll call up and start ranting about whatever subject is bothering them — the governor's latest cabinet appointment, the confusing signage that led them down the wrong exit ramp of the Garden State Parkway, the deplorable slowness of third-class mail — perhaps believing that if they just convince the reporter they're right, the newspaper will immediately launch a four-part series on the subject, written from the caller's particular point of view.

Then there are the conspiracy theorists, the ones who want us to "do some digging" into whatever fantasies they're harboring at the moment, whether it's that the local Walmart is importing illegal immigrants from Bangladesh in a garbage truck or that their town's animal-control officer is more of a dog person than a cat person.

There are also the old people who just want to talk. To someone. About anything. They'll call up with a "news tip," and of course it turns out they are the news, and the tip is that long ago — during, say, the Korean War — they nearly lost three toes to frostbite. And now, particularly on the mornings when they still feel that little tingle in their big toes, they feel the world at large needs to know about it.

Then there are the other standbys: the prisoners who use their phone time to call us, usually collect, and convince us of the gross miscarriage of justice that led to their incarceration; the paranoid schizophrenics who believe their delusions are worthy of front-page headlines; or the poor confused souls who, thinking newspaper reporters must be omniscient, will call and ask the name of the program they were watching on television last night.

As a group, they land somewhere between pitiable — particularly when they're obviously suffering from mental illness — and laughable. Except for the racists. We get a lot of those, too. They're just despicable.

Sure, Internet chat rooms and social networking have siphoned off some of our kooks over the years — there are more outlets for people to express their crazy now than ever before — but we at the *Newark Eagle-Examiner,* New Jersey's most widely circulated periodical, still get our share. Because the fact is, even with the increasing fragmentation of media, most people, even the nuts, realize a major daily newspaper like ours is still the best way to get serious attention for whatever cause or issue matters most to them.

Plus, we print our phone number in the paper.

Some reporters treat kook calls as nuisances. But most of us learn over the years to look forward to them. There's just nothing like going through an otherwise ordinary day, pecking away at some humdrum story, when suddenly you become aware one of your colleagues is talking to someone who lives off the grid and has found one of the three remaining working pay phones in the state of New Jersey to call and explicate his worldview.

If the reporter who takes the call is in a certain mood, she'll stand up in the middle of the newsroom and, for the benefit of those listening, start repeating key lines and questions in a loud voice, such as: "I realize you think Greta Van Susteren is trying to control your mind, but that doesn't necessarily mean Wolf Blitzer is going to try as well."

Or: "So you want to know if we're going to be writing about the rash of robberies in your neighborhood because someone keeps breaking into your house and moving your broom."

Or: "To make sure I understand this right, you're saying the Battle of Gettysburg didn't happen the way the history books said it did — and you know, because you were there in a previous life?"

The fun just never ends. So I have to admit I was mostly just looking for a good kook call on Monday afternoon when one of our news clerks wandered over to my desk and said, "Hey, I got a woman who says she has a big story for our investigative reporter. You want me to get rid of her?"

"Nah, I'll take it," I said.

I had just been killing time anyway, waiting for edits on my latest piece, a story about cash-strapped municipalities that were considering halting their recycling programs (corrugated waste products have seldom warranted so much attention). So when the forwarded call came through on my desk phone, I rubbed my hands together in anticipation, then answered with my most polite and officious, "*Eagle-Examiner,* this is Carter Ross."

"Hi, Mr. Ross, my name is Jackie Orr," came the voice on the other end. It was the voice of someone young, black, and determined.

"Hi, Jackie, what can I do for you?"

"Do you ever do stories about people getting sick?"

"That depends," I said. "Who's getting sick?"

"Everyone."

"What do you mean 'everyone'?" I asked. So far, so good: kooks often insisted that

17

whatever troubled them also afflicted others.

"Well, first it was just my grandmother. Or we thought it was just my grandmother. But then it turned out to be the whole neighborhood."

"Sounds like you need a lawyer more than you need a newspaper reporter," I said.

"I tried that. I tell them people are sick and they're interested. But once they hear it's not some open-and-shut mesothelioma case, they don't want anything to do with it. I talked to one lawyer who sounded a little interested, but then he wanted a fifty-thousand-dollar retainer. If we had fifty thousand dollars, we wouldn't be bothering with lawsuits. We'd just move. Our case is a little more complicated than anyone seems to want to take on."

I felt myself sitting up in my chair and paying closer attention. There are certain words kooks tend not to use. "Mesothelioma" is one of them. So while that was a little disappointing — no kook call for me today — it was also more promising from a journalistic standpoint. As a newspaper reporter, I have a certain bias toward the disenfranchised, disadvantaged masses that others, not even sleazy lawyers, want to listen to. Maybe it's because, deep down, I fancy myself a good-hearted human being who wants to help the less fortunate. Or maybe it's because the Pulitzer committee shares the same bias.

"You said it's complicated. How so?"

"Well, we don't know what's making anyone sick."

"Okay, so you don't need a lawyer. You need a doctor."

"Everyone is seeing doctors. Or at least the ones who have health insurance are. The doctors just treat the symptoms and send them home. They don't have any answers."

I didn't either. But I was intrigued enough to have Jackie assemble herself and some of her ill neighbors to chat with me that afternoon. The headline MYSTERY ILLNESS STRIKES NEWARK NEIGHBORHOOD had a lot more promise for interesting journalism than MORRISTOWN WEIGHS COSTS AND BENEFITS OF RECYCLING NO. 6 PLASTIC.

Besides, as a reporter, I had learned to trust that little assignment editor in my head to tell me when I might be onto a good story. And my assignment editor was telling me, at the very least, that Jackie Orr was no kook.

Having gained a modest amount of seniority at the *Eagle-Examiner* — eight years counted as senior at a newspaper where most of the older reporters had been forced to take buyouts — I had wrangled myself a prime desk location in the corner of the newsroom.

It was strategic, inasmuch as it meant editors couldn't sneak up on me. But more than that, it was panoramic, inasmuch as it afforded me a sweeping view of the magnificent and picturesque vista that was a daily newspaper in action. In a single glance, I could see the anguish of the photo editors who had eleven assignments to shoot and only four photographers to do the shooting; the boredom of the Web site writers who were still repurposing yesterday's news until today gave them something interesting to do; the torment of the education reporter trying to make a story about teacher-pension reform sound interesting. And, okay, maybe it didn't fit conventional standards for beauty — unless you found splendor in forty-year-old office furniture and fifteen-year-old computer terminals — but it was my view and I loved it all the same.

Along the walls were the glass offices, home to the higher editors who sometimes conspired to limit my fun but were otherwise a decent group, albeit sometimes in a cheerless, party-pooping, adjective-hating kind of way.

In the middle were the desks filled with reporters. There were a few duds among them, too, but by and large they were a magnificently contemptuous set of brilliant, irreverent, fascinating folks, the kind of people who almost always had interesting things to say and entertaining ways of saying it. And in a strange way I could never quite explain to outsiders — who didn't necessarily understand how the cruciblelike forge of putting out a daily newspaper could bond people — I considered them my extended, mildly dysfunctional family.

Just beyond them was an area of the room known as the intern pod. If kook calls were one of the immeasurable benefits of life at a newspaper, the joy of working with interns was more quantifiable. Through the years, the newspaper industry had come to rely on an ever-growing collection of young, idealistic, energetic, just-out-of-college flunkies to do much of the news gathering that used to be done by more-hardened souls. And while you had to be careful not to let some of their naïveté get in the paper, they were fun all the same. At the age of thirty-two, I wasn't exactly Father Time. But I had been in the game just long enough that I knew there was a value to seeing the world through the

21

nonjaded eyes of an intern. It helped keep me young.

Some of our interns, like Tommy Hernandez, now our city hall reporter and one of my best friends at the paper, started in this lowly post and quickly graduated to more important beats at the paper. Others had come and gone, leaving only their colorful nicknames — Sweet Thang, Lunky, Ruthie — and a smattering of stories in the archives by which we could remember them.

They were, most of all, cheap labor and eager helpmates. So it was that my eyes wandered toward the intern pod, looking for an enthusiastic aide-de-camp. Jackie Orr had promised me a room full of sick people. Interviewing them one by one, which is what I'd need to do, would take time. Having the assistance of an intern, presuming it was one who had been properly potty trained, would double my efficiency and halve my time. Plus, much like with kook calls, there was always the entertainment factor to consider. Interns were nothing if not amusing.

This being the middle of the afternoon, the pod was only partially populated. Half of them were out being good little interns, chasing stories. As I sized up the half that remained, my gaze immediately fell on Neesha Krishnamurthy, a smart — if a little too smart — young woman who had come to us from somewhere in the Ivy League. Columbia School of Journalism, if memory served. Poor thing.

Neesha's internship had thus far been distinguished only by an incident during the early days of her employment, when she stumbled across one of those only-in-Newark stories: a one-legged homeless man who had taken on a one-legged pigeon as a pet, training the bird to perch on his finger, arm, and shoulder.

Neesha somehow persuaded her editor to let her write a human-interest story about the guy — some kind of misguided effort to tug on the readership's heartstrings with a tale of man and bird, bonded by their shared disability. Unfortunately for her, our Web editors thought it had what they liked to call "viral potential," so they sent along a videographer. And he had the camera rolling during that priceless moment when Neesha got the bird on her shoulder and it confused her for its favorite statue, depositing a salvo of white glop on her arm.

One point three million YouTube hits had guaranteed that, for the rest of her days at the *Eagle-Examiner,* Neesha would be known as Pigeon.

Hence, I strolled over to the intern pod, sat down across from her, and said, "Hey, Pigeon, what's up?"

She looked stricken. "How long are people going to keep calling me that?"

"Well, that all depends on one thing," I said, faux philosophically.

"What?"

"How long you plan on being alive."

She groaned. "What if I become executive editor someday? That would mean people would have to stop calling me Pigeon, right?"

"No, that would mean we'd have to stop calling you Pigeon to your face."

"It's so unfair!" she whined.

"No, unfair is being a pigeon in Newark, New Jersey with only one leg. What happened to you is just funny."

She pouted. Pigeon could be considered attractive — lots of long, dark hair and long, dark eyelashes surrounded by rather flawless skin — but after a dalliance with the aforementioned Sweet Thang, I had promised myself to swear off interns. Plus, I had enough complications in my romantic life at the moment.

"Anyhow, I was wondering if you wanted to help me report a story," I said.

"It doesn't involve pigeons, does it? Because Buster Hays tried to trick me into a story about a —"

I interrupted her by laughing. Buster Hays was the oldest reporter left, the only septuagenarian in a newsroom whose median age was roughly twenty-four. He hung around mostly because he was far too cantankerous to give us the pleasure of seeing him quit.

"No, no. I'm serious," I assured her. "No pigeons. No birds of any sort. I got a tip about a neighborhood in Newark where apparently a bunch of people are getting sick and no one knows why."

"Oh, cool," she said.

Yes, this was one who belonged in the Fourth Estate: only someone with a reporter's sensibilities would describe mysteriously ill people as "cool."

"Anyhow, there's going to be a group of them gathered at a house this afternoon, and I was hoping you could help me interview them. You busy?"

"Well, sort of. But it can wait. Let me just go tell Matt where I'm going."

Matt was her editor. And he was a decent enough guy, for an editor, but I didn't need Matt knowing about this. There was too great a risk he would tell my editor, Tina Thompson, with whom I had a somewhat complex relationship. The less Tina knew

25

about my activities at the moment, the better.

"Don't do that," I said. She looked confused, so I continued: "Intern lesson number one: when it comes to editors, it's always better to beg forgiveness than ask permission."

"Are you sure?" she asked.

"Well, that depends. Do you want to be known around here for something other than bird poop?"

She followed me out of the newsroom without another word.

The address furnished to me by Jackie Orr was on Ridgewood Avenue, and as we made the short drive out there from downtown, I gave Pigeon a quick history lesson. Ridgewood Avenue used to be one of the South Ward's great streets, located in the Weequahic section of the city, one of Newark's great neighborhoods. Then someone got the fine idea to construct Interstate 78 through it in the late 1950s. It tore Ridgewood Avenue roughly in half, destroying the neighborhood and leaving behind a piece of the city that never quite recovered.

The house was located on the section of Ridgewood Avenue that survived just to the north of the highway, an odd wedge of real estate that had long been yearning for revitalization. It was a strange hodgepodge of residential and industrial, with everything from manufacturing and transportation companies to new public housing and old private housing, with some newly paved streets next to ones in such serious need of repaving you could see cobblestones under the asphalt.

Symbolically, nothing captured the area better than the South Ward Industrial Park. Originally conceived in the seventies as a $100 million economic engine that would employ more than a thousand residents, it was finally built in the late nineties as a $9 million facility that maybe — maybe — employed a hundred people and never did become the catalyst that anyone thought it would be.

Still, this being Newark, where urban renewal has been just around the corner for fifty years, there was a new project being touted as a neighborhood savior. Using eminent domain as something of a cudgel, the city had managed to scrape together a sizable piece of property across several city blocks, in the process leveling some abandoned factories and some houses that should have been abandoned but still had people living in them.

Then, with a variety of tax abatements and promises about streamlining approval processes, it had sold the parcel to McAlister Properties, a father-son development team who fancied themselves the Trumps of Newark. I was always a little unclear where the father, Barry McAlister, had gotten his seed money from — family? investments? bank theft? — but he and his son, Vaughn, had slapped their name on a couple of buildings in the city and, allegedly, they were going to toss up something sizable and shiny on this plot as well.

The last proposal I had heard about was for one of those mixed-use, mixed-income developments that have become all the rage among the urban-planning set. The numbers being touted by city hall always seemed to vary — anywhere from two hundred to three hundred affordable and market-rate residential units and 60,000 to 90,000 square feet of retail space — but it was, without question, going to be large. The total price tag was put somewhere around $120 million.

There were even rumors about a big-box store anchoring the retail space. A Kohl's? A Target? It was, so far, a well-guarded secret. But Newarkers got giddy when they spoke of it. That was one of the real ironies of life in a depressed city: all the people wanted was the same kind of national franchises — with their homogeneous, cookie-cutter architecture — that people in the well-to-do suburbs desperately tried to keep out.

The development was currently being called McAlister Arms — not to be confused with McAlister Center or McAlister Place, which were office buildings located downtown — and it was located just off an exit ramp to I-78. The thinking was that shoppers might be enticed into the stores by the lower sales tax of an urban enterprise zone and that commuters might be enticed to move there by the easy access to the highway.

That was another irony: the very roadway that had first rent the neighborhood asunder was now being seen as a hope for helping to bring it back. Some of the locals thought it would really turn into a boon for the area. Others thought it would be another South Ward Industrial Park, a project that promised salvation and delivered something well short of it.

Either way, it had to be better than what was there now: a big, empty lot.

It turned out the neatly trimmed single-family house where Jackie Orr had her group congregating was within shouting distance of the McAlister Arms site — or at least it was shouting distance if you could make yourself heard over the rumble of trucks and other heavy equipment that were readying the site for construction. As I pulled into a parking spot, I saw an earthmover pushing dirt into a pile that a backhoe was then scooping into a dump truck. Elsewhere, a crane was stacking steel girders. It was like watching very large Tonka trucks in action.

"So what's our plan?" Pigeon asked.

"Basically, you want to make like a doctor: ask them questions about what ouches, when it started ouching, and how it ouches. Then write down the answers. We'll sort everything else out later."

"Okay. Who's keeping the spreadsheet?"

"Who said anything about a spreadsheet?"

She looked at me like I had caught the stupid virus. "Investigative reporters keep spreadsheets," she said, as if quoting from a textbook. "It allows them to systematically track large volumes of data, identify emerging patterns, and draw conclusions based on their findings. It's how modern investigative reporting is done."

I made a show of stifling a fake yawn. "Really? Is that so? Says who?"

"Didn't you go to journalism school?"

"Thankfully, no," I said. Which is true. I had no formal training in journalism. And, frankly, I had never missed it. My undergraduate degree was from Amherst, a small liberal-arts college in Massachusetts where they had no journalism major and, in general, had tried not to teach us anything too useful. I grew more appreciative of how nonspecific my education had been with each passing year, as it became clear that in this breakneck world of ours, anything allegedly practical they might have crammed into me would have become quickly outdated anyway.

"Oh, well, I took several classes in investigative reporting and computer-assisted reporting," she said. "I'd be happy to help you set up a spreadsheet."

"Oh, no, thank you. Some of us reporters like to do their investigating a little more haphazardly."

"Why?"

"Because studies have shown reporters who use spreadsheets are seventy-two percent more likely to clog their stories with meaningless statistics," I said. "In fact, did you know that spreadsheets account for more than ninety-one percent of the deathly dull stories that get into the newspaper?"

31

She paused to consider these purely fabricated pieces of information as I turned off the engine. "You're making fun of me right now, aren't you?" she asked.

"Pigeon, you're about to meet real people, not data points," I said. "In my experience, human beings are too messy for spreadsheets. Stick around long enough and you'll learn to love them for it."

The woman who answered my knock on the door could not have been more than twenty-one. And if you told me she was fourteen, I would have believed that, too. She sort of resembled a mop held upside down: thin as the handle until her head, which exploded in a profusion of thick, black braids, loosely organized by a rubber band.

I smiled as she pulled open the wooden front door, noting she had not yet touched the clear Plexiglas storm door. She was going to size me up first, and that was fine by me. Newspaper reporters grow accustomed to being the Fuller Brush salesmen of the modern day: if we don't make a good impression on the front porch, we'll never get inside the house. For that reason, I'm always conscious of making my appearance as professional and noncontroversial as possible.

Hence, what the woman saw on the other side of her storm door was a smiling, six-foot-one, 185-pound WASP with the world's most boring haircut, pleated khaki pants, a freshly ironed white shirt, and a necktie that looked like it had been picked out by the Republican National Committee.

If she had looked really carefully, she would have noticed I double-knotted my shoes.

"Hi. I'm Carter Ross. Are you Jackie?"

She adjusted a pair of bug-eyed glasses that were too big for her small face. They were at least twenty years out of style and might have been charity giveaways. Or maybe that's just what The Kids were wearing these days. Either way, they gave Jackie an owlish look. I immediately pegged her as the girl in her high school class who spent lunchtime by herself in the corner of the cafeteria, reading fiction for pleasure.

"Yes, hi, Mr. Ross, thank you for coming," Jackie said, opening the storm door.

"First of all, please call me Carter. Otherwise you'll make me feel old. Second, this is my colleague Neesha Krishnamurthy. I hope you don't mind I brought her along to help me do some interviewing."

"That's fine. Please come in."

She showed me into a small entryway,

with stairs immediately in front of me, a small living room to the right, and a kitchen in back. Nothing in the house looked to have been added within the last thirty years or so.

"Nice place," I said, because politeness is sometimes more important than honesty.

"This is my grandma's house," Jackie said, then corrected herself: "Was my grandma's house."

Right. Was. In case I hadn't already figured it out, Jackie added, "She just died."

"Sorry for your loss. How old was she?"

"Seventy-seven. It was actually at her funeral that we started realizing how many people in the neighborhood had been getting sick. We had been so busy caring for Grandma we hadn't noticed before that."

I considered asking for more details about Grandma, but I was aware there was a room full of people just to my right. They were all from the neighborhood, which meant they were all African American, and I got the sense they were sizing up the white guy who had just walked in. I figured it made more sense to talk to the living now and get details about the dead later.

"There are more of us than what you see here," she said, pointing me to the living room. "There are about twenty of us al-

34

together. This is just who I could get on short notice."

I turned into the room and took stock. There were eight people: six women and two guys, roughly thirty to seventy years of age. They tended to be more toward the pleasantly plump side, but otherwise they looked . . . healthy, I guess. Or at least healthy for Newark, which is not an especially well city to begin with. In modern-day America, taking care of one's self requires money, good insurance, and ready access to primary care, none of which are things that people in a place like Newark tend to have.

"Hi, folks," I said. "How is everyone today?"

The replies were mostly mumbled, the faces downcast. I think people sometimes have newspapers confused with television, or at least they were acting like they were on camera. This little cadre of convalescents was ill, and they were going to play that part as long as they were in my presence. Then again, since Jackie's grandma had just died — perhaps of the same cause that was diseasing them — I suppose I shouldn't have expected a pep rally to break out just because I had asked them how they were doing.

After the introductions and a few necessary niceties, Pigeon and I divided the afflicted, went into separate quarters — me to
the kitchen, her to the small dining room
that was connected to the living room —
and began interviewing them.

What I heard four times over the next
hour or so was more or less the same story,
told in slightly different ways. People kept
getting what they thought was the flu,
except it was happening too often to really
be the flu. There was no discernible pattern
to how or when it happened. There was no
reliable predictor of when it would flare up
again.

The symptoms beyond that were a little
more scattershot, everything from puffy eyes
to aching feet to a persistent cough and
respiratory distress. And that could mean
anything from diabetes to allergies. Being
that my medical training didn't go beyond
watching *Scrubs* reruns, it's not like I could
place them as all being related to, say, a
failure in the endocrine system. Mostly
because I couldn't remember what the
endocrine system actually did. I was proud
of myself for even knowing we had one.

But there was one thing that caught my
attention: broken bones. Three of the four
people I talked to had fractured something

recently, and they said others in their group had reported the same thing. That could just be coincidence, but I doubted it. Adults just weren't that clumsy.

What I liked about broken bones, from a journalistic standpoint, was that it wasn't the flu. A bunch of people who complained they were getting flulike symptoms too often felt like it could be an imagined thing, some kind of mass hypochondria. You couldn't imagine breaking a bone. It could be confirmed with X-rays. It was incontrovertible.

Plus, it suggested something truly strange was going on.

They all had theories as to what that was. One woman swore it was the water: she noticed it was suspiciously cloudy just before the onset of her most recent outbreak. Another woman thought perhaps the local grocery store where they all shopped had applied some kind of chemical to its produce. The guy I interviewed thought it had something to do with the neighborhood's proximity to I-78, which was more or less on top of them.

It was all possible, I guess. I just knew whatever it was had to be fairly local. The people I talked to didn't really have a lot in common. They ate different diets, worked different kinds of jobs (or not at all), lived in different houses. But the one thing they all shared was the neighborhood. It didn't take an epidemiologist to speculate that something very nearby — in the air, in the soil, in the water — was the culprit.

But I understood why the lawyers Jackie had talked to wanted nothing to do with her and her motley little group. Unless you had some kind of inkling to what this peculiar pathogen might be, it would take a lot of time — and money — to figure it out. That was assuming you ever could.

After finishing with our interview subjects, Pigeon and I dismissed them one by one, making sure to get their phone numbers and addresses in case we needed to ask them more questions. Jackie promised us more people if we could come back in the morning, after she had a chance to round them up. I told her Pigeon and I would be back, with bells on.

Once the last of the visitors departed, it was just Jackie, Pigeon, and I, standing in the living room.

"So I probably should have asked you this on the phone, but: how are you feeling?" I asked Jackie. "Have you been experiencing any of these symptoms?"

"Yeah, but only once. I don't live here."

"Where do you live?"

"Well, I grew up around here. I went to Shabazz," she said, pointing vaguely in the direction of Malcolm X. Shabazz High School, a few blocks to the north. "But I live in New Brunswick now. I go to Rutgers."

I was impressed. For kids from the expensive private school where I received my secondary education, Rutgers was a respectable safety school. For a kid from Shabazz High School, making it into Rutgers was like one of my classmates making it into Harvard.

"What are you studying?" I asked.

"Pre-med."

"Better you than me. What year are you?"

"I guess you could say I'm a junior and a half," she said. "I'll probably graduate a semester early."

"How'd you swing that?"

"Summer school. I love Newark and I want to come back here someday and be a doctor — a pediatrician, actually. But for right now? I just need to be out of here during the summer. I don't want to be hanging around on the bleachers when some whacked-out banger comes after me with a machete."

I got the reference. A few years earlier,

four college students, back in Newark for summer vacation, had been sitting on the bleachers at a nearby elementary school, eating McDonald's and whiling away a summer evening, when they were attacked by a group of young men who may or may not have been going through initiation to the MS-13 gang. Only one of the four kids survived, and she still bears machete scars. One of the kids who was killed had been the drum major for the Shabazz High School marching band. He would have been a little older than Jackie. They might have known each other.

Jackie continued: "The only reason I was here so much this summer was because of my grandmother."

"Right, of course. I meant to ask you a little more about her. What was her name?"

"Edna Foster." She gave a thoughtful pause, then added, "She was the best."

"She sounds like it," I said, even though I didn't know a thing about the woman. "Do you have a picture of her by any chance?"

"Uh, yeah, sure, hang on," Jackie said. "There's one upstairs. Let me go get it."

Jackie departed the living room and disappeared upstairs for a moment, leaving me with a slightly bewildered-looking Pigeon.

"Why do you need to see what she looks

like?" she asked, quietly.

"I don't," I said.

"Then why did you ask for a picture?"

"Because every good story needs a victim, and Edna Foster strikes me as a pretty good victim. So I need Jackie talking about her grandmother in a kind, loving way. If Jackie is looking at a picture of her grandmother while she talks, we'll get better stuff. Photos can be very evocative that way. Now do me a favor and get your notebook back out and write down whatever this young woman says next, because I guarantee we'll end up using it."

Pigeon still looked to be a little circumspect — this was yet another thing that wouldn't fit on her spreadsheet — but further conversation ended when Jackie came back down the stairs and into the living room.

"This is her and my grandfather," Jackie said, handing me a framed snapshot of a man and a woman who looked to be around thirty, standing on a sidewalk. The man had his arm around the woman, who was tall and thin, like her granddaughter. If I had to put a date on the picture, I'd say 1965.

Jackie went on: "That's a picture of them the day they bought this house. My grandmother was so proud of it. She was the first person in her family to own property."

I knew enough Newark history to be able to imagine the backstory. The mid-1960s was prime time for white flight and block-busting. Whole neighborhoods changed complexion virtually overnight, thanks in part to less-than-scrupulous Realtors who roamed through neighborhoods, knocked on the doors of the white families who lived there, and said things like, "Just wanted to let you know you have new neighbors . . . Yes, it's a lovely family from South Carolina with eight kids . . . I hear they're going to plant watermelons out back."

Mr. and Mrs. Foster had probably bought this place from a nice Jewish family that couldn't wait to hightail it to Livingston.

"My grandfather got killed during a holdup a few years later. My grandmother remarried but he died of a heart attack. I still don't know how she managed to hang on to this place and raise three children by herself. She was tough."

"What kind of work did she do?" I asked.

"She worked for the city, in the engineering department. She was a secretary. She talked all the time about how she was the first black woman they ever hired, right after Gibson got elected" — Ken Gibson was the city's first black mayor — "and how it was hard sometimes, but she felt like she was going to make things better for her children and her grandchildren."

"You sort of look like her," I said, handing the picture back to her.

"Everyone says I act like her, too. She was the first in the family to buy a house. I'm the first to go to college. She just had . . . a lot of spirit."

It was the word "spirit" that got her. Jackie half blurted, half sobbed it, then immediately tried to compose herself.

"I'm sorry," she said.

"No, no, it's fine," I said.

"I just don't know what's going to happen now. My family is . . . I mean, we're no prize. I got a cousin in jail. I got another cousin who's bangin' so hard he'll probably end up there soon. But it's still my family, you know? When we get together, none of that stuff matters. It's just the family and my grandma and this house. This house is like our center. This is where we always gather, for holidays and birthdays. And now without Grandma, I just don't know . . ."

Jackie's voice trailed off again. I saw out of the corner of my eye that Pigeon was getting down every word. It's not that I wasn't absorbed in Jackie's story — I was — but I also remembered I had a story of my own

43

to write. And it was in the best interests of Jackie and her sick neighbors that I write it well.

"So had she been in good health until recently?"

"Grandma? Oh yeah. She was like a dynamo. She finally retired maybe seven, eight years ago, but she hadn't slowed down at all. She still gardened and walked and was really active with her church. And then suddenly, it was like everything went wrong."

Jackie went through the symptoms her grandmother had experienced, and it was similar to what I had heard from the other victims. The flu. The swelling. Broken leg. Broken arm. Then it progressed to kidney failure, which might have been survivable except Edna Foster was too weak to put up with dialysis. Whatever this malady was had taken all the fight out of her.

"It just didn't make any sense," Jackie concluded. "And then at her funeral, people started talking, and it was like, 'Oh, she had that? That's strange, so do I.' Or, 'Oh, she had this? That's weird, so does so-and-so.' And maybe it's because of all these pre-med classes I'm taking, but it just didn't sound right."

"So what made you want to take this on as your cause?" I asked.

"I don't know. I guess I kind of thought it was what my grandmother would have done. But she wasn't around anymore, so now it was up to me. As I told you, I called a few lawyers, but I couldn't get anywhere with them. But I couldn't just give up. So I guess I was hoping that if we got in the newspaper and got some publicity, maybe someone would take pity on us and want to help us. A big law firm that might be willing to take us pro bono. Or a doctor. Or the state, maybe. I don't know. Do you think that might happen?"

"It might," I said. "Or it might not. Obviously, I can't make any promises about what happens after a story goes in the newspaper."

"I know. I know. Look, Mr. Ross . . . Carter . . . Thanks for coming. Just to listen to those people makes them feel, I don't know, like someone actually cares. I was beginning to feel like no one did."

I looked at Edna Foster's granddaughter, with her bug glasses, mop hair, and fierce pride. She was young enough and idealistic enough that when she saw something she didn't think was right, she believed something could be done — and had to be done. And she had found a newspaper reporter who felt the same way.

"There's a notion in journalism that one of the reasons we exist is to give a voice to the voiceless," I said. "People in my business tend to forget that sometimes. But I guess I try to remember it's part of the reason we're here. It's really one of our highest callings."

Pigeon and I said our goodbyes and went back outside. The sun was getting low and I could hear the rush-hour traffic on I-78 zooming along behind me. But there was enough light that the guys at the construction site remained hard at it, their big machines making their usual racket and kicking dust into the air. I figured if they were still working, I should be, too.

"What are you doing?" Pigeon asked as I passed my car and walked in the direction of Hawthorne Avenue.

"I'm taking a walk," I said.

"Where?"

"Just getting to know the neighborhood a little better."

"But . . . why?"

I gave her a palms-up gesture. "Don't know. It's called 'shoe leather journalism,' Pigeon. Hopefully they taught you about that at Columbia."

They must have, because Pigeon dutifully

joined my tour. We walked along the side-walks, some of them new, some of them old, all of them littered with occasional mine-fields of broken glass. I had spent enough years in Newark that I had long ago stopped trying to avoid them. My shoes had thick soles. Besides, if you closed your eyes and pretended you were down at the shore, the crunchy feeling under your feet was sort of like walking on seashells.

As we explored the neighborhood, Pigeon gave me the brief version of her life story. She grew up in Edison, New Jersey, in the burgeoning Indian community there. She was valedictorian at J. P. Stevens High, where she hung out with other smart Indian kids. Then she went to Yale, where she hung out with more smart Indian kids. Her parents had made it clear they hoped she would marry a future doctor named Ranjit. You couldn't quite call it an arranged mar-riage; but he was Brahman and so was she, so it would sort of make everyone happy if she just went along with it. She said she probably would, even if she didn't really have feelings for the guy.

Yet, somewhere during this perfect, by-the-book, Phi Beta Kappa life of hers, she had been permitted one rebellion: she went to journalism school. And now it sounded like she was trying to make the most of it, in her own self-limited way.

As she wound through her little narrative, I kept my eyes peeled for . . . well, actually, I have no idea. But it is my general experience in matters such as these that you never know what you're looking for until you find it. Maybe there was some obvious source of local water contamination. Maybe one of the stoplights would be glowing radioactive orange. You never knew unless you kept your eyes open.

Except, in this case, all I really saw was a strange little Newark neighborhood that had been chopped off from the rest of the city. Interstate 78 formed a hard border to the south. The exit ramps filled the space to the east. To the west were some old brick warehouses that belonged to long-defunct companies, vestiges of Newark's manufacturing heyday. To the north was the McAlister Arms site and those clattering construction vehicles.

It created a little island on the south side of Hawthorne Avenue that was perhaps five blocks long and one block deep. And all nine of our sick people — ten, if you counted Edna Foster — lived on that island.

It brought to mind a tale I had read about in a geography class I had taken at Amherst.

It was about a midnineteenth-century doctor in London who was studying a cholera outbreak. This was in the days before germ theory had been developed, so no one understood the mechanism by which cholera spread. But by putting a dot on a map for each house that had a case of cholera, the doctor was able to determine that the outbreak seemed to be centered around one public water pump that all the houses had been using to get their water. The pump's well turned out to have been dug a few feet from a sewage pit.

That doctor, John Snow, is considered the father of modern epidemiology. And, really, all I needed to do here is what he had done: find the equivalent of the water pump and then discover the sewage pit beside it.

By the time we completed our circumnavigation of the neighborhood, it was getting to be that time of night when the only white people meandering into that neighborhood were the ones there to buy drugs. I wasn't in the market for anything stronger than pale ale, so Pigeon and I returned to my car and I got us pointed back to the office. My ride is a used — and I mean well-used — Chevy Malibu with at least 111,431 miles on it, though that may be a conservative estimate. The odometer has been broken for a while. Suffice to say that if cars could win Purple Hearts, mine would have been awarded several by now. Still, it delivered us safely back to the newsroom.

If only it could have kept me safe once I got there. I had barely stepped off the elevator when my path was blocked by the curly-headed figure that was Tina Thompson. In addition to being the managing editor for local news and my immediate editor, Tina happened to be one of the two women with whom I had recently experienced the pleasures of the flesh.

This was merely the latest development in a relationship that had a way of making me feel like I was the last person to know what was going on. Tina had, once upon a time, looked at me as the ideal mate, in a strictly biological way. She was a single woman of a certain age — that age being the last number that still begins with the digit 3 — and she had decided she was going to become a mother.

Not a girlfriend. Not a wife. Just a mother.

And I was to be her source of sperm. Not a husband. Not a lover. Just sperm.

I had always balked at that potential arrangement. I have these antiquated ideas about nuclear familyhood and, besides, I actually — this is *really* old-fashioned, I

50

know — like her. She's smart and successful and passionate about life and a little nuts, all of which I found myself strangely attracted to. I tried to tell her this, though she seemed never to believe me. Instead, she tried to make herself seem tough and invulnerable, which only made me want to discover her vulnerable side that much more, which only infuriated her, which only charmed me further.

It never seemed to go anywhere beyond that. I had this long-harbored theory that we could make a great couple. She never let me test my hypothesis. And as a result we had reached this Balkan-style settlement where everyone left the table unhappy: I didn't get a relationship, she didn't get a baby daddy.

Then, without warning, she had decided motherhood, conventional or otherwise, was no longer in her future.

Then, with the possibility of procreation off the table, and with no apparent hope for any kind of relationship, we did the obvious thing couples who want neither children nor romance do: we had sex.

We hadn't really discussed the implications of this act. She insisted there weren't any and that I had been just a one-night booty call, a convenient way to fill a momentary craving. Ever since then, relations between us had chilled to temperatures not seen in Newark since the Pleistocene epoch. I can't say I fully understood the combination of idiosyncrasies and undiagnosed disorders that was Tina Thompson, but I at least understood she liked her distance. And after our clothes-free comingling, she had decided I had gotten a little too close. She had been making a determined effort to push me away ever since.

Hence, my greeting from her was not, "Hello, Carter," or, "Nice to see you, Carter," or, "Have you had a good day, Carter?"

It was: "Where the hell have you been?"

"Out for a walk," I said. Which was, technically, true.

"Oh, go ahead and play coy if you want. I saw Pigeon scurrying away just now. You know I'll be able to beat it out of her in seven seconds flat."

"Okay, so I was out working on a story. But it's not fit for your eyes and ears as of yet."

"Yeah, well the same could be said for that recycling story you wrote," she huffed. "The unfortunate thing is that you turned it in anyway."

"What's wrong with the recycling story?"

"It's a story about recycling but it's total garbage," she said. "In its current form, it's not deserving of the fifty percent postconsumer content it would be printed on. It's in your basket with comments marked on it. And it had better be returned to me — in a lot better shape — before you even think of working on anything else."

She gave me a look people usually save for backed-up toilets, then departed.

A responsible employee — thoroughly chastened and properly ashamed — probably should have gone straight to his desk and pounded on the keyboard until his fingers were bloody. Or at least chapped.

Me? I mostly just got thirsty for a frothy, 6-percent-alcohol-by-volume beverage, preferably one that was a nice, dark amber color — especially if I could share it with someone who might provide companionship and conversation while I drank it. And perhaps side benefits later.

The person most likely to supply all those things was Kira O'Brien, so I wandered over to her desk to see if I could talk her into an evening with me. Not that it would likely take much convincing. If Tina is the Pat Benatar of my life — because she makes love a battlefield — Kira is the Cyndi Lauper. She just wants to have fun. That she also sometimes dyes her hair purple is just a coincidence.

By day, Kira is one of the *Eagle-Examiner*'s librarians. She is twenty-eight years old and looks like a proper Irish girl, with brown hair, blue eyes, and a wardrobe that appears to have been coordinated by Ann Taylor. She is quiet, conscientious, and diligent in assisting reporters with their research needs. She sometimes puts her hair up with a pencil. And even if she does it just to be ironic, it still adds to the overall effect.

Then night falls, and she leaves work and morphs back into her true form, which is ten tons of uninhibited impulsiveness packed into a ninety-eight-pound body. Among her body piercings are parts I have never heard my mother say aloud (hint: one of them rhymes with "Dolores"). She enjoys it when certain private acts are performed in areas that might make them available for public viewing. And her closet includes numerous outfits that most people would refer to as costumes. She's the only woman I've ever met who, if you ask her to dress up as a vampiress, will ask you to narrow it down.

I'm adventurous enough that I can keep up with her. Sort of. One of these days, it's entirely possible she's going to get bored by me and my white and/or blue button-down shirts — even if I am seriously thinking about adding a third color to my repertoire one of these days — and leave me by the side of the road on her way to Comic-Con.

In the meantime, I just try to hang on and enjoy the ride. I hadn't really decided what I felt about her, other than that I enjoyed her company. She had indicated that she felt pretty much the same way about me. During one of our rare serious conversations, she said she viewed her twenties as a time to have fun and "experiment." She wouldn't even think about settling down until she was in her thirties, an age she spoke of like it was a strange land she could only barely imagine visiting.

Beyond that, we had yet to have any kind of talk about where our relationship was or wasn't headed — or whether we even *had* a relationship — and I sensed neither of us was particularly uncomfortable with that. If we had to name a magazine after our arrangement, we'd call it *Vague*.

"Hey, it's good you're here," she said as I entered the library. "My shift ends at seven and I'm sort of under a time crunch to get out of here. It would help if I could get changed now, but I'm the only one here.

Could you cover the desk for a second?"

"What if someone asks a question I can't answer?" — which, in matters of library science, included just about everything.

"Just do what I do when I get stumped: pretend like the database is down and tell them you'll e-mail them when it comes back up."

"And you get paid for this?"

"Not well, believe me," she said. Then she grabbed a bag from under her desk and hustled down the hall to the bathroom.

I sat at her desk, mercifully alone. It was getting to be the time of night when reporters either had what they needed or had resigned themselves to faking it.

Perhaps five minutes later, Kira emerged from the bathroom wearing a helmet and a full-body leotard that was the color of bubble gum and festooned with various insignia and patches. She looked like a storm trooper who had fallen into a giant cotton-candy machine.

"Okay, I give up, what are you supposed to be?" I asked.

"I'm Rose, the Pink Power Ranger," she said, like it should have been obvious.

"Uh, okay?"

"I'm going to a Power Rangers revival," she said. "I really prefer to be Lily, the Yellow Ranger. But last time there were like five Lilys and no Roses, and we couldn't form into a Megazord. The forces of Dai Shi nearly defeated us. The only reason they didn't is because there's never been a *Power Rangers* episode where that actually happened. So we sort of won on a technicality. But it was a hollow victory."

"Right," I said.

"You have no idea what I'm talking about, do you?"

"Not in the slightest."

"Didn't you play with Power Rangers as a kid?"

"Guess not," I said. I have dim memories of Power Rangers coming along, but I think by that point in my development, I had already moved on from things like LEGOs to larger, more challenging toys. Like redheads. If only I had been able to master them as thoroughly as I had the LEGOs.

"Oh, then you'll totally have to come along and check it out. It starts at seven thirty but it's in Jersey City, so we have to hurry. If I'm late, they'll morph without me."

"Well, we wouldn't want that," I said. "Let's get out of here."

Kira got a few curious looks as she threaded through the newsroom in full

Power Rangers regalia. Chances were most of them didn't know it was our otherwise mild-mannered librarian underneath the helmet.

Except for Tina. She knew. Which was fine with me. I had expressed my interest in a relationship with her in every way I knew how and she had rebuffed me every time. If seeing me walk out the door with another woman made her jealous? Well, this may sound small of me, but: good.

I allowed myself a quick peek at her as I rounded the corner. All I saw was Tina shaking her head.

We took my car and within half an hour I was in the somewhat uncomfortable position of being in a room full of people in leotards, not all of whom had bodies intended for spandex. Apparently, there was an overlap between people who liked Power Rangers and people who liked cupcakes.

I had thought being the only person at the party not in costume would shield me from inquiry, but it turns out they just assumed I hadn't gotten into costume yet. As a result, I was pelted with questions about whether I was going to be one of the Jungle Fury Power Rangers or one of the Samurai Power Rangers — and what color I was going to be when that happened. My answer seemed to disappoint them. Apparently there's no such thing as the Khaki Power Ranger.

By the time it was over, I had consumed enough of this concoction they called "Power Juice" that I tossed my keys in Kira's direction and asked her to drive my zord — that's what Power Rangers call their vehicles — to my dojo. Or whatever.

I had hoped that shortly after arriving at my house in Bloomfield, I would start to be able to answer that age-old question: what *does* the Pink Power Ranger wear under her costume?

Except by the time we got there, I was just drunk and sleepy and, more than any of those things, exhausted. The day had taken more out of me than I had thought. It was all I could do to make my legs move once the car came to a halt in my driveway.

Somehow, I trudged up to the house and into my bed. I'm not sure I remember much beyond that, other than being confused. What was my problem? Had I really had *that* much to drink? Had I just not eaten enough munchies at the party to sop up the booze I had poured into my stomach?

Whatever the answer, the night was pure misery. I couldn't get comfortable. If I lay on my side, it hurt. If I lay on my back, that hurt, too. My stomach was no great shakes. The rest of me was all shakes.

I just couldn't get my temperature right. At first I was freezing. Then I was too hot. I would wake up drenched in sweat, only to fall back asleep and wake up shivering.

I also kept having these strange, awful dreams. In one of them, I kept trying to file a story, only I couldn't get my laptop to work. In another, I had been granted this exclusive interview, except I couldn't find my notebook. Then I couldn't find my pen. At a certain point, I couldn't even tell whether I was awake or dreaming. I felt disoriented, whatever state I was in.

I'm not sure I got any real sleep. But when I woke up the next morning, Kira was still there. She was dressed in librarian clothes again and was lying next to me, a damp washcloth next to her.

"Good morning," she said, when she saw my eyes were open.

"Uhhhh," I groaned.

"You had a rough night," she said, as if I weren't already aware of it.

"I can't believe I drank so much."

"Oh, baby, this isn't a hangover," she said. "You're sick. I took your temperature in the middle of the night and it was like 103.5. You have the flu or something. Do you have any Tylenol? I couldn't find any in the medicine cabinet. It would probably make you feel better."

I directed her to the assortment of pharmaceuticals I kept stashed under my sink. She returned with two pills and a glass of water. I accepted both gratefully.

"You're a total sweetheart," I said.

"I just wish you had let me know you were going to get sick. I could have brought my nurse's outfit."

"Rain check? Pretty please?"

She just laughed. As I chased the Tylenol with the water and lay back down, she began running her hand through my hair, which felt delightful. The drugs kicked in a little and I thought I might finally get some good sleep. I was just on the edge of it when a thought wriggled its way into my consciousness:

"Oh, crap," I said.

"What?" she murmured.

"I totally forgot, Pigeon and I are supposed to do an interview this morning."

I started to hoist myself out of bed, but Kira pinned me back down. For ninety-eight pounds, she was pretty strong. Either that, or I still belonged flat on my back.

"You're not going anywhere," she said. "Nurse's orders. Pigeon can handle the interview by herself. She's a big girl."

I considered this and, more to the point, tried to talk myself into exerting the effort that would be required to rise, shower, drive to Newark, and be coherent. I failed to find the will to do any one of them, much less all four.

"Okay," I said. "But let me call Pigeon and let her know I won't be able to make it."

Kira handed me the phone, and I hauled up her number in my contacts — and, yes, it was stored as "Pigeon."

The phone rang once, twice, three times. Then finally I heard a thin, strangled, "Hi, this is Neesha."

"Pigeon, it's Carter. You sound worse than I feel."

"I feel awful, too," she said. "I was up all night. I think I've got the flu or something."

I felt a small prickle at the base of my spine. And it wasn't just from the chills. What were the chances that two able-bodied, healthy young people would simultaneously come down with the influenza virus during a time of year when it was not normally known to be circulating?

Very slim. I called in my regrets to Jackie Orr, telling her I had taken ill and asking her to reschedule until the next morning.

And by the time I hung up, I was thinking, *What if this isn't the flu?*

What if it was the same thing that killed Jackie's grandmother?

Mitch DeNunzio always thought the mob got a bad rap.

Yeah, they ignored some laws. But only laws that were dumb in the first place. And, yeah, they killed people. But only people who deserved to die. And, yeah, they made money. But what's the point of being in the United States of Freakin' America if you can't make a little money?

In a strange way, he always thought some of his crime-family associates were the most principled people anywhere. They had rules and expectations — a code, as Hollywood liked to call it. They followed the code. And as long as you did, too, there was no problem.

Take, say, your friendly neighborhood bookie. Talk about a law that deserved to be broken: the ridiculous prohibition against gambling on sports, something that existed in forty-nine states (bravo, Nevada) for no other reason than that this country was founded by a bunch of Puritans. Now, sure, the local bookie was, technically, operating outside the law by taking bets on sports. But he was also providing a service that people clearly desired.

And he did it in an honorable way. He took all kinds of bets, whether he wanted to or not. If you won, he paid promptly. If you lost, all he expected was the same courtesy.

Now, if you couldn't pay? Well. In the short term, if you were a good customer, he might be understanding about a momentary shortfall. But if you still didn't pay? Well. Didn't he have the right to get upset?

He did. And there was no problem with that, where Mitch was concerned. Because the rules and expectations were clear all along. All the bookie was doing was following them.

Face it, from a moral standpoint, other industries — the supposedly legal ones — weren't nearly as clean. Take those scumbag bankers who threw the economy in the crapper with all the subprime-mortgage stuff, or the Wall Street types who gambled with people's retirement money, or CEOs who bolstered their bonuses by slashing the salaries and benefits of their workers. You want to say they're better than mobsters?

Truth was, Mitch slept fine at night. He was proud of the business he did. His old man had been what some would call a loan shark.

Mitch never called it that — "shark" was such a loaded word. Plus, it had this small-time connotation.

Mitch wasn't small-time. And he thought of himself more as a venture capitalist than as a lender. He did his research. And when he put his money in a project, it was because he knew it was going to provide the kind of return that assured the borrower would be able to return Mitch's principal to him, with a reasonable rate of interest to compensate Mitch for his trouble and risk.

McAlister Arms had attracted his eye for a while. It was just the kind of project he liked — big, complicated, and lacking in oversight. There would be money flowing into it (and out of it) for years. And jobs. And contracts. These were the kind of things that were the grease for his wheels.

He just had to make sure his piece of it was protected. Like a good venture capitalist, he wasn't going to just throw his money at it and walk away. He kept tabs on his projects, made sure they stayed on track. And if he had to do a little something here or there to nudge it toward success?

Well.

Sometimes, that's just what a good venture capitalist did.

CHAPTER 2

Upon making the startling deduction that I had contracted the Ridgewood Avenue Mystery Disease — courtesy of some as-yet-undetermined toxin that had now invaded my body — I responded in the only way I could, given the circumstances: I took a nap.

I was prepared to remain prone for the rest of the day, but several hours later I began to feel marginally better. I woke to the sound of moaning, then realized it was my own: Kira was giving me a nice back rub. That gave me enough strength to get on my feet and into the shower. When I got out, I found a note from Kira, saying she was due at work.

It was disappointing, but she had been thoughtful enough to anchor the note with a Coke Zero. Like most journalists, I am a hopeless caffeine junkie. Unlike most journalists, I hate coffee. Hence, my caffeine-delivery mechanism of choice is whatever diet beverage the Coca-Cola Company has whipped up lately. Kira and I had not known each other very long, but she already understood and appreciated how a cold Coke Zero could make everything right in my world.

Thus fortified, I was again feeling human enough to face Tuesday and the same quandary that had occupied my mind on Monday: what, exactly, was making people sick?

This time, however, I had new information, namely my own experience. And that ruled out a lot. After all, I hadn't drunk the water, eaten the food, licked the walls, or done any number of things that might have exposed me to a variety of pathogens.

All I had done was sit on the couch and breathe the air. And since I had never heard of couch-sitting leading to a pandemic — well, unless you considered watching Jerry Springer a form of disease — that left me with the air as the most likely culprit. What was fouling the skies in that tiny little piece of the South Ward?

The highway seemed like a tempting possibility, but I had to rule it out. The way Jersey people drive could make anyone sick, sure. But if there was truly something noxious being ported along Interstate 78, there would be more than just a few folks who happened to live just off exit 56 getting sick.

It had to be something industrial. And there, New Jersey in general — and Newark in particular — had a long and tainted history. Over the past three centuries or so, the city had been a world leader at making everything from leather to plastics. It was good business back in the day, but a lot of the chemicals used in those processes were still just sitting there hundreds of years later — and would be for all eternity unless someone cleaned them up. New Jersey's reputation as a toxic-waste dump is both unfortunate and, largely, unfair. But it's not entirely unwarranted.

Fact is, there was all kinds of unimaginable goo lurking under our state's surface. Was something from long ago finally working its way to the surface? Had it been on top all along and was just now being stirred up? Whatever it was, some trace amount of it must have wormed its way into people's lungs. Including mine.

By the time I arrived at work, I thought that was the worst of my problems. Then I was confronted by a more immediate one: Tina Thompson was standing in front of the elevator, waiting for it to go in the same direction as I was.

Avoiding Tina had been high on my list of things to do, for reasons more professional than personal. But it was going to be difficult to accomplish that while riding up in the same elevator car. And even though she looked terrific — from floor up: calf-length black boots, gray tights, black skirt, form-fitting white blouse, curly dark hair swept up in a clasp — I tried not to look at her too much. There was no sense in antagonizing her.

"Good morning or, wait," she said, briefly glancing at her watch, "make that good afternoon."

"Hi," I said, keeping my eyes on the numbers as they ticked upward.

"Hey, I still need you to look at that recycling story in your basket," she said, without any hint of rancor.

"Okay," I said. I was waiting for a riposte of some sort, but none was forthcoming. Instead, we reached the floor for the newsroom and she gave me a cheery "See ya!" as we departed.

Suspicious, I logged in to my computer as soon as I got to my desk and hauled up my ode to reuse. Given Tina's previous comments about the story being unfit for the paper it would be printed on, I expected to see a file awash in red, which was the color editors' notes appeared in. But there just a small parcel of red text at the top:

"Carter: This is an outstanding piece of journalism, a pleasure to read and edit. There are a few minor questions below. Please address them and ship the story back to me so we can put it on A1, where it deserves to be! — TT."

Below, there were three questions so insignificant I was able to make the fixes on the spot. I saved the story, shipped it back to Tina, then walked to her open office door. She was seated with her long, lean body in a twisted position, like a minor maharani on her throne — yoga being one of Tina's pastimes.

"Was this a trick?" I asked.

"Huh?" she said, looking up from whatever had been transfixing her on the computer monitor.

"You said yesterday the recycling story was, quote, 'garbage.' Now suddenly you're thrilled about it. What gives?"

"Oh, yeah, I . . . Look, why don't you sit down?"

I sat.

She said, "Can I be honest with you?"

"Always."

"Okay," she said, uncurling herself and placing her hands on her desk and her feet on the floor. "Last night I saw you heading out the door with your girlfriend, the human lollipop, and at first it made me feel, I don't know, angry or jealous or something."

I was going to interject that Kira wasn't my girlfriend, but I didn't want to interrupt a verbal journey that sounded like it was heading toward Apologyland.

She continued: "But then I caught myself. You've given me ample opportunity to have a real relationship, and I've turned down every one of them. Because I don't really want one — with you or anyone, for that matter. So I can hardly blame you for pursuing one with someone else. Even if the person you chose treats every day like it's Halloween, that's hardly reason to despise her. She's got herself a great guy. I shouldn't hate her for that. Or you."

"Oh," I said. "Thanks."

"You're welcome. Anyhow, I'm sorry for being in such a snit with you lately. I really would like to go back to being friends. And colleagues. I hate that I've let our personal relationship cloud my judgment as your editor.

"Which," she said, making a big show of inhaling, "brings us to your recycling story.

I went back and reread it last night and it struck me I had been guilty of malicious editing. I realized if anyone else had handed me that story, I would have been thrilled with it. The only reason I ripped it apart is because it said 'By Carter Ross' at the top. So I went back through and re-edited it more evenhandedly, and I was really quite pleased with what I found."

"Th-thank you," I stammered. I was always a bit uncomfortable when Tina was being contrite. As an editor, Tina was something of a fire-breathing dragon. As a reporter, I always fancied myself the brave and valiant knight, ready to do battle with her. But now suddenly my dragon wanted to stop and cuddle. It was enough to make me wish the fearsome lizard would just keep spitting fire. At least that way I knew to keep my shield up the whole time.

"I mean, let's be serious, I'm about to have to spend the afternoon rewriting Buster Hays. There's not enough Novocain in the world to numb that much pain. Next to him, editing you is a dream. And I ought to give you credit for that."

"Thanks," I said again.

"So what's this other story you're uncorking?" she asked. "Come on, don't make me sweat Pigeon for it."

Ordinarily, I never would have told an editor about a piece that was still such unmolded clay. There would be too much of a temptation for the editor to stick her hands in it and leave messy thumbprints all over. But given Tina's sudden softening, I made an exception to my usual policy and told her what I knew so far.

She agreed with my conclusion that Ridgewood Avenue deserved the *Eagle-Examiner*'s full attention. She gave me the official blessing to continue making use of Pigeon and to continue my search for the truth.

It would have been even better if she could have told me where to find it.

Emerging from Tina's office, I considered my options and quickly decided I needed to enlist the aid of some of my compatriots. Stick around a newspaper for any length of time and you'll realize that some of your best sources of information are the other reporters in the newsroom with you.

I immediately set my sights on Tommy Hernandez, happily clacking away on his computer. Tommy is about five foot seven, maybe 145 pounds, and gay as a box of Shrinky Dinks. He had his hair perfectly mussed and thoroughly moussed and was wearing a tailored shirt with more darts than a dive bar. He also had earbuds in. Tommy sometimes celebrates his Cuban heritage by listening to salsa music; other times, he celebrates certain stereotypes regarding his sexual orientation by listening to vapid pop music.

I couldn't say which he was indulging at the moment. He didn't appear to notice me as I approached him, but I was still a few paces off when he said, "Whatever the question you and your hideous pleated pants are coming to ask, the answer is, 'forget it.' "

Tommy is seldom shy about expressing his distaste for my fashion sensibilities. "How could you even hear me coming? You have music playing."

He looked up at me blank-faced. I pulled one of the buds from his ears. There was no sound coming out.

"You're doing the pretend-to-listen-to-music-so-people-won't-bother-you thing," I said. "You know that just makes me want to bother you more, right? Don't you at least want to know why I'm coming over?"

"No. And do you know why? One, because I'm very busy doing my own work. And, two, because you're coming out of Tina's office, which probably means she's told you not to do something that you are now going to ask me to help you do. I'm not going to be your stooge this time."

"When have I ever recruited you into an act of insubordination?"

"You mean this week? Not yet. But it's only Tuesday, so you're just about on time."

"Actually, I'll have you know, Tina is well aware of what I'm working on and I'm doing so with her full permission."

"Really?" he said, removing the other earbud. "That's sort of weird. What's her angle?"

"It's part of the new détente between us, apparently," I said. "Anyhow, if you're busy, I'll leave you alo—"

"No, I was just saying that so you wouldn't try to talk me into doing something I shouldn't have been doing. I'm really pretty free. What's up?"

I leaned against the desk across the aisle from Tommy. "I was wondering how much you knew about McAlister Arms, that new development that's being proposed in the South Ward."

As city hall reporter, I was betting Tommy would have heard any scuttlebutt surrounding such a large new project.

"Ah, Vaughn McAlister. He seems to be everyone's favorite subject lately."

"How so?"

"He's throwing money around like crazy,"

Tommy said.

"All aboveboard, I'm sure."

"Above the table, below the table . . . with New Jersey's campaign-finance laws, who can tell the difference most of the time?"

"What does he want?"

Tommy shook his hair-product-filled head. "I don't know, specifically. I think he just wants to make sure things keep moving smoothly. You know how it is with developers. Between the banks and their subcontractors and whatever options they might have on the land that are running out, they're always up against one time constraint or another. They're almost as bad as we are when it comes to deadlines. Plus, I'm hearing he has his sights set on bigger things."

"Such as?"

"I don't know. World domination."

"Seriously . . ."

"Well, the rumor is McAlister Properties is laying groundwork for something called McAlister Tower — some big skyscraper filled with Class A office space and a hotel on the top floors and all that. They'd build it right near Penn Station so they could get the PATH crowd and the New Jersey Transit crowd. It sounds like it could be really cool."

I just laughed.

"What?" Tommy said, frowning slightly.

"It's just funny that you haven't been doing this job long enough to get completely jaded yet. Ever hear of Harry Grant?"

"No."

"He was before my time, of course, but ask around. There are people around here who will remember him," I said. "He swept into town in the eighties with this plan to build the world's tallest building right here in Newark — one hundred and twenty-one stories. Everyone thought he had real money because he paid to have the dome atop city hall gilded with gold. But it turned out that was basically the only money he had."

"So what happened?"

"He built the facade for what he called the Renaissance Mall — this was the first stage of the tower — and then he went bankrupt and fled town. The facade stayed there for like two decades before someone finally knocked it down."

"So, what, you think the McAlisters are another Harry Grant?"

I didn't necessarily. Newark had come a long way from those days in the eighties, when it was so desperate for something — anything — to be developed that it was ripe to be plucked by whatever con man stopped off the turnpike. But I just said, "I don't

78

know. You tell me."

Tommy leaned back and pondered it for a moment. "I don't think so. I mean, the McAlisters seem to be legit. This McAlister Arms thing is their first residential project, but they already have a couple of office buildings downtown."

"Yeah, except they didn't build those places. They just took existing buildings and slapped 'McAlister' on them when they bought them."

"True, but they do own and manage them now. That has to count for something."

"Do you know them at all?" I asked.

"I've never met the old man. From what I'm told, he's sort of the backroom guy. Vaughn McAlister is the front man. He's usually around if you want to talk to him."

Tommy pulled his phone out of his pocket and read off a number with a 973 area code.

"You've got his phone number programmed in your phone?"

"The McAlister name comes up often enough. I've probably quoted Vaughn a half-dozen times in the last six months."

"Is he a good guy to deal with?" I asked. And here, of course, I meant it in the way reporters define a good guy. It has little to do with, say, charitable works or a magnanimous personality and everything to do with

79

whether they are quotable and return phone calls promptly on deadline.

"Yeah, good enough. He's a slut for good press. He'll pretend to be busy, but then he'll always magically be able to find time for you."

"Thanks," I said.

Tommy responded with a burst of Spanish, which he often does when he's insulting me.

"Okay, what did you just say?" I asked.

"It translates roughly as: 'Don't thank me. Just buy better pants.' "

As Tommy had predicted, Vaughn McAlister's schedule was absolutely slammed — completely and totally booked solid between now and next Labor Day, with not even a glimmer of hope that he would have time to wave hello if we passed in the hallway — except for the one small opening that happened to have popped up that afternoon. But only because the prime minister of England had canceled at the last second.

I had been somewhat vague as to why I was calling, saying only that I was writing about a neighborhood in the South Ward that was near McAlister Arms. I couldn't very well come out and say that I was worried his construction site was harboring toxic waste. Yet, it struck me during our brief phone chat — as he impressed upon me the monumental inflexibility of his colossally imposing schedule — that he didn't really care what I was calling about.

And, coincidentally, his magical opening was in twenty minutes. Which is about how long it would take me to collect myself, drive to his office downtown, park, and walk to his building.

Arriving at McAlister Place, I breezed through the downstairs security — I could have told them I was Jack the Ripper and they still would have waved me through — then faced a far stiffer inspection upon reaching the second-floor offices of McAlister Properties. A round-faced fortyish woman with shellacked brown hair and a gray skirt suit looked up at me as I entered.

"Hello, may I help you?"

"Hi. My name is Carter Ross. I'm a reporter with the *Eagle-Examiner.* I'm here to see Vaughn McAlister."

Her brow made a V shape in response to this assertion and she glanced at her computer screen. Her desk was as neat as any I'd ever seen. There was exactly one personal effect, a photo of a gawky-looking preteenage boy. Otherwise, the most prominent feature was a brass nameplate: "M. Fenstermacher." I was glad someone put in the

"M." part. Otherwise it would be easy to confuse her with all the other Fenstermachers around.

I knew, from my days of high school language class, that "fenstermacher" meant "window-maker" in German. "Fenster" comes from the Latin "fenestra," which is also the root for one of the world's greatest words, "defenestration," which *Webster's* defines as "a throwing of a person or thing out of a window." It's also what M. Fenstermacher looked like she wanted to do to me at the moment.

"I'm sorry, I don't show you as having an appointment," she said. "Is Mr. McAlister expecting you?"

"He is," I said.

This brought another consternated look and another glance at the computer screen from M. Fenstermacher. Maybe the "M." stood for "Miss," because she didn't have a wedding ring on her finger. She struck me as a woman who did not like surprises. Her immobile hairstyle, impeccable manicure, precisely applied makeup, and utterly clean desk suggested that I was standing in front of a bit of a control freak.

"Wait here, please," she said, rising from her desk.

She rose and I got a whiff of Miss Fenstermacher's perfume. I don't know Chanel from chenille, but it smelled expensive. As she walked toward a set of double doors to her right, I saw her face was not the only part of her that was rounded. She rather amply filled out her gray skirt suit. She wasn't really my type — I like them a little more natural than the painstakingly produced Miss Fenstermacher — and it's not like she was going to win any beauty pageants. But in a (thankfully) bygone era, I'm sure there were bosses who would have chased her around the desk more than a few times.

Just then Vaughn McAlister emerged from the double doors. Miss Fenstermacher brightened considerably upon seeing him. This nightmare that was an unscheduled appointment was about to be over.

"It's okay, Marcia," he announced. "There was a last-second change to the docket and I was able to squeeze Mr. Ross in."

"Thanks for seeing me on such short notice," I said, playing along.

"Thanks for coming," he said.

I smiled at him. He smiled back. I extended a hand. He grabbed it. Vaughn McAlister was a real charmer — blow-dried blond hair, perfect teeth, firm handshake. I immediately recognized the type: he charmed people simply for the sake of charming them. Even if he couldn't immediately predict the benefits, he figured there would be some eventually. It was what he did.

He fancied himself not just as a player but as *the* player — the guy who could make things happen by sheer will and personal magnetism.

What he perhaps didn't understand is that part of being a mature newspaper reporter is being immune to such things. Most of us allowed ourselves to get charmed by a player once, in our early twenties, then learned our lesson.

The only thing about him I found truly impressive was his clothing. He was wearing a sharply tailored blue pinstripe suit that had probably cost more than every pair of khaki pants I had ever bought and Italian loafers that had easily set him back five hundred bucks. Now I knew why Tommy had such a soft spot for him: shoe envy is one of Tommy's tragic flaws.

Vaughn and I tested each other a little bit, swapping a few quick ha-ha lines — about traffic, about weather — then dropping enough names so that each of us knew the other was sufficiently connected. Then we gave up trying to impress each other.

"Hold my calls, Marcia," he said as he invited me into his office.

Miss Fenstermacher would, I was sure, eagerly comply.

There were no more attempts at small talk as I followed him into his nicely appointed office and settled into a chair on the other side of his sleek desk and Cross pen set.

"That's quite a large project you have going down in the South Ward," I said, hauling out my notepad so he knew we were on the record.

"Yes, we're very excited about McAlister Arms," he said with appropriate earnestness. "It's a mixed-use development, as you may know, so people will be able to live there, work there, and shop there. We've got the commercial space pretty well sold and we're going to start opening up the residential units for sale soon as well. We've already had people inquiring about it. This is going to be a real crown jewel for Newark."

Of course it would be. You have to love developer hyperbole: what is actually a very common construction project, built to the same code standards and with the same base materials as everything else, is always a "crown jewel."

"Care to say who the anchoring com-

85

mercial tenant will be?" I asked.

"Not until the ink is dry on the contracts," he said, giving me his best Vaughn McAlister smile. "But it's a major national retailer. This is going to bring jobs to the people of Newark. We've written a first-source agreement into the lease, which means they have to use Newark employment agencies for at least fifty percent of their hires. We've also made our own promise to use eighty percent local labor during construction. This is going to bring jobs to this city. Make sure you put that in whatever you write."

It was a common gripe about development in Newark that it never ended up benefiting the people who lived there. I gave McAlister Properties credit for anticipating that criticism and doing something about it. I was about to ask another question, but I was interrupted by a knock on the door.

"Sorry," he said, then raised his voice slightly: "Come in."

It was Miss Fenstermacher. "I'm very sorry, Mr. McAlister," she said. "But this needs your signature ASAP."

Vaughn acted like he was annoyed by the intrusion, but I suspected he had told Miss Fenstermacher to interrupt, just so I wouldn't forget how Very Important he was.

He took a cursory glance at the document,

then signed it with a big, bold "Vaughn McAlister." The "V" looked like a checkmark. The "M" looked like a bird about to take flight. The rest of it was just squiggles.

"Thank you, Marcia," he said. She smiled gratefully, then departed.

We were interrupted long enough that Vaughn was able to resume the conversation at a spot of his choosing, which, as it turned out, was in a soliloquy. "You may not know this, but my great-grandparents actually lived here in Newark. They came on the boat from Ireland and lived in the North Ward. So this city is really in the McAlister bloodlines and we want to see it thrive again. McAlister Arms is going to be a model for what we can do all over Newark. And the best thing is, it's really going to benefit everyone. We've got subsidized housing for low- and middle-income families mixed in with market-rate units. People from all walks of life will be able to live there."

Ah. So the crown jewel was also going to be capable of social transformation. It was nice to know his hyperbole had lofty goals as well. Now it was time to set the bait a little.

"Wow," I said, trying to sound gee-whizzish. "I was going to speculate whether

McAlister Arms would be another South Ward Industrial Park — you know, something that doesn't live up to its hype. But it sounds like you guys have thought of everything."

"McAlister Arms is going to completely revitalize this part of Newark," he said. "And it's going to be good for the city's coffers, too. The city was willing to give us a ten-year tax abatement, but we insisted on only making it five. This is going to be a real ratables boon, and that's only going to help the city in the long run — more taxes means better schools, better police coverage, a better city."

"And this thing is really going to happen?" I asked. "You've got all the approvals and financing you need?"

He assured me he did, telling me in detail about how they were just finishing grading the property and were already moving materials on-site, and no one would be doing that if they didn't have the project green-lighted. I had already known that — after all, I had seen all the construction trucks the day before — but I wanted to make him feel like the interview was going well, like I was the skeptic who had now been won over.

I was really just setting him up for this

question, which was meant to sound like a throwaway: "I don't even want to know what you must be doing to get that site ready for construction. I know there used to be a bunch of factories down there. They must have left all kinds of awful stuff behind, huh?"

I was hoping he would give me some kind of lead for what might be making these people sick. Something like, *Oh, yeah, we found a big pool of hexavalent chromium just yesterday.* Or, *Yes, they used to make lead paint on that site.*

Instead, he just said, "Oh, well, that's all been cleaned up already."

"It has? Because I heard there were some people getting sick down there. A whole group of folks from the neighborhood, actually," I said, again as an aside.

He absorbed this information, which didn't seem to cause a single hair on his perfect head to move askance.

"Well, they're not getting sick due to anything coming from us. Our remediation process was overseen by a Licensed Site Remediation Professional in strict accordance with state Department of Environmental Protection standards. It didn't even cost us or the city anything. The DEP has grants for brownfields redevelopment. For a private

89

developer, the money can be a bit hard to get. But we had the city working with us. The DEP just loves public-private partnerships. They gave us six million dollars to clean up the site. That was done a while ago. We got it certified and everything."

I kept smiling like this was just more good news. But I was really a bit disappointed. If the remediation had been done a while ago, it meant McAlister Arms wasn't the culprit. After all, I had gotten sick the night before. It had to be a pollutant that was still active in some way.

I asked a few more questions about the development, mainly to keep my cover, then made a hasty departure. Vaughn was as charming upon exit as he was upon entrance. And he said that if I ever wanted to talk again, he would be happy to do so — assuming, of course, he could ever find the time.

It was just my luck that when I left the offices of McAlister Properties, it was three forty-five — which is known for, among other things, being close to four o'clock. And four o'clock, in Newark, meant Professor Rice's teatime.

Dr. Charles Rice was a history professor at Rutgers-Newark and was a much-loved institution in the city. Through some forty years at the university, he had perfected the art of pedantry — right down to the thick glasses and tweed jackets — and he delighted in the traditions and conventions of academia. He treated intellectual squabbles as if they just might lead to the Third World War if the wrong ideas prevailed, and he was known to weigh tenure proceedings with roughly the same seriousness as juries are instructed to consider death-penalty trials.

But he remained on enough of a corresponding basis with the outside world that those of us who lived there could still talk to him. He was eminently quotable, a man who spoke not in clipped phrases or short sentences but in full, eloquent paragraphs. And he was an absolute font of information on Newark. For time-strapped reporters who lacked the patience or expertise for serious scholarly research — self, meet self — Professor Rice was a one-stop shop for all things Newark history. If anyone would know what factory had once been down in that part of Newark, and how it might still be poisoning people now, it would be Professor Rice.

And, at four o'clock every day, he opened his humble office on the third floor of a growing-shabby university building to anyone who felt like visiting and served tea. It was his ode to eighteenth-century French salons, and he viewed it as a time for the intelligentsia of Newark to gather and discuss the important matters of the day.

Sadly, since the intelligentsia of Newark number about twelve — and most of them are busy at four o'clock — this often translated into Professor Rice sitting alone in his office, guzzling a pot of tea by himself. So he appeared to be delighted when I knocked lightly on his open door and said, "Anyone home?"

"Carter, my friend, how are you?" he said warmly.

"I'm doing fine, Professor, it's good to see you again."

We hugged — Professor Rice is a sixty-something-year-old African American man and an unrepentant hugger — and he pointed to one of the chairs in his office. It was a subtle thing, but his desk was shoved up against the wall, meaning you were never on the other side of a slab of wood from Dr. Rice. The chairs and sofas in his office, including his own, were roughly in a circle around the edges of the room. It was one small way he made his space more inviting for conversation.

"I'm so glad you came by," he said. "There's a book I've been wanting to give you."

Professor Rice was always giving me things to read. They were usually pretty good — if you didn't mind half-page footnotes — and they always had titles with colons in them. True to form, he handed me a book that would have made a fine doorstop, entitled *Marginal Color: Deconstructing Ethnicity, Race, and Class among Creoles and Non-Creoles in a Post-Revolutionary Pre-Antebellum Southeastern Louisiana Parish.*

"It kept me up all night," he said earnestly.

"Thanks," I said. "I'll try not to read it when I have any early-morning meetings."

"So what can I do for the *Eagle-Examiner* this afternoon?"

"Well, as usual, Professor, I'm hoping you can give me a quick history lesson," I said, taking out my phone and hauling up Edna Foster's address on Google Maps. "Can you tell me what kind of manufacturing used to happen in this neighborhood?"

I handed the professor my phone. He moved it around until he found the sweet spot in his bifocals, then considered it for a moment or two. He went to a larger map of Newark mounted on his wall and traced his fingers to the address I had given him. It was a modern map, complete with highways and the airport, but Professor Rice had a way of seeing through decades into what the city used to look like. It was actually somewhat uncanny.

From his wall map he went to one of his bookshelves and knelt down to the bottom level. He pulled out a platter-size, four-inch-thick book and hefted it onto a small coffee table with considerable effort.

"What's that?" I asked.

"The 1925 tax assessment of Newark," he said. "They had an extra copy at the Register of Deeds and Mortgages and they were going to throw it out. Can you imagine? Thank goodness someone had the foresight to ask me if I wanted it. Let me tell you, fella, I jumped on it. If you want a snapshot of Newark at its heyday, 1925 is about as good a year as any. The globalization that took the city's factory jobs away hadn't commenced, so all of the industry is still there. A few of the more prominent citizens had started moving out to the suburbs, but the outflow was really just a trickle. It was a good time for Newark."

Without so much as glancing at the index, he opened the enormous book to somewhere in the middle. He flipped two pages and studied it for another moment or two.

"Ah, yes," he said. "I thought so."

"What?" I asked.

"Dentures."

"Dentures?"

"Yes, come here," he said, patting a spot next to him on the couch. I joined him and he pointed to a piece of the map that was now within the McAlister Arms site.

"This was home to a company called K and J Manufacturing," he said. "This would have been a brick building several stories high which employed several hundred people. It was one of the nation's leading manufacturers of dentures."

"Huh," was all I could say.

"My friend, if I may ask, why are you curious about this?"

With any other source, I might or might not have said anything. But while Dr. Rice might be given to the usual academic gossip — like which assistant professors were sleeping and/or trying to sleep with which postdoctoral fellows — he knew when to be discreet with information. So I told him about the illness I was hunting and my suspicion that some long-ago industrial pollutant was the cause.

"Well, in that case, dentures are a good choice," Professor Rice said.

"Yeah, I guess they must have been made of, what, plastic or something?"

"Not in the nineteenth and early twentieth centuries, my friend. No, no. Back then, they were made of vulcanized rubber."

"You mean, like, tires?"

"Well, yes and no. The vulcanization process is part of making tires. But it also had many other industrial applications, including dentures."

"Think there's some byproduct of the vulcanization process that might be capable of making people sick a century later?" I asked.

Professor Rice struck an appropriately contemplative pose. "Well, chemistry isn't my area. But if I've learned nothing else about the kind of manufacturing that used to take place in Newark, it's that it's almost always unhealthy to someone somehow. You know what resource I refer to in matters such as these?"

Professor Rice was a scholar's scholar, so I was thinking it had to be some weighty academic publication. Something like, say, the *International Journal of Super-Smart Stuff Quarterly Review*.

"I couldn't even guess," I said.

"Wikipedia," he said, turning to his computer. "Let's see . . ."

He typed for a moment, then started muttering to himself, "Sulfur . . . that would smell awful, but I'm not sure it has any health effects like the ones you describe. Zinc oxide . . . I think that's part of most suntan lotions, so I doubt that's the culprit. Stearic acid? That sounds bad."

"Yeah, except I think it's found in just about every shampoo ever made, so that's not it."

"Then how about this: thiocarbanilide," he said, chewing over each syllable.

"What's *that*?"

"Well, I guess it was used starting in the early twentieth century as an accelerant in the vulcanization process."

"Is it harmful? Anything with that many syllables has to be bad for you, right?"

"I don't know," he said. "Let's see . . . Wikipedia mentions something about a lethal dose . . . huh . . . oh my."

He cleared his throat and started reading from another document: " 'May cause ataxia, analgesia, convulsions, and respiratory distress, including cyanosis.' "

I had pulled out my notebook and was writing it down. "Ataxia, analgesia . . . None of this sounds very healthy, but do you know what they are?"

"Not at all, my friend," he admitted. "Oh,

wait, look at this: 'Severe overexposure may result in death.' "

"Oh, I think I know what that is," I said. "I'm no doctor, so this is an unschooled opinion. But death . . . that's not a good thing, is it?"

"Definitely not," he confirmed. "Not good at all."

My parting gift from the good professor's office was a book called *New Jersey Makes: A Non-Marxian Sociohistory of Neo-Industrial Pre-Postmodern Manufacturing in the Garden State*. It made the doorstop of a book he had given me earlier look like a mere pamphlet. From a quick glance at the introduction, which was filled with prose as dense as it was impenetrable, it struck me as something that should have been regulated by the Food and Drug Administration as a sleeping aid.

But it did contain a chapter about K&J Manufacturing, which told the story of a son of Norwegian immigrants who rose from humble origins to become one of the most prominent men in New Jersey.

Klaus Josef Jorgensen had been the founder of K&J Manufacturing in the 1880s and perfected the process by which vulcanized dentures were manufactured. He eventually passed the business onto Klaus Josef Jorgensen, Jr., who turned K&J into a national denture powerhouse that supplied a significant portion of early-twentieth-century America's fake teeth — and compiled a significant fortune in the process.

Klaus Josef Jorgensen III took that fortune and diversified it, getting out of business — by then, dentures were starting to be made of different materials — and investing heavily in railroads, textiles, and other businesses that may have seemed like good bets in the midtwentieth century but were actually soon to go into significant decline. In the book, this was treated as more or less the end of the K&J Manufacturing story, except for one footnote.

It pertained to Klaus Josef Jorgensen IV, who recognized his father's blunder of being too backward-thinking. So, when he took over the family business in the mid-1960s, he again repositioned K&J to harness a technology that he was convinced was going to revolutionize the way data was collected and stored, leading to a flowering of information-sharing the likes of which the world had never seen. Yes, his vision was for K&J to be a global leader in the manufacture and supply of microfilm.

"By the year 2000, every American family

will have a microfilm reader in its living room," Klaus IV confidently predicted in one document cited. "And microfilm will have replaced letter-writing as the preferred method of private communication among the middle and upper classes. The market for microfilm will be limited only by our capacity to produce it."

There was no mention in the book about how this bold prophecy had turned out. All there was, at the end of the chapter, was a picture of the Jorgensen family's Madison, New Jersey estate, shot from Route 124.

I recognized the part of Route 124 where the picture had been taken — it was a bend in the road just as you got out of Madison proper, on your way to Morristown. I didn't recognize the house itself. For as many times as I had driven that road — Route 124 used to be part of my beat when I worked in one of the *Eagle-Examiner*'s suburban bureaus — I was quite sure I had never seen anything like the stately mansion portrayed in the photograph. It looked like something that had been built by one of the Vanderbilts, all limestone and marble and Gilded Era opulence.

I was sitting in my car as I finished up my assigned reading and I made the snap decision to visit the mansion. Perhaps some member of the Jorgensen clan was living there and could tell me whether K&J Manufacturing was still alive in some form — and whether it might be willing to take responsibility for the medical costs and cleanup of the poisonous legacy it had left in Newark.

If not, then K&J Manufacturing and its heirs would still fill an important role in my article. Just as every good story needs a victim, which Edna Foster had so unfortunately become, it also needs a villain. And I didn't mind admitting that it would serve my purposes quite well if the villain happened to be some spoiled, wealthy, aloof lockjaw who couldn't bother to spit the silver spoon out of his mouth long enough to give me more than a hasty "no comment" when I knocked on his door.

I was still daydreaming about that scenario when I cleared the last of the lights in Madison and reached the spot on Route 124 where the picture had been taken. I understood immediately why I had never seen any palatial homes there: the property was overgrown with a dense forest of trees and shrubs, all of which were badly in need of trimming.

I turned into the front entrance, past a magnificent stone entryway and a wrought-iron gate that appeared to have been secured into the open position by a thicket of vines and brambles. I slowed so I could make out the tarnished brass nameplate on the gate. The place was named "Masticatoria."

Mastica . . . as in "masticate"? Someone in the Jorgensen family had apparently taken the dentures thing a little too seriously.

The driveway spiraled up and to the right. It had once been paved but was now just a crumbling patchwork of moss and broken chunks of asphalt. The landscaping continued to look as if it was being tended to by a manservant who was allergic to clippers. And trimming. And mowing. And weeding. And . . . work in general.

At the top of the drive was Masticatoria itself. It had clearly seen better days. There were places where the roof had lost its terracotta shingles. One of the stone chimneys was falling down. Another appeared to have become a well-populated squirrel nest. Ivy covered many of the windows. Things that should have been straight hung at odd angles.

The joint had an uninhabited feel to it. There was just no way some blueblood would allow the family manse to fall into such disrepair. Either it was abandoned or it was now the happy abode of the Munster family.

Still, I had come all this way. It would cost me nothing to knock on the door. I pulled my car to the top of the driveway, which ended in a massive half circle — for turning around four-horse carriages, no doubt — parked, and walked up a set of marble steps to a front door that was at least twelve feet tall. I grasped an enormous brass knocker, which let out a spine-tingling creak as I brought it toward me, then let it drop.

A heavy thudding sound echoed through the inside of the house. I thought that would be the only sound coming from this enormous and empty mansion before I turned around and called it a night.

Then, surprisingly, I heard footsteps.

The man who answered the door appeared to be about my age, about my height, and about my skin color. But that is where our similarities ended.

His hair looked like it hadn't seen a pair of scissors in a decade or a comb in twice that long. His beard could have been used to hide a week's worth of foodstuffs — and, for all I knew, it was. He was wearing a threadbare T-shirt over a torso that was more bone than muscle and a pair of jeans that were torn from long wear, not in any kind of fashionable way. He was barefoot. His body odor preceded him by several arm's lengths. But other than that, he seemed harmless enough.

"Hi, can I help you?" he asked in a friendly way.

Yeah, I wanted to say, *could you please, for the love of my olfactory nerves, take a shower?* Instead I went with: "Hi, my name is Carter Ross. I'm a reporter with the *Eagle-Examiner.* This is going to seem like an odd question, but is your last name Jorgensen by any chance?"

"Yeah," he said.

"Are you . . . Klaus Josef Jorgensen by any chance?"

"People call me Quint," he said.

Quint, as in Klaus Josef Jorgensen V. He was not exactly the lockjaw I was hoping for. He looked more like a body double for Tom Hanks's character in *Castaway* — after he's been on the desert island eating nothing but coconut for a couple of years.

"Nice to meet you," I said. "This is some place you got here."

"Used to be. Now it's a real dump, huh?" he said, still grinning.

"No, no, that's not what I meant."

"Yes it is," he insisted, and his smile went

even wider, as if he was proud of it. "I wish I could sell it, but my trust explicitly states I can't. Seems like a waste to let it sit empty, so, well, this is where I live. Think it could use a touch-up or two?"

He was obviously joking, so I went along with it. "Well, maybe the trees could stand a bit of trimming."

Suddenly the smile went away. "Trim? Never! We need those trees to sequester as much carbon as possible! Come on, dude, get with the program!"

I looked at him closely to see if he was kidding. He wasn't. Not even slightly. Was it possible the heir to whatever remained of the K&J Manufacturing fortune was . . . a rabid environmentalist?

"Right," I said. "Right, of course."

I was trying to come up with something intelligent to say about global warming when he said, "Want to come in, dude?"

No, I want you to learn how to groom yourself, I almost said, but opted for: "Sure." Then, before it sounded too self-conscious, I added, "Dude."

Then I walked over the threshold of Masticatoria. As a reporter, I've been in all kinds of houses: the homes of hoarders, where there are nothing but thin trails of open floor between piles of stuff; the homes of

OCD sufferers that smell like the inside of a Lysol can; the homes of collectors, who decorate their entire abodes with stamps/butterflies/purple unicorns or whatever their fetish happens to be.

But I had never been in a place quite like this. Every room was huge, beautiful, ornate, opulent — and empty.

So my brief tour of Masticatoria included a trip through the (empty) foyer, down an (empty) hallway, past an (empty) library, and into a sitting room where there was nowhere to sit except for a few bamboo mats that had been arranged in a circle.

"Take a load off," he said, pointing to one of the mats. He caught my incredulous look, which I wasn't quite quick enough to hide, and added, "I'm not really big into furniture. It's a waste of resources."

"Yeah, I think I saw something like this on the Home and Garden Channel once," I said. "They called it 'barren chic.' "

I chose a spot that I deemed to be upwind from his aroma.

"So what can I do for you?" he asked.

"Well, I'm doing some reporting about a neighborhood in Newark that's near where one of your family's factories used to be," I said. "I was hoping you could tell me: what has become of K and J Manufacturing?"

"Oh, wow," he said, then launched into a version of the company history that was a bit more detailed — and a bit more sarcastic — than what I had read in the history book. But it ended in the same spot: Klaus Josef IV had mismanaged K&J into the ground and then died a brokenhearted early death. All that was left of the family fortune, Quint said, was the house — minus the furniture, which he gave to a museum — and something he called the 2077 Trust.

"The 2077 Trust?" I asked.

"It continues paying me a set amount a year until 2077, at which point I will turn a hundred and, the trustees assumed, either be too old or too dead to care."

He cast a sly glance to the left and right. "I tell the trustees all I do is sit around and smoke pot all day. And I always send them e-mails at four A.M. so they think I'm partying all the time. But the truth is, I've made all sorts of money that I've hidden from them. I'm currently invested in several very promising green-energy technologies. But you can't print that, because it'll ruin my fun."

"Okay," I said. "We'll make that last part off the record."

"Whatever, dude. Anyhow, I don't mean to be rambling. Why do you even want to know about this stuff?"

I was so thrown by what I was witnessing — the scion of industrialists living as a barefoot hippie in a decomposing mansion — that I couldn't even come up with a subtle way to phrase what came out next:

"Well, to be honest, I think something left behind by your family's denture-making operation is somehow surfacing and making people in the neighborhood sick."

"Really?" he said, like this intrigued him. "What are you thinking is the culprit? Do you know?"

"Thiocarbanilide."

Thinking back to the professor's rather grim warning — "severe overexposure may result in death" — I imagined that merely uttering the word would elicit a shudder from him, as if saying, "You've got thiocarbanilide poisoning" was the chemical equivalent of saying, "You married a Kardashian."

Instead, the face Quint made under his beard was more curious than menacing. "What kind of symptoms are these people reporting?" he asked.

I ran down the litany of problems, from the flu to broken bones. He was already shaking his head.

"That's not thio," he said, as if it were his

friend and he was defending its reputation.

"How do you know?"

"Because I'm a Jorgensen. When I was a kid, we used to sit around at the dinner table talking about chemistry the way other families talked about the weather. Thiocarbanilide decomposes when left open to the elements, so it's hard to imagine any of it still being around after all this time. Besides, it's organic. I'm sure it would kick your ass if you tried to eat it for breakfast, but there's no way it could cause the kind of stuff you're talking about."

I had taken chemistry in my sophomore year of high school. I remembered very clearly that Myra Merkle sat in the front row of that class. I remembered very little else about it.

"If you don't believe me, you can look it up," Quint continued. "Look, I'm not saying K and J didn't leave *something* down there that's making people sick. I'm just saying it's not thio."

"So what would it be?"

"Who knows? Could be anything. If you want, I could think about it, call some of my environmental people."

"You have environmental people?" I asked. Too bad he didn't have deodorant people.

"Well, yeah. My trust requires that I

109

donate a certain amount of money each year, but it doesn't say where. That money was made by some industries that made the Earth a pretty dirty place. It seems only right to give it away to people who are trying to clean it up. So I give it all to a variety of small environmental groups."

"Oh, that's nice."

"To be honest, I'm mostly just in it for the protests. I do love a good protest," he said, allowing his mind to drift off for a moment, doubtlessly to some picket-toting sit-in of yore. Then he snapped back to and concluded, "Anyway, when you donate fifty, a hundred grand a year to these small groups, they tend to pick up the phone when you call. Let me kick it around with them."

As tempted as I was to sit around and swap decorating tips, I didn't want to overstay my welcome. And, besides, Quint's stench was starting to make my eyes water. So we exchanged contact info and I made my way out of the odd netherworld that was Masticatoria and back into the real one of Madison, New Jersey, where people viewed their trees more as landscaping than as carbon-sequestration devices.

It was after six o'clock, a perfectly acceptable hour for a reporter not on deadline to end his working day. It was also a time when, having now fully shaken off the effects of the dread mystery flu, I was getting a little hungry. So, knowing that my hometown of Millburn was just a few minutes away, I called a very familiar phone number and said five words I knew I would probably come to regret: "Hey, Mom, what's for dinner?"

My mom is a retired schoolteacher who still cooks like she has a family of five to feed. My dad is a retired pharmaceutical executive who tells her to cut it out. She seldom listens, and I occasionally avail myself of this fact to get a home-cooked meal in my stomach.

Of the three Ross children, I am the only one to have stayed in the great Garden State, though none of us went terribly far. My brother, Tyler, is a lawyer for a big firm in Washington, D.C. My sister, Amanda, is a social worker in Philadelphia.

None of us has produced offspring yet, but my parents remain forever hopeful. Tyler was married but childless. Whenever my parents asked him when he and my sister-in-law planned to have children, Tyler would tell them, "We're thinking about it." To which my father always replied, "Well, son, you know you have to do more than think about it, right?"

Then there was me. Girls had been telling me I was "marriage material" since I was sixteen. Yet, here I was, at thirty-two, still stuck in bachelorhood. Not even dating exclusively. When my parents asked if I ever thought about having children, I made vague noises without words attached to them. The fact was, future generations of Carter Rosses were not in my immediate or even intermediate plans. They were like the promise of more-energy-efficient cars: forever five to ten years off.

Given the disappointment that was their sons, my parents' great hope for grandchild production had become Amanda. After a series of boyfriends who seemed never to last very long, she had finally gotten serious with this guy named Gary. He was a New Jersey state trooper, and while this gave me endless amounts of material for ribbing — about their uniforms being inspired by Nazis, about the whole racial-profiling thing, about that racing club some of their troopers escorted down the parkway a few years back, and so on — the truth was I had always been impressed in my dealings with New Jersey's cops. There were a few rogue idiots who occasionally gave reporters like me a lot to write about. But generally they were top-notch professionals. And Gary was, all teasing aside, a heck of a good guy.

So when Amanda announced she and Gary were getting hitched, it was a cause for great celebration — and then, at least on my mother's part, obsession. Ever since the engagement, Mom had been treating mother-of-the-bride duties like it was North Africa and she was General Patton. In a tank. And now that the wedding was this coming weekend? She was no longer recognizing the Geneva convention.

Hence, I was barely inside the door before my mother started with:

"I've been thinking about the rehearsal dinner. Cocktails start at five, which I think is too early, but this is Gary's parents doing the planning for this part, so I didn't get a say. But it would be nice if we all went over together. If we leave here at four forty-five we should get there in plenty of time. So why don't you plan on being here by four thirty on Friday?"

"Hi, Mom," I said. "How are you?"

"And you're sure you're not bringing anyone to the wedding? It's not too late you know. There's an empty seat at your table."

From somewhere inside the house, my

dad hollered, "Trish, would you leave him alone?"

"Bill, he's the only one without a plus-one. It's making the seating unbalanced," she yelled back, as if I weren't there. She turned her attention to me and said, "What about your friend Tina?"

Mom always referred to Tina as "your friend Tina." She always said the "your friend" part with this hint of collusion, like Tina and I were really deeply in love and not telling anyone, and Mom was steadfastly keeping our secret. It was clearly wishful thinking on Mom's part. She and Tina had met several times and they always hit it off fabulously.

"Sorry, Mom. That's not happening."

"She's such a nice woman and it would be so lovely to have her at such an important family gathering," she continued, as if I hadn't just spoken. "You just have to let me know by Thursday. That's when I have to give the caterer a final count."

"Mom!" I said sharply enough to get her attention. "Tina barely even talks to me anymore. We're" — I waved my arms in a frustrated gesture — "not going to any weddings, okay? Not someone else's and certainly not our own. So get Tina out of your head. She's out of mine."

114

Mom acted like she still didn't believe me, but nevertheless she said, "Well, maybe you'll meet a nice girl at the rehearsal dinner on Friday night. Maybe Gary has a cousin or something."

I hadn't told my parents about Kira yet. When I was a teenager, I learned not to give my parents too much information about my romantic life. I think there was a time in early adulthood when I started telling them more — after all, they couldn't ground me or take away my car anymore — then, after a little more time, I realized I had actually had the right idea when I was a teenager.

My parents tended to act as if our time together were a White House press briefing and I was the president. They would keep peppering me with inquiries until I finally stepped away from the podium and told them I wasn't taking any more questions. So I had learned that the less they knew when it came to relationships — call that area of my life domestic policy — the more time they would spend asking me about work, friends, or other subjects that might be called foreign policy. And, ask any president except perhaps the second George Bush: foreign policy is always easier to talk about.

Every once in a while my dad would try

to pull me aside and, man-to-man, ask me if I was getting any "mud for my turtle" — or any number of other colorful euphemisms for The Act. But I wasn't fooled: he was going to report back to Mom a sanitized version of anything I said.

So I just deflected any more talk about my romantic life all the way through dinner, a delicious and suitably WASPy meal of tuna casserole, baby spinach salad, and couscous. We were just finishing up when my phone rang. Before I could think about the ears around me, I answered it with, "Hi, Tina."

Mom just beamed.

Then came five more words I knew I would come to regret, this time not from my mouth, but from Tina's: "Hey, wanna grab a beer?"

I somehow escaped the Ross ancestral home with only minor prodding about the nature of Tina's call or the implications of her invitation. It probably helped that this was one time I wasn't being intentionally obscure: I really didn't know what Tina's agenda was.

As I drove, I found myself daydreaming that she was finally going to drop all her walls and say she was ready to give our relationship the shot it deserved. Right. And then we would fly with a flock of unicorns to a magic palace in the sky where the friendly king would insist we spend the rest of our days having sex and eating bacon.

No, there were four real possibilities. One, she really was trying to reestablish platonic, friendly relations (surely a doomed effort, given our history and chemistry). Two, she was merely pretending to be friends, and was in fact sneakily renewing efforts to entice me into being her sperm donor (which I wasn't game for). Three, she was horny and looking for another booty call (which I promised myself I would resist, with the caveat that I was incapable of doing so). Or, four, Tina being Tina, I never really would figure it out; and we would continuing drifting on a round-the-world ocean current that kept us moving in the same waters a few feet apart (which seemed the most likely scenario).

And maybe, eventually, I would figure things out well enough with Kira that I could decide, once and for all, to launch myself into a different stream. At this point, Kira was still too new to make such bold decisions. To change metaphors, it would be like deciding to transfer to the college of a girl you'd just met.

Per Tina's instructions, I went to 27 Mix, a favorite Newark watering hole of ours. She was already there when I arrived, seated at a table against the wall. She waved when I entered, not that it was hard to pick her out. It was a Tuesday night at a time when the after-work crowd had thinned and the college crowd hadn't arrived yet. Plus, she was still in the same outfit from earlier in the day, the one with the long boots and the short skirt. The only difference was she had let her hair down. A man tends to notice the hottest woman in any room, and on this night — as with many others — that woman was Tina.

I went to the bar, grabbed myself a tasty, microbrewed IPA, then joined her at the table. In hindsight, the first thing that should have set off alarms in my head was that she wasn't drinking. But I didn't notice that. Not yet, anyway. We small-talked for about twenty minutes or so, until I drained my first beer. I stood and said, "I'm getting another. You want anything?"

"I'm not thirsty," she said.

And that's when I noticed she wasn't drinking.

"What do you mean you're not thirsty?" I asked. "Last I talked to you, you were about to edit Buster Hays. That usually makes you

118

parched."

She forced out a laugh, tucked her hair behind her ear in a way she knew I loved, patted me playfully on the arm, and said, "Just go get your beer, silly."

I sat back down. "Okay, now you're trying to distract me by flirting with me. And usually that would work fine, because I'm a guy and I fall for that kind of stuff. But as you may or may not be aware, I'm also a newspaper reporter, which means I'm a trained observer of the human condition and have an inquisitive nature. So, with that in mind: what's up, Tina?"

She looked down at the table, grabbed the salt shaker, poured out a small pile, and began making patterns with the grains. I just sat there, waiting for an answer. Tina knew I wasn't going to let her dodge the question.

"So remember that night a little while ago when you came over to my house for dinner and you started rubbing me and one thing led to another?" she asked.

I was relieved: we were finally going to talk about It. The It that had been blocking any meaningful communication in our relationship like a series of strategically placed Jersey barriers. This was good. Great, actually. Maybe not as great as sex and bacon for eternity. But it was a good start.

"Yeah, I remember," I said. "I believe you said later it was a booty call."

"Right," she said. "And it was. Believe me, it was."

The unicorns and I were now hoping she was going to say that *at the time* it was a booty call, but she was realizing it was — and could be — so much more. Instead, she just played with salt a little more, mounding it into something resembling a circle and then spreading it out again.

"Tina?" I prompted.

"Yeah, right," she said, still not looking at me. "So, remember when I said I was on the pill?"

I felt the bottom of my stomach drop somewhere well below sea level. "Yes?"

"Well, they give you these little warnings about how you're supposed to take them at the same time every day, but I thought that was some kind of urban legend. I mean, how can that possibly matter as long as you remember to take it at some point, right?"

I was too stunned to say anything. She continued: "I started off saying I'd take them first thing in the morning, but it always seemed to slip my mind. So I thought I'd just take them when I leave work every night. The only problem is, sometimes I leave work at seven or eight. And sometimes, when I'm the one who's putting the paper to bed, I don't leave until one in the morning. And, well, apparently, that thing about taking it at the same time? That's not an urban legend after all."

"So you're . . ." I couldn't quite make myself say the word.

"Yeah," she said.

"How long?"

"I was supposed to get my period on Friday. By Sunday, I started getting suspicious. I've never been more than one or two days late my entire life."

"Oh," was all I could say, even if I wished I could be more articulate.

She finally looked up at me with those big, brown eyes that had a surprising amount of fear in them. Tina had been planning to have a baby for years — she was the only childless woman I knew who owned nipple shields. Even if she had recently changed her mind, I didn't figure it would take too much mental gymnastics for her to flip back to mommy mode. Yet, she looked somewhere between lost and terrified.

"I'm sorry," she said, tears welling in her eyes.

"For what?"

"I don't want you to think I . . . I don't

know, tricked you or trapped you or some- thing. I mean, there was a long time when I wanted you to, you know, get me knocked up. But I was never going to do it without your consent."

"Oh, I never thought —"

"And you should know I won't expect anything in the way of child support or anything," she said, straightening herself. "This was my fault. It's my baby. As far as I'm concerned, no one even has to know you're the father."

"Tina," I said. "I want to be the father. I want to be more than just the father. You know that."

She looked gorgeous and frightened and I just wanted to be with her. I went over to her side of the table to kiss her, hug her, do something to physically reassure her. But she jutted a flattened palm into my midsec- tion.

"No," she said. "You are *not* taking advan- tage of my vulnerability that way. Forget it. I shouldn't have told you anything."

"Tina, I —"

"Look, I know what you're thinking," she said, and began mocking my voice. " 'Oh, poor Tina. Oh, poor single mom. Whatever will she do without a big strong man like me to provide for her?' "

"That's not what —"

"You *love* to be Carter Ross on your big white horse, riding in to save the damsel. Well, guess what? This damsel doesn't need saving, okay? So you can just pack up your horse and go home."

She stood so violently she nearly knocked the chair over, grabbed her clutch off the table, and began walking with great determination to the front door.

"Tina," I said again, but she wasn't stopping. She slammed through the door and out onto the street. I gave chase until she whirled and faced me.

"Leave me alone," she yelled.

"Tina, can we —"

"I've got pepper spray in my purse," she said, reaching into her bag. "Am I going to have to use it on you?"

I stopped five feet short of her. I didn't really want to spend the next half hour of my life in agony, gasping for breath, wiping snot and tears off my face. More to the point, I recognized that, just perhaps, Tina was not yet in a place where she could have meaningful discourse on this subject.

Without another word, she turned from me, walked another twenty feet to her car, started the engine, and tore off.

■ ■ ■ ■

For at least five minutes, I stood there on Halsey Street, contemplating what had just transpired. In one short snippet of conversation — most of which I spent watching a woman make patterns with salt — I had the profound sense that everything about my life had changed, even if I didn't fully understand how.

I had observed it in other parents, though. There was a kind of wisdom that having children seemed to bestow on them. Something about replicating life put their own existences in a drastically different perspective. I had seen it in my friends who had kids, who tried to explain to me what it was like — and how it had changed them — and after tossing out a few well-worn clichés, they just gave me that look that said, *Yeah, you won't get it until you've been here.* I had also seen it in the young — often too young — parents I had written about in Newark. For as much as I exceeded them in terms of education, life experience, and worldliness, they had a certain knowledge about humanity that I plainly lacked. It felt like they knew what It — the big It — was all about. And I couldn't even guess.

Yet, here I was, suddenly thrust onto that path. For whatever Tina had to say about it, I knew absentee fatherhood wasn't an option for me. It never had been, which is why I had never taken Tina up on the offer to be her sperm donor in the first place. Once Tina cooled down, she and I could sort out what this meant for us. But I was going to have a relationship with my child. That I knew.

I also knew that meant there was a time in my suddenly immediate future when I was no longer going to be happy-go-lucky bachelor Carter. And I wasn't just going to be a newspaper reporter, either. I was going to be someone's dad. If there was a more important-sounding job title, I hadn't heard it yet.

Okay. So. Fatherhood. I had thought it was like the promise of more-energy-efficient cars, ignoring that most major automakers already offer hybrids.

I couldn't really wrap my head around it. Right now, inside my colleague, editor, and sometimes-friend Tina Thompson, there was a small seed of a human being that was one-half me. In six weeks, as I'd learned from friends who had gone through this whole thing, that cluster of cells would have its own heartbeat. Sometime a little later —

in time to be able to pick colors for a nursery, anyway — we'd know the gender. And then, if all went well, roughly nine months after an evening that started with an innocent booty call, an actual human being would come bursting out, howling and bloody and primed for a lifetime in which the world would change more than any of us could possibly imagine.

And I was going to be one of the two people explicitly charged with preparing the little bugger for it. I imagined it would start with the relatively simple stuff, like eating and pooping. Those are about the only tricks babies come out with, right? But I was reasonably sure more-complex operations would soon have to follow. Like walking. And riding bikes. And throwing balls. And being turned down for the prom. And writing college essays. And . . .

They were thoughts that, quite frankly, terrified me. I was barely a responsible cat owner, for goodness sake. Merely having to take Deadline to the vet once a year felt like an awesome burden. Was I ready for an undertaking roughly a million and fifty times more challenging? Could I honestly say, standing there on Halsey Street in Newark, New Jersey, that I possessed even one-tenth of the wisdom, patience, and stamina to deal with that?

Hell no.

The only thing that allowed me to so much as put one foot in front of another was the sneaking suspicion there were several billion other parents in the planet's relatively recent history who weren't ready for it either. Yet, it happened to them all the same. So I might as well get used to the idea that it was about to happen to me.

As best as I could see it, I had two short-term options. One, I could go back into the bar and get so mind-blowingly drunk I didn't have to remember the shame of being shoveled into a cab several hours later. Or, two, I could settle my tab and head to Tina's place in Hoboken — and make it clear to her I had arrived not on a white horse but in a used Chevy Malibu.

I have to admit, I was undecided as I stumbled, feeling a bit light-headed, back into 27 Mix and got the bartender's attention.

"Want another?" he asked.

And then it struck me: this was what fatherhood was about. It wasn't about having to figure out, right at this very instant, whether eleven was an appropriate age to get your ears pierced or whether it was okay to sleep over at Jackson's house. It was about trying your best, which you did by attempting to make one good decision at a time.

"Actually, I'll just take the check," I said.

I was feeling like a father already. That was good decision number one. Number two was going to Tina's house right now and insisting we talk about this. Yes, it was her fetus — possession being nine-tenths of the law and all that. But it was going to be my baby, too. And it wasn't fair of her to think she had the monopoly on all the worry, work, and anticipation that came with that.

Having made that decision, paid my check, and gotten back into my car, I pointed myself toward I-78 and Tina's place. There was a Devils game getting out of the Prudential Center, so I eschewed Broad Street and instead went through the neighborhoods to reach the highway.

And that was the only reason I happened to bump into the large collection of police vehicles congregated near one of the entrance ramps. I slowed when I saw that all the activity seem to be concentrated on the corner of the McAlister Arms construction site.

I glanced at the clock. I was perhaps ten minutes behind Tina — less, if she had gotten caught in hockey traffic. Deciding she could use a little more time to cool off, and perhaps a little too lost in deep and ponderous thoughts to make the more rational decision — like that this was a story I should have just sat out — I grabbed a fresh notepad and hopped out of my car.

More than likely, it would be another senseless, heartbreaking, run-of-the-mill ghetto shooting — some 'banger killing another 'banger for reasons that couldn't possibly matter as much as the value of the human life being lost. It was tragedy that was both unremarkable and unfathomable. If a newspaper actually tried to make some shred of sense out of it for its readership, we would exhaust every column inch of our news hole every single day and still barely scrape the surface. So instead we brushed it off with three quick paragraphs and a weary shrug. It would take me no more than ten minutes to gather those paragraphs and send them in.

There were floodlights up, but the police hadn't had time to set up crime scene tape. So I wandered as close as I thought I could get away with. I spied a uniformed cop who was just standing around, only slightly less guilty of loitering than me, and approached him. He was black and young, a rookie for sure. That was perfect, because it meant he wouldn't recognize me.

"Hey," I said. "What's going on?"

"Homicide," he said. "It's actually one of yours."

"What do you mean, 'one of mine'?"

"It's a white guy," he said.

"No kidding," I said. It wasn't unheard of for white people to be killed in Newark. Every once in a while, a suburbanite in town to buy drugs would be shot during a deal gone bad. Or it could be a bum who got rolled by a car whose driver hadn't bothered to stick around. But it was just unusual enough that my curiosity was piqued.

"Young guy? Old guy?" I asked.

"Somewhere in the middle," the cop said. "My partner is the one who found him. We were just driving along and we saw the body."

I was going to ask more questions, but a sergeant started steam-walking in our direction. "Hey, no reporters! This is private property," he barked.

I took three steps backward onto the sidewalk and grinned at him. "And now it's public property," I said. "Good evening, Officer."

He glared at me, but I walked away before he could invent some new reason why I was breaking the law. I continued on my way, rounding the corner, seeing if I could position myself for a better look at things.

Shortly thereafter, I got it. And it caused me to utter a phrase that would not be printed in a family newspaper. The blow-dried blond hair was the first thing I saw, followed by the sharply tailored blue pin-stripe suit and the expensive Italian loafers.

The corpse was facedown and the back of its head was conspicuously concave — an arrangement that was likely made sometime around the time of death — but there was no question in my mind:

It was Vaughn McAlister.

They set him up, then they put him down.

Vaughn McAlister had been working late, poring over some contracts, when his office phone rang. It was an internal extension, from downstairs. The front security desk at McAlister Place.

"Yes, what is it?" he said, annoyed.

"There's a courier delivery here for you, Mr. McAlister," a man said. The voice wasn't familiar to McAlister, but he didn't give it much thought. The security company he used was constantly shuffling in new people.

"Okay, just tell him to leave it with you. I'll be down later."

"He says he can't," the man told him. "It's urgent and he needs to get the signature of the addressee. That's you."

"Oh, for the love of . . . Fine, I'll be right down," McAlister said. He wasn't expecting any urgent courier deliveries and the ones that came unexpectedly were seldom good news. Especially at this time of night.

McAlister took the elevator one story down to the lobby. The moment he emerged, the back of his head became impressed with the blunt end of an old-school Louisville Slugger, the heavy kind preferred by the home-run hitters of yesteryear and the thugs of today. McAlister immediately crumpled, falling forward. Two more swings finished him off.

From there, the cleanup job started. A towel was wrapped around McAlister's head to soak up the blood. Another towel wiped down the few stray blood spatters. Then McAlister's body was tossed into a janitor's trolley and covered with trash bags — lest anyone come walking by.

Not that anyone did. It was late enough that the only people who hadn't already gone home were the workaholics who wouldn't leave their offices for a while yet. The security guard who worked in the lobby had been instructed to take a walk for a while, and he certainly wouldn't say anything. After all, he didn't see anything.

The body was loaded into a car, which soon left the parking garage. This led to the last dangerous part of the job. Ordinarily it was in the best interest of a killer to want a body never to be found. The Atlantic Ocean was invented for such things.

This killer was different. This killer wanted the body to be found — *needed* the body to be found. The world had to know Vaughn McAlister was no longer among the living. And quickly.

And there seemed no better way to make sure that would happen than by depositing the corpse on the work site that bore his family name.

CHAPTER 3

I never did make it to Tina's house that night, which was probably just as well. While we had much to discuss, I hear getting pepper spray out of khaki pants can be a real bitch.

Despite my certainty that the body I had seen was Vaughn McAlister, the Newark Police took their sweet time confirming it for us. It was sometime after midnight when they finally told me the victim was McAlister and that he had suffered a blunt force trauma to the head. I got the news into a few late editions and didn't get home until 2 A.M. I can't say the extra hours spent down at the scene helped me better understand why someone would want to bash Vaughn's blow-dried head in, but they sure did make me happy to crawl under the covers when it was all over.

I live in a two-bedroom house in Bloomfield, one of those Jersey suburbs developed at a time when they still made houses small. Up until this point in my life — which had not been marked by dependency in the form of a tiny person — it had fit me just fine. My only roommate is a somnolent domestic short-haired cat named Deadline, and his square-footage needs are not substantial. Food bowls and litter boxes take up only so much space.

As I drifted off to sleep, I wondered if, nine months from now, I would begin to understand why child-infected families moved to farther-flung parts of the world where the acreage is plentiful and the housing stock comes only in sizes XL and beyond. And when my phone rang at nine o'clock the next morning — and the caller ID told me it was Tina — I thought perhaps I wasn't the only one who had dozed off while doing the same kind of pondering.

"Hi," I said, sounding barely alive.

"Good morning," she said crisply. I thought her next words would pertain to having scouted out local Montessori schools — Tina is very proactive when it comes to things like that — but instead I heard: "Nice job on McAlister last night. None of the New York papers had a whiff of it. Their Web sites are all linking to ours. TV and radio have been giving us credit all morning and —"

"Tina, did you seriously call to talk about work? Aren't we going to talk about last night?"

There was a long pause, during which time I imagined molars were being forcibly driven against other molars. It ended with: "No."

"Come on."

"I wasn't finished. I meant to say: no, not if you value your testicles. Because I swear I'm going to have them stuffed and mounted if you bring up that topic again."

"Tina, that's not fair. I have —"

"Drop it. Just drop it," she said, and I immediately knew she really meant it. She was using her quiet voice — the scary one, the one that always made me wish she were screaming instead.

I briefly considered pushing further, but resisted. As a member of the bigger-but-dumber half of the species, I am not necessarily endowed with the greatest instincts when it comes to dealing with the smaller-but-smarter half. But I at least try to learn from past mistakes. And those many errors had taught me that when Tina used the quiet voice, it was best to table further discussion until a later time. I couldn't imagine raging pregnancy hormones made

137

this any less true.

"Okay. For now. But I reserve the right to talk about this at some later date. I'm not just going away, Tina. Whether you want to deny it or not, the fact remains that I am this child's father. And there's not going to be anything you can do to stop me from playing that role, so you might as well accept that I'm here to stay. I am fully committed to this baby."

I could barely believe the words that had tumbled from my mouth. They sounded so . . . *responsible.* What's more, Tina, in her silence, seemed to respect them. Not wanting to break this fragile win streak, I hopped off the field, concluding with: "But I understand that now might not be the right time. So let's start over with: good morning, Tina, what can I do for you?"

There was another beat of silence. Then she said, "Good morning, Carter. As I was saying, terrific work on McAlister."

"Thanks."

"The only problem is, you might have done a little too good. Brodie was so delighted he called me at seven o'clock this morning to talk about it. And he was fully engorged."

Brodie was Harold Brodie, our legendary executive editor. It had become part of

Eagle-Examiner culture that his interest in a story was often described in terms of the intensity of the erection it gave him. This, of course, was all in very metaphoric terms.

Had it been actual, it would have made Brodie the most virile seventy-year-old on the planet.

"Okay, so what does he want?" I asked.

"He wants assurances that if anyone figures how and why Vaughn McAlister died, those details will appear in our newspaper, not someone else's," Tina said. "And therefore he wants his best reporter to dedicate all his time and talents to that task."

"What does that mean for the Ridgewood Avenue story?"

"Those people will still be sick next week. This week, we're full speed ahead on Vaughn McAlister."

This, of course, was the way the news business often worked. It wasn't necessarily the most important story that got covered. It was the most pressing.

"Okay," I said. "Can I please have Tommy and Pigeon to help me?"

"Sure. But only because you said 'please.' "

"Spoken like a true mother," I said.

"Shut up, Carter," she said, and ended

the call.

As I shaved, showered, and generally made myself beautiful — and what was more pleasing to the eye than a solid white shirt, a muted-red tie, and charcoal pants made of some synthetic material that never wrinkled and may well have been bulletproof? — I kept thinking baby thoughts, until I realized that Harold Brodie probably wasn't looking for a consumer-reports piece on the hottest new convertible strollers on the market.

So I engaged my brain's moving company, put the baby thoughts in a box that I marked "OPEN LATER," and made room for the story Brodie did want. Why would someone want to give Vaughn McAlister a premature trip to the Essex County Medical Examiner's office? I went through our conversation from the preceding day and ransacked it for any hint of that kind of trouble.

By the end of a bowl of Lucky Charms — still magically delicious after all these years — I hadn't come up with any more answers. McAlister had been full of well-groomed good cheer, well-mannered optimism, and well-intentioned exaggeration.

Which is not to say he was without problems. I just hadn't found them yet. Toward that end, I placed my first phone call to Tommy Hernandez. He answered by saying, "I'm not sure I want to talk to you."

"Why not?"

"Because yesterday you asked me about Vaughn McAlister and then last night he got all dead. That's pretty creepy. What happened? He took one look at your shoes and got so mortified for you that he died of embarrassment?"

Tommy is constantly telling me that my shoes are out of style. This is one of the many ways in which I know I'm not gay: my workaday footwear consists of two pairs of dress shoes, black and brown, and for the life of me I have no clue what's wrong with them.

"Too bad I wasn't smart enough to sell short on McAlister Properties stock," I said.

"Yeah, but you were smart enough to do something else."

"What's that?"

"Give me the name Harry Grant."

"Oh?"

"Yesterday after we talked, I ended up chatting with one of my favorite city hall moles and the subject of the McAlisters came up. I guess all is not well with McAlister Arms. I said something offhanded like, 'Well, it's not like the McAlisters are going to be another Harry Grant.' And the guy said, 'I'm not so sure about that.' I pursued it a little bit but he didn't want to say any more. Maybe he'll be more talkative today."

"That sounds interesting," I said.

"Almost as interesting as if you stopped shopping for your shoes at Thom McAn," Tommy said. "I'll talk to you later."

"What's wrong with Thom McAn?" I asked, but I was already talking to a dead phone line.

On my way out the door, I gave Deadline a quick pet. I did this not because I am the world's most loving cat owner but because he hadn't moved off my bed all morning and I wanted to make sure he was still alive. Sure enough, after about three strokes, he started purring like a small outboard motor.

"See you, pal," I said. "Don't exhaust yourself, okay?"

I left him, still rattling, and began the drive to Newark. As I slalomed between some of Bloomfield's most imposing pot-holes, I placed the call I didn't feel like making: I had to cancel on Jackie Orr. Again.

"Hello?" she answered.

"Hey, Jackie, it's Carter Ross."

"Oh, hi," she said. "I'm glad you're calling. I just heard from Mr. Robertson and he's not going to be able to make it this morning. He's come down with the flu again. But we still have Mrs. Tilley, De-Andre Mickens, Mrs. Torain, plus I was able to track down Mrs. James and convince her that talking to you was worth skipping a trip to the playground with her grandchildren. So that gets you up to twelve. Do you think that would be enough to get you started on your story?"

"Actually, Jackie, I'm really sorry about this," I said, "but I'm not going to be able to make it this morning."

"Oh. Are you still sick?"

"No. Unfortunately, there was a man killed in Newark last night and I'm probably going to be working on that story for at least the rest of the week."

"The developer?" she asked. Obviously, she had either seen that day's paper or read the Web site.

"That's right," I said.

There was a silence at the other end of the line. Jackie Orr was a thoughtful young woman, not a screamer. But I knew I had disappointed her.

"So all that 'voice to the voiceless' stuff," she said. "That was just talk, huh? A rich white man gets killed and that matters more than poor black folk getting sick."

"No, Jackie, it's not like that," I insisted. "It's just . . . from a news standpoint, the story about McAlister is a little more urgent. It doesn't make the story about your neighbors any less important. I'll be able to get back to it in a week or two."

"I understand," she said. She added a hasty: "Thank you for your time, Mr. Ross," then she hung up.

And I just found out I'm going to be a dad, and I had to work until really late, and I haven't had enough bonding time with my cat, I wanted to add, just to garner what I felt was a little well-deserved sympathy. But, of course, she was already gone. And she wasn't my therapist.

I tossed my phone onto the seat next to me and pouted, feeling guilty about having to jilt her but, at the same time, powerless to do much about it. I was still pouting — and still making my way through traffic toward Newark — when my phone rang. It was Pigeon.

"Hey, how are you feeling?" I asked.

"Better today. Yesterday was awful. I don't know how you made it out of bed."

"With my legs."

"Huh?"

"Never mind. I assume you've heard about Vaughn McAlister."

144

"Yeah, Tina Thompson just called and told me all about it. Then she told me she wanted me to work with you on the story. Did you . . . did you really ask for me?"

"Yeah. Is there a problem with that?" I asked as I veered around a particularly aggressive-looking pothole. It was the kind the municipality was either going to have to patch or turn into a community swimming pool.

"No, I just . . . I mean, thank you," she said. "That's, like, the nicest thing anyone has done for me since I got here."

Yet another sign Pigeon was for real: she defined being included on a story about a grisly homicide as "nice."

"Yeah, I'm a regular prince," I said.

"So, what do you want me to do? Can I make an FOIA request?"

FOIA stands for Freedom of Information Act. It was a wonderful piece of legislation that gave citizens access to the documents being generated by their government. For voters, it was a means of keeping tabs on their elected officials. For reporters, it was sort of like unlimited access to a never-ending beer tap, because it kept the good times flowing. Still, I didn't know what Pigeon was talking about.

"Uh, what exactly do you want to FOIA?" I asked.

"I don't know. But I learned in J-school that if I did an assignment that involved FOIA-ing something, I always got an A. There's got to be *something* we can FOIA."

That was when I made a hasty decision about what to do to keep Pigeon busy. "That's all well and good. But if you want to get an A in real life, you've got to get real people to talk to you. And the person I want you to talk to is Barry McAlister."

I heard her gulping over the phone. "You mean, the dead guy's dad?"

"Yep, the dead guy's dad," I said. This was a calculated gamble on my part. I had no inkling of who had killed Vaughn McAlister or why. But if it wasn't something in his personal life — a jealous wife, an angry mistress, a boyfriend who went all Andrew Cunanan on him — it was something in his business life. Barry McAlister was the only person who was positioned to be aware of both.

And all I really knew about Barry McAlister was that he must have been a pretty private guy. Why else would he have had his son act as the front man for the family business? So, chances were, if a seasoned reporter like me came at him, he would make like a shellfish and clam up. But maybe if a somewhat-naïve young intern approached him . . .

It was worth whatever slim chance of success it had. Sometimes reporting is about instinct. And sometimes it's about getting lucky when you throw something sloppy against a wall and it sticks.

Pigeon did her share of whining and protesting, but I pep-talked her into it. What I didn't tell her was that I was fully expecting whomever we sent to talk to Barry McAlister to strike out. And I'd rather waste her time than mine.

With Pigeon thus busied, I made a quick call to my best police source. Rodney Pritchard had floated around through various parts of the Newark Police Department during his years there, and I had written a few stories about him that had inclined him to be friendly to me. Currently he was in the Gang Unit, though he had been in Homicide recently enough that I knew he'd be up on their gossip. And a little gossip could go a long way just then.

"Hey, Pritch, what's going on?"

"Uh-oh, here's trouble," he said. I heard street noise in the background, which meant he was not in the office. Sometimes, if he was at Newark Police headquarters — known informally as "Green Street," because that was their location — he'd tell me I had the wrong number. Strictly speaking, Pritch wasn't supposed to talk to me without several layers of authorization. It was understood our conversations were just between us girls.

"What makes you say that?" I asked.

"I don't know. But when you're calling, it's always trouble somewhere."

"Well, I'm sure you can guess what that is today."

I heard a horn honking through his phone. "No, actually, I can't."

"The McAlister homicide?" I prompted.

"Yeah, what about it?"

"A major developer gets killed and dumped in a vacant lot within the boundaries of your fair city. I thought that would have all of Green Street jumping."

"I'm sure the case has been assigned to someone," Pritch said. "But I was in there this morning and it was pretty business-as-usual. I don't think this one is getting any extra attention."

"That's weird."

"Why?"

"I don't know. Usually when we go big with a story, you guys follow suit."

"Yeah, but a lot of times the only reason we do that is because when you guys get excited the mayor's office gets excited. And then you-know-what flows downhill. I don't think that happened this time."

"Why not?"

"Don't ask me. Ask the mayor. Better yet, don't ask the mayor. It's sort of nice not having him up in our business."

"Noted. If you hear anything, let me know, okay?"

"Sure thing," he said. "Anyhow, I'm just a guy out on a corner, looking at fresh graffiti, worrying we're about to have another war on our hands. So I gotta go."

"All right," I said. "Good luck with that."

Upon arriving at the office, I had not even set down my briefcase when I realized there was someone sitting in the intern pod who shouldn't have been there.

It was Pigeon. She was facing away from me, slightly stooped in her chair, in a failing attempt to make herself less noticeable. I walked toward her, thinking she would turn around when she heard me. Then I cleared my throat to get her attention. But, like a puppy who had just missed the paper, she couldn't look at me. She seemed incredibly interested in a small piece of the carpet opposite me and couldn't tear her eyes away.

I walked around to the other side and stood on the spot that had transfixed her.

"Hey, Pigeon, what's up?" I asked.

She lifted her gaze about halfway up but still couldn't make eye contact. "Oh, hi," she said.

"How did things go with Barry McAlister?" I asked.

"Imuddababa."

"Excuse me?"

"Addinnaddda."

"Pigeon, I'm getting to be an old man, so you're going to have to speak up."

Finally she said, "I couldn't do it."

"Pigeon!" I said, reproachfully, drawing out the second syllable.

"I just couldn't!"

"Pigeon!" I said, this time emphasizing the first syllable. I'd never known how wonderfully adaptable the word "pigeon" was.

"I got his address and I was going to go over to his house and everything. But then, I don't know, what was I going to say? 'Hi, Mr. McAlister, I heard your son died last night. Care to tell me about it?' "

"Well, yeah, that's about the size of it. What, you think you're going over there to swap brioche recipes?"

She lowered her gaze again and said, "I feel so ashamed."

This was one of the things I loved about interns. I have dim memories of a time in my career when talking to the relatives of dead people probably made me uncomfortable, too. It felt like a long time ago, but I forced myself back into the mind-set of what it was like to be a young reporter, filled with apprehension, scared to knock on a door.

"Oh, Pigeon," I said, hefting a grandfatherly sigh and giving her a pat on the shoulder. "Sometimes as a reporter, you have to pretend that every morning you put on a suit of armor. And then you make believe that armor makes you impervious to social awkwardness. I mean, it's like doing a man-on-the-street story. Would a normal human being charge up to a perfect stranger and say, 'Gee it's cold today. What do you think about it?' No, of course not. But as reporters working on stupid weather stories assigned to us by our unimaginative editors, we do it all the time."

"Yeah, but —"

"No buts!" I snapped. "I know asking a man about his dead son is a little harder than asking someone about the weather. And it's something that as normal human beings, we could never do. But when we have our armor on, it's something we can do. It's something we have to do, because it's our job. Look at it this way: we're going to be writing about Vaughn McAlister whether his dad talks to us or not. But if you were his dad, wouldn't you want the newspaper to talk to you, just so nothing inaccurate was written about your son?"

"Well, I gue—"

"Of course you would!" I interrupted, not because it's how Socrates would have done it but because I felt like I was on a roll. "You would want nothing more than for the final words written about your boy to be a hundred-percent, spot-on perfect.

"Besides," I added somewhat philosophically, "if we don't talk to him, *The New York Times* might. And Brodie would blow a gasket if the *Times* had something on a Newark-related story that we didn't. And when Brodie blows a gasket, the rest of the newsroom leaks oil. So let's go."

"Where?"

"To Barry McAlister's house."

"You'll come with me?" she said, actually sitting up for the first time.

"Sure," I said. "What are mentors for?"

"Wow, thank you," she said, a little too gratefully. But maybe, given the emotional wattage that was charging other parts of my life, I didn't mind a little uncomplicated professional admiration coming my way.

As we made for the parking garage, Pigeon gave me the address for the McAlister household: 7 McAlister Court in West Orange. What did these guys have about naming things after themselves, anyhow? It had to be some kind of egomaniacal disorder. Trump Complex.

I unhitched the Malibu and programmed Barry McAlister's address into the GPS, which recognized McAlister Court. We got rolling and I started giving Pigeon a brief geography lesson. Even New Jersey natives get the Oranges a little confused, because they come in three different cultivations: East, South, and West. It's really quite easy to keep them straight. The farther away from Newark, the higher the real estate values.

As such, I guessed that the McAlister home in West Orange would be a decent little shack. And it was. Though it wasn't anything ostentatious. It was an older, two-story, Tudor-style home with mature landscaping, nestled at the end of a private drive. It turned out the "7" on McAlister Court was quite superfluous. There were no numbers 1 through 6.

"I guess this is it," Pigeon said as I stopped the engine.

"Okay," I said, but didn't immediately get out of the car. Pigeon and I had been yammering so much on our way out — the geography lecture had given way to a lesson about *Eagle-Examiner* history — that I hadn't given much thought to the task at hand. I usually wanted at least to try to anticipate how an interview like this might go. Would Barry McAlister be angry? Welcome us with open arms? Give us a stiff upper lip and a few bland comments?

I wasn't necessarily afraid to knock on the door of a murder victim's family like I might have been as a cub reporter, but I still wanted to feel mentally prepared for whatever I might find when I did.

"What are you waiting for?" Pigeon asked.

I grasped the handle to the car door and said, "Just taking a moment to put on my armor."

I'm not sure what I expected Barry McAlister to be, but the moment he answered the door, I understood why he had made his son the front man for McAlister Properties. Barry McAlister didn't exactly present well.

He was overweight and smelled like a Marlboro. He was dressed in a timeworn flannel shirt, shapeless jeans, and once-white sneakers that had gone yellow with age. He had a nose that filled a large portion of his face and a jawline that was almost entirely jowl. His skin was sallow and flaccid. I pegged his age as somewhere in his late sixties but his health as somewhere in his eighties.

At least by appearances, he was the opposite of his perfectly turned-out son in just about every way. The only thing he had passed onto Vaughn was his hair, which was rich and full. Barry's was gray, not blond, but it was still an impressive mane.

"Can I help you?" he asked in a gravelly, Jersey-tinged voice.

I made the rather quick determination that if Vaughn McAlister had been all about show, his dad was all about substance. So I went with the direct approach: "My name is Carter Ross. This is Neesha Krishnamurthy. We're reporters with the *Eagle-Examiner*. I know this is a difficult time for you, but we're writing a story about Vaughn and we were hoping you could talk about him a bit."

His face didn't really move. He just opened the door a little wider. "Come on in," he said.

He trudged into a darkened living room and sat heavily in a leather recliner that faced an old, round-screen television that was on but muted. There was a small folding tray next to him with a full ashtray and an empty highball glass. I could forgive him the early start.

Then I realized, to my surprise, I could do more than just forgive him. I actually understood it, in a totally new way. There I was, less than twenty-four hours into my life as a future father, and already I felt its tug. Multiply what I felt by forty-odd years' worth of memories and experiences, and then lose it all in one violent moment? Forget drinking. It would be all I could do to stop myself from wanting to play in traffic.

I shook the thought from my head and looked around. The room appeared to have been preserved in a state that might best be described as 1977. The carpet was shag. The colors were predominantly brown and orange. The couch that Pigeon and I sat on was upholstered in a paisley pattern that was outlawed the day Reagan took office. The drapes were banned shortly thereafter as well.

There were a few pictures but they were also dated. Barry was absent from them — I can't imagine the camera liked him much — so they all either featured a younger-looking Vaughn McAlister or an attractive blonde with high cheekbones and feathered hair that last looked good on Farah Fawcett.

I was looking for a gentle start to our conversation, so I pointed to a photo of the blond woman and said, "Is that Vaughn's mom?"

"Yep," Barry said. "That's her just before she ran off with another guy and left me with Vaughn. Then she died of cancer."

So much for a gentle start. He lit a cigarette and stared at the television. I sneaked a glance at Pigeon. She looked like she would have gnawed her arm off it would have gotten her out of that living room.

"Vaughn looked like her," Barry continued. "Took after her, too, even though he barely knew her. She had a real sense of style, that lady. I was the one who raised Vaughn, but he always had more of his mother in him."

"Yet he went into business with you," I said.

"Yeah, well . . ." he said, let his voice trail off.

The whole vibe was weird — weird how the guy just let us into his house, weird how everything in the place felt so stale, weird how he just started talking like we were in the middle of a conversation — but I did my best to roll with it.

"So how did you and Vaughn become partners?" I asked, pulling out my notepad.

Barry let out a wry laugh. "I guess he didn't really have a choice."

"What do you mean?"

"Long story."

"We've got time," I said.

He looked at me for a moment, then returned his gaze to the television as he started talking. "I started off with one apartment building on Avon Avenue in Newark. It was a seventy-unit building — a big place for a guy who didn't know what he was doing. I bought it for next to nothing and I still had to take out a loan to swing it. The place was a nightmare. The boiler was busted all the time. The pipes leaked sewage into the basement. There were holes in the walls, holes in the ceilings. No one paid their rent. This was in the late sixties, just after the riots, and the quality of the tenants was awful. They were all on public assistance."

He took a drag on his cigarette and continued: "I thought I was going to lose my shirt before I even had a shirt. For a year, I worked night and day on that place. I poured money I didn't even have into it, fixed everything myself, got rid of the bad tenants, got better ones. They might have feared me a little bit, because I made it clear I'd kick them out if they didn't toe the line. But I think they respected me, too. They knew I was going to give them a fair shake. And they knew I wasn't like those absentee slumlords, because I was in the building all the time, making sure everything worked okay."

Another drag. "After a year, I had the place turning a nice little profit, so I took on another building. Another nightmare. A little bigger than the last one, actually. Same thing happened. I slaved on that building until I turned it around. Then I bought another one. I was starting to make some decent money but, damn, it was hard work. People think property management is just about cashing rent checks but it's a helluva lot more than that. At least it is if you want to make money at it. By the time Vaughn was born, I was doing pretty well but my wife started complaining about the hours. Not the money, mind you. Just the hours."

He hacked into his hand, looked at his empty glass, then went on: "I had bought us this place and I thought that'd make her happy, you know. I mean, the perfect little house in the suburbs. It's what every woman

159

wants, right? But she was . . . it seemed like she was never happy. She kept complaining about me working all the time, but I . . . I guess I never took it seriously until one day she showed up at the office with Vaughn. He was maybe two. She handed me a Dear John letter, handed me the kid, and that was it."

The last cigarette wasn't quite done, but Barry wasn't leaving anything to chance. He lit another one before the first one could burn down, sucked on it until it was lit, then put it down. "After that, I tried to get babysitters for Vaughn, but I could never predict when I'd be home. They kept quitting on me that same way Vaughn's mom did. Finally I just said to hell with it and started bringing Vaughn with me everywhere. After day care, after school, Saturday, Sunday. The kid learned the business from the ground up. When you're a landlord, you see people at their best and their worst. Mostly their worst. Maybe I should have shielded him from it, I don't know. But I thought it was good for him to, I don't know, see what life really was. So if I had to clear out an apartment that had been used as a crack den, he did it with me. If I had some woman calling me hysterical because her boyfriend was trying to break the door down and the police wouldn't come, Vaughn would see that, too. He got an education, let me tell you — everything from fixing toilets to sitting in landlord-tenant court."

Barry grabbed the new cigarette, flicked the accumulated ash off the end, sucked on it briefly, then concluded, "So you asked me when Vaughn and I became partners. But the fact is, it wasn't really a decision. It was something life kind of thrust on both of us, and we made the best of it."

"So that's the residential side," I said. "I thought all of Vaughn's business was commercial."

"It was," Barry said. "Vaughn was like his mom in that he had a certain style — the clothes, the hair. He wanted everything to be fancy. He was like that in business, too. We could have both kept making a decent living doing what we were doing, but that wasn't good enough for Vaughn. He didn't want to spend his life managing ghetto buildings, chasing after deadbeats for their rent. He always had his eyes on downtown. He wanted those big, shiny office buildings. He wanted to wear nice suits to work. So he convinced me that McAlister Properties should add a commercial division and that he should be the head of it."

"How long ago was this?"

"Oh, I don't know. Ten years ago, I guess. I started selling off the residential buildings and Vaughn used it as seed money to go into the commercial side."

I felt I had gotten Barry McAlister sufficiently warmed up that it was time to ask the important question: "So, I know this isn't easy to think about," I said. "But do you have any idea who killed him?"

The television did its silent blare. The most recent cigarette sat smoldering in the ashtray. He sat stonily in his recliner, to the point where I feared I had lost him in some kind of trance.

Finally he offered, "Yeah. His secretary."

In certain ham-handed television shows, the sound technician would have inserted the sound of a record scratching, while the actors would have been instructed to stare dumbly into the camera.

"His secretary?" I said. "Miss Fenstermacher?"

"Yeah, that's her," Barry said. "Look, I don't want you writing any of this, so put your pad away. I didn't even tell the cops this, because I don't know anything for sure, but I got some history with some people at your newspaper. Some good history. I always felt like you guys worked hard to get

162

a story. Maybe if I put you on the right track you can get this one too, huh?"

"Okay," I said, putting down my pad and closing the cover. "So what makes you think she did it?"

McAlister looked longingly at his empty highball glass, then hoisted himself out of the recliner.

"Want something to drink?" he asked.

"Sure," I said quickly.

"What's your pleasure?"

"What are you having?"

"I'm a Cutty Sark man."

Scotch. I absolutely despise scotch. I'd had a bad scotch experience long ago, in college, and had avoided the stuff ever since. There mere smell of it made me a little queasy. So, naturally, I said, "Sounds great."

He turned to Pigeon and said, "And you?"

I could tell Pigeon was about to make the terrible mistake of saying no, so I quickly interjected, "It's her favorite."

He disappeared into the kitchen and Pigeon glared at me and softly said, "What are you doing?"

"Well, apparently, I'm about to be drinking scotch. And so are you."

"We can't do that! We're *working*!" she said, with utmost gravity.

"Yeah, I know. News flash: when you're in

163

this business, sometimes drinking with a source *is* working."

"But . . . I've never had alcohol before," she whispered, pronouncing the word "alcohol" like she was an international spokeswoman for the temperance movement.

"Is it some kind of religious thing?"

"No, I —"

"A health thing?"

"No, it —"

"Then live a little, Pigeon," I said as Barry returned to the room carrying three glasses filled with ice and an amber-colored liquid that didn't appear to have been mixed with anything that might lessen its potency or improve its taste. Scotch on the rocks. A Man's Drink.

He handed Pigeon and me our glasses, settled into his chair, and choked out a quick, "Here's to Vaughn."

He tilted back the drink and swallowed half of it.

"To Vaughn," I agreed. I took a less aggressive swig, but it was still enough to make my stomach feel like it had a small forest fire inside. As I brought my glass back down, I saw Pigeon was still just staring at hers. I shot her an urgent look.

"To Vaughn," she said at last, brought the rim of the glass to her lips, then took a tentative sip.

I saw the look on her face — the words "shock and awe" came to mind — but I was proud of her for resisting the urge to spit it back up all over McAlister's awful shag carpeting. It was, I could tell, a struggle.

I'm pretty sure Barry missed it. He had settled back into his chair and was fiddling with his drink, tilting it back and forth to bring more of the scotch into contact with the ice.

"This is absolutely off the record," he said. "But you know Vaughn and his secretary had an affair, right?"

"No. I can say that didn't exactly come up when he and I spoke."

"I shouldn't even call it an affair anymore. I mean, well, where do I start. . . . Vaughn was married to this girl — nice girl, good-looking girl. I really liked her. They didn't have kids yet, but I kept hoping. And Marcia had a husband and a kid, too. Anyhow, Vaughn worked some pretty long hours. Marcia was always with him. So I suppose it was kind of natural for some sparks to start flying. It's not like he's the first guy to get the hots for his secretary, but, jeez, with those two it was like a forest fire. I walked in on them one time. Doing it right on her desk."

That explained why she kept it so neat.

Barry shook his head, took another swallow of scotch, and continued: "I told him to enjoy it for a while and then go back to his wife and shut the hell up about it. But he started all this, 'But, Dad, I love her,' crap. Sometimes she'd attach a sticky note to a file he needed to look at, and it'd say something like, 'I love you with every ounce of my being.' Mushy stuff like that. I'd tell them to keep it out of the office. I mean, that's what hot-sheet hotels are for, you know? Finally one thing led to another. He left his wife. She left her husband. It was a big mess. But he kept saying it was okay. They were in love."

He said the word "love" like he didn't believe it. I didn't know if he was incredulous about it for his son and the secretary or just in general.

"So if they were in love, why would she kill him?" I asked.

"Because fires that burn hot also go out faster," he said. "Vaughn had told her they were done. I think maybe he was planning on going back to his ex-wife. He had mentioned to me she was moving back to the area. Maybe he told Marcia the same thing and she went nuts. You know what they say about a woman scorned. I always thought

166

she might come unglued a little but I never . . ."

He broke it off, overcome with emotion. He drained the rest of his scotch, actually resting his forehead on the glass for a moment.

I thought about Miss Fenstermacher, her helmetlike hair, her flawless manicure. I couldn't necessarily envision her swinging a two-by-four at someone's head. But, then again, I also knew that she wouldn't have been the first jilted lover in history to exact the ultimate revenge.

"I saw him two days ago," Barry whispered. "I was just looking at him, in the prime of his life, feeling . . . I don't know. He had everything ahead of him. I mean, we weren't . . . We didn't talk about, you know . . . I didn't say 'I love you' all the time. We were . . . too busy. We always had other stuff to talk about. But he knew how I felt about him. Maybe I wasn't always the warmest guy in the world, but Vaughn knew. . . ."

Maybe he did. Maybe he didn't. I put that away in a mental file I had already started. Things I Would Do with My Kid: make sure I said "I love you" at least once a day.

Barry gripped the glass extra hard, then gave the ice one last shake before he set it down. He looked toward the fireplace, started at it for a moment or two, then continued: "He was really excited about how his new project was shaping up. He told me he was about to land a couple of big fish."

"Yeah, who was his big mystery tenant?"

He shook his head. "I don't actually know the details. Vaughn and I let everyone think I was still doing stuff behind the scenes, because we thought that would give him some legitimacy. No one would try to take advantage of him if they knew a crusty old battle-ax like me was still on the job. But the fact is, McAlister Properties is all Vaughn. I've been out of the game for a while. Like I said, I sold my buildings. I was getting too old to be diving into the ghetto anyway. I don't really know the commercial side the way Vaughn did.

"Anyhow," he huffed, "you didn't get that stuff about the secretary from me. I'm just a tired old man who doesn't know nothing."

He grabbed the remote control off his tray table and turned up the volume. Then he lit another cigarette, never taking his gaze from the screen. I suppose I should have tried to pump a few usable quotes out of the guy, but the old joke about trying to teach a pig to dance came to mind, and I just didn't feel like annoying the pig. I nodded at Pigeon as I stood.

"Thanks for the drink," I said.

"Don't mention it," he said gruffly, eyes still on the television.

Pigeon, also now standing, said, "I'm sorry for your loss."

He looked up at her and replied, "Thanks, kid."

He returned his attention to the television and we departed without another word. Though I did notice, as I was leaving the room, that a tough old man's eyes had gone watery.

My first act, upon departing the ode to polyester that was Barry McAlister's living room and making it outside, was to take three grateful breaths of non-tobacco-saturated air. As we made it to the end of the driveway, I spied a small shrine, set off to the side and nicely landscaped.

The centerpiece was a delicate marble statue of an angel, no more than maybe ten inches tall, with an inscription on the base:

Elizabeth A. McAlister
Beloved Wife, Mother
1945–1981

"Wow," I said. "Look at this."

"Oh my . . ." Pigeon started, trailed off, then came back with: "You don't think she's . . . buried underneath there, do you?"

"Pretty small for a headstone. Besides, that's against the zoning statutes in a town like West Orange."

Pigeon just stared at it. I added, "Safe to say he still carries the torch for his wife, though, huh? The pictures inside. The shrine outside. You'd think he'd hate her for running off, but . . ."

But there was nothing more to add, other than that it was one more unusual thing about Barry McAlister. I continued to the Malibu, mostly so I could go into its glove compartment and produce something absorbent for Pigeon. She had kept her composure all through the interview but now had lost it. I was a little surprised — Pigeon didn't seem like the weepy type — but I found two unused Quiznos napkins and handed them to her.

"Here," I said.

"Thanks," she replied. Between her leaky eyes and runny nose, she made short work of it.

"You okay?" I asked when she seemed to be done. I had already gotten us moving back in the direction of Newark.

"Yeah, I'm fine. I don't normally have this problem, I just . . . That poor, poor man. First his wife leaves him. Then she dies. Then his son gets killed. It's just so sad."

"Yeah," I said, because that was about the sum total of the situation.

"And now he's just going to sit in that room and drink himself to death and . . ." Her tears started again. "Does that really not get to you at all?"

"Of course it does," I said. "I'd be less than human if it didn't. I guess I've just learned that you have to stay in touch with your feelings without letting them over-whelm you. It's a fine line. If you don't stay engaged emotionally, your stories fall totally flat and you forget the meaning of what you're writing about. Yet you have to stay detached enough that you don't fall apart and lose the ability to function. It's some-thing you learn."

"Uh-huh," Pigeon said, tears streaking down her face, like maybe she was still a little on the far side of the line.

"So, for example, we can reflect on the unusual bond between a father and a son who are both incredibly close and yet somewhat distant. Or we can talk about what kind of mental illness would drive a woman to leave her husband and son. Or we can talk about the perils of extramarital affairs. Or we can gripe about secondhand smoke because, I don't know about you, but I feel like the bottom of an ashtray right now."

Pigeon laughed a little bit at that. I continued: "But, the fact is, while all of that is important, and while all of that has its place when it comes time to start typing, none of that is going to get our story written."

She blew her nose into the napkin.

"You know what will?" I asked; then, without waiting for a reply, I finished, "A little visit to see Marcia Fenstermacher."

Pigeon was naturally dark complexioned, so it was hard to know for sure, but I'm pretty sure she blanched a little. "But . . . I thought she's the one who did it."

"Well, now, we don't know that for sure," I said. "It's innocent until proven guilty, remember? I'm sure it's possible there's some other logical explanation for how Vaughn McAlister ended up with half a head in that vacant lot, and, at risk of making a really bad pun, we should keep an open mind about it."

"That's horrible —" Pigeon started, but I waved her off.

"Anyhow, yeah, Miss Fenstermacher is our next interview."

"But shouldn't we, I don't know, wait or something?"

"Wait for what? For the police to pick her up and then we can't interview her? No way. The police aren't treating this thing like a very high priority, so they might not know about the affair yet. They'll probably hear about it soon, and when they do, Miss Fenstermacher becomes a person of interest. But for right now she's fair game. Think about it: an interview with the prime suspect in a high-profile murder case? Doesn't get much better than that."

Pigeon was biting her lower lip.

"O-okay," she said, unconvinced.

"So here's what we're going to do. Because time is of the essence, we're splitting up. I'm hitting her office. You're hitting her home. With luck, she's going to be one place or the other."

Pigeon had now taken her entire lower lip into her mouth and was gnawing on it like it was made of bubble gum. "But if she's home, what do I ask her? I can't just come right out and say, 'Hey, did you kill Vaughn McAlister?' "

"No," I said. "You probably want to be a little more subtle than that."

For the next few minutes, as we completed our drive to the office, I gave Pigeon some perhaps-helpful pointers on how to act and what to say. In truth, I was winging it a little bit. It's not like I had long experience in this area. The cops usually got to the killer before we did — it was sort of their job. Sweating confessions out of people was not something a reporter often found himself in a position to do. But I understood the general principle: get 'em talking and keep 'em talking until they slip up. Since it was the same principle that applied to any number of malfeasants — be they elected officials, public employees, or swindling businessmen — it was something I felt I could handle. I just hoped Pigeon could, too.

When we got to the *Eagle-Examiner* parking garage, I looked up the home address of Marcia Fenstermacher, thankful for her unusual name. It's not like I had to worry about sending Pigeon to the home of the wrong Marcia Fenstermacher.

It turned out Fenstermacher, Marcia and McAlister, Vaughn shared the same address in Florham Park. The house was in Vaughn's name, and it was assessed at $1.2 million, which made it quite the little love shack.

I briefly gave thought to sending a photographer with Pigeon, then talked myself out of it. At least for the time being, we wanted Miss Fenstermacher as disarmed and unsuspecting as possible. Presuming she had done it — and it was as good a theory as any at this point — it was best for her to think she had gotten away with it. Having a photographer firing away might spook her.

We'd get the photographs we needed eventually. In the meantime, we just needed to tread carefully, get as much on the record as we could, and hope that the murderer fell into our laps.

With Pigeon dispatched to Florham Park, I started the short trip to McAlister Place. I wasn't going to tell Pigeon, but I was fairly certain I'd find Miss Fenstermacher there. This was based on a guess, but I was assuming a guilty person would try to appear as nonguilty as possible. And the nonguilty-appearing thing to do would be to go into work, as if all were normal.

Or at least that was my best guess as I parked and once again traipsed more or less unbothered past the inattentive security guard.

I reached the second floor, paused briefly outside the door to gather my thoughts, then opened it.

Sure enough, there was Marcia Fenstermacher, sitting at her desk.

And she was a mess.

The hair was still perfect — nothing could budge the ultra-hold on that coiffure — but her round face was a soupy mash-up of foundation, blush, and eyeliner. It all might once have been in the right place, but that was before her tear ducts had gone into overdrive. The result was a swirl of colors and textures splattered across a blotchy canvas — like Tammy Faye Bakker in a blender.

She was clutching a Kleenex, which was obviously her preferred method of ooze containment, because her once-clean desk had at least a dozen crumpled tissues, each of them a mix of dampened pulp and smudged makeup.

She did her best to look up and pull herself together as I entered. She failed at both.

"Hello," she said, sniffing. "May I help you?"

Those were the same words she had used to greet me the day before, but the pretense of cool and calm efficiency that she had exuded then was gone.

"Yeah, hi, I'm Carter Ross from the *Eagle-Examiner.* I was here yesterday."

"Oh. Right. Of course. Sorry, I'm not . . .

functioning that well."

She returned her face to her latest tissue, which already appeared to be ready for retirement. I had to give her credit: she was either legitimately distraught or she had missed her calling as a soap opera actress.

"I'm writing a story about Vaughn for tomorrow's paper," I said. "Do you mind if I ask you some questions?"

"Uh-huh," she said.

I didn't know if she meant "uh-huh" like she minded or "uh-huh" like I could ask her questions. But I slid my notepad out of my pocket and started firing.

"So how long had you worked for him?" I asked, figuring I'd start slow.

"Three years," she said. "It's been three wonderful years. Vaughn was the kindest, smartest, most . . . most caring man I've ever met."

"He was a good boss, then?"

This gave her pause. Slowly, quietly, she said, "He wasn't just my boss."

So at least she was going to admit that. "What do you mean?" I asked, playing dumb.

"We had . . . We had . . . He was my boy-boy- . . . God, would you listen to me? Vaughn and I were together. We had been almost from the day I started working here.

He was my . . . I don't know what you'd call it. It seems ridiculous to call him my boyfriend. I'm forty-two years old, not some teenager. We lived together. He was my life partner. He was the answer to my dreams. We were . . ."

From a set of double doors to Marcia's left — the opposite side from Vaughn's office — another McAlister Properties employee appeared.

"Is everything okay, Marcia?" she asked.

But Marcia waved her off. "Yes, I keep telling you, I'm fine."

The employee and I shared a look at the wasted tissues on her desk. Yep, fine and dandy.

"Okay, well, give me a shout if you need anything," the woman said, giving me a suspicious up-and-down before disappearing behind the door.

"Anyway, as I was saying, Vaughn and I were together," she continued. "We had talked about marriage but we had both been married before. After his experience with his first wife and my experience with my husband, neither of us wanted to go through that again. But my son — I have a twelve-year-old — had started taking to him as a father figure. We were going to have him adopt Trevor so he could have some . . .

legal status, I guess. It's ridiculous when you're not married, some of the things you have to put up with. Did you know the police didn't even find me to tell me about Vaughn's murder? I'm basically his wife, but I'm still not considered next of kin. It's like I don't even count."

"So how did you learn about it?" I asked. *Other than, you know, when you heard his skull crack.*

"He was working late last night, but then he was going to come home and we were going to have a late dinner together. Trevor was with his father last night, so it was supposed to be a . . . you know, a kind of romantic thing. I was expecting him at ten and I was shocked when he wasn't home. He's never late. So I kept calling him and calling him. I swear, his phone must have like thirty missed calls on it. I never imagined . . ."

She shook her head. She was smooth enough in the delivery that I got the feeling she had rehearsed this story. Or maybe she had told it to enough co-workers that she already had it grooved in.

"Eventually, I went to bed. I thought maybe he had just fallen asleep at his desk. He did that once before, and he's been working so hard lately. I kept expecting he'd slide into bed next to me. But he . . . he never came home."

She barely squeaked out the word "home." She took a few moments to compose herself, then continued: "When he still wasn't back in the morning, I thought, okay, he slept at the office. So I came in here, ready to give him hell for not calling. But then he wasn't here, either, of course. Do you know how I learned about it?"

"How?" I asked.

She swiveled her still-perfect hair from side to side. "Google alerts. I had a Google alert that sent me any mention of Vaughn's name, so I could let him know about it. So I had this e-mail this morning with the story from your Web site."

She suffered another minor breakdown from reliving that experience, then offered a quick, "I'm sorry."

"It's understandable."

"I think I'm still mostly in shock. I mean, you see those murder victim's family members on TV who say, 'It hasn't hit me yet.' And I always used to think, 'How is that possible? What are you, some kind of idiot?' But I can tell you, absolutely, it hasn't hit me. Not really."

"Have you talked to the police yet?"

"Nope. Nothing," she said, like this still

offended her. "I still haven't heard word one from them."

Just wait, I thought. *You will.*

"So the last time you saw Vaughn alive was . . . ?"

She puffed her cheeks and let out a gust of air. "I don't know. I probably left around seven last night. He said he just had a few more things to go over and he'd be home at ten."

Right, I thought, *keep repeating that story.*

"Do you have any idea who might want to kill him?" I asked, paying careful attention to her mottled face.

But she gave no reaction, at least none that I could read. She was just shaking her head. "No. I mean, I can't . . . Who would want to hurt Vaughn? He was doing such good things for the community. Everyone was so excited about that new project. It just doesn't make any sense. Are you sure it wasn't . . . I thought maybe it was a robbery or something. We've unfortunately had some problems with break-ins. Maybe he tried to stop it, or . . ."

Right. A robbery. Sure, lady. It was time to push Miss Fenstermacher a little and see what happened.

I cleared my throat and said, "Marcia, I know this probably isn't something you want to talk about. But were you and Vaughn having any trouble?"

"No. Never. Who told you that?"

I couldn't tell her it was Barry McAlister, because he had put it off the record. "I'm afraid I can't say. But I had heard he was going back to his ex-wife."

That had merely been supposition on Barry's part, of course. But it sure brought Marcia Fenstermacher's fangs out in a hurry.

"Her?" she spit. "That's completely untrue. Vaughn and I were totally happy together. He didn't . . . I mean, we fought from time to time. But every couple fights. It was never anything serious. Even if he did leave me, he never would have gone back to *her.*"

"What makes you say that?"

"Because he didn't have anything to do with her anymore. At first she'd call and ask for money and for a while he had been giving it to her. But even that had stopped. So to suggest they might be getting back to . . . I don't know why anyone would . . . Why would that even matter?"

"Well, think about it. If there was a change in Vaughn's situation," I started, then I saw her spine straighten.

"Wait," she said. "You don't . . . you don't think I did this, do you?"

"I never said that," I said. Though it sure was interesting her brain would be so quick to reach this conclusion.

"But when you ask me if we were having problems." She let out an indignant huff. "That is just the most offensive, most horrible thing . . . As if this wasn't already the worst day of my life. The nerve you have! I'm going to have to ask you to leave, Mr. Ross. Immediately."

She looked at me with hatred in her eyes. I wondered if Vaughn McAlister had seen that face at some point before his life ended.

I escorted myself from the office and, once outside, called Pigeon and filled her in on the world according to Marcia Fenstermacher. Pigeon was already out in Florham Park by the time I was done, so I instructed the intrepid intern to case the neighborhood to see what, if anything, she could learn about the happy/unhappy couple.

Then I turned to my next task. If Vaughn McAlister had been getting ready to leave his mistress — or his girlfriend, or his life partner, or whatever we ought to call such people — and possibly rekindle with his ex-wife, it made the ex-wife my next logical contact.

Alas, whereas Fenstermacher was an

unusual name, McAlister was not, which I knew would complicate the task of finding her. I steered my car out of the parking garage to a spot where my smart phone would have decent reception and started asking my dear old friend, LexisNexis, for some help.

They say that an elephant never forgets. But, truly, pachyderms have nothing on a good digital database. If you know your way around inside them, it's amazing how much of a person's biography you can start to assemble.

Thus, I was able to find some old property records that linked McAlister, Vaughn to a McAlister, Lisa. Then McAlister, Lisa moved to Florida and reverted to her maiden name: Denbigh, Lisa.

She didn't stay long in Florida. From there, she'd gone to Arizona. Then California. Then Oregon. Without casting aspersions on Lisa Denbigh's reputation, it's fair to say she got around.

It's funny how you get a sense of a person just from the public records they leave behind. If you have someone who lives a stable life, doing dependably mature things — like buying a house, registering to vote, paying her taxes, and keeping up with her bills — she establishes a certain profile. It's neat. Tidy. Simple.

Lisa Denbigh, on the other hand, had created a swampy morass. In addition to the transient lifestyle that resulted in a dozen or so addresses across four states, she had an assortment of civil complaints against her for unpaid bills: $554 from her electricity provider in Florida; $897 from an electronics store in California; $734 from a cell phone provider; $17,554 from a credit card company; and so on. Some of them had progressed rather quickly to summary judgment, which meant she hadn't bothered to answer them.

She also had an assortment of speeding tickets, including one that had resulted in a bench warrant in California; and unpaid parking tickets, for which the county of Broward, Florida felt it was owed $570.

It was all relatively small-time — there were no felonies or violent crimes, no DUIs or drug offenses, at least not that I could find — but it didn't exactly paint Lisa Denbigh as the most fiscally responsible person in the world.

It also wasn't going to make her very easy to track down. I was able to find telephone numbers associated with some of her addresses, but not all of them. And, of course, none of the numbers was any good. Three were disconnected. One was clearly a wrong number — it led to a sandwich shop. One was for a fax machine. One forwarded to another number that was also disconnected. Another led to an answering machine that told me, "This is Roy. You know what to do. So do it."

I left a message, telling Roy if he knew where Lisa Denbigh was to have her call me. But it didn't exactly instill in me a lot of confidence. She had likely left a long trail of bill collectors in her wake, all of whom were trying to call her on phone numbers that they, too, were finding on LexisNexis. That would only make her change numbers more often — because who the heck wants to be pestered by bill collectors all the time?

Instead of attempting the impossible task of guessing where she might be now — somehow, I was thinking it wasn't Oregon anymore if she and Vaughn were getting together again — I decided to go backward. Going through her history, I went past when she was Lisa McAlister to when she was Lisa Denbigh for the first time.

I tracked her through a variety of addresses in Manhattan, then to Gainesville, Florida at a time when Lisa would have been roughly college age. And that meant more than likely she had been a student at the University of Florida. Good to know.

Going back in time even further, the earliest address I could find was on Thagard Road in Empress, Georgia, an unincorporated piece of Brooks County. The address was, as far as I could tell, still the home of Robert and Martha Ann Denbigh — presumably, Lisa's parents. Their dates of birth were about right. Their public-records profile was more of the neat/tidy/simple version. There was only one phone number associated with them, so I called it.

"Hello?" a friendly sounding southern gentleman said.

"Hi, is this Robert Denbigh?"

"It is."

"My name is Carter Ross. I'm a reporter with a newspaper in New Jersey. I'm trying to track down your daughter, Lisa."

"Oh, well, it shouldn't be too hard for you. She just moved back up your way."

"She did? Do you know where?"

"Well, no, to be honest. We just got a note from her on that Facebook thing maybe two weeks ago saying she was moving back to New Jersey. She didn't say where. We figured we'd get a note from her once she was settled down."

"Do you have a number for her by any chance?"

"Well, now, I don't know if I feel comfortable sharing that with you," he said.

"I can understand that. Could you maybe give her my number and ask her to call me?"

"I don't think she's very good about checking her messages, to be honest. When we want to get ahold of her, we usually just send her a message on Facebook. I don't have much use for it, but my wife's got an account. Why don't you do that?"

I thanked him for the suggestion and ended the call, a little embarrassed I hadn't thought of it sooner. I know there are differing opinions about Mark Zuckerberg and the phenomenon he created and/or stole, but most reporters I knew were ready to make him one of our patron saints. When it came to snooping on unsuspecting citizens — "FaceStalking," as sometimes we called it — few things were better than Facebook. It was amazing how much of their lives people would put online. Yes, Facebook has privacy controls. But a lot of people don't even bother using them.

By that point, I had enough information about Lisa Denbigh that I knew I'd find her easily, presuming she was one of the 7.5 billion people on this planet of 7 billion who have Facebook accounts. Sure enough, I came up with a Lisa Denbigh who had studied at the University of Florida and Brooks County High School.

I clicked and started chuckling. Everything was falling into place. Lisa Denbigh was a statuesque bottle blonde with high cheekbones, fake boobs, a flat stomach, and very straight, very white teeth. She actually looked a bit like the picture I had seen of Vaughn's mother, suggesting that, at least when it came to some people, maybe Freud wasn't that far off after all.

I now had the missing piece that more or less allowed me to put together a good guess at her life story. She had been head cheerleader and homecoming queen at Brooks County High School. Or maybe Brooks County Junior Miss.

No matter. Point is, she was pretty and popular. Then she went to the University of Florida, where she was in the same sorority as all the other pretty, popular girls. She graduated, went to Manhattan, and got one of those jobs that beautiful young women can always find — hostess at a high-end restaurant, receptionist at an image-conscious business, pleasing face for hire at trade shows, whatever. There were always men around to buy her clothes, buy her drinks, buy her a boob job — anything she needed.

About the time when she started realizing her youthful good looks weren't going to last indefinitely — when younger, prettier girls started showing up to replace her — she met Vaughn. He was a developer on the come who wanted some arm candy. They were a perfect couple, except for the fact that they had nothing to talk about.

After a few years, the physical attraction stopped being enough. Vaughn made a real, deep connection with his secretary and ran off with her, leaving Lisa adrift. She started moving around the country, running away from her problems. Her half of the divorce settlement had run out — which might not have taken long, since Vaughn had probably been smart enough to get a prenup. And she had never really learned how to be accountable with money. She thought beautiful people didn't have to play by the same rules as everyone else. Hence all those collection accounts I saw.

Finally she made a desperate attempt to reconnect with Vaughn — maybe on Facebook, who knows? By that point, Vaughn had grown tired of Marcia Fenstermacher, who was, while reasonably attractive, no Lisa Denbigh. And so she moved back to New Jersey and they rekindled, much to Miss Fenstermacher's consternation. And two weeks after his ex-wife showed up back in down, Vaughn had ended up dead because of it.

Or at least that was the narrative I had assembled, based on stereotypes, guesses, and certain well-honed reporter's intuition. There was only one way to find out if my version was reasonably true: I clicked on the button to compose a message to Lisa, typed out a quick request for her to please call me, and hit Send.

I just hoped she checked Facebook more often than she paid her bills.

I had more or less completed inventing Lisa Denbigh's life story when Pigeon called me, sounding out of breath.

"Hey, it's Neesha," she said, panting.

"Hey," I said. "Why do you sound like you've just run the New York Marathon?"

"Because I hate dogs," she said quickly, in between two large gulps of air.

"Come again?"

"I" — inhale — "hate" — exhale — "stupid" — inhale — "dogs," she said, with one final huff. "Sorry. I just got chased through the neighborhood by one."

"What was it, like a pit bull or something?"

"No," she said, her breathing still fast but at least not desperate. "I think it was one of

191

those . . . what was the kind of dog they had on *Full House*?"

"*Full House*?"

"Yeah, you know. That show where Mary-Kate and Ashley Olsen played the same girl, except you always knew whether it was Mary-Kate or Ashley because Ashley looks ever-so-slightly weirder than Mary-Kate?"

"Yeah, what about it?"

"They had a dog. What kind was it?"

"Pigeon . . . wasn't that a golden retriever?"

"Yeah, that's it. A golden retriever."

"So you were being chased through the streets by . . . a golden retriever. What, were you worried he would lick you to death?"

"Look, I told you, I *hate* dogs, okay?"

"Duly noted," I said. "So did you just want to tell me about your harrowing escape from this slobbering yellow menace or was there another reason for your call?"

"Oh, yeah, so I talked to one of the neighbors, and you know what she said? She said that she heard that Vaughn and Marcia had, quote, 'a big row' on Monday night."

"Really?"

"Yeah, she was kind of old — I guess that's why she used the word 'row' — and at first I was surprised that she could hear anything, because she asked me to repeat every question like five times. But she said she was walking her dog this morning — what is it with people in this neighborhood and dogs? — and she bumped into another neighbor who said she heard a lot of yelling coming from the house on Monday night."

"So this is a secondhand report of yelling," I said.

"Yeah, I guess."

"She give any details?"

"Not really. She just said everyone in the neighborhood was talking about it. The lady was a bit of a busybody, so really it might have just been her talking about it to everyone. But after what you said about Vaughn going back to his ex-wife, I thought maybe Monday night was when he told Marcia Fenstermacher and that's when she flipped out."

"Okay, good stuff," I said. "See if you can find the neighbor who actually heard this fight. And, in the meantime?"

"Yeah?"

"Watch out for wandering Pomeranians. We lost three interns just last year to those vicious brutes."

"Don't be mean," she said curtly. "That golden retriever was out to get me."

I was still laughing when she hung up on me.

Putting the Malibu in drive, I started weaving through some back streets toward the office, then decided on a quick detour to Green Street. At some point, I'd have to get a comment from the Newark Police Department about the McAlister investigation. Might as well cross it off the to-do list.

I parked at a meter and fed it — Green Street being the one place in Newark where Parking Enforcement consistently lived up to its name — then went inside the ancient and thoroughly outdated building that still housed Newark's Finest. I announced I was there to harass Hakeem Rogers, the NPD's public information officer and my occasional nemesis.

After a ten-minute wait, he came downstairs, greeting me with: "Why can't you just call me so I can have the pleasure of ignoring your message all day?"

Officer Rogers and I don't always get along very well. But at least we don't pretend otherwise. And, truth be told, I think we both enjoy the antagonism.

"Because," I told him, "I wanted to get your thoroughly unhelpful quote early on so I could have the pleasure of making fun of your bad grammar all day."

"Yeah, you're so smart. Anyway, what do you want?"

"I'm writing about Vaughn McAlister," I said.

"Yeah, I figured. What about him?"

"He was murdered in your fair city last night."

"Yeah, I heard. My comment is: Too bad it didn't happen to you instead."

"Is the Newark Police Department investigating this heinous act?"

"Of course we are," he said.

"Do you care to update the city's newspaper on the progress of your investigation?"

"Sure. You ready?"

I pulled out my pad and said, "Go."

"The Newark Police Department is actively investigating the murder of Vaughn McAlister. Anyone with information relevant to this or any other crime is urged to contact the Newark Police Department's twenty-four-hour Crime Stoppers anonymous tip line at —"

"Seriously? You're already going tips line on this one?"

Rogers usually gave us the tips-line quote when it was another thug-on-thug gang-related killing they knew they'd never be able to solve.

"That's all I got for you," Rogers said.

I debated tipping him off about Marcia

Fenstermacher, if only because it would speed things up. If the Newark Police arrested her, I'd be back to Jackie Orr and Ridgewood Avenue by the end of the week. But, maybe because I was annoyed at Rogers, I decided against it. Let the cops do their job — or not, as the case may be.

I was about to announce my departure when Hakeem Rogers did something that, while not unprecedented, was at least unusual.

"Hey, Ross?" he said.

"Yeah?"

"Put your pad away for a second."

I obliged.

"Off the record?" he said.

"Sure."

"Don't hold your breath on this one," he said.

"What does that mean?"

But Hakeem Rogers was already walking up the stairs, his back turned to me, saying more with his silence than he had with words.

Under ordinary circumstances, Marcia Fenstermacher had no trouble keeping her wits about her. She was orderly, logical and relentlessly organized. It was why Vaughn had hired her in the first place, poaching her from another developer by offering her a five-thousand-dollar raise. It was why Vaughn had become so dependent on her, relying on her to know even the smallest detail of his business. Sometimes she swore he wouldn't know where the bathroom was without her.

But, these being anything but ordinary circumstances, it took her a while to finally reach a conclusion about what to do next. There was just so much to process. Plus, everyone kept coming up to her with these big, weepy eyes, wanting to console her, inquiring how she was doing, asking if there was anything they could do. It was all well-intentioned, of course, but it kept distracting her from what she knew she really should be doing.

Yes, there was a lot to be done. And everyone would expect Marcia Fenstermacher to be the one to do it, just like always.

She needed to contact a funeral home, arrange for a viewing, find a minister to officiate at the service. Vaughn was a seriously lapsed Episcopalian who probably hadn't darkened the doors of a church since his wedding day. But it would be nice to hear some comforting words from someone in a stiff white collar. It all had to look good.

Except, of course, there was something she knew that had to be done first.

Wanting to be alone, she waited until everyone was out of the office at lunch — or at least would not be coming to bother her about anything. She quietly rose from her desk, tossing her latest overloaded tissue into the wastebasket as she stood. She walked as quietly as she could across the hardwood floor to the door to Vaughn's office.

There, she paused. She hadn't been in there since the night before, since . . .

She took a deep breath, then pulled on the handle. Everything looked the same as it had the thousands of other times she had pushed through those doors. She reminded herself she was not a superstitious person. She didn't believe in ghosts. Vaughn's spirit was not in there.

Only his files were. She walked over to the filing cabinet in the corner — the one he kept locked — and produced her key. What she needed was in the second drawer from the top.

She pulled it open and found the folder, exactly where it was supposed to be. Inside was a sealed, plain brown envelope. There was no writing on it, but she knew it was the right one.

Not bothering with a letter opener, she slid her finger under the flap, creating a series of jagged edges in her haste to get to the contents. Then she pulled out the document inside.

Her eyes paused on the words atop the first page: "Last Will and Testament of Vaughn J. McAlister."

With one last deep breath, she started reading. She went slowly at first, then started skimming as she got closer to the end. It was all there, in black-and-white.

He had left her everything. The house. Every dime in his savings account. His cars. The 401(k) — or what was left of it after he had raided it three times. His 50 percent interest in McAlister Properties. Everything.

She slid the drawer closed, her hand shaking just slightly.

CHAPTER 4

The reluctance of the Newark Police to engage in solving Vaughn McAlister's murder was curious. It's not that they were terribly concerned about what it would do to their clearance rate. With eighty or a hundred killings a year, one sliding under the boards wouldn't budge the numbers that much. Only about half the murders in Newark got solved anyway. Still, the Vaughn McAlisters of the world usually belonged in the half of the murders the Newark Police did solve. He was a regular citizen, after all — a well-known member of the business community, at that.

And yet Pritch was telling me no special resources were being put toward it, because city hall didn't seem to be making a fuss about it. And Hakeem Rogers was telling me not to hold my breath waiting for it.

Did Marcia Fenstermacher somehow possess the connections or political wherewithal to get an investigation squashed? That seemed to strain credulity. She was secretary of McAlister Properties, not secretary of state.

So was there something else about Vaughn McAlister's life or death that someone high up in the police department or the city of Newark didn't want exposed? Or was there some other actor or element out there I had yet to even discover?

It begged an explanation that I could not, at the moment, produce. So, halfway back to the *Eagle-Examiner* offices, I broke off my usual route and turned toward the Clinton Hill section of the city. My Malibu, as sensitive to the unexpected course change as any Trigger or Silver, whinnied and neighed.

"That's right, boy," I told it. "We're not going to the newsroom. We're going to visit an old friend."

When official sources don't know much, or won't say much, unofficial sources often do. And one of my best unofficial sources for all things related to the streets of Newark was a T-shirt-shop owner who more or less grew up on them.

Tee Jamison is one of those people who proves that adage about the dangers of judging books by their covers — or, in his case, brothers by their tats. Because while he's got the tattoos — and the braids, and the muscles, and a certain look that tends to make old white women nervous — he's about as much of a thug as Betty Crocker. Put it this way: I once caught him in the back of the store with a box of tissues and a bootleg copy of *Love, Actually.*

His real name is Reginald. In return for my never telling any of his friends that, he has been known to help me with an occasional story or ten. He enjoys sharing his knowledge of urban culture with me, and I'm happy to oblige by playing the part of the clueless white guy. He keeps claiming he has a second white friend, but I'm skeptical.

The street outside his store was empty, as it tended to be in the morning. By afternoon, there would be an assortment of young men that Tee semi-lovingly referred to as "the knuckleheads." They were a mostly harmless group who acted like they were in a gang — they wore gang colors, flashed one another gang symbols, affected gang attitudes — but were really just faking it. I asked them about it once, and it turns out pretending to be in a gang is a great way to get left alone by people who really *are* in a gang.

I rang Tee's doorbell and got buzzed in. From his back room, I heard, "Hey, why don't black people take aspirin?"

"Oh, my," I said. "I don't know, Tee, why don't black people take aspirin?"

"Because they're too proud to pick the cotton out of the top of the bottle," Tee said, emerging into the front of the store with a grin on his face.

"That's beyond horrible."

"Yeah, and if you told me that joke, I'd have to organize an angry mob to stomp on your pasty white face. But since it's me telling it to you, it's just funny. That's what you white people like to call 'ironic.' "

"Well, maybe Alanis Morissette would, but I was never sure she quite got the definition of that word right."

"Who's Alanis Morissette?"

"She's Canadian. And angry."

"Man, I would be too if I had to live in Canada," he said. "Ain't nothing but snow and polar bears up there. Hey, what do you get if you cross a black man and an Eskimo?"

"No. I'm not playing along this time. I can't run the risk you're an informant for the NAACP."

"A'ight," he said. "Fine. Ruin my fun. Anyhow, what's up? You never come around no more."

"I was here last week."

"You was?"

"Yeah."

"Aw, man, I thought that was my *other* white friend. You guys all look alike, you know."

"So I've heard," I said. "Anyhow, I'm actually not just here to swap racially insensitive witticisms."

"Oh yeah, what's going on?"

"You've heard about McAlister Arms, right?"

"Yeah, gonna get us a Best Buy!" he crowed.

Like I said, Tee knows stuff about Newark. "The identity of the tenant is supposedly a big secret. How do you know it's a Best Buy?"

"Because one of the knuckleheads told me they saw some dudes in Best Buy shirts walking around the property a couple weeks ago," Tee said. "It's all over the city already. Every shoplifter I know is looking forward to it."

He was kidding. I think.

"Anyhow," I said, "the property's developer got killed last night. He has a jealous girlfriend, so it might be pretty straightforward. But the cops don't seem to be doing much with it. So I was hoping you could keep an ear out for any talk about it."

"What kind of talk?"

"The usual who-done-it and why."

"Oh, well it's probably one of his workers," Tee said definitively.

I felt my head recoil. "One of his workers? What makes you say that?"

"They all getting sick."

"Sick?" I asked, getting another small jolt. Just when I thought sick people were out of my purview for the time being, here they were again. I had dismissed the possibility of the McAlister Arms site as the source of the Ridgewood Avenue mystery disease because Vaughn McAlister told me it had been cleaned up. But if construction workers were having the same symptoms as Edna Foster and her neighbors, I'd have to start digging a lot harder into McAlister Arms. Perhaps literally.

"Yeah, sick. They been hiring a bunch of people from the neighborhood down there. And at first everyone was like, 'Wow, a construction project that's actually hiring black folks.' Because usually they just bring in people from out of town, you know what I'm saying?"

"Sure."

"So they start throwing around jobs, and

then we figured out why they must have wanted black folks. It's because whatever they're doing down there is making them all sick. And, you know how it is, don't nobody give a damn about sick black folks."

"Yeah, so I've heard," I said. "What kind of sick are they?"

"I don't know. I just heard everyone working there is getting sick. But when they complain or don't show up for work, they get fired. There's enough people in this city who need jobs that there's always someone to take their place. Some of the workers figured out the score and just stopped complaining — it's good money, you know what I'm saying? But I know some other dudes who are really pissed off. One of them probably got pissed off enough that they, you know, handled it hood style."

An angry construction worker was certainly a lot more likely to be proficient with a blunt object than a secretary was. Then again, I'm not sure this simplified anything. I had seen dozens of workers down at that site. That would make for a rather sizable suspect pool.

"Do you know any of these guys who were working down there?" I asked.

"Yeah, I know all of them. But ain't none of them gonna snitch."

"No, no. I'm not looking for a snitch," I said, then told him all about the people I had met on Ridgewood Avenue and how the construction workers sounded like victims of the same malady.

"Well, I'll be damned," Tee said when I was done.

"What?"

He grinned and said, "Guess someone might care about sick black people after all."

Tee and I made arrangements wherein he'd contact some construction workers on my behalf and I'd be the beneficiary of his efforts when I got to interview them at some later date.

I was just out the door when my phone started ringing. The call was from the 973 area code, which meant it was local, but neither my phone nor I recognized the number.

"Carter Ross."

"Yo, Bird Man," I heard back. Bird Man is what people on the streets of Newark sometimes call reporters from my paper because of the more avian aspects of the *Newark Eagle-Examiner*'s banner. The person hailing me this way was young, African American, and vaguely familiar-sounding. But I couldn't quite place his voice.

"Hi, how can I help you?"

The man lowered the phone and, chuckling, announced, "He asking, 'Hi, how can I help you?' " This prompted laughter from his audience, which sounded like three or four other young men.

"Damn, Bird Man, you really do got a funny way of talking," he said.

That's when I knew who it was. "Bernie Kosar! Is that you?"

He laughed again and said to his friends, "He just asked if it's Bernie Kosar." The buddies seemed to enjoy this, too, and Bernie returned to the phone. "You too funny," he said.

"Thanks. Anyhow, to what do I owe the pleasure?"

I thought Bernie might feel compelled to repeat that line, too. But he answered, "You might want to come by Brown Town. Someone here wants to tell you something."

"Okay. I just happen to be in the neighborhood. I'll see you in five minutes."

Brown Town was the quasi-secret world headquarters of the Brick City Browns, one of Newark's more-venerated street gangs. In an increasingly partisan gang world of Bloods, Crips, Latin Kings, and MS-13 — to name just a few — the Browns had remained staunchly independent. They had their hustle and answered to no one.

Not long ago, while reporting a story, I had become an honorary member of the Brick City Browns. I had done this by earning their trust — this may have involved smoking a mildly psychoactive controlled dangerous substance — and then by giving them a fair shake in the newspaper. As a "member," I was allowed to visit whenever I pleased. Which, admittedly, was not too often.

Nevertheless, I remembered the way well enough. So it was actually four minutes later when I knocked on the door. Bernie Kosar — I had given him that name because he usually wore the retro uniform of former Cleveland Browns quarterback Bernie Kosar — answered. Except he wasn't wearing Kosar's number 19. He was dressed in droopy jeans and a brown camouflage hunting jacket.

"Hey, what happened to your uniform?"

"We ain't been wearing those lately," he informed me.

"Why not?"

" 'Cuz the Cleveland Browns football team been stinking it up so bad. It don't look good for our organization. I mean, if you're wearing Patriots jerseys, people say, 'There goes a winner.' But the Browns?

Man, the Romeo Crennel era was a joke. And don't even make me start talking about that fool Eric Mangini."

"Fair enough," I said. "Anyhow, you said someone here wants to talk to me?"

"Yeah, come on in."

I entered Brown Town, which was basically unchanged from the last time I had been there. On the outside, it was a tired-looking, three-story, wooden single-family dwelling, a genus of house Newark had in plenty. On the inside, it was one seriously pimped-out pad, with leather sofas, big-screen televisions, and enough mirrors to make you think it was being used as a set for *Feng Shui Gone Wild.*

Bernie led me into the living room, where Kevin Mack — or the guy who used to wear Kevin Mack's retro uniform, before that became untenable — was playing a shoot-'em-up video game with some other guys. Bernie nodded at him and Kevin put down the controller and said, "No fair killing me while I'm gone."

I followed the two of them into the kitchen, which was in its original, non-pimped-out condition. That meant we were sitting at a table that might be characterized as pre-Internet, surrounded by a whole lot of linoleum flooring and particle-board cabinetry. Bernie shot another look at Kevin, who started talking.

"So I was down on Peshine Avenue last night when I saw something you might be interested in," he said. "But, you know, you can't tell no cops where you heard this."

"Okay," I said. The Browns were, perhaps understandably, not fond of law enforcement. "What were you doing down there?" I asked.

Kevin glanced at Bernie.

"We've got some, uh, commercial interests in the area," Bernie said.

Back when I had gained membership, the Browns funded their activities through the sale of bootleg movies. I wasn't sure if they were still in that business or if they had moved on, and I knew better than to ask. Sometimes, even a newspaper reporter doesn't want to know the full truth.

"Anyhow, I'm, you know, doing my thing, kind of waiting for . . . someone," Kevin continued. "And suddenly this black car comes cruising down the street. I'm thinking maybe it's the dude I'm waiting for, even though that ain't his usual ride. So I'm watching it. Next thing you know, it stops, and these two white dudes get out and, real fast, haul this other white dude out of the backseat and toss him in this construction site. And then they leave real fast, and I'm like, what the . . . ? Then I look at the dude they tossed out, and I was like, 'Whoah shee! That dude is dead!' And then I got out of there real fast, because I do *not* need to be the nigga they pin that on."

He didn't need to tell me that the construction site was McAlister Arms or that the dead dude was Vaughn McAlister.

Bernie Kosar cut in: "Then we saw in the newspaper this morning you was writing about that dude. We thought you'd want to hear how it went down."

"I appreciate that. A lot," I said. "Thanks."

"Hey, man, you a Brown, you a Brown for life," Bernie said, then made some kind of hand gesture that, for as many times as I had seen it, I lacked the manual dexterity to duplicate.

"So, these two white guys," I asked Kevin. "Did you get a look at them?"

"I mean, yeah and no," Kevin said. "They sorta looked alike. They was both big. And they had they hair all slicked back. And they was wearing black leather coats. That's probably all I saw. It all happened pretty fast."

And then Kevin added what I had already been thinking: "They looked like they was from *The Sopranos* or something."

It was possible. Mobsters in Newark, once a common sight, were now more of a rarity, having retreated from the neighborhoods along with the rest of the white population. But they still made the occasional foray.

So it could be the mob. Or it could be professional killers.

Which could still mean his secretary was behind it. It could also mean it was anyone with a few grand to spend and a grudge to settle.

We chatted for a little while, though Kevin Mack didn't know much more than what he had already shared. Before long, they were extending an offer to partake in some of the aforementioned CDS, and I thought I was going to have to come up with a creative excuse as to why I couldn't when my phone saved me by ringing.

"Sorry, guys," I said without looking at it. "I'm expecting a call from my editor. I gotta take this."

They bade me a fond adieu and as I darted out I promised to visit again soon. The phone was already on its fourth ring — dangerously close to going to voice mail — when I yanked it from my pocket and saw it wasn't my editor. It was Tee.

214

I answered the way he always does: "Yeah."

"Hey, that's my line," Tee said.

"I know, but haven't you learned yet? We let you blacks invent stuff and then if it's good, we whites steal it."

"That's true. But y'all stole the Neville Brothers, too. So you can't be *that* smart."

"Well, there's no accounting for taste," I confirmed.

"Anyhow, I was going to try to round up a few of the guys who had been working on that construction site. But then one of them just walked into my store. You wanna talk to him?"

"Yeah, I'm actually close-by. I'll be there soon."

"Okay. He in the back watching a Sister Souljah tribute. So he ain't going anywhere for a while."

"I'll be right there anyway," I said, hopping into my car.

There was still no sign of any knuckleheads when I arrived. Tee buzzed me in and hollered, "We back here."

I went to the back room, where Tee was sitting on the couch with a young black man, who looked up from Sister Souljah as I walked in. He was dark skinned and neatly kept, with close-shaved hair and a thin mustache. He had a small gold earring in his left ear only, but I didn't know if that meant anything anymore — other than that he didn't feel like buying two earrings.

The far more interesting accessory was the one he had on his right leg. It was a white splint, and it ran from his ankle to his thigh. There were crutches leaning against the far side of the couch.

"Hi. I'm Carter Ross," I said. Had he stood, I would have extended a hand to shake. But he was, for obvious reasons, staying seated.

" 'Sup," he said.

"As Tee probably told you, we're writing a story for the *Eagle-Examiner* about McAlister Arms and some of the things that are going on in that neighborhood. You worked down there?"

He nodded.

"What's your name?" I asked.

"Do I gotta give him that?" the young man asked Tee.

I had told Tee enough about how my business worked that he knew how to answer. "That's how they roll. But you ain't got nothing to hide and you ain't done nothing wrong, so it ain't no big thing. You can trust him."

"Yeah, yeah," he said, like he was convinc-

216

ing himself of this fact.

"So what's your name?" I said again.

"DaQuan Richardson," he said. I made him spell "DaQuan" for me — hey, you never know — and got some of his basic information. He was twenty-three. He had lived in Newark all his life. He had gone to West Side High School. He'd done a semester of community college but it hadn't stuck. Now he was bouncing from job to job. He was going to try to get hired by United — the airline was one of Newark's largest employers — but that was on hold, on account of his leg.

"Yeah, about that . . . what happened to it?" I asked.

"I was just ballin' with some of my boys and it snapped," he said. "I wasn't even doing nothing. Just dribbling the ball and *crack*. Hurt something bad."

"When did it happen?"

"About two months ago. I had a hard cast for the first six weeks. Now it's in this thing," he said, gesturing toward the splint. "It ain't much better, but at least when it itches I can scratch it."

"And you were working for McAlister when it happened?"

"Yeah." And then he offered an unprintable word about McAlister Properties, suggesting that its bosses had a rather un-natural affinity for their mothers.

"So you're not a big fan," I confirmed.

"When I broke my leg, they just fired me. No disability. No severance. Nothing. They said I didn't qualify for nothing. It was just 'see ya later.' At first, I was pissed. But then I was like, 'Thank goodness.' "

"Why is that?"

"Because, man, I kept getting sick the whole time I was working there."

"What kind of sick?"

"Oh, you know. It was like the flu or something. You'd feel it coming on and then it would just hit you. It got so you knew when it was going to happen. I worked there three months and I probably got sick ten times. Since I quit, I been fine. It's the same with a bunch of other dudes, too. We all been getting sick. Some of them complained and they got fired. Some just quit. Some of them kept their mouth shut. They still working there, still getting sick. I heard one dude had to go on dialysis."

Just like Jackie Orr's grandmother. "What about broken bones?" I asked. "Anyone else break a bone?"

"Yeah, a couple other dudes, actually. One of them broke his collarbone on-site."

"Ouch," Tee said.

"Yeah," DaQuan said. "But that's okay, the lawyer said we gonna get us some money for that."

"Lawyer?" I said. "What lawyer?"

Fifteen minutes later, I left Tee's place armed with the name of Will Imperiale, Esquire, and some vague details about the lawsuit he was planning against McAlister Properties.

The name, I already knew. Anyone in New Jersey who had ever glanced in a telephone book, watched daytime television, or received junk mail knew the name Will Imperiale. Probably anyone who had slipped and fallen in the local grocery store knew of him, too. He was the heavily advertised king of the local personal injury lawyers.

And, according to DaQuan, he had somehow gotten word about sick construction workers and had been quietly signing them up — there were several dozen — with assurances of a quick and sizable settlement. Thousands of dollars for anyone who had been ill even once, he had said. Thousands more if someone had lost his job for any length of time. Hundreds of thousands for a broken bone. For anyone who had more serious complications? It could be even more. Plus, all their medical bills would be handled.

They were bold promises, and I was unconvinced how much he could back them up. Because, sure, in a grocery store slip-and-fall, things were relatively straightforward: there was no question how the plaintiff had gotten hurt, nor was there any doubt that the defendant had likely caused it. The lawyers would go into a conference room and come out an hour later with an agreement that a broken leg was worth, say, $200,000 in pain and suffering, $60,000 in medical bills, and $30,000 in lost wages. Not bad for an hour's work.

I couldn't imagine things were as easy in a case like this. The defendant's lawyers would know that proving the construction site was making people sick was no easy task, from a legal standpoint. Who's to say they hadn't just picked up some bug that they kept passing to one another?

You'd have to be able to find the chemical culprit, prove it was in the ground/air/water, prove it was capable of causing the maladies in question, and furthermore prove there wasn't some other toxin — from some other nearby source — at work. It would involve complicated science, painstaking documentation, a raft of expensive experts, and a whole lot of moving parts that might or might not come through for you.

Plus, you needed the rare jury that would be smart enough to understand all the science involved but still compassionate enough — or angry enough — to sock the responsible party with a large judgment. Then you needed to hope the dollar amount didn't get knocked too far down on appeal.

Oh, and the whole thing could take ten years.

I couldn't imagine Will Imperiale was mentioning any of that to his new clients. Right now, the game was just to get the maximum number of people to entrust their legal fate to him. The more clients he signed up, the more his reward grew — because he'd get a third of whatever he could ultimately collect for them.

With multiple defendants, the math got big in a hurry. Say he could sign up forty people and get them an average of $200,000 after medical bills, pain and suffering, and lost compensation were factored in. That was a tidy $8 million, of which he'd get a nice little $2.6 million slice. So it behooved him to talk big now, even if his chances of being able to deliver later were anything but assured.

If nothing else, it was, in the short term, a good follow for the next day's paper: the dead man's company was allegedly making construction workers sick and was about to be sued for it by a prominent and successful personal injury lawyer. At the very least, it was something to momentarily requite Harold Brodie's amour for the story.

I called Pigeon, told her about the lawsuit, and instructed her to stop bothering Vaughn's former neighbors — which she was more than happy to do. It didn't sound like she'd had luck finding any who were as chatty as the old lady from earlier in the day. Her new assignment, I informed her, was to start calling some of the other construction workers; Tee had given me a few names and numbers as a parting gift. I, meanwhile, was going to make an unannounced visit to the offices of Imperiale & Trautwig.

It would have made for better copy if those offices had been located in some seedy strip mall. And they may once have been. But business had obviously been good enough for Imperiale & Trautwig that they were in One Newark Center, alongside a variety of upstanding law firms, masquerading as one of them. Perhaps I shouldn't totally denigrate the practice of personal injury law. Certainly there were times when the negligence of others caused real harm to certain individuals, and they had every right to be compensated for their suffering. I just wished the whole racket weren't quite so opportunistic.

Imperiale & Trautwig took up half of the twelfth floor, and I told the receptionist just inside the main doors that I was there to see Mr. Imperiale and, no, I didn't have an appointment. This immediately became of less concern when I announced I was a reporter with the *Eagle-Examiner,* and two minutes later I was sitting inside Will Imperiale's office, across from the great man himself.

Will Imperiale was perhaps fifty, with dark hair whose color came from a bottle. The most prominent feature on him was his nose, which was large and hooked. All through our brief introductions, I couldn't help but stare at it. It was an impressive nose.

"So I met a new client of yours today," I said when it was time to stop with the preambles.

"And who is that?"

"DaQuan Richardson," I said.

With that, the nose had a smile appear underneath it. He was doing his best not to look like a man who had just hit the lottery.

He rearranged some things on his desk and tried to make his eyes seem like they were full of concern — not just dollar signs.

"Ah, yes, Mr. Richardson," he said. "How was his leg looking?"

"Just fine," I assured him. "He said it's a lot more comfortable now that the cast is off."

"He still has a long road ahead of him," Imperiale said. "He's going to be out of work for some time yet. He's a laborer, you know. Can't labor with a broken leg. Medically, there's going to be more doctor's visits, rehab, a long recovery — and that's assuming it's healed properly."

Will Imperiale was obviously hoping it hadn't. If doctors had to break it again and reset it, that would be worth, what, another hundred grand?

"All things I'm sure you'll be pointing out to the defendant's lawyers," I said. "Speaking of which, who are the defendants?"

He once again was attempting to tamp down his smile. "May I ask your interest in the case?"

"Yeah, sure. You may have heard Vaughn McAlister is no longer with us."

"Yes, I read it in the paper today."

"And I wrote it in the paper today. The thing is, we also have a paper tomorrow. So

I need to write something for that. The fact that Mr. McAlister's company is being sued — and may have been making construction workers sick — smells like news to me."

That there were also residents in a nearby neighborhood getting sick made it even more newsworthy. But I wasn't going to tell him about that yet. Nor was I ready to put it in the newspaper.

"Well, it's premature to . . ." Imperiale started, then stopped himself.

He chuckled lightly. There were obviously things bouncing around in his head, and I could tell he was having a debate with himself about how much to tell the newspaper reporter. Lawyers, personal injury lawyers especially, often have this problem. Because, on the one hand, he didn't want anything printed that might damage his case or tip off the other side as to his strategy. It was not unusual for trials to have newspaper clippings among their exhibits as the result of lawyers or clients who had said too much. On the other hand, the threat of bad publicity could be a powerful weapon for the plaintiff in any legal proceeding. Civil suits were often settled just to keep things out of the newspaper. And in a case this complex, a quick settlement benefited the plaintiff's lawyer more than anyone.

I let Imperiale have a little debate with himself. Finally, he said, "Can we talk off the record?"

"As long as I can get something on the record by the time I leave here. I'm not here strictly for the charming conversation, you understand."

"Sure, I understand," he said. "Okay, off the record: the complaint hasn't been filed yet. So, technically, there is no lawsuit. Yet."

"When were you planning on filing?"

"Soon. We were still gathering plaintiffs. You can always add more by amending the complaint after you file, of course. But I always like to feel like I've beaten the bushes pretty thoroughly before I file. I was probably going to give it another week or two. But the development with Vaughn McAlister and your interest could . . . change the timeline, I guess."

"Right, of course," I said. I understood what he was talking about: Will Imperiale didn't want to risk losing his case. If I brought attention to the fact that people were getting sick and there was no law firm of record, every ambulance chaser who had ever passed the New Jersey bar might start scouring Newark, looking for clients. But if Imperiale & Trautwig had already planted its flag in that legal ground and it was known it had already signed up a few dozen clients — perhaps all the clients there were to be had — it would become much less attractive to the competition.

"We've been writing the complaint as we went, so it's pretty much ready to go, but . . ." He stopped himself. The smile went blinding for a second, then he reined it in. "What would it be worth to you to be the first to get your hands on the complaint?" he asked.

Without hesitation, I shot back, "We're not a tabloid. We don't pay for stories."

"No, no, I'm not talking about that," he said. "No money."

"Then what?"

"I could get the thing filed by five this afternoon. No one else in the media would be able to see it until it was processed, which wouldn't happen until Thursday morning at the earliest. But I could e-mail you a copy when I filed. It would be a guaranteed scoop for you."

"And in exchange?"

"Whatever you wrote would need to say 'Imperiale and Trautwig' at least four times," he said smoothly.

Now it was my turn to smile. I got it. He didn't want money. He wanted something more valuable: free advertising. He knew a front-page story that mentioned his law firm prominently was gold. It would scare off other firms and also possibly flush out additional plaintiffs.

From a strictly by-the-book standpoint, we didn't cut deals like this with sources. And perhaps if Pigeon had been around, I would have told the guy to screw off, simply to set a good example for her. But the sausage-making enterprise that was putting together a daily newspaper could sometimes get a little messy. And while I wouldn't go bragging about this at the next Society of Professional Journalists cocktail party, I was going to mention his law firm in what I wrote anyway. So there seemed little harm in engaging in a minor gentleman's agreement that didn't involve cash considerations or anything else that would be a serious ethical foul.

"Okay, but four times is a little much. It'll start to read like a billboard for Imperiale and Trautwig," I said. "Three times."

"Three times, plus you mention our Web site."

"No Web site. It'll make me feel like your whore, plus I guarantee you the copydesk would cut it out, and I have no control over that."

He eyed me. "Okay, three times," he said,

reaching across the desk to shake my hand. "I'll send you the complaint by five. You can quote from it whatever you want."

"Deal," I said. "By the way, I assume the complaint will say what is making people sick?"

"No," he said.

"Isn't that something you kind of need to know?"

"Not really," he assured me. "Not yet, anyway. We can keep it vague for the time being. Eventually we'll get into chemical testing. For now, we just need plaintiffs with problems."

"Well, you certainly seem to have that."

"We do," he said.

As I excused myself from his office, his parting shot was: "Remember. Imperiale and Trautwig. Four times."

"Three times," I reminded him.

"Oh, right," he said. "Three."

Had to give him credit for trying.

I returned to the office, exacted a Coke Zero from the break room vending machine — Coke Zero being as necessary to my writing process as air — and hunkered down. My plan was to craft the shell of a story, then fill in the details when Will Imperiale sent me the complaint. I had barely settled

229

into my chair when Tommy Hernandez ambled my way. Well, maybe it was more of a sashay than an amble. Tommy even walked gay.

"So I'm going to tell you some things about Vaughn McAlister, but first I have a question for you: What do your shoes have in common with Hurricane Katrina?"

I looked down at my feet, still unsure what he found so offensive about how they were shod, then decided to play along. "I don't know, Tommy, what do my shoes have in common with Hurricane Katrina?"

"They both qualify as federal disaster areas."

"Okay, seriously, what is the problem with these shoes? There's nothing —"

"Laces," he interrupted.

"Excuse me?"

"Laces are what's wrong with your shoes. Unless you're trying out for the lead role in *Death of a Salesman* and you need to look like you're from the fifties, there is no need to have laces in your dress shoes. Laces are for sneakers, hiking boots, and certain avant-garde peasant blouses. I mean, those things on your feet almost look like wingtips."

"What's wrong with wingtips?"

"Are you a hipster wearing them ironically or are you playing the part of the one percent in an Occupy Wall Street protest demonstration? Then fine. Otherwise: everything. Everything is what's wrong with wingtips."

"I just . . . I don't understand."

"I know you don't," he said gravely. "Believe me, I know."

He bowed his head, moment-of-silence style, as if mourning the death of fashion.

"Anyhow," I said, "if you'll excuse me, I have a story to write."

"Oh, yeah! I knew I came over here for a reason," he said, delighted with himself for remembering. "I learned some very interesting things about the dead guy formerly known as Vaughn McAlister."

"Oh?"

Tommy sat down at the desk across from me, which was empty, and crossed his legs. "Well, remember I told you about that city hall source that likened him to Harry Grant?"

"Yeah."

"Well, I got the guy talking a little more and it sounds like Vaughn McAlister was in trouble money-wise."

"How so?"

"Apparently, McAlister Properties hasn't actually paid the city for the land that

McAlister Arms sits on. The city already deeded it over to him, but he'd yet to give them a dime."

"Oh, that's neat."

"Yeah, but there's more," Tommy said. "From what this guy says, the city sold Vaughn the land for $1.4 million, but it promised McAlister Properties $1.1 million to help clean it up."

"So he basically paid three hundred grand for a big chunk of prime real estate. But it goes in the books as $1.4 million so no one howls that the city is giving him too cozy a deal."

"Well, there's that, and also there's an accounting thing going on. I didn't exactly understand it, but I guess the money comes out of different pots, and for tax reasons, it made sense for the city to have a $1.4 million credit in one place and a $1.1 million debit in another. It's something to do with state aid."

"Okay," I said. You had to love the vagaries of municipal accounting, which were designed seemingly to keep lay people as confused as possible. The problem is, it often had the same effect on the professionals hired to understand them.

"Except here's where it gets really good," Tommy said, getting so excited he had uncrossed his legs and was now leaning forward on the desk. "The city gave Vaughn the cleanup money even though he still hasn't paid them for the land."

"So he's walking around with what is essentially a free $1.1 million loan, all while owing them $1.4 million."

"Yep. My source said no one in city hall wanted to make a big deal out of it, because they were afraid they'd end up looking as bad as McAlister. And the South Ward councilman hadn't made a fuss because he's afraid if he presses too hard, McAlister Properties will pull the plug on the project — and I guess he was planning on making McAlister Arms a centerpiece of his reelection campaign. My source said he was starting to think that McAlister might be able to get away with never paying."

"Meaning the city would have paid him $1.1 million to take ownership of a property with a fair market value of at least twice that?" I said.

That, perhaps, started to explain why city hall wasn't putting any stress on the police department to solve Vaughn's murder. Men like Pritch and Hakeem Rogers were usually antennae for political pressure — due to the aforementioned axiom about what flows downhill. But neither of them had sensed that pressure this time, because, if anything, it was being applied in the opposite direction. No one in city government wanted this murder to get much attention, and therefore no one was calling the police department to demand justice.

In short, there was a bit of a stench around Vaughn McAlister, and the less it was fanned, the fewer people would have to smell it.

"You got it," Tommy said. "So I'm thinking maybe we do a follow that says something like, 'Slain developer was broke as a joke.' You think that would be good?"

"Well, I'm all for following the money. So yeah, let's try and do a piece about McAlister's finances," I said. "But let's not put him in the poorhouse just yet. Developers are always playing games with cash flow. He might have just known he could wait a little while before paying Newark, while some of his other creditors were a little more insistent."

"Or he could have used it for bribe money," Tommy said, giggling. Tommy giggled about such wanton breaches of trust from public officials mostly because Tommy giggled about everything.

"You might want to pull his campaign contributions to see if he tried to do some of it legally," I suggested. "As for the other stuff, how much of that can we get on the record?"

"All of it. It's just going to take a little while. Now that I know what to ask for, I've requested the necessary documents from the city clerk's office. It's a question of how long they sit on it."

"What's their average these days?"

"They've been pretty good, actually. I've got a girlfriend there who helps me out."

"A girlfriend with apparently no gaydar whatsoever," I pointed out.

"Well, she's a lot older than me. So who knows? Maybe she has a son that she's just waiting to set me up with. She's Puerto Rican and she's pretty fine for an older woman. I bet if you put her mouth on a guy, it would —"

"Okay, okay. I don't want you to have to take a cold shower," I said.

"Yeah, speaking of which, *your* girlfriend is approaching," Tommy said.

It said a lot about the precarious state of my existence that I had to turn to discover whom he was talking about. But when I did, I saw Kira O'Brien slinking toward me, wearing one of her conservative work outfits — pink sweater set, gray slacks — with her hair up in a little bun. Seeing her made me feel vaguely guilty, simply because I had been thinking a lot about Tina — for understandable reasons — and quite a bit less about my favorite librarian.

"Hi, Tommy," she said.

"Hey, Keer," Tommy said.

Then she looked at me and announced, "Carter, I've given this a lot of thought and . . . I think I'm ready to take the next step in our relationship."

Sensitive interpreter of social situations that he is, Tommy took that as his cue to leave. Kira planted herself in the seat he had just vacated. I found myself wishing this conversation — wherever it was leading — didn't have to take place in the middle of the newsroom. Kira was unconcerned about public displays of, well, just about anything.

"Uh, okay, what next step?" I said, trying to keep my voice hushed.

"Well," she said, sitting up very properly, with a special twinkle in her blue eyes. "I know we haven't really talked about our relationship or put any labels on it. So I don't want this to be too sudden. And you can tell me if you think it is. You'll tell me, right?"

"Uh, yeah, sure, I guess," I said, but inside I was already flinching.

"Seriously, I want to be careful that we're not moving too fast for you," she continued. "I know how guys are with the C-word."

"The . . . C-word?" I asked. The only C-word I could think of that I had serious problems with was "celibacy."

She glanced left, then right, then whispered, "You know, the C-word: 'commitment.' "

Oh no. Not now. Not here. I suddenly felt my internal temperature rising. The last time a woman had started talking in these kinds of terms with me, it was a few years back. The girl I had been seeing at the time told me her lease was up, and she strongly suggested — to the point where one could say she informed me — that she was moving in with me. I'll spare the details and say it ended when she moved out, having strongly suggested and/or informed me that she was having an affair with a guy from her office.

And it's not that, under ordinary circumstances, I would mind having a girl as cute and spunky and smart as Kira want to progress our relationship. I mean, true, we had never really had a serious conversation about anything. But that wasn't the issue. It's just that, in matters such as these, my circumstances were T-minus nine months from changing dramatically.

"So," she continued. "I don't want you to freak out or anything but . . ."

I may have winced as I waited for her next words.

"I want to take you to the Zombie Ball," she said. Then added, "As my date."

I waited for there to be more. Like, *I want to take you to the Zombie Ball and I want you to propose to me there.* But there was nothing more forthcoming. Then I remembered: this was Kira. Simple, fun, easygoing Kira. She called it the "C-word" because she was more afraid of it than I was.

"Oh," said, feeling my body instantly cool off. "Sure. No problem. When is it?"

"Friday night," she said.

I winced again, but for different reasons. "Ugh, I can't make it that night," I said. Kira immediately looked hurt, so I explained, "My sister is getting married this weekend. Friday night is her rehearsal dinner."

"You . . . you have a sister?" Kira asked.

Like I said, we had never had a serious conversation. "Yeah. She lives in New York and I don't see her a lot, so I guess you haven't had a chance to meet her yet."

"And she's getting married?"

"Yeah. On Saturday," I said.

238

"Around here?"

"In Millburn, yeah."

"Are you . . . going with anyone?"

"No," I said.

"Oh," she said, and suddenly she wasn't looking at me anymore.

And then, with roughly the same speed as continents divide and mountains grow, it occurred to me: Kira wanted to go to the wedding. With me.

I was so proud of myself for realizing this, I didn't think about the long-term implications of what I asked next. Let me be more clear about this: I really, truly wasn't thinking. Sometimes people — and by people, I mean women — don't get this about guys. They'll get all haughty and superior and snap, *What were you thinking?* And that fact is, we weren't thinking anything at all. We just weren't.

This was one of those times. I just cleared my throat and tried to make it sound like I was still in the flow of the conversation. "You want go to with me?"

"Of course!" she said immediately, her entire face lifting upward, the twinkle back in her eyes. "I mean, it's your sister's wedding. I love weddings. Why wouldn't I want to go?"

"I don't know. I just didn't think you'd be

interested. I mean, you do know the only person at a wedding who's allowed to be in costume is the bride, right?"

"Wait, you mean I can't wear my pink Power Rangers outfit?" she said, deadpan, then gave me a wink.

"Well, as long as it's not white," I said.

She snickered and rewarded me with a genuinely happy smile. "Oh, this is going to be great. I'm so glad you asked me. I actually have the perfect dress for a wedding. I got it last year for my friend's wedding. There's just one problem with it."

"What's that?" I asked.

She rose from her chair, walked over to me, leaned in close, and whispered, "It's kind of tight. And the only way to avoid having panty lines is not to wear —"

"Carter Ross!" came a loud, female voice, jolting us both.

It was coming from the opposite side of the newsroom, from the mouth of Tina Thompson. I looked over and saw she was crooking one finger at me in a repeated motion, the internationally accepted sign for "get your ass in here."

"Excuse me," I said to Kira. "I like where this conversation is going, and I would like to continue it. But in the meantime, I do believe I'm being paged."

"Okay," Kira said. "I can't wait for this weekend. Rehearsal dinner Friday night, wedding Saturday night?"

"You got it," I said.

With her face still about two feet from mine, she gave me a devilish look that made my insides do a backflip. "We are going to have an awesome time," she said. "Weddings make me so —"

"Carter!" Tina hollered again.

"To be continued," I said, lifting myself from my chair and walking toward Tina's office.

On the way, I heard Buster Hays growl, "I miss the days when it was nothing but guys in here."

During the final twenty feet of my walk to Tina's office, I thought hard about what the source of her ire might be. Usually, I was pretty good at knowing my transgressions, a self-awareness I could use to assist in preparing a rigorous defense.

But, in this case, I was lost. I had put a good scoop in that day's paper. I was working on a story for the next day's paper that she — and, more important, Brodie — would like. I had not gone behind her back about anything I could remember. And, I mean, sure, Kira and I had just been talking in rather close quarters, but she kept insisting she didn't care about that.

Then I thought, well, maybe I hadn't done anything wrong. Maybe she was just feeling impatient because deadlines had been moved up for some reason. Maybe the pregnancy hormones were starting to make her a little nutty. Maybe this was no big deal.

"You wanted to see me?" I said with forced innocence.

"Close the door," she ordered.

Close the door. Never good. I complied.

"Take a seat," she said, taking one of the two chairs that faced her desk.

And that's when I felt what it was to be a turkey. In mid-November. With a farmer who was sharpening his ax. When Tina really wanted to take my head off, she always chose one of the chairs that faced her desk, because it pointed away from the newsroom. That way, none of the gossips in the room would be able to read her lips. Tina always liked her most serious scolding to be done without closed-captioning.

My butt had just barely met the chair when she clenched her teeth and bristled, "What the hell, Carter?"

"Uh, what hell are you referring to?"

"You didn't tell anyone my . . . condition . . . did you?" she said, fiercely.

242

"No. Why would I want to? I've barely even had the chance to —"

"No one?" she demanded again.

"No."

"Not even *your mother*?" she seethed.

"My mother? Why would I tell my mother? She's not exactly the first person I'd rush to with the news that I'm about to have a child out of wedlock."

"So you're sure she has no idea?"

"Not unless she's telepathic. I haven't even talked to her since I got the news myself. Why do you ask?"

"Because I just got off the phone with her," Tina said. "She just called and invited me to your sister's wedding. She wants me at the rehearsal dinner, the wedding, the Sunday brunch, the whole thing."

"And what did you say?"

"What else could I say? I said yes. I don't seem to be having any luck convincing you to pretend this baby isn't yours. So, unless you come to your senses, this woman is going to be my child's grandmother. Your sister is going to be the aunt. Plus, your mom has always been so sweet to me. I couldn't very well tell her to go pound sand."

"You could have said you already had plans."

"Yes, I suppose I could have. But I didn't think of that. In any event, it's too late now. It's settled."

"Yeah, I guess," I said.

I swallowed hard. The implications of my unthinking solicitation of Kira as my wedding date just a few scant moments earlier were now clear to me. For the record: it is generally unwise to ask one woman to a significant family function when another woman is carrying your seed.

"Sorry I accused you of having told your mom. The last thing I want is anyone's sympathy. But I'm still just, I don't know, a little freaked out about this whole thing. I feel like I can't get my head around it."

"Believe me, I know what you mean."

Tina's boil had already cooled to the point where it wasn't even a simmer. "Well, I guess there are worse things than going to a wedding as your date."

I gulped. "Yeah, about that . . ."

"What?"

I wanted to be honest with her and tell her I had just invited Kira so we could share a good laugh about this awkward little predicament. Except there were at least four factors to consider. One, she might not find it so laughable. Two, it wouldn't be good for the health of my unborn child to make

Mommy's blood pressure spike dramatically. Three, there was an entire newsroom full of eardrums behind me, and I had to be considerate of their pain thresholds. And, four, I'm chicken.

So I just said, "Never mind."

"Okay," she said, giving me a nice pat on the knee as she got out of her chair and went around to her normal position behind her desk. "By the way, how's the McAlister follow coming?"

I enlightened her on the most recent developments, agreed to have something filed by seven, then exited her office. But instead of returning to my desk, I peeled off down the back stairway and out the side entrance — an emergency exit whose alarm had long ago been disabled by the smokers who sneaked out that way to grab a cigarette. It seemed to be clear of loiterers for the moment, so I pulled out my phone and speed dialed the Ross family home in Millburn, with the intention of fixing this little dilemma.

"Hello," my mother answered.

"Hey, Mom, it's me."

"Hi, honey!" she said brightly; then — because I never call during the day — she quickly asked, "Is everything all right."

"Yeah, fine," I said tersely. "Except . . .

Mom, why did you invite Tina to the wedding?"

"Well, she's your friend, dear, and there was an empty seat at your table and I just thought it would be perfect."

Oh, it was perfect all right. A perfect disaster. "Mom, did it ever occur to you that if I had wanted Tina at the wedding I already would have asked her?"

"Well, I thought maybe you were just being obstinate. You get that from your father's side, you know. What's the problem? Are you two having a spat?"

No, Mom, we're actually having a baby, I wanted to say. But instead I stuck with the more immediate issue: "The problem is I just invited someone else."

"Oh, did you ask Tommy?" Mom asked. Then, before I could mount an answer, she started gushing: "Because I thought you knew I already asked him. There was an opening at your cousin Glenn's table, and I've always wondered if he might, you know, lean that way. He's never been married and he's so good-looking. Everyone says he looks just like Dirk Pitt."

"Brad Pitt, Mom. Everyone says he looks like Brad Pitt. Dirk Pitt is the guy in the Clive Cussler novels."

"Right. *Brad* Pitt. The one with all those

children. No danger of Glenn doing that." She chuckled at herself and continued: "But it really would be great if he and Tommy maybe took a shine to each other. Is that an okay word? A 'shine'? Is that what you say with gays? I really have learned to be open-minded about this sort of thing. I even voted for gay marriage on the —"

"Mom! This isn't about Tommy. It's about me. I invited a girl."

This gave Mom a hitch in her conversational stride. "A . . . a girl?" she said, and I could picture the confused, hurt look on her face. "Do you have a girlfriend, honey? You never told us anything about a girl-friend."

I started sputtering and stammering. It was amazing how, even as a thirty-two-year-old man — fully grown and independent for many years — I could still be made to feel like a blushing teenager by my mother. Finally I spit out: "I have a girl who's a . . a . . . friend. We don't really know each other that well yet. Her name is Kira. She's a librarian here at the paper. And I just invited her to be my date for the weekend."

"Oh. That is a problem."

"It sure is."

"That will unbalance the seating," she said, heavily.

247

"Among other things it will unbalance."

"Well, we'll just have to make the best of it," she said, as if she had just been informed the daffodils in one of the flower arrangements were being replaced by tulips.

"No, Mom, you'll just have to call Tina and tell her there's been a terrible mistake and you have to trim the guest list."

I could hear Mom recoiling. "Oh, honey, no! Absolutely not. That would be tacky beyond tacky. I just couldn't . . ." — she was interrupted by the click of her call-waiting — "Oh, that's the caterer! I have to go."

Then she hung up. I stuffed my phone into my pocket, then buried my face in my hands, sure that things couldn't get much worse. Then I looked up and realized I wasn't alone.

Buster Hays was sucking down the remains of a cigarette, a malicious grin on his face.

"You heard all of that, didn't you," I said.

The grin spread a little wider. "Lucky for you, my silence can be bought."

"What's the price?" I said, trying to be cagey, but knowing I was basically at his mercy.

"I got an All-Slop shift tomorrow night

that could have your name on it," Buster said.

All-Slop was our cute name for what was formally known as the NonStop News Desk — the division within the newsroom whose job it was to feed the Web site, twenty-four hours a day. We called it the All-Slop because that's roughly what we shoveled into it. There were a few reporters dedicated exclusively to the All-Slop, but the rest of us were forced to pick up the slack on a rotating basis. It amounted to about one shift a month. I am still waiting to hear where I can apply to get that time back at the end of my life.

"Fine," I said. "I'll take your All-Slop."

He grinned. I suspect if he had one, he would have lit a victory cigar.

Waiting for me upon arrival back at my desk was an e-mail from wimperiale@imperiale andtrautwig.com. The subject was "Civil suit." The message read:

MR. ROSS,
PER OUR DISCUSSION, THE ENCLOSED WAS BEEN FILED TO ESSEX COUNTY SUPERIOR COURT AT 4:56 P.M. TODAY.

SINCERELY,

WILLARD R. IMPERIALE, ESQ.
IMPERIALE & TRAUTWIG
ONE NEWARK CENTER
NEWARK, NJ 07102

I opened the document to find one of the most crowded captions I had ever seen. There were a total of twenty-eight plaintiffs, plus "John and Jane Does, 1-100." The defendants included McAlister Properties, the city of Newark, the state of New Jersey, the New Jersey State Department of Environmental Protection, the federal Environmental Protection Agency, a few corporations I had never heard of, and, strangely enough, K&J Manufacturing, good old Quint's family business. I had thought it was defunct. Maybe Will Imperiale had discovered it still had assets that could be attacked.

The document was 156 pages long, and there was no way I'd be able to read the entire thing and have my story filed by seven. So I skimmed to the end. It did not leave me terribly impressed with Imperiale's lawyerly skills. As a reporter, I had read a lot of civil complaints, enough that I had a decent sense of which ones were well-grounded in law and fact and which were long shots.

This one fell more to the Hail Mary side of things. Imperiale obviously still had a lot of work to do. Nevertheless, I grabbed some pull quotes about the gross negligence of the defendants that had led directly to the illnesses of the plaintiffs, and started cobbling together a story.

I was just getting into the flow of it when I heard a sound behind me that made my butt muscles clench. It was a pocket full of spare change being rattled around.

Which meant it could only be one person: Harold Brodie. The *Eagle-Examiner*'s executive editor almost never left his office, but when he did, he was a notorious change jangler. He always seemed to have a pocket full of the stuff — quarters and nickels to make the lower sounds, pennies and dimes for the higher registers — and it was a favorite strategy of his to walk up behind you and give it good shake so you knew he was there. Brodie had made many a tuchus tighten that way through the years.

"Hello, Carter, my boy," he said in a voice that was thin and high and belied the extent to which I feared the man behind it. I don't know why a stooped, slender seventy-year-old with overgrown eyebrows and a weak bladder intimidated me so much, but to me Brodie was the equivalent of a beefy, three-hundred-pound biker with a temper. I just didn't want to provoke him.

"Good afternoon," I said. I deliberately never address Brodie by name, because while I didn't want to call him "Mr. Brodie" — it seemed too obsequious — I also didn't have the testicular presence to call him "Harold" or "Hal."

"You did a fine job on the McAlister story," he said.

"Thanks."

"And I understand we have a follow cooking?"

"Yes, sir," I said and didn't elaborate. Long experience had taught me that the less I said around Brodie, the better.

"Have you spoken with Barry McAlister yet?"

"I did this morning, as a matter of fact."

"How was he?"

"Pretty broken up, as you might imagine. I didn't get much out of him. He was also a little drunk, to be honest."

"Ah, yes, Barry always did like the bottle," Brodie said.

"You know him?"

"He's an old friend. I was a young reporter assigned to Newark cops when I met him. Or maybe I should say he met me. I was working a story in the ghetto when a group of punks tried to mug me in front of one of his buildings," Brodie said; then, oddly, he started chuckling. "Barry McAlister came charging out of that building with a double-barrel shotgun, fired one shot in the air, and told them he'd put the other shot in one of their asses if they didn't clear off."

Brodie chuckled again and said, "He told them they could mug all the people they wanted, but they damn sure weren't going to do it in front of his building. I'll tell you, boy, he sure got me out of the soup."

"Sounds like it," I said, now understanding Brodie's interest in this story. McAlister had mentioned he had "some history" with people at the *Eagle-Examiner*. I hadn't realized the history was with our top guy.

"After that, I'd see him from time to time. He was one of those sources who you might not be able to quote, but who always knew the score. I'd buy him a drink or two, just to listen to him talk. A lot of the landlords remaining in the neighborhood were shysters, there to wring whatever money they could from their crumbling buildings without giving anything back. Barry McAlister wasn't like that. He cared for his buildings and the people inside them." Brodie shook his head. "It's a shame what happened with him and Elizabeth. He was never really the

253

same after that. She took something from him and I'm not sure he ever got it back."

Brodie was on memory lane now, a side of him I had never really seen before. He had been the top editor at the *Eagle-Examiner* for a quarter century, and it was easy to think he had come out of the womb that way. But Brodie had a past like everyone else.

"I remember Vaughn when he was just a little boy," Brodie continued. "He was a smart little fella, just like his father. This whole thing is terrible. Terrible. Any ideas who would do such a thing?"

I paused, because I wasn't sure how much I wanted to say, under the theory of The Less Your Editor Knows, The Better. But he seemed to have a personal interest, so . . .

"Well, he seems to have a girlfriend who might not be terribly pleased with him," I said. "And I talked to a not-for-attribution source who said he saw two white guys get out of a dark sedan and dump Vaughn's body on the McAlister Arms construction site. They made it sound like a professional hit."

"Were you planning on putting that in the newspaper?"

"Not with the level of sourcing I have right now," I said. "But it's definitely something to keep in mind."

Brodie closed his eyes. It was something he always did when he was thinking deeply, never minding that it was, frankly, a bit unsettling. He stayed in this contemplative pose for a long moment, then opened his eyes.

"Well, keep on it, my boy," Brodie said, giving his change one last jingle before he departed.

Will Imperiale knew how other lawyers scoffed at him. He heard their catty little comments at bar association events — cheap shots about his ads in the Yellow Pages or his billboards. He knew the disdain they had for him.

He also knew most of them couldn't have hacked it in his line of work. Say what you will about personal injury lawyers, but they worked for a living. And hard. They didn't have regular clients with recurring legal work. They couldn't bill by the hour, knowing they'd get paid no matter what the result. They couldn't pad accounts to help make up for a lean month.

All a personal injury lawyer had was his current caseload. If it was heavy with winners, he was going to prosper. If it was light or had too many losers in it, his overhead — all those paralegals and assistants on the payroll, all the money for office space and advertising — would eat him alive.

As such, good new cases were like air for

Will Imperiale. He needed them to survive.

Yeah, sometimes they came at him easy. Someone saw one of the ads and walked in with a good case. Former clients referred their cousins, girlfriends, or neighbors.

But he had learned there were other ways to get them, too.

He had emergency-room nurses on retainer at several of the local hospitals and offered them a bounty for each case they tipped him off about. He had a network of ambulance drivers with the same kind of arrangement. He was a major supporter of several of the largest police charities and he made it clear to them what would earn future donations.

Sleazy? Perhaps. Expensive? Sure. Worth it? Absolutely.

That's what made the McAlister case such a pleasure. It came at him unsolicited. One day, a man he didn't know simply made an appointment. And he refused to meet with one of the paralegals who normally did the intake work. Ordinarily, Will Imperiale wouldn't waste his time with those initial meetings. Too many of them were sob stories without a decent claim. But the guy insisted he meet with The Man himself, and Imperiale was intrigued enough to humor him.

He was glad he did. The case was an op-portunistic lawyer's dream: lots of sick people with heavy medical bills; lots of significant injuries, with very legitimate pain and suffering attached to them; and a defendant with deep pockets. Plus, the victims were poor. That always helped if it went to a jury.

Plus, poor people asked fewer questions.

The man wanted a kickback, of course. They all wanted kickbacks. And this guy was looking for a big one, much larger than Imperiale would normally even consider.

But this man was promising to serve up McAlister Properties on a silver platter. It would be guaranteed money. Plus, the guy was going to provide Imperiale enough dirt on McAlister — quite literally — that Imperiale stood a good chance of being able to go after some of the other defendants.

After all, the city of Newark had its fingers in this thing. So did the state of New Jersey. The company that had once owned the land — K&J Manufacturing — was surely still good for something. Even the Environmental Protection Agency could be liable.

It was a can't-miss case. The kickback would be worth it. There would still be lots left over for Willard Imperiale, Esq.

CHAPTER 5

There is a certain joy to being a newspaper reporter on deadline that almost makes me sorry for other types of writers. I always chuckle when novelists say they're "on deadline" and you ask them what the deadline is and they say, "October." In my world, October is not a deadline. It's a month.

In the magazine business, it's no better. They'll say they're "on deadline" because they've been told they must deliver copy in "mid-October" or "ideally by October 15, if at all possible." And, again, that's not a deadline. That's a suggestion.

No, a real deadline is something that cannot be measured in months or days. It can be measured only in hours or, better yet, minutes.

And missing it comes with consequences. The word "deadline" originally came to us from the penal system. Once upon a time, a deadline referred to an actual line on prison grounds that an inmate could not cross, or else he'd be shot dead. The newspaper business long ago took this concept and ran with it, with only slightly less drastic penalties for offenders.

When you have a deadline like that — a real deadline, a deadline with fangs — it takes on its own necessary momentum. There's no time for writer's block, to grope around for that perfect phrase or to wait for some mythical muse to inspire you. You just have to write. What comes out isn't necessarily going to be poetry. It might be downright awful. But it comes out all the same — because the alternative is to get fired. As a writer, knowing that can be very freeing.

Hence, my Vaughn McAlister follow-up story was not something I had planned on submitting to the annual New Jersey Press Association Awards. But I filed it at 6:58 — with a whole two minutes to spare — so I marked it in the win column and moved on.

I was just starting to think about Kira and Tina and the baby — and the mess my imprudence had created — when my phone rang.

The caller ID told me it was Pigeon, whom I had neither seen nor heard from in several hours. The last I knew, she had been hard at work with Tee's list of names and phone numbers of construction workers. But it suddenly occurred to me she hadn't reported back with anything. I answered with a casual, "Hey, where ya been?"

My phone's earpiece broadcast a cacophony of background noise. It sounded human, but it was all indistinct.

"Hello?" I said.

"Hey. You Carter?"

The person asking this question was not Pigeon. His voice was about two octaves too low. It also lacked the elocution and precise diction I had come to expect of the J. P. Stevens High valedictorian.

"Yes, this is Carter. Who's this?"

He didn't answer that question, just said, "You got to come get your girl."

"My girl?"

"Yeah, I told her she had a bit much and was there someone I could call. She handed me her phone and said, 'Call Carter.' She says her name is, I don't know, Mischa or something."

"Neesha?"

"Yeah, that's it."

"Uh, okay, where is she?"

"She at Pop's. You know where Pop's is at?"

I did know Pop's. It was on Springfield

Avenue and it was one of the seediest dive bars in Newark — a distinction that was not easily earned in a city where many of the drinking establishments had attained quite a low position. It was the kind of place where the proprietor had long ago resorted to serving drinks in plastic cups and beer in plastic bottles, because it made the bar fights safer and easier to clean up after.

What I didn't know was how Pigeon had gotten there.

"Yeah, I know where Pop's is," I said, already standing up and heading to the elevator.

"Good. You might want to come fast," he said.

"Why is that?" I asked.

There was no answer. Nor was there any more noise coming from the phone. Mr. Deep Voice had ended the call. So I scrambled out to the parking garage, fired up the Malibu, and made good time out to Pop's, which was only three turns and five minutes from the office. I parked a block down — there were no spots immediately outside the bar — and as I approached, I heard a lot of loud, excited, male voices. There was obviously some kind of disturbance going on inside.

Then I walked through the front door and

saw why: Pigeon was dancing on top of the bar.

Someone had found "Brick House" on Pop's ancient jukebox, and Pigeon was thrusting her body in near-rhythm to the Commodores' classic. That Pigeon's booty was perhaps not as generous as was often preferred in that ZIP code bothered none of the patrons, because she had removed her bra and was waving it over her head like a lasso.

This, naturally, was very popular with the twenty-or-so men who had gathered around the bar to encourage her. They were all black, most of them on the beefy side, and their sturdy boots and dirty jeans told me they were all employed in one blue-collar industry or another. They had finished a hard day's work and now they were blowing off steam.

One of them yelled, "Show your tits!" — most likely not for the first time — and Pigeon started playing with the hem of her sweater, lifting it just enough to show a flash of bare midriff, then lowering it.

This brought a boisterous roar from her audience, which seemed only to embolden her. She pulled up the sweater a little farther, about halfway up her torso, then kept it there for a few beats of the music before letting it drop.

The one guy who had said, "Show your tits!" kept repeating it, until soon the whole pack of them was chanting that bawdy instruction. Pigeon seemed to be of the mind to oblige them, because she brought up the edge of the sweater until it was just under her breasts and started dancing with it in that position, gyrating her hips clumsily, like some kind of intoxicated belly dancer.

And that's when I decided everyone had enjoyed enough of the show. I started shoving my way through the throng until I reached the front row, then called "Pigeon!" in a voice filled with rebuke.

But she didn't hear me. She just kept right on dancing and I feared we were mere seconds away from an entire bar full of men seeing more of Pigeon than her future arranged-marriage husband might appreciate. So I reached up, delicately grabbed the hem of her sweater, and pulled it down.

This brought a chorus of angry boos from the mob. It momentarily occurred to me that interrupting the peep show, while good for Pigeon's reputation, might end up being bad for my face. I wasn't sure I could take on one of these guys, much less twenty of them, and they were making their unhappiness with me known.

Then Pigeon solved the problem for me. She been already been knocked slightly off-balance by my grabbing her sweater. And she was probably not very steady to begin with, given the amount of liquid courage it had likely taken to get her up on that bar in the first place. So she began teetering to the left, then tottering to the right; then, in a desperate attempt at overcorrection, she ended up falling, lying full out on the bar.

Her landing knocked over a small tidal wave of beer and malt liquor. The men had been so tightly bunched there was no avoiding the deluge, and enough of it splashed into them that it quite literally doused their anger. Several of the more-enthusiastic guys in the front row, including the one who had started the chant, got a rather thorough soaking. They just stood there, half stunned and dripping. Had I been the one spilling the drink, I'm quite sure I would have gotten a beating. But since it was Pigeon, they couldn't summon much anger.

The song had ended anyway and now that the entertainment had gone down, the crowd dispersed — some to the men's room, to get paper towels, and some to other parts of the bar. I helped Pigeon dismount from the bar, then handed her a few napkins so she could at least wipe her face. She was somewhere beyond blotto and had grabbed on to my shoulders to help keep herself up.

"Oh, Pigeon," was all I could say.

"You were the one who told me to live a little," she slurred.

"Yeah, this may have been a little too much living," I suggested.

"I know, I know. It's just the guys were all so nice and they've got these things call Yay . . . Yay . . . Yaygerbuhs . . ."

"Jägerbombs?"

"Yeah! That's it! How did you know?"

I knew, because I do believe anyone of a certain drinking age — and I imagined that included anyone who had gone to a college party or a rowdy bar in the last ten years or so — had at least one run-in with a Jägerbomb. It was a combination of Jägermeister and Red Bull that, between the alcohol in the former and the caffeine in the latter, got the imbiber both buzzed and buzzing.

"Drunk on Jägerbombs," I said, shaking my head.

"Yeah! They're so much nicer than that awful drink Barry McAlister gave us earlier. It tastes kind of like cough medicine, but in a good way."

"Right," I said. "Just, in the future, try to remember they have a little more kick."

■ ■ ■ ■

As I steadied Pigeon, a man approached us. He was dressed like everyone else in the bar — a working stiff — but he appeared substantially more sober.

"You gotta be Carter," he said. I recognized this as Mr. Deep Voice, the man who had summoned me to the rescue.

"Yeah, that's me."

"Looks like you got here just in time."

"Or maybe a little on the late side," I suggested.

"Yeah, sorry about that. Your girl and some of us was just talking a little bit at the bar, having a drink. Then one of my boys bought her a shot. She liked it, so we got her another. I didn't think nothing about it, but then . . ."

"She doesn't exactly have a lot of practice handling her liquor," I informed him.

"Yeah, I see that."

Pigeon was still trying to find her equilibrium, using me as her fulcrum. Her eyes appeared not to be focusing on anything, then suddenly they zoomed in on the guy in front of us.

"Oh heyyyy! This is one of my friends!" she said, so drunkenly happy to see him that she gave his chest a thump. He was solid enough that Pigeon's hand just bounced off him.

"Yeah," he confirmed. "That's me."

"Tell him about the dirt!" she blurted.

I looked at the guy and felt my head cocking. "The dirt?" I said.

"Wait," Pigeon interrupted. "I seriously think I need to sit down. The room is getting all . . . woooo . . ."

From long experience with drunks, I knew Pigeon was about ten to twenty minutes away from communing with the porcelain goddess. But she wasn't quite ready for that, so I guided her to the nearest open table. "Won't you join us?" I asked her friend.

He complied and we sat. Now that Pigeon was no longer relying on me as her sole means of support, it was a little easier to concentrate on the guy. He was roughly my age, though I always have a bit of a hard time telling with African Americans — darn them and their unwrinkled skin. He had a plump face atop a thick body, and short black hair.

"So you're friends with Tee?" I asked, just because I wanted to establish a little rapport with the guy.

"Yeah, we go back. You know him?"

"Good dude," I said.

"Yeah," he agreed.

I stole a quick peek at Pigeon, who had slumped in the chair and settled into a semi-catatonic state. At least she wasn't feeling any pain. Yet.

"So, I'm sorry, I don't think I got your name," I said.

"Alan Sutherlin."

"And I'm Carter Ross."

"You with the newspaper, too?"

"Sure am."

"Nice to meet you," he said, and we shook hands properly.

"I assume you've worked down at McAlister Arms?" I said.

"Yeah."

"You still working there?"

"Nah, my part of the job is over."

"Are you with the lawsuit?" I asked.

"Not me. I never got sick. I know a bunch of guys who did. I just drove a truck, so I wasn't there most of the time."

"Oh," I said. "So what's this about dirt?"

Someone had put 50 Cent on the jukebox, and now we were all, officially, In Da Club. Alan was moving his head to the music a little. He seemed comfortable.

"Yeah, I was just telling your girl about it. How much you know about brownfield remediation?"

"I mean, a little. I guess. Why?"

"Well, here's how it's supposed to work, right? You take a truck full of dirt out. You dump it somewhere safe, like in a landfill or something. Then you bring fresh fill back in."

"Okay," I said. "I'm following you."

"Yeah, except with McAlister Arms, we weren't doing that."

"What do you mean?"

"First of all, we didn't have near enough trucks. Normal job, you get like ten, twenty trucks, so you can keep 'em going in and out all the time. You follow me?"

"Right."

"We had, like, two," he said, then leaned back in his seat.

"That seems . . . inefficient."

"Not for what we were doing."

"What do you mean?"

"This is what I was just telling your girl. We didn't take the dirt nowhere. We was told to just drive around with it, then bring it back and dump it like it was fresh. They told me I couldn't tell no one. Said I could get in trouble for participating in illegal dumping, or something like that. I didn't think nothing of it. I was like, 'Hey, man, you pay me union rate, I do whatever.' But then dudes started getting sick."

270

"But, wait, I'm confused. Why wouldn't they just have you do it the right way?"

"I don't know. Money, I guess."

"How so?"

"Because you got to pay a lot to get someone to take your dirty dirt off your hands. There are only certain facilities that can handle it, and most of them are in Pennsylvania, which is a long haul. That costs money. Plus, you got to pay for clean dirt. That costs more money. Plus, you got to get the right number of trucks going. That's like fifteen, twenty more trucks with fifteen, twenty more drivers. It all costs money. They wanted to make it look like we was cleaning up that site, but they didn't want to pay for it."

I thought back to Vaughn McAlister smugly telling me that the state's Department of Environmental Protection had given him $6 million for the cleanup and signed off on its completion. The city of Newark had given him another $1.1 million. He had obviously spent a small fraction of that money on the charade that was his cleanup process. I didn't know what he had done with the rest of it, but it was becoming apparent he hadn't actually remediated the site.

Which explained why people were becoming ill. Whatever chemical had been left in that dirt long ago was still there. And Vaughn McAlister had been doing the worst thing possible: stirring it up, getting it in the air so everyone — construction workers, the good people in the neighborhood, even the friendly local newspaper reporter — could suck it into their lungs.

"What a bunch of bastards," I said.

Alan nodded his head. "And then they act like the people getting sick are just faking it. That's what really pissed me off. I wasn't gonna say nothing, because I didn't know who to say it to. But then Tee told me about you, said you would know how to handle it."

I was glad Tee had that kind of faith in me. I wasn't going to tell Alan, but I didn't even know where to start.

Alan's disclosure gave me new leads to pursue, but in the meantime, I had the more immediate problem of what to do about my alarmingly blitzed intern. I escorted her into the men's room — the guys wouldn't care — and assisted her through the aforementioned purge of at least some of the poison coursing through her body.

Once that grim task was accomplished, I considered my next steps. Since she seemed incapable of walking unassisted, I figured driving was out of the question. So I helped her out into the street to my car and, with misgivings — because she was still wet from the booze soup she had spilled all over — shoveled her into the passenger seat. I momentarily lamented what this would do to the Malibu's cloth seats, which would likely end up smelling like a brewery for a week or more. But I also didn't see much alternative.

I got into the driver's seat and studied her for a moment. Her neck seemed incapable of supporting the unbearable weight that was her head.

"Pigeon," I said loudly, as if that would penetrate the haze.

Nothing.

"Neesha," I said.

She slowly swiveled her head toward me and let out a "Wa?"

"Where do you live?"

She groaned.

"Pigeon, come on, I have to take you home. Just tell me where you live."

She sank into the seat, her eyes half lidded. Realizing I wasn't going to get much of a response out of her, I started gently poking around on her person, trying to find a driver's license or something else that might have her address on it. The front pockets of her pants had been sewn shut — why twenty-first-century women put up with that kind of nonsense was beyond me — so I rolled her toward me and checked for back pockets.

She responded by flopping her arms around me, which was not exactly the response I was looking for. It got even more awkward when she buried her face in my neck and started nuzzling me. Not that I took it seriously as any kind of come-on. In her current state, she would have nuzzled Newt Gingrich.

"Easy there, Pigeon," I said, but that just made her squeeze tighter.

Still, it did make the job of checking her back pockets a little easier. Lightly, so she would not confuse it with groping, I ran my hand down her back until I found a rectangular lump that turned out to be a credit card and a driver's license. I pulled them out, untangled myself from her by gently shoving her back into the passenger seat, and found her address in Edison.

I read it out loud and said, "That's where I'm taking you, okay?"

"Noooooo," she said, moaning. "Tha's my parents' house."

I imagined her parents as a pair of strict,

traditional Indian Americans. Mom in a sari. Dad with a mustache that looked like Gandhi's. The kind of mom and dad who had raised themselves an Ivy Leaguer and then pledged her in marriage to a doctor. Then I imagined myself, a white man they had never met, showing up with their daughter, drunk and braless.

Right. Edison was out.

"Okay, so where should I take you?"

No answer. She seemed to have slipped into some lower level of consciousness. I asked the same question two more times and got nothing more than a series of incomprehensible moans. Finally I just gave up and started driving to my Bloomfield abode. It looked like a night on the couch was forthcoming.

On the way to my house, I started pondering my next move. I now knew why the McAlister Arms site had been making people ill, even if I hadn't identified the chemical agent at work. I strongly suspected that Vaughn McAlister had pocketed the money earmarked for its cleanup. The question was how Vaughn McAlister had gotten the state DEP to sign off on a remediation that clearly hadn't been done. Was the DEP just duped by the parade of dump trucks that had come and gone from the site?

Shouldn't there have been more oversight?

That was about as far as my thinking had advanced by the time I pulled into my driveway, with Pigeon now fast asleep beside me. I prodded her half awake, shucked her out of the passenger seat, and helped her stumble inside. Then I sat her down at my kitchen table and made her drink a full glass of water. I didn't know if she would remember it enough to thank me later, but operating under the golden rule of inebriation — do unto other drunks as you would have them do unto you — I thought it humane.

The water seemed to give her a little bit of life. It also seemed to make her aware of how sticky she was, because she asked if she could take a shower. I guided her into my bathroom, provided her a towel and a change of clothes. I didn't own pajamas for myself, much less for a woman, so a T-shirt and a pair of boxers — which is what I always slept in — would have to do. Then I cleared out, thankful she was functional enough to take care of things from there.

Eventually, I tucked her into my bed — in pain, but alive. Deadline was already there, and he responded to the presence of a perfect stranger by immediately curling up next to her and purring. I know there are cat owners who imagine that their pets are bonded to them and them alone. I am under no such illusions. My cat is perfectly indiscriminate about human contact. He'll cuddle with anyone whose body heat is in the neighborhood of 98.6 degrees.

I was going to find myself a hunk of couch and call it a night, but I checked my phone one last time. During all my shuffling of poor, incapacitated Pigeon, I had missed a call and had a message.

It was brief: "Hey, it's Quint. Call me."

I guess when you go by "Quint," you can get away with being first-name only. I checked the time he had left the message and it was only a half hour earlier, so there was no danger I'd be waking him up by calling at a late hour. Besides, I had the feeling Quint was a bit of a night owl.

Sure enough, he answered on the first ring. "Quint here."

"Hey, Quint, Carter Ross."

"Hey, man, didn't want you to think I forgot about you. It just took a few days for some of my people to get back to me. But it should be worth the wait, because I think I figured out what you're looking for."

"Oh yeah? What's that?"

"Cadmium," he said.

"Cadmium?" I repeated.

"Yeah, know anything about it?"

"How to spell it. But that's about it."

"Well, I tossed those symptoms you gave me off of a bunch of my people. And then finally one of them said 'cadmium' and it was a major duh moment, because I should have thought of it sooner. It's a perfect fit. Every symptom you described is a potential side effect of cadmium poisoning."

"Huh," I said. "Did K and J use cadmium?"

"Not that I know of."

"So who did down in that part of Newark?"

"Oh, I have no idea."

"But, I mean, was there a specific kind of industry that used cadmium?"

"A lot of them did," he said. "It was used in dyes, in plastic, in electroplating. Then people started figuring how bad it was for you, so it's been phased out of a lot of things. It's still used in some batteries — that's why you have to be careful about how you dispose of them. It doesn't surprise me that there's cadmium down there. What's weird is that it would now be surfacing."

"Oh, it's not so weird."

"What do you mean?" he asked.

I told Quint about Alan Sutherlin's admission to me — that all that dirt was not only still dirty, it was being freshly stirred up. "What I can't figure out is how the site managed to pass muster with the state DEP when it was only fake remediated," I finished.

Quint let out the kind of laugh that told me he didn't find anything funny. "Yeah, unfortunately, that doesn't surprise me."

"Why do you say that?"

"Because I hang around with all these environmentalists, and they complain more about the state DEP than they do about the people actually doing the polluting. All I hear about from them is how the DEP doesn't actually do its job anymore. It makes other people do it."

"Explain, please."

"This is New Jersey, right? We lead the nation in Superfund sites. And we've got a list of something like eighteen thousand other contaminated sites around the state. That's down from twenty thousand or so, but we're still finding new ones all the time. Some of them are pretty small potatoes — any place that used to be a gas station or a Laundromat is probably contaminated. It used to be, anyone who wanted to do something with one of those properties had to hire an environmental consultant who had to submit a series of documents to DEP and then wait for approval before they could go on with their project. And it could take forever, because you would, say, submit an assessment and then wait ten months for DEP to say it was okay. Then you'd submit a remediation plan and wait another ten months. You had stuff that was literally getting held up for years.

"So," he continued, "a few years back, everyone got so fed up that they changed the laws. They invented something called the Licensed Site Remediation Professional. LSRP for short. The environmental consultants had to apply to become LSRPs, but once they did, they were essentially allowed to do everything on their own. They still have to submit paperwork to DEP, but they don't have to wait for approval anymore. The LSRP's green light is enough to keep things moving forward. I guess the DEP still reads the paperwork. Eventually. Theoretically. So there's still some oversight. But, in some ways, my environmental buddies are right: the DEP is letting the LSRPs do its job for it."

"So, if I'm being generous toward DEP, I'd say they streamlined an onerous regulatory process by privatizing it," I said. "But if I'm being unkind, I say they're opening themselves up to the possibility that the foxes will be guarding the henhouse."

"More or less, yeah. The LSRP is supposed to act independently and is bound by a code of ethics that says they can't get too cozy with the developers. I'm not sure if it actually works out that way all the time. The DEP hopes it can keep the fear of God in these LSRPs because it's ultimately their ass on the line. If the LSRP certifies a site as being clean and it turns out later to be causing groundwater contamination because of shoddy work by the LSRP? The LSRP could get fined or lose his license. But otherwise? But there's nothing beyond the LSRP's say-so that a cleanup has actually been done."

I absorbed this for a moment. "But you said the LSRP does have to file a bunch of paperwork, yes?"

"Yeah, I guess. But I've seen it and I think even I could fake it. I'm sure someone who really knew what they were doing would have no problem filling in the forms in a way that passed muster. So why would that matter?"

"It matters because those are public documents, which means a nosy reporter can easily get his hands on them," I said.

"Don't get too excited. A lot of it is pretty

technical. It wouldn't necessarily make a lot of sense to you."

"Doesn't matter. As long as it has someone's name at the bottom."

"I don't follow."

"Now, Quint, you know I'm a journalist and thus prone to cynicism," I said. "But you don't suppose, here in the very righteous state of New Jersey, that perhaps an unscrupulous LSRP might, say, take a little something under the table to sign off on a remediation that didn't actually occur?"

His laugh was genuine this time. "Yeah," he said. "I suppose I can imagine that happening easily enough. But it's not like someone is going to admit taking a bribe to a newspaper reporter."

"No, but I can make it obvious enough in what I write to make it clear that's what happened."

It was one of the things that a few years in the newspaper business had taught me: readers were smarter than we sometimes gave them credit for. You didn't always need to tell them the answer to the question was four. Sometimes you just had to tell them it was two plus two and have the confidence they'd figure it out.

It was a nice thought, as I drifted to sleep on my couch, that this would be one of the times I could make the math simple for them.

The next thing I knew, there was a ringing sound. It was coming from somewhere near my front door. I was unsure what that might mean, but then, slowly, as I emerged from the grogginess of sleep, it occurred to me: someone was on my front porch, ringing the doorbell.

I opened my eyes. Light was pouring in through the window of my living room. That meant — wait, don't tell me — it was now morning.

I wasn't hungover. Or at least I shouldn't have been hungover. I hadn't even been drinking the night before. I just felt like my brain had been dipped in peanut butter. Maybe some of the alcohol Pigeon had consumed had leaked into me by osmosis.

As I got to my feet, the doorbell rang again. "Coming," I said.

I looked around for big-boy pants, but they were upstairs. Oh well. Whoever was paying me a visit at 8:00 A.M. would just have to accept me in my sleeping attire. I went over to the front door and, through the side window, saw Tina Thompson.

And this is how sleepy I was: it didn't occur to me I was doomed.

"Good morning," I said, opening the door.

She was carrying a Dunkin' Donuts bag, which had to be for me, because she ate carbohydrates only on her birthday and select holidays. She was also carrying a Coke Zero. Again, clearly for me. She was dressed for work — brown slacks, tapered white blouse that flattered her narrow figure — and had probably already been jogging. I would have told her she was glowing if I'd thought it wouldn't get me slapped.

"Good morning!" she said, brightly. "Sorry, I knew I might be waking you up. I just thought this would be a good time for us to talk about, you know, things."

Perhaps subconsciously, she looked down in the direction of her uterus.

"Great," I said, still not thinking for even half a second about my houseguest. "Yeah, definitely. Come on in."

Tina had just made it inside when, as if following instructions from the Awful Timing Handbook, Pigeon descended the staircase, rumpled and rubbing sleep from her eyes. She was wearing my T-shirt and boxers — and nothing else — and was clearly coming from the direction of my bedroom. She had gone to bed with wet hair, and it was now tousled in a way that made it appear she was coming off a very active evening.

Tina took one look at her and froze. Pigeon, likewise, stopped about halfway down the steps.

"This isn't what it looks like," I said quickly.

Tina's eyes were wide and I could practically see the synapses in her brain jumping to conclusions. What else could she think? Pigeon and I were both in our underwear — or, rather, *my* underwear — and she obviously hadn't just stopped by for breakfast.

Without a word, Tina turned and walked out the door. Heedless of my indisposed state, I went after her.

"Tina," I said, charging down the steps. She was already halfway to her car and walking with considerable determination.

"Tina, wait!" I said, having now made it to the driveway. "Let me just explain . . ."

As she reached her car, she whirled and threw the Dunkin' Donuts bag at me, hitting me square in the chest. The Coke Zero followed but, luckily, it sailed just to the right of my head.

"Explain what?" she spit. "How many different positions you used? Save it for *Penthouse Letters,* big guy."

"Tina, this isn't —"

"What? Are you about to tell me what happened in there depends on what your definition of 'is' is? Because that didn't work for Bill Clinton and it's sure as hell not going to work for you."

"She got very drunk," I said. "She couldn't . . ."

"Oh, terrific. Congratulations. So you only take advantage of twenty-two-year-old interns when they're drunk? That makes it all better, then."

"No, no. Would you please listen to me? She was drunk. I didn't know where she lived so I just let her sleep here. Nothing happened."

If Tina was listening, I couldn't tell. She was fumbling with her car keys, trying to find the little "unlock" button on the keypad — more than likely, so she could get into the car and try to run me over.

"You know, I can't believe it, but I actually feel bad for Kira," Tina said. "Because at least I know what an ass you are, and she's still going to have to find out someday."

"Would you please just come back inside? I didn't lay a finger on that girl. You can ask her, if you want. She'll tell you everything."

"Believe me, I don't want to hear it," Tina said, having gotten her car door open and taken a seat.

"Nothing happened," I insisted.

"I don't really care, Carter," she said. "Coming here was a huge mistake. Thinking that you were really serious about being a father was a huge mistake. Everything about you is a huge mistake."

She slammed the door. I had half a thought about standing behind her car to block her exit. But then I had another thought, one that involved Tina having to explain to her child someday that he didn't have a father because she had rolled over him with her Volvo.

So I let her go. She backed down the driveway, splattering the Dunkin' Donuts bag in the process, then pulled out into the street without looking back at me once.

I walked over to the bag. It appeared there had been two pastries in there, one filled with crème, the other with jelly. The insides were now oozing out of the bag, which had been thoroughly flattened.

At the moment, I knew exactly how it felt.

Over the next hour, as I readied myself for another hard day of finding news, I accepted at least seven apologies from Pigeon, both for her behavior the night before and for fouling things up with Tina. Eventually, I returned her to her car so she could go home, stop babbling at me, and change into something that wasn't imbued with ossified Colt 45.

The irony was that once I got rid of her, I immediately had to do what would have been her kind of thing: FOIA some LSRP reports from the New Jersey Department of Environmental Protection.

Technically, the New Jersey version of FOIA was known as OPRA, the Open Public Records Act. But that made it no less magnificent, in my view. I made a hasty return to the office, ready to paper the state capitol in Trenton with requests.

In my experience, there are two ways to go about this kind of thing. One, which is favored by some of my compatriots in the news media, is the Bull in the China Shop Approach. They assume that government doesn't want to give up its precious documents unless the issue is forced. They assume state employees are foot-dragging malingerers. They know the law — make that The Law — is on their side, so they storm in, making demands that they know must be met, no matter what. And they shake their angry fists until they get it.

The problem with this method is that, yes, your requests will be fulfilled. In approximately four years.

Hence, I go for a much gentler tack. Call it the Possum in the Auto Parts Store Approach. As a possum, I don't know which oil filter to use. I certainly don't have the opposable thumbs needed to install one. So I need help. And I assume the state employee actually wants to provide it — which, unfair stereotypes about government bureaucrats aside, most of them actually do. I approach with meekness, because possums are a very docile kind of animal, make it sound like I'm asking a favor (not making a demand), and thank them profusely for every small kindness they extend.

With this in mind, my call got forwarded around the DEP until I ended up talking with a nice-sounding woman named Gina, who, just my luck, happened to be the administrator of the Licensed Site Remediation Professional program. We established a quick rapport and I had already made two jokes and three self-deprecating comments about my cluelessness. Then I told her I was a reporter. She stiffened for a moment, informing me she wasn't supposed to talk with reporters. All reporter calls were supposed to go to the public affairs office. I promised her I wouldn't tell and pointed out I couldn't put her in the paper because

289

I didn't know her last name. With that, she relented. She wasn't allowed to talk to reporters but, apparently, she could talk to possums.

She said if I had the LSRP's license number I could easily request whatever documents I needed. I told her that was the problem: I didn't know who the LSRP was. And there came my big break. Gina could do a search by property-owner name. And thus she could tell me that the McAlister Arms site had been overseen by an LSRP named Scott Colston, license number 510552. She even gave me his date of birth and business address.

Gina then directed me through the maze of the DEP's Web site to the form where I could make an OPRA request for all the documents filed by that license number. She even told me what to put in certain blanks so the request would be filled quickly — in a week or so. I thanked her profusely, stopped just short of promising to name any female children I had after her, then ended the call.

That it would take a week to get the documents was not a problem. I already knew they were going to tell me that Scott Colston had signed off on a cleanup that had never happened. Now I just had to do the fun part: find him and ask him why.

I certainly planned to stop by his place of business. But there was undoubtedly more in the public record about Scott Colston. So I wandered back to the Info Palace, as our newspaper's library scientists called their lair, where Kira was staring at her computer screen like it perplexed her. She had put her hair up with a pen — they must learn how to do that when they get their MLS degree — and was wearing another one of her prim and proper sweater sets, this time in lime green.

"Good morning," I said.

"Is it?" she asked, then looked down at her watch, which appeared to have mouse ears on it. "Oh, I guess it is."

"Do you really have a Mickey Mouse watch?"

"Yeah, isn't it cool?"

I just shook my head. It was getting hard to keep up with whether there were any cartoon characters/fantasy series/superheroes she didn't like.

"So I have two favors to ask," I said.

"Shoot."

"One, Pigeon got obnoxiously drunk last night and ended up sleeping at my house. But I swear to you, nothing happened."

She took in this news without reaction.

"Uh, I'm sorry. What's the favor?"

"Just to believe me that I was pure and chaste and nothing untoward happened."

"Oh, okay. That's easy enough. What's number two?"

I slid her a piece of paper with the date of birth and business address of Scott Colston, plus a bit of background as to why I was interested in him. "Give this guy the full workup. I want everything you can legally give me on him, plus any illegal stuff, too."

"Oh, you're giving me a DOB? Hot stuff!"

"Is that all it takes to get you excited? A date of birth?"

"Well, for right now, yeah. You'll have to do a little better later."

"You trying to make me blush?"

"Would you like me to?" she asked in her I-live-dangerously voice.

Giving Kira that kind of challenge in the newsroom would be engaging in a game of chicken I couldn't possibly win. "No," I said. "Definitely not."

"Too bad," she said. "So how high a priority should I make Mr. Colston?"

"If I bat my pretty blue eyes at you, will you make it your top one?" I said, blinking rapidly and trying to look endearing.

"Let me just finish this thing I'm working on right now, then I'll get to yours. You are lucky I find nerdiness charming."

"In so many more ways than one," I said.

"Okay, let me get to work," she said, making a little shooing gesture. "Now go."

One of the many advantages of being male — or at least of being the kind of guy I am — is the ability to compartmentalize. Yes, I seemed to have more than one woman in my life. Yes, one of them was furious with me, while simultaneously being pregnant with — still trying to get my inner air-traffic controller to land this fact — my child. And, yes, they were both my date to my sister's wedding.

But as I went out to the parking garage to get my Malibu, I put those issues in separate rooms, to be dealt with at some later time. All that mattered now was Scott Colston and his business address, which was on Route 46 in Fairfield.

I enjoyed my ride out on I-280, passing a spot I had once written about. It was a patch beside the highway where authorities had found a sizable field of marijuana plants, being grown and cultivated by a group of miscreants who were, if nothing else, bold. To me, it spoke of the obliviousness of the road's travelers. According to highway-usage stats, roughly 150,000 vehicles had passed that spot every day for two years without one driver or passenger noticing anything. It was amazing what you could keep hidden in plain sight.

Leaving the highway, I merged onto Route 46, a four-lane divided road designed with collision-repair-shop owners in mind. They were the only ones who could enjoy a road so heavily trafficked with so many merges, bends, dips, and blind spots — and, hence, so many car wrecks.

My GPS eventually led me to Colston's address, which turned out to be in a strip mall on the westbound side. But I immediately became concerned that I had the wrong place. The strip mall was small, and its tenants included a cell phone peddler, a tax preparer, a dry cleaner, a tanning salon, and a pizzeria.

There was nothing that looked like the office of an environmental consultant.

I pulled into a parking spot and let the car idle while I double-checked my reckoning. Yes, I was in the right town. Yes, I had the right road. Yes, I had the right number.

It was just that the number corresponded to the pizzeria, a place called Tomaselli's, that occupied the unit on the left corner. Curious, I got out of my car to check it out. As I approached, it looked like any other server of tomato pie in a state that very well may lead the nation in pizza parlors per capita. It had a variety of come-ons in the window: Tuesday, for example, was family night, with two one-topping mediums and a two-liter bottle of soda for $13.99. It had plastic booths for seating. It had pictures of Venezia, Firenza, and Roma on the walls.

The only thing unusual about it was that when I pulled on the door, it didn't open. Tomaselli's was, apparently, closed. I checked the time on my phone. It was after eleven, a time when your typical pizzeria is gearing up for the lunch rush. There appeared to be enough of a workday crowd around here, and certainly enough traffic on the road, to justify being open.

Especially in a town like Fairfield, which a half century ago had become a repository for all the Italians fleeing Newark. Even now, it had to be close to 50 percent Italian. People in this part of New Jersey took their pizza very seriously. You could start a heated discussion by asking which establishment in town had the best crust or the best sauce. Places that couldn't compete went out of business rather quickly, and I couldn't imagine being closed for lunch was helping Tomaselli's stay afloat.

With my curiosity thus addled, I went next

door to the tanning salon. Tanning is an Olympic sport in New Jersey, and the woman at the front desk looked like a serious medal contender. I couldn't say what race she was because, to paraphrase the immortal Snooki, she was neither black nor white. She was tan.

A few years back, a woman from Nutley, New Jersey gained brief notoriety when she was accused of taking her six-year-old into a tanning bed with her. Part of what made the story go national — all the way to *Saturday Night Live* — was that the woman's skin had approximately the color and consistency of a saddlebag. The six-year-old, who was very fair skinned, also ended up getting some face time on TV. For most of the nation, the tanning mom's alleged transgression was exposing this pasty little girl to potentially harmful UV rays. For a small subset of people in New Jersey, the only sin was that Mommy had not used enough bronzer.

The woman in front of me appeared to be in that subset. She was that kind of midforties where no one had the heart to tell her she couldn't pass for midtwenties anymore. Her name tag identified her as Vicki. She was about five foot four — five nine, if you counted her gelled-up bangs. She had hoop earrings that could have doubled as stirrups and her well-developed jaw was getting a workout on a piece of chewing gum. A Jersey Girl if ever there were one.

"Hi, welcome to EverTan. How are ya?" she said, with a thick-enough Jersey accent that "are" came out more like "awe."

"Hey, I'm good," I said; then, before I could form my next sentence, she jumped in:

"Lemme guess, you're going on a cruise with your girlfriend, and you want to get a good base before you go south. I have just the right package for you. I get guys like you all the time," she said, pronouncing "all" like it was a piece of equipment that should have been found in a woodworker's shop.

"No, actually, I'm not going on a cruise, I —"

"Why not, don't you have a girlfriend?" she asked not so innocently.

"Uh," I said, because that was a deeply complicated question.

"A cutie like you doesn't have a girlfriend? What's the matter? Too many to choose from?" she asked, and I may have been imagining it, but she thrust her left hand — with its bare ring finger — a little closer to me.

"No, not . . . not exactly."

"Well, if you get one, you should take her on a cruise. Have you ever been on a cruise? I love cruises. All I do is pack a dress and two bikinis and I just tan on the deck all day. It's awesome."

Vicki was leaning halfway across the counter at me in a way that made me think that if I felt inclined to ask her to go on a cruise — or to tan with her in one of her two bikinis — she would be inclined to say yes.

"I'm sure it is. I'm actually not here to tan, sadly enough. My name is Carter Ross. I'm a reporter with the *Eagle-Examiner*. I was curious, what's with that pizzeria next door?"

"What, you doing, like, an investigation or something?" she asked, like she found it amusing.

"Something like that."

"Oh, well, what do you want to know?"

"Why isn't it open?"

"Tomaselli's? Oh it's, like, never open."

"Never?"

"Well on Friday and Saturday nights it's open, yeah," she said. "But even then, no one goes."

"So the advertisement in the window about Tuesday being family night . . ."

"Yeah. I know. Funny, right?"

"Yeah, funny. You know who owns the place, by any chance?"

This stopped her. Up until this point, Vicki had had a rather pleasant smile stretched across her bronzed face. The moment I inquired about ownership, it disappeared.

"What does that matter?" she asked.

"Do you know who it is?"

"Maybe. Why do you want to know?"

"I told you: idle curiosity," I said, trying to keep it low-key, but she wasn't buying it.

"Are you a cop or something?"

"No, as I said, I'm a newspaper reporter." I dug out a press pass and a business card and handed them to her.

"Yeah, okay, so you're a newspaper reporter," she said, taking a cursory glance at the two items. "But how do I know you're not wearing a wire for the cops or something?"

"Uh . . . I don't know. Because I have an honest face?"

I thought she was going to suggest that she frisk me, but suddenly her smile was back.

"No," she said. "I have an idea."

Her idea started with my buying the Beach-

Comber InTANsive package, which would entitle me to six twenty-minute sessions in the SuperBronzing SunBlaster 2400. It was the least expensive package they had — cheaper than the SunWorshipper FanTAN-stic package, for sure — and I was amenable to it, if a little curious as to how it would look on my expense report.

It was the second part of her idea that gave me pause.

"You want me to do what?" I asked, because I wasn't sure I had heard it right the first time.

"Tan in the nude," she said, matter-of-factly.

That, unfortunately, was what I thought she had said. "And what will that accomplish?"

"It'll prove you're not wearing a wire. That way I can talk to you. And I can tell you stuff about what goes on over there. But I don't want to end up being like Adriana on *The Sopranos.* You know, like, you're just going for a ride with your boyfriend, not thinking about anything, and then he pulls you off into the woods and, blam, that's it. And why? Because you talked too much."

The word "talk" came out as "tawk." The rest of it just came out as paranoid blabber. But there was no talking — or tawking —

her out of it.

"So I just, uh, take off my clothes and *that* will prove to you I'm not wearing a wire for the cops?"

"Exactly," she said, like it needed no more explanation.

"Uh, okay. I guess."

"Don't worry, I won't peek," she said, then threw in a quick wink.

"Right. So where do I —"

"Come on," she said, grabbing me by the arm and escorting me through a set of curtains and into a room that had four doors on either side. She went to a door on the left side that had "3" on it, pulled a set of keys off her wrist, and unlocked the door.

"Here you go," she said, holding it open. "Just holler when you're ready."

I walked inside. Vicki closed the door. As I hurriedly stripped down, I eyed the Super-Bronzing SunBlaster 2400. It looked like a coffin lined with fluorescent bulbs. I suddenly got what the 2400 signified — it was the number of places you'd get skin cancer if you spent too long in the thing.

I removed most of my clothes, then paused when I reached my boxers.

"You sure I can't keep my underwear on?"

"No," she yelled from the other side of the door. "You could have a wire hidden in there. Besides, you'll get awful tan lines."

I shook my head and went Full Monty. Then I climbed inside the tanning bed, turned it on, and closed the top.

"Okay, I'm ready," I shouted inside my crypt.

I heard the door open and close. Then, for some reason, I thought I heard what sounded like my car keys jingling.

"No offense, but I'm putting your clothes outside," Vicki informed me. "Can't be too careful."

She reentered the room. The next thing I knew, she was lifting the SuperBronzing SunBlaster's lid.

"Hey!" I said. "I thought you said no peeking!"

"Just had to make sure you didn't still have the wire on," she said. "You've got nice abs, by the way."

I groaned. She continued: "Besides, it's a good thing I checked on you. You forgot to put your glasses on."

She handed me a pair of green goggles with a black circle in the middle of each lens — like some kind of angry, black-eyed frog. I placed them on my face, feeling ridiculously exposed the whole time.

"Okay. Good," I said. "Now could you please lower the . . ."

"You know, you're pretty pale. Sure you don't want some tan accelerator? I've got this stuff called Black Storm that could really brown you up fast. I could help you put it on if you —"

"Just lower the lid, please."

She complied. As I was enveloped in simulated sunshine, I heard her pulling a chair next to the tanning bed.

"Okay, so," she started. "My girlfriend Trina has a cousin named Eddie whose best friend is this guy Tony. Now I don't really know Tony all that well, but I see him around, you know? He doesn't work but he always seems to have money. And he always pays for things in cash, if you know what I mean. And he's a little gross because whenever I see him he's like, 'Oh, baby, I could treat you so good, baby. I could buy this for you. I could buy that for you.' He makes me feel like a whore."

The word "whore" came out with an extra syllable: "who-or." She continued: "So Trina was talking to Eddie one day and she was saying, 'Oh, yeah, my friend Vicki just got a job as a manager at EverTan,' and I guess Tony was around and he just started laughing. And Trina was like 'what' and Tony was like 'nothing' and Trina was like 'no really' and finally Tony told her."

I was so blinded by the lights of the tanning bed I was finding it a little hard to concentrate. But I sensed that Vicki wanted me to contribute to the conversation, so I said, "Told her what?"

"That this whole building . . . is owned . . . by . . . the mob," she said, inserting pauses between the words to make her delivery more dramatic. "I'm not sure if the other businesses even know it. I mean, the dry cleaners are Korean, so they're, like, too busy eating rice or whatever. And the guy who does taxes is, like, I don't know, Armenian or something. The guy who owns Ever-Tan is from Iowa and people from Iowa are, like, too straight for the mob, you know? But you were asking about Tomaselli's, and . . ."

"And?" I prodded.

"Well. After Tony told Trina and Eddie and me about this building being owned by the mob, I started paying attention to Tomaselli's a little more. Because they're never open — which is weird — but every once in a while you'd see these guys just showing up there and going inside. They'd stay in there for a little while and then they'd leave. It was like they were having a meeting or something. And then this one day, I'm sitting here and I see this really nice SUV roll

304

up. It was a Cadillac Escalade. It was silver. Really nice — though I would *not* want to parallel park it. And you know who stepped out of the back?"

"Who?"

"I swear, it was Mitch DeNunzio. The boss himself. It was like something out of *The Godfather.*"

I nearly sat up so I could look at her. Then I remembered I was in a tanning bed. And naked.

So I just asked, "How did you know it was him?"

"Well, I don't know, I've seen him on the news and stuff. I told Eddie about it and he was like, 'Yeah, that's him. He rides around in a silver Cadillac Escalade.' I guess Eddie had started doing some little things for Tony — which is *so* not a good idea — and he had seen the Escalade a couple of times. It's just wild, you know? You always hear about this kind of stuff and then, wow, there it is next door. I wonder if they kill people over there at night or something."

I was quite sure they didn't, which wasn't to say there weren't other nefarious things going on there — like Licensed Site Remediation Professionals using it as a mail dump.

"Have you ever heard the name Scott

305

Colston?" I asked.

Vicki thought for a second, then said. "No. Doesn't sound familiar. Are you sure you're not with the FBI?"

"No, no," I said. "Just the newspaper."

"Yeah, I guess I believe you," she said. Then she lifted the tanning bed one more time and added, "You pretty clearly have nothing to hide."

I eventually was permitted to get dressed and leave EverTan, albeit with one more not-so-vague intimation from Vicki that we should go on a cruise together and a rather stern reminder that I should come back in a few days if I wanted my new tan to last. Also, she impressed upon me the importance of moisturizing.

As I aimed the Malibu back in the direction of Newark, my mind began churning. According to Vicki, whom I had no reason to doubt — and who had no reason to lie to me — Tomaselli's was a mob front in a mob-controlled building. It was like the former marijuana patch I was once again passing: illegal, but hiding in plain sight.

And Scott Colston, whoever he was, was having his mail delivered there, which meant Scott Colston was likely mob controlled, too.

Which raised more than a few questions about Vaughn McAlister. Had he merely paid the mob for a fake remediation? Or did his ties to organized crime run deeper? Was his entire business mob owned, with Vaughn merely serving as the legitimate face of it? Had he run afoul of the bosses in some way?

I thought about who the more likely killer was: a jilted lover like Marcia Fenstermacher or a jilted mobster like Mitch DeNunzio. It wasn't much of a contest. DeNunzio beat her on body count alone. He also was more likely to have a pair of black-sedan-driving hit men on his speed dial.

I suppose I shouldn't have been exactly flabbergasted that McAlister would have ended up involved with the mob. This was New Jersey, after all. But, in truth, I was a little surprised. For whatever New Jersey's reputation for organized crime may have been — and for whatever HBO Productions might lead you to believe — there weren't mobsters under every rock in the Garden State.

Yeah, there was probably a rumor floating around every town in the state that this pizzeria or that gas station was a front for organized crime. But the reality was that outside of a few industries — hello, waste management — the mob's influence had waned greatly, to the point where the rumors were likely all that was left.

Personally, I had never dealt with the mob. The mob to me was like an exotic elemental particle was to a physicist: I knew it was there, somewhere; and I had a variety of ways, both theoretical and experimental, to prove its existence; but I had never actually seen it.

Luckily for me, there was a staff member at our paper who had long experience with it. Buster Hays was our resident mob-beat writer. Within his several Rolodexes — Buster refused to digitize his contacts list — were a variety of old men with crooked noses and last names ending in vowels. And they were all legitimate businessmen. They just tended to have jobs that didn't involve showing up.

Buster had been writing about organized crime for us long enough that I think he knew every mobster in the state — just as they knew him. He treated them with no special deference. He was fair and forthright with them, yes. But he was fair and forthright with all his sources. The mob was just another institution he covered. It was no different than, say, the Episcopal Diocese was to the religion reporter. It was just that the Episcopal Diocese marked the bodies it buried with headstones, whereas the mob tended not to stand on such ceremony.

I tried to call Buster's office phone and cell and got no answer at either. I thought about texting him, then laughed at the absurdity: I'd have better luck texting the plant near his desk. Buster had only very recently acquiesced to e-mail as a valid form of correspondence. And even then, he still printed out all the messages he wanted to read.

Resigning myself to a far more ancient form of human interaction, I went into the newsroom and found him sitting at his desk.

"Hey," I said. "I was just trying to call you."

"I know you were," he replied in an accent that, much like Buster, came from the Bronx.

"And you didn't answer because . . . ?"

"Because I looked on the calendar and it's not Do Favors for Ivy Boy Day," he said. Buster refuses to accept that Amherst is a proud member of the New England Small College Athletic Conference, not the Ivy League. Hence, I am either "Ivy" or "Ivy Boy," depending on how patronizing he feels like being.

"What makes you think I need a favor?"

"You got that desperate look about you."

"Then I suppose it will please you to learn that you're right, as usual," I said.

Up to that point, Buster had not been looking at me — one of his favorite ways of making it clear to me I'm not worth his time. He finally turned, looked at me over the top of some drugstore granny glasses, and said, "Whataya want?"

"I want to know why the mob killed Vaughn McAlister."

He snorted. "What makes you think the mob did it?"

Without compromising Kevin's Mack's anonymity, I related to him what my reliable eyewitness had seen. Then I told him about Tomaselli's Pizza and Mitch DeNunzio.

"Great," he said. "Let's just drop by Kenilworth Heating and Air Conditioning and ask Sam the Plumber why he had the guy iced."

"Uh, okay. Where —"

"Never mind. It was before you were born," Buster said, removing the granny glasses and tossing them onto his desk. "Look, this may surprise you, Ivy, but even though I've written about them from time to time, the local crime families are not in the habit of sharing the more intimate

310

details of their operation with me."

"Yeah, but maybe you talk to someone who talks to someone who might be willing to gossip a little," I said. "I mean, how did McAlister Properties even get involved in the mob in the first place? And which mob family?"

"Well, I do have a guy who might hear some of the stuff coming out of the DeNunzio family, and . . ." Buster stopped himself. "No. Forget it, Ivy. I'm not getting involved. The mob isn't like the Department of Community Affairs. They don't have public information officers whose job it is to take our calls."

Even as he was making a fuss, I could tell his brain was already churning. He just needed a little encouragement.

"I know," I said. "That's why I need you. Come on, Buster, you're the only guy left at the paper who even has a shot at getting something like this."

It was a naked appeal to his ego. But I knew it would also be an effective one. Buster took great pride in being the last of the old guard, a staunch preserver of The Way Things Were (And Still Ought To Be).

He let out a gusty sigh and shook his head. "Okay, fine. I'll make a few calls. But the last time I looked, I'm not running a

311

free lunch program. What are you going to do for me?"

With Buster Hays, there's always a price.

In the end, it was just too much for Vicki to keep to herself. The visit from that cute *Eagle-Examiner* reporter had been the most gossip-worthy thing to happen at EverTan in months. And Vicki, who felt rather gossip starved ever since leaving her job at the health club, had to share. Just once.

Thus began the conversation chain. The first was between Vicki and Trina. It was one of those swear-to-God-you-can't-tell-anyone type conversations.

So, naturally, Trina called her cousin Eddie and told him all about it. She felt she was act-ing in Vicki's best interests — she wanted to know if Vicki could get herself in some kind of trouble for having blabbed about Tomaselli's to a reporter — and she swore Eddie to total secrecy.

Eddie hung up the phone and immediately dialed Tony. Eddie's primary concern was that Mitch DeNunzio knew where the information had come from, knew that Eddie was being loyal, and that therefore Eddie was worthy of more of the work DeNunzio had been tossing him. Tony thanked him for the information and assured him it would improve his standing with DeNunzio.

Tony had, in fact, never mentioned Eddie to DeNunzio. Not once. He was subcontracting those small little tasks he had given Eddie — paying Eddie half of what DeNunzio had paid for the jobs, telling Eddie they were being ordered by DeNunzio himself.

Thus, Tony immediately began angling for ways this information could improve *his* standing with DeNunzio. Stuff like this was gold. It would make Tony seem like he was connected. Important. Worthy of promotion, even. He relished telling DeNunzio all about it.

DeNunzio thanked him for the tip, but wasn't terribly concerned. He could avoid Tomaselli's for a while, no big deal. Scott Colston had obviously been compromised. But that was almost inevitable. He had perhaps hoped to use Colston for some other projects, perhaps turn it into another nice little sideline. No matter. Now that he had the idea, it would be easy enough to create a new Scott Colston. He dismissed Tony and didn't give it much more thought.

It was when DeNunzio heard Buster Hays was snooping around, asking questions about Vaughn McAlister, that he became concerned. He couldn't, under any circumstances, allow himself to be publicly linked to McAlister's death. No venture capitalist wants to be known for knocking off the principals of the firms he invests in. It's bad for business.

Plus, the FBI reads the paper, too. And there's nothing more the Fibbies like than a high-profile case. Mitch had associates who liked messing with the feds, but Mitch never got the wisdom of that. He prided himself on keeping himself off the FBI's list, not closer to the top of it.

Yes, he had to do something about this. Buster Hays, he didn't worry about. He had dealt with Buster before and could call him anytime and trust him to be reasonable.

But Carter Ross? He was more of a variable. He might not be as reasonable.

So Mitch made a quick phone call.

"I need you to track someone down," he said.

"Who?"

"He's a reporter for the *Eagle-Examiner*. His name is Carter Ross."

"No problem. What do you want me to do with him?"

"For now, just find him," came Mitch's reply. "We'll deal with the rest later."

CHAPTER 6

I left my negotiation/blackmail session laden with two more of Buster's All-Slop shifts — a triumph, since he was trying to pin me with four of them — then took a trip back to the Info Palace to see how Kira was doing in her search for Scott Colston.

She was sitting in almost the exact same pose as the last time I'd seen her, except she had taken the pen out of her hair, which I found mildly disappointing in a way I couldn't quite place.

"Hey, how's it going?" I asked.

She looked up at me and frowned. "Did you get so drunk with Pigeon last night that you forgot how to spell?"

"No. Sadly, I was sober last night. That's not to say my spelling is completely beyond reproach. Why do you ask?"

"Because I think you spelled Scott Colston incorrectly. Is it C-O-L-S-T-O-N?"

"Yeah, I think so. I haven't actually seen it

in print yet, because I got it over the phone. But I can't imagine there are many alternate spellings. Why?"

"Because he doesn't exist," she said. "I checked every database I know how to check. The nearest Scott Colston I found lives in Virginia. His DOB doesn't match the one you gave me. I FaceStalked him just to make sure and he's just this guy who sometimes does karaoke under the name DJ Scooter. He doesn't have a criminal record, in case you were wondering."

"I'm sure his mother is very proud of him," I said. "I hate to ask, but would you mind looking at other spellings?"

"Already did it. I looked up Collston with two 'L's, Scot with one 'T,' Colstun with a 'U,' Colsten with an 'E.' I ran as many permutations as I could think of. Nothing came up with that DOB."

"Huh," I said again.

"You want me to tell you which databases I checked?"

"No, no. I'm sure you were thorough. Thanks for making it a priority."

"My pleasure," she said.

I took a quick glance around the Info Palace, which was momentarily empty. "So," I said. "You want to tell me more about that dress you're wearing to the wedding?"

"You mean the one that doesn't have room for —"

Her next word was interrupted by my phone ringing. It was Quint Jorgensen. "Ugh, I'm sorry," I said. "Believe me, I want to hear all about it. But I do need to take this call."

She exhaled noisily. "It's probably just as well. There's no point in getting all worked up when I'm just going to have Buster Hays walk by any minute and try to hit on me again."

"Ew," was all I could say. "Sorry to have to leave this conversation on that note, but . . ."

"Yeah, go," she said. I hit the button to answer the call.

"Carter Ross."

He didn't bother with introductions. "Dude, I just read the newspaper" — having just woken up, no doubt — "and I saw your article about the lawsuit. Why didn't you tell me about it last night?"

This was as agitated as I had heard gentle Quint since I'd suggested he trim his trees. "Well, to be honest, I didn't even think about it," I said. "But I suppose I should have. I assume you figured out K and J

Manufacturing is one of the defendants?"

"No, that's not . . . It is?"

"You mean you didn't know?"

"No."

"Then why do you sound so upset?"

"Because!" he burst, like it should have been obvious. "This is a lawsuit against a major polluter? This is the perfect thing for my environmental people to protest! I'm going to call up that lawyer. I'm sure I can get him interested in a protest. I'm going to get some of those construction workers to show up. We'll get the news media. This is going to be big. Huge!"

"But . . . you sure you aren't worried about K and J being sued?"

"Oh, no," he said, dismissively.

"Why not?"

"There's really nothing left of K and J."

"So you're not —"

"You're missing the point. This isn't about K and J. It's about the protest."

"But what are you hoping to accomplish, exactly?"

"Accomplish?" he asked, like it was some kind of distraction.

"Yeah. You've got to have goals. Demands. Something like that."

"I don't know. It doesn't really matter. What matters is that we're right and they're wrong and we can use the protest to bring awareness of it. It's so perfect. Everyone is going to have such a great time."

Quint had mentioned his love of protests once before. I hadn't quite understood it back then. Now I was beginning to think maybe it was just because he was lonely.

"Right, sure. Like a party," I said. "And when are you going to have this protest?"

"Tomorrow. Ten in the morning. I've got my car charged up and I'm taking a trip into Newark to file the permits right now. This is going to be great. Can you put something in the paper about it?"

"Maybe. I don't know. I can definitely get something on the Web site. They're more desperate for content. The paper might be a little more discerning, but I might be able to slip it into whatever follow we do on the Vaughn McAlister killing for tomorrow."

"Okay. Great. You don't mind that I tell everyone the *Eagle-Examiner* is going to cover the protest, do you?"

"Quint, I'm not sure I —"

"Aw, come on, pleeeease?" he begged. "Trust me. I throw a *great* protest. We'll have two hundred people. Minimum. We'll come up with really creative placards for your photographers. I promise!"

He seemed so excited — and I felt like I

owed him, for putting me onto the LSRP thing — that I didn't have the heart to turn him down. Besides, if he really could get some of those construction workers and a decent crowd around them — and if Will Imperiale grandstanded a little bit — it might smell just enough like news that it would keep Brodie distracted.

"Sure," I said. "Count me in."

Quint's call reminded me that I had yet to follow up on his tip about cadmium. I wandered back to my desk and tried to get the computer sitting there to come to life. The computers in the newsroom are old enough that their processors are really a series of winches and pulleys, powered by running water — or at least that's about how fast they work — but eventually I got Google up on my screen.

Sure enough, a search on cadmium poisoning brought up a list of symptoms that matched what the people on Ridgewood Avenue had experienced. It often started with achiness, fever, and chills that resembled the flu, which I had experienced. It included respiratory problems, like the cough that some of my interviewees had reported. It could lead to kidney failure, like what had taken Edna Foster's life.

And it even could lead to broken bones. People who had repeated exposure to cadmium developed something called "osteomalacia" — which was a hard-to-pronounce way of saying their bones got soft. Soft enough that sometimes they just snapped.

I read about the first documented cases of cadmium poisoning, which were identified in Japan during the 1950s. A mining company had been releasing cadmium into the Jinzu River, which local farmers used to irrigate their rice fields. People who ate the rice were ingesting low levels of cadmium. But apparently it doesn't take much cadmium to have deleterious effects. So many people were suffering broken bones, the locals started calling it "Itai Itai Disease" — *itai* being Japanese for "ouch."

That soon led me to another unfortunate aspect of cadmium poisoning: there was no treatment for it. All you could do was treat the symptoms and try to stop inhaling the stuff.

Speaking of which, I realized I owed Jackie Orr a visit. She and her neighbors deserved to know what I had discovered, even if there wasn't much they could do about it. I pulled out my notepad, found her phone number, and dialed it. There was no answer, and I was in the middle of leaving a message when

323

I got a phone call from her.

"Hi, Jackie, it's Carter Ross," I said.

"Hi," she said, her tone noncommittal. I could guess she was still feeling a little betrayed by the reporter who had so quickly dropped her story for another one.

"So I think I've got a line on what's making your neighbors sick," I said. "Ever heard of cadmium poisoning?"

"No," she said. "What is it?"

I gave her my full book report on cadmium and delivered it in an authoritative voice, based on the twenty minutes of googling I had just done. At the end, she said, "So how do you cure it?"

"Unfortunately, you don't," I said. "According to what I read, there are things you can do if you swallow cadmium, but if you've inhaled it, you just have to wait until it works its way out of your system."

"That's okay. Mr. Imperiale says he's going to take care of us."

"Mr. Imperiale?"

"Yeah, that lawyer you wrote about," Jackie said. "I saw your story about those construction workers and I thought that if he was representing all of them he could represent us, too. I called him up this morning and told him about all of us. He was really nice."

I bet he was. The twenty-odd residents of Jackie's neighborhood had probably just added to his potential score by a couple of million bucks, presuming he was ever able to get a score.

"He wants to meet with all of us tonight," she said. "He said everyone just had to sign a sheet of paper saying he was their lawyer and then he'd be able to add us to the lawsuit. He said everyone could get their medical bills paid for, plus damages."

"If you win."

"What do you mean? Why wouldn't we win?"

"These kind of lawsuits can be very complex. It's one thing to think you know what's caused everyone to get sick, it's another thing to actually prove it. Take your grandmother. You said she broke her leg. Weakened bones is a classic symptom of cadmium poisoning, but it's also a symptom of aging. Who's to say it wasn't just an old lady breaking her leg? Who's to say there's even cadmium? And, if there is, who's to say where the cadmium came from? The defense is going to come in and argue that there's no cadmium anywhere on that site. Then it's going to say that even if there is cadmium, the defendant had nothing to do with it getting there. Then it will say even if the defendant was responsible, the cadmium wasn't to blame for her broken leg or her kidney failure or anything else. There are a lot of steps to proving this thing, and Will Imperiale has to nail every one of them if he wants to win. You see what I mean? So you might want to tell your neighbors not to go on any spending sprees. Even if they do eventually get something, it could be years before they see the money."

Jackie met that news with her usual considered silence. I felt like the guy who had just delivered the news that the leprechaun didn't really have a pot of gold.

"Oh," she said. "Well, I'd just as soon put my faith in Mr. Imperiale. He seems to be a lot more positive about being able to help us than anyone else. At least I know he won't run off and write about a rich developer instead."

It was a well-delivered punch to the gut. And I probably deserved it.

"Well, just try to remember that a guy like Will Imperiale is ultimately serving his own interests," I said. "That his interests and yours happen to align is merely a coincidence."

Having already delivered the body blow, Jackie went for the big uppercut:

"He's not really so different from you

then, is he?"

Hopelessly behind on all judges' cards, I had my corner wave the white towel by ending the call. I knocked together a quick story for our Web site about Quint's big protest, then my stomach told me it was getting to be pizza o'clock.

Thinking I might as well make it a working lunch, I located Tommy, who was talking on the phone. I pointed at my mouth while rubbing my belly. He gave me the finger — the polite one that Jersey people reserve for when they're not driving — and then, after wrapping up his call, started appraising me with a scowl on his face.

"Why do you look like an Oompa-Loompa?" he asked.

"An Oompa-Loompa?"

"Yeah, haven't you ever seen *Charlie and the Chocolate Factory*?"

"Which one," I asked, "the creepy one with Gene Wilder or the even more creepy one with Johnny Depp?"

"Doesn't matter. You could be cast as an Oompa-Loompa extra in either one."

"I don't understand."

"Have you looked at yourself in a mirror lately?"

I felt an instant sense of dread, like a

woman who had tucked her dress into her panties but didn't realize it until she had already walked across a crowded room three times.

"Not . . . I mean, not really," I said.

"Come on, then," he said, marching off to the men's room. I followed him, entering when he held the door for me.

"Look. See?" He pointed to my image in the mirror. "Oompa-Loompa."

I stared at myself, unsure of whom, exactly, I was looking at. The features were about where they should have been and resembled the ones I knew. It's just that they had all turned this deviant shade of orange, like something faintly reminiscent of a Creamsicle.

Or an Oompa-Loompa.

"Oh my," I said, gently poking my face. Every place I prodded, the skin momentarily reverted to its natural color, but then quickly went Oompa-Loompa again.

"Yet another tanning-bed tragedy," Tommy said, shaking his head.

"How did you know?"

"Spend as much time around gay men as I do and, trust me, you know. Tanning-related accidents are a serious problem in my community. By February it can be like an epidemic, all these orange men wandering around bars. The ones who are also on steroids have these big heads, too, so they start to look like pumpkins. It's sad." Tommy sighed wistfully. "Anyhow, what led you to the dark side?"

"Would you believe I was feeling a little low on vitamin D and I was out of milk?"

"No."

"Well, that's my story and I'm sticking to it," I said. If I told Tommy the truth — that I had stripped to get a story — it would just become another thing I could never live down. I wasn't ashamed of having done it. But only because I was the only one who knew about it besides Vicki. And Vicki wasn't telling. She was too busy helping her face make the final ascent from caramel to chestnut.

"Anyhow," I said, before Tommy could continue his line of inquiry, "let's go grab some pizza. Having radioactive skin really stokes your appetite."

He followed me out of the building and down to our favorite pizzeria. On the way, I updated him on my various findings. Once we were settled in front of a proper meal — two steaming slices and a twenty-ounce bottle of Coke Zero — I asked him what he had been up to.

"I've been trying to follow Vaughn McAlister's money," he said. "Though, to be honest, it's a little hard, because he didn't seem to have any."

"Do tell."

"Well, start with his major existing properties — McAlister Center and McAlister Place. I talked to a commercial real-estate guy who kind of walked me through some stuff. McAlister Properties is a private company, of course. So some of this is guesswork. But the guy said that Vaughn was having major problems keeping the buildings full. He had lost a couple of big tenants in the last year or two."

"Why?"

"Bad management. Bad luck. Some combination of both. My guy said there have been some security problems at both places — some break-ins, things like that. Computers stolen. Televisions stolen. The kind of heavy stuff that thieves shouldn't be able to take if the security force you've hired is even half awake. But Vaughn's wasn't. Same with cleaning. I guess his buildings had started to slip there, too. You can't go charging someone thirty-five bucks a square foot for Class A office space and then not keep it up. People have other options. And apparently all the commercial brokers in the area had started telling clients to avoid McAlister Properties buildings."

"That sounds like a problem," I said.

"Yeah. My guy did some rough math for me that said, based on the square footage of his two biggest buildings, based on when he bought them — and based on the debt service he likely had on them — that unless Vaughn had a roughly eighty-five-percent occupancy rate, he was going to start getting in trouble. Now, ordinarily, that shouldn't be a problem, because the vacancy rate for Class A office space in Newark generally isn't much more than ten percent. But I did a little undercover work. Now this, mind you, is another rough estimate. But I walked the stairways and hallways of both buildings and as best I can tell they're about sixty percent occupied. That means he's taking a bath on them."

I took another bite of pizza. "What did he pay for them?"

"McAlister Center went for forty-four million. McAlister Place was seventy-one million."

"A total of one hundred and fifteen million."

"Very good, Einstein. Now, again, this is a little bit of guesswork. But, basically, my guy said Vaughn had to come up with about six hundred grand every month just to meet his debt service. And that doesn't count staff salaries, security, cleaning, things like that. Plus, Vaughn had people working the McAlister Arms site. Even if they were just moving around dirt, that still costs money. My guy made a pretty convincing case that at sixty-percent-occupancy level, Vaughn McAlister was probably losing at least three hundred grand a month, maybe more."

I whistled, pulled out my phone, and punched up the calculator app. "So we're potentially talking about four million bucks a year," I said.

"Yeah," Tommy said, munching on pizza. "Tells you pretty fast where that cleanup money really went, doesn't it?"

"Or at least a good portion of it," I said.

"But that's not even the worst of his problems," Tommy said.

"Oh?"

"My guy said that, particularly after the financial crisis, banks are very vigilant these days about something called DSCR — debt service coverage ratio," Tommy said. "Basically, they want to know that you have enough money coming in from your existing properties before they loan you money for any new ones. And, in this case, he said Vaughn McAlister's DSCR was probably a disaster. There's no way any bank would have loaned him money for that project down in the South Ward with those other two buildings hemorrhaging so much money."

"Unless he had a couple of blue-chip tenants who might have turned his cash flow problem around," I said, then told Tommy what Vaughn had said about his supposed "big fish" and the rumors about Best Buy.

"But if he didn't have Best Buy, he was pretty much dead in the water," Tommy said.

"Yep," I confirmed. "And sinking fast."

Tommy and I batted various theories around for a while, eventually deciding that he would stay on Vaughn McAlister's finances while I would pursue other angles.

We soon settled into small talk — Tommy was urging me to continue tanning, saying it was the only way to make the orange go away — and we were just about done with our pizza repast when my phone rang.

The number came up "Restricted." Ordinary people often choose not to answer such calls. Reporters typically answer them on the first ring. An overdeveloped sense of curiosity can be annoying that way.

"Carter Ross."

"Hi, this is Lisa Denbigh. You were looking to speak with me?" she said in a southern accent that was thick as a Georgia pine forest.

"Yes, hello, Ms. Denbigh. Thanks for getting back to me."

Tommy tilted his head as soon as I said, "Denbigh." I had told him all about the former Mrs. McAlister.

"I got your Facebook message yesterday," she said. "Then I heard from my parents you had called them, too. So I thought you were probably pretty eager to talk."

"I am. Did you . . . I assume you heard about Vaughn, yes?"

A brief silence was followed by, "Yes."

"Sorry for your loss," I said.

Another silence. Then: "To tell you the truth, I'm not sure how to feel about it. There were times a few years ago when I probably would have killed the cheatin' son of a bitch myself."

Now the silence was on my end, mostly because I didn't know what to say. She quickly filled it with: "I'm sorry. That was . . . I didn't mean it like that, I just . . . We've been through a lot, Vaughn and I. And when I saw the article about him being killed, it brought back a lot of memories, some of them good, some of them bad."

"Tell me about the good first," I said, just

to get her talking.

"Are you doing some kind of obituary or something?" she asked.

"Something like that, yes."

"Well, Vaughn was . . . He was like a big, bright comet flashing through the sky. We both ran in a pretty fast crowd but he was still hard to keep up with. Everything was big, bigger, biggest when it came to Vaughn. My friends thought I fell in love with him because of his money, but I really fell in love with him not for what he was but for what he was going to be."

"What do you mean?"

"Vaughn was a dreamer. But he wasn't one of those pathetic dreamers whose dreams were never going to come true. You felt like he was the kind of dreamer who was going to work so hard he was going to force things to turn out just the way he said they would. He could . . . see things in ways that ordinary people couldn't, but he could also make them happen. He was so focused. He always said he was going to be like Donald Trump, but with good hair."

"So the money was just a side benefit?" I asked.

"Oh, honey, he never really had money. He just acted like he did, because he knew the only way people would give him money is if they thought he already had lots of it. We had a prenup that protected his share of the company but said I got half of everything else. Well, let me tell you, five years later, half of nothing was still nothing."

That certainly helped explain the variety of debts she had rung up.

"Had you been in touch with him recently?" I asked.

"Yeah, we probably talked about a week ago, actually."

"Did you talk to him frequently?"

"I guess we talked from time to time, yeah. Vaughn was the kind of guy who wanted to be friends with everyone, even his ex-wife. I think he kept in touch with everyone he ever met. It used to drive me nuts when I was married to him, because he would talk to old girlfriends. Then I just sort of realized that's who he was. He couldn't stand the thought of anyone not liking him. It was sort of sad, I guess. But sort of sweet, too."

"So you were still fond of him?" I asked, trying to circle around to the question I really wanted to ask.

"Oh, I suppose. Vaughn McAlister was hard not to like. Even when he cheated on me I couldn't hate him too much. He had a big heart, and if he was guilty of anything, it was following it everywhere it told him to go."

"Where had it been telling him to go lately?" I asked.

"What do you mean?"

Time to spit it out: "Were you two talking about getting back together?"

She didn't immediately answer my question. She just laughed. It was a real laugh: high and clear and strangely sunny, given the topic of conversation.

"Oh, shoot, honey, where would you get a crazy idea like that?" she asked.

"Someone told me you guys might be rekindling."

"Who?"

"Can't say."

"Let me guess. It was his dad, right? You don't even have to tell me. I know it was his dad."

"What makes you say that?"

"Vaughn's daddy was always sweet on me, bless his heart. He always had this joke that he was going to run off with me. I think he always hoped Vaughn and I would get back together and have a bunch of babies. But, oh goodness, no. That ship has sailed. It sailed three years and three therapists ago. I'm not saying I've got much in my life figured out. I'm probably a bit of a mess,

337

actually. But I can say this: no way were Vaughn and I getting back together. I wouldn't if he begged me, and I don't think he was going to be begging me anytime soon."

"Why not?"

"He and Fenstermonster . . . sorry, that was my little name for her. He and Marcia were really quite happy together."

"They weren't having any trouble?" I asked.

"No, they seemed pretty blissful. In a way, it made me feel a little better about how things ended between Vaughn and I. We weren't that happy anyway. He probably did me a favor by cheating on me. And at least he cheated on me with a woman he really ended up loving, not some bimbo. I think if anything he was fixing to marry her. Or at least that was how he was talking."

"So let's just say, hypothetically speaking, that Barry McAlister said Vaughn and Marcia were having trouble. What would you make out of that?"

"Probably just wishful thinking on Barry's part," she said. "He never really liked Fenstermonster that much. Sorry, he never liked Marcia that much. He was just talking out of his ass, if you'll excuse the expression."

"No, no, it's fine," I said.

"Anyhow, I'm here at the hairdresser and she's ready for me. Anything else you want to know about Vaughn?"

"That depends. Anything else you want to tell me?"

"Not really," she said.

I thought the call was going to end there, but then she added, "Except I really do hope he rests in peace."

We ended the call and I drummed my fingers on the table for a moment. It was becoming apparent that Vaughn McAlister's problems had gone well beyond a jealous girlfriend — and that the girlfriend in question probably wasn't even jealous. Weighing my sources objectively, the sober ex-wife with no real skin in the game had more credibility than the drunk father who was too distraught to think straight. I had to face that I had been a little quick to judge Marcia Fenstermacher.

"Well?" Tommy said.

"Well, I think I know what I have to do next."

"What's that?"

"Apologize to Marcia Fenstermacher for accusing her of murder."

"Why?"

"Because, one, I don't think she did it," I

said. "And, two, she might help us figure out who did."

It seemed only right that I make my apology in person, so I packed myself off for another visit to McAlister Place. The security guard appeared to have been recently anesthetized, so I walked right past him and took the stairs to the second floor, where I pulled on the door.

Except the door didn't yield. I yanked again. Locked. I knocked. Nothing.

Obviously, whoever was currently in charge at McAlister Properties had declared a day of mourning for the boss. Either that, or they all realized there was no point in coming to work at a place that was on the verge of bankruptcy.

That made Florham Park my next obvious place to look for Marcia Fenstermacher. I had the address from when I had dispatched Pigeon there the day before, and I was soon headed in that direction. I was about halfway there, having just merged onto Route 24 — not terribly far from the Millburn exit — when my mother, as if imbued with a sixth sense that her son was passing nearby, decided to call me.

And, because I knew she wouldn't call me during work unless she had a very good reason, I decided to answer.

"Hi, Mom."

"Hi, honey," she said. "Do you have a minute?"

It was never just a minute with my mother. But I said, "Yeah, sure."

"Oh, good. I have *great news.*"

"What's that?"

"Uncle Louie's gout has flared up."

"Why is that great news?"

"Because Aunt Linda says he's not going to the wedding."

"And . . . ?"

"He was sitting at your table!" she said, triumphantly.

"Yeah, still not getting why that's something to celebrate."

"Sorry, honey. I forget that you haven't spent as much time with the seating chart as I have. If Uncle Louie doesn't go, that means there's room at your table. You, Tina, *and* your new girlfriend can sit together!"

"Oh that's . . . that's just . . . super," I said. Then, to dull the pain of that news, I head-butted the steering wheel. Twice. The second one was hard enough to make the horn blow. It made me feel a little better. But only just.

"What's that?" my mother asked. "Was someone honking at you? Are you driving?"

"Yes, Mom."

"You're using a hands-free device, right?"

"Yes, Mom," I lied. My Bluetooth had been broken for three months.

"I don't want you getting a ticket. Plus, it's not safe. You know your cousin Jennifer got a ticket for that not long ago."

"I know, Mom. I was there when she told you about it, remember?"

"I just want you to be safe. Anyhow, one more thing. Do you have another minute?"

"Yes, Mom," I said, knowing her sense of time probably hadn't improved.

"Your father wants you to say a few words at the rehearsal dinner on Friday night."

"Why?"

"Well, you know the father of the groom is going to say something on behalf of his family and you know how your father feels about public speaking. So he was hoping you could say something on behalf of our family. You're really very good at that sort of thing. I'd ask your brother but he treats everything like it's a courtroom and it starts sounding like an argument. Do you think you could come up with something?"

"Okay, sure."

"It has to be something nice."

"Yes, Mom."

"And thoughtful."

"Yes, Mom."

"Maybe you could quote Auden or something?"

W. H. Auden was Mom's favorite poet. I'm not sure he ever wrote a word about love that didn't make it sound like one of life's most tortured exercises. Also, in Auden's world, it usually involved two dudes. But I said, "Okay. Auden. How about 'Funeral Blues'?"

"Carter Morgan Ross, don't you dare!"

Yes, my middle name is Morgan. It's a family name. And, yes, I know I shouldn't have given my mother such a hard time. It was my small bit of revenge for her giving me three last names.

"I'm kidding, Mom," I said.

"Okay. Okay. And you're going to be here at four thirty on Friday, right?"

"Yes, Mom."

"So we can leave at four forty-five."

"Yes, Mom."

"And get to the rehearsal dinner at five, when it starts."

"Yes, Mom."

"And you won't be late."

"Mom, you're talking to your son who named his cat Deadline. When am I ever late?"

"I know. I know. I just want everything to

go smoothly. You know how your father hates to be late for things."

"Yes, Mom."

"Okay. Remember: four thirty!" she said one more time. Then, feeling like I had sustained enough henpecking for one conversation, I hung up.

I completed my drive to Florham Park, to a neighborhood that was an even mix between modern McMansions and future teardowns. McAlister's was, naturally, one of the former — a boxy, beige thing that only went to prove that $1.2 million doesn't necessarily buy you good taste.

Before long, I was knocking on the door, ready to duck when Marcia Fenstermacher answered it and tried to kick my teeth in. Instead, the door was opened by an older woman who immediately answered the question as to where Marcia had gotten her round face.

"Hello," she said in a not-unfriendly way. "Can I help you?"

I introduced myself and told her I was hoping for an audience with Marcia. She told me her name was Sandy and that Marcia had just gone to the store for a second. But I could wait for her if I liked. I informed her I liked.

She invited me into a large kitchen and

344

pointed me to a seat at the island in the middle. The kitchen opened into a great room, where the gawky preteenage boy I had seen in the picture frame on Marcia's desk was sitting in the corner, typing furiously on a desktop computer.

"That's Trevor," Sandy said. "He's our burgeoning computer genius. Trevor, this is Mr. Ross. Please say hello."

The kid mumbled something that may have sounded like "hello." He was freckled and flat-topped and I found myself wondering who my son — or daughter, or whatever the speck in Tina's womb would eventually turn into — would end up looking like. It stood to reason the kid would be tall and dark haired. I wondered if the hair would be curly like Tina's or —

"He's on that thing constantly," Sandy said, interrupting my inner monologue. "I really don't understand what he's doing."

"I'm just coding," Trevor said sullenly, like he was tired of explaining himself.

"As I said," Sandy said, "I really don't understand what he's doing."

"Yeah, can't say as I do, either."

Trevor tore himself away from the screen for a brief moment to size me up in a way that suggested he couldn't figure out why his grandmother let a six-foot-one moron into the house.

"Well, at least he'll never lack for employment," I said, then added, "I wish I could say the same for newspaper reporters."

"Well, I just hope he —" Sandy started. But she was interrupted by two things. First was Trevor saying, "Hi, Mom." Second was Trevor's mommy giving me a scalding glance and demanding, "What do *you* want?"

Sandy and Trevor froze. This man who had waltzed into the house had seemed friendly, but Mom was obviously pissed off at him. So they were no longer sure what to make of me. Marcia was still fixing me with a face that belonged in the Nasty Glare Hall of Fame

"I wanted to offer you an apology," I said.

"What for?"

I glanced at Trevor and asked, "Is there somewhere we can go and talk?"

This turned out to be a brilliant move, because it made Marcia realize that even though I was imprudent enough to have wrongly accused her of killing the man she loved, I was not so inconsiderate as to discuss it in front of her son and mother. Plus, by the time we moved into the study, which is where she shunted me, she had cooled off a little bit. She was wearing jeans and a sweatshirt and while her hair was still perfectly immobile, the rest of her was presented more casually than when she had to play the part of Vaughn McAlister's secretary.

"Look," I said as soon as the door behind us closed, "I asked you some pretty pointed questions yesterday, and I just wanted to say I was sorry. I had caught hold of a little bit of gossip about you and Vaughn being on the rocks and him jumping back to his ex-wife. I know now it wasn't true, but it made me jump to certain conclusions. Then we heard from one of your neighbors there was loud yelling coming from the house Monday night . . ."

"Uff, probably Mrs. Peters," Marcia said. "She's a busybody of the first order but she also can't hear that well. I just . . . Trevor and I got in a little fight about his home-work."

"Yeah, anyway, I'm sorry. You were pretty clearly having the worst day of your life and I didn't make it any better. Sometimes the first quasi-plausible explanation is the one that a lazy mind seizes, but that doesn't make it right."

She had her arms crossed — I do believe they call it a defensive posture — but most reasonable people have a hard time staying too mad when someone is laying the mea culpa on three layers thick. If there's one good thing about screwing up as often as I do, it's that you become a virtuoso at apologies.

"Why are you telling me this?" she demanded.

"Well, to be honest, my executive editor knew Vaughn as a kid. So he's got a personal interest in this story, which gives me a personal interest, too. Plus, I'm more than a little curious myself at this point. So I'm hoping maybe you can help me figure out who did this."

"Why should I?"

"Well, let me ask you this: have you heard from the police yet?"

"No."

Her arms were still crossed. But at least now I had redirected some of her anger at a different target.

"Don't you think it's a little strange that they wouldn't have contacted you by this point? You're not only his significant other, you're his secretary. Wouldn't any diligent investigator want to talk to you? I mean, no one knew every facet of Vaughn's life better than you."

"Yes, I just thought . . . I thought maybe

they just hadn't gotten to me yet."

"I'm sorry to tell you this, but they might not get to you ever," I said. "Our sources are telling us no one in city hall wants to bring much attention to Vaughn's life or death due to some of his property purchases. I had two officers in the Newark Police Department tell me in different ways that the case wasn't a priority. And lord knows they've got other murders to solve. At this point, it seems like the *Eagle-Examiner* is the only institution in Newark that wants to see Vaughn's killer brought to justice. So I'd really appreciate your help."

The arms finally dropped to her sides. She flopped into one of two easy chairs in the corner of the study and pointed me to the other one.

"Have a seat," she said.

"Thanks."

She rubbed her temples and closed her eyes for a moment. Her brain had been experiencing a serious bear market, but it was doing its best to stage a rally. Finally, she said, "Okay, what do you want to know about?"

No point in sugarcoating things. "This is a hard question to ask. But please try to understand I'm trying to find the truth. And the truth isn't always pretty. Is it possible

349

Vaughn had gotten involved with the mob?"

She looked legitimately dumbstruck. "The mob? Why would he do that?"

"Maybe he needed the money? Maybe he went to them for a loan for the company that he couldn't pay back?"

"But he . . . The company had plenty of money."

"It did?"

"Well, yeah. I saw everything that crossed Vaughn's desk. One of the things that he always had to sign off on were the quarterly profit-and-loss statements we submitted to the banks where we had loans. You always have to list assets and equities. I can't pretend like I knew how to read everything on those statements. But in the last one, I swore I saw the McAlister Properties reserve account had something like eight million dollars in it."

"Seriously? Do you have one of those statements for me to take a look at?"

"Not here. But I can show you if you come into the office tomorrow."

"Okay." I was still trying to process what I had just heard as I moved on to the next topic of interest. "Another question: do you know the name Scott Colston?"

She looked down and to the right as she groped through her memory. "Yes, but . . .

why do I?"

"He's the Licensed Site Remediation Professional who signed off on the cleanup of the McAlister Arms site."

"Oh, right. Yes. I guess I've seen that name on some documents."

"Have you ever met him?"

She gave this ten seconds of thought before saying, "No. But that's not unusual. Someone like that would do his work on-site and I never . . . I never went to the site. Vaughn wanted me to stay in the office. So I wouldn't have had the chance to meet someone like that."

"Ever talked with him on the phone?"

Five seconds this time. Then: "No."

"This may seem like a strange question, but . . . are you sure he exists?"

"Well, I . . . Why do you ask?"

I told her about having traced him to a pizzeria that was seldom open and known to be frequented by mobsters, including one Mitch DeNunzio.

"Wait," she said. "Mitch DeNunzio is in the mob?"

"Mitch DeNunzio *is* the mob."

"But I thought he was — I mean, I never . . ."

"Did Vaughn have interactions with Mitch DeNunzio?"

"From time to time, yes," she said, quietly. She brought her hands to her face. They were starting to shake. "Oh my God. Oh, Vaughn, how could you?"

"Did Vaughn ever say what their meetings were about?"

"No. And it's not like I was sitting in on them. Mr. DeNunzio came to the office maybe one or two times. And there were probably another few times Vaughn went out to see him. I never really knew what it was about. I thought DeNunzio was . . . I don't know, an investor or something."

"I suppose in a manner of speaking he was," I said. "He's just not the kind you can afford to cross."

Another twenty minutes of conversation made it apparent Marcia Fenstermacher didn't know anything more about the woes that might have led to Vaughn's demise. She promised to keep pondering matters and said she'd call Vaughn's dad to see if he knew anything about Vaughn's interactions with Mitch DeNunzio. I promised to keep her in the loop about anything new I discovered. I departed with a friendly nod to Sandy and Trevor, who was still buried in his computer screen and oblivious to the world.

As I drove back to Newark, I rang up Kira, telling her about the four-thirty-or-else deadline being imposed by my mother and giving her my parents' address. I wasn't worried about her getting to the place. Kira was a librarian. She had been trained to find a children's fiction book that had been filed in the 700s, next to the books about how to draw bugs. Finding my parents' house would be no problem.

With the call completed, I settled in for a good drive-time think, trying to iron out this newest wrinkle. In some ways, it made sense that Vaughn might have had some cash in reserve. After all, he had gotten a big pile of money — $6 million from the DEP and $1.1 million from Newark — for a cleanup he'd only pretended to do. That didn't quite add up to $8 million, but maybe the business had stashed away some profits back before it started losing tenants and going into the red.

Still, that did nothing to address the main question: if Vaughn had eight million bucks in the bank, why would he feel the need to go to the mob for money? I can't say I was an expert in business financing, but in general I knew that La Cosa Nostra should be treated as a lender of last resort.

It perhaps spoke to my level of desperation and ignorance that I was starting to think my best hope for further understanding of this issue was Buster Hays. I found the newsroom's resident grouch at his desk, reading his e-mail — which he had, naturally, printed out. I wondered if he'd send his reply via the town crier.

I took measure of the newsroom clock, which read 5:48, then made my move.

"Okay, Buster," I said. "It is exactly twelve minutes until your All-Slop shift. If you expect me to be sitting in that chair in your stead when it begins, I'm going to need a little information from the organized-crime-beat writer. You got anything yet?"

"Just hold your horses, Ivy, I —" He stopped when he looked up at me. "What happened to you?"

"What do you mean?"

"You look like you took a bath in Cheetos."

"My unnatural coloring should not be an issue here," I snapped. "Don't be racist."

"Fine. Have it your way. Anyhow, I did talk to one person who might be in a place to know a thing or two about your fair-haired boy. He said Vaughn McAlister had needed a favor from Mitch DeNunzio, and that he might have been willing to provide a favor in return."

354

"What does that mean?"

"Ivy, I keep telling you, this isn't exactly an organization that prides itself on transparency."

"Yeah, but . . . a favor. So does that mean money or what?"

"No. No money. My source made it sound like a service of some kind had been performed. I don't know exactly what."

"And in return?"

"Oh, I don't know. Maybe they just wanted free office space? I kind of had to get this on the sly. The guy thought I was calling about something else and I dropped this into the conversation. If I asked too many questions, he would have stopped talking."

"So that's all I get? I'm going to spend all night chained to the All-Slop and all you give me is that Mitch DeNunzio and Vaughn McAlister exchanged unspecified favors?"

He leaned back, grinning in self-satisfied fashion. "Correct me if I'm wrong, Ivy, but that's a lot more than you could have gotten on your own. I got a few other lines in the water. I'll let you know if one of them jiggles."

"Fine," I said, feeling a little disappointed.

"Have fun shoveling," he said, then started waving me off. "Now go away, kid. You bother me."

"Trust me, it's mutual," I said, if only to offer a parting shot.

I returned to my desk. At least Buster had potentially solved one thing for me: a guy with eight million dollars did not need a loan from the mob. This, however, only renewed my curiosity as to why Vaughn McAlister was no longer breathing. Had he somehow reneged on the favor he had promised? Was that worth killing him?

I must have been lost in thought, because the next thing I knew a hand was being passed in front of my face.

"Hello? Anyone home?" Tommy was asking.

"Oh. Sorry," I said, shaking my head a little bit.

"And stop that," Tommy said.

"Stop what?"

"Chewing on that pen," he said. I hadn't realized it, but in my distracted state, I had taken a pen off my desk and stuck it between my back molars and was apparently giving it a good chomping.

"What's it to you?" I asked.

"One, it's gross," he said. "Two, never let a gay man think you've got an oral fixation. It just leads us on."

"What do you . . . Oh, never mind," I said,

suddenly getting it. I'd never look at a Bic in quite the same way. "Anyhow, what's new?"

"More bad news for Vaughn McAlister."

"Worse than being dead?"

"Well, maybe not that bad. But it was probably a serious bummer for him right before he got that way."

"And what's that?"

Tommy settled himself behind the empty desk across from me. That was one of the only good things about being in a business with ever-declining staffing levels: plenty of open seating.

"Well," he said. "I started looking into Best Buy. I called up their corporate offices in Minnesota and got the usual runaround from their spokesman about how they don't comment on their plans for expansion until the leases are signed and blah blah blah."

"Which means they hadn't signed a lease yet," I said. "That's something."

"Yeah, but that's not all. I started doing a clip search and found out the guy who brokered the deal for their store in Springfield is a guy I know."

"Better to be lucky than good sometimes."

"Yeah, so I called him and started chatting him up. And what he told me — not for attribution, of course — is that they had been in serious talks about moving into Newark. They had their advance people out on the site and everything. It looked like it was going to be green-lighted, but then it all fell apart about a week ago."

"Why?"

"He said there were serious concerns about the financing of the project," Tommy said. "Basically, Best Buy became convinced the thing was never going to get off the drawing board so they had told McAlister Properties they were pulling out."

"But that doesn't make sense," I said. "According to Vaughn's secretary, he had a reserve account with eight million bucks in it."

"Do you believe her?"

"She's offered to show me their most recent P-and-L statement when she's back in the office."

Tommy considered this for a moment. "Yeah, but that still doesn't take into account McAlister Properties' problem with its DSCR."

"Uh . . ."

"Debt service coverage ratio," Tommy reminded me. "Remember, in the postrecession world order, no bank is going to extend money to a developer unless it's convinced the business has significantly positive cash flow to be able to repay it. Vaughn wasn't even breaking even. Heck, he was *losing* money. So to a certain extent it didn't matter how much money he had in reserve. McAlister Arms was a hundred-and-twenty-million project. Eight million in the bank is vending-machine money compared to that."

"And unless he could get his existing buildings back into the black, he was never going to get another dime in financing," I said. "And he was losing roughly four million bucks a year, give or take, which means he was running out of time to turn things around."

"You got it," Tommy said. "And obviously Best Buy had decided that was never going to happen."

I wanted to keep kicking around ideas with Tommy, but I caught the newsroom clock out of the corner of my eye. It was straight-up 6:00, which meant my time was no longer my own. The next eight hours of my life were going to be spent in service to the All-Slop. I excused myself from Tommy's company and trudged over to that part of the newsroom, ready to do my part to feed the digital monster.

When I got over there, I was surprised to

see Pigeon already seated at one of the other desks.

"Hey, what are you doing here?" I asked.

"The All-Slop intern called in sick," she said. "They asked me this morning if I wanted to fill in. Since it meant I could sleep all day, I said yes immediately."

I stifled whatever sly comment I was about to make about that because Tina was walking by and I didn't want it to appear Pigeon and I were being friendly, talking, or even acting as if we were members of the same broad taxonomic family. I had successfully avoided Tina all day, and I hoped that had afforded her ample time to cool down and realize there were many explanations as to why Pigeon had spent the night at my house, and some of them might have actually been innocent.

Alas, she was eyeing me like she wished she had another Dunkin' Donuts bag to throw at me.

"What are you doing here?" she asked.

"What does it look like? I'm creating original content so it can be stolen by aggregators who profit from my hard work without paying for it."

She ignored my commentary and said, "Why is Buster's name on the schedule?"

"I suppose 'extortion' would be one word

for it. I needed his help with something, and Buster's help never comes free."

Tina shifted her glance to Pigeon, who was pretending to busy herself with a computer keyboard that had suddenly become terribly interesting.

"Cute," Tina said. "You two plan this?"

My lungs expanded with the air I would need to object, but she didn't give me the chance to let it escape. "Never mind," she said. "I don't even care. What I do care about is why you don't have a follow on Vaughn McAlister."

"I filed the thing about the protest . . ."

"I meant a real follow. With actual news in it. Something that signals to our readers we care about this story and they should, too. More importantly, something that signals to Brodie he shouldn't replace you with a twenty-three-year-old that he'll pay half as much to work twice as hard."

"Brodie would never do that."

"Spoken like a reporter who hasn't seen the latest newsroom budget," she said.

Tina wasn't serious. I knew that. And if there was any further consolation, it's what I had learned through hard-won experience with Tina: when she was out for blood like this, she didn't really mean what she said. She just wanted to make sure she cut me somehow. I decided my best tack was to appear mortally wounded and hope she felt she had gotten her pound of flesh.

"Stop trying to look pathetic. It won't work," she said. "Does Tommy have anything?"

I thought about Tommy's contributions: one not-for-attribution source saying Best Buy had pulled out of McAlister Arms; another background source, with no direct knowledge of McAlister Properties' balance sheet, doing back-of-napkin math that said it was losing money; an anonymous tipster in city hall who said McAlister was sitting on more than a million dollars of Newark's money. They were valuable additions to my understanding of Vaughn McAlister's precarious financial situation, but it wasn't really stuff I could put in the newspaper — at least not responsibly.

"We're getting there," I said. "You're just going to have to be patient."

"Oh, I'm plenty patient," she said, then jerked her thumb in the direction of Brodie's office. "It's Mr. Hot Pants who's pitching a tent."

With that rather graphic image, she left me to the All-Slop and the relative peace that was, journalistically speaking, a fairly mundane task. By that time of night, it was mostly routine stories about car wrecks, homicides, the weather, and whatever other disasters, natural or unnatural, were unfolding across the Garden State. We reacted to the stuff that seemed interesting and ignored the rest of it.

When you're on the All-Slop, you're basically hoping the news comes in at what might be called Goldilocks speed. If you get too much, it starts to feel hectic. Too little and you get bored. You're looking for juuuuuust right.

This one was a little on the fast side, so I hadn't really noticed the passage of time until around midnight, when things started to slow down. I was in the middle of some idle chitchat with Katie Mossman, one of the All-Slop's regular editors, when she took a glance at the Web feed from the fire/police incident-pager network.

"Uh-oh," she said.

"What?"

"I've been keeping an eye on this house fire in West Orange. Sounds like a big one and now, apparently, it's a fatal. Incident pager said they just found a body."

"A fatal in *West* Orange?" I said, because if there was going to be a deadly fire in the Oranges, East Orange was the most likely culprit. It had far more aging tenements, the type that tended to burn easily and catch inhabitants unaware — because the tenants stole the batteries from the smoke detectors in the hallways.

"Yeah. I'm afraid you're going to have to write it up."

"I got two hours left in this shift anyway," I said. "Might as well fill it with something. What's the address?"

She looked at the screen again and said, "It's in the one hundred block of McAlister Court."

I swore loudly. There was only one house in the 100 block of McAlister Court — only one house on McAlister Court, period. And there was only one body likely to be found in that house.

Barry McAlister.

They rode past the house twice. Any more than that and someone might notice.

There were three of them — two thick guys and a thin guy, the same crew that had been hired to do the first McAlister job.

Two passes turned out to be enough. The place was exactly as their employer said it would be: a two-story Tudor on a private lane, reasonably secluded, with enough trees that it couldn't really be seen by its neighbors. At least not until the leaves fell.

Still, they didn't want to take any chances. So they stole a car, taking it from the parking lot of the West Orange train station. It was a Buick, at least fifteen years old — the kind that are easier to steal, because the antitheft safeguards hadn't gotten too sophisticated yet. They aimed to have it back before the owner would even be aware of what had happened.

They just wanted to make sure that if anyone

saw a car turning onto Barry McAlister's private lane, it wasn't theirs.

In truth, arson wasn't really their specialty. They knew guys who were real artists at it, guys who could make it seem like a wire had shorted or an oven had been left on. Neither the two thick guys nor the thin guy knew any of those tricks.

But that didn't seem to matter to their employer, who said it didn't matter if the authorities knew it was arson. The only instructions they had been given was that Barry McAlister's house — and, in particular, his living room — needed to burn, and it needed to be a fire that would cover up as much of the evidence as possible.

Cook everything. And leave the body behind.

The body had to be found. Once again, that was key. The world had to know that Barry McAlister was dead. Same as it had been with Vaughn.

So they pulled up in the driveway in their stolen Buick and went to work. They had enough lighter fluid for a decade's worth of wiener roasts, and they used it to soak the living room. They thought about pulling some of the recycled newspapers out of the garage, so the fire would have enough fuel to get good and hot. Then they looked at Barry McAlister's shag carpet, paisley couch, and ancient drapes and decided there was enough polyester to keep things raging for a while.

The thin guy was the one who actually struck the match. The flame instantly leaped across the carpet, up the drapes and onto the easy chair where the corpse was resting.

The fire alarm started ringing shortly thereafter and that spooked them a little bit. Even though they knew none of the neighbors would be able to hear it, it made them feel like they were attracting too much attention to themselves.

So they took off, leaving a funeral pyre behind them.

CHAPTER 7

Before Katie Mossman could have much say in the matter, I told her I was heading out to West Orange. I'm not sure there was precedent for an All-Slop reporter being allowed to leave the desk. I'm also not sure there was anything Katie could have done to stop me.

It was always possible the fire had been an accident. Barry McAlister was a chainsmoker who obviously enjoyed a drink or two. He wouldn't be the first alcoholic to combine his two vices in a tragic way, dropping a lit cigarette on the couch as he passed out — to name just one way it might have happened.

Then again, it was also possible someone, perhaps some minion of the DeNunzio crime family, had killed Barry and given his house the ol' gas 'n' go, knowing that if the place was torched properly, it would incinerate enough evidence to assure the assailant of getting away with it.

I had been operating under the assumption Mitch DeNunzio had developed a serious grudge against Vaughn McAlister — for reasons I had yet to fully uncover — and had decided to take him out. Perhaps that grudge extended to Vaughn's old man. Had he seen something he shouldn't have seen? Had he known something he shouldn't have known?

Whatever it was, I wondered if Barry had even been aware of it. He was so lost he'd thought Marcia Fenstermacher had something to do with this. You would think that if Barry was aware Vaughn had been having dalliances with the mafia, that would have been the first thing he told me — not some revenge fantasy involving a jilted secretary.

When I got to West Orange, the short private drive that was McAlister Court looked like a staging ground for a disaster-training session, with an impressive assortment of firefighting equipment on hand. The municipalities in this part of the state are tiny — many just a few miles square — and yet they all have full fire departments that, on a given night, don't have anything better to do than respond to fires in other towns. I counted at least six fire departments represented.

There were also two ambulances; five marked police cars; six unmarked ones; a crime-scene-unit truck; and a K9 car, whose purpose I couldn't begin to fathom, unless they feared one of the fire departments forgot to bring its Dalmatian and would need a spare dog. There were people in uniform everywhere, most of whom were present probably only because this was the most exciting thing that was going to happen to West Orange all year and they didn't want to miss it.

There was also, front and center, a car from the Essex County Arson Squad, which perhaps began to answer my question about whether the fire had been set accidentally.

Then there was the house itself. Or, rather, what was left of it. I had covered a lot of fires in my time as a reporter, including some fatals. There weren't many as thoroughly torched as this one. What had once been a nice Tudor house was missing most of its roof. It was hard to find a place on the shingled siding untouched by flame once you got much beyond the first floor.

You generally didn't get a fire like that unless it had a little bit of help from several dozen gallons of Shell's finest 93 octane.

I got out of my car and started skulking around. The blaze had been extinguished, though the air still had that sickly, unnatural stench that house fires get from the burning of things that were never meant to be burned, like plastic and insulation. There was enough darkness and confusion that no one really paid attention to me, the first reporter at the scene. So I had free rein to cast about until I found someone who might tell me what was going on.

It didn't take long until I found him. Michael "Sully" Sullivan was the mayor of West Orange. He was a good guy — as Sullys everywhere tend to be — and I had dealt with him a couple of times before. He was a local Realtor, a better-than-average quote, and had been mayor for at least a decade, mostly because no one else really wanted the job. In a town like West Orange, being mayor was a part-time gig that paid precious little — maybe ten thousand a year — and came with more headaches than that stipend could possibly be worth.

I was glad he was there, if for one reason only: when it comes to fire and/or crime scenes, mayors are great. They have absolutely no official purpose and are as essential to any investigation as nearby manhole covers. Yet, they often get briefed and will use the information to make themselves seem important to their constituents. You can usually get them to tell you stuff the fire and/or police department never will.

"Hey, Mr. Mayor," I said as I sidled up to him. He was looking at me blankly, so I said, "Carter Ross from the *Eagle-Examiner.* Isn't this past your bedtime?"

He took a moment to recognize me, registered mild surprise when he did, then recovered with: "Hey, Carter, nice to see you again. Isn't it past yours too?"

"Ordinarily, yeah. I happened to be pulling a night shift when this went out on the incident pager. I recognized the address as being Barry McAlister's place. You may have heard about what happened to his son, Vaughn?"

"Yeah, I read about it," Sully said.

"So you understand my curiosity. What's the deal? Did whoever went after the son decide to go after the father and turn this into barbecue season?"

He shook his head and said, "More like hunting season."

Even in the dim, whirling light cast by the various fire trucks and emergency vehicles, I could still make out the pained expression on Mayor Sullivan's face.

"What do you mean?" I asked.

He pulled his hands out of his pockets,

blew on them, then shoved them back in. "Can I just talk on background and then we'll put something on the record later?" he said.

"Sure."

"Chief Delaney thinks Barry was dead before the fire started," Sully said. "We found Barry's car in the garage. The inside of it had blood all over it."

"Blood?"

"Yeah. A lot of it. Chief's theory was that someone waited for Barry in the backseat and, when he got in, reached around and slit his throat. The chief was saying the only way there could have been that much blood in the car is if someone severed Barry's carotid artery."

"Ugh," I said, flinching.

"Yeah, so basically the chief was saying it looked like Barry was killed in his car and then dragged into his living room — there were blood smears on the stairs, too. The perp then lit the body on fire, perhaps to cover evidence of the throat slashing. One of the firemen said he had never seen a body burned so badly."

"Oh, man," I said, feeling that bit of news in my stomach.

"Yeah, but the perp didn't do as good a job in the garage. I think maybe he hoped if he set a fire in the living room, the garage would catch fire, too. But there's not much about a concrete-slab floor that will burn, so most of the garage survived intact."

"So, what, he was hoping the whole house would burn to the point where no one would be able to investigate and they would just chalk it up as an accident?"

"Maybe. Who knows? Whatever his hope was, he wasn't very good at it. One of the Arson Squad detectives said the living room still smelled like lighter fluid."

We stood there for a minute or so, both of us with our hands in our pockets, looking at this singed house. There was enough here to keep some determined investigators busy for a while. The crime scene guys would work on what was left after the fire. The Arson Squad guys would determine what kind of accelerant had been used to light the blaze. The medical examiner would get what he could from the charcoaled body.

There would be more information. But none of it, I suspected, would actually help to solve anything. The answers weren't in whatever forensics were left behind in that house. They were somewhere outside. I wondered if I'd ever be able to figure it out definitely myself.

"Did you know him?" I said at last.

"A little bit. I think everyone in town knew about what happened with him and his wife — it was a bit of a scandal at the time, her just leaving like that. After that, you'd see him around, at the grocery store and that sort of thing, but he was always sort of a tragic figure. I've probably sold ten houses in this neighborhood over the years and never once seen him outside or interacting with his neighbors."

My cell phone buzzed in my pocket — most likely Katie, asking if I had anything to report. I wasn't going to answer it, but it did prod me enough to ask, "So you mind giving me that on-the-record quote you promised?"

"Yeah, sorry to ramble so much," he said. "Just put me down as something like, 'This is a profoundly sad day for West Orange and the McAlister family. Our hearts go out to them. Yet even as we mourn this terrible loss, I am confident that Chief Delaney and his detectives will bring this killer to justice.' "

I jotted the canned quote in my notebook. Just as I was finishing, Sully said, "Now, if you want to do me a favor, please make it clear in whatever you write that this poor guy was targeted for some reason and that the police believe this was an isolated crime.

I don't need everyone in town thinking there's some kind of homicidal maniac going around West Orange slitting throats and torching homes."

"Bad for property values?"

"No kidding," he said. "Just when they were finally starting to get better."

I peppered Sully with a few more questions; then, when it was clear he had told me all he knew, I called the mayor's quotes in to Pigeon, whose job it would be to immediately disseminate them to the insomnia-suffering masses surfing the Web at this hour. Before long, I started to feel like I was about as useful as all the unneeded cops hanging about. Chief Delaney, whom I was meeting for the first time, brushed me off with a "no comment." I couldn't find any investigators from the Essex County Prosecutor's Office. And I didn't know what the Arson Squad guys looked like, or if they'd even talk to me.

Around the time the last of the out-of-town fire trucks pulled away, I decided to call it a night, too. It was 2:00 A.M. My time on the All-Slop was, technically, at an end. Anything else the authorities might have to say could wait until the light of day.

The last thing I noticed before getting into my car was that the little angel statue, the one that commemorated the life of Elizabeth McAlister, beloved wife and mother, had disappeared. Maybe it had been knocked down by one of the fire trucks or shattered by an ambulance that went on the lawn or who knows. But it had somehow gone missing.

She was the last of the McAlisters. And now she was gone, too.

It took forever to get to sleep — lingering adrenaline being what it is — and morning came too fast. I had set the alarm for 9:00 A.M., knowing I had promised Quint I would cover his piddling protest. I swore that only a half hour had passed when it rang.

I dragged myself out of bed, ran the shower extra-hot, then finished it off extra-cold. It did some good, but not much. Sometimes, a shower just feels like polish on a garbage truck. I dressed in my best pleated khakis and finest white shirt and took the unusual step of packing a blazer, knowing I would likely have to go straight to the rehearsal dinner from work without time to stop at home to change.

Before heading out, I sent quick e-mails to Tommy and Pigeon. I asked Tommy to keep working on Vaughn's finances. I figured

Pigeon could handle the follow on the fire/ murder of Barry McAlister.

That left the protest for me. And not even my morning Coke Zero could generate much enthusiasm for that. I had covered enough protests to know how they normally worked: the organizers promised a big crowd of outraged citizens, only to get a dozen people, half of whom were actually there representing their own pet cause only tangentially involved with the issue in question. I could only imagine what kind of unemployed and underemployed environmentalists would crawl out from under the rocks at ten o'clock on a Friday morning for Quint's little gathering. The Society for the Preservation of the Yellow-bellied Atlantic Squid. Left-handed Ukrainians for Environmental Fairness. Friends of the Roadside Puddle by Mrs. Jones's House. I was convinced it would be a sorry assortment of souls.

Instead, as I turned down Irvine Turner Boulevard and neared the McAlister Arms site, I had to come to a halt. A long line of traffic had formed. And it wasn't moving. I saw some kind of commotion a few blocks up ahead. There were police vehicles already on the scene, parked at odd angles on the sidewalks. Some drivers were honking their horns. Others were trying to turn around and get out of the mess. A few had given up and were just standing by their cars.

I did my own U-turn, then pulled onto a side street so I could park and walk closer. As I neared the area, I saw a large collection of humanity that, if it decided to, could have turned into a very respectable mob. I'm not exactly the National Park Service when it comes to estimating crowd size, but there were at least five hundred people. And that *didn't* include the Shabazz High School marching band — in full uniform — assembled off to the side.

I heard their chanting from several blocks away. It was the old standby: "What do we want? Justice. When do we want it? Now." I found that pretty funny, since Quint had told me the day before he didn't really have a goal for his protest — meaning the people didn't even know what justice they were seeking.

It was only when I got close that I saw what was happening to snarl traffic. Roughly fifty of the protesters had linked arms and sat down in the middle of Irvine Turner Boulevard, blocking anyone trying to get to I-78.

The police on the scene were just watching them, clearly unsure of what to do.

Quint had mentioned he was going to Newark to get the permits, so I was sure the protest was legal. Blocking the street wasn't, but the cops were probably edgy about cracking down too hard. They didn't want to incite a crowd this large. Newark and riots don't have a good history together.

Out of curiosity, I sidled up to the first protester I saw. She was a young woman with long brown hair that actually had flowers in it, like she was trying to follow some sixties protest manual passed down from her grandparents.

"Excuse me," I said. "I'm a reporter with the *Eagle-Examiner.* I'm wondering: what are you here protesting?"

"I think there's some pollution or something?" she said, absent anything resembling guile. "But don't ask me. I don't actually know."

"If you don't know, why are you here?"

"I'm a friend of Quint Jorgensen's," she said, then corrected herself: "Actually, I'm more a friend of a friend. I don't really know him. I more know *of* him."

"And so you came to his protest because . . . ?"

"Are you kidding? Quint organizes the *best* protests. I never miss them. The food alone is worth coming for."

"The food?" I asked.

"Oh yeah, didn't you see? There are vegetarian sandwiches over there," she said, pointing to a long table with what appeared to be two five-foot-long sub sandwiches and a pair of volunteers behind them, cutting off pieces and passing them out. She pointed to a guy with a large foam Snickers for a hat: "That's the candy man. He passes out candy bars and that sort of thing. That tub over there has chips — don't worry, they're made from organic, locally grown potatoes. Somewhere around here, there's another lady passing out home-baked cookies. Protesting can work up an appetite, you know. Quint tries to think of everything."

As she was speaking, I had caught a whiff of marijuana smoke. I wondered if Quint had thought of that, too. I guess when you have millions of dollars and nothing better to do with it, you need not spare the extra trimmings.

I was about to ask the young woman more questions — to see just how facile her understanding of the issue at hand was — when the Shabazz High School marching band decided to add to the bedlam. With three sharp whistle blasts, the drum section began a thunderous salute. Soon every kid in the band was doing some kind of fancy

381

dance step in perfect unison with the others. They circled around the street blockers, to the encouragement and delight of the other protesters. Then they climbed a temporary stage that had been erected and began belting out the Shabazz High fight song.

It was total chaos.

And in the middle of it was Quint, holding a bullhorn, grinning at it all.

Picking my way gingerly through the crowd — a good portion of whom turned out to be smoking a substance that was not tobacco — I eventually made it to Quint, who was waving his arms in the air, acting like he was conducting the band. The kids were blaring away, not paying him any mind. He pretty clearly didn't care. The homemade cookies weren't the only things that were baked.

"Hey, you made it!" he said, clearly pleased to see me, yelling so he could be heard over the music.

"Yeah, this is . . . this is something," I yelled back.

"I told you: I throw a good protest."

"I see that."

"Please tell me you've managed to come up with some demands," I said.

"My hands?" he said. "What about my hands?"

"No," I yelled, then got closer to him so he could hear better, to the point where I was practically yelling in his ear. *"Demands. Do you have any demands?"*

"Oh, no. Not yet."

"So what are you going to do with these people?"

"I don't know, actually," he said, still seeming unconcerned. "The lawyer was supposed to handle the entertainment."

"The lawyer? Who, Imperiale?"

"Yeah. I called the dude yesterday, told him about the protest and he was all excited about it. He said he'd get some of his clients here to talk about the injuries they suffered. But now here it is game time and I don't even think he's here. You haven't seen him, have you?"

I glanced around the crowd, trying to locate a man with a big nose and fake black hair who looked like he'd be comfortable on the back of a Yellow Pages. I didn't see him anywhere.

"Nope," I said.

"Stood up by a freakin' lawyer," Quint said, shaking his head, but seeming in good humor about it. Cannabis tended to have that effect.

"Maybe he got called into court on some other matter?" I suggested.

Finally, the band stopped playing. Everyone gave them an enthusiastic round of applause.

"How the hell did you get a marching band to come?" I asked when the noise finally died down.

"Will introduced me to one of his clients. A girl named Jackie? She lives somewhere around here. She pulled some strings."

"Jackie Orr?"

"Yeah, that's her. She's right over there — the black girl with the bushy hair," he said, directing my gaze with a point until it fell on Jackie. "Anyhow, if you'll excuse me for a second, I got some work to do."

Quint walked over to the temporary stage and climbed its stairs and was soon acting as emcee, thanking the Shabazz marching band, getting another roar out of the well-fed, mildly buzzed crowd. I slid over to Jackie.

"So I understand you and Quint have joined forces," I said.

She hitched her antiquated bug glasses up her nose, readjusted the bag she had slung over her shoulder, and gave me her usual critical stare-down. "Yes," she said, and was not going to offer anything else.

"Look, I know you're upset with me, because you feel like I abandoned you. But if you had given me a little more time, I would have come back to you."

She shoved her hands into the pockets of the Aéropostale hoodie she was wearing. But something in her posture told me she was coming around, so I pressed on:

"And, besides, in some ways, things have worked out pretty well. You wanted a lawyer. You got one. You wanted attention for your neighbors' problems" — I gestured to the throngs of people around me — "and you pretty clearly have that, too. So what do you say we call a truce? I'm still going to write some kind of story about this. Even if I don't know what it's going to say or how this is going to play out, I'd like you to be a part of it."

I held out my right hand. She let it dangle there for a minute, then grabbed it and gave it a good, firm pump.

"My grandmother always told me to judge people on their intentions as well as their actions," she said. "I guess your intentions are good."

"They are," I confirmed. "They are."

Up on the stage, Quint was still revving up the crowd. He was asking if any of the plaintiffs in the McAlister Properties lawsuit were present, inviting them to give their "testimony." Obviously, Quint wanted to provide the entertainment, colorful lawyer or no.

"So what about Will Imperiale," I said. "How are his intentions?"

"Good. Really good."

"You sure? He was apparently supposed to be here this morning but he didn't show."

"Well, he showed up at my grandmother's place yesterday afternoon when he said he would," she said. "He talked us through what was going to happen, what we'd have to sign and what it said and all that. It all sounded pretty good. Everyone ended up signing with him."

That was unsurprising. Knowing how to work a living room full of potential clients was something of a necessary survival skill in the field of personal injury law.

"Please tell me you asked him some hard questions," I said. "About the timing of everything. About the difficulties of the case. About how long it might take before you got paid — if you got paid at all."

"I did. He said it was no problem. He said we'd all get paid. He promised."

Well, at least the man didn't lack for confidence. I wondered if he had somehow learned about Scott Colston, the fake

Licensed Site Remediation Professional. Maybe Quint had tipped him off. Something like that would go a long way toward proving negligence. Still, nothing was ever assured in a court of law.

"You know he can't really do that," I said. "No lawyer, no matter how sure he is about his case, can guarantee a victory. Juries are fickle. Even if he got a bench trial, where it's going to be decided by judges, he might get tripped up on some minor statutory point. The defense is going to have smart lawyers, too, you know."

"No, no, that's the thing: he said the defense has already agreed to settle."

"It has?"

"Yeah. He said the details were still being worked out. And we might not get all the money owed to us, but that if we signed with him, we'd at least get something."

"Really? How much?"

"He said even someone like me, who only got sick once, would probably get like ten thousand. He said some people would get a lot more. Maybe fifty or a hundred thousand."

"Wow, really?" I said, mostly because I was too astonished to say much more.

She nodded.

I looked up at Quint, who was railing

about the wanton negligence of McAlister Properties, the greedy corporation that cared only about its profits. Now it was starting to sound more like a stump speech for a midterm election campaign. No matter. The crowd was loving it.

"So, wait," I said, still trying to make sure I understood what was happening, "which defendant settled? There were at least fifteen of them in the complaint I saw. I mean, even Quint's family's old company was a defendant."

"This one, I think," she said, pointing to the ground. "McAlister Properties."

That was curious, to say the least. Between the construction workers and Jackie's neighbors, Imperiale had something like fifty clients, some of them with broken bones and kidney failure. One of them had even died. It was a multimillion-dollar claim if ever I'd heard one. And it's not like McAlister Properties' insurance would cover it, because the insurance company could rightly point out that its policy didn't cover negligence on the part of the insured. So the settlement would be coming out of McAlister Properties' piggy bank. Why would the McAlisters fork over millions without a fight?

Even though I knew the company had

money — that eight-million-dollar reserve — I couldn't imagine Vaughn would so willingly give up his nest egg. His only chance of surviving was to get his two main buildings profitable again, a turnaround that could take months or years, if it happened at all. He needed all the padding he could get. Why would McAlister Properties — which sounded like it was creeping toward the cliff of insolvency as it was — agree to pay a settlement that would push it over the edge? And would the settlement, which presumably was negotiated when both McAlisters were alive, hold now that both McAlisters were dead?

"Well, I still wouldn't go on any spending sprees," I said.

"He said it was as good as done."

"Did he put it in writing?" I asked.

"I don't think so."

"What do you mean, you don't think so?"

"I . . . I mean, I didn't actually read it," she said, and at least had the good sense to be embarrassed about it.

"Do you have the agreement you signed with you?"

She fished around in her shoulder bag, produced an envelope that had Imperiale & Trautwig's logo printed on it, and handed it to me.

"Thanks," I said.

I opened it and pulled out a four-page document. It all looked pretty standard. And, sure enough, there was no mention of any kind of settlement or of any kind of guaranteed payments. Imperiale was too cagey to put any of that on paper.

Really, the only unusual thing about the agreement was the part about compensation. This was usually where there was language to indicate the undersigned attorney was entitled to one-third of any reward recovered by the plaintiff. But apparently that wasn't good enough for Willard R. Imperiale, Esq.

The bastard had conned these poor people — who probably didn't know any better — into giving him 50 percent.

"Thanks," I said. "Interesting reading."

Quint had finished up his speech and had finally been joined on stage by DaQuan Richardson, the first plaintiff to testify before this mock court of revelers. But first, the Shabazz band was going to strike up another song.

This rendered further attempts at conversation somewhat pointless, so I bade Jackie farewell and wandered around the crowd for a while. One speaker after another kept coming up to the podium to complain about the malady McAlister Properties had visited upon them, each of them encouraged by Quint. It made for some odd pairings — the superrich heir from Madison and the downtrodden people of Newark — but, then again, this was an odd gathering.

Eventually, I felt like my time at the show was drawing to a close. I had enough in my notebook to file something. The crowd was growing bored and starting to dissipate. The people sitting in the street had been persuaded to let traffic go. The marching band had high-stepped its way back to Shabazz High, a few blocks away.

Not wanting to be the last princess at the ball, I meandered back to my car, only to find it double-parked by an extra-long, silver Cadillac Escalade. I stared at the car peevishly for a moment, not understanding what was happening and certainly not noticing that a rather large man had approached behind me — until I heard his voice.

"Carter Ross," he said.

I turned to see a gentleman who had about four inches and a hundred pounds on me. He was wearing a black peacoat, even though it wasn't that cold. And I don't think it was because he had a circulatory problem.

"There's someone who wants to talk to you," he said. "Get in the truck."

I looked at the vehicle and that's when it hit me: a silver Cadillac Escalade. Mitch DeNunzio's vehicle. I tried to appear unworried, even nonchalant, which is hard to do when you're worried about soiling yourself.

I cast a few furtive glances to my left and right to see if there was room for me to make a getaway. Although I couldn't have beaten this goon in a wrestling contest, I was pretty sure I could outrun him. The problem was that I couldn't outrun the bullets in his gun.

"I don't suppose I could politely decline your offer," I said, bending my knees slightly so my legs would be ready to propel me somewhere else. And fast.

Then another voice behind me said, "Not really."

It was another gentleman, a little shorter, but thicker. He was wearing a windbreaker, which meant either circulatory problems were contagious, or he was also packing. My odds of escape, which were already small, had become infinitesimal. I thought about making a break for it anyway. But then I started to think more rationally: if my choices were, basically, get shot now or get shot later, didn't it make sense to delay the pain?

"Well," I said. "Can I ask where we're going?"

"Just get in the car," Goon One said, closing in and grabbing my arm.

I couldn't believe, given that I had so recently been surrounded by hundreds of people — not to mention a full marching band — that I was now alone, with no one to witness that I was being abducted in broad daylight. But the little side street where I had parked was deserted.

Goon Two opened the door for me as Goon One shunted me inside with something less than the courtesy he might have shown his grandmother. The seats had been arranged limousine-style, with one of the benches turned backward so it could face the other one. Goon One got in behind me and planted me in the middle of that backward-facing bench. Goon Two went around and sat on the other side of me.

Facing me was a sixty-something-year-old Italian man, dressed in a silver suit that was nearly as shiny as the Escalade. His shirt collar was open and unbuttoned more than, in my opinion, a man's shirt ought to be. Not that I was going to share that reflection at the moment.

"My name is Mitch DeNunzio," he said as the SUV got moving. "That name mean anything to you?"

"I know you're, uh, probably not a big fan of the RICO statutes," I said.

He chortled. "Ha. You're funny. This kid is funny, huh?"

Having been given tacit permission to express their pleasure, Goon One and Goon Two chuckled.

I wasn't laughing. I was still looking for some kind of escape. We were trolling through Newark at a very reasonable speed, stopping at lights, obeying traffic laws. Could I overcome the six hundred pounds of meat bracketing me and hop out at an intersection? I wondered if Vaughn McAlister had been making the same calculations shortly before his head met the thick end of a baseball bat.

"So," he continued, "I understand you've been asking around about me. Having Buster Hays make some inquiries about me and Vaughn McAlister? Is that right?"

"Yeah," I said, cautiously. No sense in denying what the man already knew. Obviously, whomever Buster had spoken with had reported back to the boss. I wasn't sure how they had found me. But since I had written about the protest in the paper today, it wasn't hard to guess that I'd be covering it.

"Well, in that case, I'm glad we're talking," he said. "I know that sometimes certain . . . rumors . . . can tend to take on a life of their own with me. And I don't need bad publicity of that sort at this moment. So I want you to know: I had nothing to do with Vaughn McAlister."

Half of me wanted to say, *Great to hear. Now how about you let me out of this car and I'll go write that up?*

"You, you didn't?" I said, sounding more incredulous than was perhaps polite.

"No. Never. I actually wanted to be one of his investors. I thought McAlister Arms had a lot of promise and I know he might have needed some financing help. But we hadn't solidified anything. So why would I want to kill him when I stood to make a lot of money off him?"

"I don't know, actually," I said. "I'm told you two had some . . . meetings? And that maybe you did some favors for each other?"

"We did."

"So maybe that arrangement stopped working out as well as had perhaps been promised. And maybe you decided he didn't need to be around any longer because of it."

He was shaking his head. "Not true."

"Are you sure?" I said.

He chortled again. "You got a lot of balls. This kid has got a lot of balls, huh?"

Goon One and Goon Two followed suit and laughed. So did I. Though maybe mine was a little more nervous than theirs.

"Look, kid, I tell you I didn't kill the guy, I didn't kill the guy," he said. "We had a business relationship, yeah. That's it."

"Did this business relationship involve Scott Colston?"

This time the chortle was more of a chuckle. "Ah, Scott Colston."

"Does he . . . does he even exist?"

"Well, I'm sure I don't know," DeNunzio said, fairly winking at me with a tone that had gone appropriately sarcastic. "Because, of course, I have no association with Mr. Colston and know nothing about him. But let's just say it's possible that Mr. Colston is not very good at his job. And therefore he may have signed off on Vaughn's remediation job a little prematurely. And if that's the case, well, the state of New Jersey ought to take away Mr. Colston's license."

"Yeah, if it can find him."

"I wish them all the luck in the world," he said.

"Okay, so you may have introduced

Vaughn to Scott Colston's services. What did Vaughn do for you?"

"Nothing. He was one of my customers, actually."

"Your customers?"

"Yeah. I own a security company. We have contracts all over New Jersey. One of them is with McAlister Properties. We offered Vaughn some highly competitive rates and he took advantage of them."

My mind flashed to the last guy I had seen sitting at the front desk at McAlister Place — a guy who offered about as much security as a guard dog. A dead one.

Then I got it: Tommy had mentioned there had been a rash of break-ins at McAlister Properties buildings. Of course there had been. DeNunzio had probably been giving his goons free rein to steal anything they wanted in those buildings — which Vaughn allowed, as a way of payment for those so-called competitive rates, and as compensation for the so-called services of Scott Colston.

Mitch DeNunzio wasn't going to confirm any of this for me. But he didn't have to. I already knew. I also knew it meant it really was unlikely DeNunzio had ordered Vaughn or Barry killed. Why slaughter a golden goose like that?

"Okay, okay, I get it," I said. "So if you didn't kill Vaughn, who did?"

"I don't know. I really don't. I give you my word on that. All I can tell you is it wasn't me."

"Okay. Well. Thanks for . . . setting me straight, I guess."

We had circled back around so that we were nearing my Malibu again. The Escalade was slowing down. My ride with the boss was coming to a far more gentle end than I had ever thought it would.

"No problem, kid," he said. "And, hey, just so you know, I think that girl Vicki likes you. Cute girl. She kept talking about how maybe you'd go on a cruise with her. You want, maybe I could send you two on a cruise. Would you like that?"

"With all due respect, Mr. DeNunzio, no, thank you," I said, then added, "Trust me when I say I have enough girl trouble right now."

They had two more jobs to do. This was the second-to-last. And, in truth, they were a little disappointed. This employer had been awfully good to them, paying promptly, generously, and, of course, in cash. The employer seemed to be rolling in it.

The only real difficulty in the job is that they'd probably have to do it during the daytime, because it had to happen when the homeowner wasn't there. And time was getting tight. That's what their employer had told them.

So the three of them — two thick guys and a thin guy — rented a silver Honda Odyssey. "The silver bullet," one of them called it, jokingly. A soccer-mom car. Suburban camouflage. Perfect for a place like Florham Park. Perfect for this job, in particular.

They stole plates off a car at a local Kings supermarket and swapped them out, just in case, then parked outside the target home shortly after sunrise.

Then they waited.

All around them, the neighborhood came to life. The commuters left first. The high school kids went next. The men kept their eyes on the target house. Their employer told them there would be a woman and a kid inside — and maybe an old lady. Or maybe not.

They watched. They saw the woman. They saw the kid. There was no old lady. That was good. One less person to worry about.

A little before eight o'clock, the kid walked down the driveway and to the end of the block, where he caught a bus to school. He never once glanced at the Honda.

The three men kept waiting. An hour passed. Two. Their employer had said the lady probably wouldn't go to work, but she would definitely leave at some point.

Finally, after a few more hours, the automatic garage door opened and a minivan — noncoincidentally, a Honda Odyssey with tinted windows — backed out. It turned around at the top of the driveway and went out front-first. The woman was driving. She didn't look at them.

They waited until the minivan disappeared around the corner, then made their move. There was no time to waste. They pulled into the driveway and the thin guy hopped out. He went around to a back door and quickly jim-mied the lock.

There was a security system — they had been warned about that — but it was an inexpensive model that was easily defeated. The door had two pressure-activated sensors, one on top and one on bottom. The thin guy carefully stuck Silly Putty over them so they remained depressed the entire time. He slipped inside the house and disabled it, us-ing a device designed to trick the central monitoring computer into thinking the system was still on.

Then he hustled down to the garage and pressed the opener. The Odyssey slid inside. The thin guy closed the door behind it. From the perspective of anyone passing outside, there was absolutely nothing unusual going on at Marcia Fenstermacher's house that morning.

Once inside, they worked quickly. They were there to steal only one thing, but, of course, they knew they were going to have to turn the place inside out to find it. So they had to make it look like they were there to steal everything.

They took the kind of things a gang of home invaders — or a couple of fiending hopheads who needed money for drugs — might take, quickly throwing it all into the Honda Odyssey. All the way, they kept an eye out for the one thing they had come for.

After about five minutes, one of the thick guys found it. It was in a drawer in the office.

"Got it," he announced, loudly enough his partners could hear it.

"Great," said the thin guy. "Let's spend three more minutes trashing the place, then get the hell out of here."

CHAPTER 8

During my new-employee orientation many years earlier, I had been taken on a tour of the plant where the *Newark Eagle-Examiner* was printed. For a young reporter who had just come from a much smaller daily in Pennsylvania, the *Eagle-Examiner*'s operation was awe-inspiring, from the soaring towers used to print the color sections, to the rolls of newsprint so massive they required a forklift to move them, to the stacks of ink barrels, each one a latent source of literally millions of printed words. Newspaper economics were better back then, and the plant was cranking out something like 450,000 copies a day, employing hundreds of pressmen and a fleet of trucks to carry it all.

Seeing all the work it took to put my stories into print was both powerful and sobering, and I have long endeavored to compose articles equal to that effort. I'll never forget the chill I felt as I was ceremoniously handed a fresh, slightly damp copy of that day's edition.

Then, at the end of the tour, I was taken back outside through the employee break room, where I met Inky the Parrot, the pressmen's mascot. And when I looked down, I got a different kind of reminder of the newspaper's place in many people's lives: there, lining Inky's cage, catching his compositions, was the preceding day's edition.

It was more with Inky in mind that I wrote my story on the protest. I finished by two o'clock, at which point my lousy night's sleep was beginning to wear on me. After finessing a fresh Coke Zero from the vending machine, I returned to my desk, feeling like a new man. I was still curious about this alleged settlement that Vaughn had agreed to before his untimely demise. And, of course, I couldn't exactly ask him about it.

But I could ask his lawyer. I just had to cajole my computer's winches and pulleys into letting me search the paper's archives and figure out who that attorney was. After tripping through a few stories that led nowhere, I found a caption that went with a photo we had run of a ribbon-cutting at

McAlister Place a few years earlier. I couldn't see the photo in our archives — just the text — but it told me all I needed to know. Pictured next to Vaughn McAlister was Kevin Ryan of McWhorter & French.

And that was a break for me. McWhorter & French was Newark's biggest — and probably best — law firm. And Kevin Ryan, the partner who headed its real estate division, was a guy I knew. Newark was a big city, but like a lot of big cities, its tall buildings were just a mask for the small town that lurked underneath. And in small-town Newark, Kevin Ryan was someone I bumped into all the time, at cocktail parties, at lectures, at charity functions.

As such, when I called his office, his secretary put me through.

"Hey, Carter, how're you doing, buddy?"

Kevin Ryan was an affable sort of guy who might have overused the word "buddy." We were more acquaintances than buddies. But I suppose there are worse words to overuse.

"Hey, I'm good," I said. "How are you?"

"I've been better, to be honest. I'm still pretty shaken up about this whole Vaughn thing. Then Barry, too. And to hear the fire was arson. It's . . . it's unbelievable. I just don't know what's going on."

"Me neither," I said.

"Vaughn was . . . He was a gem of a guy. He was one of my best friends. This has been . . . This has been hard."

"I didn't realize you guys were that close."

"We really started out together," he said. "I was a young associate at McWhorter when Vaughn was getting out from under his old man's wing and starting to do his own thing. I did all his early deals for him. And it was sort of like as he grew, I grew with him. And you know what it's like when you're young. You work together a lot — long hours, that sort of thing. Then you start socializing together. I was there when he met his first wife. I was an usher at his wedding. It was . . . I mean, we started as a business relationship. But then it became more than that. I'm not sure I realized it until he died, but Vaughn was really one of my best . . . I'm sorry, I'm rambling. Is this what you're calling for? You working on some kind of appreciation piece or something?"

"Not . . . exactly. I am definitely working on a story about Vaughn. But it's less an appreciation and more an investigation at this point."

"Okay, right. Sure. Sorry. How can I help?"

"Well, I'm curious about this lawsuit

against him. The one I wrote about."

"The one filed by that sleazebag Imperiale? I haven't seen it yet. But I'm sure it's crap. A guy like that would sue his own grandmother for giving him lukewarm chicken soup."

"Yeah, so why would Vaughn agree to settle it?"

There was no delay in Ryan's answer: "What? Vaughn wouldn't have done anything like that."

"Then why is Will Imperiale is going around signing up plaintiffs by telling them he's already gotten McAlister Properties to settle? He's been promising some of them they'll get fifty, a hundred grand a pop."

"I don't know. I mean, with a guy like that, who the hell knows what he says and why? I wouldn't put it past him to lie, knowing that the bigger his class, the more he can get for their pain and suffering. But I can tell you, unequivocally, there is absolutely no way Vaughn agreed to any settlements."

"Are you sure? Could Vaughn have settled the thing without telling you? I mean, you do real estate law. Maybe he consulted an attorney who defends personal injury stuff who told him that it was in his best interests to make the thing go away?"

"No," Ryan said quickly. "I just — I mean, that would be . . . I wasn't kidding when I said Vaughn and I were best friends. We talked almost every day. You want to tell me he wouldn't have at least mentioned that he had been sued? And that he was thinking about negotiating a settlement? Even if he didn't want me to do the negotiation, which is reasonable given my lack of expertise in that area, I'm sure he would have asked me to recommend an attorney. Or at least he would have told me who he picked — whether it was someone here or at another firm. I just can't tell you enough: there is no settlement."

"Okay, I get it," I said, more confused than ever, particularly when it came to the motives and actions of one Willard R. Imperiale, Esq.

Was it possible he'd had something to do with the early demise of the McAlister boys? Had he forced them into a settlement and killed them before they could change their minds? That hardly made sense. Anyone who felt like challenging that deal later would easily win.

And yet, who else would profit from their death? Especially given that he had weaseled his way into getting 50 percent of the payout. Speaking of which:

"Got another question for you," I said. "I saw the agreement Imperiale had his clients sign. He's got them giving up fifty percent of whatever he's able to recoup. I had never heard of that before. Is that legal?"

"Good grief. That guy is unbelievable," Ryan said, and I heard what sounded like a hand slamming on a desk. "Okay. Sorry. You asked whether it was legal. The answer is: yes. Obviously, the standard is one-third. And I think it's pretty unethical to go for half under the circumstances. But the law says attorneys are entitled to 'reasonable' fees and the courts have determined that up to fifty percent is reasonable in certain circumstances."

"So there's no recourse for his clients when they realize they've been screwed?"

"Not really," Ryan said. "If he went for more than half, you could get him disbarred. But as long as he doesn't go for more than that, he can make an argument that he was taking a significant risk with a case this complex and that the higher percentage was merited. And unfortunately he could find case law to back him up."

"Okay, just wondering," I said. "Thanks."

"Don't thank me," he said. "Just nail the guy who did this to Vaughn, huh, buddy?"

■ ■ ■ ■

There wasn't much more Kevin Ryan was willing to tell me — he couldn't exactly discuss McAlister Properties' financial difficulties when he was still the company's lawyer — so we ended the call.

As I stood up and stretched my legs, I saw Tommy and Pigeon sitting at their desks, looking suspiciously unproductive. It's never good to give interns idle time, so I decided to huddle them and see what they had been able to learn. I went and collected Pigeon, then presented myself at Tommy's desk.

"Hey, we're having a team meeting," I said.

Tommy looked up at me. "My god, what's the team name? The Newark Raccoons? Didn't you sleep last night?"

"Not enough," I confirmed.

"That will take its toll on your skin, you know. That's something you need to consider. Especially at your age."

"At my *age*? I'm thirty-two."

"Brittany Murphy died when she was thirty-two," Tommy informed me. "Something you should think about."

"I feel pretty good about my chances of outliving Brittany Murphy."

410

He just shook his head. "I'm sure she thought the same thing before, you know . . ." He made a strangling sound.

"No, I'm pretty confident Brittany Murphy didn't think she could outlive Brittany Murphy."

Tommy got a far-off look, then said, "Wow. I never thought of it that way. That's deep."

Missing Tommy's mordant wit, Pigeon was looking at us like she couldn't believe she was wasting a Yale education hanging out with people like us.

"Anyhow, back to business," I said. "Either of you learn anything of note or interest yet today?"

"I just got off the phone with Kathy Carter," Pigeon said. Kathy was the spokeswoman for the Essex County Prosecutor's Office and a friend. Pigeon continued: "She said the medical examiner's office determined that Barry McAlister not only had his throat slashed, he had also been shot in the head. It has officially declared the manner of death a homicide."

"Shot *and* slashed *and* burned. Jeez. Someone wasn't taking any chances. Did the medical examiner's office also officially declare who did it?"

"No such luck," she said. "She said the

411

Crime Scene Unit bumped up the case in the queue, so they've gotten some stuff back. The blood in the car is definitely Barry's. I think maybe they were hoping Barry had put up a fight and that maybe some of the blood belonged to the perpetrator. But it was all Barry."

"My, the prosecutor's office was awfully forthcoming today, wasn't it?" I said. "We usually never get results like that this early."

"I think the Crime Scene Unit's funding is on the chopping block," Tommy interjected. "So they're taking every opportunity they can get to show everyone what a good job they're doing."

"I'll take it," I said. "What else?"

"The Arson Squad is referring all calls to the prosecutor's office. They haven't formally called it arson yet."

"Yeah, but those guys like to take their time," I said. "And we pretty much already know it's arson. So I'm not too worried about that. What else?"

"That's it," she said.

I pondered this all for a few seconds, then said, "Okay, type up what you got and send it to Tommy and me. And when you're done, why don't you go out to West Orange and work the neighborhood a little bit. See if anyone knows anything about the life and times of the former Barry McAlister that we don't. Or, better yet, ask if anyone saw anything shortly before he became the former Barry McAlister. I'm sure the police have already done that, but it'd be cool if we got it, too. And . . ."

I was trying to think of what else I could have Pigeon work on when Tommy raised his hand, as if waiting to be called on.

"Yes, Tommy?"

"She also might want to ask if there were any signs he was having money troubles," he said.

"Oh? Him too?"

"Yeah. I had sort of reached the end of my snooping on Vaughn, so I started looking into Barry," Tommy said.

"Which is exactly what I would have told you to do if you had asked. My little intern has grown up so fast."

"Yeah, whatever," he said. "Anyhow, it turns out Barry started selling off his apartment buildings about ten years ago."

"About the time Vaughn was starting the commercial side of McAlister Properties," I interjected.

"Exactly," Tommy said. "It looks like he was sort of selling them off one at a time. In dribs and drabs over the course of the last decade, he sold seven buildings for a total of $10.2 million."

"I'm sure he had loans left on some of those. But even assuming that wasn't all profit, that's not a bad little retirement account."

"Yeah, but I don't think any of it is left," Tommy said. "About a year ago he applied for a reverse mortgage on his house. And he just took out a home equity loan, too. So it seems like he was scraping around for cash."

"Jeez, what's with these McAlister boys and money?" I said. "They kept acting like they didn't have any cash, yet all the while they had lots of it."

"Yeah, are you *sure* about that?" Tommy asked.

"It's what Marcia Fenstermacher told me. And I don't think she was lying to me. She even promised to let me have a look at their P-and-L statement."

"Did you take her up on the offer?"

"Not yet. We talked at her house and she said it was at the office."

"You think she'd mind if I looked, too?" Tommy asked. "I might see something in there that lets us make sense of everything. I've done so much work on McAlister Properties' finances at this point I feel like I could apply for a job as their accountant."

"She probably won't want you to print

things that are proprietary," I said. "But I think she knows the cops aren't showing much interest in Vaughn's murder, so we're kind of her only hope. But there's one way to find out."

Interns are sometimes wont to make things harder than they really need to be, so with Tommy and Pigeon looking at me curiously, I completed the thought for them:

"Call her and ask her."

Breaking our huddle, I returned to my desk. There was no answer at the offices of McAlister Properties, so I tried Marcia's home number. It rang four times and I was thinking I'd have to leave her a message when she answered.

"Hello?" she said, breathing heavily.

"Hey, Marcia, it's Carter Ross," I said. "You okay?"

"Yeah, sorry, I was outside and I thought you were going to be the insurance company calling back and I didn't want to miss the call so I sprinted to the phone."

"The insurance company?"

"Yeah. My house was broken into this morning. The police have already been out here. The insurance company is supposed to be sending an adjuster out. It's just, ugh, like I didn't have enough going on with

415

Vaughn's funeral and now Barry and —"

"Wait, wait, slow down, your house was broken into?" I said.

It could have been a coincidence, sure. But this was another one of those things — like the fire at Barry McAlister's place — that felt decidedly un-random. There was some kind of unknown, unseen actor, constantly setting things into motion, but I still didn't know who it was or what was motivating it all.

"Yeah," she said. "Can you believe it?"

"What did they take?"

"Oh, I can barely even tell yet, they made such a mess of the place. All of my jewelry is gone, for sure. So are some of the electronics. And Trevor's computer. And the silver. They didn't take the crystal, but they grabbed pretty much anything else they thought would have quick resale value."

"And it happened this morning?"

"Yep. While I was out running some errands. The police think that maybe they were watching the place and waited until I left. It's so creepy. People always talk about how violated they feel when something like this happens, and it's true. Some of what was stolen was Vaughn's and it's like, I don't know, losing another part of him. I know it's just stuff and I should be happy no one

416

was hurt. But I don't know how much more I can take right now."

Her voice was faltering. The woman whose life had been all about control was doing her damnedest to hold it together in the face of a series of events that could have unhinged anyone. Resilience in the face of tragedy is a fascinating area of study, and psychologists are only beginning to understand why some people are more resilient than others. But, whatever the secret ingredient was, Marcia Fenstermacher seemed to have it.

"Marcia I'm . . . I don't even know what to say. I'm so sorry. That's . . . awful."

I heard her sniffle twice and breath heavily before she said, "Anyhow. Sorry to dump that on you. Were you calling about something?"

There comes a point when even the most dogged reporter has to put his humanity first. And there was no way in good conscience I could dump more on this woman. So I just said, "Yeah, but forget it. You've got enough to worry about."

"No, what is it?" she said.

"Marcia, seriously, it's just something for the story about Vaughn. It can wait."

"Please. I want to help. I . . . I . . . really could use any distraction at this point. I promise I'll have a good, long nervous breakdown when this is all over — I've got it scheduled for two weeks from now. But in the meantime, you're the only person who is trying to make any sense of what's going on. So, please, distract me."

I allowed a small pause into our conversation before saying, "Seriously?"

"Seriously," she confirmed.

"Okay. Well, you said I could look at that P-and-L statement you had at the office. I was hoping maybe a colleague and I could do that this afternoon."

"How long do you think it would take?"

"I don't know. Fifteen minutes?"

"What time is it?"

"Five minutes to three."

"All right. Why don't you meet me in the office at three forty-five."

"Are you sure it's not too much trouble?"

"Absolutely. We had all decided to close the offices for the rest of the week — it's not like anyone was getting anything done anyway — but I actually have to be in the office at four anyway. Will Imperiale's secretary called to set up an emergency meeting."

Will Imperiale. There he was again. "And what did he want?"

"I don't know exactly. She said he was going to make some kind of take-it-or-leave-it settlement offer that's going to be so good I won't be able to refuse it. But it's only on the table through the end of today."

"That's sort of curious. You know he's been telling his clients that the thing is settled already," I said, then filled Marcia in on the conflicting conversations on this subject I'd had with Jackie Orr and Kevin Ryan.

"Well, as far as I know, Kevin is right," Marcia said when I was done. "Vaughn never mentioned anything about a settlement to me, either. And it's hard to believe he would have kept something like that from me *and* Kevin."

"Yeah, I guess so," I said. "But, wait. Imperiale wants a meeting with you? Why you? No offense, but what authority do you even have to make a settlement on behalf of McAlister Properties?"

"Oh, didn't I tell you? I'm now part owner of McAlister Properties. Vaughn left his share of the company to me in his will."

"I see. So if you own half, who owns the other half?"

"Actually, that might be me, too. Barry McAlister had owned the other half. I haven't seen his will yet, but I'm guessing he left his half to Vaughn. It's not like he has any other close relatives. And if that's the case, then it's mine, too."

So the woman who had started as a clerical employee was now, perhaps, the sole proprietor of McAlister Properties. That was an interesting twist.

"You like being the boss?" I asked.

"Believe me, I was a lot more happy being the secretary. I don't really even know what to do. Vaughn used to talk to me about all this stuff, so I basically understand it. But when it comes to the banks and the tenants and all the vendors and everything . . . I don't mean to sound like an idiot, but he was always the one who made the decisions. I'm not sure . . . Well, anyway, I guess it's just one more thing I'll have to deal with before I have that nervous breakdown."

"Right," I said. "So I'll see you at three forty-five?"

"Yep. See you then."

As I hung up the phone, I was feeling pretty good about things, with the afternoon all mapped out:

I needed to be at my parents' house at four thirty, or else my mother would send out the National Guard to hunt me down. But it was only a twenty-minute ride from Newark to Millburn, twenty-five with traffic. As long as I left Newark at four, I would make it to Millburn in plenty of time.

My good mood lasted for another twenty-eight seconds, which is the amount of time that I was able to sit in my chair unharassed before I heard a loud noise coming from Tina's office.

Worse, it sounded like my name.

"Carter Ross!" she repeated.

I looked over and once again saw her standing near the entrance to her office, doing that finger-crooking thing. I complied and was barely inside when she said, "It's about the wedding. Close the door."

I shut the door behind me, then sat down. I immediately feared the worst: she had heard that Kira was coming as my date. And now I was going to get in trouble not only for that but also for not having told her. She would, of course, insist it was the second part that bothered her — she would lay it on thick about trust and communication and all that. We would never acknowledge that the first part was really the sticker, because then she'd have to actually admit she cared for me.

She was drumming her fingers and shaking her head.

"It's just a shame," she said.

"What?"

"That your baby is going to be born fatherless."

"Why?"

"Because, I swear, I'm going to kill you. Your mother called last night and asked if I could come to her house at four thirty today so we could all go over to the rehearsal dinner together."

She said "together" with special disdain. Like she was saying "anthrax" or "cholera outbreak" or "*The Bachelor:* season 18." But I was actually feeling strangely buoyed. I still had, what, ninety minutes or so to figure out how I was going to finesse the situation in a way that didn't involve Tina severing my head from my shoulders.

"And why is that my fault?" I asked. "I can't exactly control my mom. You're the one who is such good friends with her. *She* invited you to the wedding, not me, remember?"

"Yeah, but you're supposed to serve as a buffer between me and that which might be upsetting to me. I'm pregnant! I'm . . . in a delicate condition!"

"With all due respect to the future mother of my child, I'm not sure you and 'delicate' belong in the same sentence."

"Whatever. I shouldn't have to survive one-on-one time with your family without you there to run interference for me. Your mother stays on good behavior when you're around. But if you're not there, she starts asking all these questions. It might get ugly. Just tell me you *will* be there on time."

"Yeah, I'll be there. I've got a meeting with Marcia Fenstermacher at three forty-five but it's in downtown Newark at McAlister Place and it'll only take fifteen minutes. I'll be prompt. I promise."

"Marcia Fenstermacher," she said, giving her head a tilt that indicated her confusion. "I thought we were thinking she was the one who killed Vaughn."

"Yeah, that theory is now out of fashion. It's so . . . so yesterday afternoon. We've got a much more nuanced understanding of the situation now."

"And what is that?"

"Actually, I have no idea. But it doesn't look like Marcia Fenstermacher is our culprit."

"Why not?"

"Because the theory was that Vaughn was going back to his ex-wife, Lisa Denbigh, and Marcia killed him out of jealousy. But I talked to Lisa and it really sounded like nothing of the sort was happening. And, I don't know, I think Marcia and Vaughn were really in love. Besides, if this was a lovers' quarrel, Barry McAlister would still be alive, not sitting in a pile of ashes at the Essex County Medical Examiner's Office."

"So you're sure she has no motive? Nothing to gain financially by Vaughn being dead?"

"Um," is all I could say. Otherwise, I would have had to make a baaing sound, because I was feeling a little sheepish. As usual, Tina had a point.

"What?"

"Well, I was starting to think that maybe this sleazy lawyer, Will Imperiale, had something to do with this, because it seems like everywhere I turn, he's there. But now that you mention it, Vaughn *did* leave Marcia his interest in McAlister Properties in his will. And . . . uh . . ."

"Yes?"

"Well, we don't know what Barry's will says. But if Vaughn is his sole heir, that means Marcia would get that, too. So McAlister Properties would effectively become hers alone."

Tina was shaking her head at me. "Did you know that 'gullible' is not in the dictionary?"

"Aw, come on," I started, but she cut me off.

"Actually, I don't care. We're not playing

Columbo here. We don't need to crack the case. What we need is something to put in Sunday's newspaper. Brodie still has major wood for this thing. He's like a teenage boy who has found his father's stash of porno magazines."

"I think most teenage boys know how to get porn off the Internet these days."

"Don't quibble with my metaphor. Just tell me you can cobble together something for Sunday."

I sat with my chin in my hand for a moment, because I figured that would make what came next seem more thoughtful.

"Let's go big picture," I said. "Make it one of those 'The Rise and Fall of McAlister Properties,' the homegrown company that once had so much promise but now appears to be in tatters."

"That sounds kind of soft. What would it conclude?"

"It wouldn't. It would just sort of lay out what we know."

"Talk it out for me," she said.

"Okay, you go with the big doomsday opening, about how death, destruction, and apocalypse has rained down on this once-prospering, Newark-based company. Then you go to the narrative. Start with Barry's slow rise as a landlord in rough-and-tumble postriot Newark, then with him selling his buildings so Vaughn can go into commercial real estate. Vaughn acquires some nice-sized buildings downtown and slaps his name on them, but he wants the brass ring — McAlister Arms, the shiny project he develops himself and really puts him in the big time. And then things start going awry. Thanks to a rash of break-ins, his buildings start losing tenants and bleeding cash, so in desperation he pockets the money that's supposed to be earmarked for cleaning up this new property, getting a fake LSRP to sign off on it. Then people start getting sick. Then McAlister Arms loses its blue-chip tenant. Now McAlister Properties is getting sued by the sleazy lawyer and the McAlister boys are getting dead for reasons the authorities are still investigating."

"Sounds good. But can you deliver all that?"

"As long as you don't get too picky with me on the sourcing? Yeah."

"And you have time to write it?"

"I'll let Tommy and Pigeon come up with a rough draft tonight, then I'll have time to make it pretty — and you'll have time to edit it — tomorrow before the wedding."

"Okay. But why do I feel a little sick?"

"It's probably the baby."

"No," she said. "It's because, as usual, you have no real idea what's going on and I'm afraid it's going to get you in trouble."

"My soon-to-be brother-in-law Gary is a state trooper. If you're worried, just call him. I'm part of the family now. Besides, I thought you were the one who's 'in trouble.' "

"What do you . . ." she started, then the double entendre caught up with her. She just shook her head and said, "You're awful."

"Sorry," I said, grinning.

"Just be careful with Miss Fenstermacher," she said as I rose from the chair. "I know you think she's just the harmless secretary, but it's just a little too convenient how this has lined up for her."

"I promise," I said. "I won't turn my back on her."

Departing Tina's office, I gathered Tommy and Pigeon one last time to talk them through the story we were going to craft for Sunday's edition. I told Pigeon to head back out to Barry McAlister's neighborhood and see if she could gather any more string there. Then Tommy and I made our departure for McAlister Place, taking separate cars so I could make my Millburn getaway

427

at the appointed time.

As I drove, I thought through that basic story sketch I had laid out for Tina. I kept trying to pinpoint what might have been the catalyst for the murder and mayhem that had visited the McAlisters. Some of it seemed a long time coming — the business hadn't started struggling with vacancy overnight — while other factors, like losing Best Buy and getting sued, were more immediate. Those things seemed more likely triggers. But, again, until I developed a better theory on who was doing this, I was likely to be a little lost on the why.

Finally, I gave up. Thinking too hard was a dangerous thing in my line of work. I flipped on one of the local all-news radio stations, which had a mention about Barry McAlister's homicide at the top of the hour. It referred to Barry as "Newark real estate mogul Barry McAlister." I thought about the wrinkled, chain-smoking, broken old man I had visited in his unfashionably decorated West Orange home and shook my head. Some mogul.

Traffic came next, and I heard about the tractor trailer that had jackknifed and then spilled its contents all across I-280, creating an eastbound delay of eight miles — and growing — and rubbernecking delays westbound. There's a kind of schadenfreude you get from listening to New York–area traffic. You know there's going to be traffic somewhere on a Friday afternoon, and you get this perverse joy knowing it's hitting someone else. I was heading to Millburn on I-78, meaning the tractor trailer wasn't my problem.

I pulled into the parking garage with Tommy just behind me. Together, we walked past the lobby security guard, who was actually asleep.

"Do you think we should we wake him up?" Tommy asked.

"No, he looks peaceful."

"Hard to believe Vaughn was having a problem with break-ins with this kind of crackerjack security staff."

"Yeah," I confirmed. "DeNunzio Protective Services — on the job!"

We were still snickering as we reached the second floor, but the mood changed the instant I opened the office door. Marcia Fenstermacher was already inside. She was wearing business-casual clothing and a dour countenance that could have been due to at least a dozen different factors. But it seemed to be mostly the result of whatever she was looking at on her computer screen.

I introduced Tommy, then asked, "You

look troubled. What's the matter?"

"It's this," she said, pointing to the screen. "It's . . . Something's very wrong."

"What?"

"Well, this P-and-L statement is more than a month old, because we only have to file them quarterly," she said, picking up a spreadsheet printout that was on her desk. "So I wanted to get you the most up-to-date number on what's in the reserve account."

"Yeah, and?"

"Look at the number on the bottom right of the last page," she said, handing me the printout.

I flipped to the end of the document and looked at the all-important bottom line. It listed the total reserves as $8,054,772.19 — otherwise known as eight million bucks.

"Okay. What's the problem?" I said.

"Now look at this," she said.

She turned the screen toward me and I peered at it. It was the summary page for McAlister Properties, and there were several accounts listed. The largest was $35,483.22 — which, while I'm not a Fields medalist, is substantially short of eight million bucks.

"Are you sure this is the same account as the one listed on the P-and-L statement?"

"Absolutely. Look at the account numbers."

I looked from page to screen, then from screen to page. "Yeah," I confirmed. "There's definitely a problem."

"I think I'm going to have that nervous breakdown right now," she said, and I didn't doubt it. Even her immutable hair had been slightly mussed by her pulling at it.

"It couldn't have just disappeared," Tommy said. "Have you looked at the recent transactions?"

"Right, of course. I'm sorry, I'm just . . . I can't think straight."

She clicked on the appropriate button and, sure enough, there was an eight-million-dollar wire transfer that had been completed at 4:38 P.M. on Thursday.

Marcia was starting to hyperventilate and was stammering out her questions. "But this isn't . . . Who could have . . . Where . . ."

"Why don't you call the bank and ask them what's up?" Tommy said gently, casting a wary glance in my direction that I'm sure Marcia didn't catch.

"Right, of course," she said. "I'm sorry. Come on, Marcia, pull it together."

She hit the speakerphone button on her desk and dialed the bank's 800 number. She went through the prompts until she got a real human being, who identified himself as, "This is Robert in customer relations." He went through the steps of verifying Marcia's identity.

"I see you're listed on the account as having administrative privileges," Robert said. "What can I do for you today Ms. Fenstermacher?"

"There was a large amount of money transferred out of the account yesterday afternoon," she said, obviously making an effort at keeping her voice controlled. "Can you tell me who authorized it?"

"Yes, ma'am, let me check that," Robert said, and we heard him typing on his computer. "That transfer was made in person at our branch office on Broad Street in Newark. It was authorized by a Mr. McAlister."

"That's impossible," Marcia burst. "Vaughn McAlister wasn't even alive yesterday afternoon."

"Not Vaughn McAlister," Robert informed her. "This order was put in by a Barry McAlister."

Barry McAlister. So one of the last things he did before being shot, stabbed, and burned was to give away the family fortune.

"Can you tell me where the money was wired to?" Marcia asked.

"Yes, ma'am. It was sent into the escrow

432

account of Willard R. Imperiale, Esquire."

"Him?" Marcia said.

"Yes, ma'am."

"But that was never . . . Is there any way you can, I don't know, cancel the order?"

"No, ma'am," Robert said, and had nothing more to add.

There wasn't, of course. Banks didn't give you backsies. The money was gone. Maybe she could recover it eventually, but that would require time, lawyers, and figuring out why Barry had given it away in the first place. I watched as this reality landed on Marcia Fenstermacher's face.

Finally, Robert asked, "Is there anything else I can help you with today?"

"No . . . no, thank you."

Marcia ended the call and for a moment there was more silence. Marcia was seated at her desk. Tommy and I were standing on the other side of it.

"Why would Barry fork over eight million dollars to that scumbag Will Imperiale?" she asked.

"I don't know," I said. "But I'm betting the authorities in West Orange will be very interested in asking him that question."

"Oh, believe me, I'm going to ask him first," Marcia said. She looked at her watch, then said, "He's due here in less than five minutes."

As if on cue, I heard the door open behind me. I turned to see two people, neither of whom I was exactly expecting under the circumstances.

One was a woman whose cheekbones I recognized instantly, from having gazed at her Facebook photos. She was brunette now, not a blonde, but there was no question in my mind she was Lisa Denbigh.

The other was a man I couldn't quite place, but mostly because he was wearing a hat and dark glasses. Then he removed them and I realized he was someone I had seen before as well. His hair was different, too — he had dyed all the gray out of it. But there was no doubt about his identity, either.

It was Barry McAlister.

In retrospect, I should have given him the bum's rush: just lowered my shoulder, wrapped my arms around him, and kept him down there for as long as it took. I'm not the brawniest guy alive — or the bravest — but I'm pretty sure I could take out a chain-smoking septuagenarian.

Except, as he closed the door behind him and pressed the lock button, I was still trying to process it. Barry McAlister was alive? As in, not dead? Not shot, stabbed, and burned?

By the time I had put this together, Barry had already reached into the black duffel bag he was carrying and pulled out a gun — also black — and, in doing so, had taken control of the situation.

"Barry!?" Marcia said. "Where's Mr. Imperiale?"

"Mr. Imperiale is no longer with us," he informed her. "Would you like to meet the 'secretary' who set up this little meeting?"

Lisa just gave Marcia a sarcastic little wave.

Marcia was still trying to catch up to what was going on, stammering, "But what are you —"

"Shut up," Barry cut her off, pointing the gun at her. "I didn't expect you'd have so much company. You were supposed to be alone. Is anyone else here?"

Marcia didn't answer. Without taking his eyes off any of the three of us — or his aim off Marcia — he slipped the bag off his shoulder and set it down. His left hand disappeared inside for a moment and produced yet another gun.

"Here," he said, extending the second gun to Lisa. "Take this. Check the rest of the office and make sure there's no one else here."

Lisa accepted the gun. Other than her

obviously augmented breasts, she was a small, slender woman — having been underfed since puberty — and the gun looked too big for her hand. Alas, it wasn't so large that her fingers couldn't make it to the trigger.

She entered the door to my left, the side that wasn't Vaughn's old office. Barry kept his gun pointed in our direction.

"You look a lot less dead than you're supposed to be," I said.

"Shut up, wiseass," he said. "Or do you want some of this?"

He cocked the gun and trained it in the direction of my mouth, which I promptly closed. I thought back to what Brodie had told me about Barry chasing muggers away with a shotgun back in the seventies. I decided not to test if his proficiency with firearms had stayed with him in his old age.

"Yeah, that's what I thought," he said. "Okay, first things first, I want to see everyone's hands. Let's get 'em up."

Tommy, Marcia, and I complied.

"Good," Barry said. "Oh, and let's be clear, let's keep it nice and quiet, too. I don't want anyone doing any yelling or, trust me, I will make this hurt."

None of us responded. He collected our cell phones next, going one at a time, not

436

giving us any opening to make a move.

"There's no one here," Lisa said, having returned from her office tour.

"Okay, very good," Barry said. "Great job, sweetheart."

She smiled at him in a sickly sweet way, and it struck me: oh, lord, they had been sleeping together. A little part of me felt like hurling, and not because their tryst strained the acceptable limits of a May-December fling. Lisa had once been Barry's daughter-in-law. Thirty-year age difference aside, that's just nasty.

Marcia was obviously on the same wavelength as I was, because she spit out, "*Sweetheart?* Don't tell me you two are . . ."

"Zip it, bitch," Lisa said with her Georgia twang. "After what you did to Vaughn and me, I've heard enough out of you for an entire lifetime."

"After what *I* did?" Marcia fired back. "Maybe if you had actually —"

"Enough!" Barry roared. "Marcia, I keep telling you, shut the hell up. I don't want to hear anything else out of you. Now, Lisa . . ."

"Sorry, baby . . ." she started.

"Forget it. Just stay focused, honey," he said. "Don't make it emotional. Let's take care of business first."

"Yeah, this is no time for a lover's quarrel," Tommy said.

"That's enough out of you," Barry said, pointing his gun at Tommy. "Unless you want the last thing you see in this world to be a bullet heading toward your face. And you" — he swiveled the gun at me — "let's keep those hands up."

I lifted my hands a little higher.

"Now, first things first," Barry continued. "Lisa, hand me your gun back, sweetheart."

Lisa presented her gun to Barry, handle first, barrel pointed away. He closed his hand around it, and was now pointing both of them at us.

"Great," he said. "Now I need you to go in the bag. I got a hammer and a cloth bag in there."

"Okay," she said, withdrawing the requested items. "Now what?"

"I want you to put the phones in that bag and start busting them up," Barry said. "Bust 'em up good."

"Oh . . . okay," she said, clearly a little confused.

"I've read stories about some of these things having tracking devices," he said, answering the question she hadn't even asked. "Nobody needs to know where these three are."

There was a crunching of plastic as Lisa started swinging the hammer at the bag. I glanced at Tommy and Marcia. She looked calm, more calm than I'd expected she would be; he looked stricken by what was happening to his phone. I might have felt the same way, but I sensed we had even bigger problems ahead.

I couldn't figure out why Barry had asked Lisa to put the phones in the bag before crushing them. The only thing that made sense was that he planned not only to make our cell phones disappear, he planned to make us disappear. And when he did that, he didn't want McAlister Properties' employees to find little smashed-up bits of our phones on the carpet.

It also told me something else: whatever he was planning on doing to us, he wasn't planning on doing it here. We were going to be taken somewhere else. My suspicion was confirmed when Lisa announced she was done with her demolition job.

"Excellent. Now let's tie them up," Barry said, pulling an industrial-size roll of duct tape from his duffel bag and handing Lisa both guns. "Let's do Mr. Ross here first." He herded me over to the corner of the room.

"Take a seat please," he said to me. "Lisa

honey, stand right over there. If he tries anything funny, put a couple shots in his ear. We can clean up the mess later."

It was kind of surreal, watching Barry duct-tape various parts of my body together. Lisa kept a wary eye on Tommy and Marcia. As Barry went to work, unwinding a not-inconsiderable length of duct tape on my ankles and then my knees, I let my brain go to work on what, exactly, was going on.

The first, most obvious, thing was that Barry had faked his own death. He wanted to be able to disappear with no one looking for him. And, what's more, he had apparently succeeded.

"The blood," I said. "The crime scene guys said the blood was yours. They DNA tested it and everything."

He said nothing.

"The West Orange police chief said there was tons of it — enough to make it look like your throat had been slashed," I said. "How is that possible, unless . . ."

The answer hit me: "You were banking your own blood. You got yourself a big enough stockpile and then spread it around. You've been planning this for a while."

Barry allowed himself a chuckle. "Very good, smart guy," he said.

"You're sick," Marcia said.

"Can I shoot her?" Lisa asked.

"No, honey," Barry said, patiently. "Not now."

As he started in on my hands and wrists, I kept trying to put things together. Okay, so Barry had successfully played dead. And he must have found a way to take that eight million dollars with him. There seemed to be little point in disappearing broke.

So that's why he had killed Vaughn — or, rather, had Vaughn killed. The two white guys in the black leather coats that Kevin Mack had seen disposing of Vaughn's body, the two guys I had assumed were DeNunzio henchmen, were, in fact, hired by Barry.

But why had he also killed Will Imperiale? I could only presume that's what Barry meant when he'd said Mr. Imperiale was no longer with us. It stood to reason the burned body in Barry's house was Imperiale's.

For that matter, why involve Imperiale at all? If you needed a body to burn in a fire, you wouldn't grab someone like Imperiale. Sure, he was about the same height — that could help fool the medical examiner, who wouldn't test the DNA of a corpse that everyone assumed was Barry's. But Imperiale was a high-profile personal injury lawyer.

Why not grab someone more anonymous who happened to share roughly the same bone structure?

It didn't make sense. Adding a lawyer into the mix would just seem to complicate things. If you're going to steal eight million dollars, filtering it through a lawyer's escrow account wouldn't seem to give you any advantage I could think of. There had to be easier ways.

Barry finished with me and turned to Tommy next, making him sit in the corner next to me. I surreptitiously tested my duct-tape bonds and couldn't make them budge. He had done a thorough job: my legs up to my thighs, my arms up to elbows, then my forearms to my thighs. It didn't exactly leave a lot of wiggle room. And you'd be surprised how strong multiple layers of duct tape can be.

I looked outside at the street traffic one story below me — people in their cars and on foot, hurrying home on a Friday afternoon. I could see them, but of course they couldn't see in through the tinted windows. A hostage scene was playing out just a few feet from them, but they were completely unaware of it.

"You know I'm due at my mother's house at four thirty," I said. "If I don't show up, she's going to start to worry. And she's a champion worrier. I once saw her worry a coat of paint off the walls."

Barry didn't pause in his task to comment on this — not even to tell me to shut up. He was too intent on getting Tommy trussed up in the same fashion as he had done me.

When he was through, he turned to Marcia and said, "All right, before I take care of you, you've got a little paperwork to do for me, Miss Fenstermacher."

"What are you talking about?" she said, proudly. "I'm not doing anything for you."

Barry grabbed a gun from Lisa, walked deliberately up to Marcia, who was still seated at her desk, and roughly grabbed her hair. He pressed the gun to her lips, grinding the barrel into her teeth.

Marcia turned her head so that the gun was pressing into her cheek instead. "Oww, stop that!" she protested. "That really hurts."

"Let's be very clear about something here," Barry said in a low, deadly serious voice. "You're going to do what I tell you to do. You're going to sign what I tell you to sign. And you're going to do it without complaining."

He gave the gun one final jab into her face, then stood up and went to his black bag once more. He removed a legal-size manila folder that contained a thick stack of paper. As he opened it, I saw it contained five stapled documents of identical thickness. He placed the first one down in front of Marcia.

"Settlement agreement?" she said. "I'm not going to sign a settlement agreement! Barry, this is going to bankrupt the company!"

"Yeah, but not for at least a hundred and eighty days. It'll take at least that long for anyone to even figure out what's happened."

"But, Barry, you built this company," she said. "It's half yours."

"No, actually, it's all yours," Barry said. "I'm dead, remember? My will leaves everything to Vaughn. Which means, in essence, I've left everything to you. You are right now the sole owner of McAlister Properties, with total authority over the company's decisions. Let me spare you reading all that fine print: you are signing off on an eight-million-dollar settlement."

And that's when I finally got it. The settlement. The 180 days. Why Barry needed to involve Imperiale. Why Barry needed Marcia even more.

Or, more accurately, why he needed Marcia to disappear, and Imperiale to disappear along with her.

I got it then. It was twisted. But, then again, so was Barry McAlister.

As Marcia Fenstermacher signed away a fortune — all the while swearing to Barry that he wouldn't get away with it, that he was a fool, that he was going to hell, etc. — I worked it all out.

Start with the obvious: if Barry had tried to just transfer eight million dollars out of the company account and into his own, it would show up on the quarterly P&L statements that McAlister Properties submitted to its mortgage holders. Those lenders would take appropriate legal action to make sure they could still get their mitts on the money and Barry would have to fork it right back over.

But if that eight million was being paid to settle a lawsuit, the banks wouldn't be able to do anything about it. Barry would only have to pay the money back if McAlister Properties went bankrupt within 180 days. In bankruptcy court, any transaction a company makes in the final 180 days before it declares bankruptcy can be reviewed by the court and voided.

Yet, Barry was leaving McAlister Properties in such disarray, there was no way it would be filing for bankruptcy — or doing much of anything else — in the next 180 days. Of its two namesake architects, one was dead, the other one was presumed dead; and its new owner, Marcia, would be considered missing in action. The company would limp along for a year or more before anything would be decided. The settlement would be untouchable.

Enter Imperiale. The money had been dumped into his escrow account, as any good settlement money should be. It would look to all the world like Will Imperiale, sleazebag personal injury attorney, had simply gotten a big payoff, then run away rather than share it with his clients.

Once it dawned on people — in particular, those fifty or so clients who were owed 50 percent of that settlement — they would look high and low for Imperiale and never find him.

Because he was already dead.

Meanwhile, I was sure Barry had found a way to pump the escrow account dry. That money was probably already offshore somewhere. Perhaps in Switzerland. Perhaps on a little Caribbean island where Barry figured he and Lisa could live quite happily on eight million dollars for the rest of his life.

And I should have known. I should have

known the moment I saw Elizabeth McAlister's tiny angel statue was missing the night before. It hadn't been knocked over by fire trucks or anything of the sort. It had been taken by a man who was still strangely sentimental over the wife who had run off. It may well have been among Barry's last acts: lovingly wrapping up that piece of marble and packing it away for a long trip to wherever.

Around the time I got this all worked out, Marcia had signed all five copies. Barry had dumped her onto the floor next to Tommy and was wrapping her in duct tape. I watched him working, looking like a Just For Men dropout with his bad dye job.

That's when I figured out the last piece. Why Barry had dyed his hair black. Why Lisa was suddenly brunette. Or at least I had a theory. One way to confirm it:

"Marcia," I said. "Do you keep your passport in your house somewhere?"

"Yeah, why?" she said.

"Shut up," Barry ordered. "Both of you."

I didn't need to say any more to her. It would just have discouraged her.

But I knew why her house had been broken into this morning: Barry needed her passport.

These weren't just random disguises.

Barry was trying to pass as Will Imperiale. And it would work, too. They both had big noses and ridiculous hair-dye jobs. No one looking at their passport photos would be able to see beyond those things.

Lisa was a less-convincing Marcia Fenstermacher. But she was still probably good enough. While their bodies were different, you couldn't see that on a head shot. They were roughly the same age and their faces were close enough that a random customs worker or Transportation Security Administration employee — bored and tired and with a long line behind him — wouldn't bother to stop her. After all, she was just a nice woman from the suburbs going on vacation to the British Virgin Islands. Or wherever.

If investigators ever really started working on it — which was doubtful — it would appear that Willard R. Imperiale, Esq., had taken an eight-million-dollar payday and run off with Marcia Fenstermacher, the woman whose signature was on the settlement papers.

I thought about how Barry had likely snookered Imperiale into playing his part. Barry had probably waltzed into Imperiale's office and told him he was about to get the easiest payday of his life. In exchange for some portion of the proceeds, Barry was going to agree to settle this lawsuit. That's why Imperiale had been promising his clients quick money. Barry had told him that's what he was going to get.

"How much of a kickback did Imperiale think he was giving you?" I asked Barry, who was almost finished with Marcia. "That was the deal, wasn't it? You told Imperiale that McAlister Properties had eight million bucks that was ripe for the plucking and he only had to give you, what, a million? Two million?"

Barry was ignoring me. But I saw what looked like a little bit of a smile cross his face.

It all worked out. Barry was getting a comfortable retirement — and running off with a woman he'd always had a crush on. Lisa was getting her escape from all those creditors and piddling lawsuits and was being given the life of luxury that she had married Vaughn for in the first place. Plus, she was getting a pretty good slice of revenge on the woman who had wrecked her marriage.

And all they had to do to make it work was kill the man whom they both had once professed to love.

And a lawyer.

And a secretary.

And a pair of newspaper reporters.

Even though we weren't integral to the scheme, there was no way they could leave Tommy and me alive. I had known that already. Now I really understood why: the moment anyone knew Barry McAlister was not dead, the whole jig was up. The banks would never let him get away with what was obviously a scheme to pump money out of a failing business before it went belly-up. The courts would seize whatever money he had.

So Tommy and I were just the poor sots who got in the wrong place at the wrong time. I was assuming Barry was going to arrange for all three of us not to be found. Hired killers tended to be good at that sort of thing. And there was enough money on the line that Barry could afford the best.

I glanced over at Tommy, both of us looking ridiculous in our duct-tape bondage, and shook my head. "Remember what I said about outliving Brittany Murphy?"

"Yeah?"

"I take it back."

He was never allowed to say it. He wasn't allowed even to think it. He felt like some kind of deviant for admitting it to himself.

We live in a society that constantly reinforces the belief — through books, through movies, through Hallmark cards and commercials and Father's Day nostalgia — that the birth of a child ought to be a joyous, precious event, one of the great days in any human's existence.

But the way Barry McAlister viewed things, Vaughn's birth had ruined his life.

He was married to a gorgeous woman before that baby came. They lived in a nice house in the suburbs. They enjoyed themselves. He worked hard to provide for them. She had been sort of self-centered, sure. But there was enough attention and affection left over for him. And he felt the pride of having a beautiful woman on his arm. He could remember thinking how fortunate he was, how happy

451

he was. He couldn't wait to get home and see her every night. He had the perfect life.

Then, wham. Baby. And it was like a dark cloud had passed over everything. She had a difficult delivery. She couldn't nurse the child. She suffered through a horrible case of what he now realized was postpartum depression — back then they called it "baby blues" — and, in some ways, never really recovered. She was miserable all the time. She stopped paying any attention to him, stopped having any energy for him. It was like she stopped loving him. She was constantly angry. Before long, so was he. Coming home at night became like walking into a dungeon. Even her looks faded.

Then she just took off, leaving behind the kid and her feeble excuses. When he heard about her death a few years later, it was like completing the circle of agony. He had always held out hope that she might come back to him. No. More than that: he *knew* she would come back to him. Then the cancer got her. He told himself that if he had been around, she would have gone to the doctor more regularly. Or he might have noticed the lump. Instead, she was gone forever.

And maybe Barry should have resented only his wife, not his child. But it wasn't that easy to separate the two of them. All he knew was that he had been fine, and then he was miserable. And the clear dividing line between the two was the birth of his son.

Things certainly didn't get any easier when his wife left. He was a single dad at a time when there was really no such thing. He struggled constantly to find child care. He had no social life because of Vaughn — there was no going out on nights or weekends when you had a kid to watch. He had no sex life because of Vaughn — no woman seemed to want Barry when it meant also taking on his little anchor. He had nothing beyond work and parenting. Because of Vaughn.

So, yeah, Vaughn had ruined Barry's personal life. And he could sort of accept that. He could tell himself it wasn't the kid's fault.

But when Vaughn ruined his business as well, that was too much.

Barry could never understand why Vaughn hadn't been satisfied to stick just with residential. They had a good thing going with their apartment buildings. Yeah, it was hard work. And it wasn't particularly glamorous. But what was wrong with hard work? Who needed glamour? It gave them a good, steady income. They could prudently expand their holdings without too much risk.

But Vaughn was like his mother. Always concerned with appearances. Always wanting flashy things. Always having this dream of the Really Big Deal.

And somehow he persuaded Barry — against Barry's better judgment — to sell off everything and let him chase it. So that's what Barry did, putting the proceeds from his life's work into Vaughn's hands and letting him go into the high-stakes world of commercial real estate.

It worked for a while. Then Vaughn just flat screwed it up. He got so wrapped up dreaming of deals that would run into the hundreds of millions that he forgot the basic principle of property management: you need to keep the tenants happy. If you don't have tenants, you don't have anything.

His cash flow went negative right about the same time he came up with this other scheme — to take millions of dollars of cleanup money for a brownfields site, pocket it, then use it as seed money for this new project that would supposedly get him back in the black.

When Barry learned about the brownfields thing, he wanted to kill Vaughn right there. It went against everything Barry stood for in business, every principle upon which he had built McAlister Properties, everything he thought he had taught his son. They were going to get caught. He knew they were going to get caught.

Then those construction workers started getting sick. And Barry started thinking about his options. He couldn't just let Vaughn ruin everything and bankrupt them. He started coming up with a plan to save them.

It was when Vaughn lost Best Buy that Barry realized he needed to put his plan into action. The thing was hopeless. McAlister Place and McAlister Center were money sieves. Now McAlister Arms was destined be a loser before Vaughn would even be able to get a foundation poured.

They owed millions. What little equity there was in those buildings was going to go to the banks. Barry was going to lose everything.

So Barry put a plan into place to get it all back. Then he convinced the former Lisa McAlister there were eight million reasons to join him.

CHAPTER 9

As his final step in turning us into duct-tape mummies, Barry McAlister used what remained of the roll to gag us.

So there we were. Totally immobilized. Huddled in the corner next to one another. And mute.

Lisa was mostly just pacing around the room, looking at various pictures and renderings of McAlister Arms, McAlister Place, and McAlister Center — like she was just a random visitor to the office, waiting for a meeting.

Barry had taken a seat at Marcia's desk. He had put both guns down next to the keyboard and was typing on her computer. What he was doing, I couldn't see. Was there a Web site called FugitivesFrom Justice.org where he could get tips for a well-funded life on the lam? But, no; he kept swearing occasionally, like he didn't like what the machine was showing him. He kept glancing at his watch.

Every time I felt like neither of them was looking in my direction, I would test my bonds to see if I could get them to budge, even a little. If I could get a little wiggle room going, I thought maybe I could get some leverage and . . .

And, well, nothing. Even if I did manage to, say, get my hands free, my legs were still wrapped up tight. And my captors were still armed.

The only thing we had going for us — and it wasn't much — was that if Barry had planned to blow our heads off here at the office, we would have long ago been dead. He planned to kill us somewhere else. And maybe in the process of moving us, we'd have a chance to do . . . something.

This, mind you, is the equivalent of the football team down three scores thinking it still has a chance with under two minutes left. But I had to cling to something.

Barry continued looking at his watch, continued his swearing and muttering. Finally, he said, "Okay, where the hell are those guys?"

"I don't know," Lisa said. "Why don't you call them?"

"I told you, that's not how it works with guys like that," he said. "I don't even have

457

their number."

"Well, I don't know what to tell you, sugar."

Barry looked at the computer screen a little more, then decided, "We'll be fine. This is why I had us fly tomorrow morning. We're okay."

They eventually switched places, with Barry pacing and Lisa seated at the desk. I had no idea how much time was passing. I couldn't see a clock, and my cell phone, which is how I usually checked the time, was currently in about eight hundred tiny pieces inside a cloth bag. The tinting of the windows made it tough to tell how close to sunset it was getting, but the shadows cast by the buildings were definitely getting longer.

Meanwhile — and not that this was my biggest problem at the moment, but still — I was starting to get incredibly uncomfortable. I could shift positions only so much. I wanted to lie down — if only to take some pressure off my seriously numb ass — but I worried that if I went on my side, I'd never be able to get up again. So I stayed where I was, trying to battle through the various parts of my body that kept getting pins and needles. I swore my butt was never going to regain circulation.

Still, the gag was the worst. Not only did it make it impossible to talk — one of my favorite things to do — it made it hard to breathe, perhaps the only thing I liked to do more. He had left our noses exposed, but have you ever tried breathing with only your nose for an extended period of time? It's hard to fight the feeling that you're just not getting enough oxygen.

Occasionally I'd make eye contact with Tommy or Marcia. They didn't seem to be having any more fun than I was. Tommy was mostly staring at the carpet. Marcia kept intermittently closing her eyes.

"Why don't you call the guy who calls them?" Lisa said after a while.

"No," Barry insisted. "They'll be here. They must have gotten caught in traffic or something."

Maybe, if we were lucky, they — whoever "they" were — had gotten caught in the mess on I-280. Even if it was just delaying the inevitable, it was something.

I tried to distract myself by thinking about what was going on at my parents' house. I was, by now, at least an hour late. My poor mother had probably been in a full panic by 4:35 and turned into an absolute wreck when I hadn't shown up by 4:45. My brother and sister and their respective mates would have given up trying to calm her down by 4:50. At 5:00, my father would have insisted they just leave without me. Either that, or he would have found a tranquilizer gun. Tina was probably plotting a variety of creative ways to kill me — as if that weren't already being taken care of.

Thinking about Tina naturally turned my thoughts to the baby that would soon be stirring in her womb. My baby. Suddenly, I was convinced she was a girl — I don't know why — and I found myself thinking of all the things I wanted to say to her; how I would hold her when she was scared and laugh with her when she was happy; how I planned to play princesses with her or climb trees with her or braid her hair or teach her how to shoot a layup; how I was going to scare the hell out of her first boyfriend and dance with her at her wedding if she ever found a guy perfect enough to deserve her.

I imagined what she was going to look like. She would have dark hair, no doubt about that, perhaps curly like Tina's. Maybe she would get my blue eyes. She would probably end up being tall and slender — again, like her parents. I hoped she'd be smart and passionate, like her mother. And maybe my greatest gift to her would be my sense of curiosity about the world and my joy for all the things in it. Could that be hereditary?

I wasn't ever going to get the chance to find out. I felt my throat constrict and my eyes begin to water and I immediately tried to think of something else. Anything else. Turning into a teary heap wasn't going to help me get out of this.

Finally, there was a knock at the door.

"About time," Barry grumbled. He grabbed one of the guns off the desk and went over to the door. "Who is it?" he asked.

"It's the cleaning service," came a voice from the other side.

"Where have you been?" Barry said as he opened the door.

Three men walked in: two thick guys and a thin guy. They were dressed in janitor's uniforms. One of the thick guys had a radio, a bucket, and a mop. The other guy was pushing a large garbage trolley, brimming with bags full of what appeared to be shredded paper. But they were most certainly not the cleaning service.

They were here to kill us.

I'm not sure if the thin guy arrived in a bad mood, but he seemed to get into one the moment he got an eyeful of Tommy and me.

"What the . . . You said one woman," he

461

said, then gestured toward us. "You didn't say nothing about two guys. What's with them?"

"Unexpected visitors," Barry said. "I'll triple what I was going to pay you."

"Damn straight you will. But that's not the only issue. There are logistics to consider. We weren't planning on three," he said. He rubbed his jaw for a moment, then said, "Okay. Think you can get us two more carts?"

"Yeah, sure," Barry said.

"All right," the thin guy said, then turned to one of the thick guys. "We're also going to need some more garbage. Why don't you go down to the Dumpster and grab some nice, full bags."

Barry instructed Lisa how to reach the janitor's supply closet and told the thick guy where to find the Dumpster. He gave them each keys to open the doors they would encounter. As they disappeared to run their respective errands, everyone fell silent.

Then the thin guy walked over to Tommy and me and toed me with the black loafer he was wearing, like I was a dog and he wanted to see if I would snap at him. "So who are these guys?" he asked.

"Just a couple of newspaper reporters,"

Barry said.

"Newspaper reporters!" the thin guy said. "Don't you think someone is going miss them?"

"I'm sure someone will," Barry said. "But it doesn't matter, because no one is going to find them, right?"

"Yeah," the thin guy said. "That's what we do."

He stopped talking and went to work, pulling a hood out of the bucket and placing it over Marcia's head. She had been fully immobilized, so there wasn't much she could do about it as he secured the hood with duct tape. He wrapped several extra layers around where her mouth was — as if the muzzle she already had weren't enough — then started removing the garbage bags from the trolley, emptying it out. When he was done, he lifted her torso.

"Get her feet," he said to the thick guy, who complied. They dumped her roughly into the trolley and covered her with garbage bags.

So that was how they planned to get us out of the office unseen: wheeled out like so much trash.

"Give me your shirt," the thin guy said to Barry.

"Why?" Barry asked.

"Just give me your shirt," the thin guy said, lacing the instruction with an impolite word.

Barry complied, stripping down to his T-shirt and handing over his plaid, button-down oxford. The thin guy tore it into two roughly equal strips, then wrapped one of the halves around my head. It was a make-shift hood, one he secured with duct tape.

With my world now dark — and my chances for a heroic escape dimmed that much further — I could only listen to what came next. There was more duct tape being unpeeled as Tommy's head got its wrap job. Then there was a knock at the door and Lisa saying, "It's me." The door opened and I made out the jouncing of plastic wheels as two more trolleys were brought into the room.

Then there was another knock, more affirmations of identity, and I heard the rustling of trash bags. "This good?" one of the thick guys said.

"Yeah," the thin guy replied. "Help me load these guys."

I felt myself being lifted — they had no problem with my 185 pounds — then being dropped into the bottom of one of the trolleys. I was soon covered in a cascade of garbage bags. None of them was terribly

464

heavy, but they still added to the feeling that I was being smothered. As if being bound, gagged, and hooded weren't enough. I had never known myself to be claustrophobic, but I'm not sure I had ever been wedged into such a narrow space without the ability to move.

Merely breathing had now become a difficult task. There was but the smallest pocket of air surrounding me, and I could only draw at it with my nose, through a layer of what had once been Barry McAlister's shirt. It was all I could do to keep myself calm enough and to quiet the thought that I was slowly suffocating. I knew the moment I started panicking, it would only make it worse.

I heard Tommy being placed in a trolley, followed by his own blanket of trash bags.

"We good to go?" the thin guy asked.

Someone must have nodded, because the radio was turned up. It was blaring out some Journey, but with all due respect to that classic American rock band's most-revered anthem, I had definitely stopped believing.

The next thing I knew, we were rolling. And that's when I felt a deep fear settling in. Yes, it was terrifying that I could no longer see, that I couldn't hear anything over the radio, that I was enclosed in this suffocating prison, that I had no control over what would happen to me next. But it wasn't so much that my senses had been dulled or my liberties disabled.

It was that I felt suddenly and irrevocably alone. I no longer knew if Tommy or Marcia was being wheeled alongside me or if we had been separated. I was totally isolated, and my biggest fear — strange as it may sound — was that I was going to die that way. Without Tommy. Without Tina. Without my parents or my unborn child or my siblings. Without anyone who cared to take pity on me in my final moments.

It was the most terrifying way I could think of to leave this world.

All I could really feel anymore was motion. Or, sporadically, the lack of it. And all I could do was imagine where that motion was taking me. So it was — I think — we went out of the office. Then down the hall. Then into the elevator. Then down to the parking garage.

Or maybe, for all I knew, we were going up to the roof. I was quickly becoming disoriented, and for as hard as I worked to keep my brain engaged in my surroundings, it was a struggle. I wanted to scream — just in the hope someone would hear me — but the radio kept up its full-throated blaring. Plus, I couldn't really get a lungful of air. I was fearful that even trying to yell would waste what little oxygen I had.

It was just darkness. And despair. And I couldn't very well get myself free or spare myself whatever fate I had coming if I couldn't move, see, or speak. I wondered if I should start to pray. Nothing in my power was going to change my situation. Maybe I needed a higher one.

Then the soundtrack changed. Maybe I was just imagining it, but I swore I heard a sharp, percussive banging. Followed by a lot of shouting. The words were mostly blurred. But the ones that came through the loudest, clearest, and sweetest were "state police" and "get down."

My next sensation was of garbage bags being removed from on top of me.

"Hey, someone help me with this guy," a voice said.

I was being lifted. Again. But this time in a much better direction. I was being placed gently down on a hard surface. Concrete.

"Get me some scissors," the voice said again. Someone shouted something — I couldn't make it out — and the voice said, "Yeah, from the med kit."

Moments later, the tape that encircled my head was being gently cut away. "Just bear with me, sir," the voice said.

Since I was quite sure I could bear with anything that didn't involve a bullet in the head, I held still. Finally, Barry's shirt was lifted from my head.

"Oh, thank God," I heard myself say, and then I sucked in a few large gasps of air until my lungs started realizing they were going to be okay.

With that taken care of, I started looking around. The first thing I saw was a New Jersey state trooper in riot gear. The next thing I saw was a whole bunch of state troopers in riot gear.

I was underground, in the parking garage. Perhaps twenty feet away was Barry McAlister, facedown, with handcuffs securing his wrists behind his back.

The three thugs were getting the same treatment. I didn't know if they had resisted or even tried. Based on the noises I had heard, I wasn't sure if they'd had time. The troopers had been on them too quickly. The whole thing had been over in less than thirty seconds.

The trooper who removed my hood moved on to my arms and legs next, cutting the tape off me in methodical, efficient fashion.

It was around then that I saw my future brother-in-law — still dressed for a rehearsal dinner, but with his badge attached to his belt — idly strolling around, looking like he was doing nothing more taxing than considering the parked cars.

"Gary!" I said. It came out choked. And surprised. And, I hoped, grateful.

"You really ought to know better than to be late on your mother," he said, walking toward me.

"I figured she'd send the National Guard," I said. "I didn't realize she'd start with you guys first."

"The National Guard was probably next on her list. But I convinced her we could handle this."

"Yeah, I can see that," I said, as Barry and the three thugs were being led to a waiting van.

"Don't say nothing," the thin guy was warning his charges. "Don't say nothing but 'lawyer, lawyer, lawyer.' And remember, whatever they tell you is a lie."

Then he was gone. So were the two thick guys. I wasn't going to miss them.

"You were very lucky," Gary was saying. "We had a TEAMS Unit doing a training mission in Kearney this afternoon. So when we figured out you weren't just late, that you were probably in some kind of trouble, they were already decked out and ready to rumble. From there, it was just a question of getting them here."

Gary helped me to my feet. I was a little stiff but otherwise no worse off. I had never known how glorious it could feel to have blood circulating in all parts of my body again.

He continued: "That editor of yours, Tina, told us that your last known location was the McAlister Properties offices, so that was the first place we looked for you. We had our guys in the second floor of the building across the street, looking in on you with the infrared — those guys *love* having an excuse to use their infrared. They could see you had been tied up and weren't moving. It wasn't hard to figure out that something very wrong was happening, so they went on full alert."

"How long were you guys over there?" I said, still flexing various muscles that were overcoming having been seriously cramped.

"Only about twenty minutes or so," he said. "We were still assessing the situation, trying to come up with an action plan. We knew you were still alive, because of the infrared. We were fairly certain you were okay for the time being. Then we saw you were on the move. We knew we couldn't let you out of the building, so we decided to take them out down here."

"You seem to have done a pretty good job of it."

"It was a fairly straightforward operation," Gary said. "TEAMS stands for Technical Emergency and Missions Specialists. These guys train for this sort of thing."

"They're good at it," I said, still swiveling my head, taking in the scene. Then I realized someone was missing. "Where's Lisa Denbigh?" I asked. "There was a woman with them, too."

"She's over there," he said, pointing behind me. I turned to see Lisa, with her hands behind her back, talking earnestly to a state trooper with a pad in his hand. "She was begging us for a deal before we even got the cuffs on her. The first thing she said was, 'I want to testify against Barry.' "

"Yeah, that sounds like Lisa," I said. "Self-preservation runs strong in her."

"Anyhow, let's get out of here," he said.

In the coming days, I would spend no small amount of time with prosecutors from the attorney general's office, helping them assemble evidence that would send Barry McAlister to jail for the rest of his life. I would also write a series of articles that, among other things, had legislators in Trenton taking a serious look at the LSRP program and questioning the wisdom of allowing government to outsource its responsibility to protect the health of its citizens. It helped that when my Open Public Records Act request came through, the signature belonging to "Scott Colston" was an easy match for Vaughn McAlister's handwriting. He had been forging all the documents and using the pizza place as a safe mail drop.

The law firm of Imperiale & Trautwig announced it would disburse the settlement money — recovered from an account in Grand Cayman — to Newark's cadmium-poisoning sufferers and continue to pursue the lawsuit filed by Will Imperiale. Quint Jorgensen even kicked a million bucks into the fund. Not because he had to. Just because.

It would make for a busy series of days.

But first I had a rehearsal dinner to attend.

The event was being held in a large, private banquet facility. By the time I made it there, word of my imprisonment and pending death — and of the daring rescue — had spread among the guests, a portion of whom were state troopers who were, naturally, pretty charged up about it.

The first person I saw as I entered the double doors to the room was my dad.

"You're late," he said, grinning, then wrapped me in an extra-tight bear hug.

Then Mom came running up. She wept on me for a minute or two, begged me to consider a career in public relations, then dried her tears before they smudged her makeup and reminded me that I had a speech to give. And it had better be nice. And thoughtful. And she could look up some Auden on her phone if I wanted.

A guy from the banquet facility was next. He didn't cry on me, thankfully. He wanted to affix a small wireless microphone to me. I guess they took their speechifying seriously at this facility and wanted my every precious word to be heard — Gary's father had been outfitted with one, too.

As the sound guy fiddled with my blazer, I looked out at the dance floor, where Tommy and my cousin Glenn had already discovered each other. The deejay was playing a peppy pop song. Strangely, Tommy and Glenn were slow-dancing to it. They looked positively enthralled.

As soon as the mic was secure, my sister glided across the room in a very bride-to-be manner. She gave me a kiss on the cheek, then a punch on the shoulder.

"I'm putting you under house arrest tomorrow," she said playfully. "You're allowed to outshine me during the rehearsal dinner but I'll be damned if everyone is going to be talking about *you* during my wedding."

"So does that mean I can't wear white?" I asked.

"You are such a dork," she said. "You always have been."

"Thanks, Amanda. Love you, too."

My brother and his wife came next, and I took another heaping portion of good-natured ribbing — because, unsurprisingly, my family is incapable of being serious about anything for too long. Even near-death experiences.

Tina approached as soon as my family was done. My city editor/baby mama was wearing a black cocktail dress that I had seen before but that made me grateful to be male every time.

"Nice entrance, Carter," she said.

"Gotta find a way to keep it fresh."

"You're terrible," she said, but at least she was smiling.

"So from what Gary tells me, I owe you a pretty big thank-you," I said.

"Actually, you should be thankful that Pigeon is deathly afraid of dogs."

"Oh?"

"Well, I guess you told her to hit Barry McAlister's neighborhood and ask around about him?"

"Oh, right," I said, forgetting I had even done that.

"Well, apparently, she was in the midst of fleeing a particularly vicious-looking cocker spaniel when she ran into a guy who saved her from the terror. They got to talking, and he swore to her he had seen Barry at a Rite Aid in Maplewood earlier that day. The guy said he had called out to Barry but that Barry just ran away. I don't think the guy was even aware Barry had been declared a homicide victim at that point. He just wanted to ask his neighbor if everything was okay after the big fire."

"Obviously, this is someone who needs to read our Web site a little more carefully," I noted.

"Pigeon told the neighbor what was going on and the guy said he was absolutely certain it was Barry — but that he had dyed his hair."

"Worst dye job ever."

"Yeah, well, Pigeon was smart enough to realize this was a heck of a development but she didn't know what to do with it," Tina said. "I mean, a single source saying a dead guy is not dead. How do you handle that, right?"

"Right."

"Anyhow, like a good little intern, she asked her editor what to do. And then her editor called me. At that point, I was already at your parents' house and we were all wondering where you were. We had been trying to call your cell and it was going straight to voice mail. Your mother kept saying, 'He's never late, he's never late, he's never late.' And I had a hunch that if Barry McAlister was on the loose — with some kind of bad disguise, no less — he was probably up to no good and that you might be in trouble."

"Good hunch," I said.

"But I still didn't know what to do about it. It was actually that little offhand comment you made about Gary being a state trooper that saved you," she said. "I called him up, told him what was going on. He was able to locate the TEAMS Unit and send them over to Newark to check out the building. And, of course, they found you there and . . ."

She glanced over her shoulder to make sure no one was paying too careful attention, then planted a kiss directly on my lips, followed by a full-body hug that made my toes curl.

"Wow," I said when she released me.

"I really shouldn't reward behavior like this on your part," she said. "But I think a lot of stuff hit me afterward, when I thought about how close you came to not making it. I mean, if Pigeon hadn't bumped into that guy, if she hadn't made that phone call, if your sister weren't marrying a state trooper . . . I thought about how easily I could have lost you and I —" She stopped herself. "I'm sorry," she said in a raspy voice. "Would you just come out in the lobby with me for a second?"

"Yeah, just let me check to make sure I don't have to give this speech right now," I said.

I confirmed with my mother that I had at least five minutes until people would be seated for the toasts. I paused at the double doors to give the microphone guy the thumbs-up, so he would know I was heading out for a minute or two. He responded with his own thumbs-up and I slipped through the doors.

Tina and I found a private corner just outside the room, out of earshot, where she half collapsed on me, leaning in and resting

477

her head on my shoulder.

"I just kept thinking about you and the baby," she said. "I know I said I would raise this baby without you and that I didn't want you to have anything to do with it. But then I started thinking about my child *really* growing up without a father and . . . Carter, this is your baby too. I get that. And I want you to be a part of this baby's life, if that's okay with you."

"Okay with me?" I said, feeling my throat constrict. "It's the best thing you could say to me. Tina, I want to raise this baby with you more than anything."

And then, because I think we were both crying a little — and maybe both feeling a little silly about it all — we just held each other for a moment.

Not that the moment lasted long. I was suddenly hearing all kinds of noise coming from the banquet hall. The doors had been opened and a small crowd was pouring out, led by my mother — looking as wide-eyed and wild as I had ever seen her.

"Baby!" she screamed. "There's going to be a baby!?"

She rushed up to Tina and hugged her, more or less knocking me out of the way in the process.

I was just watching the whole thing,

bewildered by how my mother knew. I mean, sure, mothers have special powers and all, but I didn't realize mine had suddenly been blessed with supersonic hearing.

Then my brother walked up and clapped me on the shoulder. "Congratulations, Dad," he said.

"But how did you guys . . ."

"We heard it over the speaker system, genius," he said.

"Speaker? But —"

My brother mocked my voice: "I want to raise this baby with you more than anything!"

And that's when it occurred to me that when I had given the sound guy the thumbs-up, he had taken it as the signal to switch on my microphone. Every private word Tina and I had just shared had been broadcast to the entire room.

Well. At least no one could complain they hadn't been first to get the news.

My father and sister had joined Tina. No one was paying much attention to me — something I supposed I was going to have to get used to — so Kira came up to me and gave me a quick hug and a peck on the cheek.

"Congratulations. I'll see you later," she said, and started peeling away.

"Wait, are you leaving?"

"You have enough on your hands," she said, in a way that felt friendly. "Don't worry about me. I've still got time to make it to the Zombie Ball."

"Are you sure you're okay?"

"Oh, Carter. You're sweet. But at this stage of my life, if it comes down to babies or zombies, I'll go with the undead every time."

She waved and skipped out. I turned my attention back to Tina, who was still being mobbed by my family. There was all kinds of excited yelping and chirping — mostly from my mother — and it was making it difficult to hear. I remembered what Tina had said about needing me as a buffer, so I started trying to shuck Rosses off her.

"Okay, break it up, break it up," I said.

No one was budging. So I just leaned in and kissed Tina on the cheek.

"Love you," I whispered in her ear. "Welcome to the family."

ACKNOWLEDGMENTS

There's a shelf in my living room where I display the merry band of books I've published.

The hardcovers are the front men, propped up on their own little stands. The paperback, large print, and audio versions of those same books are arranged behind, like background singers.

I was wandering past the shelf the other day when I noticed it was starting to get a little crowded in there. And somehow, for the very first time — five books and counting into this whole mad adventure — it struck me: Wow, I *really* am an author.

Call me a slow study. But sometimes I still have to pinch myself that I get to do this for a living. And I'm endlessly grateful to all the people who make it possible.

That starts with you, o gentle reader. I consider it an incredible privilege that you let me into your life and allow me — if all goes well, I hope — to entertain you for a few hours. Each day when I sit down to write, my goal is to be the equal of the amazing opportunity you've given me.

Kelley Ragland, my editor at Minotaur Books, also deserves a heaping helping of thanks. She and her assistant, Elizabeth Lacks, do a marvelous job of keeping me out of trouble, both on the page and elsewhere. (I still get in trouble, of course, but only when I don't listen to them.)

I'd also like to acknowledge the untiring efforts of the rest of the Minotaur mafia, including publicist Hector DeJean, library goddess Talia Sherer, the marketing team headed by Matt Baldacci, the Criminal Element crew (including Claire Toohey, who I'm pretty sure meant it as a compliment not long ago when she called me a whore), publisher Andy Martin, and the big boss, Sally Richardson.

Also, I know I'm not the only St. Martin's Press author who will miss the huge presence of Matthew Shear, taken from us much too soon after a battle with cancer he kept far too quiet. He was a gem of a man whose enthusiasm for books was surpassed only by the size of his smile.

Taking my praise outside the Flatiron Building, just down the street to Writers

House, I count myself fortunate to have the counsel of Dan Conaway, the best agent in the business. It's no accident that his clientele represented 40 percent of the Anthony Award nominees this past year.

Elsewhere, Becky Kraemer of Cursive Communications is a joy to work with. But I warn my fellow authors: Hire her only if you want to get more attention and sell more books.

Speaking of selling books, I remain indebted to book peddlers across the nation, who push my work on people. In particular, I'd like to thank Kelly Justice of Fountain Bookstore in Richmond. She is a friend to me and authors everywhere.

Libraries are also close to my heart and I am constantly asking people to support their local branch. In that spirit, here's to the library scientists in my backyard: Alice Cooper at the Northumberland Public Library, Bette Dillehay at the Mathews Public Library, Bess Haile at the Essex Public Library, and Ralph Oppenheim at the Middlesex Public Library.

And, no, Lancaster County, I haven't forgotten Lindsy Gardner. I just felt like she deserved her own paragraph. Roll Tide, Miss Lindsy.

Moving on, I am nourished by friendships

in the crime fiction community, truly the best bunch of readers and writers you could ever want to be around. I will borrow the words of my friend, Erica Ruth Neubauer, who recently attended her first Bouchercon and came home gushing, "I have met my tribe." I know exactly how she feels.

On the road — a place an author finds himself in a lot — I appreciate the continuing hospitality of Tony Cicatiello, James Lum, Jorge Motoshige, and all the folks who have joined me for a meal or beverage during my travels.

Closer to home, I keep doing the bulk of my writing at a Hardees (yes, really) where Teresa Owens and the gang treat me like family and where Avis Webster provides excellent protective services. Thanks for letting me clutter up the corner all day.

And now, finally, to my actual family: a million thank-yous and a million more to my in-laws, Joan and Allan Blakely; my brother, Greg, and sister-in-law, Shevon; to my parents, Marilyn and Bob Parks, who are my anchors; and to Mary Lou Olson, to whom this book is dedicated. Sometimes we don't realize the lessons we learn from our grandparents until we have gotten along a bit in life. My grandmother is a model of elegance, grace and humility — and a thousand other traits I'm still trying to acquire. I feel blessed by the time we've spent together through the years.

Finally, I need to thank my children, both of whom, I'm proud to say, are now readers themselves (but, I hope, will not pick up this particular book for several more years yet); and my wife, Melissa, the lough of my life (private joke, don't ask). Living with a man who spends his days having conversations with imaginary people — and then killing them — is not always easy. Thanks for putting up with me, guys. I love you more than air.

The employees of Thorndike Press hope you have enjoyed this Large Print book. All our Thorndike, Wheeler, and Kennebec Large Print titles are designed for easy reading, and all our books are made to last. Other Thorndike Press Large Print books are available at your library, through selected bookstores, or directly from us.

For information about titles, please call:
  (800) 223-1244

or visit our Web site at:
  http://gale.cengage.com/thorndike

To share your comments, please write:
Publisher
Thorndike Press
10 Water St., Suite 310
Waterville, ME 04901

GETTING TO KNOW

JESUS

.

GETTING TO KNOW
JESUS

DAILY ENCOUNTERS WITH THE LORD
FROM HIS BIRTH TO HIS ASCENSION

■

ERIC KAMPMANN

For inquiries about volume orders, please contact:
Beaufort Books
27 West 20th Street, Suite 1102
New York, NY 10011
sales@beaufortbooks.com

Published in the United States by Beaufort Books
www.beaufortbooks.com

Distributed by Midpoint Trade Books
www.midpointtrade.com

ISBN 978-0-82530-790-4

Printed in the United States of America

Interior design by Elyse Strogin and Neuwirth & Associates
Cover Design by Mark Karis

CONTENTS

I fall back on the response of Bishop Ambrose, mentor of Augustine, who was asked on his deathbed whether he feared facing God at judgment. "We have a good Master," Ambrose replied with a smile. I learn to trust God with my doubts and struggles by getting to know Jesus. If that sounds evasive, I suggest it accurately reflects the centrality of Jesus in the New Testament. We start with him as the focal point and let our eyes wander with care into the margins.

By looking at Jesus, I gain insight into how God feels about what goes on down here. Jesus expresses the essence of God in a way that we cannot misconstrue.

—Philip Yancey
Reaching for the Invisible God

FOREWORD

CHUCK DAVIS

I DO NOT REMEMBER how we got started. But there we were, in my son Jordan's bedroom, which he had converted into a basic sound studio. Eric and I would read a passage of the Bible from the wisdom literature of the Hebrew Scriptures (Old Testament). Then we would have a three to five minute dialogue expounding on the text from the larger context of the entire Bible. We would complete ten to fifteen recordings per session staying a couple months ahead of the podcast schedule.

Then, one day, Eric revealed to me something that was so ingrained in my methodology that I never really thought about it. What made my message unique was the emphasis on bringing it back to Jesus— the Centrality of Christ. This led to our second year of podcasts, "Walking in the Footsteps of Jesus."

So what has the process been like for me? Friendship, gratefulness, and renewed commitment.

First, friendship. The recording sessions moved from my son's bedroom to the church basement or my study. We added Scott, a member of our church, as our new recording technician. Our friendship grew. We laughed. We rabbit-trailed. We shared life. We prayed for one another. We grew together as Christ followers around the Word and the life of Jesus.

Second, gratefulness. As Eric would ask me spontaneous and unrehearsed questions on the biblical text, I was amazed at how much of the Word of God was deep inside of me. The Holy Spirit would open files in my mind that had been stored over the past fifty-plus years of being in the text. And it was not just knowledge but heartfelt living of the Word. My gratefulness is rooted in my heritage of being raised in the Word. My parents, my Sunday School teachers, my pastors, my college and seminary professors, and my distant mentors through books, have all instructed me in the Word. And, maybe most importantly, daily reading, study, meditation, and memorization of that Word, almost every day as an adult, has transformed my life. I am sometimes brought to tears in my morning quiet times in appreciation for the life that I have been given—set apart in and unto Jesus and saturated by the Word of God.

Third, renewed commitment. Walking with Eric and knowing his story has reminded me of the power of the Word in itself. Eric's testimony points to the power of God's Word. Without help from all the crutches that I was given, Eric one day picked up a Bible, and through the reading of that Word, was transformed. This is why I daily recommit to the preaching, teaching, and simple witness to the Word of God. Eric is an incarnational reminder to me of the value and outcome of giving my life to this calling and passion.

As the prophet Isaiah declares—"as the rain brings forth a harvest, so the Word of God will not return void." Or as the writer of Hebrews declares—"for the Word of God is living and active . . . able to shape and correct us." Or as Paul reminds, the Word of God is "the sword of the Spirit" and that all "Scripture is God breathed and profitable for transforming us." And especially as Jesus reminded us, "people who build their lives on a solid foundation that will not crumble in life storms, are those who not only hear the Word but do it." Those are all my quick paraphrases of favorite declarations of the value of the written Word when experienced through the lens of a relationship with God through the Living Word, Jesus.

May your journey be as rich as mine has been through your discovery of a vibrant relationship to God the Father, through knowing Jesus, and made alive by the Holy Spirit.

INTRODUCTION

ERIC KAMPMANN

I N FEBRUARY 1991, AS I emerged from some very difficult years running my business, I discovered a "lectionary" in the back of a prayer book. I had been reading in the Bible on a pretty consistent basis during the time of my troubles, but finding a daily reading guide was a very exciting revelation for me. I began using the lectionary on a daily basis and I came to love and depend upon it more and more as time went by. In fact, *Getting to Know Jesus* would not exist if that lectionary had not been discovered that day. It became foundational for my growing knowledge and passion for the entire Bible and what it taught me about the human condition that I had not known before.

In 2007, I published a devotional called *Trail Thoughts* that the senior pastor of the church I attended, Chuck Davis, had read and liked. A few years later in 2011, we got together to produce a daily podcast on the wisdom books in the Old Testament as a way to reach members of the church who commute into New York City every day.

The podcasts were short, unrehearsed conversations that focused on a biblical verse of the day. In our response to the daily reading, we would draw attention to the historical, theological, and contemporary importance of what was being revealed through that particular verse. The central focus was the relevance of biblical wisdom literature as it related to our own secular culture. We were trying to show that the Bible is not one of many stories important to our times, but is the central narrative that helps us grapple with the very real mysteries that infuse our everyday lives.

In March 2012, I traveled to Israel with a group of twenty men and women under the leadership of Professor Bryan Widbin. Just before the trip to Israel, Chuck Davis and I began to talk about producing a new series of podcasts to follow up on the series on the wisdom books in the Old Testament.

Professor Widbin teaches Old Testament Studies at Alliance Theological Seminary and he has led trips to Israel for over thirty years. His leadership, knowledge, and passion for Jesus Christ had a profound impact on everyone on this trip; it was his remarkable commitment and authenticity that would lead to the writing of *Getting to Know Jesus*.

It was witnessing Bryan Widbin's passionate devotion to Jesus that opened my eyes to a gaping hole in my own biblical journey. For while I read the Bible daily, I had never gotten to a place where I could declare with Peter, that Jesus was "the Christ, the Son of the living God" (Matthew 16:16). It is a huge step from being an educated secular fence sitter to fully embracing Peter's revelation.

And while I had come very far from the troubles of the late 1980's, I still hesitated in committing fully in the Lordship of Jesus Christ. But through both Chuck Davis and Bryan Widbin, I saw first-hand what genuine faith looks like. It is not loud or boastful, nor does it make unsupportable claims or puffed up pronouncements. The kind of faith I witness through these two men is attractive and assured, open and vulnerable, but bold and powerful at the same time. I saw the Jesus I did not know in the men I did know and I wanted to get more of what both men had in such full measure. Thus was born the podcast series Chuck Davis and I recorded during 2013. (These podcasts will soon be available at *GettingToKnowJesus.com* or through our Getting-ToKnowJesus App available through Amazon and iTunes.)

By the time Chuck and I completed our series on Jesus, I wanted to take our efforts further by producing a devotional that would present the life of Jesus based on accounts in the four Gospels selected for the podcasts. In 2014, I began writing brief commentaries using the recorded discussions between Chuck and myself.

During the two years of recordings and writings, I built on the foundation that seemed to have begun in the late 1980's. And it was in 2012, in the shadow of Masada in the desert of Israel, that I finally made the decision to truly focus on getting to know Jesus by walking in his footsteps as given to us in the four Gospels. Not only did I want to come to know Jesus, but I wanted to do what Christians have been doing for over two thousand years: I wanted to go out into the world to help others come to know him as well.

GETTING TO KNOW

JESUS

■

When I came to you, brothers, I did not come with eloquence or superior wisdom as I proclaimed to you the testimony about God. For I resolved to know nothing while I was with you except Jesus Christ and him crucified. I came to you in weakness and fear, and with much trembling. My message and my preaching were not with wise and persuasive words, but with a demonstration of the Spirit's power, so that your faith might not rest on men's wisdom, but on God's power. 1 CORINTHIANS 2:1–5

■

WHAT DOES IT MEAN to be a follower of Jesus Christ? In his letter to the Philippians, Paul says that he considers "everything a loss compared to the surpassing greatness of knowing Christ Jesus my Lord, for whose sake I have lost all things . . ." (Philippians 3:8). In his early days, Paul was a persecutor of the young church; he stood as a witness as Stephen was stoned to death for his belief in Christ. It was on Paul's journey to Damascus that he was stopped in his tracks and transformed from persecutor to believer. But his conversion was only the beginning of a mission that would reach from Jerusalem to Ephesus, Athens, Rome, and many other countries and cities in the Mediterranean world. Paul's mission, though, came at a cost, because while he had "resolved to know nothing . . . except Jesus Christ and him crucified," the world resisted mightily: "Once I was stoned. Three times I was shipwrecked; a night and a day I was adrift at sea." He goes on to say that on frequent journeys he experienced "danger from rivers, danger from robbers, danger from my own people, danger from Gentiles, danger in the city, danger in the wilderness, danger at sea, danger from false brothers; in toil and hardship, through many a sleepless night, in hunger and thirst, often without food, in cold and exposure" (2 Corinthians 11:25–27). And yet despite all of this, Paul said that the only thing in the whole world that matters is "to know Christ and the power of his resurrection and the fellowship of sharing in his sufferings . . ." (Philippians 3:10).

BEFORE ALL THINGS

He is the image of the invisible God, the firstborn over all creation. For by him all things were created: things in heaven and on earth, visible and invisible, whether thrones or powers or rulers or authorities; all things were created by him and for him. He is before all things, and in him all things hold together. COLOSSIANS 1:15–17

■

JESUS IS ALL IN all. He made visible in human form all the attributes of God. He is the "firstborn over all creation." All things, whether visible or invisible, "were created by him and for him." Simply put, in these verses Paul is proclaiming the supremacy of Christ. From prison, John the Baptist asked Jesus, "Are you the one who was to come, or should we expect someone else?" This is a question that followed Jesus all the way to the cross. At a later time, Jesus asked his own followers, "But what about you? Who do you say I am?" (Matthew 16:15)

Many have undertaken to draw up an account of the things that have been fulfilled among us, just as they were handed down to us by those who from the first were eyewitnesses and servants of the word. Therefore, since I myself have carefully investigated everything from the beginning, it seemed good also to me to write an orderly account for you, most excellent Theophilus, so that you may know the certainty of the things you have been taught.
LUKE 1:1–4

■

IN THIS PREFACE TO his Gospel, Luke addresses a man named Theophilus (that when translated means "one who loves God"). Theophilus may have been a patron or he may have been a close friend or associate of Luke's, though he does not make an appearance in any of the other books of the New Testament. Whoever he might have been, Luke's mission was "to write an orderly account . . . so that you may know the certainty of the things you have been taught." Luke was writing to those who had not known Jesus during his three years in Galilee and Judea but had since become part of a fast-growing Christian community throughout the Mediterranean world. Luke traveled with Paul and other leaders of the Church, but false teaching was creeping in through messengers who did not know Jesus. Luke understood the importance of being true to what actually happened, though he did not claim to be an impartial observer; like Theophilus, he is "one who loves God." But his love of God created an even greater necessity to be truthful, and so Luke tells Theophilus and all readers that he has investigated everything from the beginning, including those who "were eyewitnesses and servants of the word."

In the beginning was the Word, and the Word was with God, and the Word was God. He was with God in the beginning.
JOHN 1: 1–2

■

IF LUKE IS THE historian, John is the theologian. He opens his Gospel with a statement that echoes the first words of Genesis: "In the beginning . . ." John is telling the reader that he is not just writing about an important man of his time; he is telling us that we are entering a realm of cosmic significance. He is talking about the God who, through the power of His Word, created the universe and everything in it and was moving again in a new way, not to create the world, but to restore it by sending his Son, Jesus Christ.

Through him all things were made; without him nothing was made that has been made. In him was life, and that life was the light of men. JOHN 1:3–4

∎

AS THE SPIRIT OF God hovered over creation, "God said, 'Let there be light,' and there was light" (Genesis 1:3). Jesus is the light that gives life to a dying world that has fallen away from the source of life. God sent this light into our world to give the world access to true life. While in Macedonia, Paul explained it this way: "God did this so that men would seek him and perhaps reach out for him and find him, though he is not far from each one of us. For in him we live and move and have our being" (Acts 17:27–28).

THE TRUE LIGHT

The true light that gives light to everyone was coming into the world. He was in the world, and though the world was made through him, the world did not recognize him. He came to that which was his own, but his own did not receive him. JOHN 1:9–11

■

IN CONTRAST TO THE light of God, the fallen world is colored in darker shades because sin has entered through the subterfuge of Satan with his bottomless quest to undermine mankind's relationship with God. After Adam and Eve departed from Eden, they entered a world of sin, death, and the consequences that flow from falling into the traps set by the "father of lies" (John 8:44). When Cain, their son, was tempted to attack and kill his brother Abel out of envy, God remained present and warned Cain of the costs of submitting to temptation: "Why are you angry? Why is your face downcast? If you do what is right, will you not be accepted? But if you do not do what is right, sin is crouching at your door, it desires to have you, but you must master it" (Genesis 4:8). Later, we learn that as punishment for his crime against his brother, Cain became "a restless wanderer of the earth" (Genesis 4:14). This remained the underlying condition for men and women until God determined that the time had come to send his Son into the world on a rescue mission that would open the way to a very different kind of story for the lost and weary.

The Word became flesh and made his dwelling among us. We have seen his glory, the glory of the one and only Son, who came from the Father, full of grace and truth. JOHN 1:14

■

IN THE OLD TESTAMENT, God dwelled amongst his people first in a tent and then in a tabernacle or temple: ". . . for the glory of the Lord filled the temple" (2 Kings 8:11). When John says, "The Word . . . made his dwelling among us," he uses a Greek word that also can mean tent or tabernacle. God's presence among his people was first in a tent (Exodus 40:34–35), then in a temple, and now as a person— Jesus Christ—who was an exact representation on earth of the Father.

John testifies concerning him. He cries out, saying, "This was he of whom I said, 'He who comes after me has surpassed me because he was before me.'" From the fullness of his grace we have all received one blessing after another. For the law was given through Moses; grace and truth came through Jesus Christ. JOHN 1:15–17

■

JOHN'S GOSPEL IS ALL about witnesses giving testimony about Jesus. One example is John the Baptist (John the Baptist and the author of the Gospel of John are different men): "There came a man who was sent from God; his name was John. He came as a witness to testify concerning that light, so that through him all men might believe"(John 1:6–7). John confirmed the Scriptural expectation that a prophet would come before the Messiah to make way for him. But others testify as well, including God Himself, the Holy Spirit, the disciples, and "a great cloud of witnesses" down through the ages even to the present moment. We are those witnesses called to testify before our families, friends, communities, and beyond.

No one has ever seen God, but the one and only Son, who is himself God and is in closest relationship with the Father, has made him known. JOHN 1:18

■

TOWARD THE END OF his life, Moses sought to encounter God, but even Moses could not look at God directly for "my [God's] face must not be seen" (Exodus 33:23). God was protecting Moses because being in the presence of the holiness of God would have shattered Moses or any man in his fallen state. Still, God desires to bridge the gap between himself and the creatures he created. It is the graciousness of God that caused him to step down to the human level through the incarnation of Jesus Christ and thus make himself accessible to us in our alienated condition.

> This is the genealogy of Jesus the Messiah the son of David, the
> son of Abraham . . . MATTHEW 1:1

■

WHY DID MATTHEW CHOOSE to begin his Gospel with a genealogy? He states that Jesus' lineage goes back to Abraham: "Thus there were fourteen in all from Abraham to David, fourteen from David to the exile to Babylon, and fourteen from the exile to the Christ" (Matthew 1:17). This is important because God promised David that his son will reign forever (2 Samuel 7:5–16). But there is more: Five named in the genealogy are women, and of the five, three are Gentiles. This is an early indication that no one is excluded from God's story, even if some have lived less-than-exemplary lives or possess questionable credentials. All of this suggests a very big story is unfolding, and at the center of it all is God, who through his Son is moving into the human story.

ZECHARIAH

Once when Zechariah's division was on duty and he was serving as priest before God, he was chosen by lot, according to the custom of the priesthood, to go into the temple of the Lord and burn incense. And when the time for the burning of incense came, all the assembled worshipers were praying outside. LUKE 1:8–10

■

MEET ZECHARIAH. HE WAS a very ordinary man who led a decent life. He was the husband of Elizabeth. They were in their middle years and without children. There seemed to be nothing very special about him or his wife, except that she was the cousin of Mary. Luke tells us that Zechariah had been selected by lot to serve as a priest before God in the temple. This too was an ordinary custom. But what was about to happen was anything but ordinary, because God was about to burst into the mundane world of the ordinary in a surprising and extraordinary way. Zechariah was about to become part of the birth narrative of Jesus Christ.

Then an angel of the Lord appeared to him, standing at the right side of the altar of incense. When Zechariah saw him, he was startled and was gripped with fear. But the angel said to him: "Do not be afraid, Zechariah; your prayer has been heard. Your wife Elizabeth will bear you a son, and you are to call him John." LUKE 1:11–13

■

SUDDENLY ZECHARIAH WAS STARTLED and shaken with fear. The ordinary features of his existence were shattered and blown away as the supernatural hand of God entered the natural realm. The angel of the Lord gave him a message he could not fully understand: His wife Elizabeth would be with child and he was to call the child John. Zechariah's prayer had been answered, but God had a special role for this child, which we will see as the story of Jesus unfolds.

A MIRACULOUS BIRTH

When his time of service was completed, he returned home. After this his wife Elizabeth became pregnant and for five months remained in seclusion. "The Lord has done this for me," she said. "In these days he has shown his favor and taken away my disgrace among the people." LUKE 1:23–25

∎

WITH ZECHARIAH AND ELIZABETH we see two starkly contrasting responses to God's intervention into their otherwise normal lives. Once his fear of the angel dissipated, Zechariah asked, "How can I be sure of this? I am an old man and my wife is well along in years." He expressed doubt because, naturalistically, the angel's claim made no sense. Zechariah substituted his own reasoning for God's supernatural purpose. With Elizabeth's response to the miracle of her pregnancy, we hear beautiful words of faith: "The Lord has done this for me . . . In these days he has shown his favor and taken away my disgrace among the people." When God's favor came upon Elizabeth, she did not resist it or question it; she lined up with it.

In the sixth month of Elizabeth's pregnancy, God sent the angel Gabriel to Nazareth, a town in Galilee, to a virgin pledged to be married to a man named Joseph, a descendant of David. The virgin's name was Mary. The angel went to her and said, "Greetings, you who are highly favored! The Lord is with you." LUKE 1:26–28

■

THE MARY WE MEET here was anything but a conspicuous figure in history. She was young and not yet wed, and she came from a town that was off the beaten path. From the world's perspective, Mary was very unimportant, and except for the fact that she was pledged to be married, she did not appear to have many promising prospects. But God does not judge through the eyes of the world. For the angel Gabriel told Mary that she is "highly favored." The God of the universe, the God of Abraham, Isaac, and Jacob, had chosen a young virgin to become his instrument in bringing about the salvation of all mankind in a way that defies human reason. To the world, this young woman could not possibly have been so favored by God. But the angel said otherwise.

Mary was greatly troubled at his words and wondered what kind of greeting this might be. But the angel said to her, "Do not be afraid, Mary; you have found favor with God. You will conceive and give birth to a son, and you are to call him Jesus. He will be great and will be called the Son of the Most High. The Lord God will give him the throne of his father David, and he will reign over Jacob's descendants forever; his kingdom will never end." LUKE 1:29–33

■

HOW WAS MARY TO take in what was being told to her? That she was "greatly troubled" must be read as an understatement. First she was told she would give birth to a son, but not just any son—the "Son of the Most High." He would be given "the throne of his father David," and "he will reign over Jacob's descendants and his kingdom will never end." She was told that she would be the instrument of the fulfillment of many prophecies related to the coming of the Messiah. If you are Mary, how can you possibly take this in? How can a young woman of such a lowly station in life be favored in such a profoundly significant way?

"How will this be," Mary asked the angel, "since I am a virgin?" The angel answered, "The Holy Spirit will come on you, and the power of the Most High will overshadow you. So the holy one to be born will be called the Son of God. Even Elizabeth your relative is going to have a child in her old age, and she who was said to be unable to conceive is in her sixth month. For no word from God will ever fail." LUKE 1:34–37

■

"HOW WILL THIS BE?" Mary's question is our question. How is it possible for a virgin to give birth? Almost instinctively we reject the reality of supernatural causation, and so we approach this moment with a heavy dose of skepticism. And we are not alone. Even Thomas Jefferson took scissors to his Bible to eliminate the miracles that gave intellectual discomfort to so many men and women of the Enlightenment. But should we be so swift to judge? If we open up to the reality of miracles existing all around us—starting with the existence of life itself—then the supernaturally initiated events described here by Luke do not seem so improbable.

MARY'S MAGNIFICAT

And Mary said: "My soul glorifies the Lord and my spirit rejoices in God my Savior, for he has been mindful of the humble state of his servant. From now on all generations will call me blessed, for the Mighty One has done great things for me—holy is his name. His mercy extends to those who fear him, from generation to generation. He has performed mighty deeds with his arm; he has scattered those who are proud in their inmost thoughts . . . He has helped his servant Israel, remembering to be merciful to Abraham and his descendants forever, just as he promised our ancestors."
LUKE 1:46–51, 54

■

MARY'S "MAGNIFICAT" IS HER response to what she heard from the angel Gabriel. She spontaneously breathed out praise by acknowledging through her song of worship that every blessing comes from God and she has been blessed by being a steward of those blessings. Her words of praise point to a gracious God: "My soul glorifies the Lord and my spirit rejoices in God my savior, for he has been mindful of the humble state of his servant." Her response is exemplary, a model of humility before the holy purposes of the Lord her God.

Then they made signs to his father, to find out what he would like to name the child. He asked for a writing tablet, and to everyone's astonishment he wrote, "His name is John." LUKE 1:62–63

■

OF THE FOUR GOSPELS, Luke gives the most detailed account of John's birth. In a sense, John's birth parallels the account of Jesus' nativity. There was the visitation of an angel of the Lord, the annunciation, and the promise of a miraculous birth. Furthermore, Elizabeth and Mary were relatives and both women submitted to the will of God. Suddenly Elizabeth and Mary were thrust into God's larger narrative. Neither knew what the outcome would be, but both accepted their mission in humility and faith.

A DREAM

This is how the birth of Jesus Christ came about: His mother Mary was pledged to be married to Joseph, but before they came together, she was found to be with child through the Holy Spirit. Because Joseph her husband was a righteous man and did not want to expose her to public disgrace, he had in mind to divorce her quietly. But after he had considered this, an angel of the Lord appeared to him in a dream and said, "Joseph son of David, do not be afraid to take Mary home as your wife, because what is conceived in her is from the Holy Spirit. She will give birth to a son, and you are to give him the name Jesus, because he will save his people from their sins." MATTHEW 1:18–21

■

WE HAVE FOUR ACCOUNTS of the life of Jesus, but only two of them, Luke's and Matthew's, give us a detailed picture of what happened in Nazareth and Bethlehem. It is Matthew's account that gives the most complete picture of Joseph, who eventually married Mary and served as Jesus' earthly father. When Joseph learned that Mary was with child, he did not humiliate and reject her; rather, he did the opposite by protecting her from harm and disgrace. Matthew also tells us that God intervened through the agency of an angel in a dream, who instructed Joseph on what to do because the child "conceived in her is from the Holy Spirit (who will one day) save his people from their sins." The angel of the Lord gave a very direct declaration of God's purpose both to Joseph then and to us now.

All this took place to fulfill what the Lord had said through the prophet: "The virgin will be with child and will give birth to a son, and they will call him Immanuel" (which means, "God with us"). When Joseph woke up, he did what the angel of the Lord had commanded him and took Mary home as his wife. But he had no union with her until she gave birth to a son. And he gave him the name Jesus. MATTHEW 1:22–25

■

JOSEPH HAD BEEN ON a predictable life path when suddenly he was stopped in his tracks by what was said to him in a dream. Matthew says that when Joseph woke up "he did what the angel of the Lord had commanded him and took Mary home as his wife." Joseph had retired for the night just as he must have done every night, but he woke to a new reality and a new role. He had been chosen, but he had to be willing to accept this role of protector, even if that meant shame or danger. He was obedient to the vision: he stood by Mary in her pregnancy and obeyed the angel's command to name the baby Jesus when the time came for his birth. Joseph's decision to obey was an heroic choice for a man who was not trying to be a hero.

BETHLEHEM

So Joseph also went up from the town of Nazareth in Galilee to Judea, to Bethlehem the town of David, because he belonged to the house and line of David. He went there to register with Mary, who was pledged to be married to him and was expecting a child. While they were there, the time came for the baby to be born, and she gave birth to her firstborn, a son. She wrapped him in cloths and placed him in a manger, because there was no guest room available for them. LUKE 2:4–7

■

LUKE TELLS THE STORY of real people traveling a rough and dusty road from one small town to another in order to obey an edict of the occupying Roman authorities. Through these events, a multi-dimensional prophecy was fulfilled. For the Messianic King came from the line of David: "The Lord swore an oath to David, a sure oath that he will not revoke: 'One of your own descendants I will place . . . on your throne for ever and ever'" (Psalm 132:11–12). In addition, this king came from David's city Bethlehem: "But you, Bethlehem Ephrathah, though you are small among the clans of Judah, out of you will come for me one who will be ruler over Israel, whose origins are from of old, from ancient times" (Micah 5:2). That long road between Nazareth and Bethlehem was a road known by God long before Mary and Joseph ever began to travel it.

And there were shepherds living out in the fields nearby, keeping watch over their flocks at night. An angel of the Lord appeared to them, and the glory of the Lord shone around them, and they were terrified. But the angel said to them, "Do not be afraid. I bring you good news that will cause great joy for all the people. Today in the town of David a Savior has been born to you; he is the Messiah, the Lord. This will be a sign to you: You will find a baby wrapped in cloths and lying in a manger." LUKE 2:8–12

■

WHEN A PASSAGE FROM the Bible is read and heard many times, often its significance is obscured by its familiarity. This is one of those instances where the mystery and wonder of the moment is laden with distant memories of innumerable Christmas pageants. For here something unexpected happened: The birth of the King of Kings was announced to mere shepherds on a hillside outside of a small town on the perimeter of Jerusalem. Why shepherds? John later announced Jesus as "the Lamb of God who takes away the sins of the world." We are reminded of the Passover sacrifice and the substitutionary sacrifice of the ram that God provided to Abraham in place of his one-and-only son Isaac. By the world's standards the angel of the Lord had it all wrong, but the bigger story is that the baby in the manger in Bethlehem was born to die, not as a hero or martyr, but as a substitutionary sacrifice for each one of us. As John the Baptist said much later, "Look, the Lamb of God, who takes away the sin of the world!" (John 1:29)

When the angels had left them and gone into heaven, the shepherds said to one another, "Let's go to Bethlehem and see this thing that has happened, which the Lord has told us about." So they hurried off and found Mary and Joseph, and the baby, who was lying in the manger. When they had seen him, they spread the word concerning what had been told them about this child, and all who heard it were amazed at what the shepherds said to them. LUKE 2:15–18

■

THE SHEPHERDS RECEIVED GOOD news from the angel of God, then, in an act of faith, they went to Bethlehem to confirm the truth of what they had been told, and, finally, "they spread the word concerning what has been told them about this child . . ." To receive, to go, and to tell is the Christian mission in a nutshell, and it is given to us at the very beginning of Christ's life on earth. "How beautiful on the mountains are the feet of those who bring good news . . ." (Isaiah 52:7).

HE WAS NAMED JESUS

On the eighth day, when it was time to circumcise the child, he was named Jesus, the name the angel had given him before he was conceived. LUKE 2:21

■

HEBREW TRADITION CALLS FOR the parents of a newborn to use a family name for the child, but this was not the case with either John or Jesus. In both instances an angel of the Lord provided the name. There is a hidden significance in this that has implications far beyond the family of Mary and Joseph. The name *Jesus* shares the same root as the name *Joshua*, which means God's salvation. It was Joshua who played a crucial role in the salvation history of Israel. For it was Joshua who took up the mantle after Moses died and led the desert-bound nation of Israel across the Jordan River into the Promised Land. "Be strong and courageous," God told Joshua, "because you will lead these people to inherit the land I swore to their forefathers to give them" (Joshua 1:6). As with Joshua, the infant Jesus came to fulfill God's promise to open the way to salvation, not just for Israel, but for every man and woman of every tribe and nation.

SIMEON

Now there was a man in Jerusalem called Simeon, who was righteous and devout. He was waiting for the consolation of Israel, and the Holy Spirit was on him. It had been revealed to him by the Holy Spirit that he would not die before he had seen the Lord's Messiah. Moved by the Spirit, he went into the temple courts. When the parents brought in the child Jesus to do for him what the custom of the Law required, Simeon took him in his arms and praised God, saying, "Sovereign Lord, as you have promised, you may now dismiss your servant in peace. For my eyes have seen your salvation, which you have prepared in the sight of all nations: a light for revelation to the Gentiles, and the glory of your people Israel." LUKE 2:25–32

■

SIMEON HAD BEEN WAITING for a sign. He had received a promise from God, and now the moment had arrived, but how did he know? Simeon had not charted the alignment of the stars, nor did he depend on reason or mere scholarship. No, he had been blessed with a revelation from God, and Luke makes it clear where Simeon's knowledge came from. Simeon's recognition that the Christ child was the promised Messiah came from the Holy Spirit. Luke tells us that the "Holy Spirit was on him." He uses the words "Holy Spirit" or "Spirit" three times to emphasize that Simeon was seeing the truth through God's eyes. Simeon was so sure of this truth that he praised God by proclaiming the promise fulfilled. Simeon's waiting had ended and his earthly life was complete.

ANNA

There was also a prophet, Anna, the daughter of Penuel, of the tribe of Asher. She was very old; she had lived with her husband seven years after her marriage, and then was a widow until she was eighty-four. She never left the temple but worshiped night and day, fasting and praying. Coming up to them at that very moment, she gave thanks to God and spoke about the child to all who were looking forward to the redemption of Jerusalem. When Joseph and Mary had done everything required by the Law of the Lord, they returned to Galilee to their own town of Nazareth. LUKE 2:36–39

■

WHAT MAKES JESUS' STORY so unique? In most narratives, a king would be surrounded by the rich and powerful, he would be feted by poets and songwriters, and he would inhabit palaces and fortresses apart from the teeming populace. But not here. Luke introduces us to many who are unknown, unimportant, and seemingly powerless in the eyes of the high and mighty. Luke presents us with Elizabeth and Mary, Simeon and Anna, and others who by worldly standards should be marginalized. It is a seemingly upside-down world, but as we will soon learn, Jesus came into the world for just this reason: In the eyes of God, the world was and is upside down. Jesus came to change all of that.

After Jesus was born in Bethlehem in Judea, during the time of King Herod, Magi from the east came to Jerusalem and asked, "Where is the one who has been born king of the Jews? We saw his star when it rose and have come to worship him." MATTHEW 2:1–2

■

THE MAGI, WISE MEN from Persia and regions in the east, discerned an alignment in the stars in the heavens that told of an event so monumental that they risked a long and dangerous journey to come to Jerusalem to find and worship the child born to be king of the Jews. Here we have another sign that the supernatural hand of God is at work in the natural world. Ironically, the Magi first went to the court of Herod the Great, an utterly ruthless political figure appointed by the Romans to oversee the Jewish territories. The wise men were treated well and they presented the king with the "good news" that an heir to the throne of David had been born whom they had come to find and worship.

When King Herod heard this he was disturbed, and all Jerusalem with him. When he had called together all the people's chief priests and teachers of the law, he asked them where the Messiah was to be born. "In Bethlehem in Judea," they replied, "for this is what the prophet has written, 'But you, Bethlehem, in the land of Judah are by no means least among the rulers of Judah; for out of you will come a ruler who will shepherd my people Israel.'" MATTHEW 2:3–6

■

HEROD HAD SPENT HIS entire life building up his own political power, and he was not going to take any perceived threat as good news. When the Magi told him of another king who would become king of the Jews, he was troubled. Worse, the chief priests and teachers of the law confirmed that the prophet Micah had written that the Messiah would come from David's city of Bethlehem. Furthermore, Herod's close advisors told him that this king would be no ordinary ruler because his "origins are from of old, from ancient times" (Micah 5:2). Herod was deeply disturbed by this, but he dissembled and said nothing that would tip off the Magi that he was hatching other plans for this newborn "king of the Jews."

Then Herod called the Magi secretly and found out from them the exact time the star had appeared. He sent them to Bethlehem and said, "Go and search carefully for the child. As soon as you find him, report to me, so that I too may go and worship him." MATTHEW 2:7–8

■

MARY AND THE SHEPHERDS and Simeon and Anna all recognized the hand of God at work in the birth of Jesus. The Magi came to Jerusalem to find and worship the one true king of the Jews. But a subplot developed with Herod's reaction to the news. Herod was disturbed because he sensed a threat; an enemy had appeared on the scene and Herod must act or risk losing everything. He told the Magi to search Bethlehem to find the child so that he too could worship him. But Herod had only malice in his heart; his malevolent paranoia manifested a desire to kill and destroy, not worship and praise. Herod was the first in a long line of enemies of Christ who represented the powers of the kingdoms of this world. Jesus was a threat to these enemies even as a little child.

After they had heard the king, they went on their way, and the star they had seen when it rose went ahead of them until it stopped over the place where the child was. When they saw the star, they were overjoyed. On coming to the house, they saw the child with his mother Mary, and they bowed down and worshiped him. Then they opened their treasures and presented him with gifts of gold, frankincense and myrrh. And having been warned in a dream not to go back to Herod, they returned to their country by another route. MATTHEW 2:9–12

■

AFTER PRESENTING GIFTS TO the Christ child, the Magi heeded a warning from a dream and did not return to Jerusalem as Herod commanded. But were they ever in Bethlehem? We learn from Luke that after consecrating Jesus in the temple, Joseph and Mary returned with their child to Nazareth in Galilee and not to Bethlehem. Matthew never says that the Magi followed the star to Jesus' place of birth; he only says "the star they had seen when it rose went ahead of them until it stopped over the place where the child was." Because we have merged the two Christmas stories into one, we assume that, like the shepherds in the fields, the Magi went to the place where the child was born. If we read the two accounts carefully, it is probable that the Magi arrived long after the birth, when Joseph and Mary were in a house in Nazareth. Because they did not return to Herod, he continued to believe the child was still in Bethlehem. This misconception would compound the tragedy soon to come.

When they had gone, an angel of the Lord appeared to Joseph in a dream. "Get up," he said, "take the child and his mother and escape to Egypt. Stay there until I tell you, for Herod is going to search for the child to kill him." So he got up, took the child and his mother during the night and left for Egypt, where he stayed until the death of Herod. And so was fulfilled what the Lord had said through the prophet: "Out of Egypt I called my son." MAT-THEW 2:13–15

■

MATTHEW WAS WRITING TO Hebrew followers of Jesus, so the idea of escaping to Egypt would have been seen as strange and ironic. Every Jew knew the story of Moses and the escape from Egypt through the Red Sea and the desert to freedom in a promised land. But Joseph and Mary were told by an angel of the Lord to escape back into the land of bondage. How could this be? First, Matthew tells his readers that this escape from danger into Egypt was to fulfill a prophecy of Scripture: "Out of Egypt I called my son" (Hosea 11:1). But this also indicates that the Promised Land had lost its way, symbolized by the complete corruption of Herod, who ruled over Israel as a surrogate for the Roman occupiers. Herod desired to kill the Christ child. He may have wielded power over the people of God, but he had completely lost his way and had become an enemy of God.

When Herod realized that he had been outwitted by the Magi, he was furious, and he gave orders to kill all the boys in Bethlehem and its vicinity who were two years old and under, in accordance with the time he had learned from the Magi. Then what was said through the prophet Jeremiah was fulfilled: "A voice is heard in Ramah, weeping and great mourning, Rachel weeping for her children and refusing to be comforted because they are no more."
MATTHEW 2:16–18

■

WHEN WE LOOK BACK at the unthinkable mayhem of the twentieth century, we are tempted to consider the devilish works of Hitler, Mao, and Stalin to be aberrations on the road of human progress. But aren't these modern tyrants merely political descendants of Herod, who in his corrupt rage ordered the murder of children? The truth is that a godless ruler is able to enforce terrible suffering because he has the power to do whatever he wants. He is capable of anything, including "wickedness, envy, greed, and depravity . . . murder, strife, deceit and malice" (Romans 1:29). The little children of Bethlehem were defenseless against such a man as this.

And the child grew and became strong; he was filled with wisdom, and the grace of God was upon him. LUKE 2:40

■

THE GOSPELS OF LUKE and Matthew give us a detailed picture of the birth and early life of Jesus, but less is known of the period between his return from Egypt and his early ministry. Luke does tell us this: Jesus "grew and became strong; he was filled with wisdom and the grace of God was upon him." Unlike in his earliest days, the dangers had dissipated and he participated in the usual activities of normal family life. We know he lived in the family of Joseph and Mary in Nazareth, developing skills as either a carpenter or stonemason. His time in Nazareth was a prelude to the three years of ministry that still lay ahead.

MY FATHER'S HOUSE

Every year his parents went to Jerusalem for the Feast of the Passover. When he was twelve years old, they went up to the Feast, according to the custom. After the Feast was over, while his parents were returning home, the boy Jesus stayed behind in Jerusalem, but they were unaware of it. Thinking he was in their company, they traveled on for a day. Then they began looking for him among their relatives and friends. When they did not find him, they went back to Jerusalem to look for him. After three days they found him in the temple courts, sitting among the teachers, listening to them and asking them questions. Everyone who heard him was amazed at his understanding and his answers. When his parents saw him, they were astonished. His mother said to him, "Son, why have you treated us like this? Your father and I have been anxiously searching for you." "Why were you searching for me?" he asked. "Didn't you know I had to be in my Father's house?" But they did not understand what he was saying to them. Then he went down to Nazareth with them and was obedient to them. But his mother treasured all these things in her heart. LUKE 2:41–51

■

THE STORY OF A precocious twelve-year-old boy going up to Jerusalem and impressing all the teachers in the temple court foreshadows a very different reaction to his later public ministry. A twelve-year-old boy is no threat to the established priesthood, but it is something else altogether when a thirty-year-old man comes riding into Jerusalem on a donkey with crowds of people shouting: "Hosanna to the son of David! Blessed is he who comes in the name of the Lord!"(Matthew 21:9) Even at twelve, though, Jesus was not confused about his genuine identity: "Didn't you know I had to be in my Father's house?"

REPENT, FOR THE KINGDOM
OF HEAVEN IS NEAR

In those days John the Baptist came, preaching in the Desert of Judea and saying, "Repent, for the kingdom of heaven is near." This is he who was spoken of through the prophet Isaiah: "A voice of one calling in the desert, 'Prepare the way for the Lord, make straight paths for him.'" John's clothes were made of camel's hair, and he had a leather belt around his waist. His food was locusts and wild honey. MATTHEW 3:1–4

∎

JOHN REENTERS THE STORY dressed in clothes made of camel's hair and with a leather belt around his waist, saying, "Prepare the way for the Lord, make straight paths for him." John was in a desert region away from Jerusalem, the center of political and religious power. He had taken up the role of the great prophets of Israel by warning the people to repent. One meaning of the word *Torah* is *path* or *God's way*. The people had wandered away from God's right path, or, in Isaiah's words, "We all, like sheep, have gone astray, each of us has turned to his own way" (Isaiah 53:6). The people yearned for liberation from the Roman occupiers, but John was speaking about a different kind of liberation that would lead to the Way. The moment of its arrival was imminent.

John said to the crowds coming out to be baptized by him, "You brood of vipers! Who warned you to flee from the coming wrath? Produce fruit in keeping with repentance. And do not begin to say to yourselves, 'We have Abraham as our father.' For I tell you that out of these stones God can raise up children for Abraham. The ax is already at the root of the trees, and every tree that does not produce good fruit will be cut down and thrown into the fire."
LUKE 3:7–9

■

NEVER UNDERESTIMATE THE HUMAN propensity to drift. We may begin well, but soon enough our attention is grabbed by a diversion and we wander inadvertently off the good path. We can become so transfixed by any kind of shiny bauble that we do not notice that we have become blind and lost. This was the condition of the people of Israel; they had drifted from their first love and had become no better than "a brood of vipers." John was a prophet in the great tradition of Isaiah, Jeremiah, and Elijah who, himself, was called "a troubler of Israel" by Ahab, a truly wicked king (2 Kings 18:17). John was also a troubler because he was dispensing tough love by preaching the truth that the people and their leaders had abandoned the God who favored them: "Who warned you to flee from the coming wrath? Produce fruit in keeping with repentance."

IS JOHN THE CHRIST?

The people were waiting expectantly and were all wondering in their hearts if John might possibly be the Christ. John answered them all, "I baptize you with water. But one more powerful than I will come, the thongs of whose sandals I am not worthy to untie. He will baptize you with the Holy Spirit and with fire. His winnowing fork is in his hand to clear his threshing floor and to gather the wheat into his barn, but he will burn up the chaff with unquenchable fire." And with many other words John exhorted the people and preached the good news to them. LUKE 3:15–18

■

JOHN TOLD THE PRIESTS and Levites of Jerusalem that he baptizes with water but one would appear who would baptize with the Holy Spirit. He further testified that this man "is the Son of God." John testified that God is moving in the world and something new and unexpected is about to happen. In the Semitic world, water immersion was thought of as an outward symbol of being made pure before God. But water baptism is only a shadow of what is to come, for the Holy Spirit is not a symbol but is God himself made available through the sacrificial death of his one and only Son, Jesus Christ.

Then Jesus came from Galilee to the Jordan to be baptized by John. But John tried to deter him, saying, "I need to be baptized by you, and do you come to me?" Jesus replied, "Let it be so now; it is proper for us to do this to fulfill all righteousness." Then John consented. As soon as Jesus was baptized, he went up out of the water. At that moment heaven was opened, and he saw the Spirit of God descending like a dove and lighting on him. And a voice from heaven said, "This is my Son, whom I love; with him I am well pleased." **MATTHEW 3:13–17**

■

ONCE AGAIN WE ENCOUNTER a surprise: Why would Jesus, the Son of God, require baptism from John? John said, "I need to be baptized by you . . ." but Jesus replied that he himself must be baptized "to fulfill all righteousness." This is the pivotal moment between preparation and action. Jesus fulfilled all righteousness by accepting the role the Father designated for him: "Who, being in very nature God, did not consider equality with God something to be grasped, but made himself nothing, taking on the very nature of a servant, being made in human likeness" (Philippians 2: 6–7). Jesus put his God nature on the shelf and put on his man nature. He was obedient to God's purpose for him. This is why the voice from heaven said, "This is my Son, whom I love; with him I am well pleased."

JOHN'S TESTIMONY

Then John gave this testimony: "I saw the Spirit come down from heaven as a dove and remain on him. I would not have known him, except that the one who sent me to baptize with water told me, 'The man on whom you see the Spirit come down and remain is he who will baptize with the Holy Spirit.' I have seen and I testify that this is the Son of God." The next day John was there again with two of his disciples. JOHN 1:32–35

■

THE MYSTERY BEHIND THE explosive growth of the church in the first century can be understood partially through the power of testimony and witness. John said, "I have seen and I testify this is the Son of God." John himself had a large following. He was known to be a truth teller, and people from Jerusalem pursued him and were baptized by him because many considered him to be a prophet of God. So when he testified about Jesus, people began to notice. The Gospel says that John the Baptist was sent from God to testify as a witness about Jesus so that "through him all men might believe." After John's influence decreased and Jesus' ministry grew, the testimony of witnesses increased as well. We have the testimony of God's Word through the prophets. We have Jesus' testimony about himself, we have the testimony of the early disciples, and we have the testimony of the innumerable people who received the testimony of all these witnesses and began to testify themselves about Jesus.

MAN DOES NOT LIVE ON BREAD ALONE

Jesus, full of the Holy Spirit, returned from the Jordan and was led by the Spirit in the desert, where for forty days he was tempted by the devil. He ate nothing during those days, and at the end of them he was hungry. The devil said to him, "If you are the Son of God, tell this stone to become bread." Jesus answered, "It is written: 'Man does not live on bread alone.'" LUKE 4:1–4

■

JESUS WAS LED INTO the wilderness, and he ate nothing for forty days. His hunger must have been all consuming and then, out of nowhere, he received an offer of relief. Produce a miracle, said the tempter, and I may recognize you for who you are. But by implication Satan is also saying if you accede to my offer, you will forever bow down to me. This challenge to Jesus as Lord will be repeated time and again during his three-year ministry. Here the devil was actually saying: Use your power to satisfy your bodily craving. This, of course, is a complete contradiction of God's purpose. Jesus replied by quoting from Deuteronomy, which simply declares that man, as God created him, is more than an accumulation of appetites. While not denying the necessity of food, Jesus declares that man has a higher purpose to his existence: "Man does not live on bread alone, but on every word that comes from the mouth of the Lord" (Deuteronomy 8:3).

The devil led him up to a high place and showed him in an instant all the kingdoms of the world. And he said to him, "I will give you all their authority and splendor, for it has been given to me, and I can give it to anyone I want to. So if you worship me, it will all be yours." Jesus answered, "It is written: 'Worship the Lord your God and serve him only.'" LUKE 4:5–8

■

IF THE FIRST TEMPTATION was one of provision, the second was one of power. Satan declared that all the kingdoms of the world had been given to him. But who gave him that power? Certainly God did not give over all of this to Satan. If we go back to the Genesis story, it says that God blessed the man and the woman and gave them rule over the earth and "everything that has the breath of life in it . . ." But once the fall took place, mankind ceded authority to Satan. Jesus came to defeat Satan and restore the rightful authority to those who through the power of the Holy Spirit acknowledge God and worship him and him only.

The devil led him to Jerusalem and had him stand on the highest point of the temple. "If you are the Son of God," he said, "throw yourself down from here. For it is written: 'He will command his angels concerning you to guard you carefully; they will lift you up in their hands, so that you will not strike your foot against a stone.'" Jesus answered, "It says: 'Do not put the Lord your God to the test.'" LUKE 4:9–12

■

IN THE LAST OF the three temptations, Satan's strategy to confuse and undermine Jesus has a familiar ring to it. In the Garden of Eden he created confusion by raising doubt: "Did God really say, 'you must not eat from any tree in the garden'?" God, of course, was specific about this one prohibition, but the question did its job, and soon enough both Adam and Eve chose to do the one thing God warned them not to do. Ever adaptive, Satan attempted to subvert Christ's mission through a distorted use of Scripture. His weapon was to instill doubt: If you are the Son of God, prove it to me by testing the scriptural claim that God will protect you. But the psalm does not say what Satan implies. It says, "If you make the most high your dwelling . . . then no harm will befall you, no disaster will come near your tent" (Psalm 91:9–10). Unlike Adam and Eve, Jesus was not deceived, and he simply said, "Do not put the Lord your God to the test."

When the devil had finished all this tempting, he left him until an opportune time. LUKE 4:13

■

JESUS SUCCESSFULLY RESISTED THE third temptation, but this was but one battle in a much larger war. Jesus knew this and so should we. When Luke says that Satan "left him until an opportune time," Luke merely means that Satan had retreated and will wait for another moment to subvert God's plan. Remember, the events in Eden were but a skirmish in the epic battle between the fallen angel Satan and God Himself. This battle preceded the conflicts underlining the biblical narrative (Revelation 12:7–9). And so, even though he failed here, Satan did not give up and he continued to attack throughout Jesus' three-year ministry.

JESUS CALLED PETER

Andrew, Simon Peter's brother, was one of the two who heard what John had said and who had followed Jesus. The first thing Andrew did was to find his brother Simon and tell him, "We have found the Messiah" (that is, the Christ). And he brought him to Jesus. Jesus looked at him and said, "You are Simon son of John. You will be called Cephas" (which, when translated, is Peter). JOHN 1:40–42

■

THE SETTING IS THE region of Galilee. This is where Jesus became known for his extraordinary power to heal, and it is where he met Andrew. Eventually Andrew became a disciple, but here his role was to introduce his brother Peter to Jesus in an extraordinary way: "We have found the Messiah." We do not know much more about Andrew, but we do know that at this moment he showed great insight by correctly identifying Jesus. In a sense, he is a model for all Christians who follow Jesus. We, likewise, should take on this role as conduit: Every Peter will learn of Jesus through a witness. Every Peter will have his Andrew.

Philip, like Andrew and Peter, was from the town of Bethsaida. Philip found Nathanael and told him, "We have found the
one Moses wrote about in the Law, and about whom the prophets
also wrote—Jesus of Nazareth, the son of Joseph." "Nazareth! Can
anything good come from there?" Nathanael asked. "Come and see,"
said Philip. JOHN 1:44–46

■

WHEREAS ANDREW INTRODUCED JESUS to Peter with the exclamation, "We have found the Messiah," Nathanael reacted with
skepticism bordering on intellectual contempt. Nathanael was a
learned man, and he knew that the prophet Micah had identified
Bethlehem, the city of David, as the place of origin of the Messiah
(Micah 5:2). He dismissed Nazareth with, "Can anything good
come from there?" Nathanael's initial response was to reject before
he could actually see for himself. His mind had been clouded with
layer upon layer of preconceptions as to what the Messiah would be
like. But Philip persisted, and Nathanael was about to encounter
the unexpected in a way he could never have anticipated.

A TRUE ISRAELITE

When Jesus saw Nathanael approaching, he said of him, "Here is a true Israelite, in whom there is nothing false." "How do you know me?" Nathanael asked. Jesus answered, "I saw you while you were still under the fig tree before Philip called you." Then Nathanael declared, "Rabbi, you are the Son of God; you are the King of Israel." JOHN 1:47–49

■

NATHANAEL, THE SCHOLAR AND intellectual, who had come to know things through study, suddenly, in the presence of Jesus, experienced a knowledge that flows through revelation. Apparently, Jesus revealed something that only Nathanael could know. Perhaps he was praying under the fig tree for the salvation of Israel. We will never know for sure. But in response to Jesus, Nathanael blurted out, "Rabbi, you are the Son of God; you are the King of Israel." Simeon and Anna were waiting in great expectation for the Christ child and knew him when they saw him, but Nathanael could not see the truth until God intervened to allow for clear vision. In this way, Nathanael foreshadows the conversion of Saul, who was blinded by his hatred of Christ. It was only when he accepted Christ in Damascus that "something like scales fell from (his) eyes and he could see again" (Acts 9:18).

A WEDDING IN CANA

On the third day a wedding took place at Cana in Galilee. Jesus' mother was there, and Jesus and his disciples had also been invited to the wedding. When the wine was gone, Jesus' mother said to him, "They have no more wine." "Dear woman, why do you involve me?" Jesus replied. "My time has not yet come." His mother said to the servants, "Do whatever he tells you." Nearby stood six stone water jars, the kind used by the Jews for ceremonial washing, each holding from twenty to thirty gallons. Jesus said to the servants, "Fill the jars with water," so they filled them to the brim.
JOHN 2:1–7

■

JESUS NEEDED TO KEEP God's greater purpose in view as he engaged in the events of everyday life. And so when his mother Mary turned to him to intervene to prevent an embarrassing problem from ruining an otherwise festive wedding party, he resisted, saying his time had not yet come. What did he mean? Clearly, it was not his intention to become a magician, nor did he wish to prematurely bring notice to himself. Later on, he would admonish those whom he had healed not to tell anyone. Nor did he want to fall into Satan's temptation of "proving" he is the Son of God. The stage had not yet been set for Jesus to explode onto the scene. He is both the Son of Man and the Son of God, but it was Jesus the man who needed to remain obedient to the Father's will, even if that meant avoiding public displays until his time had truly come.

Then he told them, "Now draw some out and take it to the master of the banquet." They did so, and the master of the banquet tasted the water that had been turned into wine. He did not realize where it had come from, though the servants who had drawn the water knew. Then he called the bridegroom aside and said, "Everyone brings out the choice wine first and then the cheaper wine after the guests have had too much to drink; but you have saved the best till now." This, the first of his miraculous signs, Jesus performed at Cana in Galilee. He thus revealed his glory, and his disciples put their faith in him. JOHN 2:8–11

■

IMAGINE A WEDDING CELEBRATION where the food and wine vanish. It seems inconceivable because weddings are about love, joy, and bounty. When the wine suddenly ran out in the middle of the feast, a crisis quickly developed, and Jesus' mother turned to her son for help. Though this moment was not the right time for him, Jesus was obedient and quickly performed his first miracle of turning water into wine. Most of the people attending the wedding feast did not realize what had happened, but the disciples knew, because John's Gospel says that after Jesus had revealed his glory, "his disciples put their faith in him." In a sense Jesus could not refuse his mother's intervention because he is the Son of an extravagant and bountiful God.

When it was almost time for the Jewish Passover, Jesus went up to Jerusalem. In the temple courts he found men selling cattle, sheep, and doves, and others sitting at tables exchanging money. So he made a whip out of cords, and drove all from the temple area, both sheep and cattle; he scattered the coins of the money changers and overturned their tables. To those who sold doves he said, "Get these out of here! How dare you turn my Father's house into a market!" His disciples remembered that it is written: "Zeal for your house will consume me." JOHN 2:13–17

■

WE MOVE FROM CANA in Galilee to the very seat of religious and political power: Jerusalem. We recall that Jesus had been there another time, when he was about twelve years old and the priests and leaders of the Temple marveled at his knowledge and wisdom. Now he had returned to find that the Holy Temple of God had become a chaotic marketplace where buying and selling was the primary activity, crowding out the experience of being in the presence of a holy and forgiving God. And so we see a very different Jesus, one whose righteous anger recalls the prophecies of Isaiah: "Jerusalem staggers, Judah is falling; their words and deeds are against the Lord, defying his glorious presence" (Isaiah 3:8).

Then the Jews demanded of him, "What miraculous sign can you show us to prove your authority to do all this?" Jesus answered them, "Destroy this temple, and I will raise it again in three days." The Jews replied, "It has taken forty-six years to build this temple, and you are going to raise it in three days?" But the temple he had spoken of was his body. After he was raised from the dead, his disciples recalled what he had said. Then they believed the Scripture and the words that Jesus had spoken. JOHN 2:18–22

■

LET US PAUSE TO reflect on how Jesus uses language in this passage. He says, "Destroy this temple, and I will raise it again in three days." The people listening would have heard this claim as bravado. If they interpreted his words literally, they would have missed his meaning. John interjects that Jesus was not really talking about the temple; he was speaking figuratively about his body: Kill me and I will rise in three days. Jesus was not making an exaggerated statement. He was actually prophesying that he would be crucified and then on the third day be raised from the dead.

Now while he was in Jerusalem at the Passover Feast, many people saw the miraculous signs he was doing and believed in his name. But Jesus would not entrust himself to them, for he knew all men. He did not need man's testimony about man, for he knew what was in a man. JOHN 2:23–25

■

JOHN SAYS THAT JESUS performed many miraculous signs while in Jerusalem, and they "believed in his name." But Jesus was not deceived. Jesus was not trying to win a popularity contest, nor was he trying to sway the crowd with political rhetoric. He came "to save the people from their sins" (Matthew 1:21). He did not entrust himself to the people because he knew what had become of the hearts of men. Jesus knew the nature of the world he had entered. It was a world of men and women who had fallen away from God: "The Lord looks down from heaven on the sons of men to see if there are any who understand, any who seek God. All have turned aside, they have together become corrupt; there is no one who does good, not even one" (Psalm 14:2–3).

NICODEMUS

Now there was a man of the Pharisees named Nicodemus, a member of the Jewish ruling council. He came to Jesus at night and said, "Rabbi, we know you are a teacher who has come from God. For no one could perform the miraculous signs you are doing if God were not with him." In reply Jesus declared, "I tell you the truth, no one can see the kingdom of God unless he is born again." "How can a man be born when he is old?" Nicodemus asked. "Surely he cannot enter a second time into his mother's womb to be born!" Jesus answered, "I tell you the truth, no one can enter the kingdom of God unless he is born of water and the Spirit. Flesh gives birth to flesh, but the Spirit gives birth to spirit. You should not be surprised at my saying, 'You must be born again.' The wind blows wherever it pleases. You hear its sound, but you cannot tell where it comes from or where it is going. So it is with everyone born of the Spirit." JOHN 3:1–8

■

NICODEMUS WAS A PHARISEE, a member of the ruling religious class. He came to Jesus at night because Jesus was considered an outsider, much like John the Baptist. Nicodemus was worried that his peers would consider such a visit unseemly, even dangerous. But he went anyway, bringing along all the ruling-class assumptions that pass for theological truth. It is important to note that Jesus and Nicodemus seemed to be talking at cross-purposes: Nicodemus used literal, commonsense language, whereas Jesus answered in the language of the Holy Spirit. "How can a man be born when he is old?" asked Nicodemus. Jesus replied that he is talking about a different kind of birth: "Flesh gives birth to flesh, but the Spirit gives birth to spirit." Jesus was declaring to Nicodemus (and to us) that if our philosophy does not consider the truth of the presence of the Holy Spirit of God, then it is nothing more than an intellectual construction of men; it does not come from God.

For God so loved the world that he gave his one and only Son, that whoever believes in him shall not perish but have eternal life. For God did not send his Son into the world to condemn the world, but to save the world through him. Whoever believes in him is not condemned, but whoever does not believe stands condemned already because he has not believed in the name of God's one and only Son. JOHN 3:16–18

■

IF WE EVER NEEDED an explanation for why Jesus, the Son of God, came to walk upon the earth, here it is. God sent his one-and-only Son into the world to save us. Whether we admit it or not, all men and women are in a sinful state and stand condemned before God. It is the Son, the one without sin, who stands in our place as a sufficient sacrifice for our accumulated guilt. Many will not acknowledge the necessity of the cross because they cannot see why it is needed. However, the whole weight of the biblical narrative, from Adam to Jesus, rests on the reality of the power of sin to separate us from the God who loves us. David, in his confessional psalm, explains how deep and intractable the problem really is: "Surely I was sinful at birth, sinful from the time my mother conceived me" (Psalm 51:5).

This is the verdict: Light has come into the world, but men loved darkness instead of light because their deeds were evil. Everyone who does evil hates the light, and will not come into the light for fear that his deeds will be exposed. But whoever lives by the truth comes into the light, so that it may be seen plainly that what he has done has been done through God. JOHN 3: 19–21

■

JESUS SAYS, "THIS IS the verdict," and then he unfolds in summary form the entire history of man flailing through the darkness without the light of God. He says that men loved darkness because they preferred the evil they knew to the God they had abandoned. It is the weight of guilt and shame that drives us further into the darkness. We will do anything not to be found out. Jesus says, "Everyone who does evil hates the light, and will not come into the light for fear that his deeds will be exposed." It is this fear of exposure that separates us from the light of the God who loves us. And so, rather than accept God's amazing grace, we slink away into the shadows in the company of fellow sufferers, rejecting the invitation open to all.

HE MUST BECOME GREATER;
I MUST BECOME LESS

An argument developed between some of John's disciples and a certain Jew over the matter of ceremonial washing. They came to John and said to him, "Rabbi, that man who was with you on the other side of the Jordan—the one you testified about—well, he is baptizing, and everyone is going to him." To this John replied, "A man can receive only what is given him from heaven. You yourselves can testify that I said, 'I am not the Christ but am sent ahead of him.' The bride belongs to the bridegroom. The friend who attends the bridegroom waits and listens for him, and is full of joy when he hears the bridegroom's voice. That joy is mine, and it is now complete. He must become greater; I must become less."
JOHN 3:25–30

■

DO WE TAKE JOHN the Baptist seriously when he says of Christ: "He must become greater; I must become less"? After all, John was something of a celebrity with a large following of people from all over Israel. Who willingly gives up fortune or fame? Most of us spend our productive years accumulating and achieving, but John simply says, "I am not the Christ but am sent ahead of him." He understood his role and honored it: "A man can receive only what is given him from heaven." His disciples tempted him by warning that his followers were going over to someone else. But John did not take the bait. He knew that his moment was fleeting and soon the crowds would be gone, but John had fulfilled his mission. He had been a good steward, and so he could say, "That joy is mine, and it is now complete."

The one who comes from above is above all; the one who is from the earth belongs to the earth, and speaks as one from the earth. The one who comes from heaven is above all. He testifies to what he has seen and heard, but no one accepts his testimony. The man who has accepted it has certified that God is truthful. For the one whom God has sent speaks the words of God, for God gives the Spirit without limit. The Father loves the Son and has placed everything in his hands. JOHN 3:31–35

■

JOHN THE BAPTIST'S MINISTRY may have been diminishing, but just as he was departing center stage, he left us with this powerful testimony about Jesus. He says that Jesus "comes from heaven (and) is above all," that he has come from heaven to earth to testify "to what he has seen and heard," that he "speaks the words of God," that God "gives the Spirit without limit," and that God the Father "loves the Son and has placed everything in his hands." John is making an audacious claim: The Messiah, the true King of Israel, had finally come.

GALILEE

The Pharisees heard that Jesus was gaining and baptizing more disciples than John, although in fact it was not Jesus who baptized, but his disciples. When the Lord learned of this, he left Judea and went back once more to Galilee. JOHN 4:1–3

■

WHY DID JESUS LEAVE Judea and return to Galilee? This passage does not provide an explicit reason. We do know that the Pharisees were a crucial part of the political structure beholden to the occupying Roman masters. To them, John was a troublemaker who needed to be watched and controlled; they feared that he would appeal to the people's desire for liberation from the Roman yoke. The Pharisees could not tolerate perceived threats to their power base and would move for almost any reason to quash rebellion. So when Jesus heard that the Pharisees believed he was directly associated with John the Baptist, he left to return to Galilee to teach, preach, and heal during the early days of his ministry. Jesus knew that "his time had not yet come" (John 2:4).

For Herod himself had given orders to have John arrested, and he had him bound and put in prison. He did this because of Herodias, his brother Philip's wife, whom he had married. For John had been saying to Herod, "It is not lawful for you to have your brother's wife." So Herodias nursed a grudge against John and wanted to kill him. But she was not able to, because Herod feared John and protected him, knowing him to be a righteous and holy man. When Herod heard John, he was greatly puzzled; yet he liked to listen to him. **Mark 6:17–20**

■

As Jesus' ministry began to expand, John's role had to "become less." But John did not retire. He continued to be a thorn in the side of the political, social, and financial elite in Jerusalem. He did not mince words: "You brood of vipers! Who warned you to flee from the coming wrath? Produce fruit in keeping with repentance . . . Every tree that does not bear good fruit will be cut down and thrown into the fire" (Luke 3:7, 9). John even targeted Herod, who had married his own brother's wife. She in turn proceeded to use her power and influence to force the king to act against John. Yet Herod did not immediately execute him, for even in the depths of his own venial corruption, Herod could still discern that John was a holy man. Defying his wife's pressure to kill John, Herod protected his prisoner and even "liked to listen to him." Herodias had to wait for an opportune time to exact her revenge.

THE SAMARITAN WOMAN

Now he had to go through Samaria. So he came to a town in Samaria called Sychar, near the plot of ground Jacob had given to his son Joseph. Jacob's well was there, and Jesus, tired as he was from the journey, sat down by the well. It was about the sixth hour. When a Samaritan woman came to draw water, Jesus said to her, "Will you give me a drink?" (His disciples had gone into the town to buy food.) The Samaritan woman said to him, "You are a Jew and I am a Samaritan woman. How can you ask me for a drink?" (For Jews do not associate with Samaritans.) JOHN 4:4–9

■

WHEN JESUS LEFT JUDEA to return to Galilee, he decided to travel through Samaria. This was unusual, because Jewish travellers would go out of their way to avoid Samaria and the Samaritans who lived there. Jesus stopped at Jacob's well in the town of Sychar. When a woman came to fetch water from the well, Jesus asked her to give him a drink, and what followed was no ordinary conversation. Even though she was a Samaritan and a woman of questionable reputation, Jesus went out of his way to cross social and conventional barriers to bring revelation to her and to her town. This encounter provides an early picture of Jesus reaching beyond the boundaries of a single nation. Jesus may have come to the Jews first, but his mission is to save all men and women, Gentiles and Jews alike.

Jesus went into Galilee, proclaiming the good news of God. "The time has come," he said. "The kingdom of God is near. Repent and believe the good news!" **MARK 1:14B–15**

■

WE PRAY "YOUR KINGDOM come" as part of our recitation of The Lord's Prayer, but what did Jesus mean by this? Certainly, as he began his ministry in the region of Galilee, the people would have understood this declaration in historical and political terms. They yearned for the end of Roman rule and the restoration of the glorious kingdoms of David and Solomon. But their interpretations missed the mark. Jesus was not identifying himself as a political liberator or revolutionary. He was referring to the kingdom of the Lord's Prayer—God's kingdom—that far surpasses anything men could invent or build. Jesus was announcing the restoration of the real thing and he was telling the people that his mission comes from God Himself.

Jesus returned to Galilee in the power of the Spirit, and news about him spread through the whole countryside. He was teaching in their synagogues, and everyone praised him. LUKE 4:14–15

■

NO ONE SEEMED TO expect the Messiah to come out of Nazareth in Galilee. Recall that when Philip discovered Jesus and went to tell Nathanael, Nathanael expressed the contempt felt by the educated classes toward the people in the regions surrounding the Sea of Galilee: "Nazareth! Can anything good come from there?" (John 1:46) Nathanael changed his mind when he met Jesus, and he was not the only person who experienced the grace and power of the presence of Jesus. Throughout the region, people were being miraculously healed and the news was spreading quickly. But far away in Jerusalem, only the faintest echoes were being heard about the ministry of Jesus. The region was too insignificant, and so the ruling class remained temporarily isolated from what became a gathering storm. Ironically, when the religious leaders realized that many people were following Jesus and even proclaiming him as Messiah, they countered by using Scripture to show that "a prophet does not come out of Galilee" (John 7:52). Isaiah, however, had prophesized that one would (Isaiah 9:1).

When Jesus came into Peter's house, he saw Peter's mother-in-law lying in bed with a fever. He touched her hand and the fever left her, and she got up and began to wait on him. When evening came, many who were demon possessed were brought to him, and he drove out the spirits with a word and healed all the sick. This was to fulfill what was spoken through the prophet Isaiah: "He took up our infirmities and bore our diseases." MATTHEW 8:14–17

■

WE KNOW THAT PETER had a brother, Andrew, but there is no mention of his wife or children, or if he even had children. Instead, we know that Peter was a fisherman on the Sea of Galilee near Capernaum. It would be one thing if Peter were a young unmarried man with no attachments when Jesus called him to leave everything and follow him. But Peter was attached; he had a business and family, and yet despite these relationships, he put everything aside and began to follow Jesus. This was a profoundly significant decision, and Peter made it almost instantaneously. Leaving his family, friends, and work behind was a costly decision with great uncertainty attached to it. Jesus knows there is a cost to following him and he does not want us to believe otherwise. Here is what he says to his disciples: "Still another said, 'I will follow you, Lord; but first let me go back and say goodbye to my family.' Jesus replied, 'No one who puts his hand to the plow and looks back is fit for service in the kingdom of God'" (Luke 9:61–62).

The (Royal Officer) took Jesus at his word and departed. While he was still on the way, his servants met him with the news that his boy was living. When he inquired as to the time when his son got better, they said to him, "The fever left him yesterday at the seventh hour." Then the father realized that this was the exact time at which Jesus had said to him, "Your son will live." So he and his entire household believed. This was the second miraculous sign that Jesus performed, having come from Judea to Galilee. JOHN 4:50B–54

■

WHEN WE MEET A person for the first time, we quickly begin to ascertain exactly where they fit into our categories of acceptability. Where do they live? Where did they go to college? What do they do for a living? This tendency to identify someone through certain religious and socio-economic categories is as prevalent today as it was in Jesus' time. But Jesus is a barrier breaker: Artificial boundaries do not constrict him. And so the Royal Official, who may have been a Gentile, came to Jesus in distress to ask him to save his dying son. Jesus asked him no questions, he just said, "You may go. Your son will live." Jew or Gentile, royal or commoner, Jesus responds to the human crisis, not to the identity of the suffering father. Jesus crossed boundaries all the way to the cross itself and continues to do so right up to this very moment.

When he had finished speaking, he said to Simon, "Put out into deep water, and let down the nets for a catch." Simon answered, "Master, we've worked hard all night and haven't caught anything. But because you say so, I will let down the nets." When they had done so, they caught such a large number of fish that their nets began to break. So they signaled their partners in the other boat to come and help them, and they came and filled both boats so full that they began to sink. When Simon Peter saw this, he fell at Jesus' knees and said, "Go away from me, Lord; I am a sinful man!" LUKE 5:4–8

■

WHEN PETER SAID, "GO away from me, Lord; I am a sinful man!" he acknowledged the chasm that exists between the holiness that is God and the sinfulness that is in all men and women. This is exactly what happened when Isaiah experienced a vision of God: "'Woe to me!' I cried. 'I am ruined! For I am a man of unclean lips, and I live among a people of unclean lips, and my eyes have seen the King, the Lord Almighty'" (Isaiah 6:5). Jesus did not abandon Peter; he enlisted him. Peter's exclamation was based on his realization that God is God and he is not. It was on the shore of the Sea of Galilee that Peter began the long journey of aligning himself with God's vision for his life. It was Jesus who made possible this first step for Peter.

They went to Capernaum, and when the Sabbath came, Jesus went into the synagogue and began to teach. The people were amazed at his teaching, because he taught them as one who had authority, not as the teachers of the law. Just then a man in their synagogue who was possessed by an evil spirit cried out, "What do you want with us, Jesus of Nazareth? Have you come to destroy us? I know who you are—the Holy One of God!" "Be quiet!" said Jesus sternly. "Come out of him!" The evil spirit shook the man violently and came out of him with a shriek. The people were all so amazed that they asked each other, "What is this? A new teaching—and with authority! He even gives orders to evil spirits and they obey him."
MARK 1:21–27

■

CAPERNAUM RESTED ON THE northern shore of the Sea of Galilee, not far from where the Jordan River flows down from the highlands. It was not a huge town in Jesus' day, but it was active, filled with common people earning a living off the natural resources abounding there. It was in this place that Jesus chose to demonstrate the power of his authority over nature, sickness, and even demonic spirits. The people who witnessed his miracles were astonished and perplexed: "What is this? A new teaching—and with authority! He even gives orders to evil spirits and they obey him." Who, indeed?

EVERYONE IS LOOKING FOR YOU!

Very early in the morning, while it was still dark, Jesus got up, left the house and went off to a solitary place, where he prayed. Simon and his companions went to look for him, and when they found him, they exclaimed, "Everyone is looking for you!" Jesus replied, "Let us go somewhere else—to the nearby villages—so I can preach there also. That is why I have come." So he traveled throughout Galilee, preaching in their synagogues and driving out demons. MARK 1:35–39

■

WHY DID JESUS RISE early to go to a solitary place to pray to the Father? The answer is that he had the same human needs that all people have. Jesus was on a mission: He had been traveling from town to town, preaching, teaching, and healing, and crowds gathered to follow him. His disciples said, "Everyone is looking for you!" Jesus needed to pause, he needed to reflect, and most of all, he needed to renew his energy and direction by seeking guidance from the Father. We should take heed, as we need to pause in the swirl of everyday endeavors. We need to pray for our daily bread so that we can continue to fight the good fight. We need to pray to resist temptation, to forgive and be forgiven, and to accept the authority given to us through the Holy Spirit to play the role God has gifted us in restoring God's kingdom here on earth.

A man with leprosy came to him and begged him on his knees, "If you are willing, you can make me clean." Filled with compassion, Jesus reached out his hand and touched the man. "I am willing," he said. "Be clean!" Immediately the leprosy left him and he was cured. Jesus sent him away at once with a strong warning: "See that you don't tell this to anyone. But go, show yourself to the priest and offer the sacrifices that Moses commanded for your cleansing, as a testimony to them." Instead he went out and began to talk freely, spreading the news. As a result, Jesus could no longer enter a town openly but stayed outside in lonely places. Yet the people still came to him from everywhere. **MARK** 1:40–45

■

A PERSON AFFLICTED WITH leprosy experiences an outward corruption of the skin. This disease can infect others, condemning lepers to a life exiled from the community of the healthy. As seen here, lepers also represent a visible sign of another kind of disease. Though often unseen, sin is just as lethal as physical disease and shares many of the same characteristics. Jesus did not shun the man with leprosy but felt compassion and touched him. The leper was healed, and he was sent to the priests to give thanks to God. And so it is for sinners. Jesus says elsewhere, "It is not the healthy who need a doctor, but the sick. I have not come to call the righteous, but sinners" (Mark 2:17).

Some men brought to him a paralytic, lying on a mat. When Jesus saw their faith, he said to the paralytic, "Take heart, son; your sins are forgiven." At this, some of the teachers of the law said to themselves, "This fellow is blaspheming!" Knowing their thoughts, Jesus said, "Why do you entertain evil thoughts in your hearts? Which is easier: to say, 'Your sins are forgiven,' or to say, 'Get up and walk'? But so that you may know that the Son of Man has authority on earth to forgive sins . . ." Then he said to the paralytic, "Get up, take your mat and go home." And the man got up and went home. When the crowd saw this, they were filled with awe; and they praised God, who had given such authority to men.
MATTHEW 9:2–8

■

THE PARALYTIC WAS BROUGHT to Jesus because news had spread throughout the vicinity that Jesus demonstrated an ability to heal the sick. But when he linked sin to the man's physical condition, the "teachers of the law" objected. No man can forgive sins; any man who claims this power is a blasphemer and can be condemned to death for appropriating a power only God can exercise. Jesus did not back off, though. He directly challenged the religious leaders who were questioning him: "Which is easier, to say, 'Your sins are forgiven' or to say, 'Get up and walk'?" Jesus was showing everyone present exactly who he is: As he says in another instance, "With man this is impossible, but not with God; all things are possible with God" (Mark 10:27).

FOLLOW ME

After this, Jesus went out and saw a tax collector by the name of Levi sitting at his tax booth. "Follow me," Jesus said to him, and Levi got up, left everything and followed him. LUKE 5:27–28

■

IT WOULD NOT BE difficult to gloss over this short passage. After all, it describes an event but does not explain it. Levi was a tax collector, a position that was feared and hated by the Jewish people. Not only did tax collectors have the power to take property, but they also worked for the Roman occupiers. So it defied common sense that Levi would drop everything and follow Jesus. This not only puzzles us, it must have puzzled Levi and all the people who knew him. At the same time, though, Jesus tended to call people who seemed miscast as followers and disciples. Jesus continually sought out the unlikeliest of people for his own purposes. We must remember that Jesus chose followers in conformity to the Father's will; what might look like a mistake to us was exactly in line with God's greater purpose.

While Jesus was having dinner at Levi's house, many tax collectors and "sinners" were eating with him and his disciples, for there
were many who followed him. When the teachers of the law who
were Pharisees saw him eating with the "sinners" and tax collectors, they asked his disciples: "Why does he eat with tax collectors
and 'sinners'?" On hearing this, Jesus said to them, "It is not the
healthy who need a doctor, but the sick. I have not come to call the
righteous, but sinners." **MARK 2:15–17**

■

JESUS ENTERED A "SINNER'S" house where many disrespectable
people were congregating, but in the corner were some who wore
their respectability as a garment. Their claim of righteousness
masked a haughty self-righteousness that was devoid of mercy and
love. The "teachers of the law" had exempted themselves from judgment; they were deluded, of course. No matter what height of social
and economic achievement these Pharisees had attained, Jesus im-
plied that they were no different from the tax collectors and "sinners" who had come to Levi's house. There were no genuinely
righteous men or women there, only sinners. Jesus has come for all
because all are sinners, even those who claim to be righteous.

THE INVALID

Sometime later, Jesus went up to Jerusalem for a feast of the Jews. Now there is in Jerusalem near the Sheep Gate a pool, which in Aramaic is called Bethesda and which is surrounded by five covered colonnades. Here a great number of disabled people used to lay—the blind, the lame, and the paralyzed. One who was there had been an invalid for thirty-eight years. When Jesus saw him lying there and learned that he had been in this condition for a long time, he asked him, "Do you want to get well?" JOHN 5:1–6

■

JESUS ASKED THE INVALID: "Do you want to get well?" We might reply: "What kind of question is that? Of course he wants to get well, who wouldn't?" We might recall, though, that earlier in Galilee, Jesus linked the paralytic's physical disability to a spiritual disability when he proclaimed the sick man's sin forgiven. Jesus cannot cure a man or woman who prefers to cling to his or her sickness. We need to possess the desire to recover, just as we must want to overcome the powerful impulse to sin. Paul describes this battle being waged in the human heart this way: "For what I want to do I do not do, but what I hate I do . . . What I do is not the good I want to do; no, the evil I do not want to do—this I keep on doing" (Romans 7:15,19). To begin the journey to genuine recovery, we must want to get well by acknowledging the presence of contrary desires and impulses embedded deep within our own hearts.

"Sir," the invalid replied, "I have no one to help me into the pool when the water is stirred. While I am trying to get in, someone else goes down ahead of me." Then Jesus said to him, "Get up! Pick up your mat and walk." At once the man was cured; he picked up his mat and walked. The day on which this took place was a Sabbath, and so the Jews said to the man who had been healed, "It is the Sabbath; the law forbids you to carry your mat."
JOHN 5:7–10

■

THE INVALID AT THE pool called Bethesda spent thirty-eight fruitless years trying to get to the healing waters. Jesus asked the right question: Do you really want to become well? But he received an excuse from the invalid rather than an affirmative answer. At this point Jesus acted, healing the man instantly and saying, "Get up! Pick up your mat and walk." Jesus cut through the pretense with an astonishing miracle. But not everyone was pleased; some in authority pointed out that the invalid was not keeping the Sabbath because he was carrying his mat. They disregarded the miracle to enforce a religious law. In a similar situation, as reported by Luke, Jesus had this reaction to the religious taskmasters: "I ask you, which is lawful on the Sabbath: to do good or to do evil, to save life or destroy it?" (Luke 6:9)

But he replied, "The man who made me well said to me, 'Pick up your mat and walk.'" So they asked him, "Who is this fellow who told you to pick it up and walk?" The man who was healed had no idea who it was, for Jesus had slipped away into the crowd that was there. Later Jesus found him at the temple and said to him, "See, you are well again. Stop sinning or something worse may happen to you." The man went away and told the Jews that it was Jesus who had made him well. So, because Jesus was doing these things on the Sabbath, the Jews persecuted him. JOHN 5:11–16

■

WE MUST BE CAUTIOUS about literally connecting all disease to sin. In another place Jesus was asked why a certain man was born blind: "'Rabbi, who sinned, this man or his parents, that he was born blind?' 'Neither this man nor his parents sinned,' said Jesus, 'but this happened so that the work of God might be displayed in his life. As long as it is day, we must do the work of him who sent me . . . While I am in the world, I am the light of the world'" (John 9:2–5). The man's condition might have grown out of his own sinful nature, but Jesus was unwilling to ascribe specific causation behind the condition of the blindness of the man. He makes another point altogether: God's purpose is at work in all things, including the man's blindness.

Jesus said to them, "My Father is always at his work to this very day, and I, too, am working." For this reason the Jews tried all the harder to kill him; not only was he breaking the Sabbath, but he was even calling God his own Father, making himself equal with God. Jesus gave them this answer: "I tell you the truth, the Son can do nothing by himself; he can do only what he sees his Father doing, because whatever the Father does the Son also does. For the Father loves the Son and shows him all he does. Yes, to your amazement he will show him even greater things than these. For just as the Father raises the dead and gives them life, even so the Son gives life to whom he is pleased to give it. Moreover, the Father judges no one, but has entrusted all judgment to the Son, that all may honor the Son just as they honor the Father. He who does not honor the Son does not honor the Father, who sent him."
JOHN 5:17–23

■

JESUS ANSWERED HIS ADVERSARIES by making an extraordinary claim about his unique relationship to the Father: "the Son can do nothing by himself; he can do only what he sees his Father doing, because whatever the Father does the Son also does . . ." Everything Jesus does and says comes from the Father. There is no division and no misunderstanding. Just as Jesus is to the Father, so are his disciples and followers to him. We have the same connection through the power of the Holy Spirit who dwells in our hearts. And just as Jesus speaks the language of the Spirit of God, so we, who follow Christ, must learn to understand that same language as we move through our daily lives.

FROM DEATH TO LIFE

I tell you the truth, whoever hears my word and believes him who sent me has eternal life and will not be condemned; he has crossed over from death to life. I tell you the truth, a time is coming and has now come when the dead will hear the voice of the Son of God and those who hear will live. For as the Father has life in himself, so he has granted the Son to have life in himself. And he has given him authority to judge because he is the Son of Man. Do not be amazed at this, for a time is coming when all who are in their graves will hear his voice and come out—those who have done good will rise to live, and those who have done evil will rise to be condemned. By myself I can do nothing; I judge only as I hear, and my judgment is just, for I seek not to please myself but him who sent me. If I testify about myself, my testimony is not valid. There is another who testifies in my favor, and I know that his testimony about me is valid. JOHN 5:24–32

■

MANY ARE OFFENDED BY Jesus' proclamation that "whoever hears my word and believes him who sent me has eternal life and will not be condemned; he has crossed over from death to life." This offends because it forces a choice: By rejecting God (and the one he sent), we are making a decision that will surely have eternal consequences. Jesus is talking about a time in the indeterminate future when "all who are in their graves will hear his voice and come out—those who have done good will rise to live, and those who have done evil will rise to be condemned." Jesus came down from heaven to bring about a good outcome for all who put their trust in him, for he wishes no one to die a "second death" (Revelation 21:6–8).

You have sent to John and he has testified to the truth. Not that I accept human testimony; but I mention it that you may be saved. John was a lamp that burned and gave light, and you chose for a time to enjoy his light. JOHN 5:33–35

■

JESUS SAID THAT JOHN the Baptist "testified to the truth . . . that you may be saved." Jesus knew the trajectory of John's life, from his ministry in the wilderness to his arrest and execution. But it was John's testimony to the truth that exceeded everything else in importance. For in the end John testified to Jesus' true identity and he proclaimed to all who would listen why they needed to believe in the truth of his revelation that Jesus is the Christ. "The Father loves the Son and has placed everything in his hands. Whoever believes in the Son has eternal life, but whoever rejects the Son will not see life, for God's wrath remains on him" (John 3:35–36).

I have testimony weightier than that of John. For the very work that the Father has given me to finish, and which I am doing, testifies that the Father has sent me. And the Father who sent me has himself testified concerning me. You have never heard his voice nor seen his form, nor does his word dwell in you, for you do not believe the one he sent. You diligently study the Scriptures because you think that by them you possess eternal life. These are the Scriptures that testify about me, yet you refuse to come to me to have life. JOHN 5:36–40

■

THIS EPISODE BEGAN WITH Jesus healing the invalid at the pool called Bethesda. The Jewish leaders objected on the pretense that the miraculous healing led to the breaking of the Sabbath and even to blasphemy. The opposition of the religious rulers grew out of the need to protect their tenuous power base by enforcing all kinds of religious rules. Jesus offended them because the Scripture they misused as a weapon of attack was the very same Scripture that testified about Jesus himself. The truth is that these religious leaders were devoid of the Holy Spirit, employing only their intellect to serve their corrupt purposes. Paul drew the same distinction for the Corinthians: "My message and my preaching were not with wise and persuasive words, but with a demonstrations of the Spirit's power, so that your faith might not rest on men's wisdom, but on God's power" (1 Corinthians 2:4–5).

YOU DO NOT ACCEPT ME

I do not accept praise from men, but I know you. I know that you do not have the love of God in your hearts. I have come in my Father's name, and you do not accept me; but if someone else comes in his own name, you will accept him. How can you believe if you accept praise from one another, yet make no effort to obtain the praise that comes from the only God? But do not think I will accuse you before the Father. Your accuser is Moses, on whom your hopes are set. If you believed Moses, you would believe me, for he wrote about me. But since you do not believe what he wrote, how are you going to believe what I say? JOHN 5:41–47

■

IF WE ARE SURPRISED that Jesus experienced opposition from the religious leaders in Jerusalem, we shouldn't be. C. S. Lewis called our world "enemy-occupied territory." He meant that the world has been turned upside down; a pretender has taken over, and the rightful King has returned to bring about the restoration of the kingdom of God and put to flight the rulers, authorities, and powers of this dark world (Ephesians 6:12). From the time of his birth in a stable to the slaughter of the innocents to the opposition in Jerusalem, a war was waged against Jesus, and the battle only intensified as he headed toward Gethsemane and Golgotha.

One Sabbath Jesus was going through the grain fields, and his disciples began to pick some heads of grain, rub them in their hands and eat the kernels. Some of the Pharisees asked, "Why are you doing what is unlawful on the Sabbath?" Jesus answered them, "Have you never read what David did when he and his companions were hungry? He entered the house of God, and taking the consecrated bread, he ate what is lawful only for priests to eat. And he also gave some to his companions." Then Jesus said to them, "The Son of Man is Lord of the Sabbath." LUKE 6:1–5

∎

JESUS HAD A DECISION to make. His followers were hungry, and so they began to eat kernels of grain as they passed through a field. It appears that some Pharisees were following as well, because they claimed that Jesus and his disciples were breaking the law by "harvesting" the grain on the Sabbath. To the Pharisees, it was better to starve than to break the Sabbath. But Jesus countered with an illustration from Scripture where David and his companions ate consecrated bread to stave off hunger. Then he followed with his interpretation that addressed the objections of the rules-obsessed critics. To paraphrase, Jesus said that God, in his wisdom, created the Sabbath for our rest so that we would lay aside time to be with him. The Sabbath was not created to separate us from God, but to draw us closer to him. Man-made religiosity with its endless rules and regulations can kill our relationship with the God who loves us. Jesus came to breathe life back into that relationship.

Another time he went into the synagogue, and a man with a shriveled hand was there. Some of them were looking for a reason to accuse Jesus, so they watched him closely to see if he would heal him on the Sabbath. Jesus said to the man with the shriveled hand, "Stand up in front of everyone." Then Jesus asked them, "Which is lawful on the Sabbath: to do good or to do evil, to save life or to kill?" But they remained silent. He looked around at them in anger and, deeply distressed at their stubborn hearts, said to the man, "Stretch out your hand." He stretched it out, and his hand was completely restored. Then the Pharisees went out and began to plot with the Herodians how they might kill Jesus. **MARK 3:1–6**

■

SOME IN THE CROWD questioned Jesus' authority to heal the injured man's hand on the Sabbath, but he quickly turned the table on them by asking a straightforward question: "Which is lawful on the Sabbath: to do good or to do evil, to save life or to kill?" The religious leaders had replaced principle with rules that did not promote goodness and justice. If a rule prohibits us from saving a life, then the rule prevents us from understanding God's principle behind the rule. Rules detached from God's principle of light, life, and love will not save life, nor will such rules bring about justice. Notice that Jesus' anger arose from the fact that his detractors had "stubborn hearts." Their blind adherence to man-made rules had turned them into enemies of God. This is why they decided to conspire with the Herodians to kill Jesus.

CHOOSING HIS DISCIPLES

One of those days Jesus went out to a mountainside to pray, and spent the night praying to God. When morning came, he called his disciples to him and chose twelve of them, whom he also designated apostles: Simon (whom he named Peter), his brother Andrew, James, John, Philip, Bartholomew, Matthew, Thomas, James son of Alphaeus, Simon who was called the Zealot, Judas son of James, and Judas Iscariot, who became a traitor. LUKE 6:12–16

■

JESUS NEEDED TO DECIDE who would be appointed his closest followers. It is worth noting that he did not express anxiety, nor did he seek counsel from those flocking around him. Instead, he put all the concerns and needs of everyday life aside, went to a mountainside, and spent the night praying to his Father. Remember, Jesus said he can do nothing by himself; "he can do only what he sees his Father doing, because whatever the Father does the Son also does" (John 5:19). It was through prayer that Jesus sought guidance to pursue his Father's will completely because he knew he could do nothing himself outside of the Father's will.

Aware of this, Jesus withdrew from that place. Many followed him, and he healed all their sick, warning them not to tell who he was. This was to fulfill what was spoken through the prophet Isaiah: "Here is my servant whom I have chosen, the one I love, in whom I delight; I will put my Spirit on him, and he will proclaim justice to the nations. He will not quarrel or cry out; no one will hear his voice in the streets. A bruised reed he will not break, and a smoldering wick he will not snuff out, till he leads justice to victory. In his name the nations will put their hope." **MATTHEW 12:15B–21**

■

IN TELLING HIS STORY of Jesus, Matthew references Hebrew Scripture as a way of confirming to the Jewish people that Jesus is the fulfillment of everything they had been looking and longing for over many centuries. But Jesus is not a warrior like King David, who came to finally liberate the people from the bondage of Roman occupation. Instead, Jesus traveled around healing many of their diseases while at the same time warning the people "not to tell who he was." Matthew simply reminds his readers that Isaiah prophesized that the Messiah would not necessarily be a king in the usual stereotype: "He will not quarrel or cry out; no one will hear his voice in the streets . . ." (Isaiah 42:2).

Jesus went throughout Galilee, teaching in their synagogues, preaching the good news of the kingdom, and healing every disease and sickness among the people. News about him spread all over Syria, and people brought to him all who were ill with various diseases, those suffering severe pain, the demon possessed, those having seizures, and the paralyzed, and he healed them. MATTHEW 4:23–24

■

WE COME TO AN important pause in Matthew's narrative. Jesus had been actively healing the sick, casting out demons, and teaching, but now we are going to sit on a grassy hillside overlooking the wind-swept Sea of Galilee to listen to Jesus as he opens up a radical understanding of what it truly means to serve the living God.

Blessed are the poor in spirit, for theirs is the kingdom of heaven.
MATTHEW 5:3

■

JESUS BEGINS THE BEATITUDES with a statement that throws into question the direction of our striving hearts. Many of us build our lives stone by stone, thinking that our economic well-being will relieve our thirst for something more than the riches and real estate we may acquire through a lifetime of effort. But wealth by itself cannot quench our thirst or satisfy our longing hearts. The poor are blessed because they are less prone to be blinded by the smokescreen of riches that obscures God's authentic role in this world. The poor are not blessed because they are better. God calls all men and women into relationship with himself. It is just harder for the rich to put their trust in God because they may have decided to trust in the power and position that wealth can bring. "A man who has riches without understanding is like the beasts that perish" (Psalm 49:20).

THOSE WHO MOURN

Blessed are those who mourn, for they will be comforted.
MATTHEW 5:4

■

WHEN WE EXPERIENCE THE loss a friend or a family member, we cry out from the bottom of our hearts because we know something irreversible has taken place. We mourn, but Jesus tells us that God comes beside us to mourn with us and to comfort us. We are blessed at these moments because in the midst of our profound aloneness we experience the presence of God. And when we experience his presence, we realize that when we invite God into our lives, we are not alone and will never be alone. "I will never leave you nor forsake you" (Joshua 1:5).

THE MEEK

Blessed are the meek, for they will inherit the earth. **MATTHEW 5:5**

∎

AGAIN, JESUS TAKES A counterintuitive tack when stating who will inherit the earth. In his novel *Bonfire of the Vanities*, Tom Wolfe's anti-hero, Sherman McCoy, is the "Master of the Universe," a "god" of Wall Street who exudes antipathy for the nameless swarm of humanity that surrounds him in the city of New York. Sherman is a type that can be found in all the major financial centers in the world. He is trapped in a limousine reality and would have no understanding of what Jesus is telling him and us. When Jesus points to meekness, he is emphasizing humbleness of character. The meek are meek not out of a reservoir of weakness, but through the experience of knowing God and knowing that he is God and we are not:

> O Lord, you have searched me and you know me.
> You know when I sit and when I rise;
> You perceive my thoughts from afar.
> You discern my going out and my lying down;
> You are familiar with all my ways.
> Before a word is on my tongue
> You know it completely, O Lord.
>
> (Psalm 139:1–4)

Blessed are those who hunger and thirst for righteousness, for they will be filled. **MATTHEW** 5:6

■

IF WE HUNGER AND thirst for something, we will not stop until we get it. What is your desert thirst? What do you hunger for above everything else? Jesus is using physical appetites common to all men and women to point to the one thing that will actually satisfy. Solomon asked God for the wisdom of "a discerning heart to govern your people and to distinguish right from wrong" (1 Kings 3:9). By asking for wisdom he was asking God to bless him with the righteousness that can only come from God. Jesus came down to earth to make that righteousness available to all: "Be reconciled to God. God made him who had no sin to be sin for us, so that in him we might become the righteousness of God" (2 Corinthians 5:20–21).

THE MERCIFUL

Blessed are the merciful, for they will be shown mercy. **MATTHEW** 5:7

■

AS GOD HAS SHOWN mercy to us, so we should show the same measure of mercy to others. In the Parable of the Unmerciful Servant, Jesus tells of a servant who cannot repay his master a large amount of money. The servant begs for mercy and it is granted. But soon enough, the servant demands repayment of monies owed him, and instead of showing the same kindness when the debtor cannot pay, he has the debtor thrown into prison. When the master is told of this, he asks the forgiven servant, "Shouldn't you have had the same mercy on your fellow servant just as I had for you?" (Matthew 18:23–35) Think of the master in the parable as God, and think of the wicked servant as each one of us. We have received God's mercy; in fact, we receive it everyday and we can never pay it back. But we can show it to others every time we have the opportunity. We can represent God in the world by forgiving just as we have been forgiven.

THE PURE IN HEART

Blessed are the pure in heart, for they will see God. **MATTHEW 5:8**

■

IF WE HAVE THE means, we wash away the grit and grime that naturally accumulates during our daily engagement with the world. If we don't go through the daily rituals of bathing, we begin to feel out of sorts. But outer cleanliness does not necessarily equate with inner cleanliness. Jesus compares the Pharisees to "whitewashed tombs, which look beautiful on the outside but on the inside are full of dead men's bones and everything unclean" (Matthew 23:27–28). The unclean and diseased heart infects the whole person from the inside out, making it less and less possible to "see God." Jesus is the ultimate heart surgeon who repairs and restores, beginning with the heart and working out from there.

Blessed are the peacemakers, for they will be called sons of God.
MATTHEW 5:9

■

WE HEAR PEOPLE SPEAK of peace all the time, but how can there be peace when, in the deeper recesses of the heart, we are often at war with God? It might be said that human history began with the rebellion in the Garden of Eden. One thoughtless act of defiance led directly to all the enmity, pain, suffering, murder, and mayhem that characterize so much of the historical narrative. Peacemaking, as opposed to peacekeeping, can only take root if we first make peace with God through Christ. Then genuine peacemaking can begin, one person at a time.

THE PERSECUTED

Blessed are those who are persecuted because of righteousness, for theirs is the kingdom of heaven. **MATTHEW 5:10**

■

FROM OUR EARLIEST DAYS, we expect to be rewarded for good behavior. When the opposite occurs, we feel the pain of injustice to our very core. This correlation of good behavior and reward is so pervasive that we often expect that our life will get better if we follow Jesus. But the weight of the narrative thus far suggests the opposite is just as true. Jesus' life was threatened by Herod's troops when he was a young child, he was persecuted and reviled by the religious elite for performing miracles on the Sabbath, and he was even rejected in his hometown of Nazareth. Jesus experienced persecution, his disciples experienced persecution, and the church has experienced persecution down through the ages and even to the present time.

Blessed are you when people insult you, persecute you and falsely say all kinds of evil against you because of me. Rejoice and be glad, because great is your reward in heaven, for in the same way they persecuted the prophets who were before you. MATTHEW 5:11–12

■

JESUS WARNS HIS FOLLOWERS that they will experience persecution and "all kinds of evil," but he is not just referring to one period of time two thousand years ago. Jesus is referring to every period until he returns. One contemporary example is the life and martyrdom of Dietrich Bonhoeffer. He was a voice crying out in the wilderness of Nazi Germany, warning of the coming darkness as the totalitarian plague reached even into the church itself. Bonheoffer was reviled, lied about, and persecuted because he would not abandon Jesus in order to accommodate the Nazi masters. Even when he found a safe haven in England and the United States, he did not rest until he could return to Germany to live out his faith, even to the point of death. But surely "great is (his) reward in heaven."

THE SALT OF THE EARTH

You are the salt of the earth. But if the salt loses its saltiness, how can it be made salty again? It is no longer good for anything, except to be thrown out and trampled by men. MATTHEW 5:13

■

JESUS SAYS TO PRAY that God's kingdom will come. We have been enrolled as foot soldiers in bringing about the restoration of God's kingdom, which is not yet, but will be. Jesus says we are a different kind of soldier. We are like the salt of the earth; as missionaries of the Word, we are here to reach out to a resistant world with the truth of Jesus Christ as Lord and Savior, but in an appealing and winning way. When you become salt of the earth, you take on the characteristic properties of salt: You provide flavor while preserving perishables from corruption. "Let your conversation be always full of grace, seasoned with salt, so that you may know how to answer everyone" (Colossians 4:6).

You are the light of the world. A city on a hill cannot be hidden. Neither do people light a lamp and put it under a bowl. Instead they put it on its stand, and it gives light to everyone in the house. In the same way, let your light shine before men, that they may see your good deeds and praise your Father in heaven. MATTHEW 5:14–16

■

WHEN JESUS SAYS, "YOU are the light of the world," he is commissioning his followers to go out into the world to reflect the light that comes from "your Father in heaven." In the beginning, God said, "'Let there be light,' and there was light (and) God saw that it was good" (Genesis 1:3). With the fatal choice of Adam and Eve in the Garden of Eden, that light was enshrouded but not extinguished. Jesus came to bring light back into a darkened world. The goodness of the light of God is passed through Jesus to his followers, who are to reflect that light much as the moon reflects the light of the sun. By being disciples of Jesus Christ, we are called to pass on the goodness of the Creator of that light just as Jesus passed it on to his own apostles and disciples through the gift of the Holy Spirit.

Do not think that I have come to abolish the Law or the Prophets;
I have not come to abolish them but to fulfill them. I tell you the
truth, until heaven and earth disappear, not the smallest letter, not
the least stroke of a pen, will by any means disappear from the Law
until everything is accomplished. MATTHEW 5:17–18

■

ON SEVERAL OCCASIONS RELIGIOUS rulers accused Jesus of breaking the law, but Jesus countered by reframing our understanding of
God's purpose behind his giving us the law in the first place. Jesus
is saying the law, with all its nuances and complexities, cannot be
an end in itself. Through time and tradition, the law had become
an instrument for enforcing compliance while sustaining a political
power base for an elite few. But God never intended the law to be a
rulebook. It was meant to reflect principles of life that go deeper
than a catalog of rules that need to be checked off in order to get by.
By digging down to the underlying principles, Jesus opens up for us
an understanding that includes God's purpose behind the whole-
ness, fullness, and congruency that truly shapes everything we
experience.

TEACHING AND PRACTICING
THESE COMMANDMENTS

Anyone who breaks one of the least of these commandments and teaches others to do the same will be called least in the kingdom of heaven, but whoever practices and teaches these commands will be called great in the kingdom of heaven. For I tell you that unless your righteousness surpasses that of the Pharisees and the teachers of the law, you will certainly not enter the kingdom of heaven.
MATTHEW 5:19–20

■

UNLESS WE RECOGNIZE THAT Jesus is using hyperbole, we will misread the point he is making in this teaching. He is setting up two impossibilities. First, if we break "one of the least of these commandments . . . (we) will be called least in the kingdom of heaven . . ." And then he goes further: ". . . unless your righteousness surpasses that of the Pharisees and the teachers of the law, you will certainly not enter the kingdom of heaven." Why does he do this? At the time, Jesus was teaching people who had conflated God's law with God Himself. God gave us the law as a signpost to point us in his direction and to help us stay on the good and right path. The path may vary from person to person, but it is always leading us back into relationship with God the Father through the guiding Spirit of his Son, Jesus Christ.

BE RECONCILED FIRST

You have heard that it was said to the people long ago, "Do not murder, and anyone who murders will be subject to judgment." But I tell you that anyone who is angry with his brother will be subject to judgment. Again, anyone who says to his brother, "Raca," is answerable to the Sanhedrin. But anyone who says, "You fool!" will be in danger of the fire of hell. Therefore, if you are offering your gift at the altar and there remember that your brother has something against you, leave your gift there in front of the altar. First go and be reconciled to your brother; then come and offer your gift. MATTHEW 5:21–24

■

JUST AS A DEADLY avalanche can begin with something as insignificant as a small stone, so murder can grow out of something trivial, such as calling someone a derogatory name. David's crime began when he saw a beautiful married woman bathing and ended with the premeditated murder of her husband Uriah. Envy drove Cain to lure his brother Abel to an isolated field and strike him dead. Jesus is speaking to the consequences that trailed Adam and Eve after they were exiled from the Garden of Eden. God's law against murder and adultery and other crimes, by itself, cannot stop men and women from initiating actions that sweep them up in destructive consequences. Envy, hatred, and lust cannot be weighed, but what issues forth from a malevolent heart can be heavy indeed: "He who is pregnant with evil and conceives trouble gives birth to disillusionment . . . The trouble he causes recoils on himself; his violence comes down on his own head" (Psalm 7:14, 16).

SETTLE MATTERS QUICKLY WITH
YOUR ADVERSARY

Settle matters quickly with your adversary who is taking you to court. Do it while you are still with him on the way, or he may hand you over to the judge, and the judge may hand you over to the officer, and you may be thrown into prison. I tell you the truth, you will not get out until you have paid the last penny. MATTHEW 5:25–26

■

JUSTICE AS PRACTICED IN the world is a poor shadow of the real thing. Instead of settling a matter, often the law entangles adversaries in an endless web of claims and counter claims, eating up money, time, and happiness. Instead, Jesus sets before us a stark contrast between seeking worldly justice and living the kingdom ethic that points to a way of life that goes far beyond just fulfilling the simpler aspects of the law. "Settle matters quickly with your adversary who is taking you to court."

SIN BEGINS IN THE HEART

You have heard that it was said, "Do not commit adultery." But I tell you that anyone who looks at a woman lustfully has already committed adultery with her in his heart. If your right eye causes you to sin, gouge it out and throw it away. It is better for you to lose one part of your body than for your whole body to be thrown into hell. And if your right hand causes you to sin, cut it off and throw it away. It is better for you to lose one part of your body than for your whole body to go into hell. MATTHEW 5:27–30

■

JESUS MAKES IT CLEAR that the act of adultery is the offspring of a heart filled with adulterous longings. The law is impotent in restraining the impulses of an unruly heart. If the boundaries erected by governments and religious leaders were truly effective, why would we need the police, courts, and lawyers to enforce their statutes and decrees? Jesus aims at a higher standard by pointing to the source of the problem: individual will. If I want to do something, I will often plunge ahead without considering the consequences. Law cannot restrain me. But Jesus aims at redirecting my desires and appetites to the object of my original love: God Himself.

DIVORCE

It has been said, "Anyone who divorces his wife must give her a certificate of divorce." But I tell you that anyone who divorces his wife, except for marital unfaithfulness, causes her to become an adulteress, and anyone who marries the divorced woman commits adultery. MATTHEW 5:31–32

■

"SO GOD CREATED MAN in his own image, in the image of God he created him; male and female he created them" (Genesis 1:22). After he created them, male and female, he instituted marriage as a way to bond them to build a life together, to raise children together, and to worship God the Creator together. "For this reason a man will leave his father and mother and be united to his wife, and they will become one flesh" (Genesis 2:24). The key word here is "united." The fall in the Garden of Eden fractured the relationship between Adam and Eve, and divorce is one important example of the consequences of the fall. Jesus is referring to the original relationship, not the one marred by sin and dissention. He is talking about restoring the essential goodness of the original purpose of marriage; he is talking about God's higher standard.

Again, you have heard that it was said to the people long ago, "Do not break your oath, but keep the oaths you have made to the Lord." But I tell you, do not swear at all: either by heaven, for it is God's throne; or by the earth, for it is his footstool; or by Jerusalem, for it is the city of the Great King. And do not swear by your head, for you cannot make even one hair white or black. Simply let your "Yes" be "Yes," and your "No," "No"; anything beyond this comes from the evil one. MATTHEW 5:33–37

■

IN OUR MODERN WORLD, a handshake is never enough. A "yes" or a "no" is augmented by either a battery of lawyers and accountants or is modified by innumerable qualifiers. This is the reality we accept; furthermore, we consider it naïve to risk everything on someone's word when his or her intentions are not known. But Jesus is not content to adopt the standards of this world. He focuses on kingdom standards, where the law, as constructed by man, cannot go. Jesus sets a higher standard that is built on a level of integrity that transforms word and action into a single reality: "Simply let your 'Yes' be 'Yes' and your 'No,' 'No'; anything beyond this comes from the evil one."

You have heard that it was said, "Eye for eye, and tooth for tooth."
But I tell you, do not resist an evil person. If someone strikes you
on the right cheek, turn to him the other also. And if someone
wants to sue you and take your tunic, let him have your cloak as
well. If someone forces you to go one mile, go with him two miles.
Give to the one who asks you, and do not turn away from the one
who wants to borrow from you. MATTHEW 5:38–42

■

RULES ARE NECESSARY FOR ordering a decent society. Systems and
procedures are necessary for a society to function in ways that promote the general welfare of the people. But rules can easily be corrupted and abused by those in positions of power. It is axiomatic
that rules can be used as easily against people as for them. When
Jesus says, "Do not resist an evil person," he is not setting forth a
new rule. He is giving us a higher standard that is based on foundational principles that support rules. Jesus is always concerned
with teaching deeper truths. Here he is saying that rules do not
change a person's heart. The principles of a deeper life connected to
the kingdom of God bring about genuine transformation, first in
the individual, then in families and communities, and ultimately in
society itself.

You have heard that it was said, "Love your neighbor and hate your enemy." But I tell you: Love your enemies and pray for those who persecute you, that you may be sons of your Father in heaven. He causes his sun to rise on the evil and the good, and sends rain on the righteous and the unrighteous. MATTHEW 5:43–45

■

IF POLITICIANS ARE CAPABLE of anything, it is swaying large crowds with rhetorical flourishes and visionary pronouncements and promises. Jesus is not of their ilk. He heals individuals, he chose common fishermen to be his followers, and while on earth he tried to avoid crowds and often stole away when people were seeking him. Like John the Baptist, Jesus annoyed and troubled the political and religious authorities of his time. And his teaching follows this same pattern. He does not encourage rebellion. Rather, he deals with each one of us as individuals. He miraculously healed a man with evil spirits and caused a crippled man to walk. He invited a tax collector to dine with him, and he cured a woman who had been suffering for years. He taught in the same way, keeping close to the yearnings and compulsions of the human heart. Most of those who were rich, famous, and powerful in Jesus' time vanished without a trace. But not Jesus. He continues to live in the hearts and minds of people, generation after generation.

BE PERFECT

If you love those who love you, what reward will you get? Are not even the tax collectors doing that? And if you greet only your brothers, what are you doing more than others? Do not even pagans do that? Be perfect, therefore, as your heavenly Father is perfect. MATTHEW 5:46–48

■

JESUS SAYS, "BE PERFECT, therefore, as your heavenly Father is perfect." Why would he set before us an impossibly high standard? Jesus knows that men and women, in their sinful condition, will always be short of perfection. Jesus did not want us to waste our lives wallowing in regret and sorrow. Rather he came to liberate us from that very condition, not to make us perfect, but to help us move toward the Father as we go through this life on earth, always having in view before us the perfect holiness of the Father.

ACTS OF SELF-RIGHTEOUSNESS

Be careful not to do your 'acts of righteousness' before men, to be seen by them. If you do, you will have no reward from your Father in heaven. MATTHEW 6:1

■

THE SCREWTAPE LETTERS IS a wickedly unsettling book because it is written from the viewpoint of a lieutenant of the devil himself, who is scheming to undermine a recent convert to Christianity. In one letter, Screwtape writes about the virtue of humility and how to use it to undermine the enemy (the recent convert): "Catch him at the moment when he is really poor in spirit and smuggle into his mind the gratifying reflection, 'By jove! I'm really humble,' and almost immediately pride—pride at his own humility—will appear" (*The Screwtape Letters*). As with humility, so with righteousness: The moment we become conscious of our own righteousness, pride slips in and self-righteousness chases out genuine righteousness.

GOD SEES WHAT IS DONE IN SECRET

So when you give to the needy, do not announce it with trumpets, as the hypocrites do in the synagogues and on the streets, to be honored by men. I tell you the truth, they have received their reward in full. But when you give to the needy, do not let your left hand know what your right hand is doing, so that your giving may be in secret. Then your Father, who sees what is done in secret, will reward you. MATTHEW 6:2–4

■

THE KINGDOMS OF THIS earth are but a poor representation of the genuine kingdom that is ruled by the KING of KINGS and the LORD of LORDS (Revelation 17:15). The rich and powerful of this world may give to the poor, but they often do it to show off their generosity and consolidate their temporal power. One of the three temptations Satan offered Jesus was to rule over "all the kingdoms of the world" (Luke 4:5), but what was being presented was a chimera that with time would vanish as if it never existed. Jesus rejected this phony model; instead, he says, give out the goodness and abundance God has bestowed on you. For God sees your acts of generosity and he knows your heart. To act for any reason other than mirroring God's grace is to act outside of the truth of Jesus' teaching.

HOW TO PRAY

And when you pray, do not be like the hypocrites, for they love to pray standing in the synagogues and on the street corners to be seen by men. I tell you the truth, they have received their reward in full. But when you pray, go into your room, close the door and pray to your Father, who is unseen. Then your Father, who sees what is done in secret, will reward you. MATTHEW 6:5–6

■

IN A VERY DIFFERENT context, Jesus says to Peter, "Get behind me, Satan! You do not have in mind the things of God, but the things of men" (Mark 8:33). In the Sermon on the Mount, Jesus says much the same thing about our motives behind praying. If we pray to impress people with our religious prowess, we are subverting the very reason to pray. Jesus says that prayer is about connecting with God. It is an ongoing conversation, a dialogue where we not only can speak, but we can be spoken to as well. When it comes to prayer, we need to step outside of the discourse and commerce of everyday life so that we can adjust the attitudes of our heart to hear and to be heard, to speak and to be spoken to, not in the normal way of such things, but in the intimate company of God Himself.

And when you pray, do not keep on babbling like pagans, for they think they will be heard because of their many words. Do not be like them, for your Father knows what you need before you ask him. MATTHEW 6:7–8

■

PRAYER IS THE ESSENTIAL link that connects us to God, who is not detached and foreign, but who desires to give each one of us the good things that he planned for us from the very beginning. After David fell into temptation and sin, he implored God to not take his Holy Spirit away because that would be worse than death (Psalm 51:11). God is not impersonal; he knows everything about us, and he wants us to know him. But if we fake it and babble like the pagans and puff ourselves up like the hypocritical religious leaders, we are engaging in mere pretense that in the end leaves us unhappy, alone, and dissatisfied. God is not far away (James 4:8). He is near, and it is through the power of prayer that we can draw ever closer to him. We should be confident that he hears us and longs for our eternal well-being.

THE LORD'S PRAYER

This, then, is how you should pray: "Our Father in heaven, hallowed be your name, your kingdom come, your will be done on earth as it is in heaven." **MATTHEW 6:9–10**

■

THE LORD'S PRAYER IS so familiar that it is easy to miss its depth and complexity. In the first sentence alone, Jesus includes four declarations. First, he addresses God as "Our Father," not as some stern and unfeeling taskmaster, but as "Daddy," just as a child would address his own loving and protective father. Then he says, "hallowed be your name," which sets this Father apart as holy and perfect and above the sinful and imperfect condition of men and women on earth. Then Jesus prays that God's kingdom will be restored here on earth, replacing the kingdoms that are at war with God and his people. Finally, he prays for the unity that can only exist when the original design takes root here on earth, echoing the harmony that existed at the very beginning when God created the world and all the creatures in it, and he saw that it was very good (Genesis 1:31).

DAILY BREAD

Give us today our daily bread. **MATTHEW 6:11**

■

IN THIS PLENTIFUL AND prosperous corner of the world, it is too easy to forget what would happen if all the foods we find in markets and restaurants suddenly vanished. It is difficult to imagine a world where this kind of depravation could become a reality, but for many, getting access to food is the harsh reality of daily life. When times are good, it is easy to assume provision from the endless supplies afforded by science and enterprise. But is this a reasonable position? Jesus prays to God for daily provision because he knows that God is the only true provider. As he says elsewhere in the Sermon on the Mount, "Therefore, do not worry about tomorrow, for tomorrow will worry about itself. Each day has enough trouble of its own" (Matthew 6:34). To paraphrase another prayer: "Lord, for tomorrow and its needs I do not pray . . . Please keep me, guide me, love me, Lord, just for today." Recognizing our daily dependence on God is the only way to live each and every day.

FORGIVE

Forgive us our debts, as we also have forgiven our debtors.

MATTHEW 6:12

■

WHETHER WE USE THE word "trespasses," "debts," or "sins" when praying the Lord's Prayer, we are essentially asking God for forgiveness for the countless ways we have fallen away from him. In an earlier encounter, Jesus makes his mission on earth abundantly clear: "It is not the healthy who need a doctor, but the sick. I have not come to call the righteous, but sinners" (Mark 2:17). Paul says "all have sinned and fall short of the glory of God" (Romans 3:23), so when we are praying, "Forgive us," there are no exceptions or exemptions. Everyone needs to ask for God's forgiveness because our sin causes us to betray him time and again. When Paul asks, "Who will rescue me from this body of death," he gives us the answer immediately: "Thanks be to God—through Jesus Christ our Lord!" (Roman 7:24–25) This one line of the Lord's Prayer is liberating because without forgiveness, we will never escape the destructive consequences growing out of our sin-prone nature. But it is not just about us: We need to forgive as God has forgiven us. Just as God's forgiveness cost him dearly, to forgive others as God has forgiven us can be costly. But from an eternal point of view, the cost is worth it.

And lead us not into temptation, but deliver us from the evil one.
MATTHEW 6:13

■

WHY WOULD GOD LEAD us into temptation? Perhaps it is best to think of this dilemma as fundamental to our relationship with God. Jesus seems to be requesting that God not place him in a situation where he would be tempted to betray God. When Jesus was tempted by the devil three times in the wilderness, he resisted by remaining centered in the Holy Spirit. This prayer acknowledges the existence of an evil one, who wanders the earth looking for people not able to withstand the devil's schemes. Here is the promise for those who believe: "No temptation has seized you except what is common to man. And God is faithful; he will not let you be tempted beyond what you can bear. But when you are tempted, he will also provide a way out so that you can stand up under it" (1 Corinthians 10:13).

HOW TO FAST

When you fast, do not look somber as the hypocrites do, for they disfigure their faces to show men they are fasting. I tell you the truth, they have received their reward in full. But when you fast, put oil on your head and wash your face, so that it will not be obvious to men that you are fasting, but only to your Father, who is unseen; and your Father, who sees what is done in secret, will reward you. MATTHEW 6:16–18

■

WHAT DO YOU HUNGER for? If it is food, you are seeking satisfaction from the bounty of God's beneficence. If we take the provision without acknowledging a debt to the provider, we will continue to hunger and thirst even after we have satiated our temporary need. And so we want more and more. Fasting is a way of keeping our relationship with God and the natural world in balance. Even so, Jesus warns against the imbalance that comes from using the traditional religious practice of fasting to affirm to other men and women our own godliness and righteousness. This serves only to push God away, even as it seems to lift the "hypocrites" up.

Do not store up for yourselves treasures on earth, where moth and rust destroy, and where thieves break in and steal. But store up for yourselves treasures in heaven, where moth and rust do not destroy, and where thieves do not break in and steal. For where your treasure is, there your heart will be also. MATTHEW 6:19–21

■

TREASURE IS A TANTALIZING word. One might think of rugged treasure chests filled with silver and gold coins, pirates, exotic islands, and endless adventure. Or it could be winning the lottery, or living in a luxurious house with an expensive car parked in the front courtyard. But Jesus says treasure is something else: Treasure is the outward manifestation of the inward inclination of the heart. If we spend our time accumulating wealth, then we are permitting that drive to become our ruling passion. Wealth can be a blessing, but when the love of wealth monopolizes all of our attention, then it has the power to separate us from the love of God. It is then that we become like the Rich Young Ruler who cannot abandon his love of wealth and all that it brings him for the love of Christ and all that it could have brought him (Mark 10:17–22).

The eye is the lamp of the body. If your eyes are good, your whole body will be full of light. But if your eyes are bad, your whole body will be full of darkness. If then the light within you is darkness, how great is that darkness! MATTHEW 6:22–23

∎

AT THE VERY BEGINNING of Genesis, God says, "'Let there be light,' and there was light. God saw that the light was good, and he separated the light from the darkness" (Genesis 1:3). But it is the darkness of sin that has separated us from the goodness of the light of God. Elsewhere, Jesus diagnoses the problem this way: "Light has come into the world, but men loved darkness instead of light because their deeds were evil" (John 3:19). Jesus infers that the good eye lets the light of truth pass into the heart, but the bad eye serves as a screen to filter out the goodness of God, leaving us alienated from him. Jesus' mission is to bring the goodness of the light of God into every man and woman's heart: "I am the light of the world. Whoever follows me will never walk in darkness, but will have the light of life" (John 8:12).

No one can serve two masters. Either he will hate the one and love the other, or he will be devoted to the one and despise the other. You cannot serve both God and Money. MATTHEW 6:24

■

OFTEN WE ATTEMPT TO avoid the problem of competing loves by pretending no conflict exists, but eventually we come to a fork in the road that requires that we choose one direction or the other. When it comes to the powerful attraction of money and all that wealth can bring us, it is not surprising that the draw of money has an almost spiritual hold on our affections. It is not gold or silver, however, that claims our attention; it is status, power, and the security that money buys that sucks up so much of our affection and time, leaving little room for anything else, including God. "For it is the love of money that is the root of all kinds of evil. Some people eager for money, have wandered from the faith and pierced themselves with many griefs" (1 Timothy 6:10).

WHY DO YOU WORRY?

Therefore I tell you, do not worry about your life, what you will eat or drink; or about your body, what you will wear. Is not life more important than food, and the body more important than clothes? Look at the birds of the air; they do not sow or reap or store away in barns, and yet your heavenly Father feeds them. Are you not much more valuable than they? Who of you by worrying can add a single hour to his life? MATTHEW 6:25–27

■

DAVID, THE SHEPHERD BOY, had every reason to worry, because the fate of Israel rested in his hands. Before him stood Goliath, the giant warrior of the Philistines. David was anything but a warrior, and yet he volunteered to battle the fearsome giant who petrified the entire Israel army. Even King Saul dared not take on this seemingly invincible foe. After David rejected Saul's armor for protection, he advanced towards Goliath with nothing but a sling and five smooth stones. The giant mocked him, to which David replied, "You come against me with sword and spear and javelin, but I come against you in the name of the Lord Almighty, the God of the armies of Israel whom you have defied. . . . All those gathered here will know that it is not by sword or spear that the Lord saves; for the battle is the Lord's, and he will give all of you into our hands" (1 Samuel 17:45,47). It is faith that drives out fear and stress and worry. It is living in that faith today that makes the difference. Tomorrow's problems and difficulties can be dealt with then.

FAITH CONQUERS WORRY

And why do you worry about clothes? See how the lilies of the field grow. They do not labor or spin. Yet I tell you that not even Solomon in all his splendor was dressed like one of these. If that is how God clothes the grass of the field, which is here today and tomorrow is thrown into the fire, will he not much more clothe you, O you of little faith? MATTHEW 6:28–30

■

JESUS IS TALKING ABOUT sufficient provision in these verses. He is saying, look around; if God will provide for the flowers of the field and the grass of the meadows, why do you worry that he will not provide for you? We worry, in part, because we have too little faith in the power of God's sufficiency to provide what is needed—truly needed—when it is needed. Our lack of faith expresses itself when we worry that we will not have enough, that God will not provide, and that we need to strive to provide for our own needs. This is why Jesus addresses his listeners as "O you of little faith."

So do not worry, saying, 'What shall we eat?' or 'What shall we drink?' or 'What shall we wear?' For the pagans run after all these things, and your heavenly Father knows that you need them. But seek first his kingdom and his righteousness, and all these things will be given to you as well. MATTHEW 6:31–33

■

THE KINGDOMS OF THIS earth are filled with pagans who pursue a philosophy that can be summed up this way: "Let us eat and drink, for tomorrow we die" (1 Corinthians 15:32). For them, life is fundamentally meaningless; after dealing with the needs of the body, there is only the nothingness of death and oblivion. Jesus says there is a different kingdom that feeds and clothes and attends to the whole person and not just the body. The devil would like to have us believe that his kingdoms here on earth are the only kingdoms to seek, but when tempted by Satan, Jesus declared that man is more than a bundle of physical appetites. "(God) humbled you, causing you to hunger and then feeding you with manna, which neither you nor your fathers had known, to teach you that man does not live on bread alone but on every word that comes from the mouth of the Lord" (Deuteronomy 8:3).

FOCUS ON THE NEEDS OF THE MOMENT

Therefore do not worry about tomorrow, for tomorrow will worry about itself. Each day has enough trouble of its own. MATTHEW 6:34

■

JESUS MAKES A CONCLUDING statement about what he has been teaching: Trust in God and know that he will provide. Paul puts it this way: "Do not be anxious about anything, but in everything by prayer and petition with thanksgiving, present your requests to God. And the peace of God which transcends all understanding, will guard your hearts and your minds in Christ Jesus" (Philippians 4:6–7).

JUDGING

Do not judge, or you too will be judged. For in the same way you judge others, you will be judged, and with the measure you use, it will be measured to you. MATTHEW 7:1–2

■

OFTEN, WHEN WE FIND ourselves being judgmental, we are falling into the trap of assuming full knowledge of a situation when only partial knowledge is possible. Only God can judge from the position of full knowledge, for only "he knows the secrets of the heart" (Psalm 44:21). Though partial knowledge is all that is available to us (1 Corinthians 13:12), it should not be an excuse for abandoning discernment. Jesus warns us not to place ourselves in God's position by assuming superior or complete knowledge. Instead be discerning in all your interactions with people, knowing that wisdom is a gift of God that flows out of a discerning heart (1 Kings 3:10–12).

BLINDNESS

Why do you look at the speck of sawdust in your brother's eye and pay no attention to the plank in your own eye? How can you say to your brother, 'Let me take the speck out of your eye,' when all the time there is a plank in your own eye? You hypocrite, first take the plank out of your own eye, and then you will see clearly to remove the speck from your brother's eye. MATTHEW 7:3–5

■

JESUS USES METAPHOR AND hyperbole to make a point about our willingness to judge others while turning a blind eye to our own flaws and idiosyncratic patterns of behavior. This is the willfulness of our sinful nature at work: Deflect attention from our own individual shortcomings by pointing the finger at others. But holier-than-thou posturing does not deceive Jesus. He knows that accusing and blaming go all the way back to the Garden of Eden when, after disregarding God's one prohibition, the man and woman not only blamed one another for their actions but they blamed God as well. Without redemption, nothing will ever change.

Do not give dogs what is sacred; do not throw your pearls to pigs. If you do, they may trample them under their feet, and then turn and tear you to pieces. **MATTHEW** 7:6

■

WHEN JESUS TELLS US to not give what is sacred to dogs, nor cast pearls before swine, he is drawing on the wisdom of Scripture to make the point that gifts from God can be easily squandered on those who refuse to hear and accept the truth. Because his statement seems harsh and categorical, it might be tempting to read it as an attack on gender, race, or class. But consider when, as reported in Matthew and Mark, a Gentile woman pleaded with Jesus to save her sick daughter, Jesus replied that the Jews must come first: "for it is not right to take the children's bread and toss it to their dogs" (Mark 7:27). The woman persisted because she had faith that Jesus could save her daughter, and her faith trumped everything else. Seeing the strength of her faith, Jesus responded by granting what she begged for: "For such a reply, you may go; the demon has left your daughter" (Mark 7:29).

ASK, SEEK, KNOCK

Ask and it will be given to you; seek and you will find; knock and the door will be opened to you. For everyone who asks receives; he who seeks finds; and to him who knocks, the door will be opened.
MATTHEW 7:7–8

■

FOR SOME, IT IS a surprise to discover that the Christian life is dynamic at its core; there is nothing static about it. In these verses, Jesus employs three active verbs to help us understand that God is constantly inviting us to walk with him. Jesus commands us to "ask," to "seek," and to "knock." We are being called out of spiritual hibernation and into an ongoing dialogue as we work out God's will in and through our lives. We have been invited into this dynamic relationship with the Lord, but we cannot enter into that life unless we take action by knocking to have the door opened so that we can walk through by the power of the Holy Spirit into the life and relationship God yearns for us to have with him.

Which of you, if his son asks for bread, will give him a stone? Or if he asks for a fish, will give him a snake? If you, then, though you are evil, know how to give good gifts to your children, how much more will your Father in heaven give good gifts to those who ask him! So in everything, do to others what you would have them do to you, for this sums up the Law and the Prophets. MATTHEW 7:9–12

■

WHO WILL WIN THE battle for the human heart? It boils down to whom we will follow. Who will we love? Will God be at the center of everything in our lives or will we turn to other substitutes? Can we live in a state of unresolved sin and truly love God at the same time, or are we condemned to live out a life of warring loyalties? Jesus knew that he had come from the Father to finally resolve this battle between Satan and God for the hearts of men and women. If the inclination to sin remains embedded in the human heart, then living by the principles of the Law and the Prophets will be impossible. What Jesus does not say here is that it will be his sacrifice on the cross that will open the door for every man and woman to finally resolve the battles of the heart by committing everything to a genuine relationship with the Lord through the power of the Holy Spirit. Jesus makes it possible for us to begin living out the admonition, "Be holy because I, the Lord your God am holy." (Leviticus 19:2)

THE NARROW, DIFFICULT PATH

Enter through the narrow gate. For wide is the gate and broad is the road that leads to destruction, and many enter through it. But small is the gate and narrow the road that leads to life, and only a few find it. MATTHEW 7:13–14

■

TIME AND AGAIN, THE Bible reinforces the fact the God gives men and women the gift to choose to follow or rebel, to walk the path that God has laid out for us or to go another way. God made us to be free, but Satan uses that freedom to entangle us in choices that separate us from God. If we choose the path of least resistance, we will end up living outside of the abundant blessings of the kingdom of God. God warned Moses that while he gifted all men and women with the power to choose, he also set forth the consequences that would flow from choosing unwisely: "So be careful to do what the Lord your God has commanded you; do not turn aside to the right or the left. Walk in all the ways that the Lord has commanded you, so that you may live and prosper and prolong your days in the land that you will possess" (Deuteronomy 5:32–33). In order to pass through that narrow gate, we must turn away from serving the idols of this world and choose to place our full allegiance in the one true God. Jesus invites us to do just that.

Watch out for false prophets. They come to you in sheep's clothing, but inwardly they are ferocious wolves. By their fruit you will recognize them. Do people pick grapes from thorn bushes, or figs from thistles? Likewise every good tree bears good fruit, but a bad tree bears bad fruit. A good tree cannot bear bad fruit, and a bad tree cannot bear good fruit. Every tree that does not bear good fruit is cut down and thrown into the fire. Thus, by their fruit you will recognize them. MATTHEW 7:15–20

■

IN OUR OWN TIME, false prophets proliferate using the veneer of science as their "sheep's clothing" to mask the darker purposes of their claims to the truth of their idols. Thousands of years ago it was no different: "From the least to the greatest, all are greedy for gain; prophets and priests alike, all practice deceit" (Jeremiah 6:13). Jesus warns us that not all truth tellers are truthful. It is up to us to sift through counterfeit claims to find that which is authentic. We need to be observant and discerning, and we need to weigh everything by the actual "fruit" produced. If we don't, we will be "a reed swayed by the wind," believing in every new, faddish idea that comes along instead of the truth that flows from the Word of God.

Not everyone who says to me, 'Lord, Lord,' will enter the kingdom of heaven, but only he who does the will of my Father who is in heaven. Many will say to me on that day, 'Lord, Lord, did we not prophesy in your name, and in your name drive out demons and perform many miracles?' Then I will tell them plainly, 'I never knew you. Away from me, you evildoers!' MATTHEW 7:21–23

■

HOW WOULD IT FEEL to hear Jesus say, "I never knew you"? We can claim we know Christ and we can even do all kinds of good works in his name, but if we do not do "the will of my Father who is in heaven," there is no authenticity in our claim. We remain in our sins. Following Jesus is not dependent on an outward show of religious fervor or an accumulation of achievements; it is dependent on a heart that yearns to do God's will in everything. "But if we walk in the light as he is in the light, we have fellowship with one another, and the blood of Jesus, his son, purifies us from all sin" (1 John 1:7).

Therefore everyone who hears these words of mine and puts them into practice is like a wise man who built his house on the rock. The rain came down, the streams rose, and the winds blew and beat against that house; yet it did not fall, because it had its foundation on the rock. But everyone who hears these words of mine and does not put them into practice is like a foolish man who built his house on sand. The rain came down, the streams rose, and the winds blew and beat against that house, and it fell with a great crash. MATTHEW 7:24–27

■

JESUS ENDS HIS SERMON with a teaching on the wisdom of building on strong foundations. He is asking us, what is your foundation built on? He reaches back to the wisdom literature of the Scriptures to make a final point about the very nature of the decisions we make in the way we live. Wisdom has its seat in discernment. If we choose to build our lives on the solid foundation of the Word of God, then we will be able to withstand the rains and wind that we will surely experience. But if our foundation is like sand, then, when the adversities of this life come upon us, we will be vulnerable and defenseless. It is not our strength that will ever prevail; it is the Lord's: "I love you, Lord, my strength. The Lord is my rock, my fortress and my deliverer; my God is my rock, in whom I take refuge. He is my shield and the horn of my salvation, my stronghold" (Psalm 18:1–2).

When Jesus had finished saying these things, the crowds were amazed at his teaching, because he taught as one who had authority, and not as their teachers of the law. MATTHEW 7:28–29

∎

WHY WERE THE CROWDS "amazed" by Jesus' teachings? Jesus did not come to them with titles or university degrees; he came without political or religious position; he seemed to emerge out of nowhere, and yet he "taught as one who had authority." What the people sensed was that Jesus taught under the authority of God. And the message he imparted was that the authority given over to Satan by Adam and Eve was about to be won back. Jesus came to reorder the nature of the kingdoms of the world by establishing his kingdom here on earth to replace the counterfeit kingdom erected by Satan. The Sermon on the Mount is the summation of the principles of God's authority on earth. All authority comes from God and flows through his servant believers.

When he (Jesus) came down from the mountainside, large crowds followed him. A man with leprosy came and knelt before him and said, "Lord, if you are willing, you can make me clean." Jesus reached out his hand and touched the man. "I am willing," he said. "Be clean!" Immediately he was cured of his leprosy. Then Jesus said to him, "See that you don't tell anyone. But go, show yourself to the priest and offer the gift Moses commanded, as a testimony to them." MATTHEW 8:1–4

■

THE SERMON ON THE Mount is where the principles of God are bracketed by the principles of the kingdoms of this world. And what characterizes the kingdoms of this world? Before the sermon began, Jesus was surrounded by those who were "ill with many diseases, those suffering severe pain, the demon-possessed, those having seizures and the paralyzed . . ." (Matthew 5:24). And Matthew tells us that Jesus healed them. After the sermon, Jesus encountered a man with leprosy who said, "Lord, if you are willing, you can make me clean." Jesus was willing and cured the man. Jesus not only enunciated kingdom principles in his sermon, he clearly practiced them as he engaged this needy and alienated world.

When Jesus had finished saying all this in the hearing of the people, he entered Capernaum. There a centurion's servant, whom his master valued highly, was sick and about to die. The centurion heard of Jesus and sent some elders of the Jews to him, asking him to come and heal his servant. When they came to Jesus, they pleaded earnestly with him, "This man deserves to have you do this, because he loves our nation and has built our synagogue." So Jesus went with them. He was not far from the house when the centurion sent friends to say to him: "Lord, don't trouble yourself, for I do not deserve to have you come under my roof. That is why I did not even consider myself worthy to come to you. But say the word, and my servant will be healed. For I myself am a man under authority, with soldiers under me. I tell this one, 'Go,' and he goes; and that one, 'Come,' and he comes. I say to my servant, 'Do this,' and he does it." When Jesus heard this, he was amazed at him, and turning to the crowd following him, he said, "I tell you, I have not found such great faith even in Israel." Then the men who had been sent returned to the house and found the servant well. LUKE 7:1–10

■

WHY WAS JESUS "AMAZED" at the great faith of the centurion? Jesus did not miss the contrast between the Roman pagan and the Jewish citizens of Capernaum. The citizens told Jesus to help the soldier because "he loves our nation and has built our synagogue." In other words, they were claiming grace based on works. But Jesus provided healing based on the man's faith in his (Jesus') power to heal. The soldier had seen Jesus in action and he had become a believer. He said, "I do not even consider myself worthy to come to you." The Jewish citizens believed grace could be earned, whereas the Roman pagan knew that grace is a gift of God.

Soon afterward, Jesus went to a town called Nain, and his disciples and a large crowd went along with him. As he approached the town gate, a dead person was being carried out—the only son of his mother, and she was a widow. And a large crowd from the town was with her. When the Lord saw her, his heart went out to her and he said, "Don't cry." Then he went up and touched the coffin, and those carrying it stood still. He said, "Young man, I say to you, get up!" The dead man sat up and began to talk, and Jesus gave him back to his mother. They were all filled with awe and praised God. "A great prophet has appeared among us," they said. "God has come to help his people." This news about Jesus spread throughout Judea and the surrounding country. LUKE 7:11–17

■

NAIN IS A SMALL town backed by hills and surrounded by fields that exists to this very day. It is off the beaten path that connects Nazareth and Galilee, so it seems unusual that Jesus would have used this route. But Jesus appeared in this insignificant town at just the right time to perform an astonishing miracle of raising from the dead the only son of a widow. The people understood immediately the significance of what had happened. Remembering the miracles of the great prophets Elijah and Elisha, the people exclaimed, "A great prophet has appeared among us . . . God has come to help his people." Jesus may have been rejected in his hometown, and he was attacked as a threat to the ruling class in Jerusalem, but in this small, out-of-the-way place called Nain, the people saw Jesus for who he really is.

When John heard in prison what Christ was doing, he sent his disciples to ask him, "Are you the one who was to come, or should we expect someone else?" Jesus replied, "Go back and report to John what you hear and see: The blind receive sight, the lame walk, those who have leprosy are cured, the deaf hear, the dead are raised, and the good news is preached to the poor. Blessed is the man who does not fall away on account of me." MATTHEW 11:2–6

■

HEROD WAS HOLDING JOHN the Baptist prisoner. John was in a crisis of doubt because he knew it would be only a matter of time before the executioner would appear. He even sent messengers to ask Jesus if he truly is the Messiah. Jesus replied by saying, in effect, "look beyond my words to the evidence," and then he gave six demonstrations of the power of the Holy Spirit at work through him: The blind see, the lame walk, lepers are cured, the deaf hear, the dead are raised, and the good news is preached. Jesus was telling John that he should not give in to despair: "When you proclaimed, 'Look, the Lamb of God, who takes away the sin of the world,' you were proclaiming the truth about me. I am, indeed, the one 'who was to come.'" (John 1:29)

As John's disciples were leaving, Jesus began to speak to the crowd about John: "What did you go out into the wilderness to see? A reed swayed by the wind? If not, what did you go out to see? A man dressed in fine clothes? No, those who wear fine clothes are in kings' palaces. Then what did you go out to see? A prophet? Yes, I tell you, and more than a prophet. This is the one about whom it is written: "'I will send my messenger ahead of you, who will prepare your way before you.' Truly I tell you, among those born of women there has not risen anyone greater than John the Baptist; yet whoever is least in the kingdom of heaven is greater than he. From the days of John the Baptist until now, the kingdom of heaven has been subjected to violence, and violent people have been raiding it. For all the Prophets and the Law prophesied until John. And if you are willing to accept it, he is the Elijah who was to come. Whoever has ears, let them hear. MATTHEW 11:7–15

■

JESUS TOLD HIS FOLLOWERS that, despite appearances, the kingdom of heaven is forcefully advancing. It would appear that the kingdom was under pressure of defeat and surrender because John the Baptist, who Jesus claimed was greater than all the prophets, had been imprisoned and was threatened with execution. But Jesus said to not be deceived by appearances, for God is at work to reclaim all his people since mankind's fall. It is through Jesus that God's purpose has reached a momentum that nothing in this world, including Satan, can stop. While the disciples remained mostly in the dark, Jesus knew how the story would turn out: first in apparent defeat, but then in victory over sin and death.

To what, then, can I compare the people of this generation? What are they like? They are like children sitting in the marketplace and calling out to each other: 'We played the flute for you, and you did not dance; we sang a dirge, and you did not cry.' For John the Baptist came neither eating bread nor drinking wine, and you say, 'He has a demon.' The Son of Man came eating and drinking, and you say, 'Here is a glutton and a drunkard, a friend of tax collectors and "sinners."' But wisdom is proved right by all her children."
LUKE 7:31–35

■

JESUS WAS SATURATED IN the knowledge of the Scriptures of his time. He knew the Pentateuch, the Prophets, and the wisdom literature of David and Solomon. And better than anyone, he knew that the source of all wisdom is God Himself. We have heard that Solomon asked God for discernment to help him establish right rule in the kingdom of Israel. So when Jesus says, "wisdom will be proved right by all her children," he is saying that the wisdom that comes from God for what is right and just will be proven right by the fruit that comes from the children of wisdom. Elsewhere, Jesus says that he can do nothing without the Father, and that "I am in the Father, and the Father is in me. The words I say to you are not just my own. Rather it is the Father, living in me, who is doing his work" (John 14:10). Jesus is inseparable from God, and all of God's wisdom abides in him. It is through sharing his Holy Spirit with us that we come to possess God's wisdom. And it is by the fruit of that wisdom that we will be known.

Then Jesus began to denounce the cities in which most of his miracles had been performed, because they did not repent. "Woe to you, Korazin! Woe to you, Bethsaida! If the miracles that were performed in you had been performed in Tyre and Sidon, they would have repented long ago in sackcloth and ashes. But I tell you, it will be more bearable for Tyre and Sidon on the day of judgment than for you." **MATTHEW 11:20–22**

■

JESUS PERFORMED MIRACLES IN Korazin and Bethsaida, but the people did not repent; their godlessness was comparable to the Gentile cities of Tyre and Sidon. But when Jesus speaks of the Day of Judgment, he sounds more like the Old Testament prophet Jeremiah than the "meek and mild" Sunday School Jesus of our present time. Had Jesus decided to suddenly take on the characteristics of a wrathful and judgmental God rather than a loving one? Certainly not. Jesus was stating the truth about the people of those towns. It was not that God had condemned them. The truth is they had condemned themselves by their godless actions, just as the people of Jerusalem condemned themselves in Jeremiah's time, even though they had been repeatedly warned to repent.

All things have been committed to me by my Father. No one knows the Son except the Father, and no one knows the Father except the Son and those to whom the Son chooses to reveal him. Come to me, all you who are weary and burdened, and I will give you rest. Take my yoke upon you and learn from me, for I am gentle and humble in heart, and you will find rest for your souls. For my yoke is easy and my burden is light. MATTHEW 11:27–30

■

AS JESUS IS YOKED to the Father, so we need to be yoked to him. When Jesus says, "No one knows the Son except the Father, and no one knows the Father except the Son," he is saying that he is joined to the Father in everything he does and says. Likewise, for those who choose to follow him, Jesus offers the yoke as a form of apprenticeship. When oxen are yoked together, they have double the strength to pull the load. Furthermore, Jesus offers to be the lead to provide direction and purpose. So as the Father is to Jesus so Jesus will be to us, if we will only accept the offer: "Come to me, all you who are weary and burdened, and I will give you rest. Take my yoke upon you and learn from me, for I am gentle and humble of heart, and you will find rest for your souls."

SHE IS A SINNER

Now one of the Pharisees invited Jesus to have dinner with him, so he went to the Pharisee's house and reclined at the table. When a woman who had lived a sinful life in that town learned that Jesus was eating at the Pharisee's house, she brought an alabaster jar of perfume, and as she stood behind him at his feet weeping, she began to wet his feet with her tears. Then she wiped them with her hair, kissed them and poured perfume on them. When the Pharisee who had invited him saw this, he said to himself, "If this man were a prophet, he would know who is touching him and what kind of woman she is—that she is a sinner." LUKE 7:36–39

■

THERE IS AN IRONIC juxtaposition in this account of the sinful woman and the self-righteous Pharisee. Jesus was invited to the Pharisee's house for dinner. This might seem unusual because Jesus had no obvious social cache, but word had spread about his miraculous powers of healing. Then, "a woman who had lived a sinful life" entered the picture. She brought an "alabaster jar of perfume," washed Jesus' feet with her tears, dried them with her hair, and then applied the perfume. It is not clear how the woman gained entry to the Pharisee's house—perhaps he secretly knew her—but publically he showed outrage and contempt that Jesus would allow a sinful woman to touch him. It is the nature of self-righteousness to spot sin and shortcomings in others. It is the nature of God to forgive those who genuinely seek forgiveness.

"Two men owed money to a certain moneylender. One owed him five hundred denarii, and the other fifty. Neither of them had the money to pay him back, so he canceled the debts of both. Now which of them will love him more?" Simon replied, "I suppose the one who had the bigger debt canceled." "You have judged correctly," Jesus said. LUKE 7:41–43

∎

JESUS ADDRESSED THE PHARISEE, "Simon, I have something to tell you," and then he began to teach through a short parable about debt to illustrate a larger point. Jesus asked, who would love a lender more, the person forgiven a large debt or the one forgiven a small debt? The Pharisee answered, "I suppose the one who had the bigger debt cancelled." "You have judged correctly," Jesus said. It is important to remember that with Jesus anyone can be forgiven, no matter how sinful the person has been. That is the will of God. Even the self-righteous Pharisee can be saved. Whether he applies that answer to his own condition is another matter.

Then he turned toward the woman and said to Simon, "Do you see this woman? I came into your house. You did not give me any water for my feet, but she wet my feet with her tears and wiped them with her hair. You did not give me a kiss, but this woman, from the time I entered, has not stopped kissing my feet. You did not put oil on my head, but she has poured perfume on my feet. Therefore, I tell you, her many sins have been forgiven—for she loved much. But he who has been forgiven little loves little." Then Jesus said to her, "Your sins are forgiven." The other guests began to say among themselves, "Who is this who even forgives sins?" Jesus said to the woman, "Your faith has saved you; go in peace."

LUKE 7:44–50

∎

THE WOMAN WAS FORGIVEN much because she loved much. When Jesus said to her, "Your faith has saved you; go in peace," he made a theological point that caused him trouble with the religious leaders. Earlier, when Jesus cured the paralytic in the midst of a crowd of people, the teachers of the law who were present said, "He's blaspheming! Who can forgive sins but God?" (Mark 2:7) While the repentant woman gratefully placed her faith in the Lordship of Jesus Christ, Simon the Pharisee refused to acknowledge that Jesus has the power and authority to forgive sins. He remained blinded by his adherence to his identity as a member of the ruling class.

After this, Jesus traveled about from one town and village to another, proclaiming the good news of the kingdom of God. The Twelve were with him, and also some women who had been cured of evil spirits and diseases: Mary (called Magdalene) from whom seven demons had come out; Joanna the wife of Cuza, the manager of Herod's household; Susanna; and many others. These women were helping to support them out of their own means. LUKE 8:1–3

■

IT IS TRUE THAT women were not considered nearly as important as men in biblical times, yet whether it was Mary, Elizabeth, or Anna at the beginning of Luke's account of Jesus' life, or Mary Magdalene, Joanna, or Susanna later when his ministry became public, women are identified as an irreplaceable part to the story. Luke says that these women and others "were helping to support (Jesus and the Twelve) out of their own means." They were not shadowy background figures but prominent players throughout Jesus' ministry and all the way to Golgotha and the establishment of the Church. In our own time we want to categorize women by gender, but Luke focuses on their giftedness and the importance of their participation in the events surrounding the life and ministry of Jesus Christ.

Then Jesus entered a house, and again a crowd gathered, so that he and his disciples were not even able to eat. When his family heard about this, they went to take charge of him, for they said, "He is out of his mind." And the teachers of the law who came down from Jerusalem said, "He is possessed by Beelzebub! By the prince of demons he is driving out demons." **MARK 3:20–22**

■

JESUS TRAVELED THROUGHOUT THE region of Galilee performing miracles by healing the sick, giving sight to the blind, and even raising a boy from the dead. He did things that proclaimed him to be more than just a prophet or teacher. But his actions stirred up concern even with his own family. They came to take charge of him, for they said, "He is out of his mind." Then some religious leaders slandered him by publically declaring, "The prince of demons possessed him." Who was right? C.S. Lewis said that there could be no neutral ground when it comes to our own response to Jesus. He is either Lord, liar, or lunatic. His family came down on the side of lunatic, and the teachers of the law said that he was a liar because he was possessed by "the father of lies" (John 8:44). But Jesus' actions go far beyond those performed by one who is a teacher or prophet. Later Jesus asked his disciples, "Who do you say that I am?" He is asking us as well. What will it be: Lord, liar, or lunatic?

So Jesus called them and spoke to them in parables: "How can Satan drive out Satan? If a kingdom is divided against itself, that kingdom cannot stand. If a house is divided against itself, that house cannot stand. And if Satan opposes himself and is divided, he cannot stand; his end has come. In fact, no one can enter a strong man's house and carry off his possessions unless he first ties up the strong man. Then he can rob his house." **MARK 3:23–27**

■

KINGDOMS WERE ALL OVER the place in Jesus' time, but did any of them resemble the kingdom of God? Jesus emerged out of nowhere in the early days of his three-year ministry, proclaiming, "The kingdom of God is near" (Mark 1:15). He had quietly invaded the other kingdom—the counterfeit kingdom of Satan—that became possible when the first man and woman gave up their God-given authority to him. Satan's kingdom has been in opposition to God from the beginning. Jesus makes it clear that he has come to destroy Satan's dominion. He says that "from the time of John the Baptist, the kingdom of heaven is forcefully advancing, and forceful men lay hold of it" (Matthew 11:12). We are the foot soldiers who have been authorized by Jesus to establish through the power of the Holy Spirit a new kind of rule based not on subterfuge and domination, but on love, justice, and service. We are under the authority of Christ, through the power of his Holy Spirit, to continue to build, here on earth, the kingdom of God.

Jesus continues, "I tell you the truth, all the sins and blasphemies of men will be forgiven them. But whoever blasphemes against the Holy Spirit will never be forgiven; he is guilty of an eternal sin." He said this because they were saying, "He has an evil spirit." MARK 3:28–30

∎

JESUS SAYS, "WHOEVER BLASPHEMES against the Holy Spirit will never be forgiven; he is guilty of an eternal sin." At this moment the teachers of the law were attacking and rejecting Jesus by claiming he had an evil spirit. But Jesus countered by saying that to blaspheme the Holy Spirit is to reject the true identity of Jesus. To reject Jesus by claiming he has an evil spirit is to reject God, and by doing so we remain in our chronic condition of sin and separation from the God who loves us. "The Father loves the Son and has placed everything in his hands. Whoever believes in the Son has eternal life, but whoever rejects the Son will not see life, for God's wrath remains on him" (John 3:36).

Now Jesus' mother and brothers came to see him, but they were not able to get near him because of the crowd. Someone told him, "Your mother and brothers are standing outside, wanting to see you." He replied, "My mother and brothers are those who hear God's word and put it into practice." LUKE 8:19–21

■

IF MEN AND WOMEN are category builders, Jesus is a category breaker. He asks us to think beyond the normal categories of self or group identification. He refuses to reduce our inherent complexity to what are essentially tribal relationships, such as family, gender, or age. When he says, "My mother and brothers are those who hear God's word and put it into practice," he is cutting across our self-imposed boundaries. He is saying that all people who know the Father and live a life with, through, and in Him are members of his family. He said this even before he began his public ministry, when he remained in Jerusalem after Joseph and Mary left to return home. When they realized their son was not with them, they returned to find him in the Temple with many teachers, impressing them with his extraordinary knowledge. Mary said, "Son, why have you treated us like this? Your father and I have been anxiously searching for you." "Why were you searching for me?" he asked. "Didn't you know I had to be in my Father's house?" (Luke 2:48–49) Jesus understood even then who his real Father is. He sees all relationships through the eyes of his Father.

Then some of the Pharisees and teachers of the law said to him, "Teacher, we want to see a miraculous sign from you." He (Jesus) answered, "A wicked and adulterous generation asks for a miraculous sign! But none will be given it except the sign of the prophet Jonah. For as Jonah was three days and three nights in the belly of a huge fish, so the Son of Man will be three days and three nights in the heart of the earth." MATTHEW 12:38–40

■

THE PHARISEES CONSIDERED THEMSELVES to be the final authority when it came to interpreting the Word of God. But Jesus cut through the pretensions of his inquisitors by saying that those asking for a miraculous sign were indistinguishable from the "wicked and adulterous generation" all around them. The world rather than the Word of God had mastered them. Then Jesus turned to the Book of Jonah to show what was to happen to him. He would be swallowed by death and buried for three days (as Jonah was buried in the belly of a fish in the depths of the sea), and then be raised from the dead and delivered unto life. No one in his presence understood what Jesus was actually prophesying. It was only after Peter and others looked back over their experience with the living Lord that they remembered this prophecy.

"When an evil spirit comes out of a man, it goes through arid places seeking rest and does not find it. Then it says, 'I will return to the house I left.' When it arrives, it finds the house swept clean and put in order. Then it goes and takes seven other spirits more wicked than itself, and they go in and live there. And the final condition of that man is worse than the first." As Jesus was saying these things, a woman in the crowd called out, "Blessed is the mother who gave you birth and nursed you." He replied, "Blessed rather are those who hear the word of God and obey it." LUKE 11:24–28

■

IN GENESIS IT SAYS, "the Lord God formed the man from the dust of the ground and breathed into his nostrils the breath of life, and the man became a living being" (Genesis 2:7). After the fall, however, other spirits entered the hearts of Adam and Eve, and the wickedness and corruption that ensued caused God to grieve over what had become of his creation, for "every inclination of the thoughts of (their hearts were) only evil all the time" (Genesis 6:5). Through this parable of the empty house, Jesus tells us that there is no such thing as a benign empty heart. The human heart needs to be filled up with something, and either it will be the Holy Spirit of God or it will be the "seven other spirits more wicked than (the first spirit), and they will go in and live there."

NINEVEH REPENTED

As the crowds increased, Jesus said, "This is a wicked generation. It asks for a miraculous sign, but none will be given it except the sign of Jonah. For as Jonah was a sign to the Ninevites, so also will the Son of Man be to this generation. The Queen of the South will rise at the judgment with the men of this generation and condemn them; for she came from the ends of the earth to listen to Solomon's wisdom, and now one greater than Solomon is here. The men of Nineveh will stand up at the judgment with this generation and condemn it; for they repented at the preaching of Jonah, and now one greater than Jonah is here." LUKE 11:29–32

■

AGAIN JESUS REFERS TO "this wicked generation." Then he says that no miraculous signs will be given it except the sign of Jonah. What does he mean by this? Nineveh was a large, ancient city known for its wickedness. At first, Jonah refused to go there to preach repentance because he believed there was no way the leaders and citizens of Nineveh would repent and seek reconciliation with God. But the unexpected happened and the king and all the people gave up "their evil and violent ways" (Jonah 3:8) and the city was saved. This is what God is seeking from all generations: Repentance, reconciliation, and new life. God sent one even greater than Jonah to bring restoration to the people of Israel and to all the people of the world.

Jesus spoke all these things to the crowd in parables; he did not say anything to them without using a parable. So was fulfilled what was spoken through the prophet: "I will open my mouth in parables, I will utter things hidden since the creation of the world." MATTHEW 13:34–35

■

HOW DOES GOD COMMUNICATE his story? We know our story: We are born into a family made up of a mother and father, sisters, brothers, relatives, communities, and even nations. But often ours is also a story of conflict and sorrow, sickness and separation. For the world we enter is broken and needs repentance, reconciliation, and restoration. This is where God's story intersects with human history. And that story must be told in the language of the Holy Spirit, which is God's language, the figurative language of metaphor, allegory, and poetry. "This is what we speak, not in words taught us by human wisdom but in the words taught by the Spirit, expressing spiritual truths in spiritual words" (1 Corinthians 2:13). This is the language of the mind and heart of Christ.

GOOD SOIL

Again Jesus began to teach by the lake. The crowd that gathered around him was so large that he got into a boat and sat in it out on the lake, while all the people were along the shore at the water's edge. He taught them many things by parables, and in his teaching said: "Listen! A farmer went out to sow his seed. As he was scattering the seed, some fell along the path, and the birds came and ate it up. Some fell on rocky places, where it did not have much soil. It sprang up quickly, because the soil was shallow. But when the sun came up, the plants were scorched, and they withered because they had no root. Other seed fell among thorns, which grew up and choked the plants, so that they did not bear grain. Still other seed fell on good soil. It came up, grew and produced a crop, multiplying thirty, sixty, or even a hundred times." Then Jesus said, "He who has ears to hear, let him hear." MARK 4:1–9

■

THOUGH WE MAY NOT be farmers or intimately know the cycles of planting and harvesting, we still need not stretch too far to gather the import of what Jesus is teaching. But we do need to slow down a bit so that we can hear God's voice through Jesus' words. Jesus begins by saying, "Listen!" to the crowd that has gathered on the shore of the Sea of Galilee. He wants the people to be fully engaged so that they can hear what God is saying to them through this story of planting and harvesting. Jesus draws a spiritual point from everyday reality. It is as if he is saying that the physical world around us can give us all the examples we need to understand the spiritual principles behind the everyday reality of life, if we will only be attentive.

When he was alone, the Twelve and the others around him (Jesus) asked him about the parables. He told them, "The secret of the kingdom of God has been given to you. But to those on the outside everything is said in parables so that, 'they may be ever seeing but never perceiving, and ever hearing but never understanding; otherwise they might turn and be forgiven!'" Then Jesus said to them, "Don't you understand this parable? How then will you understand any parable?" MARK 4:10–13

■

JESUS WAS PREPARING HIS disciples for ministering to a broken world. He knows that even the chosen people of God turn aside in willful blindness. After being freed from the yoke of slavery in Egypt, after experiencing miracle after miracle in the desert, the Israelites failed time and again to "perceive" and "understand" that the hand of God was guiding them toward freedom. Instead, "They forgot God who saved them, who had done great things in Egypt, miracles in the land of Ham and awesome deeds by the Red Sea" (Psalm 106:21–22). Jesus understood the extreme difficulty of the mission ahead, but he also knows that God is seeking reconciliation with a people who have abandoned him. Jesus wanted his disciples to understand that their mission was to open the hearts of men and women to the true heart of God.

SEED SOWN ALONG THE PATH

The farmer sows the word. Some people are like seed along the path, where the word is sown. As soon as they hear it, Satan comes and takes away the word that was sown in them. **MARK 4:14–15**

■

JESUS REVEALS THAT HE is talking about more than seeds. He clearly states that the seed is a metaphor for the Word of God. God extravagantly sows the earth with his Word, but it does not always land where it can germinate and grow. Sometimes the seed lands on a path where the soil has been hardened by treading feet so that the seed cannot penetrate and have time to grow. Jesus says that Satan can easily find this exposed seed and steal it away. Jesus is saying that many men and women experience the Word of God this way. The seed (or the Word) has not penetrated their hearts, and so it cannot grow. With a heart empty of God's Word, people will, nevertheless, continue to look for solace and identity and so will gather around themselves "a great number of teachers to say what their itching ears want to hear. They will turn their ears away from the truth and turn aside to myths" (2 Timothy 4:3–4).

Others, like seed sown on rocky places, hear the word and at once receive it with joy. But since they have no root, they last only a short time. When trouble or persecution comes because of the word, they quickly fall away. MARK 4:16–17

■

IT IS GOOD TO remember that Jesus was preparing his disciples for a time when "trouble and persecution" would sweep in and test their resolve, even to the point of death. If the Word he planted fell on rocky soil where it could not take root, then at the first sign of adversity, his followers would fall away. And at the moment of true testing, they did fall away. What Jesus is saying here is a prophetic warning, not only to his disciples then, but also to all generations who will face adversity in the days, months, and years to follow.

Still others, like seed sown among thorns, hear the word; but the worries of this life, the deceitfulness of wealth and the desires for other things come in and choke the word, making it unfruitful.
MARK 4:18–19

■

JESUS GIVES US A three-part warning of what can happen if we are blind to the dangers surrounding us. First, Satan can steal the word, leaving us empty and defenseless. Second, the world with all its troubles and persecutions can scatter us. Finally, the flesh, the powerful desires for the things of this life, such as the desire for wealth, power, and status, can "choke the word, making it unfruitful." The enemy of the Word is a multifaceted deceiver. Jesus was born into a warring environment, and he does not expect anything different for those who love and follow him.

Others, like seed sown on good soil, hear the word, accept it, and produce a crop—thirty, sixty or even a hundred times what was sown. MARK 4:20

■

FINALLY, WHEN THE SEED finds good soil, a crop will be produced as much as one hundred times what was sown. The miracle of the earliest days of the church is one of extraordinary increase. Out of an unlikely assortment of men and women, the church grew exponentially throughout the Mediterranean world. Paul saw himself as a conduit of the Holy Spirit as he travelled from place to place spreading the word of God in the name of Jesus Christ. He fully understood the near impossibility of the task, but neither that nor anything else prevented him from working within the design of fruitfulness God blessed him with. "What is Paul? Only servants, through whom you came to believe—as the Lord has assigned to each his task. I planted the seed, Apollos watered it, but God made it grow" (1 Corinthians 3:5–6).

UNDER A BOWL OR A BED?

He said to them, "Do you bring in a lamp to put it under a bowl or a bed? Instead, don't you put it on its stand? For whatever is hidden is meant to be disclosed, and whatever is concealed is meant to be brought out into the open. If anyone has ears to hear, let him hear. Consider carefully what you hear. With the measure you use, it will be measured to you—and even more. Whoever has will be given more; whoever does not have, even what he has will be taken from him." **MARK 4:21–25**

■

JESUS USES FIGURATIVE LANGUAGE to draw a connection between the spiritual and natural worlds. As he used seed to represent the Word of God in the parable of the sower, so here he uses light to represent the wisdom of God. If you have the light, use it. If you have seed, plant it. If we think only in terms of the natural world, we miss the spiritual reality behind everything. The natural world mimics aspects of the spiritual world. Jesus says, open your eyes and your heart to God's spiritual reality all around you and act on that reality. Paul says the same thing in his prayer to the Ephesians: "may (God) give you the Spirit of wisdom and revelation, so that you may know him better. I pray also that the eyes of your heart may be enlightened in order that you may know the hope to which he has called you . . ." (Ephesians 1:17–18).

He also said, "This is what the kingdom of God is like. A man scatters seed on the ground. Night and day, whether he sleeps or gets up, the seed sprouts and grows, though he does not know how. All by itself the soil produces grain—first the stalk, then the head, then the full kernel in the head. As soon as the grain is ripe, he puts the sickle to it, because the harvest has come." **MARK 4:26–29**

■

LIKE THE RELIGIOUS LEADERS of Jesus' time, the modern, scientific "masters of the universe" want to strain miracles out of existence by applying their naturalistic knowledge to the mysteries of the universe, the solar system, and the earth. For them, there is no need to trust in God because God is a human invention, an archaic holdover from an earlier time. But Jesus says it is otherwise. Man did not invent God; God created man, and God has not given up on us, even though we often give up on him. Without God, all explanations come up short. Jesus points to the Creator of all things for understanding the mysteries of this life. He tells us to not trust in our own understanding; rather, trust in God, just as the farmer trusts that the planted seed will produce an abundant crop. Behind all natural phenomena there exists a spiritual reality. Jesus reverses the order of our thinking. The natural world around us is a metaphor for the spiritual reality that has always been and always will be: "God is spirit, and his worshippers must worship in spirit and in truth" (John 4:24).

Jesus told them another parable: "The kingdom of heaven is like a man who sowed good seed in his field. But while everyone was sleeping, his enemy came and sowed weeds among the wheat, and went away. When the wheat sprouted and formed heads, then the weeds also appeared. The owner's servants came to him and said, 'Sir, didn't you sow good seed in your field? Where then did the weeds come from?' 'An enemy did this,' he replied. The servants asked him, 'Do you want us to go and pull them up?' 'No,' he answered, 'because while you are pulling the weeds, you may root up the wheat with them. Let both grow together until the harvest. At that time I will tell the harvesters: First collect the weeds and tie them in bundles to be burned; then gather the wheat and bring it into my barn.'" MATTHEW 13:24–30

■

IN THIS PARABLE JESUS introduces the idea of evil existing side by side with good. Just as man was created in the image of God, he is born into sin as a son or daughter of Adam (Psalm 51:5). The enemy has done his work in the night; weeds have been sowed among the wheat, leaving the owner of the field with a dilemma: Should he pull up the good with the bad? The owner answers with discernment. If he acts precipitously, he will destroy both the wheat and the weeds, both the good and the bad. But if he waits until the crops have grown, he will be able to judge correctly. He will harvest the wheat but will bundle the weeds and have them burned. Jesus says judgment will come in God's good time, but judgment, whenever it arrives, will be tempered by discernment.

Then he left the crowd and went into the house. His disciples came to him and said, "Explain to us the parable of the weeds in the field." He answered, "The one who sowed the good seed is the Son of Man. The field is the world, and the good seed stands for the sons of the kingdom. The weeds are the sons of the evil one, and the enemy who sows them is the devil. The harvest is the end of the age, and the harvesters are angels." MATTHEW 13:36–39

■

THE LANGUAGE JESUS USES to explain his parable of the weeds can create discomfort for many who hear it. He says, "The weeds are the sons of the evil one, and the enemy who sows them is the devil." Part of the problem for us is that Jesus describes the devil as an actual being who is at war with the Son of Man. In our quest to promote our culture of comfort, where conflict is papered over with feel-good thinking, the devil's existence presents an awkward intrusion into the fantasy that the devil himself is a fantasy. C.S. Lewis says that there are two dangers when dealing with the devil: The first is to think too much about him, and the second is to ignore him. Jesus never ignored him, and neither should we.

THE RIGHTEOUS WILL SHINE

As the weeds are pulled up and burned in the fire, so it will be at the end of the age. The Son of Man will send out his angels, and they will weed out of his kingdom everything that causes sin and all who do evil. They will throw them into the fiery furnace, where there will be weeping and gnashing of teeth. Then the righteous will shine like the sun in the kingdom of their Father. He who has ears, let him hear. MATTHEW 13:40–43

■

WHEN WE THINK OF God, do we think of him as love or do we think of him as judge? Most of us would prefer to think of him in terms of love because it is comforting to do so. Judgment can precipitate the fear of being punished for some imagined or real crime. Like the guilty fugitive, we are reduced to living haunted lives as we imagine being chased down for unresolved secret crimes. But God's plan permits a way out. We are all under judgment, but we are also subjects of his love. The answer lies in us: Will we be the wheat to be harvested or will we choose to be the weeds that will be pulled up and burned up before the harvest?

Again Jesus said, "What shall we say the kingdom of God is like, or what parable shall we use to describe it? It is like a mustard seed, which is the smallest of all seeds on earth. Yet when planted, it grows and becomes the largest of all garden plants, with such big branches that the birds can perch in its shade." **MARK 4:30–32**

■

AT FIRST GLANCE IT seems strange to hear Jesus compare the kingdom of God to a mustard seed. At that time, the mustard seed was the smallest of the flowering seeds, tiny in comparison to what it would become. But the people expected God's coming kingdom to be like the kingdoms that had sprouted throughout the world, with the only difference being that the warrior king would be in the line of David. The people of Israel were under the control of Rome and its armies and so they were looking for a geopolitical solution to their captivity. Jesus compared the kingdom of God to something that challenged preconceptions of what would save Israel. He did not come as the warrior king but as something as apparently insignificant as a tiny seed that grows dynamically into "the largest of all the garden plants."

LIKE HIDDEN TREASURE

The kingdom of heaven is like treasure hidden in a field. When a man found it, he hid it again, and then in his joy went and sold all he had and bought that field. **MATTHEW 13:44**

■

FOR A SECOND TIME Jesus offers his followers a better way to understand what the kingdom of God is like. Here he tells of a man who discovers a treasure, hides it, sells all of his own possessions, and then buys the field where the treasure is hidden. He gives up everything to gain something of much greater worth. Jim Elliot, a missionary who lost his life in 1956 while attempting to minister to the Huaorani Indians in Ecuador, wrote a line in his journal before his death that beautifully summarizes what Jesus is teaching us: "He is no fool who gives what he cannot keep to gain that which he cannot lose."

Again, the kingdom of heaven is like a merchant looking for fine pearls. When he found one of great value, he went away and sold everything he had and bought it. MATTHEW 13:45–46

■

JESUS IS GOING TO great lengths to draw us into his understanding of his mission here on earth. His poetic use of language invites listeners into a story and lets their imaginations develop in a way that is different from a lawyer's argument or a scientist's proof. Jesus teaches about a reality that exists beyond the natural realm, but he uses the natural world to illustrate a spiritual point of great importance. In essence, he says that the kingdom of God must always come first: "So do not worry, saying, 'What shall we eat?' or 'What shall we drink?' or 'What shall we wear?' For the pagans run after all these things, and your heavenly Father knows that you need them. But seek first his kingdom and his righteousness and all these things will be given to you as well" (Matthew 6:32–33).

"Once again, the kingdom of heaven is like a net that was let down into the lake and caught all kinds of fish. When it was full, the fishermen pulled it up on the shore. Then they sat down and collected the good fish in baskets, but threw the bad away. This is how it will be at the end of the age. The angels will come and separate the wicked from the righteous and throw them into the fiery furnace, where there will be weeping and gnashing of teeth. Have you understood all these things?" Jesus asked. "Yes," they replied. He said to them, "Therefore every teacher of the law who has been instructed about the kingdom of heaven is like the owner of a house who brings out of his storeroom new treasures as well as old." MATTHEW 13:47–52

■

JESUS USES THIS PARABLE to contrast two very different kingdoms. The kingdom of heaven might also be called the kingdom of light; it is the providence of God, a place of infinite blessings and goodness that will be fully reestablished on the Day of Judgment. But right now the kingdom of the prince of darkness has set itself up as an alternative kingdom, where people "call evil good, who put darkness for light and light for darkness, who put bitter for sweet and sweet for bitter" (Isaiah 5:20). When Jesus speaks about the good fish being chosen and the bad fish being thrown out, he is referring to the time when those who choose evil over good and darkness over light will receive their just reward. If we choose the kingdom of heaven, we will receive the blessings of eternal life with the Father. But if we choose the kingdom of darkness, we will end up where there is endless "weeping and gnashing of teeth." God never sends anyone to hell. That is our choice because God offers an alternative path to every man and woman; he offers the kingdom of heaven through the cross of his Son, Jesus Christ.

WHO IS THIS?

One day Jesus said to his disciples, "Let us go over to the other side of the lake." So they got into a boat and set out. As they sailed, he fell asleep. A squall came down on the lake, so that the boat was being swamped, and they were in great danger. The disciples went and woke him, saying, "Master, Master, we're going to drown!" He got up and rebuked the wind and the raging waters; the storm subsided, and all was calm. "Where is your faith?" he asked his disciples. In fear and amazement they asked one another, "Who is this? He commands even the winds and the water, and they obey him." LUKE 8:22–25

■

WITH THIS STORY WE move from parable to action. Jesus called his disciples to join him for a voyage across the Sea of Galilee to pagan territory. The disciples must have wondered about the purpose of such a dangerous undertaking, but Jesus showed no fear by falling asleep, even as a squall began to overwhelm the vessel and threaten the lives of everyone in it. The disciples, by contrast, experienced extreme fear as the chaos of the storm-driven sea began to swamp the boat. At the moment of greatest danger, Jesus arose and commanded the winds and the raging waters to be still, and the danger immediately subsided. This was not the last time Jesus demonstrated his authority over the dark forces of this world. The disciples did not understand the meaning of what happened on the Sea of Galilee. They asked, "Who is this?" This question continued to arise all the way to the cross. It is asked even to this very day.

AN AFFLICTED REGION

When he arrived at the other side in the region of the Gadarenes, two demon-possessed men coming from the tombs met him. They were so violent that no one could pass that way. "What do you want with us, Son of God?" they shouted. "Have you come here to torture us before the appointed time?" Some distance from them a large herd of pigs was feeding. The demons begged Jesus, "If you drive us out, send us into the herd of pigs." He said to them, "Go!" So they came out and went into the pigs, and the whole herd rushed down the steep bank into the lake and died in the water. Those tending the pigs ran off, went into the town and reported all this, including what had happened to the demon-possessed men. Then the whole town went out to meet Jesus. And when they saw him, they pleaded with him to leave their region. MAT-THEW 8:28–34

■

WHY DID THE PEOPLE of the region of the Gadarenes plead with Jesus to leave? On the surface this seems strange because Jesus miraculously cured the two demon-possessed men who terrorized the region. At the same time Jesus gave permission to the afflicting spirits to enter a herd of pigs that then rushed into the Sea of Galilee and drowned. This loss of livestock cost the people of this wild region a great deal of money, forcing them to chose between God and economic wellbeing. The people of the Gadarenes ultimately decided it was better to live among demonic spirits than risk their economic livelihood, and so they sent Jesus away. Much the same thing happened to Paul in Ephesus when those who profited by the business of creating shrines to the god Artemis discovered that Paul was subverting their business by proclaiming, "man-made gods are no gods at all" (Acts 19:28). Here again, the economy of darkness trumped the light of the Spirit of God.

EVERYTHING IS POSSIBLE FOR
ONE WHO BELIEVES

Jesus asked the boy's father, "How long has he been like this?"
"From childhood," he answered. "It has often thrown him into fire
or water to kill him. But if you can do anything, take pity on us
and help us." "'If you can'?" said Jesus. "Everything is possible for
one who believes." **MARK 9:21–23**

■

JESUS HAS AN UNCANNY ability to speak to our deepest levels of
unbelief. He says, "Everything is possible for one who believes," and
we recoil with our naturalistic preconceptions of what is possible
and what is not. The father had been living with a child afflicted
with what appeared to be epilepsy, and he couched his request for
help with the conditional "if you can" because he despaired of a
miracle. How easy it is to identify with the father's doubt. Our faith
is often circumscribed by the limits of our own idea of the miraculous. When Mary was visited by the angel Gabriel and told what
would take place through her, she replied, "How will this be?" because she was confronted with improbability upon improbability.
The father's doubts and Mary's questions resonate with all of us. We
must grapple with all the reasons for our unbelief. It is a central issue for each one of us.

Immediately the boy's father exclaimed, "I do believe; help me overcome my unbelief!" When Jesus saw that a crowd was running to the scene, he rebuked the impure spirit. "You deaf and mute spirit," he said, "I command you, come out of him and never enter him again." The spirit shrieked, convulsed him violently and came out. The boy looked so much like a corpse that many said, "He's dead." But Jesus took him by the hand and lifted him to his feet, and he stood up. After Jesus had gone indoors, his disciples asked him privately, "Why couldn't we drive it out?" He replied, "This kind can come out only by prayer." **MARK 9:24–29**

■

DO WE MORTALS SEE as Jesus sees? The answer is yes, but with this exception: Jesus sees in full while we see in part. He walked the same earth that we walk and breathed the same air we breathe, but when he encountered this afflicted son and suffering father, he brought the force and full authority of God into the encounter. The father was powerless to overcome his son's sickness. But with Jesus present, hope flooded back into the father's heart, and he exclaimed, "I do believe . . . !" The father also came to realize that alone he was powerless to bring about the good he hoped for, so he pleaded with Jesus to help him overcome his unbelief. What a profound request! This should be everyone's prayer because until we do overcome our unbelief in the Lordship of Jesus Christ, we will remain vulnerable to every false belief that passes by.

They left that place and passed through Galilee. Jesus did not want anyone to know where they were, because he was teaching his disciples. He said to them, "The Son of Man is going to be delivered into the hands of men. They will kill him, and after three days he will rise." But they did not understand what he meant and were afraid to ask him about it. They came to Capernaum. When he was in the house, he asked them, "What were you arguing about on the road?" But they kept quiet because on the way they had argued about who was the greatest. Sitting down, Jesus called the Twelve and said, "Anyone who wants to be first must be the very last, and the servant of all." He took a little child whom he placed among them. Taking the child in his arms, he said to them, "Whoever welcomes one of these little children in my name welcomes me; and whoever welcomes me does not welcome me but the one who sent me." MARK 9:30–37

■

AS JESUS WALKED WITH his disciples, he taught them kingdom principles that starkly contrasted with commonly understood earthly ways of living. The disciples strove to discern who would earn the rank of being first among the followers of Jesus. In our world, it is considered right to strive to be first, whether on the playground, in school and college, or at work. Instead of service and humility, everything comes down to achievement and self-aggrandizement. We race the race to gain the prize that will soon be won by another striver lurking in the wings. In the kingdom of God, we do not need to earn recognition. We are already there; we already belong. We have accepted God's invitation to place our identity in his hands through belief in his Son, Jesus Christ.

DO NOT STOP HIM

"Teacher," said John, "we saw someone driving out demons in your name and we told him to stop, because he was not one of us." "Do not stop him," Jesus said. "For no one who does a miracle in my name can in the next moment say anything bad about me, for whoever is not against us is for us. Truly I tell you, anyone who gives you a cup of water in my name because you belong to the Messiah will certainly not lose their reward." MARK 9:38–41

■

IF JESUS CONSTANTLY POINTS to the kingdom of God, his disciples often provide a worldly counterpoint. Listen to one of the disciples: "Teacher, we saw someone driving out demons in your name and we told him to stop, because he was not one of us." Jesus is not tribal; he does not limit himself to a small inside group. He is not a collector nor is he a possessor of things. He is the opposite, because he is always giving away. Jesus not only represents the kingdom of God here on earth, he lives it. His kingdom is not limited by social identity; he does not exclude anyone who wants to enter. His kingdom is based on the principle of multiplication, not subtraction. So he told his disciples to not exclude those who are seeking a way in, "For no one who does a miracle in my name can in the next moment say anything bad about me, for whoever is not against us is for us."

If anyone causes one of these little ones—those who believe in me—to stumble, it would be better for them if a large millstone were hung around their neck and they were thrown into the sea. If your hand causes you to stumble, cut it off. It is better for you to enter life maimed than with two hands to go into hell, where the fire never goes out. And if your foot causes you to stumble, cut it off. It is better for you to enter life crippled than to have two feet and be thrown into hell. And if your eye causes you to stumble, pluck it out. It is better for you to enter the kingdom of God with one eye than to have two eyes and be thrown into hell, where 'the worms that eat them do not die, and the fire is not quenched.'
MARK 9:42–48

■

EARLIER, JESUS SAID THAT if people are not against us, they must be considered for us, and he continues on to qualify his previous statement by saying, "If anyone causes one of these little ones—those who believe in me—to stumble, it would be better for them if a large millstone where hung around their neck and they were thrown into the sea." This sounds like an exaggeration, but only to the extent that Jesus is accentuating the seriousness of the consequences of misdirecting anyone who has found his or her way to God through belief in His Son. By this statement, Jesus is acknowledging the reality of the spiritual warfare that is always at work in both the earthly and heavenly realms.

As Jesus went on from there, two blind men followed him, calling out, "Have mercy on us, Son of David!" When he had gone indoors, the blind men came to him, and he asked them, "Do you believe that I am able to do this?" "Yes, Lord," they replied. Then he touched their eyes and said, "According to your faith let it be done to you," and their sight was restored. Jesus warned them sternly, "See that no one knows about this." But they went out and spread the news about him throughout the region. While they were going out, a man who was demon-possessed and could not talk was brought to Jesus. And when the demon was driven out, the man who had been mute spoke. The crowd was amazed and said, "Nothing like this has ever been seen in Israel." But the Pharisees said, "It is by the prince of demons that he drives out demons." MATTHEW 9:27–34

■

AFTER THE CATASTROPHE IN the Garden of Eden, much of mankind was afflicted by blindness to the reality of God and an incapacity to hear God's word. Jesus uses his divine powers to open eyes and ears to the reality of God's love, not only for those afflicted with diseases but to all who turn from sin to follow him. But the Pharisees preferred the darkness of their own condition because they saw Jesus as a threat to their comfortable well-being. It is ironic that they falsely accused Jesus of being an instrument of the devil by using the devil's favorite weapon of subversion: lies.

He went to Nazareth, where he had been brought up, and on the Sabbath day he went into the synagogue, as was his custom. He stood up to read, and the scroll of the prophet Isaiah was handed to him. Unrolling it, he found the place where it is written: "The Spirit of the Lord is on me, because he has anointed me to proclaim good news to the poor. He has sent me to proclaim freedom for the prisoners and recovery of sight for the blind, to set the oppressed free, to proclaim the year of the Lord's favor." Then he rolled up the scroll, gave it back to the attendant and sat down. The eyes of everyone in the synagogue were fastened on him. He began by saying to them, "Today this scripture is fulfilled in your hearing." All spoke well of him and were amazed at the gracious words that came from his lips. "Isn't this Joseph's son?" they asked. LUKE 4:16–22

■

THE RESPONSE OF THE people to Jesus in the synagogue in Nazareth established a recurring pattern that continues to this very day. At first Jesus was praised and admired for his gracious words. He read from Isaiah, and the words of the passage were uplifting and hopeful. The reaction was almost one of pride in the local boy who seemed to be on the road to achieving great things by preaching good news to the poor, by proclaiming freedom for the prisoners and sight for the blind, and by releasing the oppressed. Who wouldn't want to help the poor, feed the hungry, and give sight to the blind? This sounds like a program anyone would embrace. But what if the words Jesus quotes from Isaiah had a cost attached? What if Jesus inferred that those in his presence might not agree so readily if they were being asked to lift their own fingers? We will see that the reaction was not as pleasant when Jesus turned the words of Scripture on those listening in the synagogue.

NO PROPHET IS ACCEPTED
IN HIS HOMETOWN

Jesus said to them, "Surely you will quote this proverb to me: 'Physician, heal yourself!' And you will tell me, 'Do here in your hometown what we have heard that you did in Capernaum.'" "Truly I tell you," he continued, "no prophet is accepted in his hometown." LUKE 4:23–24

■

JESUS QUICKLY REJECTED THE identity imposed upon him by the people of Nazareth. They wanted him to perform the same miracles for them that he performed in Capernaum and elsewhere. But their requests had nothing to do with faith, because the people of Nazareth, including members of his own family, had defined Jesus as nothing more than the kid next door who left town and then returned as a success. They could not escape their firmly fixed idea of the boy who had lived, played, and worked among them. They could not accept his true identity because to them it was too improbable. He is the son of Joseph, not the Son of God. They could not overcome their unbelief, and so when Jesus said, "Today this scripture is fulfilled in your hearing," the crowd had no idea what he was telling them. They too suffered from blindness. They simply could not see the truth.

I assure you that there were many widows in Israel in Elijah's time, when the sky was shut for three-and-a-half years and there was a severe famine throughout the land. Yet Elijah was not sent to any of them, but to a widow in Zarephath in the region of Sidon. And there were many in Israel with leprosy in the time of Elisha the prophet, yet not one of them was cleansed—only Naaman the Syrian. All the people in the synagogue were furious when they heard this. They got up, drove him out of the town, and took him to the brow of the hill on which the town was built, in order to throw him off the cliff. But he walked right through the crowd and went on his way. LUKE 4:25–30

■

LIKE JOHN THE BAPTIST before him, Jesus turned the spotlight on the chronic condition of the people of Nazareth. To illustrate that "no prophet is accepted in his hometown," he referenced two great prophets of Israel—Elijah and Elisha—but he could just as easily have mentioned Samuel, Isaiah, Jeremiah, or even John the Baptist. The people of Israel had strayed from God's path: "There is no one righteous, not even one, there is no one who understands, no one who seeks God" (Romans 3:10–11). The people were blind to their own condition, which is why Jesus' pointed to Zarephath the widow and Naaman the Syrian. Jesus is saying that just as in previous times when the people of Israel rejected God and the prophets he sent, God would reject them as well. And as with the Syrian and the widow, both Gentiles, God reaches beyond his own people to fulfill his promise. The crowd in the synagogue reacted by trying to kill the messenger who had brought a message they did not want to hear.

Jesus went through all the towns and villages, teaching in their synagogues, proclaiming the good news of the kingdom and healing every disease and sickness. When he saw the crowds, he had compassion on them, because they were harassed and helpless, like sheep without a shepherd. Then he said to his disciples, "The harvest is plentiful but the workers are few. Ask the Lord of the harvest, therefore, to send out workers into his harvest field." MATTHEW 9:35–38

■

WHY IS THE HARVEST so plentiful? And why are the workers so scarce? It can be difficult to accept the overarching truth that this broken world (and many of the people who inhabit it) is in opposition to God. To switch allegiance from Satan to Jesus is seemingly to ask for trouble, which is what Jesus' disciples discovered. The workers are few because following Jesus can perhaps lead to some very uncomfortable and even dangerous places.

Then Jesus went around teaching from village to village. Calling the Twelve to him, he began to send them out two by two and gave them authority over impure spirits. These were his instructions: "Take nothing for the journey except a staff—no bread, no bag, no money in your belts. Wear sandals but not an extra shirt. Whenever you enter a house, stay there until you leave that town. And if any place will not welcome you or listen to you, leave that place and shake the dust off your feet as a testimony against them." They went out and preached that people should repent. They drove out many demons and anointed many sick people with oil and healed them. **MARK 6:6B–13**

■

WHEN JESUS SENT HIS disciples into the world to preach, he instructed them to travel light. For most of us, our inclination is to cram every last conceivable necessity into the most capacious bags available. We can't seem to help ourselves, because we assume that the physical things we take will, in the end, save the day. Jesus says, be counterintuitive; carry light and trust in God. For the Christian, Jesus is advancing important principles for living a productive kingdom-driven life: Do not depend on things. God will provide. He will provide food, money, and even clothing and shelter when needed. Trust in God and do the work he has called you to do with praise and thanksgiving.

I am sending you out like sheep among wolves. Therefore be as shrewd as snakes and as innocent as doves. Be on your guard; you will be handed over to the local councils and be flogged in the synagogues. On my account you will be brought before governors and kings as witnesses to them and to the Gentiles. But when they arrest you, do not worry about what to say or how to say it. At that time you will be given what to say, for it will not be you speaking, but the Spirit of your Father speaking through you. MATTHEW 10:16–20

■

PREVIOUSLY, JESUS WARNED US that enemies of God exist everywhere and will come against us in force. These enemies represent the kingdom of this world, and they will do everything in their power to stop us from advancing the kingdom of God. But Jesus also says that when we go out into the world and encounter opposition even from "friends," we will never be alone. Even the words we speak will not be our own words, but what we speak will be "the Spirit of your father speaking through you."

Brother will betray brother to death, and a father his child; children will rebel against their parents and have them put to death. You will be hated by everyone because of me, but the one who stands firm to the end will be saved. When you are persecuted in one place, flee to another. Truly I tell you, you will not finish going through the towns of Israel before the Son of Man comes.
MATTHEW 10:21–23

■

THE PICTURE JESUS PAINTS of a world of conflict and misery is troubling because we are often taught that following Jesus means a good life and an easier path, even the reward of wealth. But this idea is neither true nor biblical. The truth is that accepting Jesus will complicate your life in many ways and might even bring on expressions of enmity and persecution. We distort the truth of Jesus' teachings when we try to mold them to the prevailing cultural milieu. Jesus promised a hard road, but he also promised "that you will not finish going through the towns of Israel before the Son of Man comes." Jesus always points beyond natural realities to the spiritual reality of the presence of God working through the Holy Spirit to restore men and women to their right relationship with the Father.

The student is not above the teacher, nor a servant above his master. It is enough for students to be like their teachers, and servants like their masters. If the head of the house has been called Beelzebul, how much more the members of his household! MATTHEW 10:24–25

■

JESUS CONTINUES TO GIVE instruction with what appears to be a truism. He says that the student is not above his teacher, nor is the servant above his master. But what if the teacher is Satan (Beelzebub)? Satan is the archenemy of God; he tried to subvert Jesus in the wilderness, and his own acolytes have opposed Jesus time and again. Jesus warns the disciples (and us) to look beyond the authority of the position to the nature of the person holding that position. Watch out for imposters; they are liars and deceivers. They are wolves in sheep's clothing. They may seem harmless, but Jesus keeps making the point: Be alert and prepared, because you are behind enemy lines.

Taste and see that the Lord is good; blessed is the one who takes refuge in him. Fear the Lord, you his holy people, for those who fear him lack nothing. PSALM 34:8–9

■

WE HAVE BEEN WALKING in Jesus' footsteps now for six months. For the most part he has been developing his ministry in the regions of Galilee. While he was born in the town of Bethlehem, he returned to Nazareth with Joseph and his mother Mary and remained there for most of his youth, living a very ordinary life. But then around the age of thirty, his public ministry materialized almost instantly. We have been witnesses to his extraordinary power to perform miracles, heal the sick, and give sight to the blind. We have sat amongst his followers on a hillside above the Sea of Galilee as he opened up the mysteries of God's Word for all to hear. But now the focus begins to change as "Jesus resolutely set(s) out for Jerusalem" (Luke 9:51). We will set off with him and witness even more astonishing things as he prepares for the events that lie ahead.

Whoever acknowledges me before others, I will also acknowledge before my Father in heaven. But whoever disowns me before others, I will disown before my Father in heaven. Do not suppose that I have come to bring peace to the earth. I did not come to bring peace, but a sword. For I have come to turn a man against his father, a daughter against her mother, a daughter-in-law against her mother-in-law—a man's enemies will be the members of his own household. MATTHEW 10:32–36

■

MEET JESUS THE REALIST. He knows that most will not willingly acknowledge him. He came into a needy and broken world, and he said explicitly that the world itself needs healing because at heart it is sick with sin: "It is not the healthy who need a doctor, but the sick. I have not come to call the righteous, but sinners" (Mark 2:17). The world is at war on every level: Families feud, nations battle nations, and God Himself is warred against. Jesus descended into the middle of this maelstrom, and he knows that many will either disbelieve that he came from God or will reject him because he came from God. But not everyone will fight against Jesus; some will turn and accept "the light of the knowledge of the glory of God in the face of Christ" (2 Corinthians 4:6).

Anyone who loves their father or mother more than me is not worthy of me; anyone who loves their son or daughter more than me is not worthy of me. Whoever does not take up their cross and follow me is not worthy of me. Whoever finds their life will lose it, and whoever loses their life for my sake will find it. MATTHEW 10:37–39

■

IN THIS LIFE THERE are many loves. There are wives, husbands, parents, brothers, sisters, and friends. There is our home and community and nation, and there is even our work. But what is our first love? The second part of the great commandment says: "Love your neighbor as yourself," but this commandment follows the first: "Love the Lord your God with all your heart and with all your soul and with all your mind and with all your strength" (Mark 12:30–31). Genuine love flows directly from our love of God to our families, neighbors, and communities. Never substitute the good for the best. "Whom have I in heaven but you? And earth has nothing I desire besides you. My flesh and my heart may fail, but God is the strength of my heart and my portion forever" (Psalm 73:25–26).

WHAT DOES JESUS MEAN BY "WELCOMES ME"?

Anyone who welcomes you welcomes me, and anyone who welcomes me welcomes the one who sent me. Whoever welcomes a prophet as a prophet will receive a prophet's reward, and whoever welcomes a righteous person as a righteous person will receive a righteous person's reward. And if anyone gives even a cup of cold water to one of these little ones who is my disciple, truly I tell you, that person will certainly not lose their reward. MATTHEW 10:40–42

■

WHEN WE HEAR THE word "connectivity" we often think of the properties of electricity. Without connectivity our computers and appliances would run down and eventually become useless. Here Jesus is simply saying, if someone welcomes you, he welcomes me and also God the Father, who sent me. Jesus uses the word "welcome" to convey a connectedness between a person, a follower of Jesus, Jesus himself, and God. A simple act of kindness or hospitality has cosmic connectivity. We may not always be privy to a full understanding of the consequences of a single act, but we do believe "that in all things God works for the good of those who love him, who have been called according to his purpose" (Romans 8:28).

Now Herod had arrested John and bound him and put him in prison because of Herodias, his brother Philip's wife, for John had been saying to him, "It is not lawful for you to have her." Herod wanted to kill John, but he was afraid of the people, because they considered John a prophet. MATTHEW 14:3–5

■

EVEN BEFORE MARY GAVE birth to Jesus, John was present in the narrative, first in the womb of Elizabeth his mother and then as a prophet attracting large crowds to the Jordan River to hear his proclamation that the time to repent had come. He also came as a witness to testify that one greater than he would soon appear. He said that the one who will follow him "will surpass me because he was before me" (John 1:15). John is considered a prophet in the spirit of Elijah, but once he had fulfilled his mission, he told his disciples, "A man can receive only what is given him from heaven. You yourselves can testify that I said, 'I am not the Christ but am sent ahead of him . . . He must become greater; I must become less'" (John 3:27–28, 30).

A DAUGHTER DANCED

On Herod's birthday the daughter of Herodias danced for the guests and pleased Herod so much that he promised with an oath to give her whatever she asked. Prompted by her mother, she said, "Give me here on a platter the head of John the Baptist." The king was distressed, but because of his oaths and his dinner guests, he ordered that her request be granted and had John beheaded in the prison. His head was brought in on a platter and given to the girl, who carried it to her mother. John's disciples came and took his body and buried it. Then they went and told Jesus. MATTHEW 14:6–12

■

WITH THE BRUTAL MURDER of John the Baptist, we witness the highest level of corrupt political drama imaginable. John had offended the wife of Herod Antipas by publically objecting to her marriage to Herod, because she had been the wife of Herod's living brother, Philip. Finally, through Herodias' insistence, Herod imprisoned John, but he did not execute him. Then, in a moment of drunken folly, Herod promised his wife's daughter that she could have anything she asked for. Herodias seized this moment to exact revenge on her imprisoned nemesis. Salome, the daughter, asked for the head of John on a platter, which put Herod in an impossible position. He had to comply, for to deny the request would have been to put his own position of power in question. So Herodias' lust for revenge was momentarily satisfied. When political power and corruption intersect, human suffering invariably follows.

King Herod heard about this, for Jesus' name had become well known. Some were saying, "John the Baptist has been raised from the dead, and that is why miraculous powers are at work in him." Others said, "He is Elijah." And still others claimed, "He is a prophet, like one of the prophets of long ago." But when Herod heard this, he said, "John, whom I beheaded, has been raised from the dead!" **MARK 6:14–16**

■

THE CRIME THAT COST John the Baptist his life was the crime of proclaiming the truth of God's Word to those who hold political power. John did not deny God to avoid the wrath of a powerful political figure that ultimately cost him his life. Jesus, too, encountered opposition from religious leaders throughout his three-year ministry, but they could not stop him from making his journey to Jerusalem, the seat of political power in Israel. We see both John and Jesus walk through a world steeped in sin and under the protection of the political and religious elites. So naturally, in such a godless place, we should not be surprised that both Jesus and John experienced strong resistance from the very people they came, in very different ways, to save: "Those who hate me without reason, outnumber the hairs of my head; many are my enemies without cause, those who seek to destroy me" (Psalm 69:4).

GIVE THEM SOMETHING TO EAT

When the apostles returned, they reported to Jesus what they had done. Then he took them with him and they withdrew by themselves to a town called Bethsaida, but the crowds learned about it and followed him. He welcomed them and spoke to them about the kingdom of God, and healed those who needed healing. Late in the afternoon the Twelve came to him and said, "Send the crowd away so they can go to the surrounding villages and countryside and find food and lodging, because we are in a remote place here." He replied, "You give them something to eat." They answered, "We have only five loaves of bread and two fish—unless we go and buy food for all this crowd." (About five thousand men were there.) LUKE 9:10–14

■

THE APOSTLES EXCITEDLY RETURNED to Jesus to report on all the things that had happened since they had been sent out. But then Jesus notched it up several levels. They went with Jesus to a remote place near the small town of Bethsaida, but crowds of people followed, causing a crisis. Thousands of people gathered to hear Jesus teach about the kingdom of God, and, for those in need, to experience the miracle of healing. When the apostles sensed the danger of the moment, they advised Jesus to send the people to the surrounding villages for food. The apostles performed miracles themselves, but here their minds reverted to seeking commonsense solutions for earth-bound problems like hunger. They forgot their own history of the exodus from Egyptian slavery, where God intervened supernaturally to supply all the food and drink necessary for survival. The apostles had not fully embraced the truth that all things are possible for God and that he will provide the means. Jesus stretched the boundaries of the possible to overcome the seeming impossibility of the momentary crisis.

(About five thousand men were there.) But he said to his disciples, "Have them sit down in groups of about fifty each." The disciples did so, and everyone sat down. Taking the five loaves and the two fish and looking up to heaven, he gave thanks and broke them. Then he gave them to the disciples to distribute to the people. They all ate and were satisfied, and the disciples picked up twelve basketfuls of broken pieces that were left over. LUKE 9:14–17

■

WITH HIS FEEDING THE five thousand, Jesus shows us that we are dependent creatures. We may flee from this reality, but that does not make our dependence any less real. After conception, we are dependent on our mother's body to sustain our life, and after our birth, we are helpless without the loving protection of our parents. On a larger plain, there could be no life without the sustaining warmth of the sun. In the natural world, interdependence is searched out by scientists who want to discover the secrets behind why the world operates as it does. It turns out, though, that Jesus is that searched-for connection. But he cannot be found if we limit the search to just naturalistic phenomena and explanation. The natural world in all its beauty and complexity is a reflection of the reality of the presence of God everywhere, just as we are creatures who reflect the image of God, not in our form but in our divinely shaped nature, as it was originally given to us.

. . . and the boat was already a considerable distance from land, buffeted by the waves because the wind was against it. Shortly before dawn Jesus went out to them, walking on the lake. When the disciples saw him walking on the lake, they were terrified. "It's a ghost," they said, and cried out in fear. But Jesus immediately said to them, "Take courage! It is I. Don't be afraid." "Lord, if it's you," Peter replied, "tell me to come to you on the water." "Come," he said. Then Peter got down out of the boat, walked on the water and came toward Jesus. But when he saw the wind, he was afraid and, beginning to sink, cried out, "Lord, save me!" Immediately Jesus reached out his hand and caught him. "You of little faith," he said, "why did you doubt?" And when they climbed into the boat, the wind died down. Then those who were in the boat worshiped him, saying, "Truly you are the Son of God." MATTHEW 14:24–33

■

IF WE HAD BEEN among the disciples, would we have said with Peter, "You are the Christ" (Mark 9:29)? Alternatively, would we have said from the storm-tossed boat, "It's a ghost"? The disciples wavered because they were confronted with something that defied common sense and natural law. Men do not walk on water, nor do they feed five thousand people with a few fish and some bread. The disciples were often clueless when it came to accepting Jesus' true identity, even though they were with him almost all the time. As with the disciples, we need to cast aside our willingness to believe in almost anything as a substitute for believing in the Lordship of Jesus Christ. Our human nature demands that we believe, "It's a ghost." Only when the eyes of our hearts open up to the true identity of Jesus will we say, "It's the Lord."

Once the crowd realized that neither Jesus nor his disciples were there, they got into the boats and went to Capernaum in search of Jesus. When they found him on the other side of the lake, they asked him, "Rabbi, when did you get here?" Jesus answered, "Very truly I tell you, you are looking for me, not because you saw the signs I performed but because you ate the loaves and had your fill. Do not work for food that spoils, but for food that endures to eternal life, which the Son of Man will give you. For on him God the Father has placed his seal of approval." Then they asked him, "What must we do to do the works God requires?" Jesus answered, "The work of God is this: to believe in the one he has sent." JOHN 6:24–29

■

"THE WORK OF GOD is this: to believe in the one he has sent." This statement sounds so simple, but consider its implications. One must begin with God: Do we believe he exists, and do we believe he created the heavens and the earth and everything in it? Do we believe that he created human beings in his own image, and do we believe he placed them in an abundant garden where they would have dominion and be able to exercise their own free will with but one exception? And do we believe that the woman and the man were deceived into disobedience and by doing so introduced alienation from God through sin that has carried on through all generations, even to the present day? And finally, do we believe that Jesus Christ is the only Son of God who was sent into this conflicted world to reconcile all men and women to God the Father through the shedding of his blood on a cross? The rulers, authorities, and powers of this dark world would have us believe in anything but the Lordship of Jesus Christ. To believe that Jesus is the Son of God is very real work because so much of the world has lined up against that belief.

So they asked him, "What sign then will you give that we may see it and believe you? What will you do? Our ancestors ate the manna in the wilderness; as it is written: 'He gave them bread from heaven to eat.'" Jesus said to them, "Very truly I tell you, it is not Moses who has given you the bread from heaven, but it is my Father who gives you the true bread from heaven. For the bread of God is the bread that comes down from heaven and gives life to the world." "Sir," they said, "always give us this bread." JOHN 6:30–34

■

AS WITH MATTHEW, MARK, and Luke, John tells the story of Jesus, but with a discernable difference: the language of John's Gospel is figurative and poetic. Rather than saying that God will satisfy our physical hunger and thirst, Jesus says, "It is my Father who gives you the true bread from heaven." Jesus uses language to suggest that he is speaking about something much more important than mere bread. He says that God will provide life through his Son, who is the perfect expression of the heart and mind of God Himself. Just as he told the Samaritan woman that the water he offers is a "spring of water welling up to eternal life," (John 4:14), the bread from heaven "comes down from heaven and gives life to the world." This figurative use of language is the way that Jesus indicates the presence of the Holy Spirit of God in all things. The language of man, taken alone, is insufficient to communicate the majesty and mystery of God: "Oh, the depth of the riches of the wisdom and knowledge of God! How unsearchable his judgments, and his paths beyond tracing out!" (Romans 11:33) John not only tells us what happens, he shows us through Jesus' use of language how the living Spirit of God is the animating reality behind life itself.

I AM THE BREAD OF LIFE

Then Jesus declared, "I am the bread of life. Whoever comes to me will never go hungry, and whoever believes in me will never be thirsty. But as I told you, you have seen me and still you do not believe. All those the Father gives me will come to me, and whoever comes to me I will never drive away. For I have come down from heaven not to do my will but to do the will of him who sent me. And this is the will of him who sent me, that I shall lose none of all those he has given me, but raise them up at the last day. For my Father's will is that everyone who looks to the Son and believes in him shall have eternal life, and I will raise them up at the last day." JOHN 6:35–40

■

WHEN MOSES ENCOUNTERED GOD in the desert, he asked God what he should say when asked who sent him. God replied, "I AM WHO I AM. This is what you are to say to the Israelites: 'I AM has sent me to you'" (Exodus 3:14). By saying, "I am the bread of life," Jesus connects himself directly to the sustainer of all life. There is no equivocation here. Jesus boldly proclaims his direct kinship to God the Father, and by doing so, he subjects himself to the accusation that he is a blasphemer. Jesus reinforces this claim by saying, "For I have come down from heaven not to do my will but to do the will of him who sent me." At the same time, he tells us directly the purpose of the Father in sending him: "For my Father's will is that everyone who looks to the Son and believes in him shall have eternal life, and I shall raise them up at the last day."

THIS BREAD IS MY FLESH

At this the Jews there began to grumble about him because he said, "I am the bread that came down from heaven." They said, "Is this not Jesus, the son of Joseph, whose father and mother we know? How can he now say, 'I came down from heaven'?" "Stop grumbling among yourselves," Jesus answered. "No one can come to me unless the Father who sent me draws them, and I will raise them up at the last day. It is written in the Prophets: 'They will all be taught by God.' Everyone who has heard the Father and learned from him comes to me. No one has seen the Father except the one who is from God; only he has seen the Father. Very truly I tell you, the one who believes has eternal life. I am the bread of life. Your ancestors ate the manna in the wilderness, yet they died. But here is the bread that comes down from heaven, which anyone may eat and not die. I am the living bread that came down from heaven. Whoever eats this bread will live forever. This bread is my flesh, which I will give for the life of the world." JOHN 6:41–51

■

HOW DO YOU IDENTIFY yourself? Is it by name? Or is it by your association to family or community or even to work or wealth? It is easy for any of us to fall into the identity others have foisted upon us, but this is not the case with Jesus. He does not allow himself to be wedged into any of the normal reductionist categories. Just the opposite: Jesus constantly reframes his identity beyond the normal definitions of family and town. He wants us to see that he existed with the Father in heaven prior to the incarnation. He is the Son, and he is on a life-saving mission. Later, in Jerusalem, he confirms this relationship with the Father when he prays, "Father, glorify me in your presence with the glory I had with you before the world began" (John 17:5).

A DIFFICULT TEACHING

Jesus said to them, "Very truly I tell you, unless you eat the flesh of the Son of Man and drink his blood, you have no life in you. Whoever eats my flesh and drinks my blood has eternal life, and I will raise them up at the last day. For my flesh is real food and my blood is real drink. Whoever eats my flesh and drinks my blood remains in me, and I in them. Just as the living Father sent me and I live because of the Father, so the one who feeds on me will live because of me. This is the bread that came down from heaven. Your ancestors ate manna and died, but whoever feeds on this bread will live forever." He said this while teaching in the synagogue in Capernaum. JOHN 6:53–59

■

IF JESUS' INTENT IS to startle, then he succeeds when he says, "Whoever eats my flesh and drinks my blood remains in me, and I in them." It is important to remember, though, that Jesus often speaks figuratively. This is an instance where he is prefiguring the Eucharist, where the bread is the body of Christ and the wine his blood. Jesus says that we need to ingest this bread and this wine to become one with him, just as he is one with the Father. "Just as the living Father sent me and I live because of the Father, so the one who feeds on me will live because of me."

On hearing it, many of his disciples said, "This is a hard teaching. Who can accept it?" Aware that his disciples were grumbling about this, Jesus said to them, "Does this offend you? Then what if you see the Son of Man ascend to where he was before! The Spirit gives life; the flesh counts for nothing. The words I have spoken to you—they are full of the Spirit and life. Yet there are some of you who do not believe." For Jesus had known from the beginning which of them did not believe and who would betray him. He went on to say, "This is why I told you that no one can come to me unless the Father has enabled them." From this time many of his disciples turned back and no longer followed him. "You do not want to leave too, do you?" Jesus asked the Twelve. Simon Peter answered him, "Lord, to whom shall we go? You have the words of eternal life. We have come to believe and to know that you are the Holy One of God." JOHN 6:60–69

■

HERE WE CONCLUDE A series of passages from the Gospel of John that seem to set Jesus apart from many of his followers. These followers said, in effect, that Jesus is a crazy man speaking of crazy things, and they were put off by it. They could no longer follow him, and so they left. It is no different today. Jesus is truly revolutionary. He asks each of us to do the most uncomfortable thing in this world: Break from our past allegiances and follow him. It is hard, very hard, and we become exhausted trying to overcome our predisposition not to follow. But despite this, Jesus says, "Come to me, all you who are weary and burdened, and I will give you rest. Take my yoke upon you and learn from me, for I am gentle and humble in heart, and you will find rest for your souls. For my yoke is easy and my burden is light" (Matthew 11:28–30). Peter was right when he asked, "Lord, to whom shall we go?" He asked not only for himself, but for us too.

MERELY HUMAN RULES

The Pharisees and some of the teachers of the law who had come from Jerusalem gathered around Jesus and saw some of his disciples eating food with hands that were defiled, that is, unwashed. (The Pharisees and all the Jews do not eat unless they give their hands a ceremonial washing, holding to the tradition of the elders. When they come from the marketplace they do not eat unless they wash. And they observe many other traditions, such as the washing of cups, pitchers and kettles.) So the Pharisees and teachers of the law asked Jesus, "Why don't your disciples live according to the tradition of the elders instead of eating their food with defiled hands?" He replied, "Isaiah was right when he prophesied about you hypocrites; as it is written: 'These people honor me with their lips, but their hearts are far from me. They worship me in vain; their teachings are merely human rules.' You have let go of the commands of God and are holding on to human traditions."
MARK 7:1–8

■

ONCE AGAIN, JESUS MAKES a distinction that if applied will lead to a truly God-centered life. Jesus says, quoting Isaiah, that the religious leaders have replaced the commands of God with human traditions. He calls them hypocrites because they force their rules on the people but don't live by them themselves: "'These people honor me with their lips, but their hearts are far from me'" (Isaiah 29:13). The leaders had departed so far from God's path that they transformed God's principles for a better life into a set of impossible rules and regulations of a burdened life.

And Jesus continued, "You have a fine way of setting aside the commands of God in order to observe your own traditions! For Moses said, 'Honor your father and mother,' and, 'Anyone who curses their father or mother is to be put to death.' But you say that if anyone declares that what might have been used to help their father or mother is Corban (that is, devoted to God)—then you no longer let them do anything for their father or mother. Thus you nullify the word of God by your tradition that you have handed down. And you do many things like that." **MARK 7:9–13**

■

AS WE CONTINUE IN this passage from Mark's Gospel, we see Jesus elaborate on his teaching on the liberating nature of God's law. The law was given to guide all troubled and blinded people back to the better way, but over time, as Jesus points out, man's traditions began to become substitutes for God's Word. Jesus came from God to reestablish what has always been true: God created men and women with the free will to accept God's gift of love or to reject it. But with rejection comes tragic consequences, which all of us struggle with every day. Human traditions do not liberate, but they can enslave. Jesus does not want to abolish the law; he has come to fulfill it, and by doing so, he offers everyone a pathway to true freedom (Matthew 5:17–20).

Again Jesus called the crowd to him and said, "Listen to me, everyone, and understand this. Nothing outside a person can defile them by going into them. Rather, it is what comes out of a person that defiles them." After he had left the crowd and entered the house, his disciples asked him about this parable. "Are you so dull?" he asked. "Don't you see that nothing that enters a person from the outside can defile them? For it doesn't go into their heart but into their stomach, and then out of the body." (In saying this, Jesus declared all foods clean.) He went on: "What comes out of a person is what defiles them. For it is from within, out of a person's heart, that evil thoughts come—sexual immorality, theft, murder, adultery, greed, malice, deceit, lewdness, envy, slander, arrogance and folly. All these evils come from inside and defile a person."
MARK 7:14–23

■

NEARLY ALL THE GREAT poets and writers, from Shakespeare to Dostoyevsky to Tolstoy, draw their inspiration from biblical truth discovered in passages like this one. Jesus provides us with an insight into the condition of the broken human heart, where all kinds of evil inclinations bubble over into evil thoughts that lead to destructive action. This condition, untreated, is fatal. Jesus came to cauterize the human heart so that out of such a heart will flow thoughts and passions that mirror God's thoughts and passions. It is for this purpose that God sent Jesus into the world. The peace Jesus speaks of is not a political or societal peace, it is the peace that Paul proclaims in his letter to the Romans: "What a wretched man that I am! Who will rescue me from this body of death? Thanks be to God—through Jesus Christ our Lord!" (Romans 7:24–25)

Jesus left there and went along the Sea of Galilee. Then he went up on a mountainside and sat down. Great crowds came to him, bringing the lame, the blind, the crippled, the mute and many others, and laid them at his feet; and he healed them. The people were amazed when they saw the mute speaking, the crippled made well, the lame walking and the blind seeing. And they praised the God of Israel. MATTHEW 15:29–31

■

THE CONTRAST IS STARK. The setting is the Sea of Galilee, a place of sweeping beauty with low-lying mountains that surround the sea and a breeze that cools the land. Into such a place came people who were lame, blind, crippled, and mute to be healed by the one who came to heal all. The broken condition of man, with all of its suffering, is out of place here. It was not meant to be this way. The place and the people were meant to be in harmony with one another, and so Jesus performed the miracle of healing. The mute spoke, the crippled were made well, the lame walked, and the blind were given sight. "And they praised the God of Israel." Once again, Jesus revealed through his power to heal that he is all about the restoration of the true kingdom, where harmony exists between God and man.

A WICKED AND ADULTEROUS GENERATION

The Pharisees and Sadducees came to Jesus and tested him by asking him to show them a sign from heaven. He replied, "When evening comes, you say, 'It will be fair weather, for the sky is red,' and in the morning, 'Today it will be stormy, for the sky is red and overcast.' You know how to interpret the appearance of the sky, but you cannot interpret the signs of the times. A wicked and adulterous generation looks for a sign, but none will be given it except the sign of Jonah." Jesus then left them and went away.
MATTHEW 16:1–4

■

IN CONTRAST TO THE vision of God's kingdom that we experienced on the mountainside above the Sea of Galilee, we now see Jesus confronted by the ruling class. These were the people who expropriated all the levers of power and misused that power to take over the system for their own advantage. Jesus challenged their authority by saying that while they may have knowledge and even natural wisdom born of experience, they cannot see clearly because they look at all things through the eyes of the world they are immersed in. They had no spiritual discernment because they were part of a "wicked and adulterous generation." Spiritual discernment means that any knowledge and wisdom one possesses is always exercised in cooperation with God. The ruling Pharisees and Sadducees were in opposition to Jesus, and therefore they were in opposition to God.

Once when Jesus was praying in private and his disciples were with him, he asked them, "Who do the crowds say I am?" They replied, "Some say John the Baptist; others say Elijah; and still others, that one of the prophets of long ago has come back to life." "But what about you?" he asked. "Who do you say I am?" Peter answered, "God's Messiah." LUKE 9:18–21

■

"BUT WHAT ABOUT YOU? Who do you say I am?" Peter answered the question, but have we? Christianity is not about groups or denominations, it is built on an individual's belief that Jesus is the Messiah, the Anointed One of God. This belief is the building block of the church, and the power of this belief moves the corporate body of the church to reach out to the world, near and far, to proclaim the truth that Jesus Christ is Lord. As Jesus called his disciples to follow even before belief could become the springboard to action, so too we are called so that through our belief in Jesus as Lord, we can act with the authority of the Holy Spirit in a world that needs to hear and know the truth.

He then began to teach them that the Son of Man must suffer many things and be rejected by the elders, the chief priests and the teachers of the law, and that he must be killed and after three days rise again. He spoke plainly about this, and Peter took him aside and began to rebuke him. But when Jesus turned and looked at his disciples, he rebuked Peter. "Get behind me, Satan!" he said. "You do not have in mind the concerns of God, but merely human concerns." **MARK 8:31–33**

■

ONE MOMENT PETER WAS inspired to proclaim Jesus "God's Messiah," but then in another he went off the rails, causing Jesus to rebuke him. What happened? Peter had his own preconception of what God's Messiah was meant to be. Peter believed that the Messiah had come to liberate Israel from the iron yoke of Roman domination, but Jesus corrected Peter by saying he had reduced Jesus to a narrow, human understanding of the Messiah's mission. Peter may have been thinking of Daniel's revelation, but Jesus pointed to the suffering servant of Isaiah when he said, "the Son of Man must suffer many things and be rejected . . ." Peter moved from brilliant insight to missing the mark completely, which should serve as a cautionary tale for anyone who believes they have the inside track in discerning the mind of God by using "mere human concerns" as the basis for interpretation.

Then he called the crowd to him along with his disciples and said: "Whoever wants to be my disciple must deny themselves and take up their cross and follow me. For whoever wants to save their life will lose it, but whoever loses their life for me and for the gospel will save it. What good is it for someone to gain the whole world, yet forfeit their soul? Or what can anyone give in exchange for their soul? If anyone is ashamed of me and my words in this adulterous and sinful generation, the Son of Man will be ashamed of them when he comes in his Father's glory with the holy angels." And he said to them, "Truly I tell you, some who are standing here will not taste death before they see that the kingdom of God has come with power." MARK 8:34–9:1

■

IT IS DIFFICULT FOR us to hear these words: "Whoever wants to be my disciple must deny themselves and take up their cross and follow me." Our culture, from our families and communities to our finest institutions, preaches of pathways that promote self-advancement and self-actualization. If their assumption is that this life is the only game in town, then they might be right. But Jesus sees beyond this narrow understanding of life and death on Earth. He is thinking beyond the City of Man to the City of God. As inhabitants of this Earth, Jesus wants us to balance the necessities of this life with the necessities of the next.

LISTEN TO HIM

About eight days after Jesus said this, he took Peter, John and James with him and went up onto a mountain to pray. As he was praying, the appearance of his face changed, and his clothes became as bright as a flash of lightning. Two men, Moses and Elijah, appeared in glorious splendor, talking with Jesus. They spoke about his departure, which he was about to bring to fulfillment at Jerusalem. Peter and his companions were very sleepy, but when they became fully awake, they saw his glory and the two men standing with him. As the men were leaving Jesus, Peter said to him, "Master, it is good for us to be here. Let us put up three shelters—one for you, one for Moses and one for Elijah." (He did not know what he was saying.) While he was speaking, a cloud appeared and covered them, and they were afraid as they entered the cloud. A voice came from the cloud, saying, "This is my Son, whom I have chosen; listen to him." When the voice had spoken, they found that Jesus was alone. The disciples kept this to themselves and did not tell anyone at that time what they had seen.
LUKE 9:28–36

■

IN EXODUS, MOSES WENT to the mountain to receive the Law. Elijah received the Word of God on Horeb, the mountain of God (1 Kings 19). Here on the Mount of Transfiguration in the company of Moses and Elijah, Jesus was commissioned and strengthened to go forward with God's mission. He received everything he would need, and the voice of God proclaimed to Peter, John, and James, "This is my Son, whom I have chosen; listen to him." This is a turning point. Next Jesus set his sights on another high place, called Golgotha, where he will glorify God by giving his own life for many.

When they came to the crowd, a man approached Jesus and knelt before him. "Lord, have mercy on my son," he said. "He has seizures and is suffering greatly. He often falls into the fire or into the water. I brought him to your disciples, but they could not heal him." "You unbelieving and perverse generation," Jesus replied, "how long shall I stay with you? How long shall I put up with you? Bring the boy here to me." Jesus rebuked the demon, and it came out of the boy, and he was healed at that moment. Then the disciples came to Jesus in private and asked, "Why couldn't we drive it out?" He replied, "Because you have so little faith. Truly I tell you, if you have faith as small as a mustard seed, you can say to this mountain, 'Move from here to there,' and it will move. Nothing will be impossible for you." **MATTHEW 17:14–20**

■

INTERESTINGLY, JESUS' CLAIM THAT through faith we can move mountains may not be quite as outlandish as it first sounds. Herod, the great and brutal king of Israel, was known in his time as a prolific builder. He built the seaside city of Caesarea to honor Caesar, his political master in Rome, and he also built many other buildings and temples. But one of his greatest projects was a fortress that he called Herodium. It still stands today outside of Bethlehem, and is not far from Jerusalem itself. Herod had to literally move a mountain to construct this fortress. It stands as the highest point in the vicinity, and it would have been known to the people of Jesus' time. Rather than use hyperbole to make his point, Jesus may have drawn his example from a very real event of recent history where a mountain was moved by the will of one man who had the political and financial power to move it. The power to move mountains is even truer in the kingdom of God.

They left that place and passed through Galilee. Jesus did not want anyone to know where they were, because he was teaching his disciples. He said to them, "The Son of Man is going to be delivered into the hands of men. They will kill him, and after three days he will rise." But they did not understand what he meant and were afraid to ask him about it. They came to Capernaum. When he was in the house, he asked them, "What were you arguing about on the road?" But they kept quiet because on the way they had argued about who was the greatest. MARK 9:30–32

■

THE DISCIPLES SEEMED LOST when Jesus said that he would be delivered into the hands of men, be killed by them, and then after three days rise. Could it be that their perplexity grew out of Jesus identifying himself as the "Son of Man"? While Isaiah identified the Messiah as the Suffering Servant, Daniel described this "son of man" as a conquering warrior: "In my vision at night I looked, and there before my eyes was one like a son of man, coming with the clouds of heaven . . . He was given authority, glory and sovereign power; all peoples, nations and men of every language worshipped him" (Daniel 7:13–14). If this was the lens the disciples used to identify Jesus as the Messiah, then it is understandable why they were confused. They glossed over Isaiah's Messiah, who would come as the Suffering Servant (Isaiah 53). Jesus says the Suffering Servant must come first, then there will be a second coming at the end of times, which is described in both Daniel and Revelation. The disciples narrowed the Son of Man to their own interpretation, leaving aside the more complete picture. Their narrow lens distorted their understanding of what was actually happening.

WHO IS THE GREATEST?

An argument started among the disciples as to which of them would be the greatest. Jesus, knowing their thoughts, took a little child and had him stand beside him. Then he said to them, "Whoever welcomes this little child in my name welcomes me; and whoever welcomes me welcomes the one who sent me. For it is the one who is least among you all who is the greatest." LUKE 9:46–48

■

THE ARGUMENT AMONG THE disciples about who would be considered the greatest represents the world's point of view on almost every subject. We strive for money, position, and awards so that others will officially see the greatness that we see in ourselves. Jesus told his disciples plainly that this striving is upside down. The world can offer all kinds of recognition, just as Satan attempted to offer Jesus all the kingdoms of this world. But the kingdom of heaven is not about awards; it is about grace. It is not about what we do; it is about what animates what we do. After the resurrection, Jesus restored Peter by asking a very simple question three times: "Do you truly love me?" (John 21:16) He was not asking if Peter truly loved these other disciples or even himself. He was asking the one essential question everyone must eventually answer: Do you love the Lord your God with all your heart, with all your soul, with all your strength, and with all your mind?

DO NOT STOP HIM

He took a little child whom he placed among them. Taking the child in his arms, he said to them, "Whoever welcomes one of these little children in my name welcomes me; and whoever welcomes me does not welcome me but the one who sent me." "Teacher," said John, "we saw someone driving out demons in your name and we told him to stop, because he was not one of us." "Do not stop him," Jesus said. "For no one who does a miracle in my name can in the next moment say anything bad about me, for whoever is not against us is for us. Truly I tell you, anyone who gives you a cup of water in my name because you belong to the Messiah will certainly not lose their reward." MARK 9:36–41

■

C.S. LEWIS MUST HAVE been thinking of this passage when he wrote, "There must be a real giving up of the self . . . As long as your own personality is what you are bothering about you are not going to Him at all. The very first step is to try to forget about the self altogether" (*Mere Christianity*). Jesus continues to teach kingdom principles. The disciples fell into the trap of tribal exclusion. They said that if someone was not part of the group, then that person must be against them. Jesus cut through this artificially constructed barrier by saying, "whoever is not against us is for us." Jesus is all about inclusion; he wants no one to miss the chance for salvation.

GOD IS NOT WILLING
THAT ANY SHOULD PERISH

What do you think? If a man owns a hundred sheep, and one of them wanders away, will he not leave the ninety-nine on the hills and go to look for the one that wandered off? And if he finds it, truly I tell you, he is happier about that one sheep than about the ninety-nine that did not wander off. In the same way your Father in heaven is not willing that any of these little ones should perish.
MATTHEW 18:12–14

■

IN JESUS' TIME, WHEN a shepherd contracted to take care of a flock, it was implicitly agreed that he would be responsible for returning eighty percent of the number he began with. It was understood that some would be lost, some stolen, and some eaten by predators. Only in the rarest of cases would a shepherd leave the ninety-nine to look for one lost sheep. But God is not like the contract shepherd; he will leave the safe ones to seek and find the one lost sheep, and so it is for each one of us. The church was built for seeking lost sheep, and Jesus is the model. He excluded no one who sought to be healed. The beggar called out, "Lord, have mercy on me, a sinner," and Jesus restored his sight. The church operates on this model as well; it is the one institution that exists for its "not yet" members. Jesus' command for each and every one of us as members of his body is "go and seek the lost."

After this, Jesus went around in Galilee. He did not want to go about in Judea because the Jewish leaders there were looking for a way to kill him. But when the Jewish Festival of Tabernacles was near, Jesus' brothers said to him, "Leave Galilee and go to Judea, so that your disciples there may see the works you do. No one who wants to become a public figure acts in secret. Since you are doing these things, show yourself to the world." For even his own brothers did not believe in him. Therefore Jesus told them, "My time is not yet here; for you any time will do. The world cannot hate you, but it hates me because I testify that its works are evil. You go to the festival. I am not going up to this festival, because my time has not yet fully come." After he had said this, he stayed in Galilee. JOHN 7:1–9

■

BY DECLARING, "MY TIME has not yet fully come," Jesus told his followers (and us) that he does not operate on his own. He must wait on his Father's word. Many times before Jesus said, "I go where the Father is going, I do what the Father does and I say what the Father is saying." Jesus sees himself completely woven into his Father's narrative and will do his Father's will only when the Father commands him to act. If Jesus is commanded to wait, he will wait; if commanded to go, he will go. Apart from the Father he can do nothing.

JESUS APPOINTED SEVENTY-TWO

After this the Lord appointed seventy-two others and sent them two by two ahead of him to every town and place where he was about to go. He told them, "The harvest is plentiful, but the workers are few. Ask the Lord of the harvest, therefore, to send out workers into his harvest field. Go! I am sending you out like lambs among wolves. Do not take a purse or bag or sandals; and do not greet anyone on the road." LUKE 10:1–4

■

JESUS COMMISSIONED SEVENTY-TWO DISCIPLES to go out into a forbidding world that he compares to a place where wolves prey upon lambs. Jesus was also looking ahead to the time when others must labor in the fields of the lost. He not only commissioned the seventy-two, but also all who believe in him from that time to this: "Ask the Lord of the harvest, therefore, to send out workers into his harvest field." But it is not just about workers; it is about you and me. The workers are few; the harvest is plentiful; the time is now.

I HAVE GIVEN YOU AUTHORITY

The seventy-two returned with joy and said, "Lord, even the demons submit to us in your name." He replied, "I saw Satan fall like lightning from heaven. I have given you authority to trample on snakes and scorpions and to overcome all the power of the enemy; nothing will harm you. However, do not rejoice that the spirits submit to you, but rejoice that your names are written in heaven." At that time Jesus, full of joy through the Holy Spirit, said, "I praise you, Father, Lord of heaven and earth, because you have hidden these things from the wise and learned, and revealed them to little children. Yes, Father, for this is what you were pleased to do." LUKE 10:17–21

■

IT IS HARD TO avoid the truth that evil exists in the world. Jesus gives us a brief glimpse of how evil came to be when he says, "I saw Satan fall like lightening from heaven." Through multiple passages in the Bible, we can reconstruct a picture of what happened even before the creation of mankind. We know that Satan was an angel, that he had followers, that he rebelled against God, that he was banished from heaven, and that he fell to earth, where he began to plot his own restoration. As an angel of God, Satan existed before God created Adam and Eve and he existed before Eden. Satan entered Eden to frustrate and destroy on earth what he could not destroy in heaven. Jesus was sent to earth to do just the opposite: He came to restore the broken relationship between men and women and God. By saying that he saw Satan fall from heaven, Jesus is clearly identifying himself as the Son of God. He was there before time, as we understand it, existed.

Jesus then left that place and went into the region of Judea and across the Jordan. Again crowds of people came to him, and as was his custom, he taught them. **MARK 10:1**

■

AS LONG AS JESUS stayed in Galilee, he did not represent an extraordinary threat to the religious authorities. But then he crossed the Jordan and entered Judea, and the crowds followed him. While the Pharisees and Sadducees did not make themselves known here, it did not take long for Jesus to attract their attention. As long as he appeared to be an itinerate preacher, they dismissed him as nothing more problematic than an irritating nobody. But as he drew near to Jerusalem, their dismissive attitude was transformed into concern, and once they perceived him as a threat, they pulled all the levers of political power to bring him down.

As they were walking along the road, a man said to him, "I will follow you wherever you go." Jesus replied, "Foxes have dens and birds have nests, but the Son of Man has no place to lay his head." He said to another man, "Follow me." But he replied, "Lord, first let me go and bury my father." Jesus said to him, "Let the dead bury their own dead, but you go and proclaim the kingdom of God." Still another said, "I will follow you, Lord; but first let me go back and say goodbye to my family." Jesus replied, "No one who puts a hand to the plow and looks back is fit for service in the kingdom of God." LUKE 9:57–62

■

WHAT DOES IT MEAN to be a disciple? Jesus does not give us the answer we may want to hear. It is easy to say, "I am a Christian," but what if being a Christian means giving up the comforts of home or family? What if it means being called into an entirely new identity, where we cannot rely on the experiences of the past or the dreams of the future but must embrace the present moment with the life that Christ has called us to live? "Foxes have dens and birds have nests, but the Son of Man has no place to lay his head." This is exactly what discipleship might look like to any of us. If this is uncomfortable, then we might re-examine the things we truly value as we live the life we have been given.

However, after his brothers had left for the Feast, he went also, not publicly, but in secret. Now at the Feast the Jews were watching for him and asking, "Where is that man?" Among the crowds there was widespread whispering about him. Some said, "He is a good man." Others replied, "No, he deceives the people." But no one would say anything publicly about him for fear of the Jews.
JOHN 7:10–13

■

HERE IS A QUESTION that has challenged people from Christ's time to our own: Who is this man? Jesus asked his own disciples, "Who do you say I am?" (Mark 9:29) In Jerusalem, controversy swirled around Jesus. Some called him a good man while others called him a deceiver. The Gospel writers were not afraid to report that during the time of his ministry, as many opposed and dismissed him as embraced him. At one point even his own mother and brothers came to believe he might be unbalanced (Mark 3:31-35), and at another, the adoring crowds tried to make him an earthly king by force (John 6:15). But we need to ask, would it be any different today? Would we recognize him and praise him, or would we dismiss him as a charlatan, or even worse?

Not until halfway through the festival did Jesus go up to the temple courts and begin to teach. The Jews there were amazed and asked, "How did this man get such learning without having been taught?" Jesus answered, "My teaching is not my own. It comes from the one who sent me. Anyone who chooses to do the will of God will find out whether my teaching comes from God or whether I speak on my own. Whoever speaks on their own does so to gain personal glory, but he who seeks the glory of the one who sent him is a man of truth; there is nothing false about him. Has not Moses given you the law? Yet not one of you keeps the law. Why are you trying to kill me?" "You are demon-possessed," the crowd answered. "Who is trying to kill you?" JOHN 7:14–20

■

AT FIRST, JESUS DID not reveal himself in Jerusalem. He went up to the city from Galilee anonymously. But once there he went to the southern entrance of the temple and began to speak to the crowds. The people were amazed because, though not well known, he spoke as one with authority. While all the religious leaders and rabbis had earned their credentials through the official schools, Jesus claimed his authority from a very different source: "My teaching is not my own. It comes from the one who sent me . . . Whoever speaks on his own does so to gain personal glory, but he who seeks the glory of the one who sent him is a man of truth; there is nothing false about him." To those listening, including some of the religious leaders, this claim bordered on blasphemy. Furthermore, Jesus knew what was in their hearts and confronted them about it: "Why are you trying to kill me?" It will soon become clear that he was reading them right.

Then Jesus, still teaching in the temple courts, cried out, "Yes, you know me, and you know where I am from. I am not here on my own authority, but he who sent me is true. You do not know him, but I know him because I am from him and he sent me." At this they tried to seize him, but no one laid a hand on him, because his hour had not yet come. Still, many in the crowd believed in him. They said, "When the Messiah comes, will he perform more signs than this man?" JOHN 7:28–31

■

THE GOSPELS PRESENT US with a mystery: Who is this man? The people of his own time were confounded by a man who performed astonishing miracles but who did not meet their expectations of what the savior of Israel would be like. Was he a prophet in the tradition of Elijah and Elisha? Was he the long-anticipated Messiah, the anointed one in the line of David? Or was he a crazy man who probably needed to be locked away? Then there were the miracles that many witnessed, including some in the crowd. Whatever the crowd thought, Jesus remained certain of his own identity and teaching. And he did not take personal credit; instead he made an even more audacious claim: "I am not here on my own authority, but him who sent me is true. You do not know him, but I know him because I am from him and he sent me."

The Pharisees heard the crowd whispering such things about him. Then the chief priests and the Pharisees sent temple guards to arrest him. Jesus said, "I am with you for only a short time, and then I am going to the one who sent me. You will look for me, but you will not find me; and where I am, you cannot come." The Jews said to one another, "Where does this man intend to go that we cannot find him? Will he go where our people live scattered among the Greeks, and teach the Greeks? What did he mean when he said, 'You will look for me, but you will not find me,' and 'Where I am, you cannot come'?" On the last and greatest day of the festival, Jesus stood and said in a loud voice, "Let anyone who is thirsty come to me and drink. Whoever believes in me, as Scripture has said, rivers of living water will flow from within them." By this he meant the Spirit, whom those who believed in him were later to receive. Up to that time the Spirit had not been given, since Jesus had not yet been glorified. JOHN 7:32–39

■

JESUS TOLD THE SAMARITAN woman at the well, "God is spirit" (John 4:24). At the very beginning of Genesis we are told, "Now the earth was formless and empty, darkness was over the surface of the deep, and the Spirit of God was hovering over the waters" (Genesis 1:2). And after he sinned and prayed for forgiveness, David pleaded with God, "Do not cast me from your presence or take your Holy Spirit from me" (Psalm 51:11). So when Jesus says, "Whoever believes in me, as Scripture has said, rivers of living water will flow from within them," he means the Spirit of God who will be received later by those who believe in him. God is Spirit, but with sin, we lost access to the Spirit of God. Without that Spirit, we are nothing but "a mere phantom as (we) go to and fro" (Psalm 39:6). Jesus knows men and women thirst for the Holy Spirit. He came to earth to open the way to life through his life.

On hearing his words, some of the people said, "Surely this man is the Prophet." Others said, "He is the Messiah." Still others asked, "How can the Messiah come from Galilee? Does not Scripture say that the Messiah will come from David's descendants and from Bethlehem, the town where David lived?" Thus the people were divided because of Jesus. Some wanted to seize him, but no one laid a hand on him. JOHN 7:40–44

■

A DISPUTE AROSE: SOME said Jesus was a prophet, others said he must be the Messiah, and another, educated in the Scriptures, said he couldn't be the Messiah because he is from Galilee and not from David's birthplace. Confusion reigned because Jesus did not fit into any of the boxes people built for him. What was true then is true today. It is hard to see people and events clearly because we tend to see through a multitude of lenses that filter reality into preconceived ideas that allow us to define the world in our own narrow terms. So if Jesus does not fit, we can filter him in a number of ways that will not discomfort us. We can say he was a wise man or a prophet and we would be right as far as those definitions go, but if we filter out the mystery that is at the very center of the Jesus encounter, then we reduce Jesus to something right-sized for humans but completely out of focus as the Son of God.

A PROPHET DOES NOT COME OUT OF GALILEE

Finally the temple guards went back to the chief priests and the Pharisees, who asked them, "Why didn't you bring him in?" "No one ever spoke the way this man does," the guards replied. "You mean he has deceived you also?" the Pharisees retorted. "Have any of the rulers or of the Pharisees believed in him? No! But this mob that knows nothing of the law—there is a curse on them." Nicodemus, who had gone to Jesus earlier and who was one of their own number, asked, "Does our law condemn a man without first hearing him to find out what he has been doing?" They replied, "Are you from Galilee, too? Look into it, and you will find that a prophet does not come out of Galilee." JOHN 7:45–52

■

IT IS IMPORTANT TO note that the chief priests and the Pharisees were knowledgeable men; they knew their theology, but they did not know enough. Through their study and tradition, they knew that the Messiah would be in the line of David and would be born in Bethlehem. But everything else they claimed to know was based on hearsay and assumptions. They heard that Jesus came from Nazareth, but this was not where he was born. Ironically, their partial knowledge made the case that Jesus was the Messiah because he was of the line of David and was born in Bethlehem. But the chief priests were not looking for the truth; they were concocting reasons to arrest and condemn a man whom they perceived to be a threat to their power and privilege. To them, Jesus was a potentially dangerous troublemaker.

But Jesus went to the Mount of Olives. At dawn he appeared again in the temple courts, where all the people gathered around him, and he sat down to teach them. The teachers of the law and the Pharisees brought in a woman caught in adultery. They made her stand before the group and said to Jesus, "Teacher, this woman was caught in the act of adultery. In the Law Moses commanded us to stone such women. Now what do you say?" They were using this question as a trap, in order to have a basis for accusing him. But Jesus bent down and started to write on the ground with his finger. When they kept on questioning him, he straightened up and said to them, "Let any one of you who is without sin be the first to throw a stone at her." Again he stooped down and wrote on the ground. At this, those who heard began to go away one at a time, the older ones first, until only Jesus was left, with the woman still standing there. Jesus straightened up and asked her, "Woman, where are they? Has no one condemned you?" "No one, sir," she said. "Then neither do I condemn you," Jesus declared. "Go now and leave your life of sin." JOHN 8:1–11

∎

THE TRAP SET FOR Jesus by the teachers of the law and the Pharisees was cunning because it put Jesus in an untenable position between two irreconcilable laws. If he said the woman caught in adultery must be stoned, then he was defying a Roman law that did not permit the Jewish people to carry out death sentences. If he did not condemn her, he would have been accused of disregarding Jewish law. Instead of arguing for or against a particular outcome, Jesus wrote in the sand with his finger. What he wrote is not known—it could have been the three words of condemnation recorded in the Book of Daniel or it could have been something else—but whatever the actual words were, they put the fear of God in the hearts of the accusers, and they slowly slinked away, understanding that the finger was pointing directly at them.

When Jesus spoke again to the people, he said, "I am the light of the world. Whoever follows me will never walk in darkness, but will have the light of life." The Pharisees challenged him, "Here you are, appearing as your own witness; your testimony is not valid." Jesus answered, "Even if I testify on my own behalf, my testimony is valid, for I know where I came from and where I am going. But you have no idea where I come from or where I am going. You judge by human standards; I pass judgment on no one. But if I do judge, my decisions are true, because I am not alone. I stand with the Father, who sent me. In your own Law it is written that the testimony of two witnesses is true. I am one who testifies for myself; my other witness is the Father, who sent me." JOHN 8:12–18

■

HOW DO WE KNOW something is true? How do we validate a declaration? Truth can be hard to determine. Sometimes the evidence is unclear or there are contradictory claims. Proverbs says, "The first to present his case seems right, 'til another comes forward and questions him" (Proverbs 18:17). If we did not experience an event ourselves, we must depend on the credibility of witnesses, and this goes to the heart of how we respond to the accounts of Jesus' life, death, and resurrection. Are the witnesses credible? Luke tells us that while he was not a direct witness, he carefully investigated everything from the beginning to provide an orderly account so that the reader might know the certainty of the things that have been taught (Luke 1:3–4). In the Gospel of John, we are told that John the Baptist was sent by God to be a witness to testify about Jesus so that "through him all men might believe" (John 1:7). Down through the ages there have been countless witnesses who put aside personal well-being in order to testify to the truth of the Lordship of Jesus Christ.

Once more Jesus said to them, "I am going away, and you will look for me, and you will die in your sin. Where I go, you cannot come." This made the Jews ask, "Will he kill himself? Is that why he says, 'Where I go, you cannot come'?" But he continued, "You are from below; I am from above. You are of this world; I am not of this world. I told you that you would die in your sins; if you do not believe that I am he, you will indeed die in your sins." JOHN 8:21–24

■

SO MUCH OF THE drama of the Gospels is summarized by a distinction Jesus made to the Pharisees who gathered around him. He said to them, "You are from below; I am from above. You are of this world; I am not of this world." By "world" Jesus is not just speaking about the globe we live on; he is talking about a world system that has been set up against the world God originally created. The Pharisees moved against Jesus because they were interwoven into this system through sin. The worldly system is Satan's counterfeit kingdom. Jesus understood what he was up against just as clearly as he understood that the Pharisees and their followers were foot soldiers of the enemy. Jesus defined who the enemy is; he also declared who he is.

I DO NOTHING ON MY OWN

"Who are you?" they asked. "Just what I have been telling you from the beginning," Jesus replied. "I have much to say in judgment of you. But he who sent me is trustworthy, and what I have heard from him I tell the world." They did not understand that he was telling them about his Father. So Jesus said, "When you have lifted up the Son of Man, then you will know that I am he and that I do nothing on my own but speak just what the Father has taught me. The one who sent me is with me; he has not left me alone, for I always do what pleases him." Even as he spoke, many believed in him. JOHN 8:25–30

■

THEY ASKED, "WHO ARE you?" This question was repeated time and again and came from responses of amazement, wonder, doubt, and fear, and few were satisfied with the answers they got. Some speculated that Jesus was a prophet like the prophets of old; others believed he was a teacher filled with the wisdom of the ages; still others concluded he was a trouble-maker with political designs. They simply could not believe that Jesus was anything but a mere mortal. John reported that many believed, but many more did not, which created even more turmoil and confusion. And through all of this, Jesus was steadfast in claiming oneness with the Father: "The one who has sent me is with me; he has not left me alone." Jesus promises this same comfort to those who believe.

Jesus said, "You are doing the works of your own father." "We are not illegitimate children," they protested. "The only Father we have is God Himself." Jesus said to them, "If God were your Father, you would love me, for I have come here from God. I have not come on my own; God sent me. Why is my language not clear to you? Because you are unable to hear what I say. You belong to your father, the devil, and you want to carry out your father's desires. He was a murderer from the beginning, not holding to the truth, for there is no truth in him. When he lies, he speaks his native language, for he is a liar and the father of lies." JOHN 8:41–44

■

IN THE SECOND AND third chapters of Genesis, the devil used a question to plant seeds of doubt in the mind of Eve. God had established one clear prohibition in the Garden of Eden: ". . . you must not eat from the tree of the knowledge of good and evil, for when you eat of it you will surely die" (Genesis 2:16). The devil, knowing what God said, asked a seemingly simple question: "Did God really say, 'You must not eat from any tree in the garden?'" (Genesis 3:1) Notice the subtle twist of the truth, converting one particular tree into all trees in the garden. Later, when Satan tempted Jesus in the wilderness, he did the same thing: he changed a word or two to subvert the truth, much as propagandists do today. Jesus says the native language of Satan is the lie, for it is through the corruption of language that the liar can successfully achieve his nefarious purposes. The first lie came from Satan, and it is through that lie that he succeeded in separating men and women from God.

"You are not yet fifty years old," they said to him, "and you have seen Abraham!" "Very truly I tell you," Jesus answered, "before Abraham was born, I am!" At this, they picked up stones to stone him, but Jesus hid himself, slipping away from the temple grounds. JOHN 8:57–59

■

JESUS' STATEMENT WAS SIMPLE: "Before Abraham was born, I am!" Why did this cause the people to try to stone him? On one level, Jesus made a statement that seems to make no sense: How could he exist before Abraham when Abraham lived 2,000 years earlier? If Jesus existed before Abraham, then that could mean only one thing: Before Abraham, before Adam, and even before the creation of the world, Jesus existed with God and the Holy Spirit. He even used the revealed name of God, "I am." Jesus did not leave much room for misinterpretation and so his enemies rose up, as they would again and again, from that time until this, to try to kill him.

WHO IS MY NEIGHBOR?

On one occasion an expert in the law stood up to test Jesus. "Teacher," he asked, "what must I do to inherit eternal life?" "What is written in the Law?" he replied. "How do you read it?" He answered, "'Love the Lord your God with all your heart and with all your soul and with all your strength and with all your mind'; and, 'Love your neighbor as yourself.'" "You have answered correctly," Jesus replied. "Do this and you will live." But he wanted to justify himself, so he asked Jesus, "And who is my neighbor?"
LUKE 10:25–29

■

IS THE "EXPERT IN the law" really looking for an answer? Luke says this man asked the question to test Jesus, which means he was hoping that Jesus would be tripped up by his answer. But Jesus parried with another question: What does Scripture say? The expert answered by saying you must love God completely, and you must love your neighbor. "And who is my neighbor?" the expert asked. This led Jesus to tell a parable that would show the expert of the law just how hard it is to actually love your neighbor.

THE GOOD SAMARITAN

In reply Jesus said, "A man was going down from Jerusalem to Jericho, when he was attacked by robbers. They stripped him of his clothes, beat him and went away, leaving him half dead. A priest happened to be going down the same road, and when he saw the man, he passed by on the other side. So too, a Levite, when he came to the place and saw him, passed by on the other side. But a Samaritan, as he traveled, came where the man was; and when he saw him, he took pity on him. He went to him and bandaged his wounds, pouring on oil and wine. Then he put the man on his own donkey, brought him to an inn and took care of him. The next day he took out two denarii and gave them to the innkeeper. 'Look after him,' he said, 'and when I return, I will reimburse you for any extra expense you may have.' Which of these three do you think was a neighbor to the man who fell into the hands of robbers?" The expert in the law replied, "The one who had mercy on him." Jesus told him, "Go and do likewise." LUKE 10:30–37

■

WHO IS MY NEIGHBOR? In this parable, we are told of three travelers who have a chance to show compassion to a man who has been robbed and left for dead. You would expect the priest and the Levite to stop and help, but they don't. They pass by because they do not want to be inconvenienced by this unfortunate circumstance. Then a Samaritan happens by and he crosses over to aid the injured man. The natural reaction by the Jewish audience to the Samaritan being the good neighbor must have been disbelief. Impossible! Samaritans are the lowest of the low according to general opinion. But Jesus does not reduce his definition of a good neighbor to tribal and family characteristics. He defines neighbor from a kingdom of God perspective. What does it really mean to be a good neighbor? Jesus says it means being able to put aside provincial considerations in order to cross boundaries. It means casting aside individual imperatives to help someone who might be experiencing pain and trouble, even when doing so may be an inconvenience. The Good Samaritan accepts the inconvenience, for there is a higher call. He crosses the road and puts his own journey on hold to help, just as Jesus gives help to all of us who need his comfort and aid.

As Jesus and his disciples were on their way, he came to a village where a woman named Martha opened her home to him. She had a sister called Mary, who sat at the Lord's feet listening to what he said. But Martha was distracted by all the preparations that had to be made. She came to him and asked, "Lord, don't you care that my sister has left me to do the work by myself? Tell her to help me!" "Martha, Martha," the Lord answered, "you are worried and upset about many things, but few things are needed—or indeed only one. Mary has chosen what is better, and it will not be taken away from her." LUKE 10:38–42

■

MARY AND MARTHA INVITED Jesus into their home, but they chose different roles for the occasion. While Martha played the traditional part by preparing and serving food, Mary, like a student, sat at Jesus' feet absorbing his words. Mary's choice was unorthodox because women in the culture of that time rarely were given the opportunity to sit at the teacher's feet. Martha objected and complained that Mary was not conforming to her traditional role. Jesus, as often happens, provided an unexpected response. "Martha, Martha . . . you are worried and upset about many things, but few things are needed—or indeed only one. Mary has chosen what is better, and it will not be taken away from her." At that moment Mary chose to live outside of the cultural norm but within God's design. Martha's role is good, but Mary's role of being a student of the Lord is even better.

Then Jesus said to them, "Suppose you have a friend, and you go to him at midnight and say, 'Friend, lend me three loaves of bread; a friend of mine on a journey has come to me, and I have no food to offer him.' And suppose the one inside answers, 'Don't bother me. The door is already locked, and my children and I are in bed. I can't get up and give you anything.' I tell you, even though he will not get up and give you the bread because of friendship, yet because of your shameless audacity he will surely get up and give you as much as you need. So I say to you: Ask and it will be given to you; seek and you will find; knock and the door will be opened to you. For everyone who asks receives; the one who seeks finds; and to the one who knocks, the door will be opened." LUKE 11:5–10

■

A CHURCH BUILDING CAN be a refuge from the turmoil of everyday life. In the city, the relentless feeling of chaos often overwhelms our sense of well-being and we seek to escape the frantic collision of people and noise by ducking into the cool, calm of a church, where noise is seemingly barricaded outside the walls of the sanctuary. Jesus is calling us time and again to descend from whatever perch we are resting on to enter the everyday clamor of a needy world. And he tells us that in this world we need to be bold and audacious. We need to meet the dynamic restlessness of a dying world with a dynamic relationship with God through the power of the Holy Spirit. Jesus reminds us that we are not alone. We are to pray boldly and trust broadly. That is where we will find peace, knowing that through Christ, God has forged an unbreakable bond with us as we pursue his purpose for us and for his kingdom to come.

Someone in the crowd said to him, "Teacher, tell my brother to divide the inheritance with me." Jesus replied, "Man, who appointed me a judge or an arbiter between you?" Then he said to them, "Watch out! Be on your guard against all kinds of greed; life does not consist in an abundance of possessions." And he told them this parable: "The ground of a certain rich man yielded an abundant harvest. He thought to himself, 'What shall I do? I have no place to store my crops.' Then he said, 'This is what I'll do. I will tear down my barns and build bigger ones, and there I will store my surplus grain. And I'll say to myself, 'You have plenty of grain laid up for many years. Take life easy; eat, drink and be merry." But God said to him, 'You fool! This very night your life will be demanded from you. Then who will get what you have prepared for yourself?' This is how it will be with whoever stores up things for themselves but is not rich toward God." LUKE 12:13–21

■

MANY THREADS OF JESUS' teachings come together in this passage. Jesus does not condemn the accumulation of wealth, but he does condemn greed that might be understood as preserving that which has been gained for one's own gratification. He reminds us that life does not consist of an abundance of possessions, and often those who accumulate much become parsimonious when it comes to spending for purposes beyond self. So the rich man ends up with fat bank accounts, large estates, and fancy cars, but then is faced with the realization that all of it can vanish in an instant. Here, God calls the rich man a fool because his life was wasted in getting and not giving. He disregarded the existence of God by saying the full purpose of everything is gratifying the appetites for the things of this world: "Take life easy; eat, drink and be merry," he says. But God says, "You fool! This very night your life will be demanded of you." And Jesus concludes, "This is how it will be with whoever stores up things for themselves but is not rich toward God."

WHAT CAUSES DIVISION?

I have come to bring fire on the earth, and how I wish it were already kindled! But I have a baptism to undergo, and what constraint I am under until it is completed! Do you think I came to bring peace on earth? No, I tell you, but division. From now on there will be five in one family divided against each other, three against two and two against three. They will be divided, father against son and son against father, mother against daughter and daughter against mother, mother-in-law against daughter-in-law and daughter-in-law against mother-in-law. LUKE 12:49–53

■

WHAT DOES JESUS MEAN when he says that he will bring division, even within families? This statement might rub contemporary followers the wrong way, but it is not a new notion. From the earliest days of his ministry to his final prayer for his disciples, Jesus spoke of a world at war with God. In the Beatitudes he says, "Blessed are you when people insult you, persecute you and falsely say all kinds of evil against you because of me" (Matthew 5:11). There is no question about the condition of the world; opposition to God is prevalent and powerful. Paul preached that we must put on the "full armor of God," because the enemy of God is a powerful force operating in the shadows to obliterate the light. Immediately before his arrest, Jesus prayed to the Father to protect the disciples: "I have given them your word and the world has hated them, for they are not of the world any more than I am of the world. My prayer is not that you take them out of the world but that you protect them from the evil one" (John 17:14–15).

He said to the crowd: "When you see a cloud rising in the west, immediately you say, 'It's going to rain,' and it does. And when the south wind blows, you say, 'It's going to be hot,' and it is. Hypocrites! You know how to interpret the appearance of the earth and the sky. How is it that you don't know how to interpret this present time? Why don't you judge for yourselves what is right? As you are going with your adversary to the magistrate, try hard to be reconciled on the way, or your adversary may drag you off to the judge, and the judge turn you over to the officer, and the officer throw you into prison. I tell you, you will not get out until you have paid the last penny." LUKE 12:54–59

■

THE WORLD OBSESSES OVER forecasting the weather. The word "forecast" means to tell or predict that something will take place that has yet to happen. Jesus told the crowd that they lived in blind ignorance: "How is it that you don't know how to interpret this present time?" He then followed this question with what appears to be a non sequitur, but it is not. He is saying that all of our actions, current and past, will have consequences that from God's perspective are predictable and inevitable. We need to apply the same kind of attention to the principles of everyday living as we do to interpreting the on-coming weather. For in the end, everything we do will come under judgment, both the good and the bad.

As he went along, he saw a man blind from birth. His disciples asked him, "Rabbi, who sinned, this man or his parents, that he was born blind?" "Neither this man nor his parents sinned," said Jesus, "but this happened so that the works of God might be displayed in him. As long as it is day, we must do the works of him who sent me. Night is coming, when no one can work. While I am in the world, I am the light of the world." After saying this, he spit on the ground, made some mud with the saliva, and put it on the man's eyes. "Go," he told him, "wash in the Pool of Siloam" (this word means "Sent"). So the man went and washed, and came home seeing. JOHN 9:1–7

■

JESUS DOES NOT MINCE words. He makes a bold claim: "I am the light of the world," echoing the first words of God as recorded in Genesis: "Let there be light." By claiming to be the light of the world, Jesus links himself directly to the source of all life, and John reinforces this connection in the opening passage of his Gospel: "Through him all things were made; without him nothing was made that has been made. In him was life, and that life was the light of men. The light shines in the darkness, but the darkness has not understood it" (John 1:3–5). Jesus took some mud, the raw material of life, and he animated it with his saliva and gave the light of vision to the man born blind. John recorded an actual event that happened—Jesus gave sight to a blind man—but we can see more than a physical event that happened as reported. The story of creation, the fall of man, and God's plan for restoration are all there to see for anyone willing to open their own eyes.

I AM THE GATE

All who have come before me are thieves and robbers, but the sheep have not listened to them. I am the gate; whoever enters through me will be saved. They will come in and go out, and find pasture. The thief comes only to steal and kill and destroy; I have come that they may have life, and have it to the full. JOHN 10:8–10

■

WHAT DOES JESUS MEAN when he declares, "I am the gate"? On one level he is referring to a gate to a sheep pen. The pen itself was enclosed for protection, but there was a gate that the sheep could go through in order to get in or out of the pen. The shepherd served as steward and protector; the sheep could not leave, nor could predators break in without the shepherd allowing it to happen. Jesus also uses the image of the gate figuratively. He says that he stands at the gate as our Shepherd, and no one can enter or leave without his assent. Again, Jesus affirms his authority as Lord even though he is using an illustration drawn from every day life: ". . . whoever enters through me will be saved."

I am the good shepherd. The good shepherd lays down his life for the sheep. The hired hand is not the shepherd and does not own the sheep. So when he sees the wolf coming, he abandons the sheep and runs away. Then the wolf attacks the flock and scatters it. The man runs away because he is a hired hand and cares nothing for the sheep. I am the good shepherd; I know my sheep and my sheep know me—just as the Father knows me and I know the Father—and I lay down my life for the sheep. I have other sheep that are not of this sheep pen. I must bring them also. They too will listen to my voice, and there shall be one flock and one shepherd. JOHN 10:11–16

■

ISRAEL WAS THIRSTING FOR a Good Shepherd, one who would take care of the flock and not abandon them when it was inconvenient or dangerous. Ezekiel, the great prophet of the Old Testament, spoke of the "shepherds" of his day who had led Israel astray. God said to Ezekiel, "Tell them the Lord says, 'Woe to the shepherds of Israel who only take care of themselves! Should not the shepherds take care of the flocks? You have not strengthened the weak or healed the sick or bound up the injured . . . You have treated them harshly and brutally'" (Ezekiel 34:2,4). Jesus is the Good Shepherd; he cares for the sheep and will look after them because, "I know my sheep and my sheep know me—just as the Father knows me and I know the Father—and I lay down my life for the sheep."

"The reason my Father loves me is that I lay down my life—only to take it up again. No one takes it from me, but I lay it down of my own accord. I have authority to lay it down and authority to take it up again. This command I received from my Father." The Jews who heard these words were again divided. Many of them said, "He is demon-possessed and raving mad. Why listen to him?" But others said, "These are not the sayings of a man possessed by a demon. Can a demon open the eyes of the blind?" JOHN 10:17–21

■

THE RESPONSE TO JESUS has always been mixed, even from the beginning of his life on earth. Herod, the great king of Israel, responded to the news of Jesus' birth by plotting to kill him at the first opportunity. The shepherds in the fields near Bethlehem, hearing the good news of the birth of the Christ child, put everything aside so they could worship him: "The shepherds returned, glorifying and praising God for all the things they had heard and seen, which were just as they had been told" (Luke 2:20). To this day, those who stand in opposition respond to Jesus by lying about him or reducing him to just another teacher or minor prophet. The shepherds, though, believed what they heard and acted on it.

Then Jesus went through the towns and villages, teaching as he made his way to Jerusalem. Someone asked him, "Lord, are only a few people going to be saved?" He said to them, "Make every effort to enter through the narrow door, because many, I tell you, will try to enter and will not be able to. Once the owner of the house gets up and closes the door, you will stand outside knocking and pleading, 'Sir, open the door for us.' But he will answer, 'I don't know you or where you come from.' Then you will say, 'We ate and drank with you, and you taught in our streets.' But he will reply, 'I don't know you or where you come from. Away from me, all you evildoers!'" LUKE 13:22–27

■

JESUS SLOWLY MADE HIS way through towns and villages as he moved toward Jerusalem. In one place he was asked a question: Are only a few people going to be saved? He gave an answer that is not easy to accept because he inferred that the choice between heaven and hell is ours to make. God desires that everyone choose to enter through the narrow door, but not everyone will. Jesus says, "Make every effort to enter through the narrow door, because many, I tell you, will try to enter and will not be able to." Jesus is that narrow door, but if those trying to get through reject him, then it will not be possible to enter.

There will be weeping there, and gnashing of teeth, when you see Abraham, Isaac and Jacob and all the prophets in the kingdom of God, but you yourselves thrown out. People will come from east and west and north and south, and will take their places at the feast in the kingdom of God. Indeed there are those who are last who will be first, and first who will be last. LUKE 13:28–30

■

THE JEWISH LEADERS RECEIVED Jesus' message as a challenge to their traditions and authority. Jesus did not deny the foundations of their traditions; he explicitly referenced the patriarchs—Abraham, Isaac, and Jacob—as already being in the kingdom of God, but then he said that those in charge have sought not so much God, but position and power. Furthermore, Gentiles and many others "from east and west and north and south will take their places at the feast in the kingdom of God." And when Jesus said, "there are those who are last who will be first, and first who will be last," he was speaking directly to the arrogance and insularity of the Jewish leaders who were the ultimate excluders. Jesus was saying: Beware or you will discover too late that you will be among those who are being cast out.

Jerusalem, Jerusalem, you who kill the prophets and stone those sent to you, how often I have longed to gather your children together, as a hen gathers her chicks under her wings, and you were not willing. Look, your house is left to you desolate. For I tell you, you will not see me again until you say, 'Blessed is he who comes in the name of the Lord.' MATTHEW 23:37–39

■

IF THERE IS ONE word to describe Jesus' lament over Jerusalem, it is anguish. Jerusalem, once a shining city on a hill, had descended into a hive of corruption and godlessness. Jesus' own words echo the words of Jeremiah, who mourned the great descent and destruction of David's royal city: "How deserted lies the city, once so full of people! How like a widow is she, who once was great among the nations! She who was queen among the provinces has now become a slave" (Lamentations 1:1). Jesus was uttering prophetic words because while the city he was approaching was teeming with people and activity, soon enough it would lie deserted and ruined, as it had been once before, because its rulers and the people had abandoned God.

Large crowds were traveling with Jesus, and turning to them he said: "If anyone comes to me and does not hate father and mother, wife and children, brothers and sisters—yes, even their own life— such a person cannot be my disciple. And whoever does not carry their cross and follow me cannot be my disciple." LUKE 14:25–27

■

IT IS EASY TO fix our attention on Jesus' startling use of the word "hate" because it seems so thoroughly out of character. But Jesus intends to startle, both those who were with him then and us today. He says that in comparison to our commitment to God and his calling, our familial affections might seem like hate. But implicit in our radical commitment to God, where God is above everything, is the necessity to live out that commitment with our children, our spouse, and the people we come into contact with everyday. "And the second is like it: 'Love your neighbor as yourself.' All the Law and the Prophets hang on these two commandments" (Matthew 22:39–40). Jesus wants his followers to never forget, however, which commandment comes first: "Love the Lord your God with all your heart and with all your soul and with all of your mind. This is the first and greatest commandment" (Matthew 22:37–38).

PERSEVERANCE

Suppose one of you wants to build a tower. Won't you first sit down and estimate the cost to see if you have enough money to complete it? For if you lay the foundation and are not able to finish it, everyone who sees it will ridicule you, saying, 'This person began to build and wasn't able to finish.' LUKE 14:28–30

■

JESUS CONTINUES TO EMPHASIZE that God comes before everything else. For many of us that is difficult enough, but Jesus raises the bar even further by telling us to count the cost of discipleship. Jesus knew that many who would come after him would soften the message, but Jesus will never mislead us. He is saying that if you accept the call to follow God, wherever that might lead, there will be a cost as well as a blessing. Accepting the call means we choose to accept a reconfigured heart where God is first, others are next, and we are third.

Or suppose a king is about to go to war against another king. Won't he first sit down and consider whether he is able with ten thousand men to oppose the one coming against him with twenty thousand? If he is not able, he will send a delegation while the other is still a long way off and will ask for terms of peace. In the same way, those of you who do not give up everything you have cannot be my disciples. Salt is good, but if it loses its saltiness, how can it be made salty again? It is fit neither for the soil nor for the manure pile; it is thrown out. 'Whoever has ears to hear, let them hear.' LUKE 14:31–35

■

IN SPEAKING ABOUT DISCIPLESHIP, why does Jesus use the analogy of a king suing for peace when he recognizes the opposing king will defeat him? The connection between kings and disciples might not be evident to us at first, but it would have made sense to his disciples. Jesus was teaching them that discipleship is about abandoning yourself to another kind of King, one of far greater power and importance than a king with twenty thousand troops. Surrender to the true King, abandon yourself, and come, follow, and learn a whole new way of living. The king with ten thousand men acted wisely; likewise, the disciple who gives his life over to Christ has embraced the wisdom of living through and for the Lord.

Or suppose a woman has ten silver coins and loses one. Doesn't she light a lamp, sweep the house and search carefully until she finds it? And when she finds it, she calls her friends and neighbors together and says, 'Rejoice with me; I have found my lost coin.' In the same way, I tell you, there is rejoicing in the presence of the angels of God over one sinner who repents. LUKE 15:8–10

■

LUKE RECOUNTS THREE PARABLES, one after another, about being lost. In all three Jesus emphasizes that God will put everything aside to find and restore the thing of value that was lost, even without counting the cost. Why does the woman celebrate when one coin is found? Or why is the shepherd so joyful when the lost sheep is finally found? Jesus tells these stories because he wants us to know that we have a "Prodigal God" who will go to the furthest lengths for "one sinner who repents."

THE YOUNGER SON

Jesus continued: "There was a man who had two sons. The younger one said to his father, 'Father, give me my share of the estate.'
So he divided his property between them. Not long after that, the
younger son got together all he had, set off for a distant country
and there squandered his wealth in wild living. After he had spent
everything, there was a severe famine in that whole country, and
he began to be in need. So he went and hired himself out to a
citizen of that country, who sent him to his fields to feed pigs. He
longed to fill his stomach with the pods that the pigs were eating,
but no one gave him anything." LUKE 15:11–16

■

THIS PARABLE BEGINS WITH a son asking his father for his share
of the father's estate. This is an odd request because inheritance is
usually passed on after the death of the parent. But not here: The
father divides the property between the two sons without objection.
This generous act is also unusual because the father accedes to the
request by gifting each son, the older as well as the younger. We
know what happens next: The younger son squanders everything
that he was given and ends up more impoverished than the farm
hands around him. He lost everything—his inheritance, his self-
respect, and his family. His actions left him alienated and full of
despair. In many ways, the younger son represents the level of despair experienced by many who have experienced alienation from
the grace of a "Prodigal God."

When he came to his senses, he said, 'How many of my father's hired servants have food to spare, and here I am starving to death! I will set out and go back to my father and say to him: Father, I have sinned against heaven and against you. I am no longer worthy to be called your son; make me like one of your hired servants.' So he got up and went to his father. But while he was still a long way off, his father saw him and was filled with compassion for him; he ran to his son, threw his arms around him and kissed him. The son said to him, 'Father, I have sinned against heaven and against you. I am no longer worthy to be called your son.' But the father said to his servants, 'Quick! Bring the best robe and put it on him. Put a ring on his finger and sandals on his feet. Bring the fattened calf and kill it. Let's have a feast and celebrate. For this son of mine was dead and is alive again; he was lost and is found.' So they began to celebrate. LUKE 15:17–24

∎

SO FAR THE STORY of the lost son has followed a conventional path. The son wastes the gift of the father in wild living, leaving him in a state of want and despair. His last hope is to return home and attempt to work off his shame and his debt. But here the story takes an unexpected turn. Instead of the father banishing the son in anger, he runs to him and welcomes him back into the family. The son repents by saying, "Father, I have sinned against heaven and against you," and he has no expectation of restoration. But this father celebrates his son's return by lavishly accepting him back into the family as if the son had returned from the dead: "Let's have a feast and celebrate, for this son of mine was dead and is alive again; he was lost and is found."

Meanwhile, the older son was in the field. When he came near the house, he heard music and dancing. So he called one of the servants and asked him what was going on. 'Your brother has come,' he replied, 'and your father has killed the fattened calf because he has him back safe and sound.' The older brother became angry and refused to go in. So his father went out and pleaded with him. But he answered his father, 'Look! All these years I've been slaving for you and never disobeyed your orders. Yet you never gave me even a young goat so I could celebrate with my friends. But when this son of yours who has squandered your property with prostitutes comes home, you kill the fattened calf for him!' LUKE 15:25–30

■

NOW THE OLDER BROTHER makes an appearance. He becomes angry and accusatory and refuses to join the celebration. Why? The parable opens by saying the father "divided his property between them." The older son received his inheritance as well, but unlike his younger brother, he did not toss everything away in wild living. The good son continued to live prudently, but over time he became arrogant and self-righteous. Instead of saying with his younger brother, "I have sinned against heaven and against you," he turns the tables on the father and more or less says, "Father, your behavior is an offense to me." His self-righteousness has distorted his right reason, leaving him in as great a state of spiritual poverty as was his brother's physical poverty. The older son has been a good son in relation to family and work, but he harbors a false belief that his righteousness could be earned through works alone. Compared to the behavior of his younger brother, he has done all the right things, but his heart is full of anger and false pride. Clearly, he has not experienced the transformative power of grace, for if he had, he, too, would have accepted his lost brother with the joy of the father.

'My son,' the father said, 'you are always with me, and everything I have is yours. But we had to celebrate and be glad, because this brother of yours was dead and is alive again; he was lost and is found.' LUKE 15:31–32

■

TIM KELLER, IN HIS book *The Prodigal God*, shifts the focus away from the two sons to a God who is so abundantly generous in his capacity to love and forgive that he can cover a huge spectrum of man's sinful and godless behavior, from profligate living to miserly self-righteousness. The older son is a good person and has lived by the letter of the law, whereas the younger son has lived far outside of the boundaries of that law. But the father does not prefer one son to the other because he loves them both and wants them to love him. The deep well of gratitude expressed by the younger son is cause for celebration, just as the mere existence of the older son causes the father to say, "Everything I have is yours." Both sons are sinners; neither can earn their way back to the father. This father's grace is so wide and deep and high that his love can encompass those who think they deserve his love and those who do not.

Now on his way to Jerusalem, Jesus traveled along the border between Samaria and Galilee. As he was going into a village, ten men who had leprosy met him. They stood at a distance and called out in a loud voice, "Jesus, Master, have pity on us!" When he saw them, he said, "Go, show yourselves to the priests." And as they went, they were cleansed. One of them, when he saw he was healed, came back, praising God in a loud voice. He threw himself at Jesus' feet and thanked him—and he was a Samaritan. Jesus asked, "Were not all ten cleansed? Where are the other nine? Has no one returned to give praise to God except this foreigner?" Then he said to him, "Rise and go; your faith has made you well." LUKE 17:11–19

■

THE SAMARITAN WOMAN AT the well (John 4) was an outcast in a community of outcasts. The Good Samaritan (Luke 10) stepped in where a Levite and a priest did not. And of the ten lepers, only the Samaritan "came back, praising God in a loud voice" and thanked Jesus for healing him. Even though the leper was a Samaritan, he recognized Jesus for who he is, which is why Jesus said, "Rise and go; your faith has made you well." There is more than a hint here that the healing power of Jesus will extend far beyond the tribes and territories of Israel. Jesus has not come just for the Jew or even the outcast Samaritan, but for all who are lost and need the healing hand of God—Gentile and Jew alike.

Then Jesus told his disciples a parable to show them that they should always pray and not give up. He said: "In a certain town there was a judge who neither feared God nor cared what people thought. And there was a widow in that town who kept coming to him with the plea, 'Grant me justice against my adversary.' For some time he refused. But finally he said to himself, 'Even though I don't fear God or care what people think, yet because this widow keeps bothering me, I will see that she gets justice, so that she won't eventually come and attack me!'" LUKE 18:1–5

■

THIS PARABLE IS NOT just a story about a persistent widow or an uncaring judge: It is about you and me and prayer. Luke says at the outset that Jesus tells this parable to show that we should always pray and never give up. Prayer is not about instant gratification. It is a continuous petition, because God will answer prayer on his time, even if we plead that he come right away. Jesus says that we should persist and always be prepared for God's blessings to come, even if they come when least expected.

And the Lord said, "Listen to what the unjust judge says. And will not God bring about justice for his chosen ones, who cry out to him day and night? Will he keep putting them off? I tell you, he will see that they get justice, and quickly. However, when the Son of Man comes, will he find faith on the earth?" LUKE 18:6–8

■

THE EARTHLY JUDGE, WHO neither feared God nor cared what people thought, stands in contrast to God, who loves to bring blessings. Yet even the earthly judge relented and gave the widow justice. Jesus is telling his disciples (and us) something about the nature of God Himself. When Israel was enslaved by the Egyptians, Scripture says, "God heard their groans and he remembered his covenant with Abraham, with Isaac and with Jacob. So God looked on the Israelites and was concerned about them" (Exodus 2:24–25). God was operating on his own time, but to the Israelites, God might have seemed as heartless and uncaring as the godless judge. At the right time, though, God called Moses from the desert to return to his people to liberate them from slavery under the Egyptians. With Jesus, the Gospel of John repeats again and again, "his time had not yet come." Persist because God does hear your prayers.

LET NO ONE SEPARATE

Some Pharisees came to him to test him. They asked, "Is it lawful for a man to divorce his wife for any and every reason?" "Haven't you read," he replied, "that at the beginning the Creator 'made them male and female,' and said, 'For this reason a man will leave his father and mother and be united to his wife, and the two will become one flesh'? So they are no longer two, but one flesh. Therefore what God has joined together, let no one separate." MATTHEW 19:3–6

■

THE PHARISEES DID NOT come to learn from Jesus but to challenge him. They were minimalists who were attempting to jam the fullness of life into intellectual, theological, and cultural containers of their own making. But Jesus did not fall into their legalistic trap. He took them back to God's original design. God created men and women for relationship with him and with one another, where the "two will become one flesh." He made them male and female and then united them to become one flesh. Out of this union of husband and wife comes the structure of family. Jesus then says, because this structure is part of God's design of uniting the two to become one, God's original design supersedes the legalistic rules that were designed for the broken world of sin and death.

"Why then," they asked, "did Moses command that a man give his wife a certificate of divorce and send her away?" Jesus replied, "Moses permitted you to divorce your wives because your hearts were hard. But it was not this way from the beginning. I tell you that anyone who divorces his wife, except for sexual immorality, and marries another woman commits adultery." The disciples said to him, "If this is the situation between a husband and wife, it is better not to marry." Jesus replied, "Not everyone can accept this word, but only those to whom it has been given. For there are eunuchs who were born that way, and there are eunuchs who have been made eunuchs by others—and there are those who choose to live like eunuchs for the sake of the kingdom of heaven. The one who can accept this should accept it." MATTHEW 19:7–12

■

THE PHARISEES TURNED TO Moses as the final authority on marriage and divorce, but Jesus made a distinction that goes to the heart of the matter. He said that Moses allowed for divorce because "your hearts are hard." The rules governing divorce were designed to bring order to a people who were verging on chaos and disorder. But even when people disregard the rules, we must keep in mind God's principles behind the rules. God built men and women for relationship within the context of marriage and family. Marriage has a higher, God-originated purpose behind it, and the behavior of rule-breakers and others should not undermine God's higher purpose, even when sin and sexual immorality threaten to obliterate it.

WHY DO YOU CALL ME GOOD?

As Jesus started on his way, a man ran up to him and fell on his knees before him. "Good teacher," he asked, "what must I do to inherit eternal life?" "Why do you call me good?" Jesus answered. "No one is good—except God alone. You know the commandments: 'You shall not murder, you shall not commit adultery, you shall not steal, you shall not give false testimony, you shall not defraud, honor your father and mother.'" "Teacher," he declared, "all these I have kept since I was a boy." Jesus looked at him and loved him. "One thing you lack," he said. "Go, sell everything you have and give to the poor, and you will have treasure in heaven. Then come, follow me." **MARK 10:17–21**

■

THERE IS GREAT IRONY in Jesus' response to the young man's question: "Why do you call me good? No one is good—except God alone." The young man was looking for cheap grace. In essence, he was saying, I have done everything commanded of men—I have followed the law and have lived an exemplary life. He was not really asking; he was proclaiming his own goodness and saying that he had earned his right to eternal life. But Jesus knew the young man's heart; he knew that the young man's wealth and comfort had become his idol and that relinquishing his material well-being overwhelmed his desire for "treasure in heaven." Just as the young man could not "see" who he was addressing as "good teacher," so he could not see beyond the "good" that wealth brings compared to the "better" that God offers for all eternity.

At this the man's face fell. He went away sad, because he had great wealth. Jesus looked around and said to his disciples, "How hard it is for the rich to enter the kingdom of God!" The disciples were amazed at his words. But Jesus said again, "Children, how hard it is to enter the kingdom of God! It is easier for a camel to go through the eye of a needle than for someone who is rich to enter the kingdom of God." The disciples were even more amazed, and said to each other, "Who then can be saved?" Jesus looked at them and said, "With man this is impossible, but not with God; all things are possible with God." MARK 10:22–27

■

THE DISCIPLES SEEMED TO believe that there is a correlation between the blessings of wealth and the righteousness that leads to eternal life. But Jesus says the opposite is true: Wealth can often be a snare and a diversion that closes us off from eternal life. Wealth buys nothing but power and position: No one can earn their way into the kingdom of God, not even kings and princes. It is the grace of God that makes possible what is otherwise impossible for men and women. "For it is by grace you have been saved, through faith— and this is not from yourselves, it is a gift of God—not by works, so that no one can boast" (Ephesians 2:8–9).

Then Peter spoke up, "We have left everything to follow you!" "Truly I tell you," Jesus replied, "no one who has left home or brothers or sisters or mother or father or children or fields for me and the Gospel will fail to receive a hundred times as much in this present age: homes, brothers, sisters, mothers, children and fields—along with persecutions—and in the age to come eternal life. But many who are first will be last, and the last first." **MARK** 10:28–31

■

JESUS WAS NOT COMBATTING the Pharisees here; he was teaching his followers about the sacrifices and rewards of following him. He was reinforcing something he said in the Sermon on the Mount: Do not worry about what you will eat or drink or wear; the Father knows what you will need. "But seek first his kingdom and his righteousness, and all these things will be given to you as well. Therefore do not worry about tomorrow, for tomorrow will worry about itself. Each day has enough trouble of its own" (Matthew 6:33–34).

To some who were confident of their own righteousness and looked down on everyone else, Jesus told this parable: "Two men went up to the temple to pray, one a Pharisee and the other a tax collector. The Pharisee stood by himself and prayed: 'God, I thank you that I am not like other people—robbers, evildoers, adulterers—or even like this tax collector. I fast twice a week and give a tenth of all I get.' But the tax collector stood at a distance. He would not even look up to heaven, but beat his breast and said, 'God, have mercy on me, a sinner.' I tell you that this man, rather than the other, went home justified before God. For all those who exalt themselves will be humbled, and those who humble themselves will be exalted." LUKE 18:9–14

■

ARE YOU THE PHARISEE or are you the tax collector? There is a good test that will help uncover the answer. The next time you do a good thing, try to discern your reason for doing it. The Pharisee is proud of his "goodness." He said, "I fast twice a week and I give a tenth of all I get." These are good things; no one would deny it. But contrast this attitude with that of the tax collector. He comes before the Lord in total humility. He will not even look up to heaven but simply pleads, "God, have mercy on me, a sinner." The Pharisee thanks God for helping him to be better than all those other sinners out there. He puffs himself up, not seeing that by doing so, he is succumbing to the sin of pride. He does the right thing for the wrong reason, whereas the tax collector humbles himself before God, hoping that God is gracious and forgiving, even to a sinner like him. David was a truly great king because he did not pretend to be exempt from judgment. He prayed, "Have mercy on me, O God, according to your unfailing love, according to your great compassion blot out my transgressions . . . Against you, you only, have I sinned and done what is evil in your sight" (Psalm 51:1,3).

People were bringing little children to Jesus for him to place his hands on them, but the disciples rebuked them. When Jesus saw this, he was indignant. He said to them, "Let the little children come to me, and do not hinder them, for the kingdom of God belongs to such as these. Truly I tell you, anyone who will not receive the kingdom of God like a little child will never enter it." And he took the children in his arms, placed his hands on them and blessed them. MARK 10:13–16

■

JESUS USED THE SIMPLE faith of a little child to show his own disciples what genuine faith actually looks like. Like a child, we are dependent on the Father. He will protect us, guide us, and love us. When we put our faith in money, or position, or even family and friends, we become dependent on our own ingenuity, position, and power, all of which will certainly fail us at some point. This is what David meant when he said, "The Lord is with me; I will not be afraid. It is better to take refuge in the Lord than to trust in humans. It is better to take refuge in the Lord than to trust in princes" (Psalm 118:6, 8–9).

Jesus took the Twelve aside and told them, "We are going up to Jerusalem, and everything that is written by the prophets about the Son of Man will be fulfilled. He will be delivered over to the Gentiles. They will mock him, insult him and spit on him; they will flog him and kill him. On the third day he will rise again." The disciples did not understand any of this. Its meaning was hidden from them, and they did not know what he was talking about.
LUKE 18:31–34

■

JESUS KNEW HIS FOLLOWERS were misreading his mission. They saw him as the one who would reestablish the glorious throne of David. Jesus would be the fulfillment of God's promise that David's line will be established forever (Psalm 89:3–4). But Jesus opened another vista for them; one they had not been able to see because they had their hearts set on a different kind of Messiah. Jesus refers to the prophet Isaiah in describing what will soon take place in Jerusalem. His disciples may have known this prophecy, but their own hope blinded them from seeing the connection to Jesus: "Surely he took up our pain and bore our suffering, yet we considered him punished by God, stricken by him, and afflicted. But he was pierced for our transgressions, he was crushed for our iniquities; the punishment that brought us peace was on him and by his wounds we are healed" (Isaiah 53:4–5).

Then the mother of Zebedee's sons came to Jesus with her sons and, kneeling down, asked a favor of him. "What is it you want?" he asked. She said, "Grant that one of these two sons of mine may sit at your right and the other at your left in your kingdom." "You don't know what you are asking," Jesus said to them. "Can you drink the cup I am going to drink?" "We can," they answered. Jesus said to them, "You will indeed drink from my cup, but to sit at my right or left is not for me to grant. These places belong to those for whom they have been prepared by my Father." **MATTHEW 20:20–23**

■

JAMES AND JOHN WERE the sons of Zebedee. Along with Peter they formed an informal inner circle among the followers of Jesus. But they seemed to want public recognition of their close relationship with Jesus, and so they sent their mother to him to seek privileged positions in the coming kingdom. Whether or not the brothers were referring to an earthly or heavenly kingdom is not certain, but Jesus made his meaning clear by stating that to drink the cup he would be drinking comes with a cost, even to the point of death. John and James still did not fully understand the import of what Jesus was telling them, but soon enough the cost of discipleship became brutally clear to them and many others.

I DID NOT COME TO BE SERVED, BUT TO SERVE

When the ten heard about this, they were indignant with the two brothers. Jesus called them together and said, "You know that the rulers of the Gentiles lord it over them, and their high officials exercise authority over them. Not so with you. Instead, whoever wants to become great among you must be your servant, and whoever wants to be first must be your slave—just as the Son of Man did not come to be served, but to serve, and to give his life as a ransom for many." MATTHEW 20:24–28

■

When the ten other disciples learned that John and James had lobbied for a preferred position, they became indignant. Why? Were they also infected by the same inclination to earn or win a preferred place in Jesus' kingdom? The truth is that all the disciples used worldly standards of comparison to define their identity within the group. They were bound by a system of hierarchy where one's identity is wrapped up in one's title or position. But Jesus rejected this system and instead declared a new order for his kingdom. The mainspring of his kingdom is the inverse of the worldly system. In Jesus' kingdom, we are servants to our Master and do his will, not our own, "just as the Son of Man did not come to be served, but to serve, and to give his life as a ransom for many."

Then they came to Jericho. As Jesus and his disciples, together
with a large crowd, were leaving the city, a blind man, Bartimaeus
(which means "son of Timaeus"), was sitting by the roadside begging. When he heard that it was Jesus of Nazareth, he began to
shout, "Jesus, Son of David, have mercy on me!" Many rebuked
him and told him to be quiet, but he shouted all the more, "Son
of David, have mercy on me!" Jesus stopped and said, "Call him."
So they called to the blind man, "Cheer up! On your feet! He's
calling you." Throwing his cloak aside, he jumped to his feet and
came to Jesus. "What do you want me to do for you?" Jesus asked
him. The blind man said, "Rabbi, I want to see." "Go," said Jesus,
"your faith has healed you." Immediately he received his sight and
followed Jesus along the road. MARK 10:46–52

■

JESUS' REPUTATION AS A miracle worker must have preceded him
to Jericho because the blind man, Bartimaeus, called out to him,
"Jesus, Son of David, have mercy on me!" By calling Jesus "Son of
David," it is possible that Bartimaeus was identifying Jesus as the
Messiah. Jesus' followers tried to shun the man, but he persisted, and
so Jesus said, "Call him." Jesus had found a man of faith who wanted
to see after spending a lifetime in darkness. Jesus did not do anything; he merely granted sight to the man, saying: "Go, your faith
has healed you." Bartimaeus displayed a radical faith; he believed
that God restores sight miraculously and that Jesus is the one who
God promised would sit on David's throne. That faith healed him.

While they were listening to this, he went on to tell them a parable, because he was near Jerusalem and the people thought that the kingdom of God was going to appear at once. He said: "A man of noble birth went to a distant country to have himself appointed king and then to return. So he called ten of his servants and gave them ten minas. 'Put this money to work,' he said, 'until I come back.' But his subjects hated him and sent a delegation after him to say, 'We don't want this man to be our king.' He was made king, however, and returned home. Then he sent for the servants to whom he had given the money, in order to find out what they had gained with it. The first one came and said, 'Sir, your mina has earned ten more.' 'Well done, my good servant!' his master replied. 'Because you have been trustworthy in a very small matter, take charge of ten cities.' The second came and said, 'Sir, your mina has earned five more.' His master answered, 'You take charge of five cities.' LUKE 19:11–19

■

LUKE TELLS US THAT Jesus approached Jerusalem and that "the people thought that the kingdom of God was going to appear at once." This parable is told to keep the focus on what God is actually going to do and how he intends to do it. In the parable, the noble man goes off to "a distant country" to be appointed king. His subjects, however, do not want him to return as king. They prefer to live without him. But before he leaves, he chooses ten servants to look after his kingdom while he is gone. After he returns, he asks the servants what they have done with the minas he has given them. The first two have done well and are rewarded proportionally. But as we will learn, not everyone who says "'Lord, Lord,' will enter the kingdom of heaven" (Matthew 7:21).

"Then another servant came and said, 'Sir, here is your mina; I have kept it laid away in a piece of cloth. I was afraid of you, because you are a hard man. You take out what you did not put in and reap what you did not sow.' His master replied, 'I will judge you by your own words, you wicked servant! You knew, did you, that I am a hard man, taking out what I did not put in, and reaping what I did not sow? Why then didn't you put my money on deposit, so that when I came back, I could have collected it with interest?' Then he said to those standing by, 'Take his mina away from him and give it to the one who has ten minas.' 'Sir,' they said, 'he already has ten!' He replied, 'I tell you that to everyone who has, more will be given, but as for the one who has nothing, even what they have will be taken away. But those enemies of mine who did not want me to be king over them— bring them here and kill them in front of me.'" LUKE 19:20–27

∎

NOW WE COME TO the third servant of the parable. He falsely claims that he knows the nature of his master. He says that his master is a hard man who takes away what he did not put in and reaps what he did not sow. But we have seen the master reward the previous two servants by giving them much more than the amount they returned to their master. The third servant acted out of fear based on a wrong assumption. He buried the mina because he could not be sure that he would be able to preserve what he had been given and did not want to suffer punishment for poor stewardship. How often are we immobilized by the fear of consequences or failure? We translate risk into probability and therefore are tempted to do nothing. This kind of behavior directly results from either no faith or low faith. Fruitfulness requires a certain level of risk. It is faith itself that neutralizes uncertainty and is the mainspring of action. The third servant was unfruitful because he "knew" his master was a hard man and this "knowledge" inhibited him from acting. If he had allowed faith to drive out fear, he then could have put his mina to work, just as the other two servants had done.

INCREASE OUR FAITH!

Jesus said to his disciples: "Things that cause people to stumble are bound to come, but woe to anyone through whom they come. It would be better for them to be thrown into the sea with a millstone tied around their neck than to cause one of these little ones to stumble. So watch yourselves. If your brother or sister sins against you, rebuke them; and if they repent, forgive them. Even if they sin against you seven times in a day and seven times come back to you saying 'I repent,' you must forgive them." The apostles said to the Lord, "Increase our faith!" LUKE 17:1–5

■

QUOTING FROM LEVITICUS, PETER writes, "Be holy, because I (the Lord your God) am holy" (Leviticus 19:2). God is holy; we are not, but in so many ways we strive to attain holiness while disregarding the thing that holds us back. If we remain captive to sin, even if our sin seems harmless or inconsequential, we cannot escape the invisible chains that bind. Jesus says that if someone repents, you must forgive. He goes further: "Even if they sin against you seven times a day and seven times come back to you saying 'I repent,' you must forgive them." If we truly desire to draw closer to God, we must accept the fact that sin has infected everyone. If we ask, God will forgive us our sins as he has promised and he will keep on forgiving as long as we sincerely repent. What God is willing to do, we must be willing to do as well. Then Peter's call to us to be holy will begin to move from a possibility to an attainable probability.

Now a man named Lazarus was sick. He was from Bethany, the village of Mary and her sister Martha. (This Mary, whose brother Lazarus now lay sick, was the same one who poured perfume on the Lord and wiped his feet with her hair.) So the sisters sent word to Jesus, "Lord, the one you love is sick." When he heard this, Jesus said, "This sickness will not end in death. No, it is for God's glory so that God's Son may be glorified through it." Now Jesus loved Martha and her sister and Lazarus. So when he heard that Lazarus was sick, he stayed where he was two more days, and then he said to his disciples, "Let us go back to Judea." JOHN 11:1–7

■

LAZARUS WAS THE BROTHER of Mary and Martha, who Jesus had visited in Bethany several times. Bethany was a small village that rested on a hill across the Kidron Valley from Jerusalem itself. When Jesus learned that Lazarus was sick, he did not act immediately by leaving for Bethany, but rather he made a statement that foreshadowed what would happen in Jerusalem during Passover. He said, "This sickness will not end in death. No, it is for God's glory so that God's Son may be glorified through it." The disciples did not understand what he meant by this, but we know that he was not only referring to the death of Lazarus and the miracle he would perform through him, but also Calvary, where he himself would die "so that the Son may be glorified through it."

"But Rabbi," they said, "a short while ago the Jews there tried to stone you, and yet you are going back?" Jesus answered, "Are there not twelve hours of daylight? Anyone who walks in the daytime will not stumble, for they see by this world's light. It is when a person walks at night that they stumble, for they have no light." After he had said this, he went on to tell them, "Our friend Lazarus has fallen asleep; but I am going there to wake him up." His disciples replied, "Lord, if he sleeps, he will get better." Jesus had been speaking of his death, but his disciples thought he meant natural sleep. So then he told them plainly, "Lazarus is dead, and for your sake I am glad I was not there, so that you may believe. But let us go to him." Then Thomas (also known as Didymus) said to the rest of the disciples, "Let us also go, that we may die with him." JOHN 11:8–16

■

WHY DO THE DISCIPLES seem so dense? Jesus did speak figuratively when he said that Lazarus had "fallen asleep," which might be understood as natural rest, but they also knew that Jesus had performed many miracles. He had given sight to the blind, healed the lame, and fed thousands with a few pieces of bread and some fish. The truth is that we see Jesus very differently than they did. The world had never seen anyone like him before. The resurrection had not yet taken place, and the disciples had the optics of a world circumscribed by natural events. Their ability to understand what Jesus was saying had not yet been transformed by the experience of the resurrected Lord. And so Thomas merely resigned himself to follow Jesus to a martyr's death. He uttered brave words, but those words missed the point.

On his arrival, Jesus found that Lazarus had already been in the tomb for four days. Now Bethany was less than two miles from Jerusalem, and many Jews had come to Martha and Mary to comfort them in the loss of their brother. When Martha heard that Jesus was coming, she went out to meet him, but Mary stayed at home. "Lord," Martha said to Jesus, "if you had been here, my brother would not have died. But I know that even now God will give you whatever you ask." Jesus said to her, "Your brother will rise again." Martha answered, "I know he will rise again in the resurrection at the last day." Jesus said to her, "I am the resurrection and the life. The one who believes in me will live, even though they die; and whoever lives by believing in me will never die. Do you believe this?" JOHN 11:17–26

■

MARTHA'S BROTHER LAZARUS HAD died and been buried. If there was any hope of saving him, that hope was lost by the time Jesus arrived. He was too late, and Martha nearly rebuked him when she said, "If you had been here, my brother would not have died." But then she threw a curve ball by adding, "But I know that even now God will give you whatever you ask." Martha believed that Jesus was a man of God, but whether that belief extended to believing her brother would be awakened from the sleep of death was doubtful. Jesus turned the tables on her by declaring that he himself was the resurrection and the life. He brought future hope into the present by saying that God had granted him the power even to restore life. "I am the resurrection and the life. The one who believes in me will live, even though they die; and whoever lives by believing in me will never die. Do you believe this?"

". . . and whoever lives by believing in me will never die. Do you believe this?" "Yes, Lord," she replied, "I believe that you are the Messiah, the Son of God, who is to come into the world." After she had said this, she went back and called her sister Mary aside. "The Teacher is here," she said, "and is asking for you." When Mary heard this, she got up quickly and went to him. Now Jesus had not yet entered the village, but was still at the place where Martha had met him. When the Jews who had been with Mary in the house, comforting her, noticed how quickly she got up and went out, they followed her, supposing she was going to the tomb to mourn there. When Mary reached the place where Jesus was and saw him, she fell at his feet and said, "Lord, if you had been here, my brother would not have died." JOHN 11:26–32

∎

MARTHA PROGRESSED FROM "LORD, if you had been here" to "I believe that you are the Messiah, the Son of God, who is to come into the world." She went from mild accusation to belief by being in the presence of Jesus. When Mary learned that Jesus had arrived, she dropped everything and went out to meet him, but when she found him, she too offered a mild rebuke: "Lord, if you had been here, my brother would not have died." Death had not only torn Lazarus from his family, it had created a slight rift between the two sisters and Jesus. But Jesus had come on a mission to reveal that he is the resurrected life. Before he left for Bethany he said, "Our friend Lazarus has fallen asleep; but I am going there to wake him up." Jesus used sleep as a metaphor because he knew that "whoever lives by believing in me will never die." He would wake Lazarus from the sleep of death, and soon enough he would show, through his own death, that he is indeed the "resurrection and the life."

JESUS WEPT

When Jesus saw her weeping, and the Jews who had come along
with her also weeping, he was deeply moved in spirit and troubled.
"Where have you laid him?" he asked. "Come and see, Lord," they
replied. Jesus wept. Then the Jews said, "See how he loved him!"
But some of them said, "Could not he who opened the eyes of
the blind man have kept this man from dying?" Jesus, once more
deeply moved, came to the tomb. It was a cave with a stone laid
across the entrance. "Take away the stone," he said. "But, Lord,"
said Martha, the sister of the dead man, "by this time there is a bad
odor, for he has been there four days." JOHN 11:33–39

■

AS FAR BACK AS Genesis, we are told that God grieved because
mankind had rejected him: "The Lord saw how great man's wickedness on the earth had become, and that every inclination of the
thoughts of his heart was only evil all the time" (Genesis 6:5).
Though God's grief led to a desire to "wipe mankind, whom I have
created, from the face of the earth," he relented and called upon
Noah to build an ark that carried mankind into the future. Here
Jesus wept just as God wept because death (which is the penalty for
sin) had brought pain and sorrow to those who loved Lazarus. As
long as Satan reigns, this life will be lived in the "valley of the
shadow of death" (Psalm 23:4), but Jesus came to change that condition once and for all. "I will turn their mourning into gladness; I
will give them comfort and joy instead of sorrow" (Jeremiah 31:13).

Then Jesus said, "Did I not tell you that if you believe, you will see the glory of God?" So they took away the stone. Then Jesus looked up and said, "Father, I thank you that you have heard me. I know that you always hear me, but I said this for the benefit of the people standing here, that they may believe that you sent me." When he had said this, Jesus called in a loud voice, "Lazarus, come out!" The dead man came out, his hands and feet wrapped with strips of linen, and a cloth around his face. Jesus said to them, "Take off the grave clothes and let him go." JOHN 11:40–44

■

TRY TO IMAGINE BEING there when Jesus cried out, "Lazarus, come out!" Wouldn't you wonder if this was some kind of trick? Wouldn't this challenge everything you knew about life and death? Lazarus had been in the grave for four days. Martha warned Jesus not to have the stone removed because the decomposition would have caused a bad odor. And yet Lazarus came out bound up in grave clothes, and we are left either to believe what John reports or reject this account as impossible. The news of Lazarus' resurrection reached those in positions of authority in Jerusalem, causing the religious leaders to redouble their efforts to bring Jesus down. The forces that led to Calvary were set in motion.

Therefore many of the Jews who had come to visit Mary, and had seen what Jesus did, believed in him. But some of them went to the Pharisees and told them what Jesus had done. Then the chief priests and the Pharisees called a meeting of the Sanhedrin. "What are we accomplishing?" they asked. "Here is this man performing many signs. If we let him go on like this, everyone will believe in him, and then the Romans will come and take away both our temple and our nation." JOHN 11:45–48

■

THE RAISING OF LAZARUS was the match that lit the fuse. As Martha and Mary celebrated the return of their brother, the Pharisees called an emergency meeting of the Sanhedrin in Jerusalem to discuss the threat Jesus posed. They were afraid Jesus would attract an even larger following, bringing about the potential for greater unrest in the population. Their power rested on pleasing the Roman occupiers, and they were afraid they would lose everything if they allowed Jesus to go unchecked, and ". . . then the Romans will come and take away both our temple and our nation."

IT IS BETTER FOR YOU THAT ONE MAN DIE FOR THE PEOPLE

Then one of them, named Caiaphas, who was high priest that year, spoke up, "You know nothing at all! You do not realize that it is better for you that one man die for the people than that the whole nation perish." He did not say this on his own, but as high priest that year he prophesied that Jesus would die for the Jewish nation, and not only for that nation but also for the scattered children of God, to bring them together and make them one. JOHN 11:49–52

■

IRONICALLY, CAIAPHAS, THE HIGH priest, inadvertently revealed God's greater purpose when he said, "it is better for you that one man die for the people than that the whole nation perish." What Caiaphas intended for evil, God intends for good. It is God's plan that his Son is the sacrifice for the sin of many—one for all: "He sacrificed for their sins once for all when he offered himself" (Hebrews 7:27). Just as God found a ram as a substitute for Abraham's son Isaac (Genesis 22), so God sent his Son, not to save the temple or the nation, but to offer life through the sacrifice of his own, so that all who believe might live.

So from that day on they plotted to take his life. Therefore Jesus no longer moved about publicly among the people of Judea. Instead he withdrew to a region near the wilderness, to a village called Ephraim, where he stayed with his disciples. When it was almost time for the Jewish Passover, many went up from the country to Jerusalem for their ceremonial cleansing before the Passover. They kept looking for Jesus, and as they stood in the temple courts they asked one another, "What do you think? Isn't he coming to the festival at all?" But the chief priests and the Pharisees had given orders that anyone who found out where Jesus was should report it so that they might arrest him. JOHN 11:53–57

■

HIS TIME HAD NOT yet come, so Jesus retreated to the village of Ephraim. The crowds gathering in Jerusalem for Passover were waiting in expectation for Jesus to appear, but the Pharisees had issued orders for his arrest. The forces at work at this moment were intense. An air of high expectation hovered over the scene as if something monumental was about to happen. But whatever the people and the Pharisees expected, it had no resemblance to what God was about to bring about. It was as if the world rested on a hinge, with one door about to close and another open.

HE WEPT FOR JERUSALEM

As he approached Jerusalem and saw the city, he wept over it and said, "If you, even you, had only known on this day what would bring you peace—but now it is hidden from your eyes. The days will come upon you when your enemies will build an embankment against you and encircle you and hem you in on every side. They will dash you to the ground, you and the children within your walls. They will not leave one stone on another, because you did not recognize the time of God's coming to you." LUKE 19:41–44

■

A CITY THAT HAS abandoned God is a city at risk of complete ruin. Jesus wept because he foresaw what would take place in the not-distant future when the Roman forces cast down even the vast stonewalls of the temple. But Jesus also heard the cries of anguish and fear that had once filled the streets of David's city as the Babylonian armies invaded and destroyed the ancient Jerusalem where God had been worshipped and welcomed. In the words of Jeremiah: "Zion will be plowed like a field, Jerusalem will become a heap of rubble, the temple hill a mound overgrown with thickets" (Jeremiah 26:18). Jesus wept because the city of God had once again declined into just another city of man, where the people and their leaders were blind and deaf to the dangers of their dire condition.

Six days before the Passover, Jesus came to Bethany, where Lazarus lived, whom Jesus had raised from the dead. Here a dinner was given in Jesus' honor. Martha served, while Lazarus was among those reclining at the table with him. Then Mary took about a pint of pure nard, an expensive perfume; she poured it on Jesus' feet and wiped his feet with her hair. And the house was filled with the fragrance of the perfume. JOHN 12:1–3

■

THE SCENE WAS SET in Bethany, a small town on a hill across the Kidron Valley from Jerusalem and the temple. Below, on the side of the hill, were rows and rows of graves of whitewashed stones. Jesus was the guest of honor in the house of Martha, Mary, and Lazarus; they were celebrating the miraculous return of the brother who was dead but now alive. Then, unexpectedly, Mary took a pint of expensive perfume and poured it on Jesus' feet, and in complete humility she wiped his feet with her hair. What possessed Mary to do this act of adoration? It was as if the Holy Spirit had taken hold of her and told her to do this for Jesus as a sign of what was soon to take place.

JUDAS OBJECTED

But one of his disciples, Judas Iscariot, who was later to betray him, objected, "Why wasn't this perfume sold and the money given to the poor? It was worth a year's wages." He did not say this because he cared about the poor but because he was a thief; as keeper of the money bag, he used to help himself to what was put into it. "Leave her alone," Jesus replied. "It was intended that she should save this perfume for the day of my burial." JOHN 12:4–7

■

MARY HAD TAKEN AN expensive perfume and unexpectedly poured it on the one who had raised her brother from the dead. What Mary did was not generous in the normal sense; it was an act of worship, appropriate in ways that she could not fully imagine. But at the same time Judas Iscariot looked on in stunned exasperation. What Mary expended in worship, Judas saw as waste. Worse than that, it was revealed that he had been secretly stealing from the money used to support Jesus and the disciples. Judas was self-righteously scolding Mary out of guilt rather than concern for the well-being of Jesus and his followers. Judas had succumbed to temptation, and his greed led to a desperate place.

THE LEADERS PLOTTED AGAINST
LAZARUS AS WELL

Meanwhile a large crowd of Jews found out that Jesus was there and came, not only because of him but also to see Lazarus, whom he had raised from the dead. So the chief priests made plans to kill Lazarus as well, for on account of him many of the Jews were going over to Jesus and believing in him. JOHN 12:9–11

∎

ON THE SURFACE EVERYTHING in the city seemed normal, but behind closed doors men were plotting to smother the crisis before things got out of hand. Word had spread among the people that a great miracle had taken place, and they wanted to see for themselves that Lazarus was indeed alive. The religious leaders saw this clear expression of the power of God as a threat to their own control. The people of Jerusalem were "going over to Jesus and believing in him." And so the Jewish leaders, who were forever concerned about keeping their Roman masters contented, decided not only to rid themselves of Jesus, but also to destroy the evidence of his miracles by killing Lazarus as well.

As they approached Jerusalem and came to Bethphage and Bethany at the Mount of Olives, Jesus sent two of his disciples, saying to them, "Go to the village ahead of you, and just as you enter it, you will find a colt tied there, which no one has ever ridden. Untie it and bring it here. If anyone asks you, 'Why are you doing this?' say, 'The Lord needs it and will send it back here shortly.'" They went and found a colt outside in the street, tied at a doorway. As they untied it, some people standing there asked, "What are you doing, untying that colt?" They answered as Jesus had told them to, and the people let them go. When they brought the colt to Jesus and threw their cloaks over it, he sat on it. MARK 11:1–7

■

MARK SEEMS TO BE telling a simple story here. Jesus approached Jerusalem for the final time and asked two of his disciples to go on an unusual mission. They were to go to a village just ahead, find a colt that had never been ridden, and bring it to him. This is where the story becomes interesting. Everything happened just as Jesus said it would. Furthermore, the owner of the colt allowed the disciples to take it. But unknown to everyone but Jesus, he asked for the colt to fulfill a five-hundred-year-old prophecy: "See the king comes to you, righteous and having salvation, gentle and riding on a donkey, on a colt, the foal of a donkey . . . He will proclaim peace to the nations, His rule will extend from sea to sea and from the River to the ends of the earth" (Zechariah 9:9–10). It is here where the present moment, the historical moment, and the prophetic moment reveal in a powerful way the identity and purpose of Jesus Christ.

Many people spread their cloaks on the road, while others spread branches they had cut in the fields. Those who went ahead and those who followed shouted, "Hosanna!" "Blessed is he who comes in the name of the Lord!" "Blessed is the coming kingdom of our father David!" "Hosanna in the highest heaven!" Jesus entered Jerusalem and went into the temple courts. He looked around at everything, but since it was already late, he went out to Bethany with the Twelve. MARK 11:8–11

■

HE CAME THROUGH THE gates of Jerusalem, not as a triumphant warrior, but as Isaiah's "suffering servant," on a colt. The people shouted "Hosanna" as if half expecting King David to appear to reclaim his birthright. But it was another sort of Messiah who had returned to Jerusalem to die. Jesus knew why he was there, but the people had no idea what was about to take place. The savior they envisioned was a military leader who would release them from the political bondage imposed by the Romans, but Jesus came on a very different mission. This is how Isaiah describes this King of Kings and Lord of Lords: "Surely he took up our infirmities and carried our sorrows, yet we considered him stricken by God, smitten by him, and afflicted. But he was pierced for our transgressions, he was crushed for our iniquities; the punishment that brought us peace was upon him, and by his wounds we are healed" (Isaiah 53:4–5). This is the one who entered Jerusalem triumphantly that day.

A DEN OF ROBBERS

Jesus entered the temple courts and drove out all who were buying and selling there. He overturned the tables of the money changers and the benches of those selling doves. "It is written," he said to them, "'My house will be called a house of prayer,' but you are making it 'a den of robbers.'" The blind and the lame came to him at the temple, and he healed them. But when the chief priests and the teachers of the law saw the wonderful things he did and the children shouting in the temple courts, "Hosanna to the Son of David," they were indignant. "Do you hear what these children are saying?" they asked him. "Yes," replied Jesus, "have you never read, 'From the lips of children and infants you, Lord, have called forth your praise'?" And he left them and went out of the city to Bethany, where he spent the night. MATTHEW 21:12–17

■

JESUS ENTERED JERUSALEM, THE city of David, to find the temple courts teeming with people getting and spending, while the temple itself loomed over the scene as a rebuke to all who pursued mammon and not God. How far the people had fallen. David said about the temple, "Open for me the gates of righteousness, I will enter and give thanks to the Lord. This is the gate of the Lord through which the righteous may enter. I will give thanks, for you answered me, you have become my salvation" (Psalm 118: 19–21). But Jesus called it a "den of robbers," echoing the words of the prophet Jeremiah, "Will you steal and murder, commit adultery and perjury, burn incense to Baal and follow other gods you have not known, and then come and stand before me at this house, which bears my Name, and say, 'We are safe'—safe to do all these detestable things? Has this House, which bears my Name, become a den of robbers to you?" (Jeremiah 7:9–11) The people had drifted into a dangerous disregard for God, even in the courtyard of the temple.

Now there were some Greeks among those who went up to worship at the festival. They came to Philip, who was from Bethsaida in Galilee, with a request. "Sir," they said, "we would like to see Jesus." Philip went to tell Andrew; Andrew and Philip in turn told Jesus. Jesus replied, "The hour has come for the Son of Man to be glorified. Very truly I tell you, unless a kernel of wheat falls to the ground and dies, it remains only a single seed. But if it dies, it produces many seeds. Anyone who loves their life will lose it, while anyone who hates their life in this world will keep it for eternal life. Whoever serves me must follow me; and where I am, my servant also will be. My Father will honor the one who serves me. JOHN 12:20–26

■

AT MANY DIFFERENT TIMES throughout the Gospel of John we are told that Jesus' time had not yet come. Jesus told his mother at Cana that "My time has not yet come" (John 2:4). And when he is teaching in the temple area, John says, "no one seized him, because his time had not yet come" (John 8:20). But now, after his entry into Jerusalem on a colt, Jesus acknowledged to Philip that, "the hour has come for the Son of Man to be glorified." But by this Jesus did not mean the time had come for him to be crowned king like any other monarch. Jesus meant that the time had come for him to die by being lifted up on a cross. Philip may have been puzzled by this reply, but Jesus knew exactly what it meant when he said, "the hour had come." The mission and the moment were about to fuse.

"Now my soul is troubled, and what shall I say? 'Father, save me from the hour'? No, it was for this very reason I came to this hour. Father, glorify your name!" Then a voice came from heaven, "I have glorified it, and will glorify it again." The crowd that was there and heard it said it had thundered; others said an angel had spoken to him. Jesus said, "This voice was for your benefit, not mine. Now is the time for judgment on this world; now the prince of this world will be driven out. And I, when I am lifted up from the earth, will draw all people to myself." He said this to show the kind of death he was going to die. The crowd spoke up, "We have heard from the Law that the Messiah will remain forever, so how can you say, 'The Son of Man must be lifted up'? Who is this 'Son of Man'?" Then Jesus told them, "You are going to have the light just a little while longer. Walk while you have the light, before darkness overtakes you. Whoever walks in the dark does not know where they are going. Believe in the light while you have the light, so that you may become children of light." When he had finished speaking, Jesus left and hid himself from them. JOHN 12:27–36

■

FINALLY, AFTER ALL THOSE times when we heard that Jesus' time had not yet come, it has come. Jesus confirmed that his hour had arrived: "No, it was for this very reason I came to this hour." Should he try to avoid it? Jesus answered that question with a question of his own: Should he ask the Father to save him from this hour? Jesus had already answered these questions many times before when he told people that he could do nothing without the Father. While the people around him thought they heard thunder or perhaps angels speaking to him, Jesus heard the voice of the Father confirming the purpose and cosmic importance of the mission. Rather than the temptation to be saved from completing the mission, Jesus received confirmation that he is to glorify the name of the Father. The voice said, "I have glorified it and will glorify it again." God will glorify his name through the Son, who will begin the end of the reign of "the prince of this world." Jesus understood exactly what this means; his own followers and the people surrounding him hadn't a clue.

Even after Jesus had performed so many signs in their presence, they still would not believe in him. This was to fulfill the word of Isaiah the prophet: "Lord, who has believed our message and to whom has the arm of the Lord been revealed?" JOHN 12:37–38

■

IF MANY IN JESUS' own time did not believe, why do we think it would be any different today? If his closest followers had their doubts, why would we be dismissive when we come upon a doubter? In this age, where the scientific method is deified and technological innovation is a manifestation of science's power, why are we surprised when we hear that many no longer accept the truth of the Bible? The fact is that Christ has always been under attack, since the time of his own birth. Yet despite the skepticism of our own times, faith in Jesus Christ is alive in every corner of the world. People everywhere have answered Jesus' question to Peter, "But who do you say I am?" with "You are the Christ of God" (Mark 8:29).

For this reason they could not believe, because, as Isaiah says elsewhere, "He has blinded their eyes and hardened their hearts, so they can neither see with their eyes, nor understand with their hearts, nor turn—and I would heal them." Isaiah said this because he saw Jesus' glory and spoke about him. Yet at the same time many even among the leaders believed in him. But because of the Pharisees they would not openly acknowledge their faith for fear they would be put out of the synagogue; or they loved human praise more than praise from God. JOHN 12:39–43

■

WHAT BARS US FROM belief? Isaiah refers to intellectual blindness and a cold and hardened heart. John mentions the social or financial cost because "they loved human praise more than the praise from God." Perhaps we believe, like squirrels, that our acorn of belief will be safe if we bury it. But if our belief matters to us, if it is important enough to bury like a treasure, why can't we bring ourselves to live our faith in the open? Is it as true now as it was in Jesus' own time that we actually love human praise more than praise from God? If we profess Christ, do we proclaim him? Or do we bury our belief in him like that acorn, anticipating there will be a time and place to dig it up again?

Then Jesus cried out, "Whoever believes in me does not believe in me only, but in the one who sent me. The one who looks at me is seeing the one who sent me. I have come into the world as a light, so that no one who believes in me should stay in darkness. If anyone hears my words but does not keep them, I do not judge that person. For I did not come to judge the world, but to save the world. There is a judge for the one who rejects me and does not accept my words; the very words I have spoken will condemn them at the last day." JOHN 12:44–48

■

EARLIER JESUS SAYS, "GOD did not send his Son into the world to condemn the world, but to save the world through him" (John 3:17). The world Jesus entered was shrouded in darkness. God did not need to judge it because it stood judged already. Jesus goes on to say that mankind has abandoned love of God for love of darkness: "but men loved darkness instead of light because their deeds were evil. Everyone who does evil hates the light and will not come into the light for fear their deeds will be exposed" (John 3:20). Jesus came to change all of that because he has "come into the world as a light, so that no one who believes in me should stay in darkness." Simply put, Jesus came to reverse the order of loves. Rather than the love of self, or friends, or things, Jesus came to restore love of God as our primary love that then radiates out to love for others before love of self.

For I did not speak on my own, but the Father who sent me commanded me to say all that I have spoken. I know that his command leads to eternal life. So whatever I say is just what the Father has told me to say. JOHN 12:49–50

■

JESUS MAKES WHAT MIGHT appear to be a wild claim, but it is wild only if he is not the Son of God. While the Jews were trying to adhere to the spoken Word, Jesus came as the living Word—the exact representation on earth of God the Father. The Son speaks what the Father commands him to say and so perfectly reveals the Father through this dynamic relationship. The Father is perfectly revealed by his Son through the Holy Spirit as if they existed together eternally in complete harmony.

A FRUITLESS FIG TREE

The next day as they were leaving Bethany, Jesus was hungry. See-ing in the distance a fig tree in leaf, he went to find out if it had any fruit. When he reached it, he found nothing but leaves, be-cause it was not the season for figs. Then he said to the tree, "May no one ever eat fruit from you again." And his disciples heard him say it. MARK 11:12–14

■

AS JESUS LEFT BETHANY to return to the temple in Jerusalem, he came upon a fig tree that had leaves but no fruit. Spring was not the season for the tree to produce figs, but Jesus was hungry and the tree did not serve its purpose. Jesus' cursing of the tree may seem dis-proportional, but consider that Jesus may have been using the tree as an example to make a spiritual statement. In Jesus' time the fig tree was a symbol for Israel, a land that had abandoned the God of the patriarchs and had become unfruitful. The nation had been cursed, occupied by foreign armies, and presided over by corrupt leaders. Jesus may have been using the fig tree as a symbol of God's judgment, even as God was moving toward removing that curse through what Jesus would do on the cross.

A WITHERED FIG TREE

In the morning, as they went along, they saw the fig tree withered from the roots. Peter remembered and said to Jesus, "Rabbi, look! The fig tree you cursed has withered!" "Have faith in God," Jesus answered. "Truly I tell you, if anyone says to this mountain, 'Go, throw yourself into the sea,' and does not doubt in their heart but believes that what they say will happen, it will be done for them. Therefore I tell you, whatever you ask for in prayer, believe that you have received it, and it will be yours. And when you stand praying, if you hold anything against anyone, forgive them, so that your Father in heaven may forgive you your sins." MARK 11:20–25

∎

THE DISCIPLES WERE AMAZED that the fig tree actually withered one day after Jesus cursed it. But Jesus simply asked, why are you so surprised? Faith is audacious, and when you pray, audacious things are possible. At the same time, Jesus is not saying that God will answer every prayer and petition in just the way we want him to. In fact, we may find that God seems to be silent for a time because the time may not be right. Jesus continuously prayed to God, always knowing that in the end it must be God's will, not his (or our) will, that needs to be done. So pray boldly but trust broadly, because "we know that in all things God works for the good of those who love him, who have been called according to his purpose" (Romans 8:25).

WHO GAVE YOU THIS AUTHORITY?

One day as Jesus was teaching the people in the temple courts and proclaiming the good news, the chief priests and the teachers of the law, together with the elders, came up to him. "Tell us by what authority you are doing these things," they said. "Who gave you this authority?" He replied, "I will also ask you a question. Tell me: John's baptism—was it from heaven, or of human origin?" They discussed it among themselves and said, "If we say, 'From heaven,' he will ask, 'Why didn't you believe him?' But if we say, 'Of human origin,' all the people will stone us, because they are persuaded that John was a prophet." So they answered, "We don't know where it was from." Jesus said, "Neither will I tell you by what authority I am doing these things." LUKE 20:1–8

■

THE CHIEF PRIESTS AND teachers of the law stepped forward to question Jesus' authority to teach the people in the temple courts. They approached with confidence because they held the institutional authority of the temple itself. They had all the credentials that conferred power and protection upon them. Yet somehow they felt threatened because the people were listening to Jesus. Jesus responded to the priests and teachers with his own question, which forced them to answer, "We don't know." The irony here is that the very nature of the question cut through the pretense of the authority of the priests and teachers. If their authority was from God, they would have known the answer and not worried about the opinion of the people. All authority comes from God, including John's baptism. The religious leaders corrupted the authority they held for their own purposes. The authority God gave to John the Baptist had threatened the political order of things and therefore was destroyed. Now they saw Jesus as another threat to their power.

"What do you think? There was a man who had two sons. He went to the first and said, 'Son, go and work today in the vineyard.' 'I will not,' he answered, but later he changed his mind and went. Then the father went to the other son and said the same thing. He answered, 'I will, sir,' but he did not go. Which of the two did what his father wanted?" "The first," they answered. Jesus said to them, "Truly I tell you, the tax collectors and the prostitutes are entering the kingdom of God ahead of you. For John came to you to show you the way of righteousness, and you did not believe him, but the tax collectors and the prostitutes did. And even after you saw this, you did not repent and believe him." MATTHEW 21:28–32

■

JESUS CONTINUED TO ADDRESS the chief priests and teachers of the law. He told a story of two sons: One pretends to do the right thing but then does the opposite, while the other at first refuses to do the right thing but then ends up obeying. Jesus aimed this parable directly at those who questioned his authority. Then he added insult to injury by saying that their pretensions to righteousness belied their disbelief in the righteousness of John the Baptist. Jesus further offended them by saying that the lowest of the low—prostitutes and tax collectors—who believed John the Baptist would enter the kingdom of God ahead of them. Belief is not based on outward appearances; according to Jesus, an authentic desire to repent and turn your heart over to Jesus in joyful surrender is the only pathway to abiding in the will of God.

Later they sent some of the Pharisees and Herodians to Jesus to catch him in his words. They came to him and said, "Teacher, we know that you are a man of integrity. You aren't swayed by others, because you pay no attention to who they are; but you teach the way of God in accordance with the truth. Is it right to pay the imperial tax to Caesar or not? Should we pay or shouldn't we?" But Jesus knew their hypocrisy. "Why are you trying to trap me?" he asked. "Bring me a denarius and let me look at it." They brought the coin, and he asked them, "Whose image is this? And whose inscription?" "Caesar's," they replied. Then Jesus said to them, "Give back to Caesar what is Caesar's and to God what is God's." And they were amazed at him. **MARK 12:13–17**

■

JESUS WAS NOT DECEIVED by the flattering words of the Pharisees and Herodians. While they may have changed their tactics, they had not changed their intention. Their speech might have been as smooth as butter, but war against Jesus remained very much in their hearts (Psalm 55:21). Jesus knew this because he was not deceived by men and the things that corrupt them: "for he knew all men. He did not need man's testimony about man, for he knew what was in a man" (John 2:24–25). In answer to their loaded question, he asked for a coin, looked at it, and said, "Whose image is this?" When the Pharisees said Caesar's, he simply replied, "Give back to Caesar what is Caesar's and to God what is God's." The irony here is that the Pharisees and Herodians had given what is God's to Caesar as well, betraying God for the rewards of personal position and power.

One of the teachers of the law came and heard them debating. Noticing that Jesus had given them a good answer, he asked him, "Of all the commandments, which is the most important?" "The most important one," answered Jesus, "is this: 'Hear, O Israel: The Lord our God, the Lord is one. Love the Lord your God with all your heart and with all your soul and with all your mind and with all your strength.' The second is this: 'Love your neighbor as yourself.' There is no commandment greater than these." MARK 12:28–31

■

JESUS DISTILLED THE HUNDREDS of laws, rules, and regulations into two commandments, one drawn from Deuteronomy and the other from Leviticus. By giving just two commandments, he is not saying that all the other laws are rendered obsolete; rather, he is pronouncing the two basic principles that are foundational for all the rules and regulations that came after God gave Moses the Ten Commandments, which are themselves built on the two commandments that Jesus gives us.

"Well said, teacher," the man replied. "You are right in saying that God is one and there is no other but him. To love him with all your heart, with all your understanding and with all your strength, and to love your neighbor as yourself is more important than all burnt offerings and sacrifices." When Jesus saw that he had answered wisely, he said to him, "You are not far from the kingdom of God." And from then on no one dared ask him any more questions. MARK 12:32–34

■

THIS PARTICULAR TEACHER OF the law was an honest broker, a striver for the truth. He genuinely wanted Jesus to give an answer to his question, and he was not disappointed by what he heard. But then Jesus moved from the truth of his answer to the question of how to apply that truth. He said, "You are not far from the kingdom of God." By this he meant that knowing you should love the Lord your God is not the same as acting on that knowledge. Knowing is only the first step in acting in a way that will further the kingdom here and now. The commandment to love God and neighbor seems so simple; when we actually live it every day, we come to experience the harmonious beauty that radiates from this core into God's own purpose and design for building the kingdom that is to come.

A RIDDLE

While the Pharisees were gathered together, Jesus asked them, "What do you think about the Messiah? Whose son is he?" "The son of David," they replied. He said to them, "How is it then that David, speaking by the Spirit, calls him 'Lord'? For he says, 'The Lord said to my Lord: 'Sit at my right hand until I put your enemies under your feet.' If then David calls him 'Lord,' how can he be his son?" MATTHEW 22:41–45

■

JESUS ASKED THE PHARISEES a seemingly simple question: "What do you think about the Messiah? Whose son is he?" The Pharisees gave the partially correct answer: "The Son of David." This answer is true, but their answer was far too bound up by earthly chronology. Jesus reveals that the Messiah both precedes David and comes after David. He is from the beginning, but he will take earthly form as a descendant of David (Psalm 132:11). Immediately before his arrest, Jesus prayed this prayer with his disciples: "And now, Father, glorify me in your presence with the glory I had with you before the world began" (John 17:5). The Pharisees understood how life unfolds in its natural order, but to see the full dimensions of the mystery of God's purpose as revealed in Jesus Christ was simply beyond their capacity to believe.

While all the people were listening, Jesus said to his disciples, "Beware of the teachers of the law. They like to walk around in flowing robes and love to be greeted with respect in the market-places and have the most important seats in the synagogues and the places of honor at banquets. They devour widows' houses and for a show make lengthy prayers. These men will be punished most severely." LUKE 20:45–47

■

BEHIND JESUS' DOUBLE-EDGED WARNING was an implicit under-standing of God-directed leadership. Jesus warned the disciples not to emulate the corrupt ruling class because their thirst for the prerequisites of rule had led them away from God. Jesus warned the leaders themselves that they were only serving themselves by stealing from widows and loudly uttering vaporous prayers that served no other purpose than to strengthen their hold on political and religious power. Jesus offers a radical substitute for this earth-bound notion of leadership. Jesus' model is based on the central idea that we must serve God in whatever capacity we have been gifted and called. Jesus told his disciples, "the Son of Man did not come to be served, but to serve, and to give his life as a ransom for many" (Matthew 20:28). Jesus sets forth God's own model for lead-ership, and he tells us to beware of everything else.

Jesus left the temple and was walking away when his disciples came up to him to call his attention to its buildings. "Do you see all these things?" he asked. "Truly I tell you, not one stone here will be left on another; everyone will be thrown down." As Jesus was sitting on the Mount of Olives, the disciples came to him privately. "Tell us," they said, "when will this happen, and what will be the sign of your coming and of the end of the age?" MATTHEW 24:1–3

■

IT WAS FIVE HUNDRED years earlier that Jeremiah pronounced with much anguish that the people had forsaken God and that Jerusalem with its temple would become "a heap of ruins, a haunt of jackals" (Jeremiah 9:11). The temple itself was restored in Jesus' time, but the leaders and the people were as far away from God as ever. Instead of putting their trust in God, they put their confidence in the temple structure itself. Jesus was saying that when the people do not honor God as the centerpiece of their lives and faith, then the temple becomes a showcase of pretense and hypocrisy. And Jesus said even the temple will not stand but will be thrown down because the children of God have abandoned God just as their forbearers had forsaken him so many times before.

Jesus answered: "Watch out that no one deceives you. For many will come in my name, claiming, 'I am the Messiah,' and will deceive many. You will hear of wars and rumors of wars, but see to it that you are not alarmed. Such things must happen, but the end is still to come. Nation will rise against nation, and kingdom against kingdom. There will be famines and earthquakes in various places. All these are the beginning of birth pains." MATTHEW 24:4–8

■

JESUS TELLS US THAT there will be a period of time before he comes again when chaos and confusion will seem to reign. And he warns us not to waste our time trying to discern the exact moment when the "the end of the age" will occur. He promises he will come again, but as for the exact time and place, that is for only the Father to know (Acts 1:7). In times of wars and rumors of wars, Jesus tells us to focus on the opportunities at hand as they serve the Lord. In the Sermon on the Mount he says, "But seek first his kingdom and his righteousness, and all these things will be given to you as well. Therefore do not worry about tomorrow, for tomorrow will worry about itself. Each day has enough trouble of its own" (Matthew 6:33–34).

Then will appear the sign of the Son of Man in heaven. And then all the peoples of the earth will mourn when they see the Son of Man coming on the clouds of heaven, with power and great glory. And he will send his angels with a loud trumpet call, and they will gather his elect from the four winds, from one end of the heavens to the other. MATTHEW 24:30–31

■

As PAUL PREPARED TO depart for Jerusalem from Ephesus, he declared to the elders in a final farewell that he had "not hesitated to proclaim to you the whole will of God" (Acts 20:27). Why is this important for each of us? It is very easy, and not uncommon, to take a part of the Gospel narrative and expand it into the whole thing. Paul was obedient to the will of God through the Holy Spirit by focusing on every dimension of Jesus, from his miraculous birth to his arrest, trial, crucifixion, death, resurrection, and ascension. This is not Paul's story; it is God's story, carrying all the way back to the first words of Genesis. It can be tempting to simplify the narrative by transforming it into something other than what it is, but Paul refused to adjust the story for his own convenience. And Jesus does exactly the same thing in his prophetic teachings. While his followers wanted to know more about when "the Son of Man" would return, Jesus gave the general sweep of what will take place while keeping in place the mystery of God's timing. If we focus just on the question of when Jesus will return, we lose focus on the Jesus of the Gospels, the Jesus of Nazareth and Capernaum, of Jerusalem, and of all of the world.

But about that day or hour no one knows, not even the angels in heaven, nor the Son, but only the Father. As it was in the days of Noah, so it will be at the coming of the Son of Man. For in the days before the flood, people were eating and drinking, marrying and giving in marriage, up to the day Noah entered the ark; and they knew nothing about what would happen until the flood came and took them all away. That is how it will be at the coming of the Son of Man. MATTHEW 24:36–39

■

GOD'S KNOWLEDGE IS INFINITE; our knowledge is incomplete and often wrong. But still many of us spend hours and days looking for signs of what is to come while missing the opportunities of the moment to serve God's purpose in important ways. Jesus warns us away from this unproductive inactivity by telling us, "No one knows about that day or hour, not even the angels of heaven, nor the Son, but only the Father . . . Therefore keep watch, because you do not know on what day your Lord will come." In contrast, the religious leaders claimed a special knowledge of God's providence, but their intellectual pride was their sin. Paul looked at this foolishness from the perspective of God: "For the foolishness of God is wiser than man's wisdom, and the weakness of God is stronger than man's strength" (1 Corinthians 1:25).

When the Son of Man comes in his glory, and all the angels with him, he will sit on his glorious throne. All the nations will be gathered before him, and he will separate the people one from another as a shepherd separates the sheep from the goats. He will put the sheep on his right and the goats on his left. MATTHEW 25:31–33

■

WHEN WE PRAY THE Lord's Prayer, we say, Lord, "thy will be done." But do we walk in the way of God's will or do we turn down the "my will be done" path? God's will for each one of us is to transform the "my will" into "thy will," but for the rebellious heart, this change of direction can prove to be so hard that we give up, or, worse, fall back into the world of "my will be done." When Jesus refers to the day of final judgment, he is not necessarily looking for an accounting of all the things we have done wrong. No one will stand before the throne of God and say that they lived a life without sin. But have we chosen to live outside of the opportunities and blessings that God gifts to each one of us? Are we like the servant who doubled the value of the coins given to him by the master or are we like the servant who buried the coin out of fear rather than use it well in the service of his master? God calls each one of us to be his sheep—to follow him—not only for this life, but for all eternity.

Then the King will say to those on his right, 'Come, you who are blessed by my Father; take your inheritance, the kingdom prepared for you since the creation of the world. For I was hungry and you gave me something to eat, I was thirsty and you gave me something to drink, I was a stranger and you invited me in, I needed clothes and you clothed me, I was sick and you looked after me, I was in prison and you came to visit me.' Then the righteous will answer him, 'Lord, when did we see you hungry and feed you, or thirsty and give you something to drink? When did we see you a stranger and invite you in, or needing clothes and clothe you? When did we see you sick or in prison and go to visit you?' The King will reply, 'Truly I tell you, whatever you did for one of the least of these brothers and sisters of mine, you did for me.' MATTHEW 25:34–40

■

JESUS CONTINUES TO TEACH what it means to do God's will in this world. He sums it up this way: "Truly I tell you, whatever you did for one of the least of these brothers and sisters of mine, you did for me." To do the will of God requires us to see the image of God in every person—young and old, rich and poor, male and female. Our human categories deceive us and separate us artificially from God's will. In his first letter, John reinforces this connection between God, his children, and each one of us: "Anyone who claims to be in the light but hates his brother is still in the darkness. Whoever loves his brother lives in the light, and there is nothing in him to make him stumble. But whoever hates his brother is in the darkness and walks around in the darkness; he does not know where he is going, because the darkness has blinded him" (1 John 2:9–11).

Then he will say to those on his left, 'Depart from me, you who are cursed, into the eternal fire prepared for the devil and his angels. For I was hungry and you gave me nothing to eat, I was thirsty and you gave me nothing to drink, I was a stranger and you did not invite me in, I needed clothes and you did not clothe me, I was sick and in prison and you did not look after me.' They also will answer, 'Lord, when did we see you hungry or thirsty or a stranger or needing clothes or sick or in prison, and did not help you?' He will reply, 'Truly I tell you, whatever you did not do for one of the least of these, you did not do for me.' Then they will go away to eternal punishment, but the righteous to eternal life. MATTHEW 25:41–46

■

WHY DOES JESUS SAY to some, "Depart from me, you who are cursed, into eternal fire prepared for the devil and his angels"? He is saying that for those who claim to worship and follow God, there is a cost to discipleship. We are called to the hard tasks of feeding the hungry, providing drink to the thirsty, giving shelter to the stranger, clothing the naked, and offering hope to the hopeless. All these people bear the image of God, even if they are the most marginalized members of society. Jesus says that even the most seemingly worthless people who live wrecked and broken lives are worthy in the eyes of God because each person was created in the image of God. The Good Samaritan was good because he crossed the road to help a man who had been robbed and left for dead. He could have passed by as others had done, but then he would have been just a Samaritan, because as Jesus puts it, "whatever you did not do for one of the least of these, you did not do for me."

Now the Passover and the Festival of Unleavened Bread were only two days away, and the chief priests and the teachers of the law were scheming to arrest Jesus secretly and kill him. "But not during the festival," they said, "or the people may riot." **MARK 14:1–2**

■

TRY TO IMAGINE JERUSALEM at the moment described by Mark. The city with its closely compacted buildings separated by narrow streets was beginning to teem with people as Passover approached. The streets were noisy with crowds that had come long distances to celebrate the Festival of Unleavened Bread, which commemorated the time when Moses, responding to God's command, prepared the people to begin the journey from bondage to freedom. But hidden unseen behind closed doors, the religious leaders were scheming to arrest and execute Jesus. In a way, they had, ironically, substituted their role as descendants of Moses for the role of descendants of the tyrant Pharaoh. Jesus had come to Jerusalem on a mission from God; the religious leaders were on their own mission to subvert God's purpose, even though they had convinced themselves that they were doing God's handiwork.

Then one of the Twelve—the one called Judas Iscariot—went to the chief priests and asked, "What are you willing to give me if I deliver him over to you?" So they counted out for him thirty pieces of silver. From then on Judas watched for an opportunity to hand him over. MATTHEW 26:14–16

■

WHY DID JUDAS DECIDE to betray Jesus? Judas was a disciple, one of the original Twelve, a man who followed Jesus from Galilee to Jerusalem and showed no signs of turning on the one who had called him to follow. But Matthew tells us that at some point he went to the chief priests and asked for money to deliver Jesus into their hands. Then Matthew says, "Judas watched for an opportunity to hand him over." The word "opportunity" provides a hint to the spiritual source of this betrayal. Luke makes it clear that at the very conclusion of the time that Satan tempted Jesus in the wilderness, Satan had not given up. Instead, we are told, "When the devil had finished all this tempting, he left him until an opportune time." The prince of the kingdom of darkness found his instrument of opportunity in the person of Judas. Even though Judas was a dedicated disciple of Jesus, he was subject to the same desires and appetites that all people experience. It might even be said that the closer one is to Jesus, the more intense the temptations become. At a moment of weakness, Judas tragically gave into Satan's whisperings and turned on the Son of God. Satan found his opportune time and entered Judas' heart to capitalize on what appeared to be his final road to victory.

Then came the day of Unleavened Bread on which the Passover lamb had to be sacrificed. Jesus sent Peter and John, saying, "Go and make preparations for us to eat the Passover." "Where do you want us to prepare for it?" they asked. He replied, "As you enter the city, a man carrying a jar of water will meet you. Follow him to the house that he enters, and say to the owner of the house, 'The Teacher asks: Where is the guest room, where I may eat the Passover with my disciples?' He will show you a large room upstairs, all furnished. Make preparations there." They left and found things just as Jesus had told them. So they prepared the Passover.
LUKE 22:7–13

■

LUKE TELLS US THAT the day of Unleavened Bread is the day the Passover lamb had to be sacrificed. This is an historical fact, but behind the historical is God's supernatural intention. The angel of the Lord told Mary that she would give birth to a son and would "give him the name Jesus because he will save his people from their sins" (Matthew 1:21). Upon seeing Jesus, John the Baptist said, "Look, the Lamb of God, who takes away the sin of the world" (John 1:29). Jesus came into the world for this very reason. Isaiah describes him as a Suffering Servant who will be "led like a lamb to the slaughter . . . for the transgression of my people he was stricken" (Isaiah 53:7,8). Just as Jesus knew in advance that a man carrying water would take Peter and John to the Upper Room, so he understood how this moment was a turning point in history. God was about to open the door to redemption. He was about to provide the Lamb (Genesis 22:8).

THE LAST SUPPER

When evening came, Jesus arrived with the Twelve. While they were reclining at the table eating, he said, "Truly I tell you, one of you will betray me—one who is eating with me." They were saddened, and one by one they said to him, "Surely you don't mean me?" "It is one of the Twelve," he replied, "one who dips bread into the bowl with me. The Son of Man will go just as it is written about him. But woe to that man who betrays the Son of Man! It would be better for him if he had not been born." While they were eating, Jesus took bread, and when he had given thanks, he broke it and gave it to his disciples, saying, "Take it; this is my body." Then he took a cup, and when he had given thanks, he gave it to them, and they all drank from it. "This is my blood of the covenant, which is poured out for many," he said to them. "Truly I tell you, I will not drink again from the fruit of the vine until that day when I drink it new in the kingdom of God." When they had sung a hymn, they went out to the Mount of Olives. MARK 14:17–26

■

THE DISCIPLES GATHERED TO share the Passover meal with Jesus. They were not thinking that this was the Last Supper. When they heard that one among them would betray the Lord, they were "saddened." What a strange response. Betrayal usually evokes anger, even a desire for revenge, but the followers were only concerned about their own innocence. They said, "Surely you do not mean me?" But Jesus simply said, "It is one of the Twelve . . . one who dips bread into the bowl with me." Jesus was not necessarily singling out Judas here, because Jesus already knew that each one of the Twelve would betray him within hours, and he would be left alone to face the foot soldiers of his enemy in the Garden of Gethsemane. Perhaps Judas' sin was the greatest, but none of the Twelve were exempt, and this put each one of them in a place that would require forgiveness and restoration.

. . . so he got up from the meal, took off his outer clothing, and wrapped a towel around his waist. After that, he poured water into a basin and began to wash his disciples' feet, drying them with the towel that was wrapped around him. He came to Simon Peter, who said to him, "Lord, are you going to wash my feet?" Jesus replied, "You do not realize now what I am doing, but later you will understand." "No," said Peter, "you shall never wash my feet." Jesus answered, "Unless I wash you, you have no part with me." "Then, Lord," Simon Peter replied, "not just my feet but my hands and my head as well!" JOHN 13:4–9

■

JESUS DISCOMFORTED HIS DISCIPLES by taking on a role usually delegated to servants. Peter objected because to him (and perhaps the others) the master should never assume the role of the servant. But just as he is King, Jesus is also servant, serving the will of the Father. In the Garden of Gethsemane, Jesus struggled between his own human will and God's will. In the end he finally said, "My Father, if it is not possible for this cup to be taken away unless I drink it, may your will be done" (Matthew 26:42). Jesus modeled what it means to be a genuine servant of God. Jesus came to serve, and ultimately, he came to die so that many might live: ". . . he humbled himself and became obedient to death—even death on a cross" (Philippians 2:8).

Then Jesus told them, "This very night you will all fall away on account of me, for it is written: 'I will strike the shepherd, and the sheep of the flock will be scattered.' But after I have risen, I will go ahead of you into Galilee." Peter replied, "Even if all fall away on account of you, I never will." "Truly I tell you," Jesus answered, "this very night, before the rooster crows, you will disown me three times." But Peter declared, "Even if I have to die with you, I will never disown you." And all the other disciples said the same.
MATTHEW 26:31–35

■

THIS IS A SAD moment. The disciples all declared that they would not fall away. Peter went so far as to say, "Even if I have to die with you, I will never disown you," but Jesus knew better and declared that Peter would betray him three times before the rooster crowed at sunrise. The disciples simply misjudged the level of courage it took to stand with Jesus in his moment of greatest crisis. The kingdom of God was being established, but strong opposition was rising up to stop it. Yes, the disciples abandoned Jesus to his enemies, but this would not be the end of the story.

"Do not let your hearts be troubled. You believe in God; believe also in me. My Father's house has many rooms; if that were not so, would I have told you that I am going there to prepare a place for you? And if I go and prepare a place for you, I will come back and take you to be with me that you also may be where I am. You know the way to the place where I am going." Thomas said to him, "Lord, we don't know where you are going, so how can we know the way?" Jesus answered, "I am the way and the truth and the life. No one comes to the Father except through me. If you really know me, you will know my Father as well. From now on, you do know him and have seen him." JOHN 14:1–7

■

JESUS MADE A DECLARATIVE statement to his disciples as they partook in the Passover supper. He said, "You believe in God." This was not conditional; he was not saying, "If you believe in God." He was affirming that they were believers. But then he said something that was more difficult for them to accept: "Believe in me also." Later he would make the same statement, but in reverse: "If you really know me, you will know my Father as well." To know the Son is to know the Father. To believe in the Father sets the foundation for believing in the Son. The two are indivisible. Based on his own claim, Jesus is not a way or a truth or a life. This might apply to a prophet or a king or a great man, but Jesus is saying something very different. Because the Son is the exact human representation of the Father, he can say with complete certainty that "I am the way and the truth and the life."

ASK ME FOR ANYTHING IN MY NAME, AND I WILL DO IT

Very truly I tell you, whoever believes in me will do the works I have been doing, and they will do even greater things than these, because I am going to the Father. And I will do whatever you ask in my name, so that the Father may be glorified in the Son. You may ask me for anything in my name, and I will do it. JOHN 14:12–14

■

JESUS' STATEMENT, "YOU MAY ask me for anything in my name, and I will do it" is not an invitation to profligacy or bad behavior. The key to understanding what Jesus is driving at is the phrase "in my name." He is saying: Ask for the power to do the things I have been doing. Ask to advance God's kingdom here on earth. Ask that you may use the authority Christ has given you to work through God in this life. Ask for the power to heal, to deliver the broken into new life, and to do God's work with boldness and compassion. Jesus is affirming Scripture, not contradicting it. He is saying, Pray boldly, trust broadly, and in everything you do, work to advance the kingdom in the unique way God has granted that work to you.

If you love me, keep my commands. And I will ask the Father, and he will give you another advocate to help you and be with you forever—the Spirit of truth. The world cannot accept him, because it neither sees him nor knows him. But you know him, for he lives with you and will be in you. I will not leave you as orphans; I will come to you. JOHN 14:15–18

■

WHAT IS THIS "SPIRIT of truth" offered by Jesus? It is the same Spirit that hovered over the waters as the heavens and earth were being created (Genesis 1:1–2). It is the same Spirit that David, in his confessional psalm begged God not to take from him (Psalm 51:11). Jesus told the Samaritan woman, "A time is coming and has now come when true worshippers will worship the Father in spirit and in truth, for they are the kind of worshippers the Father seeks. God is spirit, and his worshippers must worship in spirit and in truth" (John 4:23–24). Jesus knows the Father and the Father knows him, but the Holy Spirit was not released to the disciples until Jesus opened the way on the cross of Calvary. It was on Pentecost after the crucifixion, resurrection, and ascension of Christ that the Holy Spirit came to the disciples in Jerusalem, and then in miraculous ways spread into Judea and Samaria, and to the very ends of the earth (Acts 1:8).

I will not say much more to you, for the prince of this world is coming. He has no hold over me, but he comes so that the world may learn that I love the Father and do exactly what my Father has commanded me. Come now; let us leave. JOHN 14:30–31

∎

JESUS CALLS HIM "THE prince of this world" not because he is worthy, but because he is an imposter who has drawn people away from the Father. He uses deception and lies to trade upon our gullible inclination to believe anything. Jesus says of himself that he is "the way, the truth and the life," but we are just as apt to fix on fables as believe Jesus' own declaration of who he is. God designed us to be free; he gave all men and women the power to choose, including the ability to worship false gods. From the beginning, Satan has attempted to undermine our freedom by presenting us with a continuum of choices that would detach us from our relationship with God. Satan always presents these choices as attractive alternatives, always withholding a clear picture of the consequences until it is too late. "It is for freedom that Christ has set us free. Stand firm, then, and do not let yourselves be burdened again by a yoke of slavery" (Galatians 5:1).

I AM THE TRUE VINE

I am the true vine, and my Father is the gardener. He cuts off every branch in me that bears no fruit, while every branch that does bear fruit he prunes so that it will be even more fruitful. You are already clean because of the word I have spoken to you. Remain in me, as I also remain in you. No branch can bear fruit by itself; it must remain in the vine. Neither can you bear fruit unless you remain in me. I am the vine; you are the branches. If you remain in me and I in you, you will bear much fruit; apart from me you can do nothing. JOHN 15:1–5

■

JESUS USES THE VINE as a metaphor to help us understand how God, through the Holy Spirit, infuses divine purpose into our lives. Jesus says, "I am the vine; you are the branches. If you remain in me and I in you, you will bear much fruit; apart from me you can do nothing." From the beginning God has called us to be fruitful within his design (Genesis 1:18). Each one of us has been gifted in a particular way to advance God's purpose in this world. But as branches separated from the vine, we will wither and die, producing nothing, if we don't remain in Jesus. "No branch can bear fruit by itself; it must remain in the vine." Jesus is telling his disciples and us that we must remain connected to him through the Holy Spirit to be fully fruitful in the challenges that lie ahead. His words were true then and are just as true today.

My command is this: Love each other as I have loved you. Greater love has no one than this: to lay down one's life for one's friends. You are my friends if you do what I command. I no longer call you servants, because a servant does not know his master's business. Instead, I have called you friends, for everything that I learned from my Father I have made known to you. You did not choose me, but I chose you and appointed you so that you might go and bear fruit—fruit that will last—and so that whatever you ask in my name the Father will give you. This is my command: Love each other. JOHN 15:12–17

■

AS JESUS COMMANDED HIS followers to "love each other as I have loved you," so we need to connect several dots to understand his meaning. The Great Commandment is to love God and to love our neighbor. Without the first commandment, though, living the second is not possible. Jesus says two things that open the door to living the first commandment. First, he says, "You are my friends." To be a friend of Christ is to be a friend of God. To be a friend of the Son is to be a friend of the Father. Then, Jesus defines friendship as a willingness to sacrifice for a friend: "Greater love has no one than this: to lay down one's life for one's friends." The price of loving one's friend can be costly, but not nearly as costly as the Father permitting his Son to lay down his own life for the sake of you and me. When Jesus tells his friends, "Love each other," he is telling them to conform to the very nature of the Father and the Son and to model that nature through everything they do and say.

If the world hates you, keep in mind that it hated me first. If you belonged to the world, it would love you as its own. As it is, you do not belong to the world, but I have chosen you out of the world. That is why the world hates you. Remember what I told you: 'A servant is not greater than his master.' If they persecuted me, they will persecute you also. If they obeyed my teaching, they will obey yours also. They will treat you this way because of my name, for they do not know the one who sent me. If I had not come and spoken to them, they would not be guilty of sin; but now they have no excuse for their sin. Whoever hates me hates my Father as well. JOHN 15:18–23

■

AS IF HIS DISCIPLES didn't already know the nature of the world they were confronting, Jesus repeated the warning that the path ahead would be filled with challenges, struggles, and even persecutions. He said, "If the world hates you, keep in mind that it hated me first." As we ponder the time Jesus spent here on earth, we remember that from his earliest years Jesus was threatened by the political and religious elites. Herod sent his soldiers to seek and kill the child born to be king. Throughout his three years of ministry, Jesus was challenged time and again, to the point where he asked the religious leaders, "Why are you trying to kill me?" (John 7:19) The answer is as true now as it was then: The world's system of belief and activity, permeated by the spirit of the prince of darkness, will always rise up in opposition to the threat of God's way encroaching on its way. Just as rulers of the worldly system opposed Jesus, they oppose those who follow him as well. And the opposition continues unabated even up to this very hour. So Peter in his first letter counsels, "do not be surprised at the painful trial you are suffering, as though something strange were happening to you. But rejoice that you participate in the sufferings of Christ, so that you may be overjoyed when his glory is revealed" (1 Peter 4:12–13).

If I had not done among them the works no one else did, they would not be guilty of sin. As it is, they have seen, and yet they have hated both me and my Father. But this is to fulfill what is written in their Law: 'They hated me without reason.' JOHN 15:24–25

■

THE WORLD JESUS MENTIONS here is a world that had so abandoned God that its only response was to turn on Him with an unreasoned hatred. This is a hatred that is without reason because it is unreasonable to deny God. "The fool says in his heart there is no God. They are corrupt, their deeds are vile; there is no one who does good" (Psalm 14:1). But even though men have abandoned God, God's response is not to abandon the creatures he made in his own image. Rather, he did the unexpected by sending his own Son to stand in our place and take on the punishment we deserve as payment for our own sinfulness and rebellion. God cannot just wink at our crimes of omission and commission. A price must be paid, for he is the God of both love and justice. By sending his own Son into this darkened world, God accomplished his objective by having his Son become a substitute for us—to pay the price that washes us of our unrighteousness.

When the Advocate comes, whom I will send to you from the Father—the Spirit of truth who goes out from the Father—he will testify about me. And you also must testify, for you have been with me from the beginning. All this I have told you so that you will not fall away. They will put you out of the synagogue; in fact, the time is coming when anyone who kills you will think they are offering a service to God. They will do such things because they have not known the Father or me. I have told you this, so that when their time comes you will remember that I warned you about them. I did not tell you this from the beginning because I was with you . . ." JOHN 15:26–16:4

∎

JESUS SAYS THE HOLY Spirit is the Spirit of truth. He also calls the Spirit "the Advocate," and the image this conjures is of a trial setting, with the world as a prosecutor that has built a powerful case against you. Without a Defender you will be convicted and punished, even put to death. Jesus spoke to his disciples in this way because he was warning them that the world would come after them to defeat them, so they needed to be vigilant and prepared. Then comes the promise, for the disciples and for us: He will send the Advocate from the Father, the Spirit of truth, who will strengthen and embolden us, even as the opposition tries to defeat us. In his letter to the Ephesians, Paul reinforces the truth of Jesus' words: "Finally, be strong in the Lord and in his mighty power. Put on the full armor of God so that you can take your stand against the devil's schemes. For our struggle is not against flesh and blood, but against the rulers, against the authorities, against the powers of this dark world and against the spiritual forces of evil in the heavenly realms" (Ephesians 6:10–12).

I have much more to say to you, more than you can now bear. But when he, the Spirit of truth, comes, he will guide you into all the truth. He will not speak on his own; he will speak only what he hears, and he will tell you what is yet to come. He will glorify me because it is from me that he will receive what he will make known to you. All that belongs to the Father is mine. That is why I said the Spirit will receive from me what he will make known to you. JOHN 16:12–15

■

JESUS CONTINUED TO PREPARE his disciples for a time when he would no longer be physically with them. He told them he would provide the Spirit of truth who would flood into their hearts and strengthen them to continue on. And he told them how this would happen: This Spirit would not speak on his own, but would speak only what he hears, and what he hears comes directly from Jesus and from the Father, because all that belongs to the Father belongs to Jesus. Jesus makes it clear that the will of the Father, the Son, and the Holy Spirit are one. The relationship of the Trinity to the disciples and followers of Jesus is what fueled the extraordinary growth of the young church in the first century.

I HAVE BEEN SPEAKING FIGURATIVELY

"Though I have been speaking figuratively, a time is coming when I will no longer use this kind of language but will tell you plainly about my Father. In that day you will ask in my name. I am not saying that I will ask the Father on your behalf. No, the Father himself loves you because you have loved me and have believed that I came from God. I came from the Father and entered the world; now I am leaving the world and going back to the Father." Then Jesus' disciples said, "Now you are speaking clearly and without figures of speech. Now we can see that you know all things and that you do not even need to have anyone ask you questions. This makes us believe that you came from God." JOHN 16:25–30

■

THIS MOMENT IS A foretaste of what happened to the disciples after the ascension of the Lord, when the Holy Spirit came upon them and they "began to speak in other tongues as the Spirit enabled them" (Acts 2:4). Throughout all of the Gospels, Jesus uses poetic and figurative language to communicate with others. This is especially true in the Gospel of John, where he uses words and phrases like "light" and "streams of living water" to convey spiritual dimensions of everyday realities of life. Here his disciples finally seemed to understand what Jesus has been saying all along, but it was not that the language had changed; rather, it was a new understanding of what they heard that had changed. The Holy Spirit pierced through their earthbound understanding, even if only for a brief moment, to open the "eyes of their heart(s)" (Ephesians 1:18) to the realization that Jesus "came from God." It is not language that separates us from God. It is a heart dwelling on the daily and future desires of this life that creates a wall of separation between us and the Lord.

YOU WILL BE SCATTERED

"Do you now believe?" Jesus replied. "A time is coming and in fact has come when you will be scattered, each to your own home. You will leave me all alone. Yet I am not alone, for my Father is with me. I have told you these things, so that in me you may have peace. In this world you will have trouble. But take heart! I have overcome the world." JOHN 16:31–33

■

IMMEDIATELY BEFORE JESUS SAID, "You will leave me alone," the disciples finally began to understand Jesus' true identity. But their understanding was limited to the idea that Jesus was sent by God to expel the Roman occupiers from Israel and restore David's kingdom. Jesus knew that he needed to push ahead toward the cross because that was the purpose of God's mission for him. His followers did not understand the true purpose of Jesus's earthly sojourn until after his crucifixion and resurrection. "After he was raised from the dead, his disciples recalled what he had said. Then they believed the Scripture and the words that Jesus had spoken" (John 2:22).

After Jesus said this, he looked toward heaven and prayed: "Father, the hour has come. Glorify your Son, that your Son may glorify you. For you granted him authority over all people that he might give eternal life to all those you have given him. Now this is eternal life: that they know you, the only true God, and Jesus Christ, whom you have sent." JOHN 17:1-3

■

IN THE FIRST PART of what is sometimes called his High Priestly Prayer, Jesus prayed, "Father, the hour has come. Glorify your Son, that your Son may glorify you." There is subtle irony in this request because the instrument of his glorification was the cross that was used to punish criminals. His death on a cross opened the way to his glorification, not only in his being lifted up on the cross, but also in his rising up on the third day from death to life—for himself and also for all who believe.

I pray for them. I am not praying for the world, but for those you have given me, for they are yours. All I have is yours, and all you have is mine. And glory has come to me through them. I will remain in the world no longer, but they are still in the world, and I am coming to you. Holy Father, protect them by the power of your name, the name you gave me, so that they may be one as we are one. JOHN 17:9–11

■

IN THE SECOND PART of the High Priestly Prayer, Jesus turned his concern to his disciples. While he returned to the Father, his disciples remained in the same world that has been in opposition to God since Satan prevailed over Adam and Eve. The disciples could not battle on alone; they needed protection if they were to prevail against the worldly forces lined up against them. For the disciples and for us, Jesus stands before the throne of God ceaselessly interceding on behalf of the children of God: "Holy Father, protect them by the power of your name, the name you gave me, so they may be one as we are one."

I PRAY ALSO FOR THOSE WHO
WILL BELIEVE IN ME

My prayer is not for them alone. I pray also for those who will believe in me through their message, that all of them may be one, Father, just as you are in me and I am in you. May they also be in us so that the world may believe that you have sent me. JOHN 17:20–21

■

JESUS CONCLUDED BY PRAYING for all who would come to believe through the ministry of the apostles and disciples. Jesus sees beyond the boundaries of time. He came from God and he returned to the Father, but for those who remained behind, he gave his authority to go out and spread the Good News of Jesus Christ to those who have never been with him. This prayer is perpetual; it is passed down through generations from believer to non-believer. It is as if this prayer passes through time like the concentric waves created by the action of one simple stone. But for us it is not only about the current urgencies; it is also about all those who will follow. There is great mystery in the power of this prayer for all believers; we cannot predict where it will land or even how or when it will act to transform a former enemy of God into a servant of the Lord.

Jesus went out as usual to the Mount of Olives, and his disciples followed him. On reaching the place, he said to them, "Pray that you will not fall into temptation." He withdrew about a stone's throw beyond them, knelt down and prayed, "Father, if you are willing, take this cup from me; yet not my will, but yours be done." An angel from heaven appeared to him and strengthened him. And being in anguish, he prayed more earnestly, and his sweat was like drops of blood falling to the ground. When he rose from prayer and went back to the disciples, he found them asleep, exhausted from sorrow. "Why are you sleeping?" he asked them. "Get up and pray so that you will not fall into temptation." LUKE 22:39–46

■

AS JESUS ENTERED THE Garden of Gethsemane (which means *olive press*), he felt the intense weight of the moment pressing down to the point of crushing him. He turned to his disciples twice to say, "Pray that you will not fall into temptation." He was right to be concerned about the steadfastness of his followers, but his far greater concern was his own temptation to not face the moment that was descending upon him. Luke tells us that God had not left Jesus alone at this moment, because his Father sent an angel to attend him and strengthen him. Even so, his human nature was in revolt and was directing him to flee from this trial that God had placed before him. It was here in a garden that Jesus confronted temptation head on and began to reverse the consequences that had flowed down through time from the first temptation in the first garden. He prayed, "Father, if you are willing, take this cup from me; yet not my will, but yours be done."

While he was still speaking a crowd came up, and the man who was called Judas, one of the Twelve, was leading them. He approached Jesus to kiss him, but Jesus asked him, "Judas, are you betraying the Son of Man with a kiss?" When Jesus' followers saw what was going to happen, they said, "Lord, should we strike with our swords?" And one of them struck the servant of the high priest, cutting off his right ear. But Jesus answered, "No more of this!" And he touched the man's ear and healed him. LUKE 22:47–51

■

INTO THE GARDEN CAME a posse of armed men to find and arrest Jesus. The immediate response of some of his disciples was to strike back, but Jesus knew this local fight must play out on a much larger scale. He said in prayer, "Father, your will be done." He accepted the role that he was given to play. He knew this was a drama that transcended the moment. He did not condemn Judas' betrayal but merely said, "Are you betraying the Son of Man with a kiss?" And as for fighting the crowd of men who came to take him prisoner, he said, "No more of this!" because he had already accepted the will of his Father in heaven. The battle he was actually waging was far more important than fighting the servants of the high priest. They were mere pawns in a spiritual battle that was being fought both here on earth and in the heavenly realms (Ephesians 6:12).

Then Jesus said to the chief priests, the officers of the temple guard, and the elders, who had come for him, "Am I leading a rebellion, that you have come with swords and clubs? Every day I was with you in the temple courts, and you did not lay a hand on me. But this is your hour—when darkness reigns." LUKE 22:52–53

■

IT WAS DARK IN the Garden of Gethsemane, and that darkness represented the condition of a world that had come against the Son of Man. Of course, the chief priests and their henchmen did not see Jesus as the true Messiah. They saw him as a political figure who was a threat to their own position, and so under cover of night, they came to eliminate the threat. Jesus cut through their pretense by asking, "Am I leading a rebellion . . .?" In order to carry out their scheme, the chief priests needed to brand Jesus as a political zealot and troublemaker. They believed this would convince the Roman authorities that Jesus needed to be executed. What the opponents of Jesus did not understand was that they had become tools of Satan's plan to undermine Jesus' mission here on earth. Satan's moment of victory seemed to be at hand, but here in the garden, we witness only a skirmish in a much larger cosmic field of battle.

Then the detachment of soldiers with its commander and the Jewish officials arrested Jesus. They bound him and brought him first to Annas, who was the father-in-law of Caiaphas, the high priest that year. Caiaphas was the one who had advised the Jewish leaders that it would be good if one man died for the people . . . Meanwhile, the high priest questioned Jesus about his disciples and his teaching. "If I said something wrong," Jesus replied, "testify as to what is wrong. But if I spoke the truth, why did you strike me?" Then Annas sent him bound to Caiaphas the high priest. JOHN 18:12–14, 19, 23–24

■

AFTER HIS ARREST, JESUS was bound and led to Annas, the father-in-law of Caiaphas, the high priest. Ironically, Caiaphas, very much a political figure, had disclosed the divine plan of having one die so that many might live. Caiaphas was not thinking of God; his only concern was preserving the power base he was part of. God's plan employs the same concept of one for all, but it has an entirely different application. Jesus, the Son of God, came to die so that God's original plan could be restored. When Adam sinned, he set in motion a course of events that would propel all of mankind away from the God who loves them. "Therefore, just as sin entered the world through one man, and death through sin, and in this way death came to all men, because all sinned . . . But the gift (from God) is not like the trespass. For if the many died by the trespass of the one man, how much more did God's grace and the gift that came by the grace of one man, Jesus Christ, overflow to the many . . . For just as through the disobedience of the one man the many were made sinners, so also through the obedience of the one man the many will be made righteous" (Romans 5:12, 15, 19).

Those who had arrested Jesus took him to Caiaphas the high priest, where the teachers of the law and the elders had assembled. But Peter followed him at a distance, right up to the courtyard of the high priest. He entered and sat down with the guards to see the outcome. MATTHEW 26:57–58

■

A SHORT TIME BEFORE this moment, Peter was bold. He may have been the one in Gethsemane who shouted, "Lord, should we strike with our swords?" Now Jesus had been arrested and led away to Jerusalem to stand before Annas and Caiaphas to be interrogated. Peter followed behind, and when he arrived at Caiaphas' courtyard, he sat and waited to see what would happen. Peter's world had collapsed; the triumphant entry into Jerusalem just a few days earlier must have seemed like a cruel joke. His hopes had evaporated and fear had filled the void where great expectations once resided. The disciples had scattered, and now he was alone. Little did he know that he was about to undergo the greatest trial of his life. But before that moment came, he waited.

HE HAS SPOKEN BLASPHEMY!

But Jesus remained silent. The high priest said to him, "I charge you under oath by the living God: Tell us if you are the Messiah, the Son of God." "You have said so," Jesus replied. "But I say to all of you: From now on you will see the Son of Man sitting at the right hand of the Mighty One and coming on the clouds of heaven." Then the high priest tore his clothes and said, "He has spoken blasphemy! Why do we need any more witnesses? Look, now you have heard the blasphemy. What do you think?" "He is worthy of death," they answered. Then they spit in his face and struck him with their fists. Others slapped him and said, "Prophesy to us, Messiah. Who hit you?" MATTHEW 26:63–68

■

CAIAPHAS, THE HIGH PRIEST, asked Jesus a direct question: "Tell us if you are the Messiah, the Son of God." A trap was being set because if Jesus said yes, then the religious leaders could accuse him of blasphemy. Jesus answered by quoting from the prophet Daniel, who spoke of the coming Messiah: "In a vision at night I looked, and there before me was one like a son of man, coming with the clouds of heaven . . . His dominion is an everlasting dominion that will not pass away, and his kingdom is one that will never be destroyed" (Daniel 7:13–14). The chief priest and his cohorts were infuriated when they heard Jesus reference the coming Messiah and his new dominion. They preferred to rule over the rotten kingdom that was rather than allow Jesus to establish the one willed by God. In the name of God they had chosen to war against the Son of God who came to establish a kingdom of God "that will never be destroyed."

I DON'T KNOW THIS MAN

While Peter was below in the courtyard, one of the servant girls of the high priest came by. When she saw Peter warming himself, she looked closely at him. "You also were with that Nazarene, Jesus," she said. But he denied it. "I don't know or understand what you're talking about," he said, and went out into the entryway. When the servant girl saw him there, she said again to those standing around, "This fellow is one of them." Again he denied it. After a little while, those standing near said to Peter, "Surely you are one of them, for you are a Galilean." He began to call down curses, and he swore to them, "I don't know this man you're talking about." Immediately the rooster crowed the second time. Then Peter remembered the word Jesus had spoken to him: "Before the rooster crows twice you will disown me three times." And he broke down and wept. MARK 14:66–72

■

THE CRISIS IN THE Garden of Gethsemane followed the guards and their captive to the courtyard before the house of Caiaphas. Peter hoped to hang onto his own anonymity by blending into the group of people milling about, but soon enough a simple servant girl identified him as a follower of Jesus. The moment of crisis had arrived for Peter. He had a choice: he could affirm that he was a follower of the "Nazarene," or he could deny it. Whatever his motivation, whether it was fear, confusion, or sorrow, Peter fell terribly short. His denials contradicted his claims of steadfast loyalty and love for the one he had once called "the Christ, the Son of the living God" (Matthew 16:16). Jesus had predicted that his followers would scatter in the moment of crisis, but the shock of realizing that even he, Peter, the most outspoken follower of the Lord, had betrayed the one he loved, must have been overwhelming. "And he broke down and wept."

When day came, the assembly of the elders of the people, both chief priests and scribes, gathered together, and they brought him to their council. They said, "If you are the Messiah, tell us." He replied, "If I tell you, you will not believe; and if I question you, you will not answer. But from now on the Son of Man will be seated at the right hand of the power of God." All of them asked, "Are you, then, the Son of God?" He said to them, "You say that I am." Then they said, "What further testimony do we need? We have heard it ourselves from his own lips!" LUKE 22:66–71

■

HUMAN JUSTICE IS MEANT to reflect the form and substance of divine justice, but in the early hours of the new day, a hastily convened quorum of the Sanhedrin met to place a veneer of justice on their plan to rid Jerusalem of the man they identified as a threat to their power and authority. Their assembly was nothing more than a travesty of justice. The leaders had predetermined the verdict of "guilty as charged!" Jesus said it all: "If I tell you, you will not believe; if I question you, you will not answer." The Pharisees and their partners in crime could not see that in their obsession to rid the world of this man, they had joined forces with Satan, the enemy of God.

Then they took Jesus from Caiaphas to Pilate's headquarters. It was early in the morning. They themselves did not enter the headquarters, so as to avoid ritual defilement and to be able to eat the Passover. So Pilate went out to them and said, "What accusation do you bring against this man?" They answered, "If this man were not a criminal, we would not have handed him over to you." Pilate said to them, "Take him yourselves and judge him according to your law." The Jews replied, "We are not permitted to put anyone to death." (This was to fulfill what Jesus had said when he indicated the kind of death he was to die.) JOHN 18:28–32

■

THE JEWISH LEADERS UNJUSTLY determined that Jesus was guilty of a capital offense, but they needed to shift the responsibility for his execution to the Roman authorities. So they transferred Jesus to Pontius Pilate's headquarters. Pilate was the consummate politician; he shifted the responsibility for handling this matter right back to the Jews. This was not their plan—they wanted Jesus dead before Passover, and Pilate was not playing the role they wanted him to play. As the day began, it looked like their plan might not work after all.

JESUS TAKEN TO HEROD

When Herod saw Jesus, he was very glad, for he had been wanting to see him for a long time, because he had heard about him and was hoping to see him perform some sign. He questioned him at some length, but Jesus gave him no answer. The chief priests and the scribes stood by, vehemently accusing him. Even Herod with his soldiers treated him with contempt and mocked him; then he put an elegant robe on him, and sent him back to Pilate. That same day Herod and Pilate became friends with each other; before this they had been enemies. LUKE 23:8–12

■

HEROD ANTIPAS AND JESUS are a study in contrasts. Herod's entire identity was built on maintaining rule over the territory the Romans had permitted him to control. He was corrupt, cruel, dissipated, and the ruler who had ordered John the Baptist's execution. But, at first, Herod appeared to be intrigued by the prisoner standing before him. Herod had heard reports of his ministry in Galilee and wanted to know more. But Jesus was non-responsive. He stood silently before the king, and soon enough the vehement accusations of the chief priests and the scribes influenced Herod to turn on Jesus and mock him. The entire legal, religious, and political establishment had risen up to crush Jesus, as if their entire world order depended on the death of this one man. They, of course, were right. It did.

Then Pilate entered the headquarters again, summoned Jesus, and asked him, "Are you the King of the Jews?" Jesus answered, "Do you ask this on your own, or did others tell you about me?" Pilate replied, "I am not a Jew, am I? Your own nation and the chief priests have handed you over to me. What have you done?" Jesus answered, "My kingdom is not from this world. If my kingdom were from this world, my followers would be fighting to keep me from being handed over to the Jews. But as it is, my kingdom is not from here." Pilate asked him, "So you are a king?" Jesus answered, "You say that I am a king. For this I was born, and for this I came into the world, to testify to the truth. Everyone who belongs to the truth listens to my voice." Pilate asked him, "What is truth?" After he had said this, he went out to the Jews again and told them, "I find no case against him. But you have a custom that I release someone for you at the Passover. Do you want me to release for you the King of the Jews?" They shouted in reply, "Not this man, but Barabbas!" Now Barabbas was a bandit. JOHN 18:33–40

■

PILATE SPOKE FOR MUCH of modernity when he asked Jesus, "What is truth?" In more recent times, truth has been fragmented into tiny, incoherent particles that at most might be *a* truth, but not *the* truth. Pilate was a worldly man; he dealt with the realities of the push and pull of political forces, and he knew all factions claimed that their own cause or grievance had the banner of truth behind it. But earlier, before he was taken prisoner, Jesus declared, "I am the way, and the truth and the life. No one comes to the Father except through me" (John 14:6). Pilate saw only a man standing before him, no different from the bandit Barabbas. But Pilate inadvertently touched on the central question of the New Testament: Is Jesus "the Christ" (Mark 8:35) or is he someone else? Is it really true that if you know Jesus you will know God the Father as well? (John 14:7) Or is he merely a revolutionary trouble-maker who had deeply annoyed the authorities? Pilate seemed indifferent to discovering the right answer. But we shouldn't have been because the answer to these questions makes all the difference.

But the chief priests stirred up the crowd to have him release Barabbas for them instead. Pilate spoke to them again, "Then what do you wish me to do with the man you call the King of the Jews?" They shouted back, "Crucify him!" Pilate asked them, "Why, what evil has he done?" But they shouted all the more, "Crucify him!" So Pilate, wishing to satisfy the crowd, released Barabbas for them; and after flogging Jesus, he handed him over to be crucified. MARK 15:11–15

■

IT IS IMPORTANT TO keep historic proportionality in mind here. This moment in time cannot be described in terms of hostile armies clashing in epic battles to win some territory. This was a single man standing before his accusers, waiting for his death sentence to be handed down. And yet it was at this very moment that all of human history changed course radically. Here God's divine purpose intersected with endlessly flawed world systems. Even though the world was paying little notice to the events unfolding during that Passover in Jerusalem, the greatest epic battle ever fought was being waged with supernatural intensity in the streets of the city of David.

Then the governor's soldiers took Jesus into the Praetorium and gathered the whole company of soldiers around him. They stripped him and put a scarlet robe on him, and then twisted together a crown of thorns and set it on his head. They put a staff in his right hand. Then they knelt in front of him and mocked him. "Hail, King of the Jews!" they said. They spit on him, and took the staff and struck him on the head again and again. After they had mocked him, they took off the robe and put his own clothes on him. Then they led him away to crucify him. **MAT-THEW 27:27–31**

■

WHAT HAPPENS TO HUMAN nature when it is uncoupled from love and justice and is replaced by unrestrained power? We see it here in the Praetorium, where the powerless prisoner was turned over to a company of soldiers. The soldiers stripped him, mocked him, and tortured him. They spit on him and struck him when he could not protect himself. The soldiers descended into the kind of cruel and depraved behavior that is often the default when raw political power is the sole touchstone. But the source of depravity was not the state, but the human heart: "For from within, and out of men's hearts come evil thoughts . . . murder, adultery, greed, malice, deceit, lewdness, envy, slander, arrogance and folly" (Mark 7:21–23). Those are Jesus' words. He knew that all men and women are subject to dark inclinations, but he also knew that he had come to die for people just like these Roman soldiers.

SIMON OF CYRENE

A certain man from Cyrene, Simon, the father of Alexander and Rufus, was passing by on his way in from the country, and they forced him to carry the cross. **MARK 15:21**

■

JESUS WAS CARRYING THE deadly instrument of his execution. The wood beams of the cross were heavy, and he had to drag them through the streets of Jerusalem to a small mound outside the gates of the city. Jesus had been scourged and had bled profusely. He was too weak to carry the cross, and so he faltered. It was at this moment that the Roman soldiers grabbed Simon of Cyrene to take the cross and carry it for Jesus to Golgotha. As Jesus has taken up the cross for each one of us, so Simon took it up for him. Though he did not know it, Simon became an example for the followers of Jesus. It cost Jesus everything to follow the will of the Father, and for his disciples it was costly too. Much earlier, before coming to Jerusalem, Jesus warned his disciples that the way ahead would not be easy: "If anyone would come after me, he must deny himself and take up his cross daily and follow me" (Luke 9:23). Simon of Cyrene did just that, literally.

AND THEY CRUCIFIED HIM

They brought Jesus to the place called Golgotha (which means "the place of the skull"). Then they offered him wine mixed with myrrh, but he did not take it. And they crucified him. Dividing up his clothes, they cast lots to see what each would get. It was nine in the morning when they crucified him. The written notice of the charge against him read: THE KING OF THE JEWS. MARK 15:22–26

■

MARK SIMPLY SAYS, "AND they crucified him." Four words that contain a world of meaning. It has been said before that Jesus was born to die. His life began in Bethlehem, and after a short exile in Egypt, he grew up in Nazareth. His ministry began in Galilee, but inexorably he was drawn to Jerusalem, and not just Jerusalem but Golgotha, "the place of the skull." He descended from heaven to live among us and then to be raised on a cross to die for us. "He himself bore our sins in his body on the tree, so that we might die to sins and live for righteousness; by his wounds you have been healed" (1 Peter 2:24). Even though he was in his very nature God, "he humbled himself and became obedient to death—even death on a cross" (Philippians 2:6–8).

Two other men, both criminals, were also led out with him to be executed. When they came to the place called the Skull, they crucified him there, along with the criminals—one on his right, the other on his left. Jesus said, "Father, forgive them, for they do not know what they are doing." And they divided up his clothes by casting lots. The people stood watching, and the rulers even sneered at him. They said, "He saved others; let him save himself if he is God's Messiah, the Chosen One." The soldiers also came up and mocked him. They offered him wine vinegar and said, "If you are the king of the Jews, save yourself." There was a written notice above him, which read: THIS IS THE KING OF THE JEWS. One of the criminals who hung there hurled insults at him: "Aren't you the Messiah? Save yourself and us!" But the other criminal rebuked him. "Don't you fear God," he said, "since you are under the same sentence? We are punished justly, for we are getting what our deeds deserve. But this man has done nothing wrong." Then he said, "Jesus, remember me when you come into your kingdom." Jesus answered him, "Truly I tell you, today you will be with me in paradise." LUKE 23:32–43

■

TWO CRIMINALS WERE CRUCIFIED with Jesus, one to the right of him and one to the left. One criminal joined the crowds and mockingly said, "Aren't you the Messiah? Save yourself and us!" But the other criminal saw things differently: "We are punished justly, for we are getting what our deeds deserve. But this man has done nothing wrong." It is not possible to know how this criminal came to understand that the man beside him was innocent; we have no information that he had known or followed Jesus before this fateful day. Perhaps he heard Jesus call out to God, "Father, forgive them, for they do not know what they are doing." Perhaps the Holy Spirit invaded his heart and opened his eyes to a reality that was imperceptible to all others. Whatever the case may be, this criminal received the forgiveness that Jesus granted him. His belief set him free, and so Jesus could say, "Truly I tell you, today you will be with me in paradise."

Near the cross of Jesus stood his mother, his mother's sister, Mary the wife of Clopas, and Mary Magdalene. When Jesus saw his mother there, and the disciple whom he loved standing nearby, he said to her, "Woman, here is your son," and to the disciple, "Here is your mother." From that time on, this disciple took her into his home. JOHN 19:25–27

■

JESUS WAS DYING, AND yet he spoke seven times. This was his third utterance, and it is tremendously poignant. He was looking down from the cross and saw his mother standing back from the hostile crowd. He also saw the apostle John, who the night before had fled Gethsemane. Here was Mary experiencing the unfolding of Simeon's prophetic words: "And a sword will pierce your own soul too" (Luke 2:35). Even in his moment of humiliation and suffering, Jesus remained steadfast to the great commandments of God. Of all the women in the world, God had chosen Mary to give birth to Jesus. Now Jesus turned to his disciple and said to him: This is my mother; take care of her, for the Father's love has flowed through her to me, and now it must flow from me to you and from you to her. And so it happened as Jesus commanded: "From that time on, this disciple took her into his home."

From noon until three in the afternoon darkness came over all the land. About three in the afternoon Jesus cried out in a loud voice, "Eli, Eli, lama sabachthani?" (which means "My God, my God, why have you forsaken me?"). When some of those standing there heard this, they said, "He's calling Elijah." Immediately one of them ran and got a sponge. He filled it with wine vinegar, put it on a staff, and offered it to Jesus to drink. The rest said, "Now leave him alone. Let's see if Elijah comes to save him." MATTHEW 27:45–49

■

"MY GOD, MY GOD, why have you forsaken me?" It is not just the fact that Jesus was dying on a cross; this cry to the Father was so shattering because Jesus now was carrying the entire weight of all the sin in the world. And the weight of sin is so great that it separated Jesus from the Father. Sin, of course, does that. After Cain murdered his brother Abel, God came to him and asked, "Where is your brother Abel?" Cain replied, "I don't know. Am I my brother's keeper?" (Genesis 4:9). The sin of murder alienated Cain, driving him from the land and separating him from God. He became "a restless wanderer of the earth . . ." (Genesis 4:14). Sin not only alienated men and women from one another, but it alienates us from God. Jesus took on all the sin of the world by taking our place on the cross. His pain was unbearable. He was utterly alone and experienced the deepest despair possible.

I AM THIRSTY

Later, knowing that everything had now been finished, and so that Scripture would be fulfilled, Jesus said, "I am thirsty." A jar of wine vinegar was there, so they soaked a sponge in it, put the sponge on a stalk of the hyssop plant, and lifted it to Jesus' lips. When he had received the drink, Jesus said, "It is finished." With that, he bowed his head and gave up his spirit. JOHN 19:28–30

■

JESUS SAID, "I AM thirsty," a statement describing the state of his physical condition. Then, shortly after he made this declaration, he said, "It is finished." This could be read as another statement of his acceptance of the onslaught of death, but given the sweep of the entire narrative, it is clear that Jesus was talking about the mission that began here on earth with an angel visiting a young virgin in the town of Nazareth. Matthew says that an angel came to Joseph in a dream and said, ". . . what is conceived in her is from the Holy Spirit. She will give birth to a son, and you are to give him the name Jesus, because he will save the people from their sins" (Matthew 1:20–21). The mission was nearing its earthly end, and Jesus had not faltered or turned aside. He had taken unto himself the sin of the entire world at unimaginable cost. That price had been paid once and for all. "It is finished."

THE CURTAIN OF THE TEMPLE
WAS TORN IN TWO

It was now about noon, and darkness came over the whole land until three in the afternoon, for the sun stopped shining. And the curtain of the temple was torn in two. Jesus called out with a loud voice, "Father, into your hands I commit my spirit." When he had said this, he breathed his last. The centurion, seeing what had happened, praised God and said, "Surely this was a righteous man." When all the people who had gathered to witness this sight saw what took place, they beat their breasts and went away. But all those who knew him, including the women who had followed him from Galilee, stood at a distance, watching these things. LUKE 23:44–49

■

THE CULMINATING MOMENT HAD arrived. Darkness came upon the land, and Luke reports that the curtain of the temple was torn in two. This was the curtain that separated the Holy Place from the Most Holy Place. It was the Inner Sanctum, where only a designated priest could go. It was a symbol of the separation that exists between a Holy God and a sinful people, but at the moment when Jesus called out, "Father, into your hands I commit my spirit," that division was ripped apart. Jesus had established himself as the mediator between the Father and the people. It was the moment when the prophecy of Joel began to become an actuality: "And afterward, I will pour out my Spirit on all people . . . And everyone who calls on the name of the Lord will be saved; for on Mount Zion and in Jerusalem there will be deliverance, as the Lord has said, among the survivors whom the Lord calls" (Joel 2:28, 32).

As evening approached, there came a rich man from Arimathea, named Joseph, who had himself become a disciple of Jesus. Going to Pilate, he asked for Jesus' body, and Pilate ordered that it be given to him. Joseph took the body, wrapped it in a clean linen cloth, and placed it in his own new tomb that he had cut out of the rock. He rolled a big stone in front of the entrance to the tomb and went away. Mary Magdalene and the other Mary were sitting there opposite the tomb. MATTHEW 27:57–61

■

IN THIS MOMENT OF darkness it is possible to discern tiny seeds of hope. Yes, the disciples had abandoned him, and yes, Jesus' enemies seemed to have utterly triumphed, but some light was forcing itself through. Simon of Cyrene had lifted the burden of taking the cross off the shoulder of Jesus. John, the Apostle, had returned to the foot of the cross after having fled from the Garden of Gethsemane the night Jesus was taken prisoner. Then there was the soldier, who at the moment of Jesus' death, said, "Surely this was a righteous man." And there were the women, Mary the mother of Jesus and Mary Magdalene, among others, who stood vigil as the events surrounding the crucifixion unfolded. Finally, when it appeared there would be no place to bury Jesus, Joseph of Arimathea bravely stepped forward to claim the body so that it could be buried in his own tomb. The light had not gone out completely. Darkness reigns, but light flickers on the horizon.

The next day, the one after Preparation Day, the chief priests and the Pharisees went to Pilate. "Sir," they said, "we remember that while he was still alive that deceiver said, 'After three days I will rise again.' So give the order for the tomb to be made secure until the third day. Otherwise, his disciples may come and steal the body and tell the people that he has been raised from the dead. This last deception will be worse than the first." "Take a guard," Pilate answered. "Go, make the tomb as secure as you know how."
MATTHEW 27:62–65

■

THE CHIEF PRIESTS AND Pharisees had had their way. Jesus was dead and had been laid in a tomb. It would seem that they had won, but they did not show the confidence that comes with victory. They remembered that Jesus said he would be raised from the dead in three days, and so they were concerned that somehow a deception would be perpetuated. They asked Pilate to seal the tomb and place a guard in front of its entrance so no one could gain access. The chief priests knew that Jesus was dead, but now they were driven by an irrational fear, as if their consciences were still alive to the enormous injustice they had engaged in.

When the Sabbath was over, Mary Magdalene, Mary the mother of James, and Salome bought spices so that they might go to anoint Jesus' body. Very early on the first day of the week, just after sunrise, they were on their way to the tomb and they asked each other, "Who will roll the stone away from the entrance of the tomb?" But when they looked up, they saw that the stone, which was very large, had been rolled away. **MARK 16: 1–4**

■

LUKE TELLS US THAT at the ninth hour, just before Jesus died on the cross, the "sun stopped shining." The cold spirit of death spread across the land and everything was cast into darkness. But on the third day a new spirit revealed itself. The women, who had followed Jesus even to the cross, rose in darkness to go to the tomb to anoint the body of the Lord. Mark describes their journey to the tomb this way: "Very early on the first day of the week, just after sunrise, they were on their way to the tomb . . ." The spirit of darkness had had its moment. Now the Spirit of the Lord—the spirit of light and life— was revealing itself through the natural cycle of the sun. The women thought they were heading to a place filled with the darkness of death; instead they were about to encounter a tomb emptied of death because the tomb could not possibly contain the Son of the God.

As they entered the tomb, they saw a young man dressed in a white robe sitting on the right side, and they were alarmed. "Don't be alarmed," he said. "You are looking for Jesus the Nazarene, who was crucified. He has risen! He is not here. See the place where they laid him. But go, tell his disciples and Peter, 'He is going ahead of you into Galilee. There you will see him, just as he told you.'" Trembling and bewildered, the women went out and fled from the tomb. They said nothing to anyone, because they were afraid. MARK 16: 5–8

■

"HE HAS RISEN!" JUST three words, but they will become the triumphant words of the faith that will sweep across the Mediterranean world and beyond. Confronted with this strange and unexpected turn of events, the women who had come to anoint the Lord's body lying in the tomb were told to "go, tell the disciples and Peter" that Jesus is alive, not dead, and he had gone back to Galilee where the disciples would find him. The women were instructed to act: "Go," do not stand still and do not pause, but go and tell the others what you have seen and heard. These simple words, "go and tell" become the springboard for action that will spread so quickly from person to person throughout the world. The women at the tomb were transformed from mourners into witnesses in the flash of an instant. With this encounter at the tomb of Jesus, the seeds of the faith were planted.

PETER RAN TO THE TOMB

Peter, however, got up and ran to the tomb. Bending over, he saw the strips of linen lying by themselves, and he went away, wondering to himself what had happened. LUKE 24:12

■

PETER WAS IN DESPAIR. His world had disintegrated. He had betrayed the one he loved, the one he called "the Christ of God" (Luke 9:20). Now Jesus was dead and the women had gone back to the tomb to anoint his body. This was how the world felt to Peter immediately before Mary Magdalene, Joanna, and Mary, mother of James, as well as others, brought the news that the tomb was empty. Peter did not walk; he ran to find the tomb indeed empty. While he was known for his impetuous nature, Peter did not jump to any conclusions. We are only told that he went away wondering what this meant. To fully appreciate the dilemma Peter faced here, we must put ourselves in his place. Everything that happened to Jesus had now apparently been reversed. The tomb was empty, and there were no easy explanations, leaving Peter genuinely perplexed.

When Jesus rose early on the first day of the week, he appeared first to Mary Magdalene, out of whom he had driven seven demons. She went and told those who had been with him and who were mourning and weeping. When they heard that Jesus was alive and that she had seen him, they did not believe it. MARK 16:9–11

■

WHAT WE CALL HISTORY are events in time that are witnessed or recorded through direct observation, documents, and physical evidence. Here we have an account of the empty tomb that is credible, ironically enough, because of the person who testified. To those living in the first century, Mary Magdalene was anything but an ideal witness. If the account were made up, then the last person to choose as a witness was a woman with a questionable past. And yet Mark forges ahead and reports that Mary Magdalene was the first person to encounter the risen Lord. If Mark was trying to convince people that a supernatural event had occurred when it really hadn't, he might have used a different witness. The fact that Mark does not lends credibility to the story of the risen Lord; it does not detract from it.

COVER UP

While the women were on their way, some of the guards went into the city and reported to the chief priests everything that had happened. When the chief priests had met with the elders and devised a plan, they gave the soldiers a large sum of money, telling them, "You are to say, 'His disciples came during the night and stole him away while we were asleep.' If this report gets to the governor, we will satisfy him and keep you out of trouble." So the soldiers took the money and did as they were instructed. And this story has been widely circulated among the Jews to this very day.
MATTHEW 28:11–15

■

APPARENTLY PLAN A WAS declared inoperable, and so the chief priests and other leaders hastily devised another plan to discredit any rumors that Christ was not contained by the tomb in which he was buried. The leaders enlisted the soldiers in a cover-up to protect their own political interests. The lie was necessary because the chief priests were engaged in an evil enterprise. They had conspired to convict and execute an innocent man, and they were afraid the population would rise up against them and side with the followers of the leader they had martyred. They completely missed the supernatural implications behind the fact that Jesus was no longer in the tomb.

WE HAD HOPED THAT HE WAS THE ONE
WHO WAS GOING TO REDEEM ISRAEL

Now that same day two of them were going to a village called Emmaus, about seven miles from Jerusalem. They were talking with each other about everything that had happened. As they talked and discussed these things with each other, Jesus himself came up and walked along with them; but they were kept from recognizing him. He asked them, "What are you discussing together as you walk along?" They stood still, their faces downcast. One of them, named Cleopas, asked him, "Are you the only one visiting Jerusalem who does not know the things that have happened there in these days?" "What things?" he asked. "About Jesus of Nazareth," they replied. "He was a prophet, powerful in word and deed before God and all the people. The chief priests and our rulers handed him over to be sentenced to death, and they crucified him; but we had hoped that he was the one who was going to redeem Israel. And what is more, it is the third day since all this took place. In addition, some of our women amazed us. They went to the tomb early this morning but didn't find his body. They came and told us that they had seen a vision of angels, who said he was alive. Then some of our companions went to the tomb and found it just as the women had said, but they did not see Jesus." LUKE 24:13–24

∎

THE PASSOVER HAD ENDED and people were streaming out of Jerusalem to return to their own towns and cities. Two of the travelers were heading back to the village of Emmaus when another traveler joined them. It was Jesus, but they did not recognize him. Instead they told him about the events that had ended in apparent disaster on the previous Friday: The two travelers were despondent because they had rested their hope on a political Messiah. As Moses liberated the Jewish people from the Egyptians, so Jesus, they had hoped, would liberate them from the Romans. What they did not see was that Jesus had been sent by God to liberate all people from the more insidious and intractable slavery of sin.

BEGINNING WITH MOSES AND ALL THE PROPHETS

He said to them, "How foolish you are, and how slow to believe all that the prophets have spoken! Did not the Messiah have to suffer these things and then enter his glory?" And beginning with Moses and all the Prophets, he explained to them what was said in all the Scriptures concerning himself. As they approached the village to which they were going, Jesus continued on as if he were going farther. But they urged him strongly, "Stay with us, for it is nearly evening; the day is almost over." So he went in to stay with them. LUKE 24:25–29

■

THE TWO TRAVELERS DEFINED the role of the Messiah narrowly by placing their hopes on Jesus freeing the people of Israel from the iron yoke of Roman rule. Jesus turned to the authority of Scripture to define the purpose of the Messiah as conceived by God Himself: "And beginning with Moses and all the Prophets, he explained to them what was said in all the Scriptures concerning himself." Jesus may have referred to sections of Exodus, many of the Psalms, and certain passages written by the prophet Isaiah. As Jesus taught his companions, he began to change the atmosphere of their minds and hearts. They did not want Jesus to leave, so they said, "Stay with us, for it is nearly evening; the day is almost over." As the sun declined behind the horizon and dusk began to turn to darkness, the light of understanding began to shine in their hearts. They made it clear that they did not want to let go of that light.

WERE NOT OUR HEARTS BURNING WITHIN US?

When he was at the table with them, he took bread, gave thanks, broke it and began to give it to them. Then their eyes were opened and they recognized him, and he disappeared from their sight. They asked each other, "Were not our hearts burning within us while he talked with us on the road and opened the Scriptures to us?" They got up and returned at once to Jerusalem. There they found the Eleven and those with them, assembled together and saying, "It is true! The Lord has risen and has appeared to Simon."
LUKE 24:30–34

■

A PERSON WHO LACKS compassion is often described as a person with a heart of stone. But this is not completely accurate. The unredeemed heart is more like an ember; it appears to have no life or heat, but buried deep inside, it still has the potential to ignite into flame. It just needs access to the pure oxygen of the truth of God. Walking to Emmaus, Jesus revealed the truth about himself as found in Scripture, but it was not until he was preparing to share a meal with his followers that "their eyes were opened and they recognized him . . ." Their hearts burst forth with joy, and they said, "Were not our hearts burning within us while he talked with us on the road and opened the Scriptures to us?" They left Emmaus immediately to return to Jerusalem to tell the other followers the good news: "It is true! The Lord has risen . . ."

Later Jesus appeared to the Eleven as they were eating; he rebuked them for their lack of faith and their stubborn refusal to believe those who had seen him after he had risen. **MARK 16:14**

■

THE FOLLOWERS HAD EXPECTED Jesus to transform the political landscape; they were believers in a movement that was circumscribed by the political forces of the moment. Jesus, they believed, would liberate Israel and return it to the glorious days of the kingdom of David. But now their leader had been captured and killed, and they had gone into hiding. It is not difficult to identify with their plight. By their own definition, they had lost everything and were threatened with capture and possible death. When Jesus appeared and rebuked them, he reminded them that the normal patterns did not apply, for his mission came from God and not from men. His mission was not to foment a political revolution, but to restore all mankind's relationship with God. At this moment of turmoil and apparent defeat, God's divine mission was almost impossible for them to grasp.

Now Thomas (also known as Didymus), one of the Twelve, was not with the disciples when Jesus came. So the other disciples told him, "We have seen the Lord!" But he said to them, "Unless I see the nail marks in his hands and put my finger where the nails were, and put my hand into his side, I will not believe." A week later his disciples were in the house again, and Thomas was with them. Though the doors were locked, Jesus came and stood among them and said, "Peace be with you!" Then he said to Thomas, "Put your finger here; see my hands. Reach out your hand and put it into my side. Stop doubting and believe." Thomas said to him, "My Lord and my God!" Then Jesus told him, "Because you have seen me, you have believed; blessed are those who have not seen and yet have believed." JOHN 20:24–29

■

MANY CAN IDENTIFY WITH Thomas' skepticism. Their perspective is grounded in the truism that to see is to believe. Furthermore, the followers of Jesus were in shock. Everything they hoped for seemed to have gone up in smoke. So, when Thomas heard that Jesus had risen and had been with the disciples, he must have concluded that they were blinded by grief and wishful thinking. When Jesus came to Thomas, however, he did not rebuke him. Instead, he said: Touch my hands and feel the wound in my side. Thomas responded instantly, moving from doubt to belief, and saying, "My Lord and my God!" Jesus then reminded Thomas and the disciples that they would soon face a doubting world and that their mission was to overcome that doubt by being steadfast in their own belief: "Because you have seen me you have believed; blessed are those who have not seen and yet have believed."

DO YOU LOVE ME?

When they had finished eating, Jesus said to Simon Peter, "Simon son of John, do you love me more than these?" "Yes, Lord," he said, "you know that I love you." Jesus said, "Feed my lambs." Again Jesus said, "Simon son of John, do you love me?" He answered, "Yes, Lord, you know that I love you." Jesus said, "Take care of my sheep." The third time he said to him, "Simon son of John, do you love me?" Peter was hurt because Jesus asked him the third time, "Do you love me?" He said, "Lord, you know all things; you know that I love you." Jesus said, "Feed my sheep. Very truly I tell you, when you were younger you dressed yourself and went where you wanted; but when you are old you will stretch out your hands, and someone else will dress you and lead you where you do not want to go." Jesus said this to indicate the kind of death by which Peter would glorify God. Then he said to him, "Follow me!" JOHN 21:15–19

■

AT ONE TIME PETER loudly proclaimed his undying loyalty to Jesus: "Even if all fall away on account of you, I never will . . . Even if I have to die with you, I will never disown you" (Matthew 26:13,15). Just a few hours later, Peter disowned Jesus not once but three times: "Then he began to call down curses on himself and he swore to them, 'I don't know the man!'" (Matthew 26:74). Peter had failed the Lord, and he had failed himself. He was overcome with sorrow, shame, and self-loathing, and he wept bitterly. Now Jesus had returned, and he stood before the one of whom he had said, " you are Peter, and upon this rock I will build my church . . ." (Matthew 16:18). Jesus tested Peter to prepare him for the mission ahead. Jesus asked Peter the same question three separate times: "Do you love me?" And with each affirmative answer, Jesus gave a command: "Feed my lambs." "Take care of my sheep." "Feed my sheep." Peter had been forgiven and commissioned at the same time. Now he could go out into the world to become the rock upon which the church would be built.

He said to them, "This is what I told you while I was still with you: Everything must be fulfilled that is written about me in the Law of Moses, the Prophets and the Psalms." Then he opened their minds so they could understand the Scriptures. He told them, "This is what is written: The Messiah will suffer and rise from the dead on the third day, and repentance for the forgiveness of sins will be preached in his name to all nations, beginning at Jerusalem. You are witnesses of these things." LUKE 24:44–48

■

JESUS RETURNED TO THE disciples; he ate with them, showed his wounded hands, and reminded them that everything that had happened had been foretold in the "Law of Moses, the Prophets and the Psalms." He summarized the message so that they would understand: "The Messiah will suffer and rise from the dead on the third day, and repentance for the forgiveness of sins will be preached in his name to all nations, beginning in Jerusalem." This is the Gospel message in a nutshell, and Jesus told his followers that they would be his witnesses throughout the world. This is the one reason for church: To lift up the name of Jesus through proclaiming, preaching, and declaring his Lordship to a world that has wandered onto a crooked and dangerous path. Growing the church is a vital cornerstone of God's restoration project; building the church is as simple as inviting people into that project.

Then Jesus came to them and said, "All authority in heaven and on earth has been given to me. Therefore go and make disciples of all nations, baptizing them in the name of the Father and of the Son and of the Holy Spirit, and teaching them to obey everything I have commanded you. And surely I am with you always, to the very end of the age." MATTHEW 28:18–20

■

WHEN JESUS SAYS, "ALL authority in heaven and on earth has been given to me," he means it. There are no qualifiers here. He is the risen Christ of God; obedience to the law as prescribed by the religious authorities is not the way back to God. Jesus says that following him only requires a willing desire to walk the path he walks. The message is this: Repent, believe, and be baptized "in the name of the Father and the Son and the Holy Spirit." The imperative is this: Make disciples who will become the foundation, walls, windows, and roof of the church itself. "As you come to him, the living stone—rejected by men but chosen by God and precious to him—you also, the living stones, are being built into a spiritual house to be a holy priesthood, offering spiritual sacrifices acceptable to God through Jesus Christ" (1 Peter 2:4–6).

I am going to send you what my Father has promised; but stay in the city until you have been clothed with power from on high.
LUKE 24:49

■

WE HAVE BEEN HEARING the command to "go," but now Jesus seems to reverse course and says to stay in the city and wait. Immediately before he was taken prisoner in the Garden of Gethsemane, Jesus promised his disciples that they would receive the Holy Spirit at an opportune time, but even now after the resurrection and appearances, the time had not yet come. His promise was this: "But the Counselor, the Holy Spirit, whom the Father will send in my name, will teach you all things and will remind you of everything I have said to you" (John 14:26). He also said the Counselor, the Spirit of truth, will be with them forever. Jesus would not leave his disciples as orphans (John 14:16–18). The time was coming but had not yet come when the disciples would be "clothed with power from on high." That power comes directly from the Holy Spirit of God.

TAKEN UP INTO HEAVEN

When he had led them out to the vicinity of Bethany, he lifted up his hands and blessed them. While he was blessing them, he left them and was taken up into heaven. Then they worshiped him and returned to Jerusalem with great joy. And they stayed continually at the temple, praising God. LUKE 24:50–53

■

THIS DESCRIPTION OF THE Ascension of Jesus Christ is one of two accounts provided by Luke. Here he understates what happened by only saying, "he left them and was taken up into heaven." In Acts, Luke tells of two men dressed in white who suddenly appeared after Jesus had ascended and who asked the disciples why they were staring up into the sky. Then the men in white said, "This same Jesus who has been taken from you into heaven, will come back in the same way you have seen him go into heaven" (Acts 1:11). Jesus had promised his followers that he would not leave them as orphans; now they were told he would return in the same way he left. With his departure into heaven, his followers were left with this: On the previous Friday, Jesus had died on the cross at Calvary. On the third day, the day after Jewish Sabbath, he had risen from the tomb. With his ascension into heaven, they were told that he would come back again, just as he had left. And so, with all of these extraordinary events and promises to ponder, they returned together to Jerusalem to wait for what would come next.

After the Lord Jesus had spoken to them, he was taken up into heaven and he sat at the right hand of God. Then the disciples went out and preached everywhere, and the Lord worked with them and confirmed his word by the signs that accompanied it.
MARK 16:19–20

■

THE SIMPLICITY OF MARK'S final words should not deflect our attention away from what actually happened. Usually, when the leader of a movement is killed, the movement begins to lose power. The followers, confused and afraid, scatter, and within a short time, little is left except the memory of what might have been. But with Jesus, an extraordinary reversal of ordinary expectations took place. After Jesus was taken up to heaven to sit at the right hand of God, the disciples were emboldened. They began to preach and build the church. Mark says, "the Lord worked with them and confirmed his word by the signs that accompanied it." The new kingdom began to form, and by the power of the Holy Spirit, the kingdom builders began to spread throughout Jerusalem and "in all of Judea and Samaria, and to the ends of the earth" (Acts 1:8).

This is the disciple who testifies to these things and who wrote them down. We know that his testimony is true. Jesus did many other things as well. If every one of them were written down, I suppose that even the whole world would not have room for the books that would be written. JOHN 21:24–25

■

JOHN ENDS HIS GOSPEL by stating that everything he has written is true, but then he says, even so, what has been written is but a small part of a huge story that could never be contained in books, even if those books filled up the whole world. John is saying that Jesus cannot be limited by the usual human limitations and boundaries. The Pharisees and the Sadducees and the powerful religious and political leaders in Jerusalem could not contain him. He could not be contained by King Herod or by Caiaphas or by Pontius Pilate. Even the tomb of Joseph of Arimathea could not contain him. For Jesus has risen and is seated at the right hand of God, and he has given his disciples in Jerusalem, and us, the authority through the power of the Holy Spirit to go and tell the rest of the world the good news that Jesus is the Christ.

SUGGESTED TOPICAL STUDIES

BEGINNINGS

Luke's Prologue

JANUARY 3

John's Prologue

JANUARY 4-9

Matthew Genealogy

JANUARY 10

Mary is Chosen

JANUARY 14-17, 19-21

The Shepherds as Witnesses

JANUARY 22-23

Jesus Named

JANUARY 24

Two Prophecies

JANUARY 25-26

The Magi

JANUARY 27-30

Escape into Egypt

JANUARY 31

Herod's Response

FEBRUARY 1

Jesus' Childhood

FEBRUARY 2-3

LIFE OF JOHN THE BAPTIST

John's Mission
JANUARY 8

John's Birth
JANUARY 10-14, JAN 18

John's Ministry
FEBRUARY 4-8, MARCH 12-18, MAY 14-15

John's Death
JULY 5-7

John's Importance
OCTOBER 19

SERMON ON THE MOUNT

The Full Sermon
MARCH 24-MAY 11

The Beatitudes
MARCH 25-APRIL 2

The Lord's Prayer
APRIL 17-22

STUDY OF SELECTED PARABLES

Introduction
MAY 24

Parable of the Sower
MAY 30-JUNE 5

Parable of the Weeds
JUNE 8-10

I Am the Way, and the Truth and the Life
NOVEMBER 8

Study of the Raising of Lazarus & The Aftermath
SEPTEMBER 25-OCTOBER 3

THE CRUCIFIXION AND RESURRECTION
OF JESUS CHRIST

Jesus' Arrest & Peter's Denial
NOVEMBER 23-27, 29

The Trial
NOVEMBER 28, NOVEMBER 30-DECEMBER 4

The Crucifixion & Burial
DECEMBER 5-14

The 7 Words on the Cross
DECEMBER 8-12

Resurrection & Ascension
DECEMBER 15-30